Battle Mage

BATTLE MAGE

Peter A. Flannery

BLACKHEART BOOKS

BATTLE MAGE

A BLACKHEART BOOK: 978-0-9570919-2-4

First published by Blackheart Books in 2017

PRINTING HISTORY

Blackheart Edition 2017

Contact:

Twitter: @TheFlanston

Website: www.peterflannery.co.uk

For my brother Anthony who lit the spark
For Tolkien who fanned it to a flame
For all the creative talents who keep it burning still
And for all those who love fantasy books
This is mine
I hope you enjoy it

Acknowledgements

With love and thanks to my wife, Julie, who spots so many of my mistakes and lets me know when I'm starting to waffle.
My books are better because of you.

Thanks to Kevin Arms, Judith Coulson, Megan Nagle, Fiona Seaton and Lisa Smith. You were kind enough to read this book before it was published and brave enough to give me your thoughts.

Thanks to Rob Miller, the Master Swordsmith of Skye.
I hope I did the forging of a sword justice.

(See Rob's beautiful swords at: www.castlekeep.co.uk)

LA MER
SANS FIN

CLEMENCE

Wrath

Hoffen

Le Matres

Reiherstadt

Amboss

Toulwar

Caër Dour

Navaria

The Pass of Amaethon

VALENTIA

Maiden

Caër Laison

THE BAY
OF
BARINTHUS

Tavros

ACHERON

THRAECE

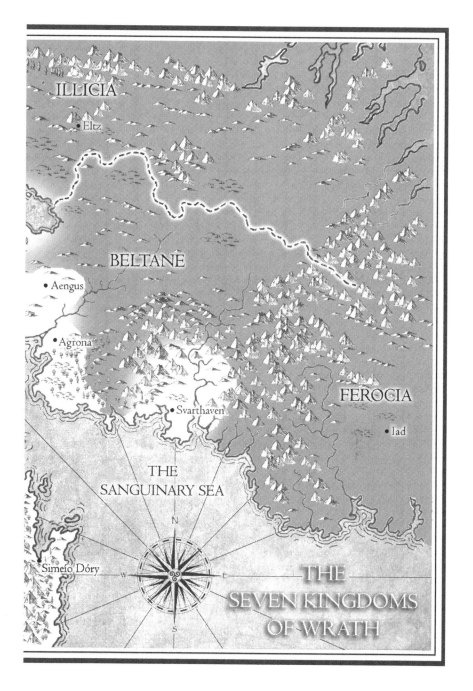

ILLICIA

• Eltz

BELTANE

• Aengus

• Agrona

• Svarthaven

FEROCIA

• Iad

THE
SANGUINARY SEA

N

Simeío Dóry

W   E

S

THE
SEVEN KINGDOMS
OF WRATH

BATTLE MAGE

The world knows no emotion to match a dragon's grief

Save perhaps a dragon's rage

Prologue

The knight blinked the blood and the tears of failure from his eyes. He wheeled his horse about and raised his visor to view the field. All across the valley the Illician forces were falling back in rout.

The battle was lost.

The knight's tears tasted bitter on his tongue. They should have been enough to defeat the Possessed army, they should have prevailed, but they had not reckoned on the demon. *It* had remained hidden, only revealing itself at the last minute and by then it was too late to request the presence of a battle mage.

No. This was their battle, and it was lost.

He felt no shame, for few could stand their ground in the presence of such a foe. And yet they had stood. For almost an hour the soldiers of Illicia had held their ground. But now the end was near.

From the crest of the hill he looked down upon his foe. The demon towered over the human warriors of the Possessed, a thing of unearthly power and hellish strength. The knight knew he could not kill it. His only hope now was to die quickly before he succumbed to the fear. With a final effort of will he urged his mount forward, hoping that his courage would not fail before the end. And yet, even as he rode to his death, he thought not of himself but of the people they had failed. The Possessed army had broken through the Illician defences. It would move into the mountains where it would be difficult to follow. It would avoid the strength of Clemoncé and move instead into the kingdom of Valentia.

Valentia had once been renowned for the courage and skill of its warriors but in recent generations its reputation had waned. As the knight gave his mount unto the charge he wondered if anything of its greatness remained.

He hoped it did.

For the sake of all their souls he hoped it did.

Part I

RUIN

I
Son of Madness

In the far north of Valentia the sun was rising on the mountain town of Caer Dour. The air was crisp and cold and the pale stone of the buildings shone brightly in the morning light. The rhythmic sound of the smithy's hammer rang above the lowing of cattle and the bleating of goats. The smell of dung from the stables mingled with that of freshly baked bread and smoke from a thousand newly set hearths.

It seemed like any other morning. There was no evidence of fear, and nothing to suggest that the town was in mortal danger. Rather, there was a sense of excitement in the air for this was the day of the trials, a special day when the people of Caer Dour got to show off their fighting skills to the Queen's emissary.

It was still early and yet there were already people in the cobbled streets, all making their way to the western edge of the town where the road to Clemoncé climbed over the craggy hill. It was from here that he would arrive, the emissary from the Court of Wrath.

Every two years he made the journey from the capital of Clemoncé to see the best of what Caer Dour had to offer in the field of combat. Those who excelled in the trials would return with him to study at the Academy of War in Wrath. It was always a time of great excitement but this year it was especially so. This year the emissary was bringing back a student who had completed his training. But this was no ordinary knight or swordsman, this was a battle mage, the first that Caer Dour had produced in over forty years, and his arrival could not have come at a more timely hour.

Barely two weeks ago the border patrols reported that a Ferocian army had broken through the Illician defences and crossed into Valentia. It had already laid waste to several villages and was now within a few days' march of the town. A demon marched at the head of the Possessed and without a battle mage the town's army would have no chance of stopping them. But today their champion was coming home and so the people of Caer Dour were not nearly as afraid as perhaps they ought to be. Instead they rose early and prepared for the spectacle of the day. People walked onto the hill and hung out of windows, all hoping to catch an early glimpse of the Queen's envoy.

On a villa near the outskirts of town two young men had gone a step further, climbing out onto the red ceramic tiles of the roof. One was Malaki de Vane, the blacksmith's son, a tall muscular youth with thick brown hair and a bright red birthmark down the left side of his face. The other was almost as tall but he was thin and frail with lank, dark hair and a pale, sickly complexion. The lines of his face were pleasing enough but his cheeks were hollow and gaunt. His name was Falco Danté, and the only thing about *him* that spoke of strength was the colour of his eyes which were a bright and vivid green.

'Be careful, Falco. You're going to fall!'

'I just want to see,' said Falco as he edged his way towards the apex of the roof.

'We'll see soon enough. Just come down here where it's safer.' Malaki despaired of his friend's foolhardiness. 'I'm not going to catch you if you fall!'

1

'Yes, you will,' said Falco with a smile. He knew his friend would never let him fall.

Malaki tried a different tack.

'You'll break the tiles,' he insisted. 'Then Simeon will have your hide.'

Simeon le Roy was the master of the villa on which they climbed. Falco had served him since the death of his father almost fourteen years ago.

'The tiles are fine,' said Falco. 'I'm not a half-ton lummox like you.'

'Well don't blame me if you get a good beating.'

'Simeon would never beat me,' gasped Falco as he swung a leg over the apex of the roof. His arms shook from the exertion of the climb and his breathing rasped noisily in his chest.

'Well he should,' said Malaki. 'I've never known a servant have it so easy.'

This of course was far from true. An easy life was the one thing Falco Danté did not have. He was a weakling in a world of warriors and worse than that, he was the son of a madman.

'Well?' asked Malaki impatiently.

'Well, what?'

'Can you see any further?'

The wheezing in Falco's chest was becoming uncomfortable. The cold morning air was not good for his lungs but still he smiled.

'All the way to the cloven rock,' he said.

'Hang on,' said Malaki. 'I'm coming up.'

Despite his size Malaki climbed the sloping roof with surprising agility. In no time at all he was sitting behind his friend on the highest point of the villa. Together they gazed towards a large split boulder where the stony path rounded the hill.

'Do you think he'll bring the magi?' asked Malaki, referring to the emissary.

'He always comes with one,' replied Falco casually. 'They'll want to review the apprentices.'

'I know that!' said Malaki. 'But do you think he'll bring more? Do you think there'll be a summoning?'

'I don't know,' Falco lied. He tried to sound disinterested but the truth was he knew the magi were coming. Somehow he knew there would be a summoning.

'I hope he does,' breathed Malaki. 'Imagine it... Not just a battle mage, but a battle mage with a dragon. The Ferocian army wouldn't stand a chance.'

'We don't need a dragon to defeat the Possessed,' said Falco. 'Darius will be enough.'

Everyone knew the way of things. A well trained army had a good chance of defeating a Possessed army of similar size but if the Possessed were led by a demon then a normal army stood no chance at all. They would be overcome by fear. Only with a battle mage could they hope to prevail.

It was not just the fighting prowess and the arcane powers of a battle mage, it was the presence of their soul, a beacon of faith, the keystone of courage by which normal men might stand. A battle mage is a mighty ally to count among your ranks but a battle mage with a dragon, well, such a thing is a force of nature.

'But wouldn't you like to see a dragon?' pressed Malaki. 'Just once.'

2

'No,' Falco lied again. He and Malaki had been friends since childhood, but he did not want *anyone* to know the depth of his yearning to see a dragon, he did not want anyone to suspect what he intended to do.

Malaki looked at his friend's narrow back, the slumped shoulders, the bowed head.

'Because of your father?' he said quietly.

Falco simply nodded. His lack of interest was a pretence, the shame he felt at the mention of his father was not. The two boys sat in silence as the sun slanted across the rooftops.

'Where *are* they?' said Malaki. 'The sun's well up. They should be here by now.'

Falco said nothing as the shadow of discomfort slowly lifted from his mind.

'Don't know why I'm so excited,' said Malaki. 'It's not as if I'll be trying out for a place at the academy.'

'You'll be fighting in the melee,' said Falco over his shoulder. 'And you're favourite to win that. Maybe they'll let you present yourself anyway.'

'Yeah,' said Malaki. 'And pigs might fly out of my arse!'

Falco laughed at his friend's modesty. As far as he was concerned there was not a cadet in the entire region who could match Malaki's skill with a sword.

'Imagine fighting in the trials,' said Malaki. 'Imagine being presented to Queen Catherine at the Court of Wrath.'

Falco was glad that Malaki could not see his face. There was a determined smile on his lips and a fierce green light in his eyes. Damn the magi and the laws of noble birth. If things went the way *he* had planned, Malaki would get his chance to impress the Queen's emissary. But he did not want to say anything just yet and he was about to change the subject when a cry of anguish made them both turn back to the house.

'What the hell was that?' said Malaki.

Falco did not answer. He was listening for any further sounds.

Another cry emerged from the villa. It was a cry of fear that gave way to an unsettling moan. Malaki was transfixed but Falco swung his leg back over the apex of the roof and started to work his way down.

'What is it?' asked Malaki as he joined Falco on the lower part of the roof.

'It's Simeon,' said Falco, walking the length of a short gully before traversing the gutters towards a veranda at the far end of the villa.

'Where are you going?'

'I just want to make sure he's all right.'

'But we'll miss the emissary.'

'I just want to make sure,' said Falco.

Malaki raised his eyes to the sky then moved to follow his friend. The moans had turned to snarls and whispers as the two youths climbed onto the veranda and peered through gaps in the shutters.

'What's wrong with him?' asked Malaki.

Falco looked down upon the shadowy form of his master.

Simeon le Roy lay sprawled on his bed, twisted in his blankets. The old man twitched and shuddered and mouthed words that neither of them could make

3

out. The moaning and crying was interspersed by snarls of aggression as if he were engaged in a struggle.

'He's dreaming,' said Falco.

'Mother of all!' breathed Malaki. 'Dreaming of what?'

'Of hell,' said Falco.

Malaki felt a shudder of fear run through him but Falco's eyes merely narrowed as the sight of Simeon's suffering roused the spectre of his own night-time terrors.

You would never have the courage

You would never have the strength

The mocking voice echoed in Falco's mind as the world seemed to darken around him.

'Should we wake him?' asked Malaki and Falco was brought out of his reverie.

'No,' he said. 'I'll wait with him. It'll pass.'

Malaki stole a sideways glance at his friend. There was something in Falco's voice that he had heard many times before, a kind of maturity, an intensity that made him feel as if he did not really know his friend at all.

'Does he always dream like this?'

'No,' said Falco. 'Some nights are worse than others.'

'Is there nothing to be done?'

Falco shook his head. 'It's the curse of a battle mage,' he said, 'but also their strength. When they meet a demon on the battlefield they do not feel the fear of other men.'

'Why not?' breathed Malaki.

'Because it's not new to them,' said Falco. 'Since they were a child they have known it in their dreams.'

Malaki wanted to know more but he knew better than to question Falco too deeply. Simeon had been a battle mage for many years, fighting the Possessed when the enemy was still a vague and distant threat. But his long service to the kingdoms of Wrath had ended abruptly some fourteen years ago when Falco's father had gone mad and killed half the magi in the town.

Malaki's gaze lingered on Falco for a moment longer then he put his eye back to the crack in the window's shutter and watched an old man wrestle with all the torments of hell.

A bell suddenly rang out in the clear morning air and both boys started at the sound.

'He's here!' said Malaki, climbing over the rail and making his way back along the gutter. The big youth climbed quickly back to the apex of the roof. 'I can see him!' he called. 'And Darius too!'

Falco looked up at his friend and smiled, but when he peered back through the shutter, Simeon was no longer writhing in his sleep. He was sitting up in his crumpled bed with his face turned directly towards the window at which Falco crouched. A shaft of sunlight fell across him, revealing a terrible mask of disfigurement. The skin of his face was scarred and burned, and the bright sunlight cast black shadows in the empty sockets of his eyes.

Simeon le Roy was blind.

4

'That cold morning air will be the death of you, Falco Danté.'

Falco smiled at his master's gentle scolding.

'And you can wipe that smile of your face, you scrawny whelp!'

The smile broadened. Simeon might have lost his eyes, but he still saw more than most. Any vestige of fear and vulnerability faded as the former battle mage rose from his bed and pulled a robe about his broad shoulders. He pushed back his long grey hair and tied it with silk cord. He was old, beyond his sixtieth year at least, and yet despite a pronounced limp and a certain stiffness in his limbs, he still possessed a warrior's bearing. He walked over to the window and drew open the shutters.

'How many magi, Master de Vane?' he called out in a voice that had the timbre of oak.

Neither Falco nor Malaki were surprised by the extent of his awareness. Not all the powers of a battle mage are dependent on the gift of sight.

'Wait!' called Malaki from his roof-top perch. 'There's a bank of mist rolled in.'

'Four,' whispered Falco so quietly that he thought it went unheard. He did not see Simeon's face turn towards him, the scarred forehead creased in thought.

There was a short pause while Malaki waited for the mist to clear. Then...

'Four,' he shouted. 'There are four magi.'

Malaki sounded disappointed, but Simeon just nodded.

'Hmm.' The sound was a low rumble in his throat. 'With the three from Caer Dour that makes seven. It seems there will be a summoning after all.'

Falco tried not to show any reaction to Simeon's words. His outward demeanour was sullen and unmoved, but inside he felt dizzy with excitement. Tonight, when all the trials were over, Darius Voltario would attempt to summon a dragon and he, Falco, would be there to see it.

2
The Balance of Friendship

'He's only brought four magi,' exclaimed Malaki as he returned to join Falco and Simeon on the veranda.

'Morning, Malaki,' said Simeon.

'Good morning, Master le Roy,' said Malaki somewhat sheepishly. Scrambling over a nobleman's house in the early hours of the morning might not be the most appropriate thing to do, but Simeon was not like the other nobles in the town. He was approachable, almost normal. Ordinarily Malaki would have shown more restraint, but in the excitement of the day he just could not help himself. 'Why only four?' he asked. 'I thought he'd bring seven to make us up to ten.'

Simeon turned to Falco inviting him to answer, but Falco refused to look at his master.

'With the proper preparation it takes only seven magi to subdue a dragon,' said Simeon.

'Subdue it?' queried Malaki. 'I thought the dragons were on our side. Why would we want to subdue it?'

Again Simeon looked to Falco, but still he showed no sign of joining in the conversation.

'Most dragons will give their lives for their battle mage, and for the free people of Wrath,' said Simeon.

'So what's the problem?'

'The problem, Master de Vane, is that there is always the chance that a black dragon will answer the summoning.'

'What's so special about a black dragon?' Malaki was enthralled. He had never known anyone speak so freely about dragons.

'Regardless of what colour they start out,' explained Simeon, 'all dragons will eventually turn black. They are the oldest and most powerful of all dragonkind.'

'Isn't that a good thing?' persisted Malaki.

'It would be,' said Simeon, 'except for one tragic fact.'

'And what's that?'

'Black dragons are mad,' said Simeon. 'Rather than fighting to the death to save a human life a black dragon will turn against them, killing at random until it is slain or it flees back beyond the Endless Sea.'

Malaki's mouth gaped open and he looked at Falco as if to say, '*Did you know this?*'

Falco turned away from his friend's unspoken question. He leaned on the railings enclosing the veranda and stared out across the town. Unlike Malaki he was not enjoying this lesson on the nature of dragons.

'It's been that way ever since the Great Possession,' said Simeon, 'when the dragons were overcome by evil. It seems that something of that Possession survives in the heart of a black dragon.'

Malaki was stunned.

'What colour of dragon answered your summoning?' he asked.

Simeon snorted softly. 'Not all battle mages are destined to fight with a dragon at their side.'

Malaki seemed disappointed. He paused for a minute as if trying to absorb what he had just learned. Then he turned to Falco.

'Is that what happened to your father?' he began. 'I've heard people say that his dragon was black.'

The moment he had said it Malaki knew he had overstepped the mark. Falco pushed away from the railings and walked through the window into Simeon's room. He had barely crossed the threshold when Simeon stopped him with a word.

'Falco!'

Falco stopped but he did not turn.

'Those are *my* chambers, Falco Danté.' Simeon too spoke without turning and Malaki's eyes flitted from one stiff back to the other. 'You can leave the roof by the way you came. And have a care about the liberties you take in my household.'

Falco made no answer but he slouched back onto the veranda and started to climb over the rail.

'I will take some bread and fruit with my wine this morning,' said Simeon in the same tone of command.

Falco was about to start along the gutter, back to the window where he and Malaki had first climbed out onto the roof. He paused. 'Yes, master,' he said quietly.

Simeon gave a curt nod of acknowledgement and Falco continued on his way.

'And Falco,' said Simeon in a more lenient voice. 'When you've seen to that, have Fossetta make up an infusion. You sound like a wizened old mule. You'll be serving no one at the trials if you're laid up in your bed coughing up a lung.'

At these words Malaki looked aghast at Simeon and then accusingly at his friend. With a few mumbled words he took his leave and followed after Falco. He caught up with him as he disappeared through the window at the top of the stairs.

'What does he mean, *serving at the trials*?' Malaki demanded as he vaulted through the window and caught Falco's shoulder before he could leave the landing.

Falco's guilty expression was answer enough.

'I've paid good money to make sure you *wouldn't* be serving at the trials!'

'I'll pay you back,' said Falco. He shrugged off Malaki's hand and started down the stairs towards the servants' quarters.

'I don't understand,' said Malaki, falling in beside him. 'Bellius will be in his element. He's bound to try and make an example of you.'

'I know,' said Falco as he pushed open the door into the kitchen.

With connections to the royal family, both in Caer Laison and Wrath, Bellius Snidesson was the region's most powerful noble *and* its most unpleasant. Apart from making other peoples' lives a misery there were just three things that Bellius cared about - wealth, power and the advancement of his only son, Jarek, a cruel and spoilt young man who had beaten Falco on so many occasions that he had lost count. Even the approach of a Ferocian army had given the nobleman the perfect opportunity to consolidate his power and Malaki had no doubt that today, of all days, Bellius would be at his insufferable best. So it was with puzzlement and annoyance that he followed his friend into the kitchen.

A waft of warm air enveloped them as they entered the large stone-flagged room. The familiar smells of cooked meats, garlic, and herbs made their mouths water. One wall was dominated by a wide open fireplace bedecked with copper pots and cooking utensils. Beside the fire was a black iron stove and standing over it a pleasantly rounded woman, her grey hair tied back beneath a white headscarf.

'Well,' said Fossetta, 'did you see them?'

Simeon's housekeeper did not look up from the pans she was tending as the two youths entered the room.

'Good morning, Mistress Pieroni,' said Malaki. 'Yes, we saw them.'

It was clear that both boys were distracted, but the lack of a response from Falco caused Fossetta to raise her eyes and follow his progress to the pantry.

'Good morning, Malaki,' said Fossetta as she watched Falco place a selection of fruit and bread on a pewter plate. 'How many magi did the emissary bring?'

'Four,' replied Malaki. The big youth had seated himself at the oak table in the centre of the room and was eyeing a platter of fresh bread and sausage.

Fossetta removed the pans from the heat. She wiped her hands on her apron as she approached the table then slid a knife and plate in front of Malaki.

'So,' she said as Malaki gave her a smile of thanks, 'there'll be a summoning after all.'

Malaki 'humphed' as he tore off a piece of bread and sliced sausage onto his plate. 'Am I the only one in this town who knows nothing about dragons?'

Fossetta placed a pewter cup in front of him and filled it with water from a jug.

'You learn a thing or two when you're house keeper to a battle mage for twenty years.'

Falco had effectively excluded himself from their conversation but, from the corner of her eye, Fossetta watched him carefully as he placed a carafe of wine beside the plate of food and went to fill a pitcher from a large pot of steaming water near the fire.

'Morning, Falco,' she said.

'Morning, Fossetta.'

Falco might be in a sullen mood but he could not bring himself to be openly rude. Fossetta was the closest thing to a mother he had ever known. He carried the pitcher of hot water back to the table, but his wheezing breath had not escaped the housekeeper's notice. Walking up behind him she placed one hand on his forehead and the other between his shoulder blades.

'Breathe,' she said.

Falco rolled his eyes and took a deep breath.

'Hmm.' Fossetta was obviously not impressed by what she felt.

'Sit,' she told him.

'But the master,' started Falco.

'I'll see to the master.'

She pushed Falco into a chair and filled a basin with water from a kettle hanging over the fire. Then she took a bottle of crushed herbs from a shelf and stirred several spoonfuls into the water. The room was suddenly filled with the sharp scent of lavender, eucalyptus and camomile. She took a large towel from a clothes rack then, bending Falco forward over the bowl of steaming water, she covered his head with the towel.

'Make sure he stays there till I get back,' she told Malaki.

With a mouthful of bread and sausage Malaki gave her a nod then the housekeeper gathered up the pitcher of hot water, the wine and the plate of food, and left the room.

Silence descended.

The only sounds were those of Malaki's chewing and the slow wheezing of Falco's breath.

'Sorry for being so tetchy.' Falco's voice was muffled by the towel.

By way of a response Malaki put some food on a plate and slid it up against Falco's hand. It was comical to see his friend's hand fumble around for a hunk of bread before disappearing under the towel.

'I still don't understand why you want to serve at the trials,' said Malaki. 'The pavilion will be crawling with nobles.'

'I have my reasons,' managed Falco round a mouthful of food.

'You're an awkward bugger at times,' said Malaki.

Falco raised the towel to look at his broad-shouldered friend.

'I know,' he smiled.

Malaki shook his head and returned the smile then, with a wave of his hand, he directed Falco to get back under the towel. The two youths sat in silence for a while until Falco spoke again.

'Red,' he said. 'The dragon that answered my father's summoning was red.'

Malaki swallowed the chunk of food in his mouth and Falco went on.

'They say that even from the start it was dark. Crimson, like the blood that flows from a vein.'

Falco sat up from the steaming infusion and pushed the towel back from his head, while Malaki held his breath. Of all the things they had talked about they had never talked of this.

'Over the years the colour deepened and the magi were watching,' Falco went on. 'Simeon says that my father knew the truth. He knew that if his dragon turned black he would have no choice but to kill it. He says that even the dragon knows what must happen and that they go willingly to their deaths.'

'So what happened?' asked Malaki quietly.

'No one knows,' said Falco. 'They say that as the colour changed my father grew withdrawn and distant. He spent more and more time in the Forsaken Lands hunting the Possessed alone. No army in support, just Aquila Danté and his dragon.'

Malaki waited for his friend to go on. He had heard snippets of the story, but no one seemed to want to talk about it. This was a chapter in Caer Dour's history that people seemed eager to forget.

'He grew increasingly angry and his anger led to confrontation.'

'Confrontation with what?'

'The magi,' said Falco. 'My father was becoming unreasonable, *unhinged.*' Falco spoke this last word as if he were quoting someone else. 'Then his dragon turned black.'

'And black dragons are mad,' said Malaki and Falco just nodded.

'The magi restrained it. But rather than helping them slay it, my father sided with the dragon.'

Malaki stared into Falco's bright green eyes.

'He killed six magi and four of the town's best knights,' said Falco. 'In the end it was Simeon who brought him down.'

'I thought Simeon and your father were friends.'

'They were.' Falco's gaze was no longer fixed on Malaki. He was staring into the past, a past that he did not remember, a past about which he had only ever been told. 'The dragon managed one last burst of fire before it was slain.'

'Simeon's face,' whispered Malaki and Falco nodded.

'The remaining magi saved his life, but the dragon's fire took his eyes before it died.'

Malaki too was staring into space as he pictured the terrible scene. Then he looked up at Falco once more.

'And you were sworn into service as payment for your father's crimes.'

'Something like that,' said Falco, wiping the condensation from his face.

Before they could say any more the door opened and Fossetta re-entered the kitchen.

'I thought I told you to stay under that towel,' she scolded.

She walked to a dresser at the side of the room and picked up a white ceramic dish then she moved to stand beside Falco and held the dish under his chin.

'Spit!' she said.

Falco let out a sigh but Fossetta was insistent. Then to Malaki's obvious disgust he hawked loudly and spat into the bowl. Fossetta studied the glob of sputum and shook her head.

'Back under you go,' she told him.

Falco knew there was no point in resisting. He gave Malaki a brief smile to say that everything was all right between them then he disappeared back under the towel.

'Shouldn't you be helping your father?' said Fossetta as she began to slap Falco's back with steady rhythmic blows. 'With the army being mobilised he must be busy.'

'He said I could look out for the emissary,' replied Malaki.

'Well, you've seen him now. And I'm sure your father could use the help.'

'But we want to see him in the town,' said Falco between slaps.

'We might get a chance to speak to him,' added Malaki.

'You two are old enough to know how it goes,' said Fossetta. 'He'll break his fast with the nobles and the magi then he'll go straight to the trials. He won't walk through the town till later in the afternoon. And if there's going to be a summoning, well, he might not do it at all.'

'I suppose you're right,' conceded Malaki. He gathered up the remaining scraps of food from his plate before rising from the table. 'As for you, wheezy,' he added, flicking a crust of bread at Falco's towel-covered head. 'I'll look out for you in the pavilion!'

Falco flinched and made an obscene gesture with his hand. Malaki laughed but Fossetta cuffed Falco smartly round the head.

'Away with you!' she said to Malaki.

Malaki started for the door, but just as he reached it Fossetta spoke again.

'Good luck in the melee.'

'Thank you, Mistress Pieroni,' said Malaki and with another smile he was gone.

Fossetta's eyes lingered on the door as she stopped slapping Falco on the back. 'He's a good boy.' She pulled back the towel and allowed Falco to sit upright.

'Yes, he is,' said Falco wiping his face with the corner of the towel.

'Good fighter too.'

Falco just nodded. The tightness in his chest had lessened and it was no longer so painful to breathe.

'Shame he can't fight in the trials,' said Fossetta.

'You know the rules,' said Falco. 'Only those of noble birth can fight in the trials.'

'He could make a challenge. If he beat one of the nobles that would earn him the right to fight.'

'Ah, but first he'd need two votes of confidence,' said Falco. 'One from the nobles and one from the warrior class. And there's not a nobleman in the entire region who would go against Bellius and accept a challenge from a blacksmith's son.'

'Well they should!' Fossetta threw the towel on the table and bent down to place her ear against Falco's back. 'Demon armies on our doorstep and we quibble over the standing of a man's birth. It's hopeless.'

'It's never hopeless,' said Falco quietly.

The housekeeper straightened up and, taking hold of Falco's chin, she raised his face to look him in the eye. 'I know that tone of voice, Falco Danté. I hope you're not planning anything foolish.'

'Who, me?' Falco's expression seemed to say.

Fossetta arched a suspicious eyebrow before tossing Falco's chin aside.

'You two boys are terrible,' she chided. 'You deserve each other.'

The housekeeper walked back over to the stove while Falco moved the bowl of steaming water to one side.

'Not sure he deserves me,' he said pensively. 'His life would be a lot easier if he didn't have me as a friend.'

There was no self-pity in Falco's tone. He was simply stating the truth.

'He's not always been the strapping good fighter he is today,' said Fossetta as she bent over the pans she had been stirring earlier. 'I remember the snotty-nosed little boy who used to cry because of the names they called him.' She dipped a finger into the smaller pan and raised it to her lips before adding a generous spoonful of sugar.

Falco filled two cups with water and set spoons and bowls ready on the table. He too remembered the name-calling on account of Malaki's birthmark.

Red Devil, they used to call him, and *Blusher*. But the one that used to upset Malaki the most was *Berry*, short for *Strawberry*. Most upsetting because it made him sound soft.

Fossetta returned to the table and poured hot porridge into the bowls.

'And I remember the skinny little runt who used to stick up for him.' She shook her head at the memory. 'How you kept coming up with those names for the older boys, I will never know.'

Falco smiled as Fossetta returned with the second pan.

'Stewed apricots,' she said, adding a dollop of the sweetened fruit to their bowls.

She took her seat beside Falco and picked up her spoon.

'You took a good many beatings for the sake of Malaki de Vane,' she said. 'I haven't forgotten, and neither has he.'

Falco stared into his breakfast. Whatever he might have done as a child, in the years since, Malaki had paid him back many times over. Sometimes he doubted that he would be here at all if it were not for the imposing presence of his friend. Yes, the scales of friendship were firmly tipped in Malaki's favour. But this was the day of the trials and Falco was determined to set the balance right.

3
The Trials

The pavilion sat on the southern edge of the tournament field where the raised platform would offer the clearest view of the trials. The white canvas was dazzling in the mid-morning sun and high above it the dragon pennant of Caer Dour rippled in the cool autumn breeze. The day of the trials was supposed to be a day of celebration, but on this occasion the excitement was tempered by a shadow of fear at the approach of the Ferocian army.

Looking out from the pavilion, Falco swept his eyes over the crowds lining the edge of the field. There was a notable absence of male faces, especially those of fighting age. Only those with family members taking part had been given leave to attend the trials. The army had been mobilised and most of the town's men were now camped further down the valley ready to engage the Possessed before they came too close to the town. The route that the enemy followed led in just one direction. Apart from the occasional goat track there was no opportunity for them to turn aside. The Possessed were heading directly for Caer Dour.

Refugees from villages and estates further down the valley had already started to arrive in the town as people fled the approaching danger. Their arrival had added to the sense of apprehension, but the people of Valentia were of warrior stock. With support from the outlying regions Caer Dour could muster an army over two-thousand strong, but few among its ranks had ever faced the Possessed, and none of them had even seen, let alone confronted, a demon.

No, the people of Caer Dour had not voiced their fears, but there was a tangible sense of relief at Darius's return. Their battle mage had returned just in time to save them and now they could enjoy the day of the trials before the last of their warriors rode off to battle.

Thinking back to Simeon's nightmares earlier in the day, Falco breathed his own private sigh of relief. The intensity of his dreams had grown more terrifying of late, though whether this was due to the proximity of the Possessed or his own imagination he could not say. Either way he was sure that they would ease once Darius had defeated the demon. For now, he brought his attention back to the present. The trials were almost ready to begin.

The tournament field lay just outside the town on a natural plateau where the craggy landscape had been levelled and covered with pale, gritty sand. The mountains of northern Valentia extended in every direction, but over to the west there was one peak that stood out from all the rest.

Mont Noir, the black mountain.

Named for the dark colour of its stone, the mountain rose like a sentinel above the town of Caer Dour. It was there that the magi kept their secret towers, and it was from there that the battle mages of the past had attempted to summon a dragon. And tonight, when everyone else was drinking and reliving the drama of the trials, Falco would climb the mountain to witness a summoning. It might be the only chance he would ever get to see a dragon up close and he was determined to take it. But the climb was not an easy one, especially for someone like him.

He must leave early.

He must leave quietly.

'Psst!'

Shaken from his thoughts, Falco almost dropped his tray of goat's cheese pastries. He backed away from the tables and moved to the side of the pavilion where one of the canvas panels had been drawn back.

'Are you serving those, or just waiting for the flies to get them?'

Malaki's arm snaked in through the side of the pavilion and deftly removed one of the tasty snacks from Falco's tray.

'You'll throw up,' Falco warned him.

'I'm not nervous,' said Malaki with his mouth full.

Falco raised a dubious eyebrow. Malaki always ate when he was nervous.

'All right, maybe a little,' he admitted. 'It's that bloody Jarek. He's been all smiles and politeness.'

Falco's expression was one of suspicion.

'Exactly,' said Malaki. 'It's enough to make anyone nervous.'

'Yeah, but you can beat Jarek.'

'I know,' said Malaki. 'But he *is* good, and there's always the chance of a lucky blow. I just don't want to make a fool of myself.'

'You won't.'

Malaki flashed him a smile then he nodded towards the crush of well-dressed people in the pavilion.

'How are things going in there?'

'Fine,' Falco lied.

Bellius had been every bit as bad as they feared. He had even used Falco's presence to cast a slur on Simeon's name. The truth was that even the other servants resented his presence. On any given task Falco took longer or carried less, but he was not complaining. If it put him in the right place at the right time then he was content.

'Have you served him yet? Has he spoken to you?'

Falco shook his head as he followed the line of Malaki's gaze. Through the press of bodies they could just see the emissary.

His name was Sir William Chevalier and he looked more 'seasoned knight' than courtly ambassador. He was tall and broad-shouldered with a number of scars on his weathered skin. His long hair was shot through with streaks of grey and there was a shadow of stubble on his jaw. His face fell short of being handsome but he had an easy manner and a warm smile that gave his strong features a certain charm. He smiled now as he talked with the nobles.

'He came into the forge,' said Malaki.

'Really!' said Falco in surprise.

'Yep,' replied Malaki. 'He left something for my dad to cast.'

'What was it?'

'A belt buckle, I think,' said Malaki. 'Something like the pendant he's wearing. Dad said it was none of my business, but he got to work on it straight away.'

Looking back Falco could see the silver pendant hanging from a leather cord around the emissary's neck. It was carved in the shape of a horse's head. Every now and then the emissary's hand would drift up to touch it as if he found its presence comforting. The emissary was still smiling, but even Malaki could see that something was wrong.

'He doesn't look happy.'

'He's not,' said Falco.

'Oh?'

'He thinks the nobles have been overconfident.'

'What? He doesn't think Darius can defeat the Possessed?'

'It's not that,' said Falco. 'It seems that Illicia sent word to several towns in the area, warning them that a Ferocian army had broken through their defences.'

'They did?' said Malaki, leaning in closer.

Falco nodded. 'Apparently the nobles were advised to request a battle mage from Caer Laison.'

Malaki snorted.

'Bellius would rather eat his own foot than ask Caer Laison for help.'

'Exactly,' said Falco as the attention of the two boys shifted to the manicured form of Bellius Snidesson. He was a tall good-looking man with glossy dark hair and a perfectly trimmed beard. Even the grey at his temples had the sheen of silver. He was impeccably dressed and, with Darius to his left and the emissary to his right, he looked the very picture of smugness.

'Well, the emissary is not impressed,' Falco went on. 'He thinks the nobles were foolish, gambling that Darius would arrive on time.'

'Well he has,' replied Malaki.

Falco gave his friend a withering look as if he were surprised to hear him siding with the nobles.

'But say he hadn't. Say he'd been delayed. The town would have been defenceless.'

Malaki conceded the point, but what did it matter? Darius was here now.

'So *this* is why you wanted to serve at the trials,' he said accusingly. 'So you could be privy to all the latest gossip.'

Falco's raised eyebrow was giving nothing away.

'Darius looks so different,' said Malaki, looking at the striking young man at the centre of attention.

'In a way,' said Falco distractedly. True, he seemed more mature and confident, but the essence of the man, that sense of spirit, that hidden fire... that had always been obvious to Falco.

'What do you mean, *in a way*?' scoffed Malaki. 'Look at him!'

Malaki was right. Darius was only in his early twenties, but he had the bearing of a much older man. In fact, for all the noble knights in the pavilion, there were only two other men who could match his strength of presence. One was the Queen's emissary, the other was Simeon le Roy.

Simeon had been placed as far down the tables as protocol would allow, but on entering the pavilion Darius had made a point of seeking him out. The two battle mages had shaken hands and something unspoken had passed between them, something that no one else in the tent could hope to understand. Their moment did not last long however, as, with a comment about 'seeing out the old and bringing in the new', Bellius had moved quickly to draw Darius back into the circles *he* had chosen to impress.

15

Caer Dour's new battle mage was of medium build with dark brown hair, chiselled features and a strong hawkish nose. He was dressed in a surcoat of green and gold with only his sword and a single shoulder guard to hint at the armour he would wear in battle. If *he* were aware of any tension in the air he did not show it. His blue eyes met the smiles of the excited nobles and he handled the attention with self-assured composure.

A great cheer suddenly rose up outside the pavilion and the awkward mood evaporated as all eyes were drawn out onto the tournament field.

'Here they come,' said Malaki.

Falco moved to watch as the cadets entered the field, each group accompanied by a relevant detachment from the army.

The first category to arrive was cavalry, escorted by five fully armoured knights from the Order of the Dragon. Tomorrow these troops would ride out to engage the enemy, but today they brought with them ten of the town's most promising youngsters. The cadets reared up on their horses, showing off their skills while the knights lowered their lances in salute to the Queen's representative.

'Who do you fancy?' asked Falco.

'Pah!' said Malaki. 'None of them would have the guts to attempt the épreuve du force.'

Falco looked at his friend and smiled. The épreuve du force, or 'trial by strength', was a gruelling test by which men of low birth could become a knight. As nobles, these young men did not need to pass a test. They would earn the title of 'knight' automatically as soon as they reached their twenty-first birthday.

'They'll be training to become officers, not knights,' said Falco. 'Now come on, Master Grumpy, who's your money on?'

Malaki looked at the ten young hopefuls and pursed his lips. Falco knew he would love to be out there with them. On horse or foot he could match any one of these privileged noble youths.

'Owen's the best all-rounder,' said Malaki, 'but Jarek's the best horseman.'

'What about Gwilhem?'

Malaki nodded. 'Tough as a mountain boar,' he conceded. 'And about as skilful,' he added with a sideways grin.

Next came the swordsmen. This was the style of fighting for which Valentia was famed - one to one combat with sword and shield.

The swordsmen wore barbute helmets, with the distinctive T-shaped visor. Their torsos were protected by mail hauberks with plate mail on the sword-arm, shoulders and the lower part of their leading leg. The two friends watched them carefully as most of these young men would be competing against Malaki in the melee. Open to anyone mad enough to enter, the melee marked the end of the trials. It was the final and most popular event of the day.

Then it was the turn of the spear and pikemen. They would be judged on strength, technique and formation, but everyone knew that the emissary would be looking for men of courage, men who could hold their ground in the face of an enemy charge. Such men could steady a line that would otherwise collapse. And, although the trials were not a real battle, Sir William Chevalier had a gift for judging the character of men.

16

Finally the archers entered the field and for some reason the cheering rose to an even greater pitch. From his slightly elevated position Falco could see the reason for the heightened enthusiasm. With a smile he nodded towards the last but one of the cadets.

'Told you she'd do it,' he said.

Malaki put a despairing hand to his forehead. Most of the twenty archer cadets were broad-shouldered young men who looked more like farmers' sons than genteel nobles. It was precisely their strength that allowed them to bend such powerful bows, and powerful bows gave them greater accuracy over longer distances. However, the figure to which Falco nodded was neither broad-shouldered nor particularly strong, and was in fact a woman.

Her name was Bryna Godwyn, only daughter of Sir Gerallt Godwyn. Her black tunic and breeches were cut from fine leather and trimmed with knot-work of red and gold. Her long red hair was tied back with a leather cord and the redness of her cheeks stood out clearly against the nervous pallor of her face. To the casual observer she appeared completely out of place. But Bryna Godwyn was an archer, and it was in the company of archers that she felt most at home.

'She's mad,' said Malaki.

'Yes,' agreed Falco. 'But you have to admire her spirit.'

Bryna was not the first woman to enter the trials, but the field of battle was generally not considered to be a suitable place for a woman, especially a noble woman. And, by the defiant set of her jaw, it was clear that Bryna was all too aware of this.

Falco looked across the pavilion to see if he could see Bryna's father.

Sir Gerallt Godwyn was a proud, but somewhat tragic figure. A knight of some renown, he had lost two sons and a wife to an illness that had swept through the town some years ago. He was one of the few nobles who had the courage to challenge Bellius Snidesson. Falco caught sight of him near the far end of the pavilion. He was being congratulated by Julius Merryweather, a large, apple-cheeked nobleman dressed in overly colourful robes. Merryweather seemed delighted that Bryna had entered the trials but it was clear from Sir Gerallt's expression that *he* did not approve of his daughter's actions.

With a final clap on the shoulder Merryweather left Gerallt and returned to his son, Tobias, who was seated in a wheeled chair by one of the tables. Falco's eyes lingered on the irrepressibly happy man as he bent down and wiped the drool from his son's sagging mouth. He could not hear what Julius said but his palsied son shifted happily in his chair and waved the small wooden 'knight dolls' that were tied to his wrists.

If the nobles disapproved of Bryna Godwyn's audacity then they verged on hostility towards Merryweather's decision to raise so disabled a son. Not that Merryweather seemed to notice. He met all adversity with jest and good humour, though how much of it was sincere and how much a well maintained front was impossible to say.

As Falco watched, Merryweather looked over the wall of bodies at the front of the pavilion then manoeuvred his son's chair down towards Falco where the pavilion was not so crowded.

17

'Don't mind if I settle him here, do you Master Danté?' he asked as if he were speaking to an equal and not a household servant. 'Can't see the wood for the trees up there,' said Merryweather with a laugh as if he had made some kind of joke.

'Not at all,' replied Falco, pushing a bench out of the way to make room for the bulky chair. It could not be said that he felt comfortable in Tobias's presence, but neither did he share the repugnance and condemnation that so many others expressed.

'Ooh, those look good!' exclaimed Merryweather helping himself to a handful of the pastries on Falco's tray before settling himself down on the bench beside his son.

Falco and Malaki exchanged an amused look before turning their attention back to the tournament field.

Flanked by their army escorts the cadets were now lined up before the pavilion. A captain from each discipline approached the pavilion and presented a scroll that was passed to the emissary and Sir William's searching eyes passed down the line as he read the names on the list. When he had finished he saluted the cadets by clapping his right fist to his chest and extending it towards them. The cadets returned the salute and the emissary took his seat beside Bellius Snidesson and Darius Voltario.

The trials were ready to begin.

Malaki and Falco watched as the cadets moved off the field. Falco's eyes flitted from one to the next but Malaki's attention was firmly fixed on the red-headed young woman in the black archer's garb.

'Why do you think she's done it?' he asked.

'Because she wants to train in Wrath I would guess,' replied Falco.

'Not to annoy her father?' suggested Malaki and Falco pursed his lips.

'It's possible,' he said. 'You know what she's like. She's always had a wayward streak.'

'But she can't compete with the other men,' said Malaki.

'She's as good as any on the shorter range,' argued Falco. 'Better than most,' he added.

'I know. But it's the timed shoot at battle range that decides the places,' persisted Malaki. 'Her bow's too light. She'll never hold a group.'

Falco had to agree. He looked at the bow that Bryna carried. It was relatively short with a pronounced recurve to the limbs. The design gave her arrows greater speed and made the most of Bryna's lighter draw-weight, but Malaki was right, it could not compete with the men's heavier bows. She could certainly reach the greater distances but her arrows would follow a far steeper arc and as a result her accuracy would suffer. She might impress the crowd with her smooth release and grouping at close and medium range but, when it came to firing under pressure at full battle range, Bryna Godwyn was quite simply outmatched.

'Still,' said Malaki wistfully. 'You've got to admire her spirit.'

Falco laughed as Malaki repeated the words that he himself had just spoken. It was a hopeless case of misplaced affection. Malaki had been in love with Bryna since the first time she had entered his father's forge as a young girl.

'I'm told you make the finest arrow points in town,' she had said in a tone that was far too lofty for her tender years.

Malaki's father had inclined his head modestly.

'I'll take two dozen,' she had continued, 'by tomorrow morning.'

Malaki's father had wiped his hands on his apron as he fought to hide the smile on his face.

'You can have your two dozen,' he told her. 'But they'll not be ready till the end of the week.'

It was clear that the ten-year old Bryna had not expected to be challenged, but she held her ground and gave a stiff little nod.

'Done,' said Malaki's father and spitting in his palm he had extended his hand.

Bryna had stared with revulsion at the smith's large grimy hand but not wanting to appear shaken she had spat in her own palm and sealed the deal with a handshake. Then, with a flick of auburn curls, she had left.

Malaki's father had turned to his son. He had raised his eyebrows in amusement then laughed at his son's enraptured expression as Malaki watched her walk out of the forge.

'She's not even that pretty,' teased Falco.

Malaki blushed and punched Falco in the side of the knee.

'And she's a noble,' Falco went on, being careful to move out of range. 'And she barely knows that you exist.'

Falco had to dodge as Malaki reached for him again, and in doing so he lost half the remaining pastries on his tray.

'Danté!'

The harsh cry preceded a tall skinny servant with a pudding bowl haircut and a small severe mouth. It was Ambrose, Bellius Snidesson's personal manservant. He had been appointed the day's Master of Service and until now Falco had managed to keep out of his way.

'You're a disgrace, Danté!' snapped Ambrose in a fierce whisper. He cast a venomous glance in Malaki's direction, but today the pavilion was his domain and he was not about to be intimidated by the blacksmith's son. 'Clear up this mess!'

Here he actually yanked Falco down to the floor by the arm of his tunic. He might have done more, but Malaki pulled back the flap of the pavilion and made it clear that, Bellius's man or not, he was well prepared to give him a good hiding. Ambrose took note of the threat and stepped back from Falco.

'Go through to the back when you're done,' he said. 'Wine, cold meats and cheese. If you have to be here you might as well try and make yourself useful.'

And with that Ambrose melted back into the crowds, smiling and talking in a sickeningly obsequious tone.

'Ugh!' said Malaki, disgusted. 'Now that's enough to make me throw up.'

Falco laughed as he gathered the scattered food back onto his tray. But as he got back to his feet he felt the weight of someone watching him. He turned to see Simeon leaning back in his chair. His master's face was not happy, his scarred brow creased in a disapproving frown.

19

'I should go,' said Falco, feeling suddenly guilty that he might have let Simeon down.

Malaki nodded. 'See you after the melee,' he said.

For a moment Falco just held his eye. 'Good luck,' he said. 'And when you get the chance, be sure to fight with all your heart.'

Malaki frowned at his friend's earnestness. Then he smiled.

'I always fight with all my heart,' he said. 'It's what makes me so damn good.'

Falco flicked a crust of pastry at him and the flap in the side of the pavilion closed.

Ballymudge

Falco was kept so busy over the next couple of hours that he saw little of the trials. However, by early afternoon most of the guests had finished eating and were settled in their seats, enjoying a fine display of martial skill. It had been a good day for Caer Dour, with four of the spearmen being invited to train at the Academy of War. With them would go three of those who fought with sword and shield and not one, but two of the cavalry cadets who had just completed a thrilling bout of mounted combat.

Falco's back ached as he stood to one side of the pavilion trying not to spill the drinks on his tray. His chest had started to tighten and he was desperate for a rest but Ambrose seemed determined that he should not get one. Falco's lip curled in dislike as he watched the manservant fill his master's cup with wine for the fifth time. If Bellius had been annoying before then he was fast becoming insufferable. His son was one of the two cavalrymen chosen to return with the emissary to Wrath.

It had come down to a head-to-head clash between Jarek and Owen. Despite ten minutes of intense fighting, neither youth had been able to land a clear blow. Then Jarek's horse had lost its footing and the contest appeared to be over. Any other rider would have been thrown, but Jarek held his seat and launched a counter attack as his horse surged back to its feet. The fight resumed and was only brought to an end when the emissary rose from his chair and raised a hand to stop it. He called the exhausted cadets forward and asked them the question that they longed to hear.

'The Queen of Wrath has need of such as you,' he began. 'Will you give up your wealth and privilege and return with me to Wrath?'

The youths' faces had glowed.

'I will,' they answered together.

The crowd was still muttering excitedly and the field was being cleared in preparation for the archers when Falco felt the presence of someone standing behind him.

'Jarek fought well.'

Falco did not turn round at the sound of his master's voice. Simeon spoke as if he had seen every exchange of the contest and, for all that he detested Bellius's son, Falco had to agree that Jarek deserved his success.

'He did,' was all he said.

'And what about you?' Simeon asked. 'Are you still determined to go through with this?'

Falco's heart skipped a beat. He had two secret plans for the day. Simeon knew of the first, but no one knew of the second.

'I am,' he said quietly.

'Then you need to rest,' said his master. 'You look like you're about to collapse.'

Simeon called another servant over but Falco was reluctant to give up his tray.

'Ambrose will have my guts.'

'Ambrose is not your master,' said Simeon. 'Now sit.'

Falco surrendered as Simeon pressed him into a chair. Then the old battle mage placed his hand in the centre of his back and Falco felt a familiar tingling sensation as something of Simeon's power flooded his body with warmth.

'Thank you,' he said as the tightness in his chest eased.

'Just be sure to choose your moment carefully,' said Simeon. 'When the melee is over you will only have a minute in which to act. You must announce your challenge before the trials are called to an end.'

Falco nodded his understanding and Simeon moved away to retake his seat.

Taking a few deep breaths, Falco looked out onto the field. The archery targets had been set in place and the shooting lines drawn with powdered chalk. Then, as he watched, the archers were invited to take up their positions. People in the pavilion were going back to their seats and Falco found himself looking across at Merryweather's son.

The two of them were of similar age. Tobias's disability made people feel uncomfortable but Falco had always liked him. Despite being trapped in a body that robbed him of dignity he always appeared cheerful and happy. Even now, as the archers took their places he rocked back and forth excitedly, waving his dolls and bashing them together in mock combat. But then one of the dolls came loose from his wrist and dropped under the table.

Falco looked up to see if Tobias's father had noticed, but Merryweather was engaged in a lively conversation with a group of nobles, so Falco left his seat and ducked under the table to retrieve the wooden knight himself. When he got back to his feet Tobias was looking at him, a dribble of saliva running down his chin. He smiled and laughed as Falco struggled to tie the knight back around his wrist.

'Ankh oo, Ballymudge,' mumbled Tobias and Falco could not help but smile.

Ballymudge was the pet name that Merryweather's son had given Falco when they had first met as children. Everyone had tried to correct him, but Tobias was insistent and it was a small indulgence to grant the crippled child.

'Ah, Falco. That's uncommonly kind of you.' Merryweather's deep voice was full of warmth as he took over the task of securing the knight to his son's twitching wrist.

'Ballymudge,' said Tobias, holding up the restored knight.

'Yes,' said his father, wiping his son's face once more. 'You and your Ballymudge.' Merryweather looked at Falco. 'Talks about you all the time,' he said. 'Even does a good impression of your wheezing.'

Falco smiled tightly.

'He means no offence of course,' laughed Merryweather. 'He's fond of you, that's all.'

Falco smiled and backed away to his seat.

'Now,' said Merryweather, settling himself down beside his son. 'Let's see what Mistress Godwyn has to offer the Court of Wrath.'

It was quite obvious that Merryweather was relishing Bryna's decision to enter the trials, but Falco could empathise with her father's embarrassment. As much as he admired her courage, Falco had no wish to see her make a fool of

22

herself. He looked out onto the field as the archers lined up on the shooting line, examining their equipment to hide the nervous tension.

Favourite to win was Allyster Mollé, a young nobleman of at least six foot two. Challenging Allyster were several others, chief among which was Brachus de Goyne, a black haired youth with an unpleasant set to his bearded jaw. There were nods of acknowledgement from the archers to either side of Bryna but no one expected her to be a contender so it was easy to be polite.

Finally the range was set at fifty yards and the marshals cleared the field. The archers would fire sixty arrows each before their scores were compared. The arrows would be shot in rounds of six, so each of them selected six arrows that were as closely matched as possible. Then they stepped up to the firing line and straddled the slender line of chalk.

There was a sheen of sweat on Bryna's face but she looked composed and determined as she nocked her first arrow to the string. At the end of the firing line, his black flag raised in the air, the marshal waited for their attention. When all the archers were ready he called out for all to hear.

'Archers. In your own time. Loose!'

The black flag came down and the archers turned their attention to the small gold circles at the centre of each target.

Like everyone else in Caer Dour, Falco knew what the discipline of archery required: good technique, concentration and consistency. Bryna Godwin possessed all three qualities and, as her arrows began to thud into the target, it was clear that she was not here on a whim. Shaft after shaft leapt from her bow to find the gold. Not every arrow found its mark, but of the twenty archers standing on the line, not one of them was holding a group as tight as Bryna's.

Falco watched as she nocked another arrow and raised her bow. There was no stiffness in her back or shoulders and her right elbow was raised high as she drew back the string until one finger nestled in the corner of her mouth. She held the draw for just a second and then, at the very point of release, she actually closed her eyes, as if for that last crucial moment she wanted to shut out every possible distraction.

It was clear from the whispers in the pavilion that Falco was not the only one to spot this peculiar trait and, as the first shoot came to an end, the audience showed their appreciation as Bryna was awarded the gold ribbon for the highest final score. Falco leaned back to see if he could catch a glimpse of Sir Gerallt's reaction to his daughter's success. He caught sight of the stern-faced knight and despite his continuing embarrassment there was an unmistakable glow of pride in his eyes.

Falco smiled and turned to watch as the targets were being moved back to one hundred yards. Once again the marshal's black flag came down and the archers let their arrows fly but now, when the five dozen had all been fired, the shortcomings of Bryna's lighter bow were beginning to show. She had dropped from first to fourth place. That would not be enough to secure a place at the academy and the greatest challenge was yet to come.

There was something like disappointment in the murmuring of the crowd as the shooting lines were swept away and the targets moved even further back. Still standing in a vaguely straight line, the archers milled about as they waited for the marshals to set the targets down. No one knew what the final range would be. They would have to use their judgement to gauge the distance as best they could. This was one of the elements that made the final shoot so challenging. The other was the imperative of time.

The rules were simple... Fire twenty arrows as quickly as you could. The first to finish would end the shoot and the highest score would win. Yes, the rules were simple but the reality was not. Fire too quickly and your aim would suffer, fire too slowly and you might lose the chance to score with all your arrows.

Among the archers the mounting tension was clearly visible. They filled their quivers with twenty arrows then watched as the marshals finally set the targets down.

'What do you think, Master Danté?' said Merryweather leaning across to speak to Falco. 'Must be close on two hundred yards?'

Falco nodded in agreement.

The archers waited while the field was cleared. Some of them took a few steps forward, some a few steps back as they tried to estimate the distance to the targets. Bryna however, did not move. She stood staring intently at the target, her bow held firmly in her left hand. Then she turned to watch as the marshal raised his flag,

Falco felt a flutter of nervous excitement as the marshal's flag hung in the air. *'Just do your best,'* he thought. *'The people will understand.'*

'This shoot is at unmarked battle range,' the marshal called out. 'The first to fire twenty arrows will end the shoot. Arrows loosed after the white flags have been raised will not count.'

He waited for all the archers to give their acknowledgement and Falco held his breath as the marshal paused. The archers were ready, hands poised above their arrows.

'Archers, in your own time.'

The marshal waited another second.

'Loose!'

The flag came down and a great gasp of astonishment exploded from the crowd. Of all the twenty archers nineteen quickly snatched an arrow from their quivers, but there was one among them who did not reach for an arrow.

When the marshal's flag came down Bryna dropped her hand from her quiver and started to run, sprinting down the range towards the targets. Her actions obviously confused the other archers and she was thirty yards ahead of them before the first arrow arched over her head. The crowd was in uproar.

Was that allowed?

Was she allowed to do that?

There had been no reaction from the marshals. There was no marked shooting line so there was nothing to say exactly where the archers had to stand. The rules had not been broken and Bryna ran on.

A second volley of arrows arched over her head as Bryna closed on the targets. She had to get close enough to negate the advantage of the men's more powerful bows. Only then would it come down to the two things in which she excelled... speed and skill. Most of the archers had fired three arrows by the time Bryna skidded to a halt. She dropped to one knee and stole another moment to gain her composure. Then she reached back over her shoulder, grabbed an arrow and began to fire. And now the crowd began to cheer.

Bryna's hands moved in a blur as she nocked her arrows, drew and loosed with blinding speed.

Falco had never seen anyone fire so quickly and it seemed only a few seconds before she leapt to her feet and thrust her hand into the air. Seven arrows traced an arc over her head, but the white flags had gone up and the marshals were watching. Not one of those arrows would count. Bryna had fired her twenty. The timed shoot at battle range was over.

The pavilion was in shock. Nobody had ever seen anything like it and yet no one could say that Bryna had broken the rules. It was just that no one had ever thought to do such a thing before. Bellius was predictably furious and many of the other nobles were indignant, but there were just as many who were amused and some who were even impressed. And there was at least one who was clearly delighted by Bryna's unconventional tactics.

'Bravo!' shouted Merryweather excitedly. 'Bravo!' The jolly rotund man was on his feet and clapping for all he was worth.

Falco shook his head as he watched the marshals come together in a huddle. The scores had been tallied. There was a tie. After a prolonged discussion that set the crowd muttering, two of the archers were invited to come and stand before the pavilion. One was the favourite, Allyster Mollé. The other was Bryna Godwin.

The muttering turned to cheers as the victors approached the pavilion and the emissary stood to receive them. He looked at Allyster and gave the young nobleman a nod of congratulations. Then his attention shifted to Bryna and his expression became more severe.

'You would be in dire trouble if you let the enemy get that close in a real battle, Mistress Godwyn,' he said.

Bryna swallowed hard and her flushed face grew a shade redder.

'But if they ever did get that close,' the emissary went on, 'I'm sure you would make them pay.'

'I would, my lord,' said Bryna with a slight tremor in her voice.

Finally the emissary's expression softened. The weathered creases of his face broke into a smile, but when he addressed them it was in a tone of grave solemnity.

'The Queen of Wrath has need of such as you,' he began. 'Will you give up your wealth and privilege and return with me to Wrath?'

'I will,' they said together.

Allyster was clearly elated by the emissary's favour, but Bryna's eyes searched the pavilion for another face. The face of one whose approval she valued so much more.

Falco leaned back until he could see Bryna's father. Then he watched as they shared a private, unspoken moment. Sir Gerallt's expression remained stern as he looked down upon his daughter, but then the corner of his mouth lifted almost imperceptibly and he gave the smallest of nods. Bryna's composure almost slipped as her bottom lip began to tremble, but she would not embarrass her father with tears. She did, however, allow herself a smile, a smile that lit up her face like a sunrise.

'All right,' breathed Falco as if Malaki were sitting beside him. 'Maybe she is quite pretty.'

5

The Challenge

For the first time in the day Falco had gone out of his way to look for a job, but not just any job. He wanted something that would require him to be near the front of the pavilion as the trials drew to a close. And so, as the archery targets were cleared away, he found himself standing just ten feet to the emissary's left with a tray of sweets and heady-smelling liqueurs.

The day of the trials was almost over. Only one event remained, the chaotic free-for-all known as the melee. There was no coveted place at the academy of War for the winner, but the melee was still the most eagerly anticipated spectacle of the day and the reason for this was obvious. The melee was open to anyone, noble and low-born alike. Anyone who fancied their chances was invited to enter. This was a contest for all the people of Caer Dour so it was no surprise to see young men ambling into view from every corner of the field.

Each was armed with a round-shield and longsword. Forged from a white metal alloy, the edge of these blades was rounded and dull. They might not cut like a live blade but they could still break bones and bruise unprotected flesh. The pale alloy had the added advantage of leaving a silvery mark wherever it struck, an invaluable aid to the marshals whose job it was to identify the 'wounded' and the 'slain'.

Falco scanned the figures, looking for his friend's distinctive blue-steel armour. Malaki's armour was not burnished to a mirrored finish. It was not engraved or inlaid with silver or gold. Except for a light sheen of oil it looked just as it did when it was drawn from the forge's fire. The distinctive blue lustre of the steel told the armourer when the metal had reached just the right temperature, retaining flexibility while adding a hardness that would turn all but the most violent of blows.

Malaki had made the armour himself and it was clear to all where his future lay.

'Yes,' thought Falco as he continued to scan the crowd. 'Malaki would make a good blacksmith, but he would make a better knight.' All Malaki had to do was win the melee and *he* would do the rest. Finally his friend strode onto the field and Falco drew a calming breath.

Malaki's arrival was noted by all. Some gave a friendly, if somewhat wary smile, others simply returned his nods of acknowledgement, while many of the nobles tried a little too hard to pretend that they had not seen him at all. Bellius's son Jarek simply stared at Malaki with open contempt. Unlike most of the others on the field he believed he was a match for Malaki de Vane. He was wrong of course, but he was too conceited to know it.

The young men continued to weigh each other up as a large anvil was brought forward and set down just a few yards in front of the pavilion. The striking of the anvil would mark the various rounds of the melee. This was an age-old tradition and, with the anvil in place, the marshals called the melee to order.

The assembled men came forward and the crowd seemed to lean in closer as the marshals' spokesman addressed them.

'Men of Caer Dour,' he began. 'You all know the rules of the melee.'

'There are none!' roared the crowd in what was clearly a long-standing joke.

The marshal smiled indulgently before he went on. 'This is an open contest where every man fights for himself.'

There were jeers from the crowd as if they thought the marshal's rules were altogether too boring.

'The melee will be split into four rounds,' he continued, 'with each round being marked by the sounding of the anvil.'

Everyone looked at the anvil and the burly man standing behind it with a large hammer in his hand.

'Anyone spending more than five seconds on the ground will be removed from the melee.'

'Boo!' screamed the crowd.

'Anyone suffering a significant injury will be removed from the melee.'

'Boo!' cried the crowd and even the contestants smiled at their appetite for blood.

'And...' the marshal added, being sure that they were all paying particular notice, 'Anyone showing a strike to a critical area at the end of a round will be removed from the melee.'

'Boo!' cried the crowd but now the smiles and the laughter were fading away. The marshals had moved into position ready to observe the fighting from every possible angle.

Falco felt a familiar presence at his shoulder.

'It's all down to Malaki now,' said Simeon.

Falco nodded. His stomach was churning with nerves.

'He'll do it,' he said. 'There's no one out there to match him.'

Simeon nodded his concurrence. Falco was not the only one who thought well of Malaki's fighting ability.

Finally the melee was ready to begin. The contestants had spread out evenly across the field with just a few yards between each of them. Their positions were essentially random and Falco was satisfied to see that Jarek was on the far side of the field.

Helms were settled, shields were armed and swords were raised but, as the final manoeuvrings took place, Falco began to sense that something was wrong. The contestants around Malaki seemed just a fraction too close. Malaki had clearly chosen one or two that he would engage from the start but others, who 'seemed' to have chosen different targets were actually angled more in his direction. Falco frowned and the drinks on his tray clinked together ominously.

'What is it?' asked Simeon.

'It's the spacing,' said Falco, raising a hand to point. 'It doesn't look right. It looks as if they're going to...'

Falco's words were cut off as the hammer came down on the anvil and the melee burst into a storm of combat.

Falco watched as Malaki darted forward. He blocked a blow with his sword then charged his first target with his shield. The poor man was thrown off balance and Malaki swept his feet from under him before delivering a 'fatal' blow to his downed opponent.

It all happened incredibly quickly and Malaki was already turning to his second target when the first unexpected attack took him off guard. He reacted swiftly and parried the blow with his shield, spinning round to launch a counter-attack, but as he did so three other contestants rushed at him simultaneously. He engaged one sword with his own but two others found their mark. One struck him hard on the back of his leg while the other slashed him in the side just below his armoured breastplate. He whirled away and tried to launch an assault of his own, but the damage was done. There were two silvery marks on critical areas of his body. His attackers retreated, seeking out new opponents, opponents who were still in with a chance of winning.

Malaki's chances were over. He was out.

'They jumped him!'

Falco could not believe his eyes.

'Four of them jumped him, all at the same time.'

Falco felt someone relieve him of his tray as sweets and liqueurs spilled onto the floor. He stared out across the field to where Malaki stood amid the chaos of the ongoing struggle. For a moment the big youth remained there as if he did not know what to do. Then one of the marshals reached him and drew him clear of the fighting. Clearly in a daze Malaki allowed himself to be led to the side of the field where his father, Balthazak de Vane, was waiting for him.

Falco's heart ached as he watched Balthazak remove Malaki's helm and take his son into a tight embrace. Somewhere, in the far distance he heard a loud metallic ring as the hammer marked the end of the first round. Three more times the anvil sounded dimly in Falco's ears and still he could not quite believe it. His great plan, his great gesture of friendship, it had all come to nothing. Malaki was supposed to win. How could it all have gone so wrong?

'I'm sorry, Falco.'

Falco felt Simeon's hand on his shoulder and slowly his senses returned to normal. He looked out from the pavilion as the winner of the melee was being brought forward by the marshals.

It was Jarek.

Bellius stepped forward to applaud his son who was surrounded by a gaggle of his friends. They were all celebrating his victory but they were also laughing uproariously. Something had obviously tickled their fancy.

Jarek stepped away from his friends and, looking up at his father, he raised a finger as if he were scolding a naughty child. Bellius placed a hand on his chest and raised his eyebrows as if to say, *'who, me!'*

Realisation dawned on Falco.

Bellius had planned it all along. One way or another he had contrived to have several of the contestants 'choose' Malaki as their first target in the melee. By the time they realised what was going on it was too late. Malaki was out.

Falco's thin hands clenched into fists, but as he turned towards Bellius he felt Simeon's grip tighten on his arm.

'No, Falco,' said the old battle mage. 'It would serve no purpose.'

Falco tried to pull away, but even in his sixties Simeon had no problem restraining his feeble servant. Falco bit down on the frustration and turned away from the celebrations. He did not see the anger on Darius's face nor the disgust on the face of Sir William. All he could feel was his own disappointment and that of his friend. Even the crowd seemed more subdued than was usual at the conclusion of the trials.

Finally Bellius stepped forward to address them and he could not have been more full of himself.

'People of Caer Dour,' he began. 'Today is a great day. Not only have eleven of our finest been chosen to train at the Academy of War, but one who has finished his training has returned home to us.'

The crowd cheered as Darius rose to his feet.

'It is many years since the shadow of madness darkened the reputation of this town.'

Here more than one person cast a look in Falco's direction.

'But today that shame is wiped clean. Today we welcome home our new champion, the greatest battle mage that Caer Dour has ever known. Darius Voltario!'

Darius was clearly embarrassed by Bellius's exaggerated praise but he raised his hand to acknowledge the crowd's enthusiasm as Bellius's voice took on a more serious tone.

'And how timely is his return.' Bellius nodded gravely. 'Surely we see the hand of fate at work. For even now a Ferocian army closes on our town, an army of the Possessed with a demon at their head.'

The crowds cheerful enthusiasm evaporated as Bellius reminded them of the danger that was advancing on their homes.

'Yes,' said Bellius. 'Surely fate is smiling upon us. For now we have a warrior who can stand against the demon that would claim our souls.'

Bellius was getting into his stride, but Falco was deaf to his words. He felt no rousing of the blood. He felt only the bitter pain of disappointment and a growing sense of hate.

'The Ferocian army broke through the Illician defences,' Bellius went on. 'But it will not break the men of Valentia, and today we have seen why. The warriors of Valentia are the finest in all the Seven Kingdoms. Today we fought in a spirit of comradeship and competition. But tomorrow many of you will ride out to fight for our very survival. So I declare this a day of special celebration, a day of triumph. And I declare the trials ov...'

'Wait!'

The single word carried the weight of conviction and people looked round to see who it was that had spoken. They looked to Sir William Chevalier, to Darius and even to Simeon, but no one looked in the direction of Falco Danté.

Clearly annoyed at being interrupted Bellius was about to speak once more.

'Wait!' repeated Falco and now there was no mistaking the speaker.

People looked at him in disbelief, but Falco was beyond caring.

'The trials are not over,' he said, holding Bellius's seething gaze. 'I have a challenge to make.'

'You?' said Bellius in a tone that could not have been more scornful. '*You* have a challenge to make?'

'I do.'

Bellius was clearly furious at what he saw as a ridiculous proposition, but everyone knew that, servant or not, Falco was within his rights.

'Let us hear it then,' said Bellius with a mocking grin. 'Who do you wish to challenge?'

'The challenge comes not from me,' said Falco. 'I speak on behalf of another.'

'Who?' snapped Bellius and his tone made it clear that his patience was nearing its end.

'Malaki de Vane,' said Falco.

'The blacksmith's son?' sneered Bellius, but now his grin seemed just a little forced. 'The one who was just knocked out in the first round of the melee?'

'The same.'

'Well,' laughed Bellius as if he expected everyone to agree that this was utterly preposterous. 'Well,' he said again when people simply waited for him to continue. 'To make such a challenge you will need two votes of confidence, one from the warrior class and one from the nobles.'

Now his smile grew more confident for he could think of no one who would sanction such a challenge. He was about to dismiss the whole affair when Simeon stepped forward to stand at Falco's side.

'I vote for the challenge of Malaki de Vane.'

The pavilion was suddenly filled with gasps and whispers of surprise and the muttering spread outwards as word of the challenge reached the crowd.

From the corner of his eye Falco saw Malaki's father leading his son forward to stand before the pavilion. Malaki still looked utterly dejected and when he glanced up at Falco his expression seemed to suggest that he did not relish the idea of being made to look a fool twice in one day. But Falco ignored his friend's silent entreaty.

'Fine!' snapped Bellius, who could not believe that this farce had been allowed to go so far. 'That's one vote from the noble class. Now all you need...'

'You mistake me!' said Simeon, cutting him off. 'I do not speak as a noble. I vote as one from the warrior class.'

'But your house?' objected Bellius. 'Your wealth and lands?'

'A gift,' said Simeon, 'from a friend, long dead.'

Bellius laughed as if he were surprised to have been so duped. But now his laughter and his smile were genuine.

'Well then,' he said. 'All we need now is a vote from the noble class.' Here he looked round at his fellow nobles with a thinly veiled threat in his eyes. 'Who will second this challenge?'

'I will!' said Falco.

Stunned disbelief echoed round the pavilion as all eyes turned once again to Falco.

'What?' said Bellius. 'You! A servant!'

Many of the nobles had begun to laugh as if this was all some kind of ill-judged joke but then Simeon spoke again.

31

'Once again you are mistaken,' said the old battle mage calmly. 'Falco Danté is not a servant, but the son of a noble lord. He has merely chosen to serve.'

People were speechless. Even the whispers had ceased, but Bellius was beside himself with indignation.

'He was sworn into service to pay for his father's crimes!'

'No, Bellius,' said Simeon. 'He was not. He passed into my care as part of a promise that I made to his father.'

'But this is ridiculous,' gasped Bellius. 'Everyone knows that he has served in your household for years.'

'That is true,' replied Simeon. 'But he served out of choice and not out of obligation. Falco is of noble birth and his vote will count.'

Bellius's dark eyes flashed from Simeon to Falco. He looked like a cornered animal and for a moment it seemed like he might lose his composure. But then the smile returned to his face.

'So be it,' he said. 'Your challenge is noted. Let the challenger come forward.'

Falco turned away from Bellius as Malaki's father propelled his son towards the pavilion. Balthazak was as surprised as anyone to hear that Falco retained his noble lineage, but he was not about to pass up on this chance to improve his son's prospects.

Malaki was clearly in shock as he stumbled forward to stand before the pavilion. He seemed unaware that he was now the absolute centre of attention. Instead he stared up at the person he *had* thought he knew, the person who had been his friend for as long as he could remember. There was an unsettling frown on his brow and a dangerous light in his dark brown eyes. But then he seemed to see something in Falco's face that smoothed the frown and softened the light in his eyes.

What he saw was fear. Not fear of repercussions from the nobles, but fear that his judgement might have been in error. It was the fear that he might have lost his friend.

Falco's breath was locked in his chest as Malaki stared up at him, but then the frown faded from his friend's face and something like a smile appeared in his eyes. It was a smile that said, *'You're an idiot Falco Danté. And when this is over I'm going to bloody kill you!'*

'So Master de Vane,' drawled Bellius unpleasantly. 'Will you choose a knight to answer your challenge or will your sickly lordling do it for you?'

Malaki's eyes moved from one noble face to the next. There were some fine warriors among them but Malaki could not imagine any of them going against Bellius to accept his challenge. Sir Gerallt Godwin might but Malaki had no wish to put Bryna's father in an awkward position.

Once again it was Falco who broke the silence.

'I will choose,' he said.

Bellius smiled and gestured with his hand as if it made little difference who did the choosing. When it came to the nobles of Caer Dour, Bellius Snidesson simply wielded too much power.

32

An uncomfortable silence followed in which all eyes were on Falco. He cast a final glance in Malaki's direction then turned back to Bellius, but the nobleman said nothing as he waited for Falco to speak. The pause became strained and Bellius raised his eyebrows impatiently, but Falco's mouth had gone suddenly dry. Then he licked his lips and spoke.

'I choose Sir William Chevalier,' he said.

'I choose the Queen's emissary.'

6
Servant or Noble Lord

If people had been surprised by what went before they were struck dumb by what Falco now proposed, that the royal envoy from the Court of Wrath would accept a challenge of combat from the son of the town's blacksmith. Even Bellius was speechless.

'Wha... I... this...' he blustered incoherently.

He gave a nervous little laugh but any trace of humour had vanished from his face. He seemed about to speak again when a tall figure loomed behind him and every one turned to look at Sir William.

The emissary moved past Bellius until he stood just a few feet in front of Falco. Until now Falco had not realised just what an imposing figure the emissary was, but he held his ground and forced himself to look up into the man's hard grey eyes.

'What is your name, boy?'

'Falco, my lord,' said Falco, feeling more intimidated than he ever had in his life. 'Falco Danté.'

'Danté?' repeated the emissary as if the name were not unknown to him.

'Yes,' said Bellius from behind him. 'This is the son of Aquila Danté, the man who brought dishonour on this town.'

The emissary's eyes slid to one side, but apart from this small gesture of annoyance he ignored Bellius's remark.

'And why do *you* not fight in the trials?' he asked.

'Hah!' scoffed Bellius and his scorn was echoed by many of the nobles in the pavilion who laughed as if the very idea was unthinkable.

'Falco is not without skill,' said Simeon at Falco's shoulder.

'No,' said Bellius. 'Not so long as the sword is a willow switch and the contest lasts no more than a second or two.' Again Bellius's unkindness found support and Falco hung his head in shame. 'Master Danté suffers from poor health,' explained Bellius. 'I understand his condition has a name, though it could more easily be described as feebleness.'

Again more laughter, but there were also many who bowed their heads at Bellius's cruelty.

'Falco is cursed with scarlet consumption,' said Simeon and his sightless gaze made it clear that Bellius would do well to cease his taunting. 'He has been afflicted with it since childhood.'

At the mention of this disease the emissary's gaze flicked up to Falco's brow where a distinctive rash was just visible beneath the line of his hair. The corners of his mouth turned down and his eyes narrowed suspiciously as if he had reason to doubt this diagnosis.

The emissary's apparent doubt hurt Falco more than any of Bellius's taunts, but he had come to terms with his physical shortcomings long ago. Doubt and derision were nothing new to him so he raised his face and met the emissary's eyes once more.

'And what do you hope to gain from this challenge, Master Danté?' asked the emissary.

'For myself, nothing.'

'And for your friend?'

'Only that you judge him as you would any other man who fights today. And if he wins, that you might consider taking him with you back to Wrath.'

There were gasps of astonishment from every direction but the emissary simply smiled.

'If he wins?' he said with genuine amusement.

Falco nodded indignantly.

'He wouldn't keep his sword a minute,' said the emissary with a glint in his stone-grey eyes.

'It'll be at your throat in two,' said Falco and even he was surprised by his boldness.

The emissary's smile returned as he acknowledged the boast.

'And what makes you think that the Queen's envoy would accept your challenge?' he asked.

This at least was one question that Falco was prepared for. Unlike Valentia, where the laws of noble birth applied, Illicia was a meritocracy. That is to say that effort and accomplishment were valued above the chance fortunes of a man's birth.

'You are a man of Illicia,' he said. 'You would not think it beneath you to accept a challenge from even the lowliest of peasants.'

For a moment the emissary held Falco's gaze. Then the smile faded from his face.

'I'll give you your two minutes,' he said. 'If your friend still holds his sword at the end of the challenge I will *consider* him for a place at the academy.'

Falco's heart soared.

'However,' cautioned the emissary. 'We shall not fight with round tip blunts. It would be no great achievement for him to keep his sword in the face of a sword that cannot kill. We fight with live blades or not at all.'

Falco had not anticipated this but it was too late to back out now. Without even looking at Malaki he gave a decisive nod.

'So be it,' said the emissary, unpinning his cloak. Then he turned to Bellius as if the matter were decided. 'Have a taper cut to two minutes.'

'But... but...' stammered Bellius but things had gone too far for even him to stop.

The emissary walked to the edge of the pavilion while the people of Caer Dour crowded round, forming a natural arena for the two men to fight in.

'Who will lend the blacksmith a blade?' said the emissary as he unbuckled his sword belt.

'He can use mine,' said Simeon, removing his own belt and handing his sword to Falco.

Falco smiled at his master and walked to the edge of the pavilion. The sword seemed to resonate in his hands as if it were ringing with a high clear note. For a moment he hesitated and Simeon gave him searching look.

Bringing his attention back to the task in hand Falco looked down from the pavilion and threw the sword to Malaki but it landed short and people laughed as

Malaki bent to retrieve it from the ground. As he straightened up the big youth nodded his thanks to Simeon. Then his gaze shifted to look at Falco.

And when you get the chance, be sure to fight with all your heart.

'So this is what you meant...'

Malaki's brown eyes shone and it was clear that he did not intend to waste this opportunity to regain some measure of pride. With something approaching reverence he drew Simeon's sword and placed the belt and scabbard on the raised edge of the pavillion. Then he moved to take up his position in the 'arena'.

The emissary moved to the middle of the platform where two broad steps led down onto the tournament field. Then, as he switched his sword from one hand to the other, Falco caught sight of something that caused the breath to catch in his throat. It was a small insignia carved into the blade just below the hilt. No one else seemed to have seen it, or if they had they did not know what it meant. The design showed the stylised form of three mountain peaks. It was the emblem of an order of knights whose reputation was legendary.

It was the emblem of the Knights Adamant.

William Chevalier belonged to one of the most fearsome military bodies that the world had ever known.

'Oh, shit!' thought Falco. *'What have I done!'*

The blood drained from his face as he watched the emissary walk out to face his friend. Malaki looked surprisingly calm and Falco resisted the urge to shout a warning. Maybe it was better that Malaki remained ignorant of what he faced. Two of the marshals came forward with pieces of armour but the emissary waved them away. He would fight with no more protection than his normal clothes might provide. In response Malaki declined the helmet that his father was holding out to him, a gesture that was clearly deemed foolish by the crowd.

Finally the two men stood opposite each other and the emissary looked across to the pavilion. Two of the marshals stood ready with a candle and a thin waxed taper suspended on a slender metal tray. The taper would burn for exactly two minutes and they waited only for the emissary to give them the word.

'In your own time,' he told them before turning to face Malaki.

'This is a free challenge between Malaki de Vane and Sir William Chevalier of Eltz,' the marshal's spokesman announced. 'This is a time-limited challenge,' he added. 'If, after two minutes, Master de Vane still retains his sword then the challenge will be judged a success.'

The people of Caer Dour held their breath.

'Combatants, are you ready?'

Two nods gave the spokesman his answer.

The candle was brought in and the taper began to burn.

'Fight!' the spokesman shouted and the two men charged each other with a speed that took everyone by surprise.

The first clash of swords was so fast and violent that Falco was certain his friend was doomed. For all his size Malaki was still young but if anyone thought the emissary might go easy on him they were wrong.

Sir William pressed forward with a series of blows that had Malaki retreating so fast that many in the crowd were forced to scramble out of harm's way, but then the blacksmith's son launched an attack of his own. He aimed a

36

blow at the emissary's neck then switched low as if he meant to take his opponent's leg off at the knee.

Each blow was met with a sure and certain parry but even so, Malaki's attacks were so powerful that it was now the emissary who was forced to give ground. He backed away slowly as the crowd shifted to give them space.

Falco smiled with satisfaction. Malaki was in his element and for a moment it looked as if he might be getting the upper hand. Then the emissary suddenly stepped forward to meet Malaki's attack. Sparks flew as he caught the younger man's blade with his own. Then before Malaki could disengage the emissary rotated his blade and swept it viciously to one side.

The crowd gasped as Malaki was spun off balance, but the emissary's first attempt to disarm him had failed. Malaki turned his recovery into an attack but the emissary anticipated it and tried once again to whip the sword from Malaki's grasp.

Falco flinched as it seemed certain that Malaki would lose his blade but somehow he held on. He even managed a feint that caught the emissary by surprise. The emissary ducked and Malaki tried to strike him with the hilt of his sword, but the emissary leaned back from the blow and caught Malaki's arm with his free hand. Then before anyone knew what was happening, he spun Malaki round until he had his left arm round his throat and his sword across the big youth's wrist.

Malaki became still as the sharp steel rested against the pulsing veins of his wrist.

A great cry of surprise rose up from the crowd as the scintillating action was suddenly brought to an end. Then, still holding him close, the emissary spoke into his opponent's ear.

'You fought well for a blacksmith's son,' he said, tapping Malaki's wrist meaningfully with his blade. 'Now. Drop your sword!'

Falco clenched his fists and screwed up his face in frustration. He watched as Malaki's sword dipped and his head bowed forward in defeat. He was just closing his eyes with disappointment when Malaki's grip suddenly tightened on his sword and he slammed his head back into the emissary's face.

The crowd gave a collective cry of shock as blood burst across the emissary's face and he staggered back from the heavy blow that had broken his nose. Malaki spun free and whirled to re-engage his opponent. The emissary was clearly shaken by the unexpected attack but when Malaki tried to bring his sword to bear the emissary somehow managed to block it. Still giving ground he parried another attack and another as he blinked the blood and the 'stars' from his eyes.

Malaki tried to press home his advantage but the emissary suddenly stopped retreating and charged forward. The two combatants locked swords and strained against each other but then the emissary shoved Malaki off balance and hammered his elbow into the big youth's mouth. Malaki stumbled backwards, spitting blood, and now the emissary attacked in earnest.

Falco had never seen anyone attack so fast and so hard and Malaki simply crumbled before it. He blocked blows with sheer desperation and for the first time he looked vulnerable and afraid. But the emissary did not stop until Malaki was forced to his knees. Finally he drew a rapid circle with his blade and

Malaki's sword went flying from his grasp. Then the Queen's envoy brought his sword down with lethal swiftness.

The blade came to a halt just an inch from Malaki's neck and the big youth could do nothing but kneel there in the face of defeat. He was spent. He was beaten.

Falco looked on in shock. It was over and the crowd was silent. There was no cheering, no applause. No one knew how to respond. They simply watched as the emissary stood over Malaki with his blade still hovering above his shoulder.

'Ahem!'

The discreet call for attention drew all eyes back to the pavilion.

'Pardon, my lord,' said the marshal's spokesman. 'But... ahh...'

'What is it?' asked Sir William without taking his eyes from Malaki.

'It's the taper, my lord. The two minutes...'

The emissary did not remove his sword but he averted his eyes and angled his head towards the spokesman.

'The disarming came outside the time,' the marshal explained apologetically. 'The challenge counts as a win.'

There was an expectant hush from the crowd as everyone waited to see what the emissary would do. They might have expected indignation. They might have expected embarrassment. They did not expect laughter, soft deep laughter.

Slowly Sir William stood up from his killing stance. He withdrew his sword and wiped his bloody nose on his sleeve. Then he looked down on his opponent and held out his hand. Still dazed and trembling from the exertion Malaki grasped the extended hand as the emissary helped him to his feet. Then to the crowd's huge satisfaction the emissary took Malaki's wrist and held his arm aloft.

Now the crowd could cheer and oh, how they did.

Malaki was dumbfounded but the emissary turned him about to acknowledge the applause on every side. Finally the cheering subsided and the emissary released Malaki's wrist, standing back to look at him.

'You have much to learn, Malaki de Vane,' said the emissary. 'But you fight well, for one so young... Very well,' he repeated, raising a hand to his broken nose.

Malaki looked mortified at what he had done but he was also deeply pleased by the emissary's words. Everyone was entirely satisfied by this wonderful end to the trials but the emissary was not quite finished yet. He watched as Malaki shifted awkwardly under the praise and admiration of the crowd then he caught the young man's eye and held it fast.

'The Queen of Wrath has need of such as you,' he began.

A lump formed in Malaki's throat and tears sprang to his eyes. Everyone knew what was coming next

'Will you give up your wealth and privilege and return with me to Wrath?'

For a second Malaki could not speak. He had neither wealth nor privilege, but everyone knew that the words were merely a formality.

'I will,' he croaked and the crowd's jubilation erupted once more.

The emissary gave a nod of satisfaction and stepped back as people pressed forward to congratulate a hero they could truly call their own. Malaki staggered under the crush of well-meaning enthusiasm. He laughed as his father took him in a great embrace and lifted him from his feet. Then, as his father set him down, he looked over the surrounding wall of people, up into the shadowed light of the pavilion, up into the eyes of his friend.

All the commotion seemed to fade away as the two boys looked at each other. They both knew that this changed everything, that after this day nothing would ever be the same again. Malaki's dreams had just come true, and as for Falco, well he was going to lose the only real friend he had ever known. Both of them knew it, and they both accepted it. And although it went unspoken the message in Malaki's deep brown eyes was clearly understood.

'I am your friend, Falco Danté,' the message said. *'Servant or noble lord, I will always be your friend.'*

Falco's green eyes shone brightly in reply then he watched as the blacksmith's son was hoisted aloft and carried away to join the rest of the cadets who had been victorious in the trials.

7

The Magi

And so the trials were over but not everyone was pleased by the way the day had ended. Many of the nobles shared the view of Bellius Snidesson that the rules had been stretched too far. To think that nobles like Jarek should have to share their glory with the son of a blacksmith. Wearing a scowl of anger Bellius stood to one side of the pavilion and the direction of his gaze made it clear whom he held accountable for the unacceptable events of the day.

Falco tried to ignore the wave of ire directed towards him. All he wanted to do now was to go down and congratulate Malaki and then to leave the pavilion as quietly as he could. He took Simeon's sword from one of the marshals and replaced it in the scabbard that Malaki had left on the edge of the pavilion then he turned to where his master stood at the end of the table.

'Congratulations Falco,' said the old battle mage as he fastened the sword belt around his waist. 'Your harebrained scheme was a success.'

'Thank you master,' said Falco with a self-conscious smile.

'Master?' queried Simeon. 'After today's revelations?'

'If it please you.'

'Is the shame still so great?' asked Simeon quietly.

'I would feel more comfortable,' answered Falco. 'For a while at least.'

'For a while then,' said Simeon. 'But you cannot hide in service forever.'

Falco nodded his understanding.

'Now, go and congratulate your friend.'

Falco turned away and headed for the small flight of steps at the centre of the pavilion, but before he could go any further the emissary appeared at their foot and climbed the steps towards him. He had a white towel pressed to his bloody nose and Falco hoped that he might pass by without stopping. For a moment it appeared that he would, but then the emissary stopped. Taking the blood-stained towel from his face he looked at Falco.

'You have done your friend a great service today,' he said quietly.

Falco averted his eyes as the emissary looked around the pavilion, taking in the tangible hostility that was clearly directed towards him.

'I hope it was worth the price.'

'It was,' said Falco, his green eyes flashing up to meet the emissary's gaze.

The emissary nodded and seemed about to move away, but once again he paused.

'I never met your father,' he said. 'I only ever heard of what he did.'

Falco's face burned with humiliation.

'But I can tell you this, Falco Danté. In his years as a battle mage your father saved many thousands of lives,' the emissary waited until Falco met his gaze once more. 'You can be proud of the way he lived,' he said. 'If not perhaps of the way he died.'

Falco swallowed hard and bowed his head awkwardly.

The emissary ignored his discomfiture and looked instead to Simeon who stood a few steps behind him.

'Scarlet consumption, you say?'

'Since the age of five,' replied Simeon.

The emissary pursed his lips as if he remained unconvinced.

'You have some knowledge of the condition?' asked Simeon as if he could see the doubt on the emissary's face.

'A little,' the emissary said. 'The rash,' he went on, pointing to Falco's scalp, 'is it worse in the winter or the summer months?'

Falco shifted awkwardly as the two men discussed his condition.

'The cold aggravates his lungs,' answered Simeon. 'But the hot days of summer are worse.'

The emissary nodded as if this confirmed his suspicions.

'Was he ever caught in a fire?'

'He was.'

Once again the emissary nodded slowly.

'My sister suffered from a complaint that was mistaken for the crimson lung. By the time we learned the truth she was too weak to survive the cure. Had her true complaint been recognised earlier, she might not have died so young.' He looked at Falco once more as if the sight of him brought back sad and painful memories. 'You might want to speak again with his physician,' he said. 'Ask them about the spores that are released when silver pine trees burn.'

Simeon inclined his head respectfully.

'Thank you,' he said. 'I will do as you suggest.'

The emissary gave Falco a final searching look. Then he pressed the towel back to his nose and moved away.

Falco turned to his master and the old battle mage could sense the question in his eyes. He held up a cautionary hand.

'We'll see Heçamede in the morning. Now go.'

Falco stumbled down the steps in something of a daze. Heçamede Asclepios was one of the town's healers. She had treated Falco since he was a child.

Not scarlet consumption.

Proud of his father.

Could either of these things be possible?

In spite of the injuries he had suffered during their final encounter, Simeon had always spoken in defence of Falco's father, but to hear it from someone outside the town, from the Queen's own representative no less. Well, that was something altogether different. That was something that he could almost believe.

'Falco!'

Falco looked up to see Malaki's father walking towards him.

'Malaki,' Balthazak shouted over his shoulder. 'Here he is! Here's the crazy fool who almost got you killed!'

Falco grimaced then winced as Balthazak swept him into a bear hug and planted a bristly kiss on his cheek.

'My, but you always were a free spirit,' said the blacksmith holding Falco at arm's length. 'Just like your father.'

Falco lowered his eyes then looked up as Malaki appeared beside them. Well-wishers continued to clap him on the back and ruffle his hair but the worst of the crush was over. People were beginning to disperse.

'How's the mouth?' said Falco.

41

'Sore,' said Malaki, taking a bloody cloth from his mouth.

'Well, if you will go challenging one of the Adamanti?' said Balthazak.

'Yeah, right!' scoffed Malaki, but his father just raised his eyebrows.

'You didn't know?'

Malaki looked horrified. 'No,' he said, fixing Falco with an accusing glare. 'I did *not* know.'

'Don't look at me!' said Falco. 'I didn't know either. Well, not until it was too late,' he added ruefully.

'Hah!' laughed Balthazak as if the whole thing were hilarious.

He grabbed them both round the back of the neck and brought their heads hard against his own.

'Marvellous!' he said. 'Bloody marvellous!'

Then he kissed them both and with a final laugh he went off to join the people streaming from the field.

A strange silence fell about them as the two boys watched him leave.

'So,' said Falco, trying to recapture something of the celebratory mood. 'You're off to Wrath.'

'So,' replied Malaki. 'You're a bloody nobleman!'

For a few seconds they looked at each other, then great smiles spread across their faces and they fell into a tight embrace.

'I'll not forget what you did today,' Malaki breathed into Falco's neck.

Falco ignored the crushing pressure that threatened to break his ribs. There was something satisfying about his friend's great strength, something deeply reassuring. He was going to miss it.

'Just a shame you couldn't put up a better fight,' said Falco as the two friends stepped back from each other.

'What would you know, Pastry Boy!' said Malaki giving Falco a shove that sent him stumbling backwards.

'I know he whooped your ass,' said Falco rubbing his shoulder.

'I know!' said Malaki as if he were delighted to have been beaten so convincingly. 'Did you see the way he fought? And he wasn't even trying, not really. Can you imagine if he'd really been trying to kill me?'

Instead of answering Falco just raised his eyebrows and pointed behind Malaki. Someone else had come to congratulate the blacksmith's son, someone whom Falco was certain he would not want to overlook.

'What? Oh,' said Malaki as he saw Bryna Godwyn standing there.

Bryna had taken the leather cord from her hair and her red curls spilled around her face and shoulders. Falco turned to his friend and was not surprised to see him looking terrified.

'Typical,' thought Falco. *'You face one of the Knights Adamant without flinching and yet you quail before a young woman who barely comes up to your chin!'*

'Congratulations Malaki,' said Bryna, holding out a slender hand.

'You...you...' stammered Malaki and Falco just knew he was about to say, *you know my name!* 'You too,' he managed at last.

Falco smiled as the two shared an awkward handshake but then something drew his attention back towards the pavilion. People in the tent were no longer

42

looking out onto the tournament field. They were facing the other way, moving aside to make way for three figures in dark magisterial robes.

The magi had arrived.

Their preparations must be complete. It was time for Darius to get ready for the summoning.

Feeling a flutter of nervous excitement Falco glanced quickly at his friend. Malaki and Bryna were doing their best to hold a normal conversation. This would be an ideal time for him to slip away without being missed. He dodged through the thinning crowds and made his way quickly back to the pavilion. He climbed the steps and moved to one side where he would be able to hear what was being said without being noticed. The magi possessed powers beyond the understanding of normal men and Falco was certain that if he got *too* close they would instantly 'know' what he intended to do.

Of all the people in the world, the magi were the most learned and the most mysterious. Their arcane abilities granted them tremendous power and even Queen Catherine could not escape the influence of the magi. They commanded both respect and fear and most people viewed them with a measure of distrust, some even blamed them for the Great Possession, a terrible event in history when all the battle mages of the time had been killed when their dragons had become Possessed and turned against them.

Until that time it was believed that dragons were immune to Possession and it had come as a terrible shock to find that they were not. Some believed that the magi had known that dragons were susceptible, known and said nothing. They had always been jealous of the battle mages' power and people wondered if they had allowed the Great Possession to occur, only realising the depth of their mistake when all the battle mages and their dragons were dead.

Some still talked of uncovering the truth but no one wanted to risk upsetting them because the magi play a critical role in the training of a battle mage and without the battle mages they would all be lost.

Moving carefully, Falco edged his way closer as the three robed figures moved through the pavilion. The first was Morgan Saker, Caer Dour's senior magi. The second was one of the magi from Wrath, while the third was not a fully-trained mage but an initiate, an apprentice mage who has yet to complete his training. The initiate was Meredith Saker, Morgan's son.

Falco watched as they stopped to talk to Bellius Snidesson and, as ever, Falco found himself mesmerised by the presence of the senior mage.

It was Morgan Saker who had slain his father's dragon. But it was also Morgan Saker who had pulled Falco from the blaze when, as a child, some vengeful soul had set fire to his family home. Falco could still remember looking up to see the tall figure of the mage striding towards him through the flames and clouds of smoke.

He should have felt grateful, but then, as in all the years that followed, he had only ever felt afraid.

For all his years Morgan Saker's hair was still as black as coal. His skin was pale like Falco's, but there was nothing sickly about *his* complexion, and his dark eyes were like fathomless pits giving onto the depths of all that he had learned. In every sense of the word he was a formidable man and for all their wariness, the people of Caer Dour were relieved that it was he who would be standing guard when Darius went to summon his dragon.

From the corner of his eye Falco watched the three robed figures take their leave of Bellius and move to the front of the pavilion where Darius and the emissary were waiting to greet them.

'Is everything ready?' the emissary asked.

'It is,' said Morgan Saker.

Falco saw Darius fill his lungs with a great indrawn breath, the first sign of nerves that the young man had displayed.

'How long do we have?'

'There's a little over three hours before sunset.'

The emissary nodded. 'And the walk?'

'An hour and a half, perhaps,' said Morgan. 'We have plenty of time.' He looked at Darius as if he were gauging whether or not he was up to the challenge. 'Are you prepared?' he asked.

'I am,' replied Darius.

'And if a black should answer?'

'We shall kill it,' said Darius.

For a few seconds Morgan's gaze searched Darius's face for any sign of weakness or uncertainty. Finally he seemed satisfied.

'Then let us go,' he said.

A sombre calm had descended on the tournament field. By now just about everyone had noticed the arrival of the magi. They knew why they were here, but the last time a dragon had come near the town of Caer Dour it had brought death and destruction. The excitement of the trials seemed to evaporate in the cool evening air. In a few days time their army would engage the Possessed. With Darius at their head they could defeat the demon and its army, but the presence of a dragon would ensure that many more survived who would otherwise be lost. So, despite their fear and reservations, the people of the town wanted Darius to be successful, to ascend the slopes of Mont Noir and send out his call, and to have it answered by a dragon.

They watched as the young battle mage followed the magi out of the pavilion. They watched as Sir William fell in beside him, a solid presence to calm their hero's nerves. They watched as the small group of men wound their way up towards the mountain before disappearing round a bend in the path. What they did not see was a slender figure leaving the pavilion and cutting away on a smaller track to the left of the path.

If it took Darius Voltario an hour and a half to reach the 'Dragon Stone' it would take Falco at least twice as long. But he had three hours to make the climb, three hours before sunset. Even then he would never make it if he took the normal route. Instead he would go by Crib Goch, a narrow ridge that cut out almost two miles of the path that Darius would follow.

He would need to move slowly, he would need to conserve his strength, but Falco had set his will to the task and, unlike his body, his will was not so weak.

8
The Summoning

It took Falco an hour to traverse the knife-edge ridge known as Crib Goch. The peak of the ridge rose some six-hundred feet above the valley floor but Falco was unaffected by the dizzying height. He moved with care, resting frequently to catch his breath and look across the valley for any sign of Darius and the magi.

A sudden gust of wind blew up around him and he tightened his grip on the stone. The air was growing colder and he glanced up at the sky. A ceiling of low cloud had rolled in and the light was starting to fade, but he was not concerned. The clouds were not threatening, but they did herald a change in the weather. Cooler air was moving in from the north. Autumn was bidding farewell to the last warmth of summer. It was the harsh cold of winter that lay on the horizon now.

'But not tonight!' thought Falco. *'There will be no freezing rain tonight.'*

Confident that the weather would not break for a day or two Falco continued to pick his way along the ridge. As his thoughts drifted he found himself going over what the emissary had said about his illness and his father. He had never felt proud of his father and was even ashamed of the deep sense of love he felt for him. And as for his 'condition'... Well, it had always been assumed that he would die an early death. Few people with the Crimson Lung lived to see thirty.

Could Heçamede be wrong?

Could his illness be cured?

Falco had known the healer all his life. Indeed, she had been present at his birth, a difficult birth that should have claimed both mother and child. Heçamede had managed to save Falco, but the life of his mother was beyond the skill of any physician to save and Eleanora Danté had died just two hours after the birth of her son.

Falco paused near the top of the ridge. Thoughts of his mother always evoked a complex mixture of emotions. There was a strange sense of detachment as if the story involved someone other than himself. But then a hot surge of sadness and guilt would rise up inside him, cooled only by an overwhelming sense of loss.

'Strange,' he thought. *'To miss so deeply someone you have never known.'*

Another gust of wind made Falco's eyes water and as he blinked away the tears he saw movement on the mountainside ahead of him. Ducking down behind the top of the ridge he peered out as three robed figures came into view with Darius and the emissary behind them. They walked in single file, making steady progress up the mountain where four other magi would be waiting for them.

Falco had timed it perfectly.

They had another half hour's climb to go, and that would take Falco more than an hour, but he still had time. He would be at the dragon stone before the sun started to set. He watched as Darius and the magi moved into a gully and disappeared from view. The entrance to the gully was a quarter of a mile away, but still Falco paused before breaking from cover. The ridge continued for a while before merging with the main body of the mountain and Falco tried not to rush as he scrambled over the crags to rejoin the main path.

45

He slowed as he approached the gully through which the summoning party had passed. The steep-sided valley led to the far side of the mountain where the accessible slopes gave way to the dramatic crags and precipitous cliffs of Mont Noir's western face.

The minutes passed and it was not just the exertion of the climb that made Falco's heart beat so wildly. It was the fact that he was drawing close to the dragon stone, that great slab of black granite from which the battle mages of Caer Dour had always summoned their dragons.

He moved cautiously now. Up ahead the path cut through a landscape of jagged boulders and huge slabs of stone. The jumble of rocks marked the highest part of the climb and beyond them he would be able to look down into the Castle of the Winds, a natural amphitheatre of fractured cliffs surrounding the dragon stone.

Falco tried to calm his breathing as the path wound its way between the enormous monoliths. The air took on a cavernous quality, exaggerating the quietest sounds until even the light shuffling of his feet seemed to echo loudly around him. Just a few more yards and he should be able to see the dragon stone itself. He was just rounding a great buttress of rock when he felt the edge of a steel blade at his throat.

'Don't move!'

Falco froze, his heart thumping loudly in his chest.

The stern words had been spoken at his ear, so close that he could feel the speaker's breath on his neck.

'What is your business here?'

Falco did not answer at first. He was still recovering from the shock. He had heard nothing. The speaker had simply appeared out of nowhere behind him.

'Well?'

The pressure of the knife increased a fraction against Falco's skin.

'I just wanted to see,' he said.

'No one is permitted on the mountain during a summoning,' said the speaker and now Falco recognised the emissary's voice. 'You of all people should know that, Falco Danté.'

Falco let out a relieved sigh as the emissary removed his knife and pressed him back against the rock.

'What were you thinking?'

'I just wanted to see,' repeated Falco quietly. He could not bring himself to meet the emissary's eyes.

There followed a moment's silence and Falco's eyes flicked up to the emissary's face. The fingers of his hand still rested against Falco's chest but now he was looking up at the sky, trying to gauge how much time was left before sunset. A robed figure suddenly appeared beside him and Falco found himself looking into the shining black eyes of Meredith Saker.

Meredith showed every promise of following in his father's footsteps. Or at least he would have done had he been more convinced of the path that lay before him. He had his father's intelligence and his father's gift for scholarship. He had his father's strong features and shining black hair, but unlike his father, Meredith's black eyes shone as if his thoughts reflected what he saw in the world

46

instead of drawing all things into the lightless depths of his mind. And yet, despite the more moderate aspects of his nature, Meredith still possessed his father's ability to convey scorn with nothing more than a look.

'There is no time to take him down,' he said. 'And I would not trust him to go of his own accord.'

'We cannot interrupt the summoning,' said the emissary.

'No,' agreed Meredith, looking at Falco as if he were nothing more than a foolish child.

'And we cannot leave him in plain sight.'

Meredith paused for a moment in thought.

'We shall take him with us,' he said.

'Are you sure?' asked the emissary. 'You would need to conceal all three of us.'

Falco had no idea what the emissary was talking about, but Meredith simply nodded.

'Come,' he said. 'We do not have much time.'

The emissary removed his hand from Falco's chest.

'You stand where you are told to stand,' he said and the look in his eyes made it clear that Falco would be wise to do exactly as he was told. 'You do not move. You do not make a sound.'

Suitably intimidated Falco managed a tight nod of concurrence.

With a final disparaging look Meredith turned and continued down the path while the emissary stood back, inviting Falco to go next.

The disturbing echoes continued as they entered the Castle of the Winds. Rising up around them the cliffs formed a great semicircle, a natural auditorium that opened out to the west where the sun was just beginning to sink beneath the ceiling of the low clouds that stretched almost to the horizon.

At the base of this great arena was a flat expanse of rock some forty feet in diameter. Roughly circular it looked like a single slab of polished stone, an altar or a stage, maybe. But this was not a place built by men, it was a place formed by the mindless forces of nature. Yet even the architects of Wrath could not have conceived a more fitting place from which to summon a dragon.

This was not the first time that Falco had entered the Castle of the Winds and now, as before, he was entranced by the harsh beauty of the place.

'Down here,' urged Meredith when Falco failed to follow him.

'That ledge,' said the emissary, pointing over Falco's shoulder. 'There, in the lee of the cliff.'

Falco nodded and worked his way along a channel in the rock before clambering over a series of dark granite blocks.

The ledge on which they now stood was one of many that rose up around the walls of the 'amphitheatre', but theirs was set back to one side, a place to watch the proceedings, but not a place from which to take part.

Looking down from the ledge Falco could see Darius standing at the centre of the dragon stone. He was now fully clad in the dark, enchanted armour of a battle mage. He stood with his sword and shield held ready but with his head bowed as if he were listening.

From Darius, Falco's gaze moved up the surrounding cliffs. And there they were, the seven magi, each one occupying a broad rocky ledge positioned evenly about the Castle of the Winds, each one standing with their heads bowed in concentration and their arms held rigid by their sides, their hands spread, the fingers tensed as if with some intangible effort.

'They look strange,' said Falco as his eyes moved from one ledge to the next.

'What do?' asked the emissary coming to stand beside him.

'The magi. They look veiled, somehow, as if they are cast in shadow.'

'You can see them?' asked the emissary as Meredith came to stand with them.

'Can't you?' asked Falco.

The emissary shook his head with a frown.

'Can you?' Falco asked Meredith.

'If I concentrate,' said Meredith, looking at Falco with a strange searching expression in his eyes. 'What about my father?' he asked. 'Do you see him too?'

'The shadow about him seems darker,' said Falco, turning back to the rising walls of stone. 'But yes, he is there in the centre, directly above Darius.'

He pointed in the direction but the two men just continued to look at him. The emissary seemed concerned while Meredith looked as if he were trying to figure out what this meant. As the light of the setting sun suddenly fell upon them, it was the emissary who broke the unsettled mood.

'Quickly,' he said. 'It's almost time.'

Falco looked out to the west where the sun had now dropped below the ceiling of low cloud. It was a deep yellow colour and the dark rocks of the Castle of the Winds now appeared to be edged with gold.

'Come away from the edge,' said Meredith. Again there was that note of disapproval, but his tone was somehow less condescending than it had been before.

The three men came together behind a spur of rock that extended out from the cliffs behind them. It formed a low wall over which they now looked west. The sun was deepening in colour as it sank towards the horizon and now, just as it had lit up the rocks of the mountain, it set the clouds aglow with ridges of bright, luminescent orange.

Beside him Meredith closed his eyes in concentration and Falco sensed a subtle change in the quality of the light.

'He is casting a cloak of concealment,' said the emissary in answer to the question in Falco's eyes. 'Should a dragon appear, it will be unaware of our presence.'

Falco looked back at Meredith. He was surprised by the speed with which the apprentice mage had cast his spell. He turned to the emissary.

'I thought it took the magi ages to cast their spells,' he whispered.

Everyone knew that one of the differences between a mage and a battle mage was the speed with which they cast their spells. The magi were capable of powerful magic, but their preparation could take hours, days or weeks - little use in the frenzied chaos of a battle. By contrast, the power of a battle mage could be unleashed with the speed of thought.

The emissary arched an eyebrow as if he were surprised at how quickly Falco had forgotten the instruction to be silent. But then his expression softened.

'He started preparing the spell at sunrise,' he said.

'Ah...' breathed Falco, almost apologetically.

'It is no easy thing to conceal yourself from a dragon,' said the emissary. 'Not to mention you and I.'

Meredith suddenly opened his eyes and turned towards them.

'It is time,' he said.

The orange disk of the sun began to disappear below the horizon of distant mountain peaks and Darius moved to the edge of the dragon stone. Below him was a sheer drop of a thousand feet. It was as if he stood on the edge of the world and Falco looked on in awe.

Darius lowered his sword and shield to his side then he bowed his head and...

Boom!

Falco felt a sudden compression of the air and in his mind he heard a sound like a mighty clap of thunder.

Once... twice... three times the subsonic boom reverberated around the Castle of the Winds before travelling out across the world. Darius waited until the last of the silent echoes had died away and then he raised his head and retreated to the centre of the dragon stone to wait.

'How do they know?' asked Falco, hardly realising that he had spoken his thoughts out loud.

'Who?' asked the emissary in a whispered voice.

'The dragons,' said Falco. 'How do they know to come here at the precise time of the summoning?'

The emissary just looked at him.

'They live beyond the Endless Sea,' whispered Falco. 'How can they possibly get here so quickly?'

It was Meredith who answered him.

'No one knows,' he said. 'Some say that the call goes out long before the actual act of summoning, at the time of the battle mage's birth or the moment at which they recognise the true nature of their calling.' Looking down at Darius he paused. 'But how they come to be here at the very hour of the summoning... no one knows.'

Falco looked across at Meredith. It was clear that this was not the first time he had pondered this question.

'What do you believe?' he asked.

Meredith looked at him suddenly as if Falco were trying to trick him into speaking his mind. He glanced at the emissary before answering.

'I believe...' he said, as if he wanted to make it clear that this was only his opinion, 'that it has something to do with the dragon's memory.'

Falco frowned in puzzlement.

'How can they remember something that hasn't happened?'

Meredith lowered his gaze.

'I do not know,' he replied awkwardly.

The emissary looked at Meredith before turning to Falco.

'Only the most senior magi are permitted the study of dragonkind. Is that not so, Lord Saker?'

Falco noticed that the emissary used the title normally reserved for fully fledged magi.

'It is easy to be seduced,' said Meredith. He spoke as if he were repeating what he had been taught, but it was clear that he had a strong sense of fascination for the creatures that dwell beyond the Endless Sea.

'We need the dragons,' said the emissary quietly. 'But the magi believe it is dangerous to forge too deep a bond. As far as they are concerned, all we need to know is how best to use them, and how to kill them when they turn against us.'

The emissary's tone betrayed what he thought of this ignoble attitude but Falco was no longer listening. He stood beside them, staring into space. There was an intense expression on his face and unmistakable fear in his gaze. He was turned to the west and the red light of the setting sun was reflected in his eyes.

'Something is coming!' he said.

Meredith and the emissary followed his gaze into the glowing band of light on the horizon, but they saw nothing. The sun was no longer visible and the low clouds had begun to glow pink.

The emissary looked down at Darius and sure enough, he too seemed to have sensed something. The tension in the Castle of the Winds soared and they could all imagine the mounting energy held tight in the grasp of the gathered magi. This was the moment that they had hoped for, the moment they had feared. The emissary looked once more at Falco then turned to gaze into the furnace of the sky. At first he saw nothing, but then a tiny speck appeared above the distant horizon.

Beside him, Falco was cleaved to the spot. He was about to come face to face with the creature that had brought about the death of his father. Caer Dour's battle mage had been successful. The call of Darius Voltario had been answered.

9
The Dragon Stone

They watched as the small dark fleck seemed to hover over the horizon. It did not waver. It did not soar. There was no chance that it was just an eagle or a raven. This was a dragon and it was flying directly towards them. The only question that remained was what colour would it be?

Would it be blue like the steel of Malaki's armour or swathed in scales of emerald green? It might gleam like gold or burnished bronze or shimmer white like the hardest frost. It might be red like the blood that flows from a vein but not black, please the Fates, let it not be black.

'It looks dark,' breathed Meredith.

'They always look dark against the sky,' whispered the emissary. 'We're seeing it in silhouette.'

Meredith glanced back nervously into the Castle of the Winds, looking for any sign of concern from Darius or the magi. But the battle mage and the magi simply remained tense and still, ready and waiting for whatever it was that now closed upon them.

For the longest time the dark shape seemed to remain the same, but then it began to grow. It grew until they could almost make out its shape; almost see the beating of its mighty wings.

'It looks dark,' Meredith said again.

'Just wait,' insisted the emissary, but even his voice held a note of uncertainty that had not been there before.

Beside them stood Falco, unmoving, entranced. He could not take his eyes from the approaching shape. As he gazed up at it he began to imagine that he could sense something of its presence. He knew this was impossible, but he could not shake the feeling that something of fury was descending upon them.

The shape seemed to grow higher as it grew closer but still it appeared dark against the glowing clouds.

'It really does look da...' the emissary began but Meredith cut him off.

'Red!' he gasped with obvious relief. 'It's red!'

The emissary glanced at him before looking back at the approaching dragon. It was so big now that they could make out something of its shape, the massive wings beating slowly, the long neck and tail and the solid bulk of its body. The emissary shielded his eyes as he stared up into the sky.

'Red,' he echoed with a smile.

Now it was clear to see. The dark shape of the dragon gleamed with the unmistakable sheen of red.

Once again Meredith turned to look into the Castle of the Winds and even from their vantage point he could sense the relief of Darius and the magi. They too could see that the dragon was red. The tension had gone out of their arms and he could almost sense them letting go of the energy that they had held in readiness for the worst.

A rare smile spread across Meredith's face as he turned back to the emissary. Smiling in turn the emissary clapped him reassuringly on the shoulder.

'Black,' said Falco beside them.

51

'No,' said Meredith. 'You can clearly see it's red.'

The apprentice mage looked up at the winged shape that now appeared so close.

'Black,' said Falco once more and the certainty in his voice was chilling.

The emissary frowned as the smile on Meredith's face began to slip. He glanced towards his father and suddenly he noticed how the dark rocks of Mont Noir were shining with the red light of sunset. Quickly he looked back into the sky and sure enough, the red sheen on the dragon's scales was fading to the deepest shade of night.

Meredith spun round to face Castle of the Winds. He closed his eyes and the heads of seven magi snapped up suddenly to look at him.

'Black,' he whispered, speaking quietly across the space between them. 'The dragon is black!'

Darius and the magi looked up into the sky to see the terrible truth for themselves. With desperate swiftness they tried to re-establish the spells that had started to seep from their grasp. Likewise Meredith reasserted the cloak of concealment around himself and his two companions. They had no way of knowing if they were too late, if the dragon was now aware of the trap that lay in wait for it. All they could do was hold their nerve and hope for the best.

As it descended towards them the hammering of Falco's heart seemed to slow until it matched the measured beat of the great beast's wings. Lower it came until it hung in the air before the dragon stone, scornful of the yawning gulf below it. Its black scales shimmered with a dark pearlescent lustre, rippling over the great muscles that moved beneath its skin. Eyes the colour of molten gold stared into the Castle of the Winds, the black slits of its pupils sweeping back and forth as if it knew that something was there, even if it could not see it.

The spells of concealment had prevailed, the dragon was unaware of their presence.

Falco held his breath as the dragon glided forward over the dragon stone. Then, with astonishing grace, it unfolded its limbs and alighted on the massive granite slab. In all his life Falco had never imagined anything so beautiful and so terrible.

The dragon was smaller than he thought it would be, its body no bigger than a slender horse. Its neck was fully four feet long, while its sinuous tail came to a sharp, spear-like point. Its limbs were heavily muscled, its movements fluid and powerful. Its entire body was covered in scales with armoured plates across its chest and shoulders and down the leading edge of its limbs. The horns on its head swept out from a brow that spoke of intelligence, and the expression in its eyes was laced with the promise of violence.

This was no creature of myth and legend, no fantastical beast born of the wild imaginings of man. This was a living, breathing animal and all the more impressive because of it.

The dragon took a few measured steps towards the centre of the stone. Then it stopped. Enormous talons tensed against the rock, gouging into the granite like spikes of hardened steel. Sharp teeth were revealed as the dragon curled its lip and took a breath.

Yes... It knew there something was here, it just did not know what.

As Falco grew accustomed to the sheer physical presence of the dragon he became increasingly aware of the force that the creature was exerting on his thoughts. Feelings and emotions began to ripple through his consciousness, glimpses into another frighteningly powerful mind.

There was suspicion and confusion as if the dragon was not sure why it had come to this place. It had been expecting to meet something, one of its own kind maybe. But there was nothing here. Or at least that was how it seemed.

Falco's eyes shifted to a point just a few yards in front of the dragon where the shadowy figure of Darius stood ready to strike. Just a few more steps and the dragon would be in reach of his blade. To Falco's senses the battle mage's sword had begun to hum with magical force as if steel itself were not enough to cleave a dragon's hide. Even beside such an awe-inspiring creature Darius did not appear daunted and Falco had a sudden revelation as to what it meant to be a battle mage.

Darius stood with his shield raised and his weight shifted forward onto his leading foot. His right arm was extended behind him, his sword angled back, ready to swing forward for a killing stroke.

Still the dragon held its ground as if it sensed the folly of taking another step. If Darius was going to strike the first blow he would need to close the distance that stood between them.

Falco felt the hum of Darius's sword rise to a searing whine. He felt the combined strength of the magi closing round the dragon. They would wait for Darius to make the first move, but together they were almost ready, almost ready to slay the dragon.

As the truth of what was about to happen became real Falco had a sudden sense of what a tragedy it would be to kill such a magnificent beast. To strike from behind the veil of magic, like an assassin. Again the alien presence of the dragon's thoughts intruded upon his mind. The creature was not in a place it would wish to be. It had come here for reasons it did not understand. This was a place of tragedy and death.

This was a place of humans.

Again the dragon took a breath as if it could smell what it could not see.

This was a place of humans.

Falco could feel the dragon's hatred, as hot and black as its own obsidian heart. The force of it crushed all other thought from Falco's mind. How could anything live with such loathing and not be driven insane?

Suddenly Falco knew that it was true.

Black dragons were mad.

He found himself wishing that Darius would strike. That he would cut down this apparition of dragonkind before it killed them all. But then, just when he thought he had plumbed the depths of the dragon's malice, he sensed a hot spark of sadness burning at the creature's heart. It was a spark of grief so terrible that tears instantly welled in Falco's eyes and he paused in his wish to see the dragon dead. As he struggled with the overwhelming sense of desolation he found himself thinking of an ancient proverb.

The world knows no emotion to match a dragon's grief,
Save perhaps a dragon's rage.

Through his tears Falco saw Darius edging forward, taking slow and steady steps to bring the dragon within the reach of his pulsing blade. From the cliffs around him the magi had cast their web of energy. As long as the dragon remained unaware of their presence it would not be able to break free, but still it seemed to sense something. It tried to step back but the magi's invisible force restrained it. It tried to spread its wings, but found them fettered. Confusion and fear flared in its mind as Darius prepared to strike. Just one more step and the dragon's head would be cloven from its neck.

'*Wrong!*' thought Falco. '*This is wrong!*'

Darius was about to strike, but before he knew what he was doing Falco leapt forward.

'NO!' he cried, and even as the word left his lips he knew he had made a terrible mistake.

The dragon's head snapped up towards him and the fury in its gaze was like a physical force.

'What have you done?' cried Meredith beside him. 'You have broken the spell of concealment! By the stars, what have you done?'

Falco could not answer; he could not move. He could not look away from the creature staring up at him. At the edge of his vision there was a sudden rush of movement as Darius lunged forward, but Falco's warning had broken the spell that blinded the dragon.

There were humans here.

It could see them now.

With astonishing speed the dragon lurched back as Darius's sword flashed towards it. The battle mage's blade sliced through the scales at the base of the dragon's neck, but the cut was shallow, the dragon was barely wounded. Darius tried for a second stroke but the dragon lashed out with its tail, the spear-like tip whipping towards the battle mage with lethal speed.

Darius parried the tail with his shield and ducked away from the dragon's savage jaws. But then the dragon attacked in earnest and Falco could not believe that anyone could survive such a savage onslaught. The dragon attacked with the speed of a panther, the talons on its front paws swiping with such violence that any one of the blows would have killed a normal man, but Darius simply gave ground, whirling backwards until it was his turn to attack.

Smacking aside the dragon's muzzle with his shield he tried again to open the creature's neck. The dragon twisted to avoid the deadly blade then, with a sudden flick of its paw, it sent the battle mage's sword flying from his grasp.

The dragon's teeth reached for him once more but Darius extended the palm of his hand and a bolt of searing energy burst forth. The dragon reared back in pain as flesh and steel-hard scales were blasted from the base of its jaw and Darius made a dash for his sword. He was just closing on it when the dragon caught him with a swipe of its taloned paw.

Darius took the blow on his shield but even so the force of it sent him tumbling across the dragon stone. He grabbed his sword and spun to his knees just as the dragon sent a gout of searing flame towards him. Darius raised his shield and the flames seemed to writhe across the surface of a bubble that had formed around him.

With its foe cowering behind its shield the dragon sought to rise into the air, but as it did so it encountered the restraining power of the magi and was thrown back down onto the slab of black granite.

For a second the mighty beast appeared beaten, forced to its belly on the stone, but dragons are not easily subdued and the strength of the magi's spell had been undermined by Falco's warning. With a great effort the dragon pushed itself up from the ground and stabbed its gaze into the shadowed ledges rising up around it. And now, with its will focussed, it could see its shadowy assailants, seven magi staring down upon it, the fear and the strain showing on their faces.

Now on its feet the dragon looked up as if it was trying to decide which of them it would kill first. Maybe it sensed weakness as it settled on one to its right. Expanding its chest it took an enormous breath then opening its mouth it exhaled a jet of writhing flame. The column of fire shot towards the terrified man and the mage raised his hands in a futile attempt to ward off the flames, but there was no need.

Back on the dragon stone Darius had reached out and formed a dome of protective light over the man. The dragon's flames slammed into the dome before dissipating harmlessly into the cool evening air. The mage breathed a sigh of relief, but the damage was done, his concentration had been broken, his contribution to the restraining of the dragon had ended.

The dragon's head snaked round to look once more at Darius while, on the ledge directly above them, Morgan Saker's lips were moving rapidly as he tried to summon enough power to kill a dragon. He knew he did not have enough time. The last time he had killed a dragon it had taken him two weeks to prepare.

But still he had to try.

Darius stepped to the side as the dragon turned to face him. Then suddenly it leapt into the air, and this time the energy restraining it was not enough to hold it down. It rose up above Darius and was about to cover him in flames once more when the battle mage suddenly laid his sword across his shield. Inside his helmet his eyes closed with a sudden frown of effort and from the edge of his shield an arc of light shot forth. The dragon convulsed to one side in an effort to avoid the attack, but the shining blade of light scored its chest and burned a foot-long slash in the membrane of its right wing.

Darius darted forward as the dragon crashed to the ground but before he got close enough to strike, the point of the dragon's tail slashed across his leg finding a gap in the armour at his knee. Pitching forward the battle mage turned the fall into a roll and as he came back to one knee he swung his sword inflicting a deep cut across the dragon's shoulder. The dragon roared and leaned back to avoid another attack and Darius's blow went wide.

Rising to his feet Darius stumbled on his injured knee and the dragon caught him with a massive blow that struck him full in the chest. The battle mage was sent flying through the air. He slammed into the rocks at the edge of the dragon stone and fell flat on his face. Blood flowed onto the black granite and Darius did not get up.

With a single beat of its wings the dragon swooped in for the kill. The injury to its wing made its flight awkward but its adversary was going nowhere. Darius Voltario was about to die when the emissary attacked the dragon from the rear.

With all his might the Knight Adamant hacked at one of the dragon's hind legs. The strike was a good one and the emissary's blade bit into the creature's flesh. The dragon gave a terrible roar and swung round to face this new foe.

Standing on the ledge beside Falco and Meredith, the emissary had watched the battle unfold. But when it became clear that the fight was turning against them he leapt down from the ledge and descended the rocks as quickly as he could. He had been too late to prevent the attack that felled Darius but now he braced himself as the dragon spun to face him. As a knight of Illicia the emissary had faced several demons but this was the first time he had faced a dragon and, while it did not radiate the same crushing sense of evil, the dragon was every bit as terrifying.

The emissary held his sword in two hands. He had no armour, no mystical powers to call upon. If the dragon chose to attack with fire he would burn like a living torch. The dragon's tail whipped forward and the emissary ducked as it sliced the air above his head. He dodged back as the dragon tried to fell him with a ferocious swipe. Twice the dragon's talons scoured the air around him, but as it went for a third swipe the emissary attacked with his sword. The blade cut into the tough webbing between the fingers of its paw and the dragon hissed in pain. It was expanding its chest, ready to incinerate the emissary, when a ball of blue flame exploded against its ribs. A second burning sphere punched into the side of its face.

The magi had given up on their attempts to restrain the dragon and had finally conjured enough energy to launch an attack. But they were not battle mages and the damage they inflicted was pitifully weak. The dragon was simply enraged to further heights. It turned its back on the emissary, took three bounding steps, and leapt into the air towards the nearest of the magi. The man tried to summon another attack but the dragon flapped its wings and was on him in an instant. With its great jaws it tore the man's head from his shoulders and threw his headless body down onto the dragon stone.

More burning projectiles struck the rock around it, but the dragon seemed to know that they could not harm it. It kicked off from the ledge and soared towards the next magi. The man turned to run for cover but the dragon opened its mouth and flooded the rocky ledge with flame. The Castle of the Winds echoed loudly with screams of agony as the man was consumed by fire. Moving on, the dragon was swooping towards the unflinching figure of Morgan Saker when a bolt of significantly greater power slammed into its side.

In mid-flight the dragon keeled over to see where this new and unexpected threat had come from. It came to rest on a pinnacle of rock and focussed its burning gaze on two young humans standing on a ledge. One wore the robes of a magic user, the other looked pale and pathetically weak.

Both were about to die.

Falco looked down as the dragon's head swung round to look at them. Beside him Meredith stood gasping and exhausted, as shocked as any by the

56

energy he had just unleashed. They had watched the battle like the unwilling audience of some terrible play, but now the dragon was looking at them and they knew the violence that had held them spellbound was about to fall upon them.

'RUN!' shouted the emissary as the dragon launched itself towards the two youths. 'FALCO... RUN!

Falco turned from the apparition of death surging towards them. There were deep cracks in the rocks behind them. If they could get into them before the dragon arrived they might just escape the flames. He made to run then stopped. Meredith was frozen to the spot. The apprentice mage just stood there, too terrified to move.

With the strength of desperation Falco grabbed Meredith and shoved him towards the deep crevices behind them. Meredith stumbled in a daze as Falco drove him towards the safety of the cracks. He had barely managed to thrust him inside when he heard the, 'whoomph... whoomph' of the dragon's wings.

Hearing the rush of a great indrawn breath he ducked inside the crack, pressing himself in as far as he could go. For a second he was aware of Meredith's sobbing breath close to his ear then the world exploded in a fierce roar and Falco screamed as a terrible burning pain flayed the skin from his exposed shoulder, the flames writhing around his neck and face.

The emissary looked up in horror as the dragon spewed flames over the ledge on which Meredith and Falco had been standing. But the flames were suddenly extinguished as the dragon was yanked backwards and thrown once more to the dragon stone, cast down by the force of a father reaching out to protect his son.

The black eyes of Morgan Saker bore down upon the dragon as if he had the strength to kill it by the sheer force of his will. Unfortunately he did not. He knew it, and so did the creature looking up at him. In truth, there was no one now who could stop the dragon. It was going to kill them all.

Falco slumped to the ground as the brightness of the dragon's fire was suddenly quenched. He knew they should be dead but somehow they were not.

His mind was flooded with pain and he shook uncontrollably, but still he had to see. It was he who had ruined the trap that would have seen the dragon dead. He could not hide away in darkness while others faced the death that he had brought upon them. Too faint and nauseous to stand, he crawled slowly back to the lip of the rocky ledge and looked down upon the dragon stone.

To one side the corpse of the headless mage lay near the edge of the thousand-foot drop. At the base of the rocks on the opposite side lay the armoured body of Darius, lying in a pool of blood, unmoving. Thirty feet above the lifeless battle mage Morgan Saker looked down and his eyes burned with a hatred to match the dragon's own.

The dragon advanced with slow deliberation. It glanced at the emissary who moved to stand in its path and Falco wondered what kind of courage it must take to stand your ground in the face of certain death.

Even through the pain that wracked his body Falco could sense something of the dragon's mind. It was going to kill the emissary, but what it really wanted was the mage that stood on the ledge above. Morgan Saker was the embodiment of everything it hated, everything that had driven it to the point of insanity. It would revel in the mage's death, but the emissary blocked its path.

Falco watched as the emissary lifted the silver pendant from around his neck. He raised it to his lips, kissing it lightly before allowing it to fall. Then he readied his blade and prepared to meet his end. The dragon surged forward, its jaws gaping, its talons spread wide to strike down its human foe, and Sir William stepped forward to meet it, but before the combatants could clash a crackling bolt of energy shot past the emissary's shoulder and slammed into the dragon's chest. The dragon roared in pain as its ribs were laid bare by the attack that left a smoking hole in its flesh.

This was not the feeble power of the magi, this was power of an altogether greater magnitude. This was the attack of a battle mage.

Feeling like he was about to pass out Falco looked behind the emissary to see where the attack had come from. At the back of the dragon stone, Darius was getting to his feet. The young battle mage had shed his helm. His sword and shield were gone, but he had never looked more dangerous. One side of his face was covered with blood and he was hunched over several broken ribs. He limped on his wounded knee, but still he advanced.

Recovering from the attack the dragon looked past the emissary to the enemy it had thought vanquished. Its rage soared to a blinding pitch and it opened its mouth to cover him in flames, but Darius extended his hands and unleashed another fearsome bolt. Again the dragon stumbled back coming ever closer to the edge of the dragon stone and the sheer drop behind it, and still Darius came on. He ducked as the dragon's tail whipped towards him, opening a gash on his cheek.

The dragon was badly wounded now but it was still a formidable foe. Moving past the emissary Darius tried for another attack but the dragon ducked and the battle mage's fire shot over its back. Then the dragon took a rapid breath and flames burst from its mouth.

The emissary dived aside as the protective shield sprang up over Darius once more, but the battle mage was weakening. Steam rose up around him as the wet blood on his face began to boil.

But still he came on.

As the flames died away the dragon took another step back until it stood on the very edge of the dragon stone. Darius was now directly in front of it and the dragon drew back a massive paw to crush him, but the battle mage met the attack with his open palm. There was a pulse of light and the dragon screamed as the bones of its right forelimb were shattered. It reared up on its hind legs and grabbed the battle mage with the talons of its left paw. Darius cried out as the dragon's claws sank into his neck and shoulder. The dragon tried to bite him but Darius grabbed its great head and somehow held the jaws at bay. Unable to reach him with its teeth the wounded beast opened its mouth once more.

Dragon fire engulfed Darius as the opponents grappled on the edge of the abyss, and finally his strength began to fail. His hair ignited and the flesh of his face began to blister and crack. The battle mage was burning alive but even at the last he placed his hand against the dragon's chest and with a final detonation of magical force he ruptured the dragon's heart.

The flames vanished and there was a moment of stillness as the two mighty combatants stared into each other's eyes. Had the dragon been any other colour they would have fought side by side, each willing to sacrifice themselves to save the other's life. But the dragon that Darius Voltario had summoned was black and black dragons are the enemies of humankind.

Black dragons are mad.

For a second the dragon stood erect, its talons hooked over the edge of the dragon stone then the light went out of its eyes. As it fell backwards its mighty wings wafted forward, folding around Darius as if enclosing him in a last embrace. Then, still locked together, the dragon and the battle mage fell from the dragon stone and were gone.

Every Living Soul

Falco managed barely a mile down the mountain before he collapsed from pain and shortness of breath. Following close behind him the emissary bent down to lift him from the rocky path. As he gathered him into his arms Sir William was surprised at how light he was. Falco stood six feet tall, but he seemed to weigh little more than a child. This was just as well for they still had several miles to go before they reached the town and Morgan Saker was leading them at an unforgiving pace.

The seething mage did not even notice that Falco had fallen. If it were down to him they would have left him weeping and delirious in the Castle of the Winds. Indeed, there had been a point when it seemed that Falco would follow Darius over the cliff.

'Do you realise what you have done?' Morgan had bellowed as he held Falco at the very edge of the dragon stone, pushing him so close to the vertiginous drop that his heels rested on nothing but air.

'I didn't save you from the flames so that you could damn us all!'

Only Falco knew that this was a reference to his childhood and not to the dragon's fire of this tragic night. Morgan's hands were locked in his tunic and such was the guilt that now consumed him that he would not have cared if Morgan had let him go.

'Father!' cried Meredith. This was the first word that Meredith had uttered. 'Father,' he said again and the sense of utter misery in his voice seemed to reach the incensed mage.

With an animal snarl Morgan pulled Falco back from the brink and threw him across the dragon stone. Then, without another word, he strode away and began to climb back out of the Castle of the Winds.

'What about the dead?' asked one of the magi.

'We have no time for tending the dead,' said Morgan without turning.

The magi turned to the emissary but his expression was every bit as dire.

'The dead are beyond our power to help,' he said. 'The people of Caer Dour are not.'

And with that he hauled Falco to his feet.

'Can you walk?' he asked, and the fact that Falco remained on his feet seemed answer enough. He steered him towards the steps leading out of the amphitheatre and the others had no choice but to follow.

Now they walked with stumbling haste down the slopes of Mont Noir. It was dark and they could see the lights of the town shining below them. By the time they reached the outskirts there was a crowd waiting for them, but as they came closer the anticipation on the peoples' faces quickly changed to alarm. They saw the ailing figure in the emissary's arms and noted the absence of Darius and two of the magi. They knew something had gone terribly wrong.

'Where's Darius?' they asked.

'Did he summon a dragon?'

'What's the matter with the boy?'

'Where's Darius?'

Morgan Saker ignored all the questions and the people parted to let them through. He spotted someone in the crowd and waved the wiry man forward.

'Where's Bellius?' he asked without so much as slowing down.

'He's in the gardens,' said the man. 'Hosting a party for Jarek.'

'Find him,' said Morgan. 'Have him meet me in the square immediately. Tell him to bring as many of the nobles as he can find.'

The man frowned at the seriousness in the mage's voice.

'Quickly man!' snapped Morgan. 'As if your life depended on it!'

Without another word the man sprinted away down the cobbled street and Morgan marched on. The crowds fell in behind them as they continued on their way to the centre of town. Their route took them close to Simeon's villa and as the bustle of the crowds grew louder the old battle mage came out onto the front steps of his home. With him were Malaki and Fossetta.

'Falco!' cried Malaki, catching sight of his friend in the emissary's arms.

He started forward, but Simeon reached out a hand to restrain him.

'What is it?'

'It's the summoning party,' said Malaki. 'Something's wrong. Falco looks hurt.'

Fossetta too felt the urge to go to Falco, but she waited to see what the master of the household would say. The muscles in Simeon's jaw bunched and he lowered his head as if he did not need Morgan Saker to tell him how things had gone on the mountain. Then he drew a breath and squared his shoulders.

'Fossetta,' he said. 'Go and find Heçamede. Tell her she is needed.'

'It looks like they're heading for the square,' said Fossetta.

Simeon nodded. 'Then tell her to meet us there if she can.'

The housekeeper did not even bother to remove her apron before descending the steps and hurrying away down a small cobbled lane.

Simeon reached out to take Malaki's arm. 'Let's go,' he said.

It was not until they had reached the square that they finally caught up with the emissary.

'I'll take him,' said Malaki, reaching out for Falco.

'He needs a healer,' said the emissary.

'She's on her way,' said Simeon.

Malaki held his friend in his arms as more people flooded into the square. 'He's burning up,' he said as Falco's sweating brow came to rest against his neck. 'What happened?'

The emissary did not answer but the look in his eyes filled Malaki with fear as he looked down at his friend.

'Oh Falco,' he thought. 'What have you done now?'

Falco's pale cheeks looked grey and clammy. The crimson rash, which was normally hidden by his hair, was now visible across his brow and temples. His breath came in weak, juddering gasps and there was a blue tinge to the flesh around his lips. Malaki had witnessed many of Falco's 'episodes', but he had never seen him as bad as this.

'Quickly Heçamede,' he pleaded silently. 'Please, come quickly.'

Morgan Saker marched across the square and climbed the steps to a raised area of stone with fountains at each corner. People pressed forward, eager to know what had happened, but the magi waved them back. Saker was not going to say anything until Bellius and the nobles arrived.

'Lay him down here,' the emissary said to Malaki, indicating the broad steps beside one of the fountains. He tore a strip of cloth from the hem of his shirt and soaked it in the cold water before wiping it over Falco's head and neck. 'We need to cool him down,' he said.

Malaki held Falco while the Queen's envoy mopped his brow and soaked his tunic.

'Chevalier,' said a deep voice as Simeon appeared beside them.

The emissary looked up then stepped back as Simeon dropped down to one knee beside Falco. The old battle mage placed one hand on his ward's chest and the other on his brow then he bowed his head in concentration. For a few seconds there was no change. Falco continued to shake, straining for even the most meagre of breaths. Then suddenly he arched his back, drew in a rasping breath and screamed out a single word.

'DARIUS!'

The uneasy murmuring of the crowd was suddenly silenced as everyone turned to see where the terrible cry had come from. People moved away from the small group gathered beside the fountain. The anxiety in the air was now turning to fear.

Just what *had* happened on the mountain?

As people began to whisper and stare Fossetta suddenly appeared, shoving her way through the growing crowd. Behind her came Heçamede Asclepios, one of the town's most gifted healers. She was a tall woman with the dark looks that spoke of Thraecian heritage. Together they made straight for the fountain and when Fossetta saw the state of Falco's condition she put both hands to her mouth and choked back a sobbing cry. Heçamede put a hand on Simeon's shoulder and the old battle mage came back to his feet.

'What happened?' she asked, feeling the heat of Falco's forehead and holding his wrist to check his pulse.

With a quick glance at the surrounding crowds the emissary leaned down close to the healer's ear.

'Dragon fire,' he whispered quietly.

Heçamede frowned and lifted her hand to observe the rash on Falco's brow. Then she opened his shirt and sure enough the crimson rash was spread full across his chest. Somehow the dragon's fire had unleashed the full virulence of Falco's illness. Simeon's powers had allowed him a few life-saving breaths, but his throat was closing up once more. If his condition could not be stabilised he would die of asphyxiation.

Heçamede quickly opened the leather satchel that hung from a strap around her shoulder. She removed a curious silver tube with a mouthpiece at one end and a small, lidded bowl half way down its length. Then she took out a bottle of whitish powder and tapped a small amount into the bowl.

'What's that?' asked Fossetta.

'Ephedra powder,' said Heçamede. 'It will reduce the swelling in his airways.'

The healer took the instrument and placed one end in Falco's left nostril before putting her lips to the mouthpiece. Then, closing his other nostril she gave a series of sharp puffs, each timed to coincide with Falco's indrawn breath. With every puff Falco gave a weak choking cough, but the coughs grew steadily stronger and his breaths steadily deeper. The blue tinge faded from his lips and some semblance of colour returned to his cheeks.

The healer removed the tube and felt his pulse once more. Slowly Falco's breathing eased and the feverish shaking of his body grew less. The healer let out a sigh of relief and was just turning her attention to the burns on his shoulder when a commotion rose up on the far side of the square. Bellius Snidesson had arrived with a dozen of the town's nobles. He made directly for the war memorial and people scurried to get out of his way. Everyone watched as he climbed the steps and fell into hushed conversation with Morgan Saker.

'Help me turn him,' said Heçamede focussing once more on her patient.

Malaki drew his eyes from the imposing huddle gathered on the raised dais and bent down to help her. He eased Falco over and tore open his scorched shirt so that Heçamede could examine the extent of his burns.

'Is it bad?' asked Simeon. Only he knew the indescribable pain of being burned by dragon fire.

Heçamede raised an eyebrow. 'He was lucky. Only the surface layers have been damaged. The fire must have barely caught him.'

Looking down at the area of red and weeping flesh Malaki could not think of his friend as being lucky. Falco had lost the skin from his shoulder and the flames had licked up the side of his neck and face. The skin might heal but he would bear the scars for life.

Heçamede removed a small atomiser from her satchel. She filled it with a dilution of herbs, spraying a fine mist onto the wound before covering the area with a panel of oiled silk. She bound Falco's shoulder with clean bandages before applying a silvery ointment to the lesser burns on his neck and face.

Finally she laid Falco back in Malaki's arms and gave him a draught of something to ease the pain. Falco swallowed the sweet-smelling medicine and, as his body drew back from the brink of death, his mind was free to acknowledge the misery that lay in wait for him. Drowsily he opened his eyes. For a second he gazed at the people looking down at him then he buried his face in Malaki's shoulder and began to cry.

Heçamede turned to Fossetta and Simeon.

'The dressings will need to be changed daily,' she told the housekeeper, who gave a tearful nod. 'And if you could help with the pain, Master le Roy... Your powers will also help the burns heal more quickly.'

'Of course,' said Simeon.

'What about the consumption?' asked Fossetta. 'I've never seen it so bad.'

'No,' said Heçamede examining the rash on Falco's chest. 'And I'm not even sure it *is* consumption. Scarlet lung does not react to heat like this. This is something different.'

Behind her the emissary nodded his agreement. He was about to say more when a furious voice called out from above them.

'Where is he?' cried Bellius, coming to the edge of the raised area. 'Where is the mad man's spawn?'

A shocked silence descended on the square as all eyes turned to see the focus of the nobleman's rage, but Falco was too distressed to heed the venom in his words. Nothing that Bellius said could make him feel worse than he already did.

Standing beside Bellius was Morgan Saker and the four surviving magi. Behind them stood many of the town's most powerful nobles, the shock written large upon their faces.

'What is it?' cried a voice from the crowd. 'What's going on?' All across the square this appeal was taken up until the crowd was clamouring to know what had happened on the mountain.

Morgan Saker raised his arms and waited for the murmurs to die away. For a second he looked down on them with his black eyes and then. 'Darius is dead,' he said.

There was a collective intake of breath, the stunned silence of disbelief, and Morgan Saker continued.

'The dragon he summoned was black. We were unable to restrain it.' His eyes flicked down towards Falco. 'The dragon killed two of the magi and would have killed us all had Darius not struck it down.' Morgan paused. 'He fought with courage and killed the beast, but he was consumed by the dragon's fire. They fell from the mountain together. Our battle mage is gone.'

The people of Caer Dour were in shock. Summonings were not supposed to end like this. Everyone knew that there were three ways that a summoning could end. First, the summoning would go unanswered and the battle mage would return alone. Second, the call would be answered and the battle mage would have his dragon.

And finally, yes... a black dragon might answer the summoning. But on such rare occasions the beast was slain. That was why the magi were present. Seven magi to restrain a dragon and a battle mage to kill it, that was the way it was supposed to be. The dragon might be slain, but the battle mage would always return to fight the Possessed. That was the way it was supposed to happen.

Not like this.

Summonings were not supposed to end like this.

This had begun as a day of celebration, now it was ending in tragedy. For a while no one spoke. More people were coming into the square and a hubbub of conversation rose up as the dreadful news was relayed to the newcomers.

'Simeon,' said a familiar voice. 'Whatever's happened?'

Simeon turned as Julius Merryweather put a hand on his arm. The two men clasped each other's forearms while Merryweather's bright eyes flashed around trying to take in the scene.

'Darius is lost,' said Simeon.

'Great heavens!' said Merryweather. 'And your boy?' he whispered looking down at Falco with concern.

Simeon's lips tightened.

'Burned by dragon fire,' he said quietly. 'Heçamede has secured him for now, but his chest... his lungs...' Simeon shook his head.

Above them Morgan Saker was fielding a growing number of questions from the increasingly agitated crowd.

'What had happened?'

'Why hadn't they been able to subdue the dragon?'

'Were the magi too few? Were they too weak?'

'Weak!' said Morgan dangerously. 'We were not weak!' He was about to speak again when Bellius thrust himself to the fore.

'How dare you blame the magi,' he railed, 'when the reason for this tragedy is lying there in front of you.'

Everyone turned to follow the line of his trembling finger and people moved back, clearing a space around Falco and his companions.

'*He* is the cause of this calamity,' snapped Bellius. 'Him! The feeble son of Aquila Danté. He warned the dragon before Darius could strike. He sided with the dragon.'

'That's not true,' began Meredith Saker, but his father silenced him with a look.

'First the father, and now the son,' spat Bellius and suddenly the sense of shock gave way to a new and altogether more unpleasant mood. The eyes of the people looking down at Falco grew hard and unfriendly. Suddenly there was anger in the air, anger and blame.

'What about the Possessed?' someone called out.

The anger evaporated as people were reminded of the terrible danger that was moving up the valley towards them. With dizzying swiftness they switched their attention back to Bellius and Morgan Saker.

'What about the demon?'

'What about the Possessed?'

'Who's going to fight them now?'

Bellius held up his hands to quieten this new wave of anxiety, but he looked nervous and uncertain.

'We should send to Caer Laison for help,' said one of the nobles.

'It is too late for that,' snapped Morgan, and even the great mage looked distinctly uncomfortable.

'But, the Possessed... the demon... without Darius...'

'We are lost!' said Meredith Saker.

Morgan glared at his son, but it was too late. Meredith had spoken the truth. Without Darius their army had no chance of defeating the Possessed.

'We should call the army back to the town,' said one of the nobles. 'Man the walls at the head of the valley. Surely we could hold them there.'

Bellius nodded. 'Yes,' he said. 'There's no need to meet them in the field. We could shore up our defences. Hold them at the valley's head until help arrives.'

'Help!' said Morgan with more than a touch of scorn in his voice. 'There is no *help* that can reach us now.'

'But we can still fight,' said one of the other nobles. 'Surely with help from the magi.'

'Magi are no use on the battlefield,' growled Morgan. 'That's why we need a battle mage. Only they have the power to shield an army from the fear that flows out from a demon. And we have no battle mage.'

His eyes settled on the prostrate figure lying in Malaki's arms. He waited until Falco opened his eyes and turned to look at him.

'We have no battle mage, because of you.' He spoke as if they were the only two people in the square.

Once again the people of Caer Dour turned to look down at the weak and injured figure of Falco Danté. There was no pity in their eyes, no sympathy for his suffering. There was only a growing sense of fear. People began to speak all at once as they tried to quell the rising tide of panic.

'We could muster more troops from the outlying regions,' suggested someone from the crowd.

'We could arm the townsfolk,' said another. 'The people would fight to save their homes.'

'We could attack them from the cliffs before they reach the town.'

The murmur of conversation rose to an enthusiastic pitch as the people of Caer Dour tried to think of ways to defeat the Ferocian army. Still standing on the memorial, Bellius began to look more confident as he conferred with the nobles. He looked pompous and self-satisfied as if it would be down to him and his powerful friends to save the town. But the people of Caer Dour paid him no heed. They were talking themselves into a frenzy when a new figure climbed the steps onto the raised area.

'Wait!' cried the clear strong voice of Sir William Chevalier. 'People of Caer Dour, wait!'

The crowds slowly quietened as they turned to see what the Queen's envoy had to say. If they had hoped for support and encouragement they were disappointed. The emissary looked out across the mass of faces and there was a deep sadness in his eyes.

'You cannot fight,' he said at length.

The people in the square bridled at this as if he were questioning their ability or resolve.

'You cannot fight a demon army,' the emissary said. 'Not without a battle mage.'

'We can field an army more than two thousand strong,' said Bellius. 'Many more if we call up every man of fighting age.'

The emissary gave a pained sigh.

'But how many of them have faced a demon before?' he asked. 'How many have even fought the Possessed?'

Bellius gave a dismissive sniff and turned away. In all the town there was barely a handful of people who had ever fought in the war against the Possessed. The very name sounded like something drawn from the annals of history, a newly awakened threat that had ravaged the kingdoms of Beltane and Illicia, terrible and tragic but distant, the scourge of other people's lives. Only in recent years had the effects of the war been felt in Valentia, only as the strength of those other kingdoms had begun to fail.

The emissary nodded slowly. There was no judgement in his eyes. He did not blame the people for their innocence.

'You cannot fight,' he said again. 'And it is too late to call for help.'

'Then what must we do?' asked someone from the crowd.

'You must withdraw,' he said. 'You must withdraw and hope that you can reach a place of safety in time.'

'But that would leave the town undefended,' scoffed Bellius as if the idea was ludicrous. 'Do you really think the fighting men of Caer Dour would retreat and simply hope that the demon army would leave our families in peace.'

Sir William looked Bellius dead in the eye.

'You mistake me, sir,' he said. 'It is not only the army that must flee.'

Bellius Snidesson began to frown.

'The army of the Possessed will move up the valley until it reaches the town and then it will kill or claim every living thing that it finds. And it will find anyone who is foolish enough to remain.'

The crowd began to murmur once more as the full ramifications of what he was saying slowly dawned on them. The emissary paused a moment to let his point sink home.

'Let the children sleep tonight,' he said. 'But come the morning, every man, woman and child must be ready to flee into the mountains.'

'But where will we go?' asked a woman from the far side of the square and the emissary searched the crowd to see her face.

'We shall make for Clemoncé,' he said as if he spoke to all the mothers of all the children asleep in their beds that night. 'We shall make for Clemoncé and hope that we reach a place of safety before the demon can overtake us.'

'But this is madness!' said Bellius. 'We can't uproot an entire town and move it into the mountains by morning.'

'It would be madness to stay,' replied the emissary.

'But what about our homes? What about our land?'

'Homes can be rebuilt. Land can be reclaimed.'

Bellius threw up his hands in exasperation and looked to Morgan for support, but the mage seemed to look straight through him and the emissary turned back to the crowd.

'People of Caer Dour,' he called out. 'We cannot change what has happened here tonight and we have no time for grief.' The people watched him in silence. 'Go back to your homes and prepare for a journey into the mountains,' he went on. 'Pack only what you need. Take nothing that will slow you down.'

The mood of the crowd sobered as they began to accept the reality of their predicament. The thought of taking their families into the mountains was daunting but they were people of Valentia. They would not shrink from trial and hardship.

'Speed, food and shelter,' said emissary. 'Let these be the thoughts that guide you. Speed, food and shelter, but the most important of these is speed.'

He waited until he was sure that the people understood.

'There is a rocky plateau,' he went on, 'just outside the town on the road to Clemoncé. Tell your friends and your family. Tell everyone you know that we shall assemble there at sunrise tomorrow morning.'

He gazed at their faces a final time.

'No one must be left behind,' he said. 'If there are people who need help, help them. If there are people who need persuading, persuade them. By sunrise tomorrow the town of Caer Dour must be empty of every living soul.'

II

Regret

Slowly the crowds dispersed and the leaders of Caer Dour retired to discuss the plight of their people. Simeon went with them for there was no one who knew more about the Possessed than he. Their discussions went on for some time and it was well after midnight before the old battle mage finally returned home.

Malaki had carried Falco back to the villa and made him as comfortable as possible while Fossetta set about preparing for the journey into the mountains. When she had done all she could she returned to relieve him.

'You should be getting home,' she said. 'This is going to be a busy night and your father will need all the help he can get.'

'Maybe I should...' Malaki began but Fossetta cut him off.

'I'll keep an eye on Falco,' she said. 'Best thing for him now is sleep.'

Malaki nodded, albeit somewhat reluctantly. As he rose to his feet Fossetta put a hand on his arm then she stood on her tip toes to plant a kiss on his cheek.

'You were magnificent in the trials,' she said with sudden tears in her eyes.

Malaki smiled. 'Thank you,' he said, although the events of the day now seemed distant and insignificant.

Fossetta watched as he left the room then she moved to take his place beside Falco. The flame from a single lamp filled the room with a soft orange glow but still Falco's skin looked as pale and grey as stone. He twitched and moaned, his throat rasping with every indrawn breath.

'Darkness,' muttered Falco, lost in the grip of fever and delirium. 'Darkness in the deep. Darkness on the hills.'

Fossetta felt a shadow of fear fall across her heart. It was many years since she last heard Falco mention the 'darkness' in his sleep. His condition *must* be bad if his dreams had drawn back to that tortured place in his mind. Often when he spoke of the darkness he would mumble about other things. Fossetta and Simeon had never been able to tell if it was a place with three hills or three imaginary friends that seemed to bring him comfort.

'It doesn't matter,' Simeon had told her. 'Anything that helps him fight the nightmares is good.'

Hoping he might find some comfort now, Fossetta brushed a strand of dark hair from Falco's face. She checked his fever and leaned down to kiss him before retiring to the chair across the room. It was some time later when she stirred at the sound of the door opening.

'How is he?'

Fossetta stood as Simeon came into the room. 'Not good,' she said and Simeon could hear the anxiety in her voice.

'Stronger than he looks,' he told her. 'Isn't that what you've always said?'

Fossetta smiled at her master's kindness.

'Is everything decided?' she asked.

'As much as can be,' replied Simeon. 'We'll make for the city of Toulwar. That is the nearest place that would see us safe.'

'Does it have a battle mage?'

'It will,' said Simeon. 'It's a staging point for armies moving into Illicia. A battle mage has been assigned to join the latest army before it leaves the city at the end of the month.'

'But that's only nine days from now!'

Simeon did not answer. Everyone at the meeting had shared Fossetta's concern. The city of Toulwar was more than a hundred miles away and the mountain path was not an easy route. There was no way an entire town of people could cover that distance in nine days.

'We'll send out riders,' said Simeon. 'The people of Toulwar will learn of our plight. The army will ride out to meet us.'

'And what about those who cannot flee?' asked Fossetta and here Simeon bowed his head.

'They will be given the means to decide their own fate.'

Fossetta raised a hand to her mouth. 'Heaven help us,' she breathed.

Simeon placed a hand on her arm. 'Is everything ready?' he asked, trying to bring her thoughts back to the practicalities in hand.

Fossetta nodded, tears standing in her eyes. She knew of several people who were too ill or too old to venture into the mountains.

'I've had Davis make up loads for the pack horses,' she said, dabbing at her eyes with the sleeve of her blouse. 'There'll be plenty of people who won't look beyond the first day,' she added. 'We must be prepared to share what we have.'

Simeon nodded and smiled. 'Get some sleep,' he told her. 'I'll sit with him for a while.'

Fossetta looked down at Falco, the expression on her face a mixture of concern and pity. 'Heaven help us,' she said again and with that she left the room and Simeon settled himself down in the chair.

An hour passed and the flame in the lamp was but the smallest bead of amber fire.

Falco opened his eyes.

Across the room he could see the vague outline of Simeon sitting in the chair. It seemed that he was sleeping and Falco was relieved. He had no desire to speak to anyone. His chest ached and his shoulder burned with a terrible pain. He was just trying to shift into a more comfortable position when Simeon spoke.

'Why?'

In the dim light Falco could just make out the scarred mask of Simeon's face.

'I had to see,' he said in a quiet voice. 'I had to know.'

'Know what?'

'What it was that he died for,' said Falco. 'What it was that drove him to it.'

'And did you find your answers?' asked the old battle mage.

'No,' said Falco. 'The dragon was mad and my father was mad to side with it.'

Simeon gave a low sigh. He seemed almost disappointed. Maybe he too had hoped to find some explanation for the actions of Aquila Danté.

There were a few moments of silence.

70

Falco stared up at the ceiling and his tears were those of a son grieving for his father. The last hope of his father's redemption had died in the blind rage of the dragon's fire. 'I'm sorry,' he said.

Simeon bowed his head at the remorse in Falco's voice. He did not blame him for what had happened. The entire town might have been doomed by Falco's actions, but Simeon did not see it as Falco's fault. He knew the urge that had driven him to enter the Castle of the Winds, that desperate need to know. Indeed Falco could not have done otherwise.

'Try to sleep,' he said. 'You will need your strength in the days to come.'

'Sleep,' thought Falco. He would find no peace in sleep.

And as for strength... Falco almost laughed.

Strength was for the living. He had no need of strength.

12

Into The Mountains

The next morning saw six thousand people assembled on the broad expanse of rocky ground to the west of the town. On a cold autumnal day it was a bleak and desolate place with nothing to dull the biting wind that blew in from the north. The sun had barely risen but still it found the town of Caer Dour all but deserted.

The people had taken heed of the emissary's words and only a handful remained in the town. Most would be able to follow before it was too late, but there were also those who had been 'helped on their way' and there was a haunted expression in the eyes of the people. They stood in groups, huddled together against the cold and clutching satchels of food and whatever personal items they had decided to bring. Many had horses or mules laden with provisions or carrying those too young, too old or too infirm to walk. They looked wretched and lost, but then the emissary appeared over the edge of the plateau and the mood lifted like the grey mist rising from the valleys.

Sir William rode a beautiful smoke-grey Percheron, a warhorse favoured by the knights of Illicia. He did not smile at the people as he moved onto the plateau, but there was something in his bearing that gave them comfort. It was not confidence exactly but a kind of calm, as if he had experienced events such as this before and was living proof that they could be survived. Beside him, on a black horse of similar size, came Simeon le Roy. Despite his age and hollow-eyed blindness the old battle mage possessed the same kind of reassuring presence as the emissary, and the people of Caer Dour began to feel a faint glow of hope.

But behind them, on a horse of considerably lighter build, came a smaller figure, hunched and bowed and swaying in the saddle. He wore a fur-lined cloak of slate-grey, but even with the hood pulled down over his face the people knew who it was.

It was Falco Danté, son of Aquila Danté, the mad battle mage, the traitor. *He* was the reason why they were fleeing their homes. *He* was the reason they were standing in the cold.

Falco felt like he was moving through a nightmare. People who the day before would have greeted him with a smile now looked at him with hard, unforgiving eyes. He could barely cope with the pain that wracked his body. He had no strength for the enmity that cut through him more keenly than the scything north wind. He bowed his head as two horses drew up alongside him.

'Don't look at them,' said one of the riders in a gruff voice.

Falco glanced to his left. It was Balthazak de Vane, Malaki's father.

'Just keep your eyes on Simeon,' said Balthazak.

He did not look at Falco. He kept his gaze fixed straight ahead.

Falco turned to see Malaki riding close on his right. Both father and son were now wearing their blue steel armour with warm cloaks cast about their shoulders. They looked strong and dignified, more like knights than the town's blacksmith and his son. Falco felt a great surge of love for them quickly followed by a black wave of guilt. He did not feel worthy of their kindness. Even when Malaki gave him a furtive grin he could not bring himself to smile.

The strength of Falco's escort deterred many from openly glaring, but the looks and whispers persisted as they made their way towards the group of nobles gathered at the centre of the plateau.

'Good,' said Malaki, nodding towards the nobles. 'Heçamede is with them.'

Glancing up Falco could see Heçamede watching them as they approached. He could not say that he was pleased to see her.

Malaki and his father fell back as they reached the group while the emissary dismounted to speak with Bellius and Morgan. Simeon remained on his horse and Falco's mare came to a gentle halt. Behind him Fossetta dismounted from one of the pack horses. She had watched anxiously as they made their way up the trail, trusting more to the horse's good sense than to Falco's wakefulness to keep him in the saddle. Now she came forward to join Heçamede at Falco's stirrup.

'How is he?' asked the healer.

'No better,' said Fossetta. 'His chest hasn't cleared and the rash is worse than ever.'

Heçamede nodded slowly and reached up to turn back the hood of Falco's cloak. 'The emissary is right,' she said. 'This is not scarlet consumption.'

'Is that good or bad?' asked Fossetta.

'Only time will tell,' said Heçamede evasively.

The emissary had made a point of seeking her out last night. The condition he spoke of was very rare in these parts but the symptoms certainly seemed to fit. She would speak with him again if she got the chance. Right now he was surrounded by nobles all trying to speak to him at once. As she watched he raised a hand to calm them.

'What news of the army?' he asked.

'The first riders reached us an hour ago,' replied Morgan.

'Two hours,' corrected Bellius sourly.

Morgan gave him a withering glance, but Bellius just rolled his eyes and put a hand to his forehead. Like so many standing there he had the strained look of a man who had not slept.

'The army is on its way,' he said, taking a flask of wine from his manservant Ambrose. 'They should catch us up some time later today.'

'Good,' said the emissary. 'And the Possessed, what is the latest on them?'

'They're barely two days from the town,' said Bellius.

The emissary's gaze drew inward and his jaw bunched. 'Then we had better be on our way,' he said grimly. He turned back to Morgan. 'Are the riders ready?'

Morgan gestured to one side where four horses stood in a line, their riders standing nervously by their sides. Each one of them had a leather dispatch tube slung over their shoulder. The emissary worked his way down the line. The first three were men of light build and weathered faces; the fourth was a young woman.

The emissary paused.

'She is of age,' said a man standing to one side with his arm around a woman who had the same dark eyes and black hair as the young rider. Both looked anxious but resolute.

'She is fast,' said the woman. 'And brave.'

The emissary nodded to the young rider's parents. 'What is your name?' he asked her.

'Anwyn,' said the young woman.

The emissary placed a hand on her shoulder then turned to address them all. 'Ride swiftly,' he said as the riders swung lightly into the saddle. 'And deliver your message safely. Our fate lies with you.'

With a last nod of farewell the riders dug in their heels and galloped away.

'Will they make it?' Sir Gerallt Godwin voiced the question on all their minds.

The emissary watched as the riders disappeared beyond the edge of the plateau. 'Yes,' he said at last. 'They will make it.' He stepped up into the saddle and looked down at the sea of upturned faces. There was nothing more to be said. It was time for them to leave. With a sigh he brought his horse onto the path and started along the road to Clemoncé.

Simeon urged his mount forward and the black warhorse automatically fell in beside the emissary's grey. Likewise, Falco's horse required no direction it simply followed on behind.

As Falco reached the path Malaki led his horse over to ride beside his friend. Behind them came Fossetta on one of the packhorses, her arms wrapped round a young boy who chatted away incessantly. Then came Balthazak with Sir Gerallt and Bryna Godwin. Merryweather was behind them with Tobias securely tied to the horse beside his father. The ebullient nobleman was declaring to his son that, despite the cold, this was the most exciting adventure. Beside him Tobias lifted a crooked arm to gesture up the line towards Falco.

'Ballymudge...'

'He'll be fine,' said Merryweather reaching over to pat his son's withered leg. Tobias turned his wobbly head to look at his father. There was a frown of doubt on his lopsided face. 'He'll be fine,' insisted Merryweather with a smile. His optimistic nature would not allow him to consider anything else.

And thus the envoy to the Queen of Wrath led the people of Caer Dour into the mountains. They made surprisingly good time and by midday they had covered almost seven miles. The oppressive clouds had broken and apart from a few sweeping showers the refugees remained mostly dry. It was still cold but the blue sky raised their spirits and the mountains of northern Valentia looked beautiful in the afternoon sunlight. The long caravan of people had stopped for food and rest when a rider arrived to say that the army was closing on them and should catch them up shortly after sunset.

'That's good,' said the emissary. 'Tell Lord Cadell that we look forward to hearing his council.'

Without pausing for food or drink the rider simply turned about and picked his way back down the crowded trail.

The emissary watched him go before returning to discuss the practicalities of the army's arrival with Bellius and Morgan. They were deep in conversation when Simeon's voice demanded their attention.

'Chevalier!'

The old battle mage was on his feet, his ravaged face turned up towards the sky.

74

'What is it?' asked the emissary, coming to stand beside him.

'Something watches us,' said Simeon.

Falco felt a cold shiver run through him. He too had the sense of something watching, some insidious presence hanging in the air above them. He *had* put it down to the dark cloud of guilt and paranoia that was engulfing his mind. But now as he turned his eyes to the sky he could discern a distinct presence above them, distant and dark, a hot mote of evil.

Shielding his eyes the emissary gazed into the sky while around them others began to look upwards.

'There!' said Bryna suddenly. 'Near that thin line of cloud.'

She was right. They could all see it now, a tiny dark shape hovering over them.

'It has wings,' said Bryna.

'A bird,' suggested Merryweather hopefully.

'It's not a bird,' said Simeon.

'Schwarz engel,' said the emissary in the language of Illicia. 'A dark angel. A lesser demon of the Possessed.'

'Will it attack us?' asked Sir Gerallt.

'No,' said the emissary, climbing onto a stand of rocks. 'They are strong but they are not known for their bravery.' Once more he peered into the sky before looking down along the route which the riders had taken. 'They would not attack a mass of people, but they could pick off those who venture out alone.' He gritted his teeth in frustration. 'The demon must be gaining in strength if it is bringing through lesser minions.'

'Will it go after the riders?' asked Sir Gerallt.

'It will return to its master first,' said the emissary, 'to inform the demon of our flight. But then...' The unfinished sentence left them in little doubt.

'Then we must warn them!' said Bellius, seeming more animated than he had all day.

'It's too late,' said Morgan. 'They were our fastest riders and they have several hours head start.'

'We shall just have to hope for the best,' said the emissary. 'They might be overlooked.'

'And if they are not?' asked Bellius.

'Then they should seek the cover of rocks or trees,' said the emissary. 'If they hold their ground they might just stand a chance.'

All around him people were switching their gaze from the sky to the mountain trail along which they had come. Until now the demon army had seemed faceless and abstract but now a creature of darkness was actually looking down upon them. Suddenly the threat of the Possessed seemed horribly real.

'We should get moving,' said the emissary, and his tone had the force of command.

People packed away their food and the ripple of preparedness travelled down the long caravan of refugees. Within a matter of minutes the people of Caer Dour were on their way once more. At times the trail was too narrow for two horses to walk abreast but at others it widened out and as the afternoon sun made feeble attempts to warm them Malaki drew alongside his friend once more.

'Did you see it?' he said, keeping his voice low so that the people around them would not overhear.

Falco did not answer.

'It looked like a bird to me,' persisted Malaki. 'But Bryna's eyes are better than most. She says it was the wrong shape, more like a man with wings.'

Falco gave his friend a sideways look.

'You've been talking to Bryna?' he wheezed.

Malaki smiled with pride, but also with relief. It was the first time Falco had spoken all day. Surely that was a good sign.

'A little,' said Malaki. 'We've been discussing arrow points.'

'Arrow points,' said Falco as if that were entirely reasonable.

He glanced across at his friend and the blush on Malaki's cheeks made his birthmark stand out more clearly than ever.

Falco's mouth curved into a smile and the two boys laughed.

They continued on in silence and the sun disappeared once more behind the clouds. The landscape was craggy, the grey rocks interspersed with heather, gorse and twisted stands of mountain pine. The sound of startled birds accompanied them as they made their way along the remote winding track. Rounding a curve they could see that the trail led down to a river valley. It was wide and sheltered, a good place to make camp.

The light was fading by the time they reached the floor of the valley and Malaki reached up to help Falco down from his horse. He laid him down in a sandy hollow and set about making a fire. Darkness brought a certain calm to the camp with people cocooned in the reassuring glow of firelight. The fear and shock were still present but they were on their way, one day closer to the city of Toulwar, one day closer to safety. The night was still young but many had settled down into bedrolls and blankets, exhausted by the tension and the miles of difficult travel.

All Falco wanted to do was sleep. Instead he found himself hunched forward and sweating as Fossetta removed the silk dressing from the burns on his shoulder.

'Good,' said Heçamede who was kneeling beside the housekeeper. 'There's no sign of infection. Now, clean the edges and spray it with the atomiser.'

She handed Fossetta a clean swab and Falco choked back a cry as she cleaned the edge of his wounds. Even the gentle misting of herb infused water burned like fire and Falco stared straight ahead, trying to shut out the pain as Fossetta applied a fresh piece of oiled silk. Finally the dressing was changed and Falco was allowed to relax back into a more comfortable position. Then, just when he thought he could close his eyes and shut out the world the emissary appeared at Heçamede's shoulder.

'How is he?' he asked, crouching down beside the healer.

'I think you're right,' said Heçamede and Falco looked away as she drew back his garments to expose his chest.

'See how the rash is spreading, and it does not pale when compressed.'

'Yes,' said the emissary. 'This looks more and more like the disease that took my sister.'

'If it's not crimson lung then what is it?' asked Fossetta. 'And can it be cured?'

'It's an infection caused by the spores of a fungus,' said Heçamede.' The spores are released when certain types of wood burn. In rare cases the fungus can invade the body.'

'In Illicia it is treated with the resin from the Silver pine but I'm told this tree does not grow in Valentia,' said the emissary.

'We could use the resin from Corros pine trees,' said Heçamede.

'But that's caustic,' said Fossetta. 'Just touching the sap can cause burns.'

'We have no choice,' said Heçamede. 'The infection is spreading. Soon the tissue will begin to break down.'

Fossetta blanched. She knew what Heçamede was saying. The infection was not only spreading across Falco's skin. It was in his lungs too. If it was not stopped he would be consumed from within. Her jaw bunched and tears sprang to her eyes as she looked up and down the valley for signs of Corros pine trees. Then she turned to Malaki.

'Come!' she said. 'You will help me look.'

Malaki had never heard such a tone in Fossetta's voice before.

'Of course,' he said, rising to his feet and fastening on his sword. There had been no more sign of the dark angel but still, it would not be wise to venture into the darkness unarmed.

'We'll start on the northern slopes,' said Fossetta. 'Corros pine prefers the shade.' And with that they were gone.

Slumping back onto his bedroll Falco turned his face away from the fire. Why were they bothering? Why did they even care? It was all his own fault anyway. All he wanted to do now was sleep. It did not matter to him if he never woke again.

13
Dark Angel

The army caught up with them shortly after nightfall and Lord Cadell immediately fell into conference with the emissary and the leaders of Caer Dour. Drifting in and out of sleep Falco could hear the murmur of their discussions. It was getting late when he woke to see Simeon and the emissary returning to their bedrolls. The two men sat down and Malaki rose to fetch them each a bowl of soup and a hunk of bread.

Hovering on the edge of sleep Falco watched as they quietly ate their supper. His eyes slid across the rocky ground, picking out the dim shapes of people in the firelight. Bryna Godwin lay not far away and Falco watched as Sir Gerallt settled down beside his daughter. Close to them was Merryweather, his great heavy body curled around his son who was sleeping soundly in his father's embrace.

Heçamede's bedroll was spread within the encircling light of the fire, but she was tending to the needs of the people while Fossetta had taken herself off to one side to prepare the needles from the Corros pine trees that she and Malaki had collected. Even from here Falco's eyes watered as veils of the acerbic fumes wafted across the campsite.

As Simeon and the emissary finished their late supper Balthazak took something from his saddle bag and approached the emissary. Crouching down he handed him a small bundle wrapped in a soft white cloth.

The emissary looked surprised. 'I can't believe you found the time,' he said.

Balthazak inclined his head as if it were nothing. 'It still needs to be cleaned and the leather needs to be polished and braided. I have a finished belt if you need it.'

The emissary waved the suggestion away.

'I'd like to do it myself.'

Balthazak nodded. 'Just let me know when you need to set the rivets.'

'Thank you,' said the emissary. He opened the bundle to reveal a needle file, several lengths of black leather cord and a silver belt buckle in the shape of a horse's head.

'You've a nice touch,' said Balthazak.

The emissary snorted softly. 'This was my fourth attempt.'

'I hope she's worth it.'

'She is,' said the emissary.

With a smile Balthazak returned to his bedroll. He drained the last of the wine from his cup then he drew up his cloak and fell asleep. Within a matter of seconds he was snoring loudly. The people gathered around the fire looked at each other in mild embarrassment. Malaki shook his head despairingly.

'He does that every night,' he said and people laughed then one by one they followed the blacksmith's lead.

It was some time later when Falco stirred from sleep. Heçamede had finally returned to her bedroll and Falco thought that everyone was asleep until he saw movement from across the fire.

The emissary lifted the belt buckle and blew away some of the detritus that he had scraped off with the file. In the faint glow of the fire Falco could see that the silver metal was beginning to shine. Seeming to sense that someone was watching him, the emissary turned to look at Falco, his grey eyes dark and shadowed. For a moment the emissary held him with his searching gaze then he gave him a slow nod of acknowledgement and Falco lowered his eyes to the fire. His gaze sank deep into the glowing embers and slowly he fell asleep once more.

He woke to the feel of rain on his face.

It was barely daylight and yet the people of Caer Dour were breaking camp. All around there was the bustle of activity interspersed with the crying of children. The dry night had turned wet and cold and people steamed as they prepared for another difficult day of travel.

Falco tried to raise himself but even the effort of sitting up put a strain on his chest, the damp weather only compounding the problem with his breathing. Fossetta crouched beside him with a bowl of porridge.

'Not yet,' said Heçamede who was leaning over a copper pan set above the fire. 'He wouldn't keep it down.'

Fossetta nodded and watched as Heçamede reached for the clay jar that she herself had prepared. As the water in the pot began to boil Heçamede spooned a small amount of a brown tar-like substance into the pan. The effect was immediate and the healer screwed up her face and turned away from the plumes of acrid steam.

Falco felt a sense of foreboding as Fossetta put down the porridge and cradled him against her chest. Holding it at arm's length Heçamede brought the pan forward with a blanket to go over Falco's head. The anxiety on her face did nothing to allay Falco's trepidation, but he did not resist as they set the pan on a stone and leaned him towards it. Heçamede threw the cloth over his head and Falco was shrouded in darkness. The fumes stung his eyes and made his skin prickle and burn, but as he drew a breath the pain exploded in his chest. It felt like he was drowning in acid.

Despite his illness and inherent weakness he lurched back, butting Fossetta in the cheek and spilling the pan of boiling water onto the earth. The people around him cursed at the foul biting fumes and Falco slumped onto his side coughing and choking and trying desperately to fill his lungs with clear cold air.

Heçamede bent down to see if Fossetta was all right but the housekeeper seemed more concerned about Falco. After all, it was she who had made the preparation that had caused him so much pain. Malaki threw aside the blanket and helped Falco into a more comfortable position, staring down at the rash which extended beyond his hairline.

'Heçamede!' he called.

Seeing that no real damage was done Heçamede left Fossetta to see what had caught Malaki's attention. He pointed to Falco's brow. The leading edges of the rash had turned from crimson to black.

'It works,' said Heçamede. 'The fumes are killing the fungus. This could cure him.'

'If it doesn't kill him first,' said Malaki.

'He is dying already,' said Heçamede. 'At least this way he has a chance.'

Conceding the point, Malaki helped Falco into the saddle and handed him a flask of water. Falco gulped it down as if the water could quench the burning pain in his chest and throat.

'Can you ride?' asked Malaki.

Falco gave him a nod as he took the reins and gripped the pommel of his saddle. As the people climbed out of the valley so the army came down, moving with the strength and speed of a disciplined force. They formed up on the flat river valley and waited for the leaders to speak to them.

Lord Cadell stood in the huddle of nobles with Bellius, Morgan and Simeon but it was the emissary who came forward to speak. He climbed onto a stand of boulders so that they could see him more clearly.

'Men of Caer Dour, and women,' he added, for there was more than a handful of women's faces staring up at him from the ranks of the army. 'We have learned from Lord Cadell that the demon army is closer than we had thought.' He paused. 'If the Possessed continue to advance at such a rate then the people will have no chance of reaching safety. They will be overtaken.'

Grim faces grew a shade grimmer. They knew what the emissary was going to ask of them.

'We must find a way to slow their advance,' the emissary said. 'Small forces of mounted troops to fall back and slow the enemy. Not to stand and fight,' he added quickly, 'but to harry, to make them pause, to give us more time.'

Everyone looked to the soldiers on horseback. Only they had the speed to attack with any hope of retreating from harm.

'We are looking for forces of a hundred,' said the emissary. 'And we will need officers to lead them.'

Without exception the officers urged their mounts forward, their troops standing firm behind them. There were almost three hundred horses in the Caer Dour cavalry and it seemed that all of them were willing to volunteer for this most dire of tasks. The emissary smiled grimly, but his satisfaction was tempered by caution. How many would volunteer once they had looked into the bone-white eyes of the enemy.

Falco looked across to see Malaki talking to his father. After a brief exchange he saw Malaki's head droop forward and Balthazak reached out to embrace him. With this simple farewell Balthazak left his son to join the volunteers.

The first one hundred were chosen and once again the emissary stepped forward.

'Be careful,' he told them. 'Do not try to make a stand. Attack and fall back. When the fear becomes too great withdraw before it claims you. Every hour that you can buy us is precious. Every hour brings us that much closer to safety.' He looked at them a final time. 'Have faith, and come back safely. Farewell.'

And with that they left, a small contingent of men riding back down the trail to face the demon and the two thousand warriors of the Possessed. Falco watched them go and a piece of him went with them. He did not need Bellius to accuse him, he knew he was responsible.

With the first rearguard detachment on its way the army set off to follow the people. Falco's horse fell in behind Simeon's once more and another long day of travel began. The steady rain did not let up and by midday the refugees were drenched and miserable. As the day wore on Falco felt that his breathing was a little easier. He was not sure if it was just his imagination, but the tight feeling of slow suffocation seemed a fraction less.

As the path widened Malaki drew up alongside. His father had not been selected for the first detachment, but Balthazak had chosen to ride with the rest of the cavalry, bringing up the army's rear.

'How do you feel?' asked Malaki. He noticed the way Falco was now holding the reins and not clinging to the pommel in an exhausted stupor.

'Sore,' said Falco. 'And wet.'

Malaki smiled. Falco still sounded weak, but even a despondent response was better than none at all. They rode on in silence for a while, the rain falling in a slow and steady drizzle. Turning in the saddle Malaki peered back down the trail.

'I wonder how long before they meet the Possessed,' he paused and Falco could sense his anxiety, his doubt. 'Do you think you would have the courage to stand?'

Falco looked into his friend's deep brown eyes.

'It's the fear,' said Malaki. He nodded towards Simeon and the emissary. 'They talk about the fear as if it were an actual force, something that could reach out to devour us.'

'It is,' said Falco. 'It could.'

Malaki stared across at his friend but Falco just hunched forward pulling the hood of his cloak down over his face. The wind had strengthened and the rain was angling towards them. It was going to be a long and miserable afternoon.

*

Thirty miles ahead of them, four riders were picking their way down a steep rocky slope. Since leaving the townsfolk the riders had grown close. They rode together as a single unit, measuring their pace to cover the difficult ground as quickly as they could. They had been charged with a great responsibility and yet they were enjoying the challenges that the mountain path laid in front of them.

They smiled now as they left the rocky slopes and raced along the flat expanse of a river valley, a rare chance for the horses to show their speed.

Anwyn looked back as her horse, Deneb, tore through a rivulet of sparkling water. She had reached the valley first and was determined to beat the men to the other side. Her heart sank as she saw Godfrey coming up hard behind her. Altair, his magnificent black stallion, stood a full hand taller than her own chestnut mare and never seemed to tire. Even as she watched they thundered past her, Godfrey whooping with delight and Altair straining forward, revelling in his own strength.

'Ok,' thought Anwyn, gritting her teeth. 'You, but not the others.' She gave a light tap with her heels and Deneb surged beneath her with a renewed burst of speed.

Smiling, she looked back once more. Gareth and Dylan were thirty lengths behind. There was no way they would catch her now. She was about to look away when she caught sight of a black shape in the sky behind Dylan.

Deneb whinnied in protest as Anwyn pulled the horse to a sharp halt. She wheeled about, her heart suddenly filled with a dreadful sense of foreboding. The dark shape was falling from the sky, heading straight for Dylan. Anwyn had the impression of dark wings and a body like that of an emaciated man, the skin a dark mottled grey. She caught a flash of teeth and shining claws and then the creature swooped down, slamming into both horse and rider and dragging them to the ground.

Lying on its side the horse thrashed in the shallow river. It gave a sudden, horrible scream and became still. Trapped beneath it, Dylan was lying in the cold water. The creature was hunched over him, its talons hooked in his chest. It bent down over Dylan and when it straightened up its teeth were dripping with blood.

Anwyn felt as if the breath was locked in her chest. She could only stare as the creature fixed her with black eyes that shone like orbs of polished marble. Its face was almost human but with the nose of some hellish bat and a mouth filled with sharp teeth like dark points of steel.

A shower of water splashed Anwyn's face as Gareth pulled up beside her. He reached over to grab her arm. 'Ride on!' he cried. 'Anwyn!' he screamed when she did not respond. 'There's nothing we can do. Ride on!'

With a last look at Dylan's body lying in the river Anwyn turned away from the angel of darkness and raced for the far side of the valley where Godfrey was waiting for them, shock and fear written large upon his face.

'What happened?'

'Something took Dylan,' said Gareth. 'We must go on.'

Gareth seemed calm, but there was a tremor in his voice that suggested he was only just clinging to some level of control. Without another word he turned his horse up the rocky slope and began to climb out of the valley. In a state of shock Godfrey and Anwyn followed but they had not gone far when an inhuman cry echoed around the valley.

Looking back they saw the creature rising from its prey, its dark wings beating the air as it rose into the sky. The creature would not attack again, not while they were ready and waiting for it. Instead it climbed higher until it disappeared among the clouds.

Checking the leather dispatch tubes that hung across their backs the three remaining riders pushed their horses hard up the slope. Ahead of them lay the highest part of the mountain path and beyond that the trail led steadily downwards.

Being raised in Caer Dour, the mountains had always seemed to offer security but now they felt dangerous and exposed. And so they pushed their horses hard, anxious to leave the mountains and find some cover on the forested pathways of Clemoncé.

14

Rearguard

Falco's spittle was flecked with blood. It was the morning of the third day since leaving Caer Dour and it was raining. It was still early but they had already been moving for three hours and it was time for the first rest break of the day. Falco leaned against a boulder while Fossetta and Heçamede examined a gobbet of his sputum in a small ceramic bowl. The phlegm was streaked with red and their expressions were grim. There had been no evidence of blood until Falco started taking the Corros pine infusion.

'It's not as thick as normal,' offered Fossetta. 'Not as dark either.'

Heçamede nodded but her expression remained grave. 'But the infusion is damaging the tissue, and that will make him more vulnerable to the infection.'

'And what then?'

'Then we shall see which is stronger,' said the healer, 'the infection or the son of Aquila Danté.'

Heçamede placed a hand on Falco's brow. Her face was stern but slowly her expression softened and she stroked his cheek before removing her hand.

Fossetta reached out to help Falco down into a seated position but he waved her away. 'Try to eat something,' she said and Falco gave her a half-hearted nod.

He did not like to admit it but in a strange way he was feeling better. The burns on his neck and shoulder still hurt terribly and his lungs felt like they had been scoured with shards of glass, but his breathing definitely felt easier. He glanced over to a nearby pool where Malaki was watering the horses. Further up the trail the townsfolk were already walking again but the pace had slowed. People were cold and miserable and the impetus of the first two days had given way to a dreary trudge.

His gaze drifted in the other direction towards the army. There was tension in the air as everyone waited for the first rearguard to return. They had been gone for almost a day and people were anxious for news of their fate. Falco could see the concern on the soldiers' faces as they talked in low voices. Closing his eyes he leaned back against the boulder. This was the first time in three days that he had stood upright and his back felt like it had fused into a permanent stoop. Still, he did his best to straighten his spine, turning his face up into the rain and wincing as he drew the cold air into his lungs.

'I swear you look an inch taller.'

Falco looked over as Malaki returned with the horses.

'No, really,' said Malaki. 'And you've got some colour in your cheeks. Either that or you've been using Fossetta's rouge again.'

Falco turned away to hide the beginnings of a smile. 'Fossetta doesn't wear rouge,' he said.

'She does when she's down at the Hoof and Horn.' Malaki raised his eyebrows meaningfully.

Finally Falco laughed. The Hoof and Horn was an ale house of dubious reputation and the thought of Fossetta wearing rouge for the benefit of its bawdy patrons was actually quite funny. He tried to adjust his stance but he slipped on the wet rocks and stumbled to the ground, biting back a curse as his shoulder brushed against the rock.

'Easy there,' said Malaki, helping him into a more comfortable position.

Falco pushed him away and Malaki settled back on his haunches. 'Seriously though, you are looking better. The potion is working. You just have to stay under a bit longer. It's like Heçamede says, the fumes have to penetrate deeply otherwise the infection will come back worse than ever.'

Falco averted his eyes. Breathing that stuff was almost impossible. Three times now he had drawn the corrosive steam into his lungs and each time the effect had been the same, a paroxysm of painful retching. Malaki might have pressed him further but their attention was suddenly drawn to a ripple of activity moving up the line towards them.

'It's the rearguard,' said Falco.

'Thank the stars,' murmured Malaki.

They watched as the mounted troops advanced, making their way towards the leaders at the head of the army. As they rode past, Malaki spotted a friend of his father, a big man on a great warhorse. 'Marcus!' he called out.

Catching sight of the blacksmith's son the man drew his horse over. His face was wet with rain but even so they could see that he had been crying and this simple observation seemed to unsettle Malaki more than anything else.

'Where's your father?' asked Marcus.

'Further back,' said Malaki. 'With the main body of the army.'

Marcus nodded. He looked lost, confused.

'So few,' said Malaki, looking at the small number of men moving past them.

'We lost only seven,' said Marcus. 'The rest are being cared for.'

'Are they badly hurt?' asked Malaki but Marcus just stared.

'Not wounded,' he said. 'Undone.'

Malaki stared up at the big man, an expression of puzzlement on his face.

Slowly Marcus turned his head to look at Falco.

'You're the one from the dragon stone,' he said. 'The one from the summoning.'

Falco felt cowed by the desolation in the man's gaze.

'You have done us great harm,' said Marcus, and such was the look in his eyes that Malaki actually took a protective step forward.

Finally Marcus raised his eyes.

'I must go,' he said. 'The others must be warned.' And with that he urged his horse on.

Malaki blew out his cheeks with relief as the big man moved away. He had been surprised by the tension and confused by Marcus's comments. 'Undone,' he said turning to Falco. 'What does he mean, undone?'

Falco did not answer. He understood the darkness in Marcus's eyes; he knew what it meant to be undone by fear.

Beside him, Malaki's gaze turned inward as the poisoned flower of doubt bloomed in his heart. Like most Valentians, Malaki had grown up to accept the fear of battle, the fear of injury and death, but this was something different. This was the fear of eternal darkness and despair, the fear of something that you could not fight. Falco had lived with *this* fear his entire life but now it was seeping into the real world and his heart ached to see the effect it was having on his friend.

They managed a few mouthfuls of food while the officers finished giving their report and then it was time for the second rearguard to assemble. The two youths climbed back onto their horses to watch as the men chosen for the second force came forward.

'That's Bryna's father,' said Malaki as Sir Gerallt Godwin joined the group.

The regal looking man brought his horse forward to stand with the common soldiers. He would be one of the officers leading them. Falco looked back to see if he could see Bryna. She had been walking with the healers, and yes, he could see her now, standing with Heçamede on a low promontory. Her complexion seemed a shade paler as she watched her father take his place at the head of the small force. And then, beside him Malaki stiffened as another rider moved out to join Sir Gerallt and the others.

It was Balthazak.

Falco glanced at his friend but Malaki's eyes were fixed firmly on his father as the blacksmith took his place behind Sir Gerallt, both men staring straight ahead, their minds fixed on the task ahead of them.

Finally they were all assembled and without further ado the second rearguard disappeared back down the trail. Riding quickly, it might take them as little as six hours before they encountered the Possessed.

The enemy was closing fast.

There was a sense of discomfort in the air as the army prepared to move on. It was not easy to watch your comrades ride into danger while you marched in the opposite direction. Falco felt the guilt more keenly than any and now Malaki's father was among those paying the price for his actions. He looked around uneasily only to find that people were looking at him, staring at him as Marcus had done with dark unsettling eyes.

'Yes,' they seemed to say. 'That's him. He's the one that sided with the dragon.'

Falco bowed low in the saddle. He cast a worried glance in Malaki's direction, frightened of what he might see, but his friend was absorbed in his own thoughts, his eyes downcast, his face tight with anxiety. In silence they turned back onto the trail. The healers had already started walking and with the second force on its way the army resumed its march.

A few soldiers were sent ahead to spur the townsfolk onward. They could not afford to be slowed by lethargy. Lunch was eaten on the move, people travelled in silence and by early afternoon they had reached the flat expanse of a river valley. Ahead of them they could see the path winding steeply up the far side, rising towards the highest part of the route to Clemoncé.

As they rode out onto the floor of the valley they became aware that the line of people was being diverted around something that lay in the river beside the path. Malaki rose up in his stirrups but he could not see what was causing the obstruction.

'Something's not right,' he said.

People ahead were beginning to look back, staring at Falco. One of them looked directly at him and spat on the ground. Malaki glanced at Falco, concerned at how this open display of hostility might affect his friend but Falco was more concerned with what it was that lay in the river. He felt a shiver of dread at what it might be, but when the leaders went to investigate Falco went with them.

'It's one of the riders,' said Malaki as he pulled up behind Falco.

Falco barely heard him. He felt like he was looking down from a great height, staring at the body lying in the river. The rider lay trapped beneath the body of his horse. His throat had been torn out and flaps of ragged flesh rippled in the clear cold water. The veins on the rider's body showed black beneath his skin as if he had been infected by some kind of necrosis and his eyes were open and staring, leeched of colour and frosted with cataracts, his expression frozen in a moment of terror.

'What about the others?' said Bellius Snidesson. 'What if they're all dead?'

'There's no sign of that,' said the emissary, crouching down beside the man. 'We must hope that they are still alive.'

'And if they are not?'

The emissary silenced Bellius with a contemptuous glance but his words echoed in Falco's mind

What about the others?

If the riders did not make it through then no one would be coming to help them. The demon would catch them in the mountains and it would kill them all. Falco looked at the line of people winding up the hillside ahead of them, the men, the women, the children.

'*By the stars,*' he thought. '*What have I done?*'

*

Anwyn kept her eyes on Gareth as the three remaining riders made their way down the exposed narrow path. To their left the mountain dropped away sharply, falling several hundred feet to the river below. But they were getting lower. Spurred on by Dylan's death they were making good progress. The mountains were behind them; ahead they could see the green valleys and sprawling forests of Clemoncé. Anwyn glanced over her shoulder to see Godfrey keeping pace with them, a solid presence bringing up the rear. His thin face was shadowed with fear but he gave her a reassuring nod, patting Altair's neck to steady him. The great black stallion was not comfortable at the back of the line. He wanted to be at the head, leading from the front.

She drew her attention back to the path. A few lengths ahead Gareth glanced back at her, a quick look to make sure she was all right. He was just looking away when the creature took him. It flew down so fast that she never saw it coming. Just a sweep of dark wings and Gareth was gone, torn from the mountainside, his horse screaming as it tumbled from the path.

Anwyn was almost unhorsed as Deneb careered to a halt. The terrified horse skittered towards the edge of the path but then Altair slammed into her, Godfrey driving him forward, pushing Anwyn away from the dizzying drop.

Deneb calmed and Anwyn looked out to see the winged creature rising higher into the air, Gareth dangling beneath it like a scarecrow plucked from a farmer's field. He made no sound but she could see him clutching at the talons locked in his neck and shoulders. The dark angel stared down at them as it lifted its prey higher into the sky, but then suddenly it ripped its claws free and Gareth's body plummeted towards the river below. The creature flexed its talons and then it let out a soul-piercing cry and dove towards them.

It was almost upon them when Godfrey drew Altair up onto his hind legs. The black stallion flailed at the air, catching the creature with a solid kick from one of his steel-shod hooves. The creature gave a shriek of pain and tumbled away, falling swiftly before recovering itself and disappearing away up the valley.

For a moment they could not move. The horses trembled with fear, ears laid flat and nostrils flared. Godfrey recovered first, reaching over to place a hand on Anwyn's arm.

'We'll never make it,' said Anwyn, her eyes glazed and her young voice choked with fear.

'Oh, but we will,' said Godfrey. 'We'll make it together.'

Slowly Anwyn gave him a nod and Godfrey smiled.

'Now, let's ride!' he shouted and Altair leapt away down the path.

Without a moment's hesitation Anwyn followed after him and they flew down mountainside as if the demon itself were at their backs. As they descended, the craggy peaks gave way to grassy hills. Tomorrow they would ride for the cover of Clemoncé's forests and the city of Toulwar.

15

Sacrifice

The people of Caer Dour walked long into the night. The Possessed were now so close that they could not afford to rest for long. It was almost midnight before they settled down to camp on a rocky plateau bordered by cliffs that fell away into darkness.

Huddled once more on the stony ground Falco watched as the emissary came to speak with Simeon and the other leaders. They were all exhausted but veryone was busy; everyone had a job to do. Malaki was tending to a horse that had thrown a shoe, Heçamede moved from one needy patient to the next, while Fossetta was busy brewing another infusion of Corros pine.

Things were looking grim and Falco could hear the leaders discussing their plans for making a stand. The army could not win but they might be able to survive long enough for help to reach them. Falco heard the deep voice of his master.

'I should be able to hold the demon back for a while,' said Simeon. 'But I do not have the strength I once had.'

'Then we must make it count,' said the emissary. He turned to the captains of the army. 'Simeon is the key,' he told them. 'If he falls then we are all lost. We must protect him. And in turn he will shield us from the worst of the fear.'

He turned to address Morgan, asking if there was anything that the magi could do to help but Falco did not want to hear it. He sank down into his cloak. Fossetta had almost finished the infusion and soon he would be choking and retching once more. He was just closing his eyes for a few minutes rest when he became aware of a commotion moving through the army.

Wincing at the pain he raised himself up to a seated position and looked out over the people sitting round the scattered campfires. A group of riders was moving through the camp, picking their way towards the leaders. Malaki suddenly appeared beside him, wiping his hands on a rag.

'What is it?' he asked.

'Riders from the rearguard,' said Falco.

Malaki reached down to help him up as Falco struggled to his feet. Something was wrong. As the riders drew closer they could see that there were several shapes slung over the saddles of the horses... bodies.

A sudden sense of horror swept over Falco as he looked at one of the bodies draped over a horse. Malaki saw it too and, still wiping his hands, he took a few steps forward. A hubbub of whispers rose up from the soldiers in the army and slowly they turned, looking at Malaki with veiled eyes.

Malaki began to walk forward, his steps becoming quicker as the light of the moon glinted off blue-steel armour.

'*No!*' thought Falco, even as the murmur of a name began to settle on the air. '*No!*'

'De Vane.'

The wave of hushed whispers spoke the name, de Vane.

Suddenly Falco recognised the figure standing beside the body in blue-steel armour. It was Sir Gerallt Godwin, Bryna's father. Cords were cut and Sir Gerallt lowered the blacksmith's body to the ground. Eyes followed Malaki as he took a few more steps through the crowd.

Sir Gerallt moved to intercept him but Malaki pushed him aside, stumbling forward to look down on the body of his father. The smith's armour was battered and torn, his face awash with blood. Malaki did not notice the injuries, it was the grief that crushed him. He slumped to his knees, gathering his father's body into his arms, his strong muscles bunched as if he could somehow squeeze the life back into his father's corpse.

Sir Gerallt knelt beside him.

'He never succumbed to the fear,' he said as if this were of critical importance. 'Some of the men had become trapped in a gully and your father led a charge to break them free. His horse was injured and Balthazak was cut down, but he didn't succumb to the fear.' Sir Gerallt laid his hand on Malaki's broad back. 'The Possessed will never claim his soul,' he said. 'Your father is at peace.'

Finally the tension went out of Malaki's body and his broad shoulders heaved with great silent sobs.

Falco could not bear it. He looked down at his friend holding the broken body of his father. Malaki had loved him dearly but so had he. Like Simeon, the blacksmith had always been kind to him, never judging, never suggesting that Malaki should forego his troublesome and sickly friend. Falco had always been welcome in the forge, and always found it comforting, the warmth, the smell, the sound of the hammer and the bellows. The grief tore at his soul. And if so great for him, how much greater must it be for his friend.

Falco could not bear it.

Blinking through his tears he turned away, stumbling through the camp, desperate to escape the waves of despair that swept through his mind as the voice from his nightmares mocked him.

You would never have the courage
You would never have the strength.

People cursed as he stumbled past them but Falco did not care. He barely saw them, barely heard their protestations. No matter what the voices said, he would have the courage to end this pain.

'Ballymudge!'

Somewhere in the distance Falco registered Tobias's voice as the crippled boy saw him staggering past. And then there was the voice of Merryweather, filled with concern.

'Falco... Falco, are you all right?'

Falco ignored them, these were phantom voices, they held no meaning for him. All he knew was pain and grief.

'Fossetta! He's over here,' called out Merryweather.

Falco staggered on until he reached the edge of the camp but he did not stop, instead he struggled on into the night. The ground continued for a while but then the shadowy rocks gave way to a yawning blackness. That was where he needed to be. Maybe in the darkness he would find some peace.

Feeling as if he were floating rather than walking Falco moved towards the darkness. He was almost upon it when something slammed into him and pulled him to the ground. His shoulder screamed with pain but that was nothing compared to the frustration he felt at being denied the darkness. With desperate strength he lashed out at the thing that held him. His fists made contact with flesh and bone and slowly he heard someone crying.

'Falco, stop!' the voice was crying, a woman's voice, a voice he knew. 'Please, stop.'

It was Fossetta.

All the strength went out of Falco's body. He slumped back on the ground, Fossetta's arms still locked around his waist, shoulders hunched against the blows that Falco had rained down upon her. Light bloomed around them as people arrived with torches. In a daze Falco felt himself raised into the air. Beside him yawned the edge of the cliffs and he made one last lunge for oblivion but strong arms held him fast.

'No,' said the voice of the emissary. 'You will find no redemption there.'

The emissary carried Falco back to his bedroll and laid him down. They offered him water but Falco turned his head. They tried to make him breathe the Corros fumes but he overturned the bowl. He did not sleep, he only drifted in and out of a nightmare where Malaki stood over the body of his father with Darius and the dead rider from the river. There were flames in the dream and a shadowy figure that might have been his father or it might have been the demon coming to claim his soul.

Falco could not tell.

The morning dawned misty and wet, but nothing had changed. Falco still sought the oblivion that would end his pain. They had tried to make him eat but he refused and now they were trying to make him take the fumes once more.

'You will die if you don't,' said Fossetta, kneeling down to beseech him.

'Let him die,' said someone nearby and Fossetta hung her head in despair.

'What's the matter?'

Falco stiffened at the sound of Malaki's voice.

'He won't take it,' said Fossetta. 'He won't breathe the fumes.'

Slowly Falco peered upwards. Malaki's shoulders were bowed. His brown eyes were red-rimmed and the crimson birthmark on his face stood out starkly against his deathly pale skin.

'Won't take it,' he repeated menacingly.

'So what!' said a nameless voice.

'It's all his fault anyway,' said another.

'Let him die.'

Malaki's jaw bunched as people called for Falco's death. Then suddenly he started forward. Falco lurched back in alarm but Malaki reached down and grabbed him, hauling him out of his bedroll and dragging him across the rocks to where the Corros infusion simmered by the fire. Then, throwing him down, Malaki crouched behind him, clamping one massive arm round Falco's skinny chest. Finally he grabbed a fistful of Falco's long black hair and thrust his head forward.

'Bring it!' he snapped.

Heçamede hesitated while Fossetta stood clutching the blanket. They had never known Malaki behave so harshly. Slowly Heçamede nodded and reached for the steaming pan.

Falco began to struggle as they came forward but Malaki held him fast. Heçamede set the pan down and Falco would have dashed it aside but his arms and legs were pinned. Malaki gave Fossetta a nod and she threw the blanket over Falco's head as Heçamede removed the lid from the pot.

Falco went limp as the fumes engulfed him but slowly he began to squirm. Finally he could hold his breath no longer and he began to buck and thrash but there was no way he could break free of Malaki's strength. He coughed and gagged but Malaki did not let him go. Fossetta and Heçamede exchanged anxious glances. Falco had never stayed under as long as this.

'Malaki,' said Fossetta at last, but still the blacksmith's son held on.

'Malaki, that's enough,' said Heçamede. She was just reaching out to remove the blanket when Malaki released his hold. He cast him aside and Falco collapsed, choking and rasping for breath.

Everyone was shocked. People looked down at the pitiful figure writhing on the ground. Fossetta was crying but Malaki seemed not to care. He stood there, staring down at Falco and then, in a harsh throaty voice, he spoke.

'They might want you dead,' he said, stabbing a finger at the nearby townsfolk. 'But I don't.' Finally his composure broke and his words gave way to tears. 'I don't.'

Fossetta reached out to comfort him but he waved her away and stumbled off into the camp. The housekeeper knelt beside Falco, who was crying like a child, and even his tears were red with blood.

*

Anwyn and Godfrey were galloping at full stretch. After so long picking their way through the mountains it was a relief to maintain such speed. Anwyn was just beginning to believe they would make it when a shadow passed over the fields ahead of them.

'Just ride,' shouted Godfrey keeping pace beside her.

They rode together through a grassy meadow. Ahead of them, barely half a mile distant, was the edge of the forest.

If they could just reach the trees...

'We're not going to make it,' cried Anwyn, craning her neck to scan the skies. She could not see the creature but she knew it was there. She could feel its presence. She glanced across at Godfrey and it was clear from his face that he could feel it too. They knew the creature was about to strike and Godfrey's head seemed to droop in resignation. Then he steered Altair a little closer.

'Ride for the trees,' he called out suddenly. 'Anwyn,' he shouted, waiting until she looked across at him. 'Ride for the trees.'

She nodded, confused. They were already riding for the trees. But then Godfrey spoke a command to Altair and the great black stallion sprang away, leaving Deneb in its wake. For a moment Anwyn felt betrayed, abandoned, then she saw the shadow of the creature rippling over the grass and she knew what Godfrey was doing.

'No!' she called out. 'Godfrey, no!'

Godfrey pulled away from her, racing towards the safety of the trees. He knew that the creature would try to stop them. And he knew it would take the quickest one first. At least this way he might buy Anwyn enough time to reach

91

the forest. Then away from the right the creature streaked towards him, sweeping across his path with terrible speed. With the talons of its feet it grabbed Altair's head, the momentum of its attack breaking the horse's neck as it was yanked aside. The creature swung around, beating its wings as Altair went down. Godfrey was thrown from the saddle. He landed badly and did not get up.

Anwyn could not breathe, her chest felt tight with fear. For a moment she closed her eyes trying to focus on nothing more than keeping Deneb riding straight. Behind her she heard a chilling shriek and glancing back she saw the creature surge into the air, beating its wings, driving towards her. Her heart was racing and her eyes were awash with tears. Ahead of her the trees looked blurred and indistinct. She could not tell how close they were.

'Faster Deneb! Faster my love!' The words came out as a breathless sob but Deneb seemed to sense the urgency in her voice and somehow the chestnut mare found an extra burst of speed.

Suddenly the fringe of trees was growing larger, rising up to meet her. Anwyn's heart soared but then she heard the whistle of something scything through the air towards her. With desperate strength she yanked the reins to one side and Deneb snorted in protest as she tried to react. It was only the perfect union of horse and rider that saved her.

The dark angel screamed in frustration as the horse jinked to one side and its talons slashed at nothing but air. But the creature of darkness was surprisingly agile. It swept round and gave chase once more.

Anwyn glanced back to see it closing fast. She would not surprise it a second time. She braced herself for the attack then blinked as something whipped across her face. A shadowy darkness engulfed her and branches whacked against her body as she plunged headlong into the forest. She had made it to the trees and the cries of the creature's frustration sounded suddenly muffled and distant.

Slowly the terror subsided and Anwyn drew back on the reins as she picked her way through the trees.

'Thank you,' she wept, leaning down to place her cheek against Deneb's sweating neck. 'My brave, brave girl. Thank you.'

Deneb whinnied nervously in reply.

'We're going to make it,' said Anwyn, her eyes picking out the line of the little used path. She reached back to settle the dispatch tube across her back and then she urged Deneb onwards. They were both exhausted but there would be time to rest when they reached Toulwar.

They were in the cover of the trees.

There was nothing that could stop them now.

*

The dark angel rose up high above the trees. Fury burned in its blackened heart, fury at being denied. But evil is ever a patient thing. And so it would wait. It could feel the woman through the trees. It could feel her fear and the pathetic hope in her tepid soul. It swept over the forest canopy picking out the broken line of the path. In the distance it could see the grey shadow of a city but there was much space in between.

Time yet to claim the human's soul.

16

Cowardice, Courage and Cunning

For the first time on the journey Falco was riding alone. Ahead of him were the sick and injured, behind him the leaders at the head of the army. Malaki was nowhere to be seen. The events of the previous night seemed vague and distant, like a half-remembered nightmare. However, something of the darkness had passed from his mind, leaving behind a kind of numbness. Falco had plumbed the depths of despair, now he just felt lost.

Slowly he became aware that someone was riding beside him. He glanced across to see the emissary.

'I am sorry about Balthazak.'

Falco bowed his head and after a while the emissary went on.

'We cannot change what has happened in the past. All we can do is look to the future.'

Falco looked across at him. He could not understand why the emissary afforded him so much attention.

'But it's not easy,' the older man went on. 'It takes courage.' And for just a second he held Falco's gaze. 'Whatever happens here, there are dark days ahead. All any of us can do is decide how to meet them. Will we fight? Will we try to make things better? Or will we lose hope and give in to despair?' He paused. 'This is your choice Falco Danté, and it is a simple one.'

He gave Falco a last meaningful look. Then with a parting nod he urged his mount forward and the grey warhorse trotted on.

Falco watched as the Queen's envoy moved along the line, offering a smile here, a word of comfort there. There was much in him that a young man could admire and Falco found himself wondering if his own father had ever offered such hope to the people he had led before everything ended in tragedy. In his heart he was certain that he had.

He began to look about. He saw the way Heçamede moved through the hospital train, Fossetta and Bryna helping where they could. That was worthy work. Surely that was something he could do.

A sudden bout of coughing doubled him over. The pain was bad but it was the pain of a raw wound, not the sickening ache of diseased flesh. When he wiped his mouth there was blood on his hand but it was fresh and bright. Falco looked at it in wonder. There was barely a trace of the mucous that had been so much a part of his life. His eyes filled with tears, a cleansing rain that somehow soothed his soul.

*

The blinding fear was just beginning to lift from Anwyn's mind and she began to take in more of her surroundings. It was obvious that the path was rarely used but still it was clear enough to ride at decent speed. Beneath her she could feel Deneb beginning to relax, falling into an easy gait, resting after the desperate race to reach the forest. Anwyn wanted to stop and rest but she was trying not to think of Godfrey and riding helped to divert her thoughts. Besides, as she continued she saw signs of the path being used. Surely now she must be getting close.

Ahead of her the way opened up as the trees gave way to a wide clearing. The path followed the shore of a lake, edged with reeds and dotted with ducks and other water fowl. Beyond that a golden meadow led back toward the trees.

At a steady canter Deneb emerged into the clearing and Anwyn closed her eyes as the warmth of the sun fell upon her face. They skirted the water and were almost at the meadow when something startled the birds on the lake. Anwyn was just wondering what might have frightened them when a dark shadow fell across her. She had time for a fleeting moment of terror before the dark angel hit her.

Pain stabbed into her sides as she was torn from the saddle and carried aloft. Talons, like hot spikes of iron pierced her ribs and she found herself looking back into the vile face of the creature. It stared over her shoulder, its breath scalding her neck and its black eyes glinting with triumph. A bead of silvery saliva dripped from its teeth and fell onto Anwyn's neck, fizzing and burning like acid. She did not cry out. She was already half way between this world and the next.

Dimly she reached for the dispatch tube that hung at her side. The strap was caught between the creature's talons but she managed to slip the buckle and pull it free. Her breath came in short gasps as her lungs filled with blood but she held on to the tube as the demon carried her higher. Looking down, Anwyn saw Deneb disappearing beneath the trees. She smiled to see her beloved horse safe but then she focussed on the dispatch tube and tears filled her eyes.

'I'm sorry,' she whispered, thinking of her parents and all the people she had failed. As her mind filled with darkness Anwyn let the tube slip from her fingers, a final effort to discharge the duty bestowed upon her.

The creature carried her out over the water and then, with a shriek of victory, it let her fall. Anwyn was dead before she hit the water, the splash muffled by a thick clump of reeds. For a moment the creature hung in the air looking down at its fallen prey, then with a final cry it soared upwards and disappeared east, back towards its master.

*

Again they walked into the night, pausing now for just a few short hours. People settled where they stopped, exhausted by the difficult miles and the growing weight of fear. And yet despite this there was a sense of excitement among the refugees. By now the riders should have reached Toulwar. Some spoke of the dark creature they had seen in the sky but most were convinced that, by the morning at least, help would be on its way.

Falco was not so sure but even this fragile hope was better than none. He steered his horse over to where Fossetta and Davis were setting a fire. Malaki did not come to help him down from his horse tonight but Falco could see him a short distance away, checking the horses' hooves. So, grabbing the pommel, Falco swung out of the saddle and dropped to his feet. He felt shaky and weak but he had relied on the help of others for too long. It was time he started to take care of himself.

Rising from the fire Fossetta came over and placed a hand on his brow. 'Will you take some soup?'

Falco nodded. 'Thank you,' he said.

Fossetta's face creased with emotion and she moved her hand to his cheek. The black despair had gone from Falco's eyes. Somehow the boy she loved had come back to them. Turning away, she busied herself with fetching soup.

Falco looked down to see Heçamede preparing another infusion by the fire. The healer did not look at him. She was still annoyed at his refusal to take the remedy. Falco's stomach churned with dread at the thought of breathing the fumes again and Heçamede's mouth tightened as he walked away, turning his back on the one thing that could save him. The treatment was working, but it would take several more doses before the infection was eradicated completely. If they did not wipe it out it would come back with a vengeance.

Turning away from Heçamede Falco walked slowly over to where Malaki was still examining the horses. He stood close but Malaki chose not to notice him. Falco stepped forward as his friend moved to the next horse in the line and the big youth was forced to stop. He straightened up, still refusing to look at his friend.

'It hurts too much to do it by myself,' said Falco, swallowing a sudden tightness in his throat. 'But if you could help me...'

He left the words hanging and after an awkward silence he nodded and turned back to the fire. Still walking unsteadily he took up the blanket they had been using for the infusion then he moved back to the fire and knelt down beside Heçamede.

Fossetta's eyes glittered as she looked from Falco to Malaki. For a moment the big youth remained stiff and unyielding but then his head bowed and he turned towards them. Without a word he walked over to Falco and crouched down behind him.

Falco handed Fossetta the blanket then, just as he had that morning, Malaki wrapped a powerful arm around his chest and grabbed a fistful of his hair. Heçamede placed the pan in front of Falco and, fighting every instinct of self-preservation, Falco leaned towards it. Fossetta covered him with the blanket and Heçamede removed the lid. The effect was the same as ever, but however much Falco struggled Malaki held him in a relentless grip.

After what seemed an eternity Heçamede gave a nod and Fossetta snatched away the blanket. Gasping for breath Falco straightened up but Malaki did not relax his grip at once. For a moment he held Falco tight, pressing his face into his friend's neck. Finally he released his hold and stood up, stumbling off into the camp.

Still retching Falco reached out towards him but Fossetta knelt down.

'Give him time,' she said, wiping Falco's face. 'Give him time.'

Falco watched Malaki disappear into the night. The darkness that had filled his mind might be growing less but the pain and grief would be slow to fade. He allowed them to help him back into a more comfortable position and tried not to cry out as they changed the dressing on his burned shoulder. Finally Heçamede began to pack things away in her satchel.

'Thank you,' said Falco.

'You're welcome.' The healer's reply was curt and Falco wondered if he had said something wrong. Then, getting to her feet, Heçamede left before Falco could see the tears shining in her dark Thraecian eyes.

Feeling a little confused Falco watched as she too melted into the night.

'Here,' said Fossetta, smiling. She handed Falco a bowl of soup and a slice of bread. 'How do you feel?'

'Hungry,' said Falco. He had hardly eaten anything in the last few days.

'Good,' said Fossetta. 'But take it easy,' she added. 'It'll take you a while to regain your strength.' Straightening up she turned back to the fire.

'I'm sorry,' said Falco quietly and Fossetta turned back to look at him.

'I know you are, my love. I know.'

Falco finished his soup and devoured his bread. Then, with a last look at the people around him, he closed his eyes to sleep. He slept deeply for almost two hours and woke to a familiar sense of warmth suffusing his body. Simeon was kneeling beside him, his hands extended over his chest.

'Lie still,' said the old battle mage and Falco settled back down. 'The rash has all but gone,' said Simeon.

'I feel different,' said Falco, wondering, as he often did, how Simeon could know things that he could not see. 'Sore but not sick, if that makes sense.'

Simeon nodded and shifted round to sit on a rock. 'It makes perfect sense.'

Across the fire Falco could see the emissary standing beside Malaki. They were leaning forward, intent on some task and over the distance he heard the metallic sound of small hammer blows.

'Has he finished it?' asked Falco, referring to the belt that the emissary had been working on.

'Almost,' said Simeon. 'Malaki's just helping him set the rivets.'

'Is it for his wife?'

Simeon pursed his lips. 'I'm not sure he's married. Not so far as I know, at least.'

Falco nodded slowly, looking at the man who had come to them in their hour of need. He paused before speaking again. 'Do *you* think he can see into the hearts of men?' he asked.

Simeon smiled. 'I think he sees more than most,' he said. 'There's a reason why the Queen chose him.'

Falco continued to stare at him and then his attention slid across to Malaki.

'People were always going to die,' said Simeon, as if he could sense the direction of Falco's gaze. 'Even with Darius, people would have died fighting the Possessed.'

'I know,' said Falco. 'But Balthazak...' he could not finish the sentence.

'You must not torment yourself with such thoughts,' said Simeon. 'You did not bring the demon down upon us.'

They were silent for a while and Falco watched as the light from the fire played over Simeon's scarred face. Having felt the touch of dragon fire he could only imagine the agony that Simeon had been through.

'Will we make it?' he asked.

Simeon did not answer, he only snorted softly, a dark smile playing on his lips. The Possessed were closing quickly and no one knew if the riders had made it through or not.

'And if we do?' asked Simeon, deflecting the question. 'What will you do then?'

'I don't know,' said Falco. 'Return home, I guess.'

Simeon gave a hollow laugh. 'Home,' he repeated. 'I'm afraid there will be nothing left to return home to.'

Falco nodded sadly. 'Then I suppose I'll stay in Toulwar,' he said. 'Maybe in time we can rebuild Caer Dour.'

'You could go with Malaki to Wrath,' said Simeon. 'Maybe there you will find the answers that you seek.'

Falco looked up, waiting for him to continue.

'I knew your father,' said Simeon. 'There was darkness in him for sure. But he was not mad. There is a reason why he turned against us.'

Falco stared at his master.

'I believe your father's death had some meaning,' said Simeon. 'Maybe in Wrath you will find some meaning of your own.'

Falco was speechless. In the last few days he had felt his world collapsing, closing down to a dim and clouded future and now Simeon had punched a hole through the clouds and the light of possibility shone through.

Maybe in Wrath he would find some answers.

Maybe in Wrath he would find some purpose to his life.

Simeon left him then and despite the thoughts swirling through his mind he managed to sleep once more, but not for long. They woke in darkness and began to walk well before it was safe to travel. The Possessed were now just a few hours behind them and there was no time to tarry longer. Falco had eaten a little bread and fruit for breakfast and now, as he swayed in the saddle, he could feel a semblance of strength returning to his limbs. Ahead of him he saw a mother standing to the side of the path, struggling to rouse one of her children, a boy no more than six.

'Tarran, curse you. We cannot stop!' Tugging at the boy's arm the woman was frantic with concern.

'He can ride with me,' said Falco, pulling up beside them.

The woman looked up, torn between the need for help and the thought of accepting it from the very person who had brought disaster upon them. Finally necessity prevailed and with a muffled word of thanks she swung her son up into the saddle. Falco wrapped his cloak around the tearful boy.

'Don't worry,' he said. 'The riders have made it through. The knights of Toulwar are already on their way to help us.'

The boy twisted round to look at him, his stark blue eyes searching for any trace of falsehood. Something in Falco's heart told him that the riders had *not* made it through. And yet his words did not have the feeling of a lie. With a small smile the boy turned away, leaning back against Falco's bony chest.

*

Captain Reynald de Roche of the Toulwarian Royal Chasseurs dismounted as he approached the horse. The chestnut mare was trembling with exhaustion and clearly terrified. He offered his hand, talking in low soothing tones as he edged his way closer. Finally he was able to take hold of the bridle and the horse pressed its head against his shoulder, its ears flicking back and forth.

'Easy there,' said Captain de Roche, stroking the horse's sweat-soaked neck. It had clearly been ridden very hard but there was no sign of its rider.

Slowly he led the horse back to his men. The patrol was four days out of Toulwar and was just heading back to the city when they came across the frightened horse.

'It came from this direction,' said one of his men. 'From the road to Valentia.'

Captain de Roche turned his head. Had not the Queen's emissary taken that road not two weeks ago?

He left one of his men to care for the horse then mounted up alongside the other lightly armoured chasseurs. 'We'll follow the trail back to the edge of the forest.'

He paused before setting off. They had all heard the stories about the breach in the Illician defences, and even on this patrol they had come across a woodsman who spoke of a 'dark creature' plying the skies above the forest. They *had* put it down to a velvet eagle venturing down from the mountains but now Captain de Roche was not so sure. 'Be on your guard,' he told his men. 'I fear there is evil abroad.'

With that they galloped away. Their own horses were tired and thirsty but the captain knew of a lake not far along the trail. They could water the horses there.

*

The people of Caer Dour were stumbling in their haste, cursing the officers from the army who spurred them on.

'Faster... Keep moving... Faster...'

Falco looked at one man who clearly did not relish the task he had been given. But still he chivvied the people on, glancing back frequently to see if there was any sign of the latest rearguard. Something was wrong. The Possessed were now so close that the defensive forays had been returning quickly but the latest was overdue.

Daybreak had brought cold showers sweeping across the mountains but now the clouds were breaking and broad patches of blue sky became a welcome sight. But then someone ahead cried out pointing up to the sky and a ripple of dismay swept towards Falco. Looking up he could see what was causing the disturbance, the dark angel flying high above them, casting its shadow of fear.

'Come closer,' thought Falco, staring up at the creature. *'I know some who would smite you from the sky.'* As if in answer the creature soared over them, scouting the mountains in the service of its master.

Still seated in front of him the young boy quailed against his chest and beside him the boy's mother cowered down, gathering her other two children into her arms. Falco brought his horse to a halt. He stroked the boy's hair and looked down at the mother.

'Don't be afraid,' he said.

Slowly the mother looked up and Falco could read the dread in her eyes.

'The enemy knows you love them,' said Falco, looking down at her children. 'He sees it as a weakness, a way to break your faith.' He looked back at the woman and a hint of fire burned in his bright green eyes. 'Let it be your strength.'

The woman frowned as if confused by the authority in his voice but slowly she straightened up. She gave Falco a brief nod, then she wiped her eyes and bid her children walk on.

'You're starting to sound like me,' said a voice and Falco turned to see Simeon pulling up alongside him.

'I've heard you say as much,' said Falco, feeling strangely self-conscious.

'That's because it's true,' said Simeon with a smile.

They rode in silence for a while and the boy, Tarran, jumped down to walk with his mother. Falco kept glancing back, looking for signs of the latest rearguard. 'Something's wrong,' he said. 'They should be back by now.'

Simeon nodded then he raised his head, turning his blind face up ahead where some of the leaders were coming back down the trail.

'What is it?' he asked as the leaders pulled up beside them.

'Some of the nobles have fled,' said the emissary. 'Bellius Snidesson among them.'

Falco gaped but Simeon just bowed his head.

'Seventeen knights and forty members of their households,' said Morgan Saker.

Falco began to speak but Simeon raised a hand to stop him.

'Do not judge them too harshly. Others would do the same if they had swift horses for all their loved ones.'

Morgan Saker seemed about to object when several things happened at once.

First, riders from the latest rearguard came into view, forging their way up the path to speak with the leaders.

'The demon is on our heels,' said the captain with an edge of panic in his voice. 'They stopped for a while and something happened that we did not see, but now they come on faster than ever.'

Lord Cadell's face was set as he tried to fathom what this might mean but then they noticed the line ahead of them had stopped. People on the path began looking back as one of the forward scouts came galloping down the line.

'Well?' snapped Lord Cadell as the breathless scout struggled to form his words.

'The enemy is in front of us, my Lord. The way ahead is blocked!'

Falco looked from one anxious face to the next. It seemed that Bellius had made his escape just in time. Not only had the enemy caught up with them it had done the unthinkable. Somehow the army of the Possessed had overtaken them. The people of Caer Dour were cut off. There was no way they could reach safety now.

17

A Message in the Reeds

'How could they *possibly* get ahead of us?' exclaimed Lord Cadell.

'The demon has gated them through,' said the emissary who had experienced this phenomenon before. 'If a demon is powerful enough it can tear a rift in the fabric of reality and send a small number of troops from one place to another. The demon that follows us must be gaining in strength.'

The people of Caer Dour looked at him aghast.

'How many?' asked Simeon.

'Enough to stop us in our tracks,' replied the emissary, looking at the path ahead which was now choked with hundreds of frightened people running back towards them.'

'And how long before the demon catches up to us?'

'Three hours, maybe less.'

The muscles in Simeon's jaw bunched.

'Can we break through?' asked Falco.

'Perhaps,' said the emissary. 'But by then the enemy would be upon us. The last thing we want is for the Possessed to catch us on the path.' He shook his head. 'No. Our only chance is to look for a defensible position and hope that we can hold out long enough for help to arrive.'

Falco's blood ran cold. They were trapped in the mountains and they still did not know if the riders had made it through.

'There's a valley a little way back,' said one of the scouts. 'Steep sides, with a line of low cliffs that would be easy to defend.'

'Good,' said the emissary. 'We shall make our stand there.'

*

Captain Reynald de Roche stared at the tracks on the ground. They did not make sense.

'The horse was startled here,' said one of his men, a man called Francois, one of the finest trackers in Toulwar. He was bending low over the ground, pointing out the line of hoof prints. 'Here you can see the gait is steady, the horse is being ridden.' He walked forward. 'And here the ground is churned up as if there was a fall or a collision.' He straightened up shaking his head. 'But there is only one set of prints and no sign of a fall. From here the tracks become erratic, heading on towards the trees. It makes no sense.'

Captain de Roche gazed down at the ground. He looked back along the path and forward to the trees. It was as if the rider had vanished into thin air.

'Sir!'

He turned to see one of his men walking towards him with a brown leather dispatch tube in his hands.

'It was lying in the grass beside the lake,' said the man, handing over the tube.

Captain de Roche gazed at the lake which was calm and quiet and dotted with birds. Then he opened the tube and slid out the message that was furled inside. Handing the tube to one of his men he began to read. As he did so a frown creased his brow and his men watched as their captain's face grew pale.

'What is it, Captain?' asked one of his men.

'The people of Caer Dour,' said Captain de Roche, folding the message and tucking it into a pouch at his belt. 'They have been forced into the mountains, pursued by a demon army of the Possessed.'

The men looked at him in disbelief. To them the Possessed were an abstract threat, the nightmare menace of distant lands.

'Mount up!' snapped Captain de Roche. 'Their fate lies with us.' His harsh tone broke through the shock and the chasseurs leaped into action. Within seconds they were galloping down the trail towards the city of Toulwar. However, they had not gone far when Captain de Roche turned onto a smaller trail heading to the south of the city.

'Captain!' called out Francois as small branches whipped across their path. 'This is not the quickest way to the city.'

'I know,' cried Captain de Roche.

He was not heading for the city. He was heading for a small retreat perched on an outcrop of rock where certain 'visiting warriors' and their mythical creatures were known to stop. The army from Toulwar would never reach the people of Caer Dour in time. They needed help that came on swifter wings and Captain de Roche could only hope that his gambit would pay off; that the person he sought would still be at the retreat when they arrived.

Meanwhile, behind them, the body of a young woman lay face down in the dark waters of a forest lake. Her mortal remains would never be laid to rest and yet her soul might have found some comfort in the knowledge that the message, for which she had given her life, had reached its goal at last.

*

The people of Caer Dour streamed into the steep sided valley. There were no paths leading out and only the most nimble had any chance of scaling the cliffs that surrounded them. This then would be their fortress and may yet become their tomb.

The mouth of the valley was level and flat but as it narrowed it was cut across by a series of low cliffs. It was a good place to make a stand, allowing the army to block the entrance to the valley, keeping the people safe until the last possible minute.

It had taken them an hour to get the people into the valley and Falco watched as the last of the families were escorted in. He was doing his best to be helpful although he found the effort exhausting. Heçamede had given him a small pot of ointment for Tobias. Being strapped to a horse for several days had left the crippled boy with terrible pressure sores and the ointment would ease the pain and help them to heal.

'At least it's not raining,' said Julius Merryweather as Falco handed over the ointment. Merryweather had already cleaned his son's sores and he wasted no time in applying Heçamede's remedy. Tobias looked up and Falco blushed. He had not meant to stare. The boy studied him for a moment, his watery eyes strangely penetrating then slowly he began to smile.

'Ballymudge better now.'

Falco snorted softly and smiled in turn.

'And how are you Tobias?' he asked.

'Hurts like a bathtard,' said Tobias, flinching as his father clipped him round the head.

'What have I told you about your language,' said Merryweather, clearly delighted by his son's enduring spirit.

Falco smiled at the bond of love between them but his smile was tinged with sadness. Despite his father's best efforts Falco could see that some of Tobias's sores had become infected. He glanced at Merryweather and the expression in the big man's eyes said it all.

If only they could live long enough for Tobias to die from infected wounds.

And so the day drew to an end. After all their efforts they had been overtaken and now they were trapped in the mountains. Their only hope was to hold out as long as possible and that meant keeping Simeon alive. The significance of this had already been explained to the army. Sitting beside his master, Falco now listened as the emissary talked to the parents and the elders of the community.

Dressed now in the mail hauberk and armoured boots of a cavalryman, the emissary crouched down among them. People gathered close about him, away from the main body of the people so that the children could not hear what was being said.

'While Simeon lives the army will be able to fight,' the emissary told them. 'His presence will keep the fear at bay.' He paused. 'But Simeon's strength is not what it was. We will do what we can to support him. But if he falls...'

The emissary stopped and people looked down at the knives that had been handed round, knives sharpened to a razor's edge, knives that could end a life with as little suffering as possible.

The emissary's tone was hard and uncompromising as he continued.

'If Simeon falls the end will come quickly.' He looked into their faces. 'Whatever happens, you must *not* let your children be taken by the Possessed.' He waited for this message to sink in. 'The enemy will try to prevent you. He will fill your mind with promises and lies. Do not believe him. If Simeon falls then end it quickly, before your courage fails.'

The parents' faces were pale and grim but they were also calm and resolved. They would do what was necessary.

A horn suddenly sounded and everyone looked up. One of the sentinels on the cliffs had sounded the alarm. The enemy had been sighted.

The parents returned to their children and Falco followed Simeon and the emissary as they went down to join the army. The sun had set and they stared out to the west where the last light of day was fading. In the distance the mountains cast a dark silhouette against the sky but the craggy outline shimmered and swam as if from the heat of a hot summer's day. Falco could actually feel the warmth of it on his face.

'It is the Possessed,' said Simeon, guessing his thoughts. 'They carry the heat of Hades with them.'

In the sky behind them the bloated disk of a full moon was just rising and in its pale light they caught their first glimpse of dark, unearthly steel. Even at that first glance the fighting men of Caer Dour took a step backwards but the blind old man that was Simeon le Roy took a step forward and with him went Sir

102

William Chevalier, the Queen's emissary from the court of Wrath. Falco stood at Simeon's shoulder. He knew he could not fight like Malaki or the emissary but neither would he flee. The fear held no thrall over him. He had mastered that long ago.

Then Lord Cadell came forward and Sir Gerallt Godwin and others, and slowly the defenders advanced to the edge of the low cliffs. Falco remained with Simeon as he took up position on a broad expanse of rock some fifty yards behind the front line. This was where he would make his stand. From here he could hold the entire army in his mental embrace.

With Simeon in place the emissary went to mount his horse.

'Easy there, Tapfer,' he said as the horse shifted beneath him.

Bred for war, the smoke grey Percheron recognised the tension that came before a battle and the proud stallion's blood was up. The horse's flanks were now covered by a leather flanchard while a plate chanfron and segmented crinet protected its head and neck.

The plan was to let the Possessed come forward and then to hold them at the cliffs. The cliffs were not high. In places they were no more than a rise in the ground but they provided a defensible position and Lord Cadell would make the most of it. He positioned his greatest concentration of troops where the cliffs were lowest, flanking them with ranks of archers. Behind them the remaining cavalry had been divided into two groups where they could quickly respond to any breaches in the line. The remaining troops were deployed along the line of cliffs; a thin line of sword, shield and spear.

As Falco watched the army take up its positions he saw Bryna Godwin joining the ranks of archers to the right. And there, standing with the powerful men at the centre of the line, was the armoured figure of Malaki. The big youth was about to don his helmet when he seemed to sense Falco's gaze. He turned around and their eyes met. The two young men exchanged a brief and sorrowful moment then Malaki gave a slow nod and turned away.

Falco had never felt more alone, more useless. He bowed his head, staring down at his weak and bony hands.

'There is more than one way to fight.'

Falco looked up at Simeon.

'Go to Fossetta,' said Simeon. 'Show the people you are not afraid. That will help them more than you can know.'

Dejected, Falco turned to go but Simeon reached out to stop him, his rough hands tracing Falco's features as if to memorise his face.

'I have loved you Falco Danté,' said the old battle mage gruffly. 'As I did your father. As I would a son.'

Falco looked into the scarred face of the man who had raised him. His throat was tight with emotion.

'Promise me you will go to Wrath,' said Simeon. 'If you live to see the dawn. Find your place in the world, Falco. And find out why I had to kill the finest man I ever knew.'

Falco nodded and Simeon drew him close.

'Don't lose faith,' he breathed. 'Whatever happens, don't lose faith.'

103

Lost in Simeon's embrace Falco could only nod then slowly he turned away from the army of Caer Dour and walked instead towards her people. He found Fossetta sitting with the sick and injured on the west side of the valley where the tall cliffs rose up into the mountains. Wiping his eyes he took a seat and listened as Julius Merryweather tried to distract a group of children with a series of amusing tales, but for once the jolly man's humour had deserted him and the children seemed unconvinced.

Falco saw the young boy Tarran coming towards him.

'The older boys are saying we won't live the night,' said Tarran.

Falco looked up to see a host of people waiting to hear what he would say. He drew Tarran forward.

'Nonsense,' he said. 'I happen to know that Fossetta has a goose egg, three strips of bacon and a juicy pear squirreled away in her backpack. Isn't that right Fossetta?'

Fossetta held up four fingers.

'Four strips of bacon actually,' she said with a smile.

'There you go,' said Falco. 'No way I'm missing *that* breakfast.'

Tarran smiled and the people nearby found some of the fear lifting from their hearts. Falco looked up to see Heçamede staring at him, her dark eyes shining with approval.

All day they had been trying to calm the fears of the people, and all day the fear had grown deeper. Until *he* came to sit with them. He was pale and skinny and weak, and it still wasn't clear if he would survive the infection in his lungs. But at least now he stood a chance.

'Strong,' thought Heçamede. *'Like his father.'*

She remembered arriving in Caer Dour with a handful of refugees from the war in Illicia. She had been little more than a girl at the time; a young healer swept up in horrors she could barely have imagined. The people of Caer Dour had welcomed them and she had been invited to stay at the home of Eleanora Danté, the wife of a nobleman who also happened to be a battle mage. It was her patience and enduring compassion that allowed Heçamede to come to terms with the nightmares that haunted her dreams and she could still remember the intensity of the woman's bright green eyes.

'And gentle,' she thought, remembering the tragic night of Falco's birth. *'Like his mother.'*

Horns suddenly echoed off the nearby cliffs, a last defiant call to arms.

Falco stood up and looked down the valley. In the light of the moon they could see the vanguard of the Possessed approaching, dark shapes in the deepening night shining dully with the glint of steel. Behind him he was aware of parents gathering their children to them and Falco thought of the hidden knives that each of them held.

Parents forced to kill their own children?

Falco gritted his teeth at the prospect of such horror. Then, pushing Tarran behind him, he stared down at the jagged figures of the Possessed, and in the dim light his green eyes burned.

18

The Possessed

The Possessed came on with the slow certainty of a nightmare but this was just the vanguard. The demon, with its full strength, was yet to reach the valley.

Standing with the other men, Malaki watched as the enemy emerged from the gloom. They looked human but he knew that such a description no longer applied. They were both more and less than ordinary men. They were lost souls, people plucked from the bosom of humanity, baptised in the fires of hell and reborn in darkness.

They wore the armour of Ferocia: breastplates, round-shields and open-faced Hoplite helms, dark steel with a sheen of bronze. The very look of it conveyed an impression of brutality. And it glowed, dimly, like metal heated in a fire. Malaki could feel the heat of it on his face. He looked around and from the expressions of uncertainty he could see that the other men could feel it too.

Malaki tried to swallow but his mouth was suddenly dry. He felt the fear rising up inside him but he clenched his teeth and pushed it down. His father had not succumbed to the fear and neither would he. With a trembling hand he drew his sword and couched his shield, a great round-shield that covered his body from shoulder to knee. Almost subconsciously he shifted his weight to a fighting stance and noticed that the men to either side did the same.

Lord Cadell had placed his finest warriors at the centre and Malaki had come to join them. If the front line was threatened they would rally around Simeon, forming a bodyguard of steel. Whatever the cost it was their job to protect him and even Malaki was prepared to give his life to keep the battle mage alive.

Slowly the Possessed drew closer. In the cold light of the moon Malaki could see their skin, ashen grey and blotched with bruise-black markings. Closer and he could see their eyes, like orbs of wet bone and filled with malice. They knew that he was afraid and the knowledge made them stronger.

This same terrible realisation was repeated all along the line of the cliffs as people came face to face with the Possessed. How could they win? How could they possibly win?

Malaki turned back to look at Simeon but the old battle mage seemed to be lost in concentration then he bowed his head and Malaki felt a strange sensation in his chest, a prickling light that seemed to flood his body and surge up into his mind. He found the fear lifting and turned back to face the enemy.

This then was the power of a battle mage, to give back to men the hope and courage that the enemy would otherwise take from them. Then, away to the right, Malaki heard the emissary's voice.

'Archers, ready...'

Malaki held his breath. The Possessed were almost at the foot of the low cliff, moving forward with slow deliberation. Then, with a sudden rush, they charged forward. Malaki heard the emissary call, 'Loose!' and a hail of arrows shot down from the cliffs.

*

Bryna Godwin watched as the arrow leapt from her bow. It struck one of the Possessed in the chest and the shaft splintered as the arrow failed to pierce its breastplate. Within a second she had another arrow ready but her hands were shaking so badly that she could not set it to the string. That first volley had checked the initial charge of the Possessed but it did not stop them. Many of the arrows had found their mark, stabbing into arm and leg, but still the Possessed came on.

In that moment Bryna Godwin learned two things.

The first was that pain and injury were not enough to stop the Possessed.

The second was that she was nowhere near as brave as she thought she was.

For several frantic seconds she tried to nock her arrow, while from the corner of her eye she could see the Possessed getting closer, clambering over the rocks of the low, sloping cliff.

Finally the arrow gave a little tick as it clicked onto the string and Bryna raised her bow. She saw a group of the Possessed climbing up towards her. Two of them fell back, pierced by many arrows but three came on. They were Sciritae, the light infantry of the Ferocian army and they moved with frightening speed. They looked up at the young girl with a terrifying hunger in their eyes and Bryna's shot went wide. She reached for another arrow but one of the Possessed had gained a narrow shelf near the top of the cliff and Bryna recoiled as it tried to vault up the last few feet to reach her.

There was a twang from beside her and the Sciritae fell back with an arrow in its face. Bryna glanced to her side to see 'Old Man Reese,' a wizened old man with only one eye.

'Slow your breathing,' said Reese in a voice like an old door creaking. 'Aim for the face or throat if you can.'

He loosed a second arrow and the next Sciritae toppled back with an arrow in its throat. The third was scrambling over the edge of the rise when a young spearmen rushed forward and began stabbing downwards. It was their job to protect the archers if the Possessed got too close.

'They can be stopped,' creaked old Man Reese. 'You just have to keep on shooting.'

He did not smile. He did not even look friendly but Bryna found his words comforting beyond belief. With a concerted effort she calmed her breathing and nocked an arrow to the string. She looked up to find a target just as the young spearman cried out. Two more Possessed had lunged forward and grabbed the spearman's ankles.

Acting on impulse Bryna slung her bow and reached down to help him. She grabbed the first things she could reach, the shoulder of his jerkin and a handful of his thick black hair. Being so close to the Possessed was terrifying and Bryna could feel her mind becoming distant with fear. She could smell the stench of their rotting bodies and she flinched from the searing heat that seemed to emanate from them. She felt as if the world was tumbling into chaos.

And this was only the vanguard.

Beside her Old Man Reese pulled a long knife from his belt and began hacking at the Possessed. He had almost severed the creature's arm when a Ferocian blade stabbed up into his belly. The old man gave a wheezing cry and pitched forward over the cliff. Beside herself with fear Bryna strained to keep her grip on the young spearman. Part of her mind was screaming to let go, to fall back before she too felt a hot blade sliding into her belly but she could not. The thought of the Possessed pulling this young man to his death was just too awful. She could hear his desperate pleas as he tried to pull himself free.

Bryna pulled with all her strength but just then the Possessed yanked him down and the young spearman disappeared from view. The last thing that Bryna saw was the expression of horror in his eyes. And then he was gone.

Hands pulled Bryna back from the edge of the cliff as more spearmen came to repel the Possessed but it was too late. Bryna looked down at her hands. The left was open and empty while the right still held a bloody clump of the young man's hair. Feeling suddenly vague and distant Bryna crawled away from the fighting. Behind her she heard the horrible commotion of battle, the clash of steel, the snarls of the enemy and the screams of pain. The battle had only just begun and already it was too much.

Bryna Godwin curled up in the shadow of a boulder and began to weep.

*

Malaki felt sick with anticipation. To either side he could see soldiers fighting to keep the enemy from reaching the higher ground, but the Possessed seemed to be avoiding the area around Simeon. Looking along the cliffs Malaki could see places where the Possessed were attacking on mass. The archers to his right had suffered a heavy attack and he edged forward hoping to catch a glimpse of Bryna.

'Hold your position,' said one of the men beside him and it was only then that Malaki realised he had moved out of the line. Suitably chastened he glanced back at Simeon but the old man's brow was creased in a frown, his face moving back and forth as if he could sense the approach of some new impending danger.

Then, quite suddenly, the Possessed stopped fighting and withdrew from the cliffs, fading like wraiths into the cold moonlit night.

Malaki followed the line of their retreat and away down in the valley he saw a greater spread of darkness with a deeper shadow burning at its heart. Here then was the reason they had fled their homes. Here was the embodiment of the evil that threatened all of humankind.

A demon from the seventh plane of hell.

*

Even before the shadow of it appeared in the valley Falco felt the approach of the demon. From his slightly elevated position he could see the line of the army strung out along the cliffs, shifting nervously, glancing back to see if they had permission to flee.

Falco pitied them.

To see their loved ones facing an eternity of suffering and to know that they did not have the courage to save them. They were indeed pitiable but they were not alone. The intangible glow of Simeon's presence spread across the valley. Although they might not know it, the army of Caer Dour was bathed in it, suffused by it.

Falco gazed down at the figure of Simeon, the man who had been both master and father to him. Wracked with age and disfigurement, Falco could not imagine how anyone so diminished in body could yet remain so strong. He turned to look at the people who lay behind him, the sick and the injured, the children and the old. They too could feel the cloak of Simeon's faith. They did not understand it but still it gave them comfort.

A battle mage stood with them.

Surely there was hope yet.

*

The demon stopped at the mouth of the valley. To its eyes the world of humans appeared weak and fragile, a thin veneer over the greater realm from which it came. This was a place to be defiled, a place to fill with suffering and despair. This was its mission and it was an easy one.

There was but one thing that gave it pause, the presence of a soul that did not quail in fear. There, in the midst of armoured flesh, a Defiant. The only thing of humankind that could challenge the demons of the Possessed.

The demon paused, holding in check the rabid appetites of its minions. It paused while it gauged the strength of its adversary. And then it smiled.

The Defiant was old and withered, a shadow of strength that once was great.

It smiled, a gesture which on its unholy features was more animal snarl than any expression of pleasure. It smiled and a drop of black saliva dripped from its massive jaws, the hot leathery skin drawing back from fangs that shone like pitted lead and yet were harder than any tempered steel.

It smiled and brought its army on.

*

Simeon relaxed as he felt the demon withdraw its gaze. It had taken all his will to conceal his strength from the creature's hellish mind. Let it think that he was old and weak. It would learn its error soon enough, and that might just give them a chance. The demon's strength was terrifying, both physical and mental. No wonder it had broken through the Illician defences.

Simeon felt the urge to turn to the west, to look in the direction from which help might come but he clenched his jaw against the temptation. He must bury such hope. The demon would perceive it as a weakness and it would be right.

He was the only thing that could save the people now.

*

Falco watched as Bryna was brought to join the sick and injured. It was deeply saddening to see such spirit reduced to a trembling wreck of nerves. He tried not to stare as Heçamede drew her gently to the fire.

'Sit here,' said the healer. 'I'll find you something to drink.'

Falco was about to look away when he saw the young boy Tarran run up with one of his friends. Tarran was holding Bryna's bow, while his friend clutched her quiver, still full of arrows.

Tarran laid the short, recurved bow across Bryna's lap while his friend stood the quiver beside her. Bryna gazed down at the bow as if she had never seen it before. Her eyes flitted to the quiver of arrows before rising to look at the youngsters. Her expression was dull and distant but then she focussed on the boys and began to cry.

The younger boy found the experience too distressing and ran away, but Tarran stepped forward and laid his hand on Bryna's knee.

108

'It's all right, mistress,' he said. 'The army of Toulwar is on its way to save us.'

Bryna's crying showed no sign of lessening and Tarran's conviction seemed to waver. He stood there uncertainly until Fossetta appeared beside him.

'Come away now,' she said. 'Go and find your mother.' Gently she turned the young boy and sent him on his way. For a moment she watched him go then she turned to look down at Falco who looked dreadful.

'You should rest.'

Falco nodded. He had found great satisfaction in helping out but he was still incredibly weak and the pain in his chest and shoulder still burned. Turning away from Bryna he raised his eyes to the west, gazing up at the cliffs in the direction of Toulwar. He was just wondering if Tarran might be right when the night was split by a piercing shriek.

'The dark angel' whispered Fossetta gazing into the sky.

They could not see the hellish creature but they knew it was up there. The shrill cry of the lesser demon was answered by a bellowing roar that shook the very ground beneath their feet. The demon had issued its challenge. The battle for the soul of Caer Dour had begun.

19

Simeon

The Possessed surged forward like a dark wave of steel and rotting flesh. First came the lightly armoured Peltae, or Pelts. Armed with short javelins and long knives, these were the skirmishers of the Ferocian army. They swarmed up the cliffs with rapid jerky movements. The speed of their attack caught the defenders by surprise but the warriors of Caer Dour stood firm.

The Pelts struck at the defenders and many fell but the line held. Next came the main body of the Ferocian army, the Sciritae. They came with shields raised against the arrows that stabbed down at them. The Possessed had been stripped of their humanity and robbed of their own volition, but they were not mindless and they were controlled by a demon which, for all its evil, was still shrewd and cunning. Quickly the Sciritae stormed the low cliffs and the fighting began in earnest and Malaki was in the thick of it.

Somehow he had lost his helm and now he twisted as a Ferocian blade stabbed towards his ribs. He threw up his shield as a second blow arced down from above. Two Sciritae were pressing him hard and he stumbled backwards over the rocky ground. He blocked several attacks but as the Possessed warriors continued to push forward, Malaki lost his footing and fell with one of the Sciritae landing on top of him.

Having dropped his sword he was now trapped beneath his own shield with the weight of the Sciritae bearing down on his chest. Its face was just inches from his, snarling over the rim of his shield, while the second struck down at Malaki's head.

Malaki lurched to one side as the sword threw up a shower of sparks from the rocks beside his head. Meanwhile he grappled the sword hand of the Sciritae still lying on top of him. He was suddenly aware of the terrible heat emanating from the enemy and as the fear grew so did the heat. Panic surged in his belly as all his fighting experience seemed to count for nothing, but then the Sciritae on top of him was thrown aside, kicked in the face by an armoured boot. Several figures forced the other Sciritae back and Malaki looked up to see a large man standing over him. It was Marcus, the man from the first rearguard, the one who had spoken so coldly to Falco.

'Try to stay on your feet,' said Marcus. He pressed Malaki's sword back into his hand and then he was gone, returning to the fray with the two other men at his side.

Fighting raged all about them and for a moment Malaki just stood there. This wasn't how he had imagined battle would be. This was no contest of skill. This was chaos. He felt sick and tearful but more than anything else he just felt young. For all his size and strength he was a boy pretending to be a man.

But then, just yards to his right he saw a man stumble to a slash across his thigh. The man dropped his guard and was about to die but somehow Malaki closed the distance between them and raised his shield to block the blow. He did not even remember moving his feet but the sound of the Sciritae's blade clanging against his shield broke the spell and he returned to the present.

Sweeping his shield aside he brought his own sword round in a horizontal arc that glanced off the Sciritae's armour. The creature raised its sword to attack but Malaki kicked the inside of its knee and rammed the rim of his shield into its throat. The Possessed warrior gave a strangled snarl before Malaki's sword bit down into its neck.

Black blood sprayed into the air and Malaki closed his eyes as the burning fluid splashed across his face. He spat the vile stuff from his lips and looked down at the man he had just saved.

The man looked at him in awe.

In the cold light of the moon Malaki's brown eyes looked black. One side of his face was slick with dark, oily blood. The other flared bright red with the birthmark that had cursed him as a child. Reaching out a hand Malaki pulled the injured man to his feet.

'Go to the healers,' he said.

Still staring, the man just nodded then he turned and hobbled away to get his injured leg stitched up.

Malaki was just turning back to the fight when horns sounded the call to rally. The men of the front line struggled to close their ranks while the warriors of Simeon's bodyguard fell back into a defensive formation in front of the battle mage. Malaki found himself shoulder to shoulder with Marcus.

'What is it?' he asked the older man.

'Kardakae,' said Marcus. 'Ferocian heavy infantry. The demon is trying to break through to Simeon.'

Malaki nodded, surprised at how calm he felt, while Marcus glanced at him in surprise. It was no longer the good-natured boy from the forge who stood beside him.

It was a man of Caer Dour.

And strong.

*

Falco needed to rest but he could not tear his eyes away from the fighting. He saw brief flashes of blue light where the magi were trying to help, but their power was of little use in a battle and the clean line of defence began to look more ragged as small groups of the Possessed broke through to the higher ground.

As horrific as it looked Falco longed to join the fight, but even the thought of it made his heart beat more quickly. His head grew fuzzy and his legs almost gave out. He might have fallen had Fossetta not reached out an arm to steady him.

'I thought I told you to rest,' she said, taking his weight and leading him over to a bed roll.

'Now, stay there and rest.'

Weariness flooded his body but as he lay back Falco saw shapes moving on the cliffs high above them. He raised himself up on one elbow.

'What is it?' asked Fossetta following the line of his gaze.

In the moonlight they could see figures scaling the cliffs, trying to escape the valley. The climb was treacherous but there was many a nimble youngster who could manage it. Some of them had almost reached the top, nearly a hundred feet above them.

'The fools,' breathed Fossetta.

'You can't blame them,' said Falco. 'Some of them might make it through.'

As they watched they saw two more figures begin the climb. Falco recognised one of them, and by the sudden tone of her voice, so did Fossetta.

'Tarran Dahoolie! Come down here at once!'

Fossetta strode to the foot of the cliff and grabbed the young boy's ankle before he could climb out of reach.

'Does your mother know what you're up to?'

Tarran hung his head.

'No, I didn't think so,' said Fossetta still holding onto his sleeve.

'But the others are nearly safe,' grumbled Tarran.

The three of them looked up and it was true. Four of the climbing figures were almost there. They were within a few feet of the cliff top when Falco felt a shadow fall across his heart.

A moment later a real shadow rippled across the rock face.

'Dark angel!' someone cried and suddenly everyone's attention was fixed on the cliffs and the demonic shape stooping down towards it.

*

Bryna heard the cry of alarm but it seemed to come from a long way off. She had no idea how she had come to be sitting beside people who muttered and moaned in pain. Her bow and quiver were lying on the ground at her feet and in her hand was a clump of bloody hair. A feeling of revulsion swept over her and she made to drop it but somehow she could not bring herself to let it go.

'Dark angel!'

The cry went up again and Bryna raised her eyes for the first time. She saw people standing and staring, pointing up to the cliffs that towered over them. As her eyes adjusted she could make out people clinging to the rock far above the ground. Then she saw a shape in the sky, a winged shape, dark and frightening.

As if in a dream she saw the winged creature swoop towards the cliff and pluck one of the clinging figures from the rock. For a moment it held the figure's weight before letting it fall towards the watching crowds. On its way down the figure struck the rocks, flopping and tumbling like a doll made from rags.

The body of the fifteen year old boy landed just twenty feet from Bryna. His clothes were torn and his arms and legs were strangely twisted but his face was unmarked except for a single bead of blood running down across his brow.

It took Bryna a moment to realise he was dead.

There was a scream and Bryna looked up. Another figure had been torn from the cliff and cast down onto the rocky ground. The remaining figures now began a frantic retreat, desperate to get down from the cliffs before the dark angel could pull them to their deaths.

Bryna looked down at her hands then carefully, almost tenderly, she tucked the bloody clump of hair into her jerkin.

*

112

'Light preserve us,' sobbed Fossetta, the awfulness of the scene was too much for her. She grabbed hold of Tarran and pressed his face into her apron to prevent him from witnessing any more horror.

Falco's jaw ached with fury. For all his weakness his hands were clenched in bone crushing fists. Like everyone else he felt completely helpless. Even as they watched they saw the dark angel closing in on another victim. The young boy was backing down the cliff with reckless speed but there was no way he could escape.

Talons outstretched, the dark angel was reaching for him when something shot into its side, just below the joint of its wing. With a piercing cry it lurched away from the boy. Hovering in the air it turned its gaze on the people standing at the base of the cliff. Its eyes seemed to fix on something or someone and it gave a terrifying scream. The scream seemed to promise pain and suffering but then...

Thunk!

An arrow took it squarely in the chest.

The creature screamed again but this was a scream of pain and it beat its wings in an attempt to flee.

Thunk... Thunk!

Two more arrows found their mark and the dark angel fell from the sky. Its ash-grey wings flapping as it dropped like a stone.

In the silence that followed Falco turned to see Bryna Godwin standing a few yards behind him, bow in hand, another arrow already on the string.

Slowly she walked towards them. She gave them a brief nod then looked down at Tarran who had his face buried in Fossetta's skirts. Slowly the young boy emerged and Bryna placed a gentle hand on his tear-stained cheek.

'Don't worry,' she said. 'The army of Toulwar is on its way to save us.'

There was no humour in her voice. It was as if she did not remember Tarran speaking the exact same words to her. She looked him in the eye, tousled his hair and turned away to rejoin the army.

*

As gaps appeared in the line of battle so the units of cavalry came into their own. The Possessed forced a breach to the right of Simeon but the emissary's cavalry were well placed to meet it. With a sudden charge they forced the Possessed from the higher ground and slowly the infantry was able to reform the line. The emissary had just given the order to withdraw when he heard the horns sounding the call to rally.

Wheeling his horse about he stared towards Simeon. In the cold light of the moon he could see a solid block of dark warriors marching straight for the old battle mage. They were Kardakae, the shock troops of Ferocia, and behind them a towering bestial figure, all darkness and searing heat.

The demon was making its move.

The emissary looked at the mass of dark warriors driving forwards. Even the heavily armoured troops of Simeon's bodyguard could not hold off that assault. They needed cavalry support.

'Cavalry, to me!' he called above the tumult. 'Lancers to the front.'

He was impressed by the way the mounted troops responded and within moments they were back in formation and ready to charge once more. He brought them forward slowly, waiting for the Kardakae to gain the rise. In the distance he could see Lord Cadell's cavalry forming up on the left flank. They too must have spotted the danger. The emissary allowed himself a grim smile.

If they could strike the Kardakae on both sides...

He raised his sword, gave the order to charge and a hundred horses surged forward with a hundred more coming from the opposite side of the valley.

*

Malaki watched as the Kardakae forced their way onto the higher ground and drove directly towards Simeon. Clad in black armour these huge warriors smashed through the lighter troops on the front line, but the men in Simeon's bodyguard had been chosen for a reason. To a man they were big and strong and covered in the best armour that Caer Dour had to offer. They would not easily fold and now Malaki stood with them. Flanked by the more experienced men he swallowed hard as the Kardakae advanced but still he raised his shield and gripped his sword. No matter their size and strength, they were the enemy and he would fight them.

Behind him he felt a sudden breeze as if a fierce squall had blown up around Simeon. Glancing back he saw the old battle mage standing there, sword in his left hand while his right was balled into a tight and trembling fist. He was frowning as if his hollow eyes were tightly shut. His entire body was wrought with tension but his hair flew up around him as if a torrent of air was rushing up from the ground at his feet. As he tore his eyes away Malaki had a sudden sense of just how dangerous Simeon could be. He was gathering energy to himself, energy that was about to be unleashed.

Malaki had no more time to watch, the Kardakae were upon them and he barely had the chance to brace himself before they struck. He raised his shield as a heavy blade swung down towards him. The impact sent shock waves through his entire body but he managed to stay on his feet. A series of heavy blows almost drove him to his knees but then Malaki caught his balance and struck back.

With all his strength he struck at the Kardakae's helm. The attack drew no blood but it must have dazed the Possessed warrior and before it could recover Malaki rammed the rim of his shield into the face of its helm before hacking down at his opponent's leg. The Kardakae staggered forward as something in its knee gave way and Malaki thrust his sword into the gap between its helm and the neck of its breastplate. The powerful warrior fell at his feet but then Malaki was forced to leap back as another took its place.

Simeon's bodyguard was being driven back and there was nothing they could do to prevent it. Despite the relentless brutality of the Kardakae's assault Malaki continued to defend himself, but then a dark blade skipped off his shoulder guard and glanced off his temple. Stumbling back Malaki thought he heard the command to 'retreat to flank' but he was too stunned to respond. Then someone grabbed hold of his armour and hauled him aside.

Struggling to stay on his feet Malaki turned to see that the men of bodyguard had retreated to the sides. The Kardakae advanced towards Simeon and not a single man of Caer Dour stood between them. Blinking blood from his eyes Malaki started forward but someone caught hold of him.

'Stay back!' screamed a voice in his ear, but Malaki could not bear to see the old battle mage standing there undefended. Breaking free, he was about to attack when Simeon thrust out his hand and a ferocious burst of energy slammed into the Possessed. The powerful Kardakae were blown apart as a great hole was blasted in their ranks.

'Now!' called the voice in his ear and the warriors of the bodyguard charged forward to re-engage the Possessed. At the same moment the cavalry of Lord Cadell and the emissary struck the Kardakae from both sides.

Malaki was carried along by the momentum of the charge but he had little idea of what was going on. As good a fighter as he was, he had never been a part of the army, never spent hours repeating drills and exercises in preparation for battle. The older men responded instantly to commands whereas Malaki felt as if he were taking part in a dance for which he barely knew the steps.

However, the impact of the combined attacks stopped the Kardakae in their tracks and the tide of battle seemed to be turning in their favour, but then Malaki became aware of a shadow rising up at the edge of the cliffs. A new wave of fear seemed to ripple along the front line then Malaki saw something fly through the air above the heads of the embattled troops. He only caught a glimpse and it took him a moment to register what it was. It was the upper half of a man's body, no legs, just a torso with arms flailing as it cart wheeled through the air.

*

The combined cavalry charges had almost split the Kardakae in two and the emissary was at the heart of the fighting. Beside him he saw one of his mounted knights go down, his horse literally cut out from under him. But they had done it. They had broken the momentum of the Ferocian shock troops and gained the advantage. But then a huge shape climbed up onto the higher ground and any glimmer of hope was extinguished.

Standing fully ten feet tall the demon stood on two back-bent legs like those of a monstrous goat. Its powerful torso was of human form, the muscles clearly defined by the ruddy glow of its internal heat. Its head was more akin to a bull's with great downward curving horns and teeth like those of a ravening hound, and its silvery eyes shone like molten lead.

Rooted to the spot with fear, the men of the front line froze before this abomination of the underworld, while the emissary simply stared at the demon in horror. He had seen demons before of course but the sheer force of their presence always came as a shock and he wondered what they could possibly do to stop it. He had never heard of cavalry bringing down a demon but still they had to try. Simeon's magical attack had been surprisingly powerful but he was aging and blind. He could not fight like a battle mage in his prime. It was down to them to keep him alive for as long as possible and if that meant attacking the demon then so be it.

He gave the command to disengage and noticed that Lord Cadell had already done the same. The cavalry would form up and charge again but this time they would choose a different target. This time they would aim directly for the demon.

20

Great Soul

The army of Caer Dour was on the verge of collapse. Only Simeon's presence prevented them from throwing down their weapons in despair. At the centre of the line, the men of Simeon's bodyguard were struggling to hold the Kardakae at bay. Without cavalry support the dark warriors were pushing them back once more, driving ever closer to the battle mage. To either side the cavalry had withdrawn. Their numbers had been depleted during the charge on the Kardakae, but now they wheeled about looking for a line of attack to the demon.

On the left flank, Lord Cadell's route to the demon was almost clear, while on the right the emissary found his way blocked by a mass of Sciritae. If there was going to be an assault on the demon it would be Lord Cadell who led it.

The focus of the fighting was now centred on the demon and the man who stood against it. On the right side of the valley a small group of Sciritae broke through the line and sprinted up the valley towards the people. Fortunately a unit of archers were stationed nearby and the Possessed were brought down before they got too far. However, one of them fell into a shallow gully and disappeared from view. An arrow had pierced its leg, but that was not the kind of injury to stop one of the Possessed. The archers turned their attention back to the front line and no one noticed as the injured Sciritae got back to its feet and continued up the gully, a gully that led directly towards those people in the care of Heçamede and Fossetta.

*

Falco looked on in horror as cracks began to appear in the line of defence. The fear had risen to a new pitch and Falco turned to look at the people cowering beside Heçamede and Fossetta. Beside him were a number of soldiers from the front line. Many of the injured had been patched up and returned to the fight but these man lay silent or groaning softly, the extent of their injuries too great for them to rise. He saw Julius Merryweather raise himself up on one elbow as he lay beside his son. Tobias seemed agitated and Merryweather did his best to calm him but the boy refused to quieten down. Barely able to sit up he gestured urgently towards Falco with a wavering arm.

'Ballymudge!' he slurred as if trying to warn Falco.

'It's all right,' said Merryweather.

'No!' insisted Tobias, still pointing in Falco's direction. 'Bad!'

Falco frowned at the determined note in Tobias's voice.

And then he felt it too... an evil presence behind him as if something from beyond the grave was emerging from the shallow gully that opened up nearby. He turned just in time to see the Sciritae rise into view not fifteen feet away.

There was a collective gasp of shock from the people behind him, closely followed by a flurry of activity. Julius Merryweather struggled to his feet, snatching up his walking stick before moving to stand protectively over his son, while Fossetta grabbed a long handled frying pan from beside the fire. As for Falco, he moved slowly to one side, reaching down to take up a sword from one of the injured soldiers. He did not take his eyes off the Sciritae which looked at him with a kind of wariness.

Straightening up Falco stared into the creature's bone-white eyes. For a moment the Sciritae followed his movement and then the expression in its eyes changed from uncertainty to hate and it charged forward.

Falco saw the creature surge towards him. He saw its blade rise up for a downward strike. He knew what he needed to do, but the sword in his hand felt impossibly heavy. As a young boy he had been every bit as good as Malaki, but now his body was too weak to obey the commands flashing through his mind. He barely had time to raise his sword before the Ferocian blade was slashing down towards his head. He staggered from the blow and almost dropped his sword, but somehow he held on. He parried another attack, but then the Sciritae smashed him in the face with its shield and Falco's knees buckled beneath him as the creature moved in for the kill.

For a split second Falco had a vision of it dead, cut down by an arc of incandescent fire, but the power of the vision terrified him more than the thought of death and so he only stared. He saw the blade begin to fall but one of the injured soldiers crawled forward and grabbed the Sciritae's ankle and the attack went wide. The creature killed the man with a stab to the chest but then a stone clanged into the side of its helm, quickly followed by several more.

Shaking off the dead man's hands the Sciritae started forward, raising its shield as people pelted it with stones. Still on his knees Falco swung his sword at the creature's legs but it blocked the attack with ease and would have killed him had Julius Merryweather not smacked it round the head with his stout walking stick. The Possessed swung at the portly man and Merryweather cried out as the blade cut a gash in his belly.

The Sciritae turned back to finish Falco just as a large frying pan slammed into its face. Staggering from the blow the creature struck out again and Fossetta dropped the pan as its blade slashed her upper arm. The Sciritae would have killed all three of them but more people rushed forward. Two men and three women threw themselves at the hellish creature, wrestling it to the floor. The creature fought with a frenzy and two more people were injured before it was finally killed by a large rock that caved in the side of its helm.

Gasping for breath Falco struggled to his feet and staggered over to Fossetta.

'I'm all right,' said the housekeeper, gripping her upper arm as blood seeped between her fingers.

They turned to look at Merryweather.

'Julius!' gasped Fossetta when she saw the dark stain on the ground.

The large man was down on one knee, a bloody hand clutching at his belly.

'Heçamede!'' called Fossetta.

She helped Merryweather down onto his back. His normally red cheeks looked deathly pale in the moonlight.

Falco collapsed to the ground beside Merryweather staring at the large wound that gaped just above the waistband of his trousers. Feeling sick from the exertion of the fight he reached forward and laid his hand over the dreadful injury, trying to stem the bleeding.

'Ah, Falco, my boy,' said Merryweather like a man waking from sleep. 'That's better. That's much better.'

Falco did not know what to say. He gazed down at the big man then looked back to where Tobias was sitting up. The crippled boy's head wobbled on his thin neck but his eyes were clear. Falco looked away as a wave of regret swept over him. Then Heçamede was there beside him.

'Move aside, Falco,' said the healer as she knelt down to examine the wound. Her mouth grew tight at what she saw but she undid her bag and misted the wound with her atomiser before reaching for a needle and thread.

Too exhausted to get to his feet Falco crawled away on his hands and knees. Struggling to breathe he moved to the edge of the hospital camp and pulled himself up against some rocks. With the black clouds of guilt returning to his mind he looked down at the battle raging across the valley, the heaving violence lit by the cold light of the moon.

The line of defence was still holding but only just. The enemy had taken the low cliffs and was pressing the defenders back. At the middle of the line the Kardakae had advanced to within a few yards of Simeon. Falco saw the emissary's cavalry brought to a halt by a mass of Sciritae and he saw the towering shape of the demon laying waste to all who stood before it.

But then, away on the left he saw Lord Cadell's cavalry begin their charge. Feeling like he might collapse at any moment Falco watched as the mounted knights thundered towards the demon.

*

Even as the emissary tried to cut his way through the Sciritae he saw Lord Cadell begin his assault on the demon. The commander of Caer Dour's army formed his troops into a wedge and brought them up to full charge.

Glancing around, the emissary could see that the main line of defence was slowly failing. Their only hope was to kill the demon, but he knew this was beyond their power. They might still be fighting, but in his heart he knew the battle was lost.

Into his mind flashed the image of a woman's face and a horse's head carved in wax, cast in silver, and fixed to a black leather belt. She would have liked it. It would have made her cry, but she would have liked it.

With a clear mind and an aching heart Sir William Chevalier prepared himself for death.

*

Lord Cadell's cavalry ploughed into the line of Possessed that stood between them and the demon. Most of his remaining knights were stopped or brought down but Lord Cadell broke through with Sir Gerallt Godwin just a length or two behind him. Both knights carried lances and it seemed that nothing could stand against the force of their charge, but then the demon paused in its slaughter and turned towards them. It tilted its great horned head as if surprised by the temerity of their attack then it lowered its head and spread its arms to meet them.

The two knights bore down upon the demon, lances driving straight for its heart, but at the last moment the demon lunged forward. With one hand it grabbed Lord Cadell's horse by the throat, forcing it up into the air and spilling its rider to the earth, with the other it swept Sir Gerallt from the saddle with a massive blow that broke his horse's neck and crushed the nobleman's chest. Sir

118

Gerallt's lance had caught the demon in the shoulder but the tempered point barely grazed the skin.

Lord Cadell fell badly and looked up in horror as the demon held his horse aloft, the animal's front legs flailing in the air while its rear hooves skipped and smacked against the rocky ground. For a moment the demon looked down at Lord Cadell as if trying to fathom how such a creature could dream of harming one of the Faithful. Almost absently it crushed the horse's throat and dropped the animal's carcass to the floor. With a single stamp of a massive hoof, it killed the leader of Caer Dour's army then it turned towards Sir Gerallt. The veteran knight was trying to free his sword from its scabbard, but his ribs were shattered and his breastplate was red with the blood he had already coughed up. Barely an inch of naked blade was free before the monster loomed over him.

The demon was reaching for Sir Gerallt when a savage bolt of energy slammed into its side. The towering monster staggered from the impact as dark flesh was blasted from its ribs. With a roar of fury it turned in the direction of the attack.

Blind though he was, Simeon le Roy was staring directly at it.

*

Simeon almost stumbled under the force of the demon's gaze. It saw him clearly now and there was no chance of further deception. The demon knew the limits of his strength and it knew they were lacking. Its shoulders hunched as it lowered its head and started towards him.

Powerful Kardakae were thrust aside as the demon strode forwards but then Simeon attacked again and another ball of searing blue light shot from his hand. The demon reeled as the magical attack struck it in the shoulder, but this second attack was less damaging than the first. Simeon's powers were not what they were but still the demon's advance was stalled. It stopped and, spreading its arms, it summoned its own form of dark magic.

'Down!' cried Simeon as he felt the infernal energy building in the demon's grasp.

The warriors in his body guard ducked behind their shields as a storm of red-hot shards shot out from the demon's hands. The stream of burning shrapnel would have torn through the men's armour but instead it slammed into the protective barrier that Simeon had summoned before them. The demon's chest expanded as it sought to conjure a greater burst but then Simeon drew up his sword. He brought it round in a rapid sweep and an arc of blue energy leapt from the blade, scything through the air towards the demon.

The demon threw up its arms to fend off the attack and the arc of energy parted around its hands, but one small segment got through, opening a gash in its cheek and slicing off the point of one great curving horn. Enraged to new heights the demon raised a massive fist high above its head before slamming it down into the earth. A shockwave of energy punched through the air and the ground bucked violently as the men of Simeon's bodyguard were thrown to the floor. Simeon himself stumbled to his knees as the earth seemed to kick out from under him.

Towering over the sprawling humans, the demon started forward once more. It came on slowly as if it knew that nothing could stop it now, but then Simeon raised himself to one knee and thrust out a hand in a gesture of denial.

The demon stopped as if someone had placed a restraining hand on its chest. It tried to come on, leaning forward as if into a strong wind, but it could not.

Still with one arm raised Simeon gripped his sword and struggled to get to his feet. The effort of restraining the demon showed in every sinew of his body but the blind old man continued to rise as the demon strained to reach him.

The men of his bodyguard had been thrown aside and nothing now stood between Simeon and the demon. His scarred face was creased with effort but then he gripped his sword with both hands and drove the point down into the rock at his feet. It was a statement of defiance, a line drawn in the sand.

The demon staggered as if from an invisible attack. It took two steps back on its massive goat-like legs before regaining its balance and looking at Simeon with an appraising gaze. Yes, it had misjudged the strength of its opponent but now it was time to end it.

As the fighting raged across the valley the demon closed its eyes, spread its hands and the very earth beneath its hooves began to burn. Low flames of angry red and putrid green began to spread forth, creeping across the ground in a slow wave of unearthly fire, a wave that crept inexorably towards the lonely figure of Simeon.

Lying twenty feet away, Malaki stared in horror at the encroaching flames. Like the rest of the men he had been thrown aside when the demon struck the earth. Still stunned from the force he tried to get back to his feet but the flames seemed to be draining him of strength. He could feel the heat of them on his face but the heat seemed to go deeper. It seemed to penetrate his flesh and scorch his mind. He wanted to rush to Simeon's defence, but the slow advance of the flames was more than his courage could bear and he knew that all was lost.

As the last of any hope gave way to despair Malaki de Vane began to weep.

*

The emissary picked himself up from the rocky ground. He had been thrown from the saddle when Tapfer stumbled from the impact of the demon's blow. He could see the smoke grey Percheron backing away, pawing at the ground in terror. The emissary's sword lay nearby and he lunged for it as one of the Sciritae charged in to attack him. He dispatched the creature quickly and killed two more before he got a clear line of sight to Simeon.

And what he saw made his stomach clench with fear.

The Kardakae had fallen back, flanking the demon on either side while the ground before them burned. The livid flames were low and fierce and spreading towards Simeon. Even from here the emissary could feel their heat. But these were no ordinary flames.

This was Baëlfire from the depths of Hell and no one could stand before it.

*

Simeon did not need eyes to see the flames. He could feel the terrible heat upon his face. He remembered the inconceivable pain of being burned by dragon fire but this was worse. These were flames to consume one's very soul. He fought against the fear but his will was weakening. And as his willpower faltered the flames crept closer.

Injured men lay in the path of the fire and as the flames reached them they began to scream, horrible screams that tore at the mind of all who heard them.

This was the torment that awaited every soul in the valley. Young, old, sick and hale, if the demon claimed them they would burn in agony for all eternity.

Simeon knew this and so he stood his ground. Even as he felt his strength failing he stood his ground and gripped his sword, determined to buy the people every possible second of life... of hope.

*

The emissary heard the screams of the men caught in the fire. They writhed in agony and still the flames came on. Simeon was using all his strength to resist the demon and the mental cloak protecting them from the fear was failing. The old battle mage was still standing but he could not stand alone.

The emissary could feel the fear clawing at his mind. Clinging to the strongest, most precious memories he could muster he started towards Simeon. If he had the strength... if he had the faith... he could get to the battle mage and help him in his struggle. Just to know he was not alone would give Simeon strength. But the presence of the demon was like a physical force. Every step forward took a tremendous effort of will and all the time the flames grew ever closer.

The emissary felt the sweat pouring down his face. He felt his soul cringing from the promise of eternal damnation, but he forced himself on, past the men of the bodyguard who could not bring themselves to move. He forced himself on until he was just a few yards from Simeon, but finally he could do no more.

With his strength spent and his courage crushed, Sir William Chevalier bowed down and pressed his face into the earth.

*

Falco stared down as the terrible flames spread out from the demon. He felt the fear mounting as Simeon's protection began to fail. The line of defence was finally crumbling and the moment of utter collapse was at hand. He turned to look at the people gathered in the valley behind him. They were huddled close, reaching for the knives that would save their children from a fate infinitely worse than death. Looking back to the battle he saw the strong men of Simeon's bodyguard laid low by the power of the demon. Only one man had the strength to advance.

He watched as the Queen's emissary staggered forward, trying with all his courage to reach Simeon. He knew the emissary would fail. He knew that Simeon would be left alone to face the torment of the fire, and he knew that even Simeon's strength would not be enough. For years Falco had listened to the doubts that haunted his master's dreams. The old battle mage had been weakened by betrayal and grief. In the end, Falco knew his faith would fail and he could not bear it.

As if in the grip of some terrible nightmare Falco felt his own feet moving as he made his way down towards the battle.

The people watched as their army began to collapse. They watched as the proud figure of the emissary was brought to his knees. They watched as the fire crept forward and the old man sagged lower and lower, clinging to his sword as if it were the only thing holding him up. The end was close and the words of the emissary echoed in their minds.

'If Simeon falls then end it quickly, before your courage fails.'

121

The valley held its breath as sharp knives inched their way towards innocent throats, but then they saw a new figure upon the valley floor, the figure of a thin and sickly youth. And the knives of mercy paused.

Falco stumbled over the rocky ground. His head spun, his lungs ached and the burns on his neck and shoulder felt raw and naked. His vision swam but he was dimly aware of the fighting as the soldiers of Caer Dour clung to the last vestige of hope. At the centre the battle was already lost. The low carpet of fire had almost reached Simeon and only the faint glimmer of his will prevented him from being consumed. He was no longer standing tall. He was down on one knee, clinging to the hilt of his sword like a man about to be washed away in a flood.

The men of the bodyguard were oblivious as Falco staggered past them. Some tried to crawl away from the flames, but most were simply bowed in defeat, the humps of broken men. Falco was dimly aware of Malaki and the emissary. Both were still straining to reach Simeon but their efforts were little more than a scrabbling in the dirt.

None had the strength to stand in the presence of the demon.

None save Falco Danté.

He was the weakling of the town, the object of an entire generation of derision. He was the victim of a wasting disease, the son of a madman but he was also the son of a battle mage and somehow he found the strength to face the flames. He staggered forward with one thought in his mind, to reach Simeon and to let him know that he was not alone. To hold him as he died. To hold him as he burned. If they were doomed to suffer the fires of Hell then they would suffer them together.

And with this single aim Falco forced himself onwards. The demon's presence was like an invisible barrier. It tried to stop him, snarling, clawing and tearing at his mind. It was unthinkable that any human could bear such evil and yet Falco did. He pushed forward and it was Simeon's words that resounded in *his* mind.

'*Don't lose faith... Whatever happens, don't lose faith.*'

Clinging to his master's words Falco came up behind Simeon and knelt down to embrace him. The old battle mage was almost spent. He still gripped the handle of his sword but his fingers were slipping.

Reaching around his master's broad shoulders Falco closed his own hands over Simeon's and held them fast. He pressed his face into Simeon's sweat-drenched hair and listened to the coarse breathing that was growing fainter with every heart beat. And as he held his dying master he realised that there were words clenched within his shallow breaths. Soft and fierce, more a thought than a spoken voice but still Falco heard them.

'Aquila Danté was my friend... Aquila Danté was my friend.'

Falco's heart lurched in grief. So this was the nature of the demon's attack. This was the doubt it used to bring an old man down. Falco wanted to tell Simeon that he did not blame him for his father's death. He wanted to tell him that he loved him, but he had no strength for words. He held on to Simeon with every shred of will that he possessed.

Don't lose faith.

Don't lose faith.

The people of Caer Dour looked on in awe as the thin figure of Falco Dante knelt down to embrace Simeon, two figures of age and frailty kneeling before the towering might of the demon. Somehow they felt something of the emotion in that embrace and for a moment they seemed to imagine the fear lifting from their minds.

Was Simeon regaining his strength?

Could the support of Falco bring him back to his feet?

For just a second it seemed that the flames halted in their advance.

*

The demon felt the presence of the mind that had joined the Defiant and it was perplexed. There was weakness, guilt, grief and fear. More than enough to crush a human soul and yet somehow it endured. Such a soul was dangerous; such a soul could not be allowed to live. With renewed effort the demon drew upon its deep reserves of hate and drove the fire on.

*

The last mote of hope was extinguished as the people saw the flames advance once more. The pause had been nothing more than a trick of the light, a gust of malicious wind sent to tempt them at the last.

Standing beside the prone figure of Merryweather, Fossetta was weeping openly. She had not noticed Falco's absence until people began to murmur and point, and then it was only with difficulty that she was prevented from rushing down to save him. Of course she could not. She could barely think for the fear coursing through her mind.

A dreadful hush had fallen over the people behind her as parents prepared to kill their children. Falco's brave gesture had bought them a few precious moments, but now the end was upon them and it was worse than Fossetta could possibly have imagined. Then, from right beside her, she heard Tobias speak.

'Ballymudge.'

Fossetta could not look at him. She could not take her eyes from the pathetic and glorious figures of Simeon and Falco. As for Merryweather, he was barely conscious, but the impulse to respond to his son penetrated his stupor.

'It's all right,' he said. 'Falco's going to sleep soon. We're all going to sleep soon.'

'No!' spat Tobias. 'Ballymudge!'

Fossetta glanced at the crippled boy but, unlike everyone else, he was not looking down at the battle. He was staring up into the mountains.

Slowly he raised a withered arm, his crooked finger pointing up to a high ridge.

'Ballymudge!' he said again.

Slowly Fossetta followed the line of his finger and finally she saw what he was pointing at. There, on the ridge, was a shape, a strange shape silhouetted against the sky and something chimed in her memory. She had seen a shape like that before and finally she put a name to it.

Dragon.

Perched high up on the ridge and staring down into the valley was a dragon.

And on its back a rider.

A battle mage.
A ballymudge.

*

The battle mage gazed down upon the people of Caer Dour, their anguish and terror rending at his heart. He closed his eyes and opened his mind and gathered their fear unto himself. They were almost broken, almost lost, almost but not quite yet.

Opening his eyes he looked upon the warriors still fighting the Possessed. He looked upon the two bright figures hunched before the flames. And he looked upon the demon, the vile transgressor of their world. He looked upon the demon and his eyes began to flare. He felt his dragon move beneath him and he did not hold her back. He leaned in close as she kicked away from the rock and began to fall. She rolled onto her back, wings folded like a stooping hawk and together they fell like a bolt out of the clear moonlit sky.

*

Falco had lost all sense of the real world. All he knew was the close press of Simeon's body held tight within his arms. The old man's breath was little more than a dry scrape but Falco refused to let him fall. He felt the overwhelming force of the demon's malice trying to crush them and still he held on. Slowly the flames of Baëlfire surrounded them and finally Falco's will began to fade.

Images flashed through his mind and he knew that he was losing his sanity. He saw his childhood home burning, and the dark eyes of Morgan Saker staring at him through the flames. He saw the exquisite beauty of a black dragon alighting on the Dragon Stone and Darius blasting it with searing bolts of blue. He felt the grief and the hatred in the dragon's mind and saw them fall together into the abyss. He heard himself screaming and through the screams he saw Malaki walking towards him, his father's broken body in his arms.

Falco's grip faltered on the sword. But then the strangest thing occurred. Part of his mind knew that it was night-time, still several hours before the dawn and yet somehow he felt the sunrise. In his mind he saw it shining above a mountain ridge to the west. He felt himself lofted far above the valley, looking down upon the battle as through the slits in a helm of steel. Beneath him he saw a ripple of yellow scales and the great sweep of a golden wing. Then he felt himself falling, the sound of the wind whistling in his ears. But this was just a fancy, the fleeting dream of someone who was about to die.

Finally he saw the outline of a face blurred by tears. He felt a rough hand upon his cheek and a tender kiss upon his brow, a kiss that lingered then and lingered still within his heart. Too young to know it at the time, it was the last kiss of a father saying farewell to his son. Falco could feel the gentle strength in his father's hand, the scratchy bristles of his beard and the wet touch of his father's tears. He knew that if he gave in to the demon's spite he would lose this memory for ever.

And so, even as Simeon died and the darkness closed upon his heart, Falco held on.

*

124

The demon exulted as it felt the Defiant's heart give out and its lip curled as it prepared to dine upon the weakling's soul. But then it stopped and a stab of doubt flashed across its blackened heart.

Draconis.

There, falling from the sky was one of the despised wyrms with a pure Defiant clinging to its back.

The demon gave a snarl of rage and hate, frustrated that even at the last, it might be denied the prize of seven thousand souls. With a shake of its head it drew the Kardakae forward into a protective wall of heavy blades and dark steel. Then it summoned such a storm of brimstone as could kill a dragon.

*

The dragon came in low and fast, a beautiful creature with scales of deep yellow and shimmering gold. Wings drawn in for greater speed it streaked across the valley, rolling to one side as the demon unleashed a lethal stream of volcanic shale. The deadly burst missed its target and a moment later the great yellow dragon slammed into the towering demon of the Possessed.

Just before the moment of impact the battle mage leapt from the saddle, turned in the air and landed in the midst of the Kardakae. He swept his blade from its scabbard and killed the first of the dark warriors with a single upward cut. He turned and slew another, the edge of his sword seeming to glow as it sliced through the black armour of the huge warriors. The Kardakae rushed to attack him but found themselves beset by the men of Simeon's bodyguard.

All across the valley the men and women in the army found the weariness fading from their limbs and the fear lifting from their minds. For the first time since they fled their homes they believed that they could win and so, even in the face of defeat, they found again the strength to fight.

The demon was almost thrown off its feet by the force of the dragon's attack, but it was a thing of impossible strength. Even as it staggered back it grabbed hold of the dragon and slammed it into the ground. The earth shook as the mighty creature was brought down. The demon rose over it, the flesh of its shoulder was torn to the bone but still it raised a fist ready to strike a blow that would crush the dragon's ribs. It never got the chance.

Recovering with amazing speed the dragon opened its mouth and hit the demon full in the face with a burst of fire. The monster roared as its skin began to peel away. It kicked out with its steel-hard hooves but the dragon twisted clear. It was reaching for the dragon's throat when the battle mage struck, severing the tendons at the back of one enormous goat-like leg. The demon staggered and turned to face the Defiant, but before it could mount another attack the dragon reared up behind it, pulled its horned head to one side and sank its teeth into the base of the demon's neck. Roaring in pain the monster reached back to grab its assailant but then the battle mage hit it in the chest with a bolt of energy that illuminated its ribcage from within.

Slumping to its knees the hellish fiend tried to summon one last explosion of fire that would consume them all, but the dragon dug its talons into the monster's face, drew back its head and the battle mage's blade whipped across its throat. The battle mage stepped clear as a flood of burning fluid spilled down the demon's chest. The dragon released its hold and the massive creature of the underworld pitched forward onto the ground.

The demon was dead and the battle mage and the dragon turned their attention to the Possessed. Before the sun rose in the valley not a single one of them remained alive. The people of Valentia had come to the very brink of desolation, but finally the battle for the soul of Caer Dour was won.

21
The Marchio Dolor

Deep in the Forsaken Lands of Beltane a demon of far greater power closed its eyes as it felt one of the Faithful depart. The vanquished demon had been cunning and strong but new to the earthly realm and rash. It had pushed too far, too fast and now it had paid the price for its zeal. But no matter. It was but one of many unlike *he*, who was a thing of singular power. In the realm of perdition they had no need of names but here, in the charnel world, they called this demon the Marchio Dolor, the Marquis of Pain.

He was not displeased by the name.

The Marchio Dolor turned to the northwest. Yes, somewhere there, near the border with Clemoncé. Of all the seven kingdoms Clemoncé was the smallest and yet, in some indefinable way, the strongest too. Their Defiants gave hope to others and where there was hope it was not so easy to break the faith of common souls.

The armies of the Faithful were sweeping across the land. There were just two places where their advance had been stalled. In the north, around the Illician city of Hoffen, and in the south where the Faithful were being thwarted by the Beltonian general Vercincallidus. Even now the Marchio Dolor himself was moving south to crush the troublesome general.

What they needed was a demon of similar power to break the resistance in the north.

The Marchio turned to the supplicants weeping in the night. The pitiful fools longed for death but death would not save them. Death would only deliver them into the hands of others far crueller even than he. They existed now only to suffer and every day would be a new revelation of agony. But tonight he would use them for a higher purpose. He would use their pain to reach into the heart of the infernal realm and call forth a demon to slay the Defiants and cleave the wyrms asunder.

With utter indifference he looked upon the supplicants, men, women and children. They cried and sobbed in ragged snorts, terrified in the certain knowledge that worse was yet to come.

His lip curled in disgust at their weakness then he closed his eyes and knelt down upon the earth to pray. He prayed until the supplicants rose into the air as if each were suspended from a butcher's hook snagged within their chest. He prayed until the rock beneath them split apart and the flames of Baëlfire rose up around them, until their flesh turned black and their tortured screams filled the night. They would writhe in agony until his prayers were answered and then their crozzled souls would descend to suffer the eternal torments of hell.

Finally satisfied, the Marchio Dolor came back to his feet. It might take months for such a demon to rise from the deepest planes of hell but still he ordered the Enlightened to stand ready to make whatever tools this new manifestation of darkness might require.

Many years ago the Enlightened had made the armour that covered his flesh, armour that could deny the power of a Defiant and turn the point of a wyrm's claw. Now the Enlightened stood around the burning pit like ghosts, the

127

light of the flames playing across their pale skin and bone white eyes. Unlike the Marchio however, they were not inured to the screaming of the damned. Deep within their withered hearts something of their humanity still remained and the light of the flames glistened in the tears upon their cheeks.

The Marchio paid them not another thought. The suffering would continue until a new demon rose from the pit and then the Defiants would pay for the sins of their resistance. For now he turned his mind back to the kings and queens who stood against him, to Osric the proud, Ernest the weak, Vittorio the fool, and Catherine the bitch queen of Clemoncé. He would break them all and feed upon their screaming souls. And then he would move on to Acheron and Thraece, and what sublime satisfaction there would be in humbling their great strength.

Had *he* possessed anything in the way of humanity he might have smiled in anticipation, but tonight one of the Faithful had been slain and there was no room in his heart for anything more than hate. He looked down on the bleak land stretching out below him. In the distance he could see a faint glow of orange light, the torches and campfires of those who fled before him. He flexed the muscles of his mortal flesh and his eyes burned like pits of molten bronze. Tonight they had suffered a defeat but tomorrow they would be avenged. The nations of Wrath were divided and weak, the Defiants and wyrms too few.

There was nothing in the world that could stop them now.

Part II

WRATH

Solace
ILLICIA
Hoffen
Le Matres
Reiherstadt
Wrath
Ville De Pierre
Maidstein
Amboss
CLEMÉNCE
Hertzheim
Seeburg
Toulwar
Caer Dour
Lake
Viegal
Ruaen
Navaria
The Pass of Amaethon
BELTANE
Maiden
VALENTIA
Caer Laison
Távros
THE BAY
OF
BARINTHUS
ACHERON

22

Toulwar

Falco woke to the smell of herbs. It was daytime and he was lying in a bed with clean linen sheets. Blinking slowly, he gazed up at the dark wooden beams on the ceiling. For a moment he thought he was back in Simeon's villa and a feeling of deep relief washed over him but then he noticed the ceiling was different and the sense of relief vanished as memories of all that had happened swept through his mind. He closed his eyes and turned his face into the pillow.

'It's all right. You're safe.'

He felt a soothing hand on his forehead and opened his eyes to see Fossetta sitting on the edge of his bed.

'There, now,' she said, smiling as she saw the recognition in his eyes.

Falco tried to sit up but he was too weak.

'Here,' said Fossetta, raising him up and placing another pillow behind his back. She offered him a glass of water but Falco waved it away.

'Dizzy,' he said, closing his eyes once more.

'That'll pass. You've spent the last eight days flat on your back. It'll be a while before you find your feet.'

Falco nodded but his mind was struggling to make sense of things.

Eight days?

He had dreamlike memories of being carried through the mountains; of the sky giving way to a canopy of trees. He remembered waking to the feel of rain on his face, images of people tending him, of food and drink being coaxed down his throat then the echoing sound of walls around him and candles burning in a darkened room, people sitting beside his bed.

Once again he opened his eyes and this time the room did not tilt around him quite so much. He looked up at the woman he had known his entire life.

'Toulwar?'

Fossetta nodded but her smile was laden with a sadness that Falco had never seen before.

'We're in the citadel. You were brought here after the battle.'

'The battle,' said Falco, clearly confused as to what the outcome had been.

'We prevailed,' said Fossetta, although her expression did not speak of victory. 'One of the riders got through. A battle mage managed to find us.'

'With a dragon,' breathed Falco, frowning as he remembered the strange images streaming through his mind.

'Yes,' said Fossetta while Falco took in his surroundings.

The plainly furnished room was built from a pale stone softened by carpets and wall hangings. A pair of heavy turquoise curtains hung to either side of a balcony that extended from the room. Falco had no idea where he was but the light outside the window gave the impression of height. He looked back at Fossetta.

'Simeon?'

The housekeeper shook her head.

'We buried him in the mountains. With the others who fell.'

Falco nodded. He had already known that Simeon was dead. He remembered the sense of departure when his heart gave out and could only hope that the old battle mage was now at peace.

'It's funny,' said Fossetta, removing a handkerchief from the sleeve of her blouse. 'Sometimes I can still hear him calling for me.' She smiled at her own silliness and Falco reached out to take hold of her hand. He had to swallow several times before he spoke again.

'Malaki?'

'He's fine,' said Fossetta, brushing the handkerchief across her cheek. 'A bit battered and quiet but he's fine. He's been spending a lot of time with Bryna.'

Falco smiled but Fossetta lowered her eyes.

'Her father died in the battle too.'

Falco's smile faltered.

'He charged the demon, with Lord Cadell,' said Fossetta.

'I know. I saw them.'

They were silent for a while as their thoughts were drawn back to the terrible night in the mountains.

'And Merryweather? He was hurt...'

'The wound refused to heal,' said Fossetta. 'He died shortly after we arrived here.'

Falco's heart clenched in grief.

'What about Tobias?'

'Better than you might think. The people here are very kind and the emissary thinks he might be of some service to the Queen.'

Falco was too upset to enquire what this service might be.

'So many dead.'

Fossetta gripped his hand.

'Hey, now,' she said in a sterner tone. 'There would have been a lot more if you hadn't gone to help Simeon.' She waited until he looked at her, the expression in her eyes warning against any further self pity.

Falco looked suitably chastised and Fossetta bent down to kiss him.

'Welcome back, my love,' she breathed.

He leaned his head against the soft flesh of her cheek. He could not remember a time when she had not been there to ease away his fears.

'And now,' said Fossetta, letting go of his hand and rising to her feet. 'I think there's someone else who would like to see you.'

Falco watched as she moved to the door.

'He's been sleeping in the corridor,' she said in a disapproving tone. 'Seemed nervous about being in here in case you woke up.' She raised her eyes despairingly as she reached for the latch. Falco heard her speaking to someone outside then she stepped back and Malaki appeared in the doorway. Shoulders slumped, the big youth ambled into the room, his downcast eyes looking everywhere except at his friend.

Falco's eyes began to smart and an ache that he had forgotten closed around his heart. Fossetta looked at Malaki and despite her earlier tone there was an expression of understanding in her eyes. She gave him a smile and nodded him on.

Falco eased his legs over the side of the bed and slowly got to his feet, clinging on to the bedstead to prevent himself from falling. He swayed a little and Malaki lurched forward to catch him but Falco caught his balance and suddenly the two boys were standing face to face. The silence stretched as they struggled to find something to say.

'So,' began Falco. 'Are you still going to the Academy of War?'

Malaki nodded.

'Good... I'd hate to think you broke the emissary's nose for nothing.'

A snort of laughter escaped from Malaki before he could restrain it.

'I thought I might go on as well.'

Malaki looked up and now it was Falco's turn to avert his eyes.

'Shall we go as friends, do you think?'

'No,' said Malaki. 'We'll go as we have lived... as brothers.' And before Falco knew what was happening Malaki swept him into a bone crushing embrace. The dam holding back their tears burst and the two boys held each other as they cried. Falco's tingling legs gave out and the only thing holding him up was his friend's great strength. He buried his face in Malaki's shoulder.

'I'm sorry about your father.'

The tightness of Malaki's embrace increased.

'And I'm sorry about yours.'

Fossetta watched as the two boys healed the rift that had opened up between them. She tried to speak but her throat felt suddenly tight. The two youths moved apart as she gave a cough from the door.

'I'll have some food sent up,' she managed, looking at Falco. 'But try not to eat too much.'

Falco nodded and Malaki's face brightened at the mention of food. Fossetta looked at them for a moment longer then with a tearful smile she left the room. The two youths grinned at each other, then a wave of vertigo coursed through Falco and Malaki reached out to help him back onto the bed.

'Blades,' said the big youth. 'And I thought you were skinny before the battle.'

'Up yours, smithy!' said Falco as he flopped back onto his pillows.

Malaki perched on the edge of the bed while Falco made himself more comfortable. 'How do you feel?'

'Knackered.'

Malaki smiled but then his gaze shifted to the burns on Falco's neck and shoulder. 'That still looks sore.'

'Doesn't hurt like it used to,' said Falco, raising a hand to touch the raw-looking skin.

'Heçamede's been keeping an eye on you. And the healers here are pretty good too.'

The skin had been treated with some kind of ointment and Falco caught the smell of comfrey as he rubbed the herbal residue between his thumb and fingers.

'And how's the chest?'

Falco was suddenly surprised that he had not noticed before. His chest felt clear, with only a vague hint of discomfort. He breathed deeply and Malaki nodded in appreciation.

133

'Heçamede says you should be fine. You might feel some tightness and maybe a burning sensation and headaches if you try to do too much. But apart from that she thinks you're pretty much back to normal.'

Falco raised an eyebrow at his friend's detailed prognosis.

'They didn't always shut the door properly,' said Malaki, blushing.

'And how are you? How's Bryna.'

Malaki's blush deepened but there was no mistaking the satisfaction in his eyes. 'She's well, considering.' He gazed down at his hands. 'Bit quiet, cries a lot. Like the rest of us. No one's quite the same as they used to be.'

Falco understood what his friend was saying. This was the first battle that they had known but it was also their first experience of the Possessed. The reality of their world had been shaken and they would never be the same again.

'Still bossy, though?'

'Hell, yes!' said Malaki and the two boys laughed.

They talked for a while and Falco learned about everything that had happened since the end of the battle, how they had buried the people in a communal grave, with Simeon in a separate plot facing the mouth of the valley, watching over them in death as he had done in life. He told Falco how the emissary would not let them burn the Possessed until words had been spoken over the piles of stinking corpses.

'He said they were just as much a victim as anyone else who fell,' said Malaki.

Falco learned just how close he had come to death and how it was only the healing powers of the battle mage that saved him. Finally he learned how the army of Toulwar had arrived just two days later and led them gently down to the city.

'And what about Bellius,' asked Falco. 'Did he make it through?'

'Oh yes,' said Malaki. 'Even managed to make himself look like a hero. Like he'd risked everything to come and get help.'

'But he knows the truth and it won't be easy for them, knowing they fled to save their own skins.'

'That's not going to bother a tosser like Bellius,' said Malaki. 'He's probably in Wrath already, lording it up with his 'royal cousins'.'

They talked about the people of Clemoncé and the city of Toulwar, which sat on the shore of a great lake surrounded by forest. Falco was just beginning a second round of questions when there was a knock on the door and one of the orderlies leaned into the room.

'Pardon, my lords. Two men to see Master Danté.'

Falco gave him a questioning look.

'Sir William Chevalier of Eltz and Dominic Ginola, battle mage from the southern city of Ruaen.'

'Yes, of course,' said Falco, trying to sit more upright in his bed. He felt suddenly nervous. He would be pleased to see the emissary again but he wondered how another battle mage would react knowing that he was Aquila Danté's son. Trying to feign some semblance of dignity he watched as the two men entered the room.

134

The emissary's familiar face was marked by several newly healed cuts and Falco noticed a slight limp but apart from that he seemed fine. The other man was just as tall with dark, shoulder-length hair and a lean face only marred by a nose that had clearly been broken several times.

The emissary walked straight up to Falco and shook his hand warmly.

'You're looking better,' he said with a smile.

There was something about the emissary's presence that spoke of security and continuity. Falco gave a shy smile and turned as the battle mage held out a bottle.

'In Clemoncé it is customary to bring a gift to those in healing.' The man's voice was deep, with the tuneful fluidity of the Clemoncéan dialect.

Falco took the bottle and turned it to look at the brown paper label, which bore the name 'Marceneu' and a woodcut picture of grapes.

'From the vineyards of Ruaen,' said the battle mage. 'It might help you sleep.'

Feeling deeply self-conscious Falco mumbled a few words of thanks and handed the bottle to Malaki who placed it on the table beside his bed.

There followed something of an awkward silence.

'Malaki says you saved me after the battle,' said Falco.

The battle mage inclined his head. 'I did what I could. And what you did was no small thing,' he went on. 'There are few that can walk into the storm of a demon's mind.'

Falco lowered his eyes.

'Simeon was like a father to me,' he said as if this explained everything.

There was no false modesty in Falco's voice. He simply did not realise just how extraordinary his actions had been.

'What will you do now?' asked the emissary.

'I'll go on to Wrath,' said Falco. 'I would like to train as a healer. If they will have me.'

Malaki and the emissary laughed but the battle mage just frowned in confusion.

'He doesn't know?'

'Know what?' asked Falco, confused and embarrassed by their reactions.

'If you go to Wrath it will not be to train as a healer,' said the emissary.

'Then what?'

'A battle mage,' said Malaki and Falco stared at his friend as if he were speaking gibberish. 'It seems Tobias has a gift for picking them out, even as a four year old child.'

Falco continued to stare at him blankly.

'Ballymudge,' said Malaki.

'That's what he calls me,' said Falco as if this explained nothing. 'That's what he's always called me.'

'He calls me the same thing,' said the battle mage.

Falco's expression hardened.

'You want me to become a battle mage. Like my father?'

He looked at Malaki as if to say, you should know better.

135

'You have the *potential* to become a battle mage,' said the emissary. 'Only time will tell if that is to be your destiny.' He placed a reassuring hand on Falco's shoulder. 'Now, try to get some rest. In a few days time we will be leaving for Wrath.'

Falco nodded distractedly as the two men took their leave. They paused at the doorway looking back at the thin figure lying in the bed.

'The magi will never agree to train him,' said the battle mage.

'Maybe they shouldn't,' replied the emissary and the battle mage looked at him sharply.

'The war is going badly. Another Aquila Danté would certainly help.'

'Not if *he* turns against us too.'

The battle mage frowned and looked at Falco with an appraising eye.

'And will he?'

'I don't know,' said the emissary and with that he quietly closed the door to Falco's room.

'Will he turn against us?'

The Queen would ask him the same question and he would give her the same answer. William Chevalier had a gift for seeing into the hearts of men but in the case of Falco Danté he simply did not know. All he knew was that when everyone else had been laid low by the demon, this thin and sickly boy had walked into the very face of evil. If he could do that at the lowest ebb of his strength what could he do at its height?

Falco was far too weak to attempt the Rite of Assay, and Dominic was right, the magi would never agree to train him but if the Queen *was* to ask his opinion then he would say yes, Falco Danté should be trained as a battle mage. The only question that then remained was how.

23

A Meeting of Minds

Falco was lying in bed. It was after midnight and he could not sleep. Soon they would be leaving for Wrath. He was trying to picture the capital city when there was a quiet knock on his door. He sat up as one of the orderlies entered his room, a brass candle holder held in the crook of his finger.

'Pardon, Master Danté,' said the young man. 'Your presence is requested on the north tower.'

'By whom?'

'The battle mage, Dominic Ginola.'

Surprised and suddenly nervous, Falco swung out of bed, dressed quickly and grabbed the sheepskin coat that lay on a chair beside the door. Five minutes later he emerged from the stairwell of the north tower. The battle mage stood in the centre of the wide open space, a small torch burning in his hand.

'Thank you for coming.'

Falco gave him a self-conscious nod of acknowledgment.

'There's someone who would like to meet you.'

'Who?' asked Falco but the battle mage did not answer.

He just smiled and placed a reassuring hand on Falco's shoulder then he crossed the open space and disappeared down the dimply lit stairwell. More intrigued than ever Falco pulled his coat close against the cold autumn air. Clouds drifted across a starry sky and far below he could see a scattering of lights in the sleeping city. He checked again to make sure he was alone, wondering who might want to speak to him in the middle of the night.

Before he had the chance to get impatient he felt a presence, not from the stairwell, but from the sky above. He looked up and there, against the starry sky, was a shape, a winged shape descending quickly towards him.

Falco took several steps back as the dragon alighted on the paving stones. It landed with exquisite composure, no sound, just a powerful gust of wind as its massive wings arrested its decent. Falco's heart was hammering in his chest and yet he felt no fear. The dragon stood five feet at the shoulder but its head rose high above him. It looked down upon him and Falco was transfixed by the intensity of its gaze. Even in the darkness he could see the sheen of its golden yellow scales. It was magnificent, a creature of power and grace.

For a moment the two beings looked at each other and Falco had the sense that he was not looking at an animal but a creature of intelligence and nobility. It was strange but he felt as if he were in the presence of a knight. But there was something in the dragon's demeanour that spoke of discomfort and Falco had the sudden revelation that the dragon was nervous.

As they continued to look at each other Falco found images surfacing in his mind. He saw the black dragon in the Castle of the Winds and felt again the sense of power, hatred and grief. He remembered the horror of seeing it fall; the shame he felt at his part in its death. Then he looked at the dragon standing before him and was amazed to see the same emotions shining in its eyes.

Shame and grief.

The dragon grieved for the loss of its brother but it was also ashamed. It could not comprehend how one of its own kind could ever come to harm a human being and it was looking to *him* for answers. Falco shook his head. He had none.

Feeling as if he had somehow let the dragon down Falco bowed his head. For a moment the dragon looked down at him then it moved closer and lowered its own head until its scaled brow came to rest against Falco's forehead.

Falco was overwhelmed. This was so different to his encounter with the black dragon in the Castle of the Winds. Despite the yellow dragon's size he felt no sense of danger. Somehow he knew that he could trust this creature absolutely. With a liberating sense of abandon he closed his eyes and opened his mind as the dragon's scent wafted around him. It was a strange and complex smell like fresh leather, hot metal and pine trees.

He could hear the deep flow of her breathing and, just below the reach of hearing, he could feel the percussive beat of her mighty heart. Slowly he reached up to touch her. The dragon's scales felt hard like enamelled steel and yet, even in the bitter chill of midnight, they were warm. He pressed his hand against the dragon's cheek and felt it move beneath his touch. She might be encased in armour but she was a creature of flesh and blood.

Finally he removed his hand and the dragon raised her head. For another minute she looked down upon him then slowly she backed away and spread her wings. She bowed her head in a final gesture of respect then reared back on her hind legs and launched herself into the air. Falco swayed in the force of the downdraft and watched as the dragon lofted into the dark sky unaware that he was not the only one who saw it disappear into the night.

*

Across from the citadel two men looked out from a high window of the city's mage tower. One was Morgan Saker, the other was the tower's Veneratu, the Master of the Toulwarian magi.

'Does he know?' asked the Veneratu.

'No,' said Morgan Saker. His eyes fixed on the north tower of the citadel where the small figure of Falco Danté had now disappeared from view. 'He was too young. He knows nothing.'

The Veneratu seemed unconvinced.

'The dragon paid him homage.'

Morgan nodded slowly, wondering what such a show of respect might mean.

The two men stared out from the balcony.

'He must not be trained!' said the Veneratu.

'He would never endure the Rite of Assay.'

'But if he did...'

'Yes,' said Morgan. 'He would win the right to a summoning.'

'We cannot allow that to happen.'

'He might not form the same bond with *his* dragon,' said Morgan. 'His father took many years to grow so close.'

'Are you willing to take the chance?'

Morgan's black eyes glinted in the darkness. He was not thinking of what might come to pass, he was thinking of what had gone before, of something that had happened when Falco was just a child. He remembered the small boy standing in the midst of the burning building and he remembered forging his way through the flames to save him. At the time he had considered it an act of compassion. Now he knew it for what it was, a moment of weakness that could lead to their ruin.

'No,' he said, in answer to the Veneratu's question. 'I am not.'

'Then let us send word to our brothers in Wrath. Danté's son is not to be trained, no matter what pressure the Queen might bring to bear.'

Morgan nodded but his mind was still distracted. He found himself thinking of something Bellius Snidesson had said back in the town square of Caer Dour.

'First the father and now the son.'

Doubt gnawed at Saker's heart. Why had he saved the child? It would have been so much easier to let him die, so much easier to kill him as they had killed his father. With a deep sigh Morgan followed the Veneratu from the balcony. They would summon a quintet to the chamber of discourse. It would take five mages several hours to send even a short message to the capital but that would be enough.

By sunrise the magi of Wrath would be warned.

Falco Danté must not become a battle mage.

*

Meredith Saker moved into the shadows as his father and the Veneratu swept along the corridor and disappeared from view. They were heading for the chamber of discourse at the heart of the tower. For several moments he stood staring after them, wondering what could be so important that they needed to send a message at this late hour.

He turned back to the window and looked across to the north tower of the citadel. He too had witnessed Falco's meeting with the dragon but unlike Falco it brought him no satisfaction. He felt only conflict in his heart and he could not escape the feeling that he was spying on his father.

But why?

For as long as he could remember, there had been a shadow in his mind, a seed of doubt that told him all was not right in the world. In the Castle of the Winds, it had begun to grow. It had no form and he could not put a name to it but it had something to do with Falco Danté and his strange affinity with dragonkind.

Meredith closed his eyes and cleared his mind. He would find no answers in vague suspicions. Instead he would employ the oldest of all magi disciplines - contemplation.

Through contemplation the nature of any shadow could be unmasked.

*

Falco did not remember returning to his room. He did not remember getting into bed. All he could think of was the gentle pressure of the dragon's head pressing against his own, the deep bellows of its breathing and the incredible warmth of its inner heat. All his life he had wanted to see a dragon, as if somehow it might help him understand his father's death, and now he found that they too were looking for answers. But for now Falco was content. He had stood

139

in the presence of something powerful and pure. The Possessed might threaten their world but they would not do so unopposed.

Feeling a deep sense of peace Falco closed his eyes to sleep. In two days' time they would leave Toulwar and set off on the road to Wrath.

24

The Great Possession

After having woken, Falco recovered quickly. In an ideal world they would have given him more time to regain his strength but disturbing reports had been coming in about a growing sense of fear and even some sporadic attacks along the eastern border of Clemoncé, small forces of Possessed that appeared out of nowhere to attack in the night. The emissary seemed to find these reports deeply troubling.

'It is a sign of the enemy's influence,' he told them one night as they sat together in the citadel's dining hall. 'The main battle front is still many miles from Clemoncé but as the shadow creeps closer cracks open up and the evil of the Possessed bleeds through.

'I have been away too long,' he said. 'And besides, the Queen will be eager to meet *you*.'

'Me?' exclaimed Falco.

'The son of Aquila Danté?' said the emissary. 'Oh, yes.'

Falco still found the idea of becoming a battle mage ridiculous and more than a little unsettling. People had already suffered for the flaws in his father's character. He had no wish to test the limits of his own. He turned to Fossetta and Malaki for support but neither of them seemed in the least bit surprised.

'You've your father's fire and your mother's good grace,' said Fossetta.

'But I can barely lift a sword, never mind swing one in battle.'

'Aye, but you know what to do,' insisted Malaki. 'You were just as good as me when we were boys.'

'But that was years ago,' said Falco, remembering how he had been forced to stop practicing as his health deteriorated.

'It never goes away,' said Malaki sagely. 'You just need building up a bit. A few months in a blacksmith's forge, that's what you need.'

The emissary's expression was thoughtful but he smiled at Falco's exasperation and raised his eyebrows as if to say, 'they know best'.

They talked for a while until the emissary rose to his feet.

'I will send word of our departure to the Queen,' he said and with a bow he left them.

Falco had felt a flutter of anxiety. He had been excited about the prospect of seeing Wrath, but now that it came down to it he found himself reluctant to leave, especially as Fossetta had decided to remain in Toulwar to look after Tobias. The crippled boy had agreed to the emissary's unusual suggestion. Using his special 'gift' Tobias would travel the land looking for other youngsters like Falco who possessed the hidden fire of a battle mage.

'Tobias needs me,' Fossetta explained later that evening as they sat beside the fire in Falco's room. 'It's time for you to find your own path and you can't do that with me clucking around your heels.'

Neither of them tried to hide their tears as they hugged each other close.

'If you ever need me...' said Falco.

'I know, my love. I know.'

Now they gathered on the outskirts of Toulwar to say their goodbyes. The families and friends of the cadets were there, along with a small crowd of people from the city. Like Fossetta, Heçamede had also decided to stay in Toulwar. The people of Caer Dour needed their healer more than ever.

'Live long and true,' said the healer, quoting an old Thraecian proverb.

'Thanks to you,' said Falco, embracing her warmly and thinking of all the times she had saved his life.

And there was Tobias, sitting in his chair with Fossetta standing behind him.

'Goodbye, Tobias,' said Falco, crouching down to take his hand. 'Take care of Fossetta now, won't you?'

Tobias's head wobbled on his thin neck as he looked at Falco.

'Guh'bye, Ballymudge. Mek sure you hummon a big hragon.'

Falco gave a wry laugh.

'And good luck in finding more ballymudges. I hope they're not all as weedy as me!'

Tobias laughed as if this were quite the funniest joke. Finally he came to Fossetta but they had said their true goodbye in the privacy of Falco's room and so they parted with a hug and a kiss as if Falco was off on a camping trip with Malaki.

'Take care of each other,' Fossetta told them. 'And remember, when you meet the Queen it's, Your Majesty, in the first instance and then ma'am after that.'

The two youths nodded and with more than one backward glance they led their horses to join the emissary and the other cadets waiting on the road.

'I wish *they* weren't coming with us,' said Malaki, nodding towards the small group of magi who were also waiting beside the road. Among them were Morgan Saker and his son Meredith. They too would be travelling with the emissary to the capital.

Finally the emissary invited them to mount and they waved to the people that had come to see them off. Falco kept looking back until a bend in the road meant that he could no longer see Fossetta. It was a strange feeling to be riding away from everything he had known and he was glad to have his friend beside him. He glanced across but Malaki was laughing quietly with Bryna.

'Just as it should be,' thought Falco with a smile.

And so they had set off through the forested land of Clemoncé, threading their way through woods of oak, beech, chestnut and pine. At times they passed through villages and towns and even here the peoples' sleep was troubled by nightmares and a growing sense of fear.

'The enemy is getting closer,' said the emissary. 'It was the same in Illicia when I was a boy.'

The grim expression in his eyes offered them little in the way of comfort but there was nothing for them to do but journey on. By day they maintained a steady pace while at night they camped beside rivers, lakes or clear forest pools.

The cadets tended to keep to themselves with the magi making their own camp close by. For the most part the conversation was of small things but as the journey progressed they began to reflect on what they had been through and so their thoughts turned to the Possessed. It was nightfall on the ninth day of the journey when someone asked the question...

Just where did the Possessed come from?

'Do they not teach history in Valentia?' asked the emissary, sipping a cup of spiced wine as they sat on logs beside the fire.

'I think we'd like to hear it from you,' said Malaki and the other cadets nodded in agreement.

The emissary paused and steam obscured his face as he took another sip of his wine.

'All we know is that they first appeared in Ferocia.'

The sun had set and veils of grey mist began to gather in the darkening gloom. The cadets were gathered close around the fire with the magi sitting in a separate group a short distance away but even they seemed to be listening as the emissary gathered his thoughts.

'The nations of Wrath have always warred amongst themselves,' he began. 'But only Ferocia seemed to enjoy the slaughter.'

The emissary sighed, his gaze focussed inward as he remembered hearing the story from his father.

'Time and again their armies would cross the Scythian Mountains, sweeping down into Beltane and Illicia. And do not think the more distant kingdoms were safe. Ferocia boasted a huge navy and their warships raided the coasts of Valentia, Thraece, Acheron and even Clemoncé. Nowhere was safe and everywhere people feared the sight of the black wolf on the red Ferocian flag.'

'But we fought back,' said Bryna who was sitting beside Malaki.

'Yes we did,' said the emissary. 'For the first time the kingdoms of Wrath put aside their differences and fought together. They drove the Ferocians back over the Mountains and pursued them to the capital city of Iad itself. But then something happened.'

He paused.

'Some say the Ferocian magi called upon the forces of the underworld; others that their King made a pact with the lord of darkness. All we know is that the free armies of Wrath were suddenly overcome by fear. But what did it matter. They thought they had defeated the enemy, but they were wrong. All they'd done was drive the Ferocians to the edge of desperation and somehow this opened the gates of hell.'

Beyond the firelight the very air itself appeared black.

'It did not happen all at once and for many years people thought that Ferocia had indeed been tamed. But then the nightmares began.'

Here Falco's head became bowed. He knew the nightmares of which the emissary spoke.

'It was only certain children who were afflicted,' said the emissary. 'Most were driven mad, killing themselves or clawing out their own eyes, anything to escape the terror.'

No one said a word. Their experiences in the battle had given them some insight into what these children might have suffered.

'The nightmares were a warning, a portent of what was to come, but it wasn't until eight years later that a new army crossed the mountains of Scythia. It wasn't as large as previous forces but somehow the Ferocian warriors had been changed. They felt neither pain nor fear and it seemed as if their minds had been taken over by some dark, malicious force. People began to refer to them as 'The Possessed'.

'Survivors spoke of the dead coming back to life, of terrible demons fighting alongside them but however outlandish the reports, one thing was clear. This new Ferocian army could not be stopped. Armies sent to destroy it found themselves overwhelmed by fear, and those that did not flee were cut down or taken by the enemy, and so their numbers grew.'

'But we did stop them,' insisted Malaki.

'Yes. Eventually,' said the emissary. 'It was in Beltane, that a young man led an army against the Possessed, and won.

'His name was Telamon Feyn, the first battle mage. He was one of the few children who survived the nightmares, now grown to a strong and quiet man. The stories tell of a glowing sword and fire shooting from his hands but it was the courage...'

'Why are they always men?' interrupted Bryna with more than a touch of annoyance.

Falco and Malaki exchanged an awkward glance but the emissary gave a wry smile.

'In fact, they are not,' he said. 'The queen has a female battle mage in her service, as does Prince Ernest of Illicia. But you are right, battle mages, for the most part, are men.'

He looked at her, noting the way her face lifted at this news, but realising he had not really answered her question.

'The truth is we don't know, but we believe it is down to the response of the children. When faced with trauma girls tend to look inward, while boys are prone to aggression. Neither response will save the afflicted. Only boys who are able to master their aggression and a rare few girls survive the nightmares. And not all of them go on to become battle mages.'

'But many did,' said Malaki, and Falco smiled at his enthusiasm. He had always loved tales of old wars and glorious battles, they both had.

'Well, not many, perhaps,' said the emissary. 'But a few at least. The magi began to train them, honing their powers and helping them to realise their potential. For a while they were able to hold back the Possessed but the number and power of the demons only increased. It wasn't until Telamon took to wandering in the mountains that we learned where our salvation would come from.'

Now it was Falco's turn to look interested.

'The magi criticised him for turning away from the battlefield but Telamon insisted that they needed help. He went up into the mountains and remained there for days without food or sleep. He knew that people were dying but still he waited for something.'

The emissary paused.

'They say that a summoning is like the sounding of a great bell, a tolling of the spirit, loud enough to cross the Endless Sea.'

He thumped his fist against the log on which he sat, three times, just as he remembered his father doing on the dining table in the Great Hall of Eltz.

'A silent call sent out into the void. And it was answered.'

'The dragons,' breathed Malaki and the emissary nodded.

'No one knows where they come from, or why, but somehow they hear the call of a battle mage and come to fight alongside us. At first it was just Telamon. But then others followed his lead and a summoning became the final part of a battle mage's training. In those days all summonings were successful.'

'Were any black?' asked Falco quietly.

The emissary shook his head.

'We don't know. The colour of the dragons is rarely mentioned in the records. But whatever the colour, it was enough. The tide was turned. With a battle mage and a dragon the soldiers of Wrath were able to defeat the demon armies of the Possessed.'

He paused and they were silent for they all knew what was coming next. It was the greatest tragedy ever to befall the world, the last desperate act of an enemy on the brink of annihilation, a terrible event known as The Great Possession.

The emissary drained his cup and shook out the dregs before he went on.

'The Possessed were defeated and the battle mages were the champions of humankind. They took it upon themselves to watch over the land and hunt down the last remnants of the enemy.'

He paused.

'Peace reigned. The years went by and the vigilance of the battle mages seemed unnecessary but still they insisted on keeping the armies of Wrath in a state of readiness. Such readiness is costly, however, and the kings of Wrath began to protest. The magi too were unhappy with the power afforded to the 'great souls'. As far as they were concerned they were no longer needed but the battle mages insisted that they needed to remain on their guard. Tensions grew until the leader of the magi began to speak of an impending disaster.'

The emissary stared into the fire.

'His name was Syballian, The Prophet, Grand Veneratu of the magi. He surprised everyone by siding with the battle mages, saying that they were right; the enemy was not gone and was simply waiting for one last act of vengeance.

'Once again the people were gripped by fear, wondering what this last evil gesture might be. Then came the night of Syballian's vision. He sensed a convergence of evil in a place called the Cazan or Cauldron, a high valley in the mountains not far from the remote mage tower of Ossanda. The Enemy was opening a new rift into the world, said Syballian, and must be stopped.'

Everyone was captivated now, imagining this last chance to stop the evil of Possession for good.

'At this time there were nineteen dragon mounted battle mages in Wrath and, as one, they flew to the Cauldron determined to destroy whatever horrors might be waiting for them. Nineteen dragon mounted battle mages, plus a host of magi from Ossanda. Surely nothing could stand against such a force.

'But they were all mistaken. It was not the legions of hell or a host of demons that awaited them but the power of Possession itself. Only this time it

145

would not be humans overcome by evil. This time the force of Possession would claim the dragons.'

Falco felt a shadow of horror pass over his mind. He remembered the fury of the dragon in the Castle of the Winds. Could it be that black dragons were still susceptible to Possession?

He breathed a sigh as the emissary continued.

'Reports from the magi speak of dragons going mad and attacking their battle mages before they had the chance to react. In the end it was hopeless. Even with the help of the mages the dragons were too powerful. By the time they were slain they had killed every single battle mage plus half of the mages who had been there to help them. It was a catastrophe but at least it was the end. The corrupting power of Possession was gone from the world.'

The night was dark and deathly quiet. Even the wind had grown silent in the trees.

'That was four hundred years ago,' concluded the emissary, his tone wistful and disbelieving.

'And now the Possessed are back,' said a voice out of the darkness.

Everyone looked up to see Meredith Saker standing at the edge of the firelight.

'Yes,' said the emissary, watching Meredith as though he expected him to say something more.

Falco could see the uncertainty in Meredith's eyes. They had all known something of the emissary's tale, how the last gasp of the Enemy had robbed them of the battle mages, and how many people blamed the magi for not realising that dragons were open to Possession. Even now, some four hundred years later, some people still blamed the magi. But what did it matter? The Enemy had been vanquished. People had gone back to their ordinary lives and the balance of power between the magi and the kings of Wrath had returned to its uneasy state.

For several seconds Meredith held the emissary's gaze but then he lowered his eyes and glanced in the direction of his father and the other magi. Then, without another word, he turned away and disappeared into the night.

'What was all that about?' whispered Malaki.

Still staring after Meredith, Falco just shook his head.

An awkward silence descended until the emissary rose to his feet.

'Come,' he said. 'Time for sleep.' He kicked back a few embers that had spilled from the fire. 'If we make good time tomorrow we should reach the coast and from there it's just two more days to Wrath and your meeting with the Queen.'

The young cadets glanced at each other nervously but the emissary gave them a reassuring smile and slowly they began to prepare the camp for the night.

Falco helped to clear the supper things away then, while Malaki went to check on the horses, he laid out their bedrolls with Bryna. The sky was clearing and Falco caught the flicker of stars between the clouds. He was just turning back to the task in hand when his attention was drawn to the magi, now gathered around a small fire of their own. Swathed in their dark robes they cast a forbidding shape in the darkness and Falco felt a shiver of unease run down his spine. He had always been wary of the magi's power but there had been

146

something in Meredith's bearing that spoke of doubt and Falco found this strangely unsettling.

'What're you staring at, dreamer?'

Falco jumped as Malaki returned from the horses.

'Nothing,' he said but Malaki followed the line of his gaze.

'Do you think they knew about the dragons?' said Falco, nodding in the direction of the magi.

'Who knows?' said Malaki. 'I'm more worried about meeting the Queen! I'm bound to do something I shouldn't.'

Falco nodded distractedly while Malaki settled down onto his bedroll. He made some comment to Bryna and got a punch in the ear for his trouble. Still laughing, he bade them all goodnight. He pulled his blankets up over his broad shoulders and then, just like his father, he fell instantly asleep. Bryna glanced at Falco and they shared a moment of amusement before they too settled down.

Falco listened as the camp grew slowly quiet but sleep continued to elude him as he reflected on the emissary's tale.

Had the magi known that dragons were at risk?

Could they have warned people?

Could they have prevented the Great Possession?

The question kept on repeating itself and he thought he would never drop off. But then another thought began to spread across his mind. Tomorrow they would reach the coast and for the first time in his life he would see the sea, the Endless Sea beyond which the dragons were said to live.

Dragons... Magi... Possessed... The sea...

Dragons... Magi... Possessed... The sea...

Such was the rhythm of Falco's thoughts. He could not imagine a body of water that seemed to go on forever but somehow he found the notion deeply comforting and so, by degrees, he fell asleep.

25
Journey's End

The west coast of Clemoncé possessed a wild and rugged beauty. The rich forests of the interior gave way to windswept hills of grass, gorse and bracken with just the occasional stand of trees, bowed and contorted by the relentless persuasion of the wind. But if it was the wind that painted this landscape it was the sea that carved it. From the towering cliffs and jagged rocks to the broad sweeps of soft white sand, everything was shaped by the sea and Falco never tired of looking at it. He gazed at it now as they rode along a hard-packed grassy path that followed the line of the cliffs.

The morning air felt fresh and clean, just as it did in the mountains, but the wind that came off the sea was seasoned with salt. Falco could smell it on the breeze and taste it on his lips as he rode with Malaki and Bryna. They were nearing the end of their journey and their thoughts had turned to what would happen when they finally arrived in Wrath. The emissary had dropped back to join them and they took the opportunity to ply him with questions.

'We don't even know where we'll be staying,' said Bryna.

'You'll be housed in the academy barracks,' said the emissary. 'And then you'll go through selection.'

'I thought we'd already been selected,' said Malaki and Falco smiled at the anxiety in his voice.

'Indeed you have,' said the emissary. 'But we still need to decide how to make best use of your skills.'

'He makes a good stew,' said Falco. 'I'm sure they could use him in the kitchens.'

It was a measure of Malaki's nervousness that he did not retort with some quip of his own.

'It's an important job,' said Falco relentlessly. 'An army marches on its stomach.'

The emissary laughed and even Bryna grinned at Falco's teasing. She was still coming to terms with the humour of common folk and often found it difficult to tell when they were joking and when they were not. Early in the journey she had been appalled when they teased one of the cadets for pissing himself during the battle.

'Why would they joke about such a thing?' she had whispered to the emissary.

'Why would they not?' answered the emissary, smiling as he saw the young man's embarrassment washed away in a wave of good humoured banter.

Now Bryna looked sideways at Malaki waiting to see how he would react to Falco's jest. Fortunately the emissary came to his rescue.

'I'm sure he would make an excellent cook but I think Master de Vane's destiny lies elsewhere.'

Malaki cast Falco a withering look then smiled at Bryna who found herself strangely moved to realise that she was now included in their friendship.

'At the academy you will be trained as officers,' said the emissary in answer to Malaki's question. 'The selection process simply decides which units you will

148

get to command. And of course, those wishing to become a knight will be invited to attempt the épreuve de force.'

'Is that how you came to join the Adamanti?' asked Falco.

The emissary inclined his head modestly. 'I was chosen in Illicia. But the process is just as demanding and not one I would care to repeat.'

Falco and Bryna looked suitably daunted but Malaki's chin came up as if he relished the opportunity to test his strength. He seemed about to ask another question when the cadet at the front of the line called out, his arm extended to point ahead of them.

Rising up in his stirrups Falco saw a rider appear over the hill, surging down the slope and heading straight for the unmistakable figure of the emissary.

'Sir William,' said the man, bowing in the saddle, as he pulled up his horse beside them.

The emissary inclined his head.

'I was dispatched to find you, although I did not expect to encounter you so soon.'

'The road has been clear and the weather kind,' said the emissary.

The rider nodded, glancing round at the people in the party. The glance was cursory but Falco could tell that he had just made an accurate count of their numbers.

'Will you be making directly for the capital?'

'Yes,' said the emissary. 'Is the Queen in residence?'

'She is, my Lord.'

'Then you can tell Her Majesty that we should arrive in the city tomorrow morning.'

The scout gave a shallow bow and took up his reins as if to leave but the emissary raised a hand to stall him.

'What news of the war?'

'Nothing good, my Lord,' said the scout, his face dropping as if he were personally responsible. 'Fear grips the eastern border and yours was the only victory we have learned about of late.'

'Has the Fifth Army returned?'

'Three weeks ago, my Lord. The Queen rode out to meet them, as is her custom, but now she has sent forth two more.'

'*Two* more?'

'Yes, Lord. The Third Army was dispatched to the south east from Toulwar.'

The emissary nodded. He had already known about this deployment.

'And the First Army now marches to support the Illician forces around Hoffen.'

The emissary frowned and the rider looked concerned.

'I could stay a while if your Lordship would like to know more. We have little news from the front but I will tell you what I know, if you wish.'

'No,' said the emissary. 'I will attend the councils on my return and the Queen will be eager for news of our arrival.'

The scout laid his right hand across his chest and bowed low in the saddle, a gesture that the emissary returned and then, with a final look of satisfaction, he was off.

Falco saw the expression in the man's eyes. He was pleased to be able to carry back good news but more than that, he was clearly relieved by the emissary's return. Falco glanced across at the man who had led them since they left Caer Dour.

'*Yes*,' he thought. '*Certainly more than just a simple emissary of the court.*'

'Is that bad?' asked Malaki as the scout disappeared over the hill. 'That the Queen should deploy the First Army?'

'Not bad, in itself,' said the emissary distractedly. He waved to those at the front of the line to continue. 'But I'm surprised that things have reached such a pass.'

'Does that mean things are going badly in Illicia?' asked Bryna. Their anxiety over the details of their training suddenly seemed selfish and trivial.

The emissary gave a grim laugh. 'Things have been going badly in Illicia for many years,' he said. 'This just means that they are getting worse and the danger is moving closer to Clemoncé.'

'How many armies does Clemoncé have?' asked Malaki.

'Five. Not counting provincial forces,' replied the emissary as they continued along the grassy hillside. 'Then there's the Queen's Irregulars, the Légion du Trône and the new mage army, although that doesn't fall under the Queen's command.'

'Then who commands it?' asked Falco.

'The magi,' said the emissary, making no attempt to conceal the tone of disapproval in his voice. 'Or more particularly Galen Thrall, Grand Veneratu of the magi.'

'Do they fight with swords or magic?' asked Malaki.

'Both.'

'I thought only battle mages fought in battle,' said Bryna.

The emissary gave a soft snort of derision. 'A perception the magi are eager to change.'

'Are they powerful?' asked Falco.

The emissary gave him a sideways glance as if it pained him to answer. 'I have only seen them in training, but yes, they are powerful.'

'Then we should welcome their efforts,' said Bryna somewhat haughtily. Coming from the noble class she was not so inclined to be distrustful of the magi.

'Maybe we should,' said the emissary with a diplomatic smile.

Falco and Malaki exchanged a quick look but there was no point in arguing. For all they knew an army of mages *might* be enough to tip the balance in the war against the Possessed.

'What about the Légion du Trône?' asked Falco. 'I've never heard of them.'

The emissary nodded, mindful of the way Falco had changed the subject.

'The Légion du Trône does not foray abroad,' explained the emissary. 'It is charged with the defence of the capital.'

'And the Queen's Irregulars?' asked Malaki.

The emissary inclined his head with a smile of some fondness on his lips. 'Not every soldier who journeys to Wrath is of the standards required by the Academy of War.'

'So they're not very good,' said Malaki.

'To say so would be unkind,' replied the emissary and Malaki looked embarrassed. 'But no,' he continued with a laugh, 'they're not very good.'

They all smiled and for a while they rode in silence. It was a beautiful autumn day, cold and bright with white clouds scudding swiftly across a blue sky. They had almost reached the summit of the hill when the emissary tapped Falco on the arm and pointed up into the sky ahead of them. At first Falco saw nothing but then he saw a small dark shape emerge from behind a cloud, moving across the sky towards the mountains in the distance. Malaki and Bryna had now seen it too.

'A dragon?' asked Malaki.

The emissary nodded. 'They used to be a common sight in the capital. Now most are abroad, fighting the Possessed.'

Falco was mesmerised by the distant speck that slowly dwindled and was lost again among the clouds.

'And there,' said the emissary as they reached the crown of the hill, 'is the port city of Wrath.'

The view opened out before them and there, still some miles away, was a great expanse of grey stone reaching inland from the coast. Falco had thought the forest city of Toulwar large but it was nothing compared to this.

The entire city was enclosed by a double curtain wall, the crenelated line of battlements punctuated by guard towers and barbicans. Beyond the walls they could see towers, spires and domes rising above the terracotta roof tiles of the city's normal buildings, the bright ochre adding a touch of warmth to the imposing fortifications of the city.

'You can see that the city walls are extended to protect the harbour,' said the emissary as the Cadets crowded forward to see. 'Then, towards the centre, you can see the citadel rising over the city.'

'Where's the academy?' asked one of the cadets.

'On the plateau behind the city,' said the emissary. 'That's where you will find the Academy of War, the training fields and the towers of the magi.'

'And what's that pale stone building to the left of the citadel? The one with all the flags?'

'That's the palace,' said the emissary, pointing to a structure at the very edge of the cliffs. 'The home of Queen Catherine herself.'

They gazed in wonder at the huge city, lying with the sea to the west and the snow-capped mountains to the north and east. They could almost imagine the pale blue and turquoise of Clemoncé's colours but the flags were too far away to make out the horse head insignia of the Queen.

'What's she like?' asked Bryna.

The emissary looked at the youngsters, their eyes alight with anticipation, but he offered them no answer. Instead he only smiled.

26

The Queen of Wrath

Standing at the balcony of her chambers, Queen Catherine de Sage looked out over the bustling city of Wrath. She had been away from the palace for several days and was glad to be back despite the backlog of issues that required her attention. There were a dozen pressing matters to be dealt with but all she could think of was the small pile of letters lying neatly on her writing desk. Cyrano had brought them to her earlier, his expression giving nothing away. although she knew for a fact that he would have read them.

'How many replies?' she had asked her advisor.

'All of them, Majesty.'

The Queen raised an eyebrow. She had not expected the other monarchs to reply so soon and some of them not at all. Another sign of just how bad things had become. She felt a shudder run through her. The midday sun was bright but her gown was light and the sea breeze felt cold upon her skin. Folding her arms against the chill she raised a hand to the black velvet choker that encircled her neck. Crudely embroidered with the royal monogram, it was a symbol of the forces that shaped her life: duty, grief and love. It was the first thing she donned each morning and the last thing she removed each night but now it was getting a little threadbare and she wondered how long it would be before the stitching came loose or the clasp gave way. It was a reminder that she could not remain in mourning forever. Sooner or later she would need to give Prince Ludovico an answer.

'*But not this year,*' she thought with a determined smile. '*And Fates willing, not the next.*'

With a sigh the Queen put aside such thoughts as she gazed out over the city that her forebears had founded more than twelve hundred years ago. It looked safe and serene but the safety, she knew, was an illusion.

Her father King Philip II had always taught her that peace was a transient thing. Plague, drought, famine, war... shadows on the landscape. They all pass with time. It was their job as sovereign, he told her, to limit the times of shadow and embrace the times of light. Her father had been the wisest person she had ever known but now she feared that he might be wrong. The shadow of the Possessed was not one that would pass with time. If they were not stopped the darkness of the enemy's reign would last forever.

Their only hope was to stand together but the kingdoms of Wrath were not united. Illicia and Beltane were on their knees. Valentia floundered under the rule of an idiot king. Acheron revelled in its singular might, while the King of Thraece had been laid low by a stroke, his rule usurped and his son denied accession by the machinations of the Thraecian magi.

It was hopeless.

And yet she clung to hope.

It was in the spirit of hope that she had written to the other kings. And now they had replied. Would they come together as they had done in the past or would they continue in isolation, denying the horror that threatened them all?

The answer lay in the letters on her desk and with a sigh of resignation she turned away from the window. Her mind was buzzing with the minutiae of running the city but if the kingdoms could not come together then food shortages and anxiety over the number of refugees would be the least of their concerns. Sitting down at her desk she looked at the collection of letters, each one bearing the royal crest of the king who had sent it.

But which one to read first?

Hesitating for just a moment she decided to read them in the order she had written to the kings. Picking up the first letter she untied the crimson ribbon and noted the dragon seal of the King of Valentia.

From Vittorio Tristis, King of Valentia, to Her Majesty Queen Catherine of Wrath

Caer Laison would like to thank Your Majesty for her concern about the Ferocian army which recently entered our domain to the north. Initial reports did indeed suggest that the force was significant and marched with a demon at its head, but we have since learned that the brave people of Caer Dour were able to defeat the demon in the mountains before it could pose any threat to the Kingdom of Clemoncé.

So Your Majesty need not have worried. We have many such stalwart towns in the northern reaches and I am quite sure that, had they needed any help, they would have first called upon their king. In Valentia we have a proud history of victory against the Possessed, unlike Her Majesty's kingdom which, being bordered by greater realms, has been spared the danger of such assaults.

As to your other request, we have opened the border with Beltane only to find our cities swamped with refugees. However, with regard to sending forces abroad, we must decline. We deem it more important to keep our armies and our Great Souls close to the capital, the defence of which must be our primary concern.

If Your Majesty has resources to spare we suggest she send them east to bolster the Illician forces who allowed the enemy to slip through in the first instance.

Cordially yours
Vittorio Tristis, Lord of Caer Laison and Sovereign King of Valentia

The Queen shook her head at Vittorio's arrogance. Valentia deserved better. Brief as it was, the Chevalier's report from Toulwar had told the real story of what had happened in the mountains. She had not intended to send him into danger. It was only after he left that they had learned of the threat and there was no way of knowing that the demon would move into that particular valley. Besides, the Queen thought with a smile, even had he known, she suspected her emissary would still have insisted on visiting this town, which seemed to produce more than its fair share of exceptional warriors.

Sir William Chevalier was her subject and servant but over the years she had learned to value his council and she would be glad when he returned to the royal court. Only this morning she had dispatched a scout to see when he might arrive. The emissary's report from Toulwar had contained some intriguing points of interest, including the fact that he travelled with the son of Aquila Danté.

The Queen smiled indulgently. What she would not give to see the faces of the magi when *he* rode into town. Putting aside such thoughts, she lay down Valentia's reply and reached for the next letter in the pile. Slipping off the ribbon she recognised the flame seal of Beltane and drew an apprehensive breath before beginning to read. She could not think it held anything in the way of good news.

From Osric, King of Beltane, to Her Majesty Queen Catherine of Wrath

Madame

Some months ago Your Majesty made a generous offer of support which, in our arrogance, we chose to decline. Now events have progressed in the manner of your fears and pride is a luxury we can no longer afford. Our attempts to drive the enemy back have failed and only the efforts of the great general Vercincallidus save us from complete collapse. The Possessed have cut off the area around Svarthaven and our forces are now divided. Nårothia and Estånia are lost while the people of Serthia are retreating to the fortress cities of Aengus and Agrona. We shall make our stand in the heart of Veåst. But we are failing.

The demons are growing in strength and number and we do not have sufficient battle mages to hold them. King Vittorio has finally opened the border and our people flow like a river into Valentia but he is afraid. There are reports that a dåmon army laid waste to some of his northern towns and so, like Acheron and Thraece, Valentia is looking to its own defences.

We are informed that things fare no better in Illicia and that you are committed to their aid but, if it is still within Your Majesty's power, then we would humbly ask for the support of any Great Souls that you can spare. Without them the Fires of Beltane will surely be extinguished.

With deep respect, your friend and ally.

Osric Goudicca
King of Beltane and Chieftain of the Nine Tribes of Eldur

The Queen felt her chest tighten with concern. Osric was a great and proud king. She knew how much it would have cost him to write such a letter. Things must be ill indeed. Most of her own battle mages were fighting in Illicia but she would speak with Marshal Breton to see if any could be spared.

With a sigh she reached for the next letter on the tray and her expression remained one of concern. The letter was from Illicia and, as with Beltane, its contents were unlikely to bring her any comfort. Her own grandmother had come from that great kingdom and she steeled herself against the likelihood of bad tidings as she unfolded the cream coloured parchment.

From Ernest of Festunthron, Crown Prince of Illicia, to Her Majesty Queen Catherine of Wrath

Dear cousin,

How does one say thank you for an army (again)? I fear Duke Friedrich of the Ceraton League does not share my gratitude. His pride might never recover but he is ever a practical man and your troops are now helping to secure the area east of Hoffen. I am only sorry that I declined your earlier offers of assistance. Had I listened to your advice we might have prevented the breach in our lines south of Amboss.

I do not need to tell you that the war continues to go badly here and I fear that I am ill equipped to deal with it. I cannot help thinking that my father would have held the Possessed at Coburg. I know what you would say to that, and in moments of doubt I cling to your words of encouragement, but such doubts are not easily dispelled.

But now, to other matters...

I am pleased to hear that you are keeping well and managing to abide the relentless ambitions of the magi (your father would have been proud). Is it true that the mage army is almost ready to enter the field? How full of himself Galen Thrall must be.

And how is our friend? I miss his council but I know that you need him more than I. The Adamanti continue to honour him. Please convey my regards next time you see him.

Stay strong, dear cousin. The world of Wrath needs you, even if some are slow to realise it.

I will write again soon, hopefully with better tidings.

Ever your humble and loving servant, Ernest

Queen Catherine smiled, her eyes pricking with tears. Ernest was such a gentle soul. He had the heart of a poet and yet despite his doubts his character was every bit as strong as his father's. The responsibility might well have come too soon, and too harshly, but he was learning to become a leader of men. Indeed he had no choice. With a sigh she put down the letter from her cousin and stared at the remaining two.

Acheron and Thraece...

Would they join her?

Would they mobilise for war?

As she reached for the letter from Acheron her heart told not to hope for too much.

From Tyramimus Kthénos, King of Acheron, to Her Majesty Queen Catherine of Wrath

My dear mikró Queen.

It was with some surprise that we received your latest entreaty for the might of Acheron to become embroiled in the wars of the East. We thought our position plain but it is clear that Your Majesty is cursed with the same weakness of sentiment that afflicted your father. One suspects it is weakness of a similar kind that has resulted in Beltane and Illicia surrendering so much of their territory to the Possessed. Had they followed the example of Acheron and remained strong, they would surely have enjoyed more in the way of victory instead of calling on the strength of other nations to make up for their own short comings.

So, at the risk of repeating ourselves, let us be clear.

Acheron answers only to Acheron.

We will not press Valentia to allow passage of our armies.

We will not instruct Admiral Navarchos to release the Acheron fleet.

And we will not allow our battle mágos to risk their lives in the defence of lands other than our own (although it is my understanding that some have already disobeyed our commands in order to engage the Possessed in Beltane).

If Your Majesty would take our advice then we would suggest that Clemoncé cease its meddling in the affairs of other states and garner its strength for its own defence. If reports are to be believed then it shall soon have need of it.

Yours
Tyramimus, King, and Lord High Protector of Acheron

Mikró queen... Mikró queen!

Queen Catherine took a deep breath and let the tension go out of her jaw. Then despite her annoyance, she laughed. Beside the massive bear-like figure of Tyramimus maybe she was a 'little queen'. In person, he could be the most charming of men but in matters of state he postured like a prized fighting bull. She forgave the comment about her father. She happened to know of the deep regard in which they held each other. But she could not forgive his stubbornness. How many lives could have been saved if Acheron had joined the fight a year ago? How many towns and cities that now lay in ruins?

What would it take to make them understand that they could not stand alone?

Once more the sense of hopelessness threatened to overwhelm her but she pushed it aside and prepared herself to read the letter from Thraece. However, she had not read more than two words before she closed her eyes in frustration. Veneratu was the title given to the leader of a magi tower. After months of trying in vain to reach the King of Thraece she had addressed her latest letter to his son, Cleomenes the younger. But her gambit had failed. Her message had been intercepted by the magi. With a sigh of resignation she raised the letter and read on.

From Veneratu Ischyrós, on behalf of Cleomenes Vari, King of Thraece, to Her Majesty Queen Catherine of Wrath

Majesty

Once again the King's illness prevents him from replying to you in person but he has asked us to convey his disappointment that you would address your correspondence to his son and not to the monarch himself. Had it not been for the vigilance of the magi this letter might not have come to his attention at all. But let me assure you that the King's position has not changed. His primary concern is for the safety of his people, which is why he has entrusted the governance of Thraece to the wisdom of the magi. Perhaps Your Majesty would be wise to do the same.

It is our belief that she places too much faith in her precious battle mágos. History has shown that they are not enough to defeat the Possessed. They failed in the past and we have no reason to believe that they will save us now. Their numbers are declining and only last month we were forced to slay another black drákon during a failed summoning.

No... the age of the battle mágos is over. It is time for the pure magi to take over the governance of Wrath and to lead its armies to victory. We are informed that the training of the Clemoncéan mage army is almost complete and then we are quite sure that Your Majesty will be convinced. Till then we must decline your requests for support.

The Thraecian armada will remain in Thraecian waters. Thraecian spears will remain on Thraecian soil and any battle mágos leaving Thraece to risk their lives in the defence of other lands will be deemed a traitor.

As one who bears the responsibility for the safety of a Kingdom we are quite sure you will understand.

In the hope that Your Majesty's wisdom will prevail

Veneratu Ischyrós, Worshipful Master and First Servant of the Thraecan magi

The Queen crushed the Thraecian reply in her slender fist, the parchment trembling with pent fury. Curse the magi and their relentless drive for power. Why could they not work in concert with the royal courts instead of always trying to prove their supremacy. She thought of the army mentioned in the letter, an army of mages, a thousand strong. It was her late husband who had granted them permission to raise such a force. Poor Stephan. He had been too weak to deny their incessant requests, his resolve eroded by the fear of failing their people. And now he was gone, taken by a wasting disease that killed him in less than a month, and she was left to rule alone.

No, not alone. Her hand drifted again to the black velvet choker. No, she was not alone but neither was she free to rule as she would like. She was not free to appoint a new king of her own choosing and she was not free to deny the magi when they offered something that might be able to save them.

157

An army of mages. It sounded like a good idea but still she had her doubts. The magi were men of knowledge and power. They had never been warriors. And yet Ischyrós was right. The battle mages might not be enough. Maybe an army of mages *was* the answer. Their success would further their ambition and diminish her rule but she would gladly give up power to save the people of Wrath.

The sense of hopelessness returned and she went to stand at the balcony once more.

The people of Clemoncé had always filled her with hope. Only yesterday a new batch of recruits had arrived to train at the Academy of War. Young people travelling far from home to fight in her name. She had ridden out to greet them, as she always did, an idea the Chevalier had first suggested. As a young queen she had not understood the importance of such a gesture but now that she had seen the shattered bodies and broken minds of battle she knew.

To be a Queen was not to be above the people. It was to be daughter, sister and mother to a nation. And as such she would love them and protect them and grieve for those who fell. It may well be impossible to stop the Possessed but she was the Queen of Wrath and she would not despair.

Her eyes watered as she stared out across the sea then a movement near the southern gate caught her attention. She gazed down at the distant streets and yes... there it was again... the mottled travelling clothes of a scout, the same scout she had sent out only this morning. His swift return could only mean that the Chevalier was close.

Trying not to seem too desperate for news she moved through to the parlour and busied herself with the latest reports from the city administrator. It was a thoroughly annoying six minutes before Cyrano knocked on her door to announce the scout's return.

'Your Majesty,' said the Queen's advisor, ushering the mud spattered scout into the room. 'News of the Chevalier's return.'

'Your Majesty,' said the scout dropping to one knee and bowing low.

'Please,' said the Queen. She motioned for the man to rise. 'You have news of our emissary?'

'Yes, Ma'am,' said the scout. 'I found him just south of the River Denier.' He asked me to tell you that he should arrive in the city tomorrow morning.'

'Does he look well?'

'Very well, Ma'am.'

'And the people of Caer Dour?'

'Better than I expected,' said the scout. 'After the stories we've heard.'

The Queen nodded her understanding and smiled.

'Thank you, er...'

'John Pierre, Ma'am,' said the scout, clearly overwhelmed that the Queen should want to know his name.

'Thank you, John Pierre. Please convey the news to Marshal Breton and Lanista Magnus at the academy.'

The scout gave a nod and bowed low before backing away and turning to leave the room. The relief on the Queen's face was clear to see and Cyrano graced her with an indulgent smile.

158

'Oh, don't look at me like that,' she snapped. 'You'll be glad to see him back too.'

'Indeed I will, Ma'am,' said the advisor. 'The Fourth Army is almost ready for its next rotation. We can hardly send them off to war without their commander.'

The Queen narrowed her eyes and gave her advisor a sour faced scowl.

'Be quiet, you miserable harbinger. Tis several months before the Fourth is due for deployment. Besides, you read his report. It seems the Chevalier wishes to resume his duties as an instructor.'

'And will you grant his request?' asked Cyrano. He too had been surprised by the Chevalier's request. There must be something very particular about the cadets from Caer Dour if Sir William wanted to oversee their training in person.

'I'm not sure,' said the Queen. 'We will wait to hear what he has to say. For now we will just be thankful for his safe return.'

Cyrano nodded his concurrence. 'Will you be riding out to meet them?' he asked.

'Of course,' said the Queen indignantly.

'The stables will have your horse ready at sunrise.'

'Good,' said the Queen. 'Now, how long do we have before the meeting with the Navarian Ambassador?'

'The consul should be arriving with him shortly. We have a little time, at least.'

'Then tell me everything you know about Aquila Danté.'

'Yes, Ma'am,'

'And when we are finished with the Ambassador have Jarnac meet me in the pommeraie. I will take some instruction before I listen to the evening petitions.'

'Perhaps the great hall would be a more suitable...'

'Am I some delicate flower to wither at the first touch of winter's chill?'

'No, Ma'am. I only...'

'Then do as I say.'

'Yes, Ma'am,' said the royal advisor, duly cowed.

Cyrano's family had served the royal court for seven generations but he had never known a sovereign like the Queen and he had always struggled with the notion of royalty venturing into public places. It was her father, King Philip 'The Commoner', who had begun the tradition, insisting that the gates be left open and that no one should be denied access to the palace. A younger Cyrano had objected, arguing that the gates kept them safe and without them any brigand would be free to enter the palace. The King's daughter had been inclined to agree.

'Locking the gates places a barrier between the people and the throne,' her father had explained to the ten year old princess. 'And denying them entry to the palace only shows the people that we do not trust them.'

The King had laughed at the doubt in his daughter's eyes.

'Set yourself apart from the people and they will serve you out of duty,' he told her. 'Trust them and they will claim you for their own.'

Her father's words echoed in her mind as the Queen gazed at her advisor and finally she took pity.

'I'll be back in the palace before sunset.'

Cyrano bowed his head at this concession. He knew she was in no danger, not even in the darkest corner of the city. She was not a perfect woman, not a perfect queen. As the letters from the other kings had illustrated she was meddlesome, arrogant, sentimental and naive but she placed her trust in the people of Clemoncé and for this reason, more than any other, they loved her.

27

As The Eagle, So The Falcon

It was late afternoon and the city of Wrath now dominated the landscape before them. The city itself was still some three miles distant but they had already passed several outlying 'villages', temporary settlements consisting of tents and wooden huts with people milling about in the makeshift streets.

'Refugees,' said the emissary. 'More arrive every month.'

Falco looked at the people who, like themselves, had been displaced by war. In their eyes he saw the same uncertainty that haunted the people from Caer Dour. They had no idea what the future might hold for them.

Despite being so close to the city the emissary had begun to lead them inland believing that the bridge on the main road was impassable. However, the local people assured him that the bridge had been repaired and so they turned back, heading down a gentle slope to a river where a host of men were working on a stone bridge.

'But you told the scout we'd be arriving tomorrow,' said Malaki.

'That was before I knew they'd repaired the bridge,' said the emissary. 'When I left, the central span had been brought down by heavy flooding and without the bridge we'd have another two hours up to the Ford of Garr.'

Falco gazed at the impressive structure that strode the river in five great arches.

'This way we'll be in the citadel before the sun goes down. Unless you'd rather spend another cold night in a lumpy bedroll.'

'No, said Malaki. 'It's just...'

'Don't worry,' said the emissary. 'She's not as scary as her name suggests. Unless you make her angry,' he added with a smile.

The workers on the bridge cleared the road to let them pass. Many of them doffed their soft caps or greeted the emissary with a bow and Falco noticed the easy manner with which he met these gestures of respect. The city now loomed large before them. The great expanse of the double curtain wall stretched out to either side and the main gate was crowded with people flowing in and out of the city.

'I think we'll enter by the harbour gate and come up to the palace through the gardens,' said the emissary.

'We're going to the palace *now*!' exclaimed Malaki, his voice an octave higher than normal.

'The Queen likes to greet cadets on their arrival,' said the emissary and Falco smiled at Malaki's sudden show of nerves.

'That includes you too, Master Danté.'

The smile died on Falco's lips.

'You may not have won a place during the trials,' said the emissary. 'But battle mages also train at the Academy of War. Besides, it is my job to decide who is presented to the Queen. You will come with us.' His expression made it clear there would be no debate.

Falco was about to protest further when Morgan Saker drew up alongside them.

'We will leave you here,' said the senior mage as the rest of the magi continued towards the main gate.

'You are not coming to the palace?'

'Our duty is to the Grand Veneratu. It is to him that we should first report.'

The emissary was clearly not impressed by this show of disrespect but he maintained his dignity and bade them farewell as the magi filed past. He directed the cadets down towards the harbour and was about to join them when he noticed that Meredith had paused, looking at Falco as if there were something he wanted to say. For a moment the apprentice mage hesitated but then he bowed his head, urged his horse forward and followed his father up into the city.

The emissary watched him leave, his eyes narrowed in thought. Watching Meredith disappear among the crowds he gave the smallest of nods then he turned away, leading the cadets down towards the harbour where ships and boats of all sizes were moored up against the wharf or anchored in the calm lagoon behind the breakwater.

Falco found the harbour a dizzying place of sights and sounds. There was the keening of gulls and the creaking of timbers, the tolling of ships' bells and the shouts of harbour hands and market traders, all against the slap and boom of breakers beyond the harbour wall. And then there was the smell, the overwhelming smell of fish mingled with tar and sweat, with the occasional waft of exotic spices that Falco could not identify. He did not find it unpleasant and yet he was grateful when they slipped through the gate and left the harbour behind.

Now they entered a quiet quarter of the city where gardens led down to the coast and green lawns spread up towards the rocky hillside on which sat the citadel and the palace itself. There were people around but it was not crowded. Some swept leaves or tended the gardens. Others were gathered in groups as if this were just a pleasant place to meet.

They heard the steely ring of combat and were surprised to find a number of groups engaged in training. Some were obviously formal training sessions with an instructor and students but others seemed to be informal sessions between small groups of individuals sparring with sword and shield and spear.

'The desire for martial excellence spreads well beyond the academy walls,' said the emissary.

Continuing on their way they passed through a second gate beyond which the gardens changed again. The trees on these southern slopes were planted more closely and Falco noticed that most of them were fruit trees. Here and there he could see people on ladders, gathering the last of the autumn pears and packing them into boxes.

As they moved more deeply into the orchard they heard the clack and retort of wood on wood and suddenly they came upon a clearing where another couple were engaged in a sparring contest. One was a woman of perhaps thirty years, wearing leather breeches and a white blouse, over which she wore a green dress which was split to the silver cord at her waist. Her blue eyes flashed with concentration and her chestnut hair flew wild about her shoulders, sticking in damp strands to her sweat-soaked skin. The other was a man with a lithe but

162

powerful build. His dark hair was sleek and silky and although he was out of breath he moved with the strength and deliberation of a seasoned warrior.

They fought with wooden sword and metal shield and Falco was impressed by the ferocity of their exchanges. This was no pretence at swordplay. This was an exercise in mortal combat. The combatants' fight brought them a little closer to the path and suddenly the woman noticed their presence. Her eyes swept across them as she continued to attack and parry but then she caught sight of the emissary and for just a moment her concentration was broken. Her shield dipped and the man's wooden sword struck her cheek with a whack that made them all wince.

The woman gave a cry and spun away. When she turned back her face was livid and a bead of blood ran down her flushed cheek. She shot a quick look at her opponent, cast a fleeting glance over the people in the travelling party, then fixed the emissary with an indignant glare.

Falco saw anger in her deep blue eyes but there was embarrassment too. Without a word she threw down her sword and shield and ran through the trees to a black horse that was calmly cropping the grass at the base of an apple tree. She swung lightly up into the saddle and, with a kick of her heels, she was gone.

All eyes turned back to the man with the silky black hair. His face was proud with the dark cast of Acheron or Thraece. There was no apology or embarrassment in his expression but there was a certain nervousness as he looked up into the grey eyes of the emissary.

'Why did you strike the lady?' asked the emissary in a dangerous voice.

'Because she lost concentration and dropped her guard, my Lord,' said the man.

'Do you think she will forgive you?'

'Quicker than she forgives you, I think,' said the man with the hint of a smile.

'I fear you are right, my friend,' said the emissary with a sudden laugh.

The cadets looked from one to the other, while in the distance they could just see a black horse climbing up the hillside path.

'Do you know that woman?' asked Falco.

That,' said the emissary, staring after the now distant figure. 'Is the Queen of Wrath.'

Ten minutes later an even more nervous group of cadets followed the emissary through the high archway and into the central courtyard of the palace. Their horses had been ushered away by stable hands and each of the travellers had been offered a towel and a bowl of rose scented water to wash before their introduction to the Queen. Malaki gazed at the bowl in despair. It would take more than a little sweet smelling water to make him presentable.

'Don't fret,' said the emissary with a laugh. 'You have come to swear your lives to the Queen. Do you think she'll worry about a little dirt and grime?'

Malaki did not look particularly reassured.

With hands and faces duly washed, they proceeded across the courtyard where they were met by a tall man in an impeccably tailored doublet of black chenille with a faint sheen of silver brocade. He wore a short cloak of turquoise silk, draped from one shoulder to denote a servant of the court. And on his head he wore a black velvet cap with a blue trim as a mark of his authority. Beneath the cap his short-cropped hair was white, while his well trimmed beard and heavy eyebrows were surprisingly dark. His hawkish eyes were a deep brown and they swept across the youngsters with a keen intelligence.

'Sir William,' he said, in a tone that conveyed a wealth of meaning, and not all of it good.

'Master Cyrano,' replied the emissary with a respectful bow of his head.

'Another boyish prank?'

'No, my lord,' said the emissary with a laugh. 'I did not expect to find her outside the palace.'

'Not that you ever discouraged *that*,' said the Queen's advisor with a disapproving glance.

The emissary's smile was writ with guilt.

Cyrano turned to the cadets.

'Welcome to Wrath. In a few minutes time you will be escorted to the barracks at the Academy of War.' He nodded to a squire standing to one side of the courtyard. 'However, the Queen likes to greet all cadets upon their arrival in the city.' His eyes swept over them and, just for a moment, it seemed as if his keen gaze lingered on Falco but then he gave a satisfied nod as if everything was in order.

'The Queen will meet you on the western terrace. The Chevalier knows the way.' And with that he turned and climbed the short flight of steps into the palace.

The cadets breathed an audible sigh of relief.

'Not the friendliest of men, is he?' said Malaki.

'No,' said the emissary. 'But he is perhaps the truest.'

With that he led the cadets through a short tunnel in the west wall of the courtyard. This led to a lawned terrace with a gravel path running down its length. To the right loomed the palace while to the left the walls followed the line of the cliffs, looking out over the sea where the sun had disappeared into a bank of cloud on the horizon. It was cold but the evening sky was clear and bright.

As they continued along the terrace they saw the lawn rise up to a low mound. The mound was crowned by a bower cast in bronze and fashioned in the shape of three trees coming together to form a roof of interlacing branches. The weathered metal was bright with verdigris and standing beneath it was a tall woman with long chestnut hair.

The cadets gazed up in awe as they followed the emissary.

'She's beautiful,' whispered Bryna and Malaki nodded but Falco gave no answer.

Was this the same woman they had just seen, flustered and sweating in the gardens below?

Now she stood tall and slim. Her gown a single fall of turquoise silk, edged with gold thread and tied at the waist with a slender golden chain. About her shoulders she wore a pale blue cloak with a wolf fur mantle to guard against the evening chill, and at her neck a black velvet choker, threadbare and rustic beside the refinement of her other clothes.

The emissary led them round the foot of the mound until they were lined up against the wall and then they watched as he climbed to kneel before the Queen. The contrast between the slender woman and the rugged knight could not have been more stark but when it came to presence Falco could not have said which had the stronger of the two.

The Queen looked down at the man kneeling before her. Her gaze was imperious and something of her earlier anger still remained in the set of her jaw and the narrowing of her deep blue eyes. But then her expression softened as if she could not sustain her ire in the face of such humility. Finally she extended her hand and the emissary raised his head to kiss it.

'You,' she said as the emissary came to his feet. 'Are a day early.'

Although spoken quietly the wind carried the Queen's words towards the cadets and they smiled at the guilty look on the emissary's face.

'An entirely innocent mistake, Your Majesty,' he said.

The Queen's gentle snort suggested this was not the first time she had been required to forgive her emissary an 'innocent mistake'. They looked at each other for a moment and something unspoken passed between them then the emissary turned to the waiting youngsters.

'Your Majesty,' he said in a louder voice. 'May I present the academy recruits from the Valentian town of Caer Dour.'

The Queen turned to face them and any trace of anger faded from her eyes.

'Welcome,' she said, her voice richer and deeper than they might have expected from one so slight of frame. 'I have heard something of the trials you have endured but now you are safe. The city of Wrath is your city, the people of Clemoncé your people.'

The youngsters of Caer Dour were deeply affected by the compassion in the Queen's voice and some of them lowered their faces to hide a sudden swell of tears.

The Queen turned to the emissary and, stepping outside the bower, he called the name of the first Cadet.

'Allyster Mollé.'

Almost in a dream the young archer ascended the mound to meet the Queen. She shook his hand and exchanged a few softly spoken words before he descended the other side to wait beside the palace wall.

When it came to Bryna she climbed the gentle slope with her chin held high and her face set like stone. Falco did not catch what the Queen said to her but Bryna's shoulders suddenly sagged. Her head drooped and the Queen reached out to gently raise her face. Again the words were carried away on the breeze but Falco saw the warmth of the Queen's smile and the tears on Bryna's cheek.

When Malaki was called he climbed the mound with the easy movement that marked him as a natural fighter but when he bowed to the Queen he dropped his right foot back in something resembling a curtsy. When he straightened up his entire face was as crimson as the birthmark on his cheek. The Queen smiled kindly but there was no mistaking the amusement in her eyes.

'My Lady,' mumbled Malaki, completely forgetting the correct way to greet the Queen.

She extended her hand and Malaki raised it gently to his lips.

'So you're the one who broke my emissary's nose?'

'Er, yes, Your Majesty,' said Malaki, his face growing an even deeper shade of red.

'Oh, I wish I'd been there to see that!'

Malaki glanced up, surprised that the Queen would make such a jest. Her eyes flicked in the emissary's direction and suddenly Malaki did not feel quite so much the fool as he made his way down to join the others beside the palace wall. The remaining cadets were introduced until only Falco was left. There was such a contrast between the hale young people introduced thus far and the tall waif-like figure of Falco.

He was painfully aware of the eyes watching him as he ascended the low mound. When he glanced up, the friendly warmth had gone from the Queen's gaze, replaced, not by hostility, but by a keen and searching interest. He bowed low, kissed her hand then straightened up to look her straight in the eye.

The Queen raised an eyebrow as if she were surprised by the directness of his gaze.

'And why have you come to Wrath, Master Danté?' she asked.

Falco paused. He had not expected to be challenged in this way.

'To do what I can,' he said.

'Nothing more?'

Falco found himself wondering just how much the Queen knew about his father. For a second his eyes narrowed as he became more guarded. Yes, a part of him was hoping to find some answers, some kind of purpose. But the real reason for him coming to Wrath was far simpler than that.

'To be honest, Your Majesty, I just wanted to be with my friend.'

The Queen let out a gentle sigh as if she had been holding her breath.

'I can think of no better reason,' she said and finally she smiled.

Falco lowered his gaze and bowed once more. He did not see the Queen glance to one side and give the emissary the slightest of nods. In something of a daze he ambled down the slope to stand beside Malaki and Bryna.

'I can't believe she was so nice,' whispered Bryna, still dabbing her eyes.

'A curtsey,' muttered Malaki. 'I don't believe it. A fecking curtsey!'

Bryna laughed and took Malaki's arm but Falco barely heard them. All he could hear were the words of the Queen echoing in his mind.

And why have you come to Wrath, Master Danté?

Looking up he saw the emissary move back into the bower to stand before the beautiful woman that was the Queen of Wrath. They could no longer hear what was being said but Falco saw something in the emissary's bearing that he had never thought to see... nerves.

They spoke quietly for a while and Falco noticed the way their eyes never made contact for long and yet despite a certain awkwardness there was no doubting the intimacy between them. The cadets were now gathered close, all staring up at the man and the woman framed against the brightness of the westering sky.

'They love each other,' said Bryna quietly.

'Yes they do,' said a deep voice and the cadets turned to see the Queen's advisor standing behind them.

'Then why don't they marry?' asked Bryna, emboldened by the advisor's candour.

'They can't,' said Cyrano. 'Politics and the line of accession dictates that the Queen should marry Prince Ludovico of King Michael's Mount. To refuse him would divide the nobles and weaken the Queen's standing with the magi.'

'Is that why she is still in mourning?'

Cyrano nodded.

'As long as she wears a token of black she can avoid giving the Prince an answer, and they,' he nodded towards the emissary and the Queen, 'can keep alive an illusion of hope.'

They watched as the couple spoke quietly together. Just once the Queen extended her arm as if to find the emissary's hand but he drew back and reached into his tunic to reveal a bundle wrapped in plain white cloth. The cadets edged forward as the emissary drew back the wrapping.

'The belt,' whispered Malaki.

Up on the mound the Queen looked at the object lying in the emissary's large rough hands. A belt of interlacing leather thongs with a silver buckle formed in the likeness of a horse's head, the same design that fluttered on the flags above the palace. But it was not the design that caused the breath to catch in her throat. It was the fact that the leather thongs were black.

She reached out a hand to touch it.

'I can't believe you found the time,' she said, her voice thick with emotion.

'I picked it up at a market stall down by the harbour.'

'You did not!' scolded the Queen and here she actually shoved him in the shoulder.

'No,' said the emissary. 'I did not.'

'It's beautiful,' said the Queen and for a moment they held each other's gaze before the Queen turned and drew her long hair back from the nape of her neck.

The emissary paused and took a breath as if to steel his nerves before reaching up to unclasp the worn velvet choker from around the Queen's throat, the velvet choker that he had made for her more than a year ago. He folded it and slipped it into the same pocket from which he had drawn the belt. And then, reaching beneath her cloak he slipped the belt around the Queen's slender waist. He did not linger in fastening the clasp but to the cadets, watching from the base of the mound, it seemed like an embrace.

'Time for a little privacy, I think,' said Cyrano, breaking the spell that held the cadets entranced.

He led them back down the path and through the tunnel in the palace wall. In the courtyard he passed them into the care of the squire who took them back to the stables before leading them through the busy streets of the capital towards the gates in the northern walls where a path climbed up to the plateau and the Academy of War.

*

The Queen and the emissary had moved round the palace to watch as the line of cadets wound up through the city towards the northern gates. Their gaze was focussed on the skinny figure at the back of the line.

'Are you sure he is strong enough?' asked the Queen.

167

'No,' replied the emissary.

'The magi will not agree to train him.'

'There might be another way,' said the emissary thinking of the way Meredith had looked at Falco. 'Besides, Aurelian might help.'

'Aurelian is a cantankerous old bastard,' said the Queen.

'True. But he is all we have.'

The Queen looked less than convinced.

'And you still wish to take part in their training?'

'For a while at least.'

'Marshal Breton will not approve.'

'Marshal Breton will be relieved,' said the emissary. 'You know he finds my presence irksome.'

'That is because the men look to you and not to him.'

'Perhaps,' said the emissary.

They watched as the line of cadets climbed the winding path and disappeared over the lip of the plateau. For a while she was silent and then the Queen asked the question that the emissary had been expecting.

'Will he turn against us?'

'I don't know,' he said and the Queen sighed as if it were foolish to expect such certainties.

'So be it,' she said at length. 'As the eagle, so the falcon. Let the madman's son be trained.'

*

Morgan Saker looked down from the balcony of the mage tower as the last of the cadets came into view.

'Is that him?' asked the man beside him, a man who radiated even more power and authority than Saker himself. His name was Galen Thrall, Grand Veneratu and Worshipful Master of the Clemoncéan magi.

'Yes,' said Saker. 'That's him.'

'Then we have nothing to fear,' said Thrall with all the certainty of a diktat.

'You did not see him face the demon.'

Thrall's eyes narrowed in thought.

'He is a child,' he said. 'Besides... without a mage to guide him he will never become a battle mage. The matter is ended. We stay the course and keep our will focussed on the army. Once the people see what an army of mages is capable of there will be nothing to stop us from dissolving the thrones and assuming the governance of Wrath.'

With that he turned away from the balcony and walked back into the heart of the tower where a council of elders had been called.

Overlooked, unnoticed and deep in contemplation, Meredith watched them leave. The Grand Veneratu spoke with absolute certainty but Meredith was confused. What did it matter if Falco became a battle mage? Surely they would all benefit from that. He moved to the balcony and looked down at the cadets. For some reason his father hated Falco and the Grand Veneratu talked about him as if he were a threat, but Meredith could not understand it. He had never liked Falco but he could not ignore the fact that he had saved his life, saved him from the torture of the dragon's fire. It was a debt that lay between them and somehow it must be repaid.

He turned from the balcony to face the dark interior of the tower. Tonight he would retire to a chamber of solitude to contemplate the disciplines of lore that would form the basis of his study, one of which, he had already decided, would be history. This tower was the centre of the magi's power. At its heart lay the knowledge and history of two thousand years. Somewhere amongst the shadowed archives of the past lay the source of his father's hatred. And Meredith was determined to find it.

*

It was twilight as the cadets made their way up the winding path to the plateau. Falco was only dimly aware of his surroundings as they crested the rise and rode towards a series of low square buildings. He was thinking of the question that the Queen had put to him. He had not lied but he knew in his heart that there was more to it than that. Wrath had come to symbolise more than just the home of the academy, more than just the capital of a great kingdom. It represented the chance of a new beginning and the possibility of finding answers to the questions that had dogged his life. And so, as the others talked in nervous excitement, Falco's head was bowed in thought. He was only shaken out of his reverie when they climbed onto the plateau and Malaki and Bryna drew up alongside him.

'What did she say to you?' asked Malaki.

'She asked me why I'd come to Wrath.'

'That's easy,' said Malaki. 'You're here to become a battle mage.'

The certainty in Malaki's voice struck a chord in Falco's soul and with a sudden thrum of revelation he knew that it was true.

Whatever his doubts, whatever challenges lay ahead, the truth was suddenly clear. He was here to become a battle mage.

Boom!

28

The Hermit, The Healer
& The Fisherman

It was twilight in the remote Illician mountains and the boy's heart began to beat faster as he drew closer to the cave, not because of the steep and rocky climb, but because he had never seen the hermit before. The other boys spoke of a wild man with rotten teeth and ragged clothes, his eyes fierce and staring and his skin made filthy by the black dirt on the floor of his cave. They told the tale of one boy who had dropped the basket of food but finished the climb to apologise for his mistake. He was never seen again and, while the other lads did not say as much, their vague hints suggested that the hermit had eaten him in place of the food that the village sent as tribute. And so the boy was truly frightened as he ducked under the Hanging Rock and caught his first glimpse of the cave, a dark gash in the craggy cliffs of the mountain.

Fighting against his fear the boy hugged the basket of food to his chest as he made his way up the crude steps on the final part of the climb. His hands trembled as he placed the basket under the ledge of rock and rang the small brass bell that stood in a crevice.

'Wait until he comes to take it,' the elders had told him. 'Otherwise the rooks and ravens will spill it down the cliffs.'

The boy's heart thumped in his chest and the sound of his breathing echoed back from the bleak rocks around him. Finally he saw movement. He took an involuntary step backwards then stopped as a man emerged from the cave. They had lied!

Yes the man looked wild with his thick grey hair, tattered clothes and weathered skin but he was not black with dirt and his eyes were not wild and staring, rather they were blue and calm and filled with a sadness that the boy could not begin to comprehend. Without a word he placed his hand on his chest and gave the boy a bow of thanks. Confused and strangely saddened the boy gave him a nervous nod before turning to race back down the path. If he was quick he might make it back before it became fully dark.

With an expression of utter detachment the hermit watched the boy run headlong down the mountain path. Then with no more interest than if it were filled with leaves he picked up the basket of food and walked back in to the cave.

Boom!

The hermit stopped. He turned. The calm dispassion gone from his eyes, replaced by shock and something akin to fear. He put down the basket of food and stood at the mouth of the cave, staring out across the slowly darkening landscape, his heart beating every bit as fast as the young boy who had just delivered the food.

Had he been mistaken?

Had he heard it... felt it?

He waited...

Nothing.

Breathing rapidly he bent to pick up the basket but as he straightened up his eyes were drawn to the darkest recess at the back of the cave. Fear rose up in his mind and a terrible sadness closed around his heart. Nearly twenty years he had lived in this cave and in all that time he had only once ventured into that recess. He peered into the deep impenetrable shadow.

He would not venture to the back of the cave.

He could not.

He dare not.

*

It was twilight as the young Thraecian girl sprinted through the olive grove with all the speed she could muster. The healer was not at home but her father had taken a turn for the worse and she simply had to find him.

'I saw him heading up the slope,' Phineas the goatherd had told her. 'Towards the cemetery beyond the olive groves.'

And so she raced between the ancient trees hoping to find him and get back to the house before her father was beyond help. The girl skidded in the dusty earth as she emerged from the olive grove. There he was, the finest healer in the entire district, crouching at the foot of the nameless grave. Some said his wife was buried in the grave. Others said it was the first patient he ever lost. Whatever the case it had robbed the healer of any trace of happiness and left him a hollow man. He healed the sick and tended the injured but he never smiled or acknowledged his patients' thanks with anything more than a distracted nod. He was a source of curiosity and sadness to the town.

For all her haste the girl hesitated before coming forward but the healer seemed to sense her presence and, rising to his feet, he turned to face her.

'My father,' gasped the girl now charging forward. 'The pain is worse than ever and now he cannot breathe.'

The healer reached into a cloth bag slung across his shoulder. He pulled out a small pouch and handed it to the girl.

'A pinch of this in a little warm water,' he told her. 'Keep him calm and tell him I will be with him shortly.'

With tears of gratitude standing in her eyes the girl nodded her thanks and raced away.

The healer watched her go, knowing he was needed and yet reluctant to leave. He had no idea what had brought him here this evening. He used to come here all the time but over the last few years he had tried to stay away. He looked down at the grave and the familiar grief rose up in his heart, the shame as black and poisonous as ever. Then with a sigh he turned to leave.

Boom!

The healer froze.

With something approaching dread he turned back to face the grave. His heart was suddenly pounding as if he expected to see something clawing its way out of the earth. Coming here had been a mistake. He had been right to stay away.

He looked around listening... waiting...

171

Nothing.

Feeling every bit as breathless as the girl's father, the healer turned from the graveyard and stumbled away. He might have buried his past but that did not mean he could escape it.

*

It was twilight as the small fishing boat rounded the remote headland on the coast of Beltane. The nets were in and there were just a few more baskets to check before they headed for the safety of the harbour. The fisherman was at the tiller, steering the boat with practiced ease while the two fishing hands gripped long handled hooks ready to snag the sealskin bladders that marked the location of the baskets. The older of the two gave his younger brother a brief nod of encouragement. This was his first time out and he was eager to make a good impression.

As they reached the first bladder the fisherman let the sail go slack and turned the prow of the boat into the waves. This allowed the younger brother to catch the mooring rope and haul the basket up from the sea bed.

'Well done,' said his brother as he came to help.

They emptied the lobsters into the holding tubs, put new bait in the basket and threw it back over the side. The fisherman drew the sail tight and brought the small craft about and the two brothers turned their attention to the baskets ahead of them.

'We missed one,' said the younger brother as he noticed a pale bladder lying close to the rocky cliffs.

His brother gave him a sharp look and shook his head.

'Not that one,' he hissed. 'We never collect that one.'

He glanced at the fisherman but the master of the boat seemed not to have noticed. No one knew why he never checked that basket or what the sealskin bladder marked. Rumour had it that he had once killed a man and weighed his body down with rocks. But it made no sense to mark the scene of such a crime. Others said that he had lost a shipmate in a storm and the bladder marked the spot where the fisherman's friend had drowned. The truth was that no one knew.

The fisherman was aware of their eyes upon him. He was also aware of the tales that people told. It mattered not. One of these days he would cut the tether and let the marker float away. Then perhaps, he could forget.

His face impassive, he steered the boat towards the next marker.

Boom!

The fisherman turned the boat so rapidly that the two brothers clung to the sides as the small craft pitched and rolled on the choppy sea. Suddenly frightened they looked up at the man standing in the stern wondering what had made him stop the boat.

The fisherman stared into the depths as the pale bladder bobbed on the water.

Had he heard something? Had he felt it? Or was it just a freak wave sounding in some hollow of the rocks?

He waited, while the ship danced drunkenly beneath him...

Nothing.

The two brothers watched as the fisherman turned back towards them. His expression was dark but there was also a deep sadness in his eyes. Suddenly it was easy to believe that he had killed a man and marked his grave upon the sea. Nervously they took up their hooks but the fisherman ignored the remaining baskets and steered them straight for home. There would be no more fishing done tonight.

Leaving the subdued brothers to sort the catch the fisherman left the harbour and walked back along the coast to the place where the pale marker bobbed in the darkness just a few boat lengths from the cliffs. A bead of salt water ran from his eye.

Time and tide, it seemed, were not enough.

Indeed, an ocean of water was not enough to drown his guilt.

*

In a distant land, far beyond the Endless Sea, a creature raised its head.

And three that never answered too.

Boom!

29

A Familiar Reception

If Falco had been surprised by the intimate nature of their audience with the Queen he was less surprised by the wall of silence that greeted them as they entered the long dormitory of the academy barracks. The squire who had served as their guide gave a nervous bow before making a quick exit, leaving the new arrivals facing the stern gaze of at least thirty strong young men. Their collective expression was one of disdain as they weighed up the competition from the provincial town of Valentia. For the young noblemen of Caer Dour it was not a problem. After a moment's pause they simply moved towards empty bunks as if they were perfectly entitled to be there.

This left Falco, Bryna and Malaki.

A weakling, a woman and a common blacksmith.

Some of the cadets looked with interest at Bryna but Falco noticed how most of them seemed to focus on Malaki as if they could gauge something of his ability simply from the way he stood. Yes, the one with the birth marked face had been singled out from the start. Falco gave an inward smile, secretly relieved that for once he was not the centre of attention. However, his anonymity did not last for long.

'Hah!' said a voice from half way down the room. 'If it isn't the traitor from Caer Dour. Come to polish his friend's armour, no doubt.'

The cadets turned at the voice and a natural channel opened up between them. Falco's heart sank as he saw the speaker come forward. It was Jarek Snidesson.

'So you survived,' he said in an accusing tone. 'You bring destruction to our town, death to our people and yet *you* survive.' He walked forward, the familiar swagger in his lofty poise. Behind him came three or four stout supporters, one of them a huge Beltonian, bigger even than Malaki.

The other cadets watched him come forward. They did not understand the history between them but they could see that one held power and the other did not. For nobles whose fortunes depended on choosing the most advantageous ally the question of which side to take was an easy one.

'At least we didn't run,' said Malaki, stepping slightly ahead of Falco.

'Ah, the blacksmith's son,' said Jarek in the same patronising tone that came so easily to his father. 'And a girl who is only here because she cheated in the trials.'

His eyes flickered to one side and Falco saw Bryna put a hand on Malaki's arm.

'But run, you say?' said Jarek, addressing himself to the cadets in the room. 'You would have died in the mountains if my father and I had not ridden to get help.'

'Shame on you,' said Falco, his face set like stone. He did not go into the details of the riders who had given their lives. He did not need to. The quiet conviction in his voice was more than enough to cast doubt on Jarek's boast.

For a second Jarek's eyes flared with a murderous light but then his lip twitched in a sneer as he quickly changed the subject.

'We would not have been there at all if not for him.' He paused to stare directly at Falco. 'You did alert the black dragon that killed the town's battle mage, did you not?'

Falco said nothing but it was clear from his silence that, in this at least, Jarek spoke the truth. The mood in the room hardened and Jarek smiled, victorious, although his eyes still held the promise of violence.

Suddenly the door to the barracks opened and two men walked in, each wearing surcoats of black with a white horse's head motif, marking them as academy instructors. One of them held a parchment scroll and both radiated a sense of authority well beyond any of the young princelings in the room. The older of the two men stepped forward. He was heavily built and his bald head was raked with dents and scars. He wore a thinly trimmed beard on a solid jaw, his eyes set deep beneath a heavy brow. He cast a hard eye over the room and it was clear that he had just made an accurate assessment of what was taking place. It was ever the same, young stags establishing the order of dominance.

'The academy welcomes the cadets from Caer Dour.' His voice was surprisingly mellow with a strong Clemoncéan accent. 'My apologies for not meeting you upon your arrival. We had not expected you until tomorrow.'

His gaze quickly took in the new arrivals, both those already standing beside beds and the three who stood apart.

'My name is Lanista Magnus,' he went on. 'This is Lanista Deloix, warden of this barracks.'

He gestured to the man standing beside him, a tall muscular man with dark skin, braided hair and pale brown eyes like those of a wolf. His face and arms were also marked with scars and the tip of his left ear was missing, severed, it seemed, by a single clean cut.

'We are not expecting any more cadets to join us and so your training will begin in two days time but for now please introduce yourself and your chosen discipline.' The Lanista unfurled the scroll and scanned it quickly before his eyes settled on Jarek.

'Jarek Snidesson,' said Jarek. 'Officer training, cavalry.'

The Lanista's gaze moved on.

'Allyster Mollé. Officer training, archer.'

He continued around the room until he came to the three people who still stood apart from the rest. His gaze came to rest on Bryna.

'Bryna Godwin,' said Bryna. 'Officer training, archer.'

A faint murmur rippled through the cadets and two of them sniggered at some jest from a black haired youth near Falco. Falco did not hear the comment in full although he knew it related to bowstrings and certain parts of Bryna's anatomy.

The Lanista's eyes turned to Malaki.

'Malaki de Vane, officer training, knight,' said Malaki and a new murmur ran around the room.

Falco caught a distinct, 'Humph' from Jarek but several of the larger cadets looked at Malaki with renewed interest. So they would not be the only ones to attempt the épreuve de force this month.

175

Finally the Lanista's eyes settled on Falco and many of the cadets laughed as if he were making some kind of cruel jest. Jarek gave a snort of derision.

'And Falco Danté,' said the Lanista, referring to his scroll. 'You will also bunk here until a decision is made about your training.'

'What decision?' blurted Jarek. 'Surely this 'servant' has not been awarded a place at the academy!'

Flushed with indignation Jarek had started forward but the Lanista stopped him with a look.

'There are some questions to be answered before Master Danté can begin his training as a battle mage.'

'A what?!' exclaimed Jarek as the room erupted in disbelief. Surely the Lanista could not be serious but the senior instructor did not smile. He simply looked at Falco for a moment before giving a brief nod as if he were satisfied, for now.

Jarek blustered and laughed but the humour was forced and the smile refused to settle on his lips.

Lanista Magnus raised a hand and the room slowly quietened.

'In two days time you will be woken at dawn to begin your training,' he said and the cadets grew still once more. 'And you are honoured,' he added in a tone of particular significance. 'I have just received word from the palace that we shall be joined by a new instructor. Or rather an old instructor will be coming back to join us. This year Sir William Chevalier of Eltz will take part in your training. At least until the Fourth Army is deployed in a few months' time.'

A buzz of excitement ran through the cadets and Falco felt a huge sense of relief at the realisation that the emissary would not be leaving their lives just yet.

Once again the Lanista called for quiet.

'Get some rest,' he told them. 'You are going to need it.'

The cadets began to talk excitedly but the Lanista had not quite finished. The powerful man moved through the cadets until he stood before the young man with dark hair who had joked about Bryna. For a moment he just looked at him and the youth smiled uneasily then without warning Lanista Magnus slapped him round the side of the head. The blow was so hard that it spun the young man off his feet. He landed face down on the floor and the Lanista turned back to address the room.

'Disrespect for our female cadets will not be tolerated,' he said as the young man was helped up from the floor. 'That is the kind of behaviour I expect from the Irregulars, not from elite cadets sworn to the service of the Queen.'

Many of the cadets lowered their eyes.

'Anyone forgetting this message will be asked to leave the academy. There will be no second chance. Do I make myself clear?'

This was met with surly nods and mumbled grunts while Jarek's mouth worked as if he had eaten something bitter. It was clear that being told what to do did not come easily to most of these privileged young men.

The Lanista turned to Bryna.

'Here in the barracks you will have curtains around your bed and a separate latrine but there will be times when such niceties cannot be afforded.' His gaze was hard and unflinching. 'If you can't tolerate the thought of baring your arse to take a piss in front of a hundred horny men then you had better leave now.'

Bryna blushed but she did not waver. Malaki seemed embarrassed but Falco saw this for what it was, a salutary warning to Bryna, yes, but also a test of what the Lanista had just told them all. He noticed that not one of the cadets laughed at the prospect of Bryna dropping her drawers. It seemed the Lanista's first lesson had not gone unheeded.

A faint smile of approval appeared on the Lanista's face and he gave a small nod before turning back to the cadets.

'If you have any questions ask for Lanista Deloix at the instructors' quad.' He paused. 'Sunrise, two days time,' he said again. 'Until then, I bid you goodnight.'

With that the two instructors turned and left the room.

Jarek waited until the door had closed.

'You... a battle mage?' he snorted. 'Surely this is some kind of sick joke.' He moved forward to stand directly in front of Falco. 'After your father, after what you did to the town, how can you possibly believe that they will let you become a battle mage? As if it were even possible. I mean, look at you...'

Here he actually grabbed Falco's arm as if he were nothing more than a lifeless scarecrow.

'Skin and bones,' he sneered with a cautionary glance in Malaki's direction. 'Not exactly the stuff of a great warrior.' He turned back to his small cohort of followers. 'Wait till my father hears of this. He'll wet himself with laughter and then he will inform cousin Ludovico of your family history. The prince will have you dismissed from the academy and sent from the city in shame.' Jarek walked away dismissively then stopped as Bryna's voice rang out.

'It is the Queen and not Prince Ludovico who decides such matters in Wrath,' she said, her face hot but her voice steady and clear.

Jarek turned slowly, a knowing smile of menace on his lips.

'For now,' he said. 'But just wait until the mage army of Galen Thrall enters the field. It was the prince and his nobles who supported them, while the Queen resisted the magi every step of the way. The age of the 'Great Souls' is over and the magi will not forget those who stood against them.'

The newcomers from Caer Dour knew little of such political manoeuvrings but Bryna held her ground. She was of noble birth too. She was not about to be browbeaten by the likes of Jarek.

Finally Jarek walked away and Bryna turned back to Falco and Malaki.

'Shit wipe!' she cursed under her breath.

The boys gaped to hear such language on her well-spoken tongue but then she looked up apologetically and they laughed quietly together. They looked around for some empty bunks but the only ones left were singles in different parts of the room.

'Here, take these two,' said Owen, picking up his stuff and carrying it over to an empty bed on the far side of the room.

Falco nodded his thanks. He was aware that most of the cadets were still looking at them. Many of them had revelled in Jarek's taunting, practised bullies enjoying a familiar scene. However, he noticed that the cadets from Caer Dour had averted their eyes. Unlike Jarek they had seen Falco walk towards the demon to stand at Simeon's side. And they had travelled with him on the journey to Wrath. They had not become friends exactly but they had developed a certain respect even if they might not admit it.

Owen's gesture left two empty beds together and Falco was looking for another close-by when a young man nudged his neighbour and gestured for him to move his things along. With their dark hair, blue eyes and square jaw Falco could tell they were brothers. The smaller of the two had a mischievous twinkle in his eye while his brother's expression was calm and steady. Falco waited while the larger brother moved his belongings before depositing his bags on the bed.

'Thank you.'

'Alex Klingemann,' said the younger brother, as he came to stand at the foot of Falco's bed.

Falco shook his hand, somewhat surprised by such open friendliness.

'And this is my brother, Quirren,' said Alex, moving forward to shake hands with Malaki and Bryna. 'He's the quiet one,' he added with a grin.

Quirren stood on the other side of the bed but he gave each of them a stoic nod of acknowledgement.

'Is it true you travelled with the Chevalier?' asked Alex.

Falco nodded, noting that he spoke with the same Illician accent as the emissary.

'And you actually saw a demon?'

Again Falco nodded.

'Bryna shot one from the sky,' said Malaki. 'Well, a dark angel at least.'

'A schwartz engel,' said Alex, looking at Bryna with new appreciation. 'A lesser demon but even so...'

Falco noticed that some of the other cadets were also listening. They glanced from Bryna to Jarek, the expression in their eyes less certain as if they were beginning to realise that the story they had thus far been told might not be the whole truth.

'What's he like?' asked Alex, with obvious reference to the emissary.

'Alex!' said Quirren in a low voice before Falco had a chance to answer.

'All right,' said Alex, rolling his eyes and giving his brother a 'spoilsport' look. 'You get settled in,' he said, turning back to Falco. 'And if you need anything...'

'Thanks,' said Falco.

With a smile Alex turned away but he had hardly gone a step when he turned back to face Falco.

'In Illicia he is considered a great man.'

Falco smiled, surprised to see a certain nervousness in Alex's eyes as if he feared the shattering of long held illusions.

'He is,' said Falco and Alex's smile returned, clearly delighted that Falco was able to confirm the emissary's reputation.

Falco watched him go and heard Quirren mutter a low chastisement.

'What?' said Alex. 'I was only asking.'

Still smiling, Falco turned back to Bryna and Malaki who were staring round the room entranced. It was only now that they had the chance to fully appreciate their surroundings.

Their beds were three of fifty in the long stone built room. There were small windows set at regular intervals but night had now fallen and the only light came from lanterns hanging from the ceiling beams or the small pot-bellied stoves that sat against the walls.

The wooden floor was planed smooth with a scattering of coarse woven rugs. The walls were whitewashed stone adorned with tapestries showing various forms of fencing and military formations but it was the weapons that really captured their attention. It seemed that every nation and troop type in the world was represented on the walls of this room.

Falco could see spears and curved kopis swords from Thraece, leaf-bladed lakonia from Acheron, heavy broadswords and bearded axes from Beltane and longswords from Clemoncé and Illicia. And from Valentia... the mongrel, some say the refinement of all swords, the bastard. Blades that were neither long nor short, not slender pointed nor overly wide, heavy enough to block an attack but light enough to allow for maximum speed. There was no set length or design. In Valentia swords were made to match the person who would wield them. It was this ambiguity of design and lack of discernible heritage that earned them their dubious name. Adherents of the refined fencing schools treated them with disdain but in the heat of battle, when you might be confronted by any kind of foe, there was nothing to beat a well matched bastard.

Finally they had surveyed the entire room and Malaki came to stand at Falco's shoulder.

'I've heard of all these weapons,' he said in a low voice. 'But I've never seen half of them in the flesh. Did you see that zweihander on the far wall?'

'An absurd weapon,' said Falco with a smile.

'Yeah, but bloody impressive,' said Malaki while Bryna just raised her eyes to the ceiling.

'Boys and their swords,' she said and with that she began to unpack her saddle bags onto the wooden shelves that stood beside her bed.

The boys grinned at each other and began to do the same. Beside each bed was a low table with a single drawer and a tall wooden unit with three deep shelves and pegs from which to hang weapons and armour, while at the foot of each bed lay a large wooden chest. Malaki gave a satisfied nod and began to unpack his blue-steel armour onto the three shelves of the unit while Bryna hung up her bow and quiver. She put her bracer and shooting glove into the small drawer along with a leather pouch that contained spare arrowheads, white goose fletchings and stag-horn nocks for repairing arrows.

Watching them Falco felt a twinge of anxiety. Both extremely skilled in their chosen disciplines, they were clearly meant to be here but what about him? He felt a strong connection to the weapons and armour in the room and the sight of a well forged sword had always struck a chord in his soul, but if he were honest, he shared Jarek's misgivings. He looked down at his skinny hands and thin wrists.

Not exactly the stuff of a great warrior.

Still, he would not let the likes of Jarek tell him what he could and could not do. He would trust in the confidence of the emissary and in the instincts of a crippled boy who had never learned to walk. He stared back at the distrustful glances cast in his direction. If for no other reason he would become a battle mage just to spite them. In the dim light of the lanterns Falco's green eyes flashed with a light that was anything but weak and one by one the onlookers turned away.

He gave a soft snort of satisfaction. 'Shit wipes,' he breathed, and smiled.

30
Darkness Rising

Deep in the Forsaken Lands the night was illuminated by a patch of glowing earth. The rock was fractured and split apart by unearthly flames that burned in the darkness. Above the flames the blackened bodies of a dozen tormented souls turned slowly in the air, their bodies horribly burned and mutilated by the flames. But they were not dead. The unholy power of the Possessed would never allow them the blissful escape of death. They moaned and wheezed through seared throats and the fat dripped from their flesh like tears.

Around them stood half as many cadaver-like figures known as the Enlightened, pale, thin and utterly desolate. Their skin had a waxy, translucent quality and their eyes glistened like orbs of wet bone. Apart from a few scant rags they were naked and in their hands they held the tools for working metal, tongs and files and hammers. In their former lives they had been swordsmiths and armourers. Now they were spared the worst of hell's afflictions in return for the service of their skills.

For weeks the Enlightened had stood beside this rift in the fabric of the world but now the servant of darkness was rising and it was time for their work to begin. In the boiling maelstrom of hell the entity possessed no earthly form but here in the charnel world it would become a thing of flesh and it was their task to create the tools that would serve it best.

Slowly the Enlightened began to form an impression of its nature. Would it be encased in heavy armour, slow and heavy, a thing of unstoppable force? Or would it be nimble and fast, furnished with light armour and a slender blade?

The Enlightened leaned over the terrible flames eager, despite themselves, to know what weapons they would forge. They stared into the glaring heat as they sensed the needs of the emerging demon and then, as one, they settled back and let out a dry sigh of precognition. They saw what was rising and they saw what they must make for it...

A helmet, with layered sides and a high narrow ridge.

Plate for shoulders, chest and arms.

And blades, large, curved and cruel.

Blades to cleave a dragon's scales.

In the cold dark of a bleak Forsaken night, the Enlightened set to work.

31

The Academy of War

Despite the nerves, the hostile reception, the snoring, farting and seemingly endless coughing of the other cadets, Falco slept surprisingly well. There was only one moment in the night when his dreams had been particularly bad and he could only hope that he had not cried out or made any sound that might draw attention to himself.

He woke to the combined miasma of bodily aromas, coffee and the camphor smell of liniment. People were talking in low voices and, blinking through the half-light of morning, he saw that most of the cadets were already up. As promised, curtains had been erected around Bryna's sleeping area and as Falco swung his legs out of bed he saw her emerge, towelling her hair as she drew the curtains back. Her skin had the bloom of someone who had recently bathed.

'I swear the piggeries in Caer Dour smelled better than this,' she mumbled but Falco could see the satisfaction in her eyes. Smelly men or not, she was definitely happy to be here.

'Good morning to you too,' he said and Bryna replied with the flash of a smile.

Falco was amazed by the change that had come over her since the battle. She no longer seemed haughty and unapproachable, although she could still silence you with a look that made you feel about two inches tall.

'He's up!'

Falco turned to see Malaki at the bottom of his bed. He too had a towel draped over his shoulder and his thick brown hair was still damp and uncombed.

'They've got amazing baths,' said Malaki, rubbing his head vigorously with the towel. 'Hot water and everything.'

'They look after us pretty well.'

Alex Klingemann appeared at Malaki's side. 'Good morning,' he added with his customary smile. 'Quirren and I thought we might show you round, after you've had some breakfast, of course.'

Falco exchanged a look with Malaki and Bryna. Alex possessed a natural friendliness but it was also clear that he was hoping to learn more about the emissary and their encounter with the Possessed. However, the chance of having a helpful guide was not one to be missed.

'We'd appreciate that,' said Falco.

In addition to the other smells of the barracks he now caught the distinct smell of freshly baked bread and frying bacon. His stomach growled and he realised just how hungry he was.

While Bryna finished getting ready Falco dug out his cleanest clothes and followed Malaki to the baths. In the fading light of the previous evening he had not really appreciated the shape of the building. Now he could see that the sleeping quarters formed the west side of a large quadrangle built around an open courtyard of gritty sand containing numerous training aids and combat mannequins. The bath house was on the east side, while the kitchens and dining hall were to the north. Falco took it all in as they made their way across the courtyard.

As they entered the bath house he was amazed to see a dozen tiled baths set into the floor just as they had been in some of the wealthier houses of Caer Dour.

Malaki smiled at his friend's expression.

'We'll meet you in the dining hall,' he said, as Falco began to undress.

'Just make sure you save me some bacon,' said Falco with an indulgent groan as he lowered himself into the hot, steaming water.

For all that it was warm and luxurious Falco did not linger in the bath. Jarek Snidesson had just entered the room with several of his followers and unlike the Klingemann brothers the glances they shot in his direction were far from friendly. Trying to appear unconcerned he dressed quickly and made his way through to the dining hall where Malaki and Bryna were waiting for him.

Bryna shook her head as she watched him demolish a huge plate of bacon, eggs and fried tomatoes with several slices of fresh bread and a fat juicy pear. He washed it down with a large cup of water. Since waking up in Toulwar Falco's appetite had increased so dramatically that he could now give Malaki a run for his money.

'Told you he'd finish it,' said Malaki and Bryna narrowed her eyes at his triumphant grin.

As soon as Falco had finished eating they cleared away the things and returned to the sleeping quarters to meet Alex and Quirren before leaving the barracks through the main entrance in the south wall. The morning was cold but the clouds were lifting from the mountains and the sun was beginning to shine through.

As it turned out, Alex proved to be an excellent guide. The two brothers had been in Wrath for several weeks, waiting for the last of the cadets to arrive. They also had an older cousin who had trained at the academy so their knowledge was fairly comprehensive.

In his mind Falco had always pictured some kind of castle or university but it turned out that the Academy of War was not so much a building as a military camp currently bustling with thousands of soldiers from the Fourth Army as they prepared for their next campaign.

'I thought the academy was just for cadets,' said Falco as they passed a series of enormous stables.

'Working with the main armies is part of our training,' said Alex as if this were common knowledge. 'Some of the cavalry manoeuvres can have as many as five hundred horses.'

'What kind of formations use five hundred horses?' asked Bryna.

'Depends what discipline you choose. But we all have to train in the traverser manoeuvre.'

The three newcomers looked at him blankly.

'It's a term they use here in Clemoncé,' said Alex giving them a meaningful look. 'It means 'passing through'. We've never done it but it looks bloody terrifying.'

Before they could enquire further they had to step aside as a line of mounted troops emerged from a complex of stables and rode up a short rise onto a higher level of the plateau. Each of the riders wore half plate armour and carried a lance, not the extravagant lances used for jousting, but a simple spear, ten feet long.

'Knights from the Fourth Army,' explained Alex. 'Heading up to the tournament field for lance practice.'

They climbed the short rise onto the upper level of the plateau which offered a much better view of their surroundings. There were numerous buildings: workshops, forges and food stores along with rows and rows of white canvas tents, most of which seemed to be occupied by soldiers from the Fourth. Beyond the buildings and tents were a number of training grounds, enclosed fields of grass or sandy shale.

'That's where we'll do most of our training,' said Alex, pointing to a central field covered with wooden posts and combat mannequins similar to those in the courtyard of the barracks. Even from a distance they could see the wooden posts were hacked and dented, shaped by many seasons of practice.

'What's that one?' asked Falco, pointing to a further field where the ground began to rise towards the mountains. It too was dotted with posts but unlike the closer field, where the posts were made of wood, these uprights appeared to be made of some kind of black stone.

'That's the magi training field.'

'Stone training posts?' said Malaki.

'Shards of fortissite,' said Alex. 'It's the only thing that magical force can't damage.'

Falco stared at the small forest of octagonal pillars. The black stone reminded him of the dark rocks of Mont Noir and the Castle of the Winds.

'Battle mages use them too,' said Alex, glancing cautiously in Falco's direction.

They had not said as much but neither he nor Quirren actually believed that Falco was here to train as a battle mage.

'Do they train with the cadets?' said Malaki. 'The battle mages I mean.'

'I think so,' said Alex. 'But they also train in the crucible.'

They looked at him blankly.

'It's an arena sunk into the ground like an amphitheatre,' said Alex. 'They say it stops any stray attacks from doing unwanted damage but I just think they like to train in secret.'

'Can we see it?' asked Malaki.

'Oh, I don't know,' said Alex with uncharacteristic gloom. 'It's a bit of a way.'

'We've never been,' said Quirren, smiling at his brother's discomfort. 'He's frightened of the magi.'

'I'm not frightened,' said Alex. 'They just make me nervous.'

'It's up there,' said Quirren, pointing up the rocky slopes behind the academy.

The others looked to where he was pointing, but then their eyes were drawn over to the right, to the dark tower of the Clemoncéan magi, which stood tall and imposing against the backdrop of the snow-capped mountains.

'We can head up there later if you like.'

184

Malaki and Bryna nodded but Falco could sympathise with Alex. He too felt nervous in the presence of the magi.

'Come on,' said Alex, drawing their attention away from the tower. 'I'm sure Bryna would like to see the archery ranges.'

They skirted the training area until they came to a series of fields furnished with all manner of targets. There were the normal round bosses made from straw but there were also narrow padded posts and targets made to look like warriors of the Possessed. A group of some fifty archers were doing some range practice, shooting at clouts, brightly coloured strips of cloth pegged to the ground at specific distances.

'What range do they go up to?' asked Bryna, casting a critical eye over the ranges.

'Three hundred yards,' said Quirren, who was standing beside her. 'But only the heaviest bows can reach that far.'

'They say a Beltonian longbowman can hit a man at three hundred yards,' said Alex.

'Nonsense,' said Bryna. 'At that range they might just be able to hit an army.'

Alex looked a little crestfallen while Falco and Malaki just smiled. When it came to archery they knew better than to argue with Bryna.

They continued to explore until they came back around to the tournament field where the men from the army were now well into their exercise. The knights had split into two groups and were taking it in turns to launch attacks against a thick straw target set on three poles.

Alex led them over and they watched as the mounted troops cantered around the field in two lines before peeling off one at a time to begin their attack. Watching them were two cavalry instructors known as écuyers, or squires, who called out commands as the exercise continued.

'They call this en passant,' said Quirren who was standing next to Malaki. 'They use it against the larger bestiarum of the Possessed.'

Malaki watched as one of the riders began his attack only to veer away at the last moment at a command from the écuyer.

'The idea is to draw the beast's attention without getting hurt so that the next knight can make a successful attack,' said Alex.

'They measure the timing in hoof beats,' added Quirren.

He gave a slight smile and nodded as Malaki looked at him in disbelief. Surely no cavalry could achieve such precision as to measure an attack in hoof beats.

'That's the kind of thing they'll teach us if we become knights.'

Falco looked on as Malaki turned back to watch the impressive display of control. He could see the hunger to learn in his friend's deep brown eyes.

Finally one of the écuyers called out, 'en vérité,' and the current rider drove his attack home and speared the straw target to the ground.

'It means 'in truth',' said Quirren.

'Sometimes they just shout vérité,' added Alex. It was clear that both were in awe of such feats.

The morning drew on and despite Alex's continuing reluctance they decided to climb up and take a look at the crucible.

Leaving behind the training fields, they climbed the rocky slopes to another flat area of ground. The mage tower rose up to their right and Alex kept glancing nervously up at it.

'Are we allowed to be here?' asked Malaki as they walked out onto the level ground.

'As far as I know,' said Quirren.

Despite this, there was a distinct note of tension in the air as they approached the sunken arena. Suddenly the ground opened up before them and they found themselves looking down into a great oval depression fully forty feet deep and some eighty yards long. The sloping sides were cut into rock steps that descended to a floor of pale sandy gravel. It really did look like a great amphitheatre.

'It looks old,' said Bryna, gazing into the amazing space which looked like it had been there for centuries.

The more they looked the more it appeared that Alex might have been right. The rock-hewn steps appeared scarred and scorched. It was easy to believe they had taken the brunt of countless battle mage attacks.

'What's that?' asked Falco. His attention had been drawn to a dark archway set into the eastern side of the arena. They could not see very clearly but the archway gave onto a tunnel that seemed to lead in the direction of the mage tower.

'I don't know,' said Alex in a whisper.

'We could go down and take a look,' said Malaki but Falco shook his head.

'No,' he said. 'Let's go and look at something else.'

There was something about the mouth of that tunnel that made him feel distinctly uncomfortable, something that spoke of nightmares and the whisper of nightmares.

'Yes,' said Alex. 'Let's go.'

They turned away from the crucible and walked back to the edge of the rise. The sun had started to come out and the unsettling fear that Falco had felt seemed to dissipate in the cold clear light. They stood at the edge of the rise and looked out over the plateau. From here the academy was spread out below them and beyond it the city rose like an island against the backdrop of the sea.

Falco let his eyes roam from the rugged coastline in the south to the towering mountains in the north. As his gaze returned to the plateau he saw a row of stone-built cottages. Smoke was rising from one of the small chimneys and a man was standing in the middle of a vegetable plot at the end of the row. Although quite bright it was still cold but the man wore only a light shirt over pale brown trousers. He seemed to be staring at something high in the sky behind them.

Falco followed the line of his gaze and there, in the gaps between the clouds he caught sight of a dragon. This was much closer than the one they had seen on their approach to the city. Now he could make out much of its shape and the way its wings moved to catch the air. As he watched, Falco saw it draw in its wings and fall sharply before spreading them wide and wheeling up and away out of view. His heart soared and he looked down to see the man in the shirt staring up into the sky as if he could still see the dragon. There was something strange about the way he stood, something that reminded Falco of the men who had taken part in the rearguard sorties during their flight from the Possessed. It was a kind of distractedness, a disassociation with the world around them.

Then from out of the cottage another man appeared but this one walked with a pronounced limp, his body was hunched and Falco could see that he had only one arm. He ambled over and laid his one good hand on the other man's shoulder. For a moment they just stood together then the man in the white shirt bowed his head and allowed himself to be guided back to the cottage.

'The Crofters,' said Alex, coming to stand by Falco's side. 'At least that's what the people in the city call them.'

Falco half turned but he could not take his eyes off the two men. The others moved across to see what he was looking at.

'They're actually retired battle mages,' said Alex.

'The older one looks injured,' said Malaki and Alex nodded.

'That's Aurelian Cruz, a living legend. He and his dragon were crippled by a pair of demons in the north of Beltane.'

Falco watched as the maimed man disappeared into the cottage with his companion.

'He killed one of the demons but the other almost bit him in half before his dragon pulled him free. Even then he would have been killed by the demon's fire if his dragon hadn't got in the way. They say it covered him with its body and took the flames upon itself.'

As Falco watched he saw the man stop and reach out a hand to something that lay beside the door and he suddenly realised that what he had taken to be a deeper patch of shadow, was in fact a dragon lying in the shade at the base of the cottage wall.

'There's a dragon there,' said Falco.

'That's Dwimervane. Aurelian's dragon,' said Alex. 'Crippled and half blind. It can't fly but sometimes it climbs up into the mountains.'

'It looks black,' said Malaki.

'Dark blue,' said Quirren. 'They say it won't live long enough to turn black.'

They were silent for a while and the man at the door still paused as if he were talking to a friend. Then quite suddenly he turned to look up at them and it was clear that his gaze was fixed on Falco. For a moment he continued to stare then he too ducked into the cottage and disappeared.

'Who was the other man?' asked Bryna.

'I don't know his name,' said Alex. 'But he was also a battle mage. The dragon he summoned was black and he was forced to kill it. Now his spirit is broken.' He paused. 'They call such men the Disavowed.'

Falco felt a familiar grief tighten around his heart. For all its terrifying violence and hate he had been deeply saddened by the death of the black dragon in the Castle of the Winds. He could imagine how killing such a creature might destroy a man's faith.

'Come,' said Alex. 'Let's go into the city and find something to eat.'

An hour later they found themselves sitting on the battlements of the city wall, gazing out over the harbour and the sandy beach that stretched away towards the River Denier in the south. Alex picked at the thick pastry on his beef and potato pie and finally he could restrain himself no longer.

'So, have you actually seen him fight?'

There was no need to ask who he was talking about.

'Malaki fought him,' said Bryna and Alex scowled in disbelief. 'In the trials,' she continued. 'Someone,' she glanced accusingly at Falco, 'issued a challenge and the emissary accepted.'

Alex stared at Malaki with unbridled envy.

'You didn't win,' he said as if the very notion was unthinkable.

'No,' said Malaki, blushing with embarrassment.

'No,' repeated Bryna. 'But he did break his nose.'

Alex and Quirren simply gawped and the three Valentians laughed before proceeding to tell their tale in full. The story moved on to the summoning and the battle in the mountains. By the time it was finished the Klingemann brothers were stunned into silence. They *had* taken the three friends as simple country folk from the mountains, but as the afternoon wore on they realised that, for all their knowledge of Wrath and the academy, it was they who were the novices.

The day had proven to be an exhilarating treat of exploration with a fair exchange of knowledge on both parts. By the time they returned to the barracks in the early evening their legs felt leaden from wandering the streets of the city.

'Wonder what they've got for supper,' said Alex as they approached the quadrangle building of the barracks.

'Smells like stew,' said Quirren, heading off to the sleeping quarters. 'I'll get the herbs from home.'

'They never add enough seasoning,' explained Alex, starting after his brother. 'Save us a table by a window,' he called back over his shoulder.

'I'm going to change,' said Bryna.

'And I could do with a...'

'Thank you!' said Bryna, raising a hand and closing her eyes with a little shake of her head. She opened her eyes and looked imploringly at Falco. 'Has he always had this habit of announcing his bodily functions?'

'He's always been disgusting, if that's what you mean,' said Falco with a smile.

'Ugh... Boys!' said Bryna and, rolling her eyes once more she left to freshen up before dinner.

Falco and Malaki exchanged an amused look.

'I'll see you in there,' said Malaki heading off towards the latrines.

Still smiling, Falco continued through the arched entrance and into the central courtyard of the quad. There were a number of cadets present. Some looked exhausted, with flushed faces and sweat soaked shirts. They had obviously spent the day in training, but as soon as they caught sight of Falco they gathered up their clothes and moved through to the baths. Falco thought little of it as he started across the sandy courtyard but then several of the other cadets turned round and he recognised two of the dour looking youths who had stood beside Jarek the previous evening.

'You bring shame to this place.'

Falco's heart sank as he saw Jarek emerge from the covered area at the side of the courtyard. It was almost as if he had been waiting.

'You know you're not welcome here.' Jarek moved to block Falco's path, a wooden training sword held casually in his hand.

'That depends on who you ask,' said Falco, eyeing the five well built young men who now surrounded him.

'Why don't you leave now and save us all the disgrace of being associated with you.'

'I'm not going anywhere,' said Falco, his heart beating heavily.

He pushed his way forward but Jarek nodded to one of his cronies, a huge youth with the red hair and heavy jaw of a Beltonian. With no discernible effort the Beltonian gave Falco a shove that sent him flying into one of the wooden training dummies. He tried to stop himself but the force of the shove took him by surprise and he pitched face first into the hard wooden post. Reeling with pain and shock Falco tried to right himself but before he could regain his balance one of the other youths kicked his legs out from under him and he fell heavily on his side.

Images of what he *should* do flashed through his mind but his body was simply not up to the task and all he managed to do was curl into a ball as the kicks and punches slammed into his body. He grunted in pain then gasped as Jarek grabbed a fistful of his long black hair.

'The Academy of War can be a dangerous place,' he said in a low menacing tone. 'It's not unheard of for cadets to be killed in training and your big friend won't always be there to save you.'

Falco winced as Jarek wrenched his head back to look in his eyes.

'If you ever accuse my family of cowardice again I will see you dead and buried in a pauper's grave.' His voice was now a tight and sibilant whisper. 'Do I make myself clear?'

With that he let go of Falco's hair and turned away.

'I didn't say you were a coward,' said Falco, raising himself up on one elbow and spitting out a mouthful of blood. 'I merely suggested that you were wrong to claim the courage of others as your own.'

Jarek stopped, the training sword hanging loosely in his hand. His head bowed forward but then his fingers tightened on the hilt of the wooden sword and he spun round to whack Falco in the side of the head.

Such an uncontrolled blow might have caused significant damage but it seemed that Falco's skull was harder than it looked. Even so, he collapsed on the gritty sand and a trickle of blood ran into his eye. Dazed and blinking he looked up as his attackers walked away. For just a moment Jarek looked back. His eyes were filled with loathing but Falco noticed something else, something that made the hatred in Jarek burn more fiercely than ever. Shame.

'What the hell happened to you?' said Malaki as he caught sight of Falco in the dining hall a few minutes later.

Bryna was bathing a cut above his right eye.

'We found him in the courtyard,' said Alex as Malaki slid a huge plate of stew and dumplings onto the table.

'Tripped on the steps,' said Falco.

'Snidesson!' spat Malaki. 'The little...'

Falco motioned for Malaki to sit then winced as Bryna pressed the cold cloth to his head.

'It's going to need a stitch,' she said.

'Why would he do this?' asked Quirren, his normally calm face dark with anger.

The three Valentians looked at each other but offered no answer. There was no way they could sum up the history of animosity that existed between Falco and the noble family of the Snidessons.

'We should tell someone,' said Alex. 'Lanista Deloix, perhaps.'

Falco shook his head.

'That would only make things worse.'

'I can't wait to meet him in training,' said Malaki.

'Is he not skilled?' asked Quirren.

'Oh, he's skilled all right,' said Malaki. 'But I'm still going to kick his arse.'

Falco laughed. He was surprised to find that he felt no anger towards Jarek. Jarek had Bellius for a father, and a mother who cared more for her moneyed reputation than she did for her son, while he had had Simeon and Fossetta. No, it was not anger he felt towards Jarek but pity. He pushed away Bryna's hand and held the cloth to his own head before swiping Malaki's plate and stuffing a fat dumpling in his mouth. He winced as the hot gravy stung his bleeding lips.

'Guess I'll go and get another plate,' said Malaki sourly and despite his cuts and bruises Falco smiled.

So, Jarek and his cronies had given him another beating. So what? After all the excitement and trepidation, it seemed the Academy of War was just like home.

32

The Disciplines of Lore

It was midnight in the hidden depths of the Clemoncéan mage tower. Meredith Saker had just spent the last twenty-four hours meditating in one of the cells put aside for just such solitary purpose. Now it was time to emerge and reveal to the Grand Veneratu the disciplines of lore that would form the basis of his study. Meredith was nervous. He suspected his father would not approve of the choices he had made. But so be it. That was the whole point of this meditation, to find the true nature of one's calling. He had lived his entire life in his father's shadow. It was time to cast a shadow of his own.

The door to the cell opened and a mage stood in the opening, an oil filled torch in his hand.

'They are ready for you.'

Meredith nodded and slowly rose to his feet. His body was stiff from kneeling so long but he made no complaint as he motioned for the attending mage to lead on.

The cell opened onto a long corridor of dark stone that seemed not to have been built but rather carved from the bedrock of the mountains. Set into the walls were numerous doors, each leading to a cell similar to the one that Meredith had just left, a small windowless room with a simple cot and a bucket for bodily waste. They reminded Meredith of the prison cells back in the main keep of Caer Dour.

'This way,' said the attending mage, directing Meredith to the right where the passageway was lit by flames burning in dish-like sconces protruding from the walls.

For some reason the man seemed nervous and he kept glancing down the corridor to the left where the unlit passageway disappeared into shadow. Meredith followed his gaze and a distinct feeling of unease rose like a chill through his body. At the far end of the corridor he could just make out another cell, and even though there was no grill or opening in the door, he had the distinct impression that he was being watched.

Unnerved by a sudden pall of fear he turned to follow the attending mage. As they progressed along the corridor Meredith became aware of quiet noises coming from some of the occupied cells, whispers, chants and softly muttered refrains. They were about to leave the corridor when the air shook as if someone had just struck the door of a cell with a battering ram.

Meredith flinched as the sense of fear grew more intense than ever. Then three other mages appeared in the corridor, each one powerfully built and stern. Over their robes they wore the dark shawl of wardens. Meredith sensed their tension and the sudden concentration of energy in their hands. All three of them were holding powerful spells in their minds.

Another boom reverberated through the air and Meredith realised that the noise was coming from the cell at the far end of the corridor.

'Did you disturb him?' asked one of the wardens.

'No,' said the attending mage. 'We came away quietly.'

The wardens cast them a suspicious look before turning away. They had just started down the corridor when a voice seemed to creep through the air towards them.

'Eu pot auzi tu, fiul lui Saker' said the voice in low sinister tone. 'Pot mirosi tu.'

Meredith felt an unpleasant shiver run down his spine. Even among the magi there were few who understood the old language of Ferocia but Meredith had studied it in depth.

'*I can hear you, son of Saker,*' the voice had said '*I can smell you.*'

'Go on,' said one of the wardens. 'We'll see to brother Pacatos.'

Meredith and his attending mage had just turned to go when the voice spoke again.

'Am miros trădare în tine.'

'*I smell the treachery in you.*'

Meredith stopped. He turned then flinched as the great booming sound shook the corridor once more. It sounded like the door to a cell was being pounded off its hinges.

'Come,' said the attending mage, clearly anxious to get away. 'The Grand Veneratu is waiting.'

'Who *was* that?' asked Meredith, as they climbed the stairs to the upper levels of the tower.

The attending mage seemed reluctant to answer but Meredith caught his arm.

'It was Brother Pacatos,' he said at last.

'What's wrong with him?' asked Meredith. 'Is he a prisoner?'

'He is... confined.'

'Why?'

'They say that he's unbalanced,' said the attending mage in a hushed tone. 'That he is powerful but that he finds it difficult to exercise control.'

Meredith glanced back the way they had come.

'Do not go down there,' said the attending mage. 'Do not approach his cell. And *never* alone!' Having stressed the point he turned and continued up the stairs.

Deeply unsettled Meredith paused for a moment before hurrying after him with the words of Brother Pacatos echoing in his mind.

'Am miros trădare în tine.'

I smell the treachery in you.

Reaching the top of the stairs they passed through a doorway and so they did not hear the horrific scream that echoed through the tunnels they had just departed. A little further and they reached a large set of double doors.

'The apprentice mage, Meredith Saker, to declare his chosen disciplines,' announced the attending mage as they entered the Grand Veneratu's chamber.

Still shaken by what had taken place in the cells Meredith gazed at his surroundings. He was standing in the centre of a circular room built from smoke grey marble. Doors of black wood led to other rooms and an arched passageway gave onto darkness. From the movement in the air Meredith guessed it led outside, to a balcony perhaps. On the far side of the room a raised dais followed the curve of the wall and, sitting on what could only be described as a throne, was Galen Thrall, Worshipful Master and Grand Veneratu of the Clemoncéan magi. The throne was a great seat of black marble with a high back and arms carved in the likeness of ravens.

'*So much for our vows of humility,*' thought Meredith.

To the right of the throne stood his father, Morgan Saker, and Meredith chided himself for the carelessness of his reaction. They might not be able to read the details of his mind but they could certainly gauge the tone of his thoughts. Making a mental note to be more careful he bowed deeply to the Grand Veneratu before turning to acknowledge his father.

'Is your meditation complete?' said Thrall. 'Have you chosen the disciplines you will study?'

'I have,' said Meredith, looking at the Grand Veneratu properly for the first time.

Galen Thrall was a man of senior years. At first glance one might take him for a kindly figure until one realised that the smile in his eyes was only there by choice and the benevolent set of his narrow mouth was but a twitch away from a sneer. His oiled hair was long with a slight curl to the flaxen grey. His skin was pale with a patina of creases and small scars of indeterminate and slightly disturbing nature. And his eyes, a waxy greenish grey with pupils just a fraction too small to be explained by the subdued light in the room.

He was a man that made one nervous and Meredith could tell that even his father felt uncomfortable in his presence. Suddenly he began to doubt the choices he had made. To court his father's disapproval was one thing, to invoke the displeasure of Galen Thrall was quite another.

'And your choices are?'

Meredith had the unsettling impression that Thrall already knew. Maybe he *could* read minds after all.

'Communication... History and... Dragonkind,' said Meredith.

'Nonsense!' barked his father but Galen Thrall just nodded as if these were entirely worthy areas of study.

'You have a gift for concealment and conjuration,' his father continued. 'And surely politics has more relevance than history. I thought you wanted to make a difference in the world.'

At this Galen Thrall arched an eyebrow as if he found such ambition amusing and Meredith flushed with embarrassment. Despite his earlier resolve his father still had the ability to make him feel like a child. But still, this was his right. The completion of these studies would mark him as a fully fledged mage.

'This is my decision to make,' he said, summoning all the dignity he could muster. 'These are the disciplines I have chosen.'

'Yes, yes,' said Galen Thrall. 'And we shall help you in your studies. But not dragonkind. There is little to be gained in the study of wyrms. They are a fading and tragic species, soon to disappear from the world entirely, I fear. But history... Knowledge of what has gone before is always of value. I see no problem with this.'

He smiled magnanimously but the pupils of his eyes seemed to narrow even further. Thrall was wary of anyone who 'wanted to make a difference'.

'Go now,' he went on, dismissing Meredith before he could say anything more. 'Chambers have been made ready for you. When you are rested I will have someone escort you to the archives. And may your studies bear the fruit that you desire.'

Meredith's face burned with mortification at Thrall's dismissing his chosen subject of dragonkind but there was no way he could contradict the Grand Veneratu. Pointedly ignoring the heated glare of his father he bowed low, turned to leave and left the room.

*

'History!' snorted Morgan as the door to the chamber closed. 'What a waste!'

Thrall said nothing for a moment, his brow lowered in thought.

'Can we trust him with the truth?'

'I don't know,' replied Morgan. 'Ever since the summoning he's been withdrawn, confused... He has too much of his mother's weakness.'

'Then he must not read the chronicles of the Eighty Fourth.'

'But he is studying history and he is gifted in concealment. If you remove them or try to hide them he will know.'

'We will not hide them and we will not remove them,' said Thrall with a smile. 'I will have Brother Serulian installed in the archives. He is a master of obfuscaria. Your son could read the chronicles of the Eighty Fourth a hundred times and never remember a word.'

'He will become suspicious.'

'Ha!' spat Thrall with a rasping laugh. 'He will not even notice. The knowledge will be swallowed up in darkness. He will simply believe there was nothing new to learn.'

'So be it,' said Morgan.

'So be it,' said Thrall.

*

Burning with anger, and dizzy with hunger and fatigue, Meredith followed the attending mage through the tower to the chambers that had been put aside for him. He had expected to feel some satisfaction at defying his father but all he felt was a boiling resentment and the familiar weight of disappointment. As the attending mage left the room Meredith swore to himself that he would not be diverted from his chosen disciplines. No matter what persuasion the Grand Veneratu and his father brought to bear he would study the history of Wrath and somehow he would learn about dragonkind.

Am miros trădare în tine

Was this the treachery of which Brother Pacatos spoke?

With a terrible sense of foreboding Meredith suspected it was not.

194

33

The Training Begins

None of the cadets slept half so well the following night. The knowledge that they would be woken at sunrise kept most of them tossing and turning until well after midnight. Falco expected them to be roused by some hideous din as they did in the army barracks of Caer Dour. Here Lanista Deloix had simply appeared with a junior assistant. He stood at the end of the barracks while the assistant rang a brass bell, which hung from one of the wooden posts running in pairs down the centre of the room.

'Ding, ding, ding!'

Three modest chimes, then three times again, more than enough to rouse the restless cadets from their beds.

'Good morning. I trust you slept well' he said, taking in the puffy faces and red eyes of the cadets. 'You have twenty minutes to dress, relieve yourselves and report to the central training field. Clothes and boots have been laid out for each of you.' He gestured to the clothes now lying on the chests at the foot of each bed: trousers, tunic and boots with a sheepskin jacket and a waxed cotton cloak. The Lanista gave a nod to show that he was finished and the barracks burst into activity.

Falco winced as he got out of bed, the bruises had coloured over night and his ribs felt stiff and sore. He put a hand to his face and explored the cut in his mouth with his tongue then looked up to see Lanista Magnus standing beside his bed. The senior instructor passed a critical eye over Falco's injuries before he spoke.

'The matter of your training will be decided this afternoon,' he said, his face stern and unreadable. 'Until then you will be treated the same as any other cadet.'

Falco nodded and watched as Lanista Magnus turned to leave. There was something unsettling in his tone as if he knew more than he was willing to say. With a sense of foreboding Falco reached for the cotton shirt at the end of his bed, wincing at the pain in his ribs.

'Are you all right?' asked Malaki.

'I'll be fine,' said Falco.

At the far end of the barracks he could see Jarek and the others who had attacked him the previous night. He did not want to give them the satisfaction of seeing him struggle, so gritting his teeth against the pain, he dressed quickly and finished his ablutions.

'What did Lanista Magnus say to you?' asked Malaki as they headed out of the barracks with Bryna.

'Just that they'll make a decision about my training this afternoon.'

'Sounds ominous,' said Malaki.

'I'm sure it'll be fine,' said Bryna.

Falco was not particularly reassured. He made no reply as they followed the rest of the cadets up to the training field where they were met by Lanista Deloix. The sky was still dark and there was a smirr of rain in the air, so despite their cloaks and sheepskin jackets the cadets shivered in the grey light of a damp morning. Autumn was giving way to winter.

Lanista Deloix directed them to a large white tent at the side of the field. As they entered they were met by assistants who took their cloaks and presented each of them with the weapons of their chosen discipline. Bryna was given a bow, a quiver full of arrows and a shortsword in a belted leather scabbard, while Malaki and Falco were presented with a Valentian bastard sword and a steel alloy round-shield.

Feeling more than a little self conscious Falco adjusted the straps on the shield to account for his skinny arms. Glancing up he noticed the scornful looks from Jarek and several of the other cadets, but he did not care. Once again he felt that sense of satisfaction at being in the presence of weapons, of holding a sword. He was tempted to think it was a male thing but he saw the relish with which Bryna fastened the shortsword around her waist before slinging the quiver over her shoulder and picking up her bow. No. It was about identity and how you saw yourself. He might not look the part the way that Malaki did, but as Falco gripped his sword and couched his shield it felt somehow right.

When they were all suitably equipped they followed Lanista Deloix outside where Lanista Magnus was now waiting for them. The senior instructor raised an arm and pointed up towards the mountains.

'Up there, in the mist,' he began, 'is a stone they call the Pike, a great slab of granite poking out from the side of the mountain. Every morning you will climb to the Pike before returning here to break your fast and prepare for the day's training.'

The cadets gazed up into the low cloud hanging over the mountain. They could just make out the pale line of a path snaking its way up into the mist.

'It's two miles and a thousand feet to the Pike,' said Lanista Magnus. 'It should take you about an hour,' he added as the other instructors returned to the shelter of the tent.

Some of the cadets hovered uncertainly but it was clear that some of them were familiar with this ritual and hefting their weapons they set off at a jog.

'Come on,' said Alex, urging Falco and the others to follow. 'It's quite a climb and it's more than two miles.'

'You've done it already?' said Falco as he, Malaki and Bryna fell in beside the two brothers.

'We did it the other day,' said Alex. 'Our cousin told us about it. It's not supposed to be a competition but he says it always turns out that way.'

Malaki's eyes lit up but Falco's spirits dropped. He was already feeling breathless and after just a few more minutes he had slowed to a walk.

'You go on,' he said when they held back to walk with him.

Alex and Quirren nodded but Malaki seemed reluctant to leave.

'Go on, you great oaf,' said Falco giving him a shove. 'You can't let that bastard Jarek beat you.'

Finally Malaki smiled and with a nod to Bryna he sprinted off up the track. Falco saw Quirren step up to match his speed while Alex and Bryna followed at a more leisurely pace.

To Falco the two miles felt like ten but he tried to keep going, only pausing to let those coming back down go past. One of these was Jarek who made a point of forcing Falco off the path. However, Falco soon forgot this affront when he saw that Malaki and Quirren were now right behind him and closing fast. He only wished he could be there when Jarek realised that a blacksmith had beaten him back to the tent.

With a smile he pressed on and eventually came to the 'Pike', a massive slab of stone that jutted out from the rocky slope like a finger pointing into the void. The top surface was flat and Falco took a moment to walk along its narrow length, unaffected by the significant drop that opened up below him. Standing at its tip he felt the cold mist swirl about him. It reminded him of being back in the mountains of Caer Dour. He took a breath and smiled. Yes, he had struggled but he had done better than he thought he would, and he even found the exertion quite satisfying. He turned round and, feeling strangely invigorated, he began to run back down the path.

The hour candle had long since burned down when Falco returned to the training field. He found the cadets milling around in the pale, drizzly morning. Some of them were finishing their breakfast while others were talking in groups, comparing weapons and going through manoeuvres and techniques. One of the assistants took Falco's sword and shield before handing him a plate of food and a beaker of what smelled like chamomile tea.

'So you made it,' said Malaki as Falco sat down at one of the benches.

Falco showed him a finger as he put a huge dollop of orange conserve on a hunk of bread and shoved it into his mouth.

'Did you beat him?' asked Falco, nodding towards a group of cadets gathered round Jarek.

'What do *you* think?' said Malaki with a grin.

Falco smiled and gulped down a mouthful of hot tea as the cadets were directed to move outside.

Lanista Deloix led them to a series of wooden benches arranged in a semicircle beside the large white tent. He motioned for the cadets to take a seat then went to stand in the open space before them. A moment later a dozen instructors with at least as many assistants emerged from the tent and a ripple of excitement ran through the cadets.

Falco nudged Malaki as he saw who was leading them out. There, with Lanista Magnus at his side, was the unmistakeable figure of the emissary dressed in the black surcoat of an instructor. He gave no sign of recognition and Falco felt a twinge of disappointment as he cast his gaze over the cadets with neutral equanimity.

From the corner of his eye Falco caught sight of Alex and Quirren both trying hard not to let their nervousness show. He turned to look at Malaki who was sitting beside him. They had come to know the emissary quite well and the only nerves they felt came from the fear of letting him down. Falco gave Alex a smile of reassurance then tensed as someone leaned in close behind him.

'So, the Queen's pet knight has come to watch over you, has he?'

Falco closed his eyes as Jarek whispered in his ear.

'Well... Prince Ludovico has now heard of this farce. It seems the Fourth Army may be deployed earlier than planned. You won't enjoy the emissary's protection for long.'

197

Jarek leaned back and Falco glanced round at the youths on the back row. It was clear from their contemptuous glances that they expected him to receive preferential treatment from the emissary.

'What did he say?' asked Malaki but Falco just waved him to be quiet. The day's training was about to begin.

The academy assistants had set out a series of tables full of training weapons and armour. They had also erected a number of wood and straw training mannequins dressed in the black armour of Ferocian Kardakae. The very sight of them made Falco shudder.

Everything was ready and the emissary turned to face them.

'Why are you here?' he asked.

The question was quiet, almost introspective and at first no one answered. Then a heavy-set young man with a dark complexion spoke up to Falco's left.

'To learn to fight,' he said. 'To be the best that we can be.'

The emissary nodded as if this was a perfectly good answer.

'Yes...' he said. 'But more than this. You are here to become leaders of men. When you leave the academy you will return to your people and teach them what you have learned. In this way the knowledge of the academy can be spread across the world. But why would the elite school of Clemoncé want to share its secrets with the other kingdoms, kingdoms with which it has fought countless wars over the centuries?'

'To defeat the Possessed.'

Falco looked to his right. It was Alex who had spoken.

'And why is that so important? What makes them so special?'

'Because they threaten us all,' said one.

'Because they are so cruel,' said another.

'Cruel?' The emissary gave a bitter laugh. 'When the Illician army captured the Beltonian town of Guerthang, they slaughtered every man, woman and child. My own kinsmen murdered more than a thousand people.' He frowned as he spoke, as if he could barely believe what he was telling them. 'Are the Possessed any crueller than that?'

The cadets were silent. They all knew stories of massacres, torture and death within their own kingdoms. The history of Wrath was littered with such horrors, some of which still went on today. Were the Possessed really any different? The emissary let them ponder that question for a moment before speaking again.

'What is the worst thing you can imagine?' he directed his question to a blond-haired Illician youth in the front row. 'What is the worst thing that one person can do to another?'

'Murder,' said the young man and the emissary snorted as if this barely qualified as an answer.

'Torture,' said another.

'And what is the worst kind of torture?'

'Hot irons...'

'The rack...'

'Flaying...'

The emissary pursed his lips, still unimpressed.

'And what if someone you loved was being tortured in such a way and there was nothing you could do to save them? What would you hope for then?'

The cadets stared at him in horror.

'That they might die quickly,' said a young man from the back.

The emissary fixed him with a stone hard stare.

'And what if they could not die?'

The young man looked at him, confused.

'What if their pain and suffering could not be ended by death? What if the skin was peeled from their flesh and that was but the start of their suffering?'

He stared at them all, not allowing any of them to avoid the implications of what he was saying.

'Those taken by the Possessed are not killed, they are claimed. They will never be allowed the luxury of death. Even when their bodies are consumed their souls will remain in torment forever. The people who fell to the Possessed five hundred years ago are not dead. They writhe in agony still.'

Silence.

'Is there no hope for them?'

The question was spoken softly and the emissary paused before answering. He knew that many of these youngsters would have lost people to the Possessed.

'If they died without losing faith then the enemy cannot claim them. If the demon that claimed them is slain then their souls may be saved. But if they were captured or died in despair then no. Their only hope lies with us. Some believe that if we defeat the Possessed and drive the darkness from our world then perhaps their souls can be redeemed.'

The cadets stared at him. Until now they had thought only of themselves and their own advancement. They had seen the academy as a way to improve their skills and status. Now the emissary was telling them that the fate of countless souls rested with them.

Falco thought of the people *they* had lost to the Possessed.

Balthazak... Sir Gerallt... Simeon.

Were they at peace or did they also suffer the torments of hell? Glancing to one side he saw that Malaki and Bryna sat with their heads bowed.

'So I ask you again. Why are you here?'

This time no one was willing to answer.

'You are here to learn how to fight,' said the emissary. 'To be the best that you can be.' He glanced at the young man who had just given this answer and gave him a nod. 'That is all that any of us can do.'

The cadets stared up at him and even Jarek Snidesson was not unaffected by the force of his presence.

'So,' said the emissary.

And now he smiled.

'Let us fight.'

The cadets were split into small groups with an instructor and several assistants. Falco found himself in a group under Lanista Magnus with Malaki and Bryna plus a number of Beltonians and several young men with the dark complexion of Acheron or Thraece.

'But I'm here as an archer,' said Bryna as one of the assistants handed her a training sword and shield.

'You each have your chosen discipline,' said Lanista Magnus. 'But you will also train in others. Archers will fight with sword and shield and learn the basics of spear formations, while spearmen will learn how to use a bow in ranks without shooting their companions in the back. In this way you will come to appreciate the strengths and limitations of different units on the battle field. Invaluable experience when you come to take command.'

The cadets glanced at each other. They had just begun their training and already the instructors were talking about command. Then, without further ado, they too were kitted out with a training sword, a shield and padded leather armour and the training began in earnest.

They trained for a couple of hours going through some of the basic fighting styles that most of them were familiar with but, after only twenty minutes, Falco's arms felt like dead weights. Since waking up in Toulwar he had definitely grown stronger but he was still weak compared to the others. He struggled on until one of the assistants rang a bell and the instructors called them back to the benches where the emissary addressed them once more.

'For sparring we use wooden swords or the metal blunts that most of you are familiar with.' He nodded to the blunt training swords that each of the cadets held. 'But we also train with live blades.' In his hands he held a one-handed Illician 'arming sword' and a metal round-shield. 'Has anyone here trained in the fencing forms of Liberi or the Gladiatoria?'

Fully half the cadets raised an uncertain hand.

Falco glanced at Malaki. Simeon had owned an ancient copy of the Gladiatoria and the two boys had loved nothing better than to sneak into his study and look at the pictures, and later to read the text, of this revered fighting manual.

The emissary nodded to a clean jawed Clemoncéan youth with sandy blonde hair. He handed him the sharp longsword and shield and invited him to take up position in front of the training mannequins which had been made to look like Kardakae. The mannequins had been furnished with swords, each presenting the blade to replicate various types of attack.

'On the bell I would like you to dispatch the enemy,' said the emissary, giving the young man a smile to assuage his nerves.

The cadet nodded then as the assistant rang the bell he lunged forward, the point of his sword finding the gap beneath the Kardakae breastplate. He stepped to his left engaged the next mannequin's blade with his own and retained it to deliver a precise stab into the unprotected armpit. The next he cut across the neck, then it was the elbow and finally he moved past the last dummy, parrying with his shield before turning to deliver a 'lethal cut' through another gap in the Kardakae's heavy armour.

He stood, panting, while the mannequins wobbled and rocked from his attacks. Each had been dispatched by a precise strike, delivered with great accuracy and skill. The cadets were impressed and the emissary nodded in appreciation. He indicated for the young man to take his seat.

'Now,' he said. 'Has anyone here actually fought the Possessed?'

200

The cadets shook their heads slowly, all save those from Caer Dour who had fought the Possessed in the mountains.

The emissary moved to stand in front of Malaki. Malaki's head had been bowed but now he looked up, the expression in his eyes dark as if he had no wish to remember how it felt to face one of these warriors in the flesh. The emissary extended the hilt of the sword and slowly Malaki took it. With some reluctance he got to his feet and took the round-shield on his arm. Slowly he moved to take up position.

'These are Kardakae of the Possessed,' said the emissary. 'I want you to defeat them.'

Head still bowed Malaki looked at the emissary before turning to face the lifeless mannequins. He appeared cowed and withdrawn but Falco noticed the blade of the sword lift slightly as Malaki's hand tightened on the grip.

The bell rang and Malaki powered forward. His first attack came up inside the Kardakae's guard, forcing the black breastplate up and slicing through the straw body that tied it to the post. His second attack was a continuation of the first and the Illician blade hacked down into the Mannequin's shoulder, severing the sword arm as Malaki moved past. The next was felled by a massive blow from the rim of his shield and finished by a sword strike that took a great chunk out of the thick wooden post. Two left... Malaki snapped the post of one with a powerful kick and demolished the last with a series of blows from sword and shield. The final mannequin collapsed to the ground in several pieces, the black helmet rolling free.

Malaki stood there, tense but poised as if he were ready to fell a hundred more and the cadets looked on in shock. Lanista Deloix gave a small nod while Lanista Magnus wore a grim smile of satisfaction.

For the most part the cadets looked at Malaki with newfound respect. Only Jarek and a few of his followers seemed unimpressed. He gave a scornful snort at Malaki's display, while the big Beltonian looked at Malaki with a distinct challenge in his eyes.

The emissary turned to the cadets.

'One of the main things we teach you here at the academy is the difference between sparring and genuine combat.' He waited for Malaki to retake his seat. 'A well placed hit might score you a point in a fencing match, but in order for an attack to be effective in battle the enemy must fear for their lives. It takes real force to cut through leather armour, or break an arm through chain, and it's not so easy to find gaps in plate armour when your opponent is trying to kill you.'

He nodded his thanks as one of the assistants handed him the breastplate from the first of the Kardakae dummies. He held it up so that they could all see the impressive dent from Malaki's sword.

'This was an attack that was going to do some damage no matter where it struck. It *demands* a response from your opponent. When you defend you must defend against such as this, an attack that is intended to kill.'

He looked at the young man who had given a fine display of accuracy.

'I'm not suggesting you abandon finesse but you need to understand that it is not enough. You will need both skill and brutality to defeat the Possessed.'

The point was made and the training continued. The assistants attached armoured pads to the training posts so that the cadets could see just how much force it took to penetrate different types of armour. It soon became clear that their fast flicks and clever cuts were nowhere near enough to damage an armoured opponent. All of a sudden the training that most of them had done so far seemed like little more than playing.

As the morning progressed Falco could see that the instructors were slowly assessing them, watching the way they fought and moved but also the way they responded to instruction and how they behaved towards each other. But it was too much for him. Even though the training session was fairly light his arms felt so pumped with blood that he could barely hold his sword and his chest ached with exertion. The instructors did not berate him, they simply focussed their attention on others until Falco was ready to try again. He was extremely relieved when they finally returned to the benches to watch groups of cadets sparring in pairs. He nodded his thanks as one of the assistants handed him a steaming cup of broth.

It was still cold but it was almost midday and the early mist had lifted from the mountains. Feeling more than a little disheartened, Falco shook his head as he looked down at his weak arms and thin wrists.

'They fight well.'

He turned to see the emissary sitting beside him.

'Yes, they do,' he said, lowering his hands and sipping his drink to hide the self-pity he had been indulging in.

'What about Owen?' said the emissary. 'He's fast...'

'Yes, said Falco, realising that the emissary expected him to comment. 'But he reacts too quickly. It makes him vulnerable to a feint.'

'And the Acheronian fighting Quirren?'

Falco looked at the dark-skinned youth. He moved like a natural fighter with the powerful build for which Acheron was famous.

'Predictable,' said Falco. 'He always retreats to the left and he signals an attack with his foot.'

The emissary pursed his lips, nodding.

'And what about your friend, the blacksmith?'

Falco glanced at him as if he were joking. Surely there was little to criticise about the way Malaki fought. But there was no jest in the emissary's eyes and so, frowning slightly, he turned his attention to Malaki. At first he just saw plain fluid ability but as he watched he became aware of small things he had never noticed before.

'He carries too much weight in his shoulders and he over commits on the attack,' said Falco. 'If he wasn't so good it could leave him open.'

'He isn't so good and it does leave him open,' said the emissary with a laugh.

He was silent for moment.

'Strength is just time and effort,' he said and Falco bowed his head, embarrassed by the transparency of his thoughts. 'But what's in here.' The emissary touched his temple. 'And here,' he tapped his fingers against his chest. 'This cannot be taught.'

'So am I to be trained?'

The emissary paused and it was clear that he had something difficult to say. Falco waited to hear his fate.

'There's to be a court martial,' said the emissary at last. 'The Queen has granted permission for your training but her consent is being challenged.'

'By whom?'

'The Lords Snidesson and Saker. They are citing a charge of treason for what happened on the dragon stone.'

Falco closed his eyes.

'When?' said Falco

'Soon,' said the emissary. 'I've just heard that the constables are on their way.

'And who will judge me?' asked Falco, his pulse suddenly quickening.

'Normally it would be the Queen. But it's her decision that's being challenged so Prince Ludovico will take the chair. Snidesson will be there to represent Darius while Galen Thrall will sit on behalf of the magi who fell.'

'Will you represent me?' asked Falco.

The emissary shook his head.

'I've been called as a witness along with Lord Saker and his son Meredith. Don't worry,' he went on when he saw the despair on Falco's face. 'Prince Ludovico will not uphold a charge of treason. They seek only to block your training with the magi.'

'Then they have succeeded,' said Falco. 'There's no way Galen Thrall will agree. Not if Saker has anything to do with it.'

'Don't be so sure,' said the emissary. 'It might not be down to Thrall.'

Falco looked at him sharply. Galen Thrall was the Worshipful Master of the Clemoncéan magi, surely everything was down to him.

'Besides... There's someone else who might be able to help.'

'Oh?'

'Yes,' said the Emissary, rising to his feet as a line of riders came into view. 'Assuming he likes you, that is.'

'And what if he doesn't?'

'Then he might just kill you,' said the emissary and Falco was hard pushed to tell if he was joking or not. Feeling suddenly sick he stood beside the emissary as the four constables skirted the training field before coming to a stop beside Lanista Magnus. He noticed that they had brought a spare horse.

The cadets ceased their sparring and gathered round to watch

'What's going on?' asked Malaki but there was no time to answer.

The constables had finished speaking to the trainers. Wearing an expression that suggested he did not appreciate anyone interrupting his training sessions, Lanista Magnus led the constables over to where Falco and the emissary were now standing.

'Falco Danté,' said the constable in charge. 'You have been charged with treason in relation to the death of the battle mage Darius Voltario. You will come with us to the Chamber of Council to hear your fate.'

Malaki gaped in disbelief just as Bryna came over to join them. The other cadets looked on with a mixture of interest and suspicion. Alex and Quirren appeared concerned while Jarek Snidesson smiled as if he had just thrashed Falco in a fencing match.

'Go with them,' said the emissary softly. 'I will join you shortly.'

Trying to calm the turbulence that swirled in his belly Falco walked forward and mounted the horse that Lanista Deloix was now holding for him. The constables gave the emissary a stiff nod then, with two in front and two behind, Falco was led away.

34
Defiance

The Chamber of Council was an oval shaped building in the northern part of the city, a large covered amphitheatre used for lectures, court rulings and public strategy meetings. Built of pale brown stone the impressive walls were decorated with reliefs of great debates and orators of the past and crowned by a low domed roof, a tribute to the skill of Clemoncé's stone masons and engineers.

There were four main entranceways to the chamber but the constables escorted Falco to a small archway and a stone staircase that led down into a tunnel. They emerged from the tunnel onto the floor of the amphitheatre, a large area of polished marble that was covered by an enormous carpet portraying some kind of map. This central area was surrounded on all sides by tiers of stone seats rising up to the roof and providing all parts of the building with a clear view of whatever was taking place on the floor. It reminded Falco of the crucible and like the crucible it was more than a little intimidating.

The constables directed Falco to a wooden chair at one end of the floor. Two of them stood guard beside him while the others went to stand at the far end where two tables had been set out, one directly facing Falco with a smaller one to the side. As the constables took up their positions one of them nodded to the main entrance and Falco watched as two men emerged. The first was clearly a scribe while the other appeared to be some kind of magistrate. They seated themselves at the smaller table to one side of the floor.

Next came the witnesses: Morgan Saker, with his son Meredith, and the emissary. The two magi crossed the floor before settling themselves on the lowest tier of seats to Falco's right. The emissary took a seat opposite them on the left. He did not look at him but still Falco found his presence deeply comforting.

Finally the three men who would sit on the panel emerged. The first was Bellius Snidesson; the second could only be Galen Thrall. And, judging by the splendour of his clothes, the third was Prince Ludovico of King Michael's Mount, a tall and noble looking man of middle forty years with an axe-blade of a nose and long black hair which was heavily etched with grey. Like Bellius, he wore a neatly trimmed beard and moustache but unlike Bellius, he did not look upon Falco with naked hatred. Instead the expression in his clear brown eyes was serious and thoughtful.

The three men took their seats behind the main table with Bellius on one side, Thrall on the other and the prince in the middle. Galen Thrall swept his gaze round the chamber before fixing Falco with a jade green stare that made him feel naked. Prince Ludovico, on the other hand, looked at Falco as if he found it hard to believe that so slight a figure could be the source of so much ire.

To one side the scribe took up his quill, the prince gave a nod and the magistrate called the court martial to order.

The hearing did not take long but to Falco it seemed to go on for an age. He gave his own testimony in something of a daze and for the rest of it he felt numb and detached as if he were watching the proceedings from a high vantage point somewhere near the ceiling. Finally the various accounts and arguments were heard and Falco watched as the three members of the panel leaned in close to decide his fate. He felt light-headed and the sounds of their muted conversation echoed strangely in his ears.

'Don't worry,' said a quiet voice and Falco turned to see the emissary standing beside him. He looked to the constables before handing Falco a cup of water. 'You spoke well and the prince is a fair man. He will not be swayed by Snidesson's bile.'

The emissary spoke in a lowered tone so as not to be overheard by Bellius Snidesson who kept shooting venomous looks in Falco's direction. Galen Thrall, on the other hand, focussed all his attention on the prince who sat at the centre of the table wearing a frown of concentration. The emissary had assured Falco that *he* would not support a charge of treason but it seemed unthinkable that he would go against the will of Galen Thrall.

Looking away from his gaze Falco took a drink, his hands shaking so badly that some of the water spilled down his chin.

As they continued their discussion Falco took the opportunity to glance around the room. To his right Morgan Saker was watching the panel's discussion while Meredith continued to stare straight ahead. Along with the emissary they had each given vivid accounts of what had happened on the dragon stone.

Falco was just looking back towards the panel when he realised that what he had taken for a shadow, on the uppermost tier of seats, was in fact the figure of a man. Vaguely he remembered seeing the shadow on entering the chamber. Silent and swathed in darkness the mysterious figure had been present during the entire proceedings. Before he had a chance to look any closer his attention was brought back to the floor. Finally Prince Ludovico had heard enough. Bellius and Thrall sat back in their seats as the prince raised a gloved hand.

'The court wishes to thank the witnesses for their honest testimony of this terrible event.' His voice was deep with a heavy Clemoncéan accent.

With a nod to Falco the emissary returned to his seat and the prince went on. 'There can be no doubt that Master Danté alerted the dragon and broke the concealment that would have ensured its death.'

At this, Bellius smiled in satisfaction while Galen Thrall simply nodded sagely, the hint of a smile in his lipid green eyes.

'However, the matter of treason must come down to intent.'

Bellius shifted in his seat while the pupils in Thrall's eyes suddenly narrowed.

'There is no evidence to suggest that Master Danté *intended* to cause the death of Darius Voltario. Testimony suggests it was an involuntary outburst. Foolish and tragic but lacking in malice.' He paused before delivering his verdict. 'On the count of treason I find the defendant, not guilty.'

Falco let out the breath he had been holding, surprised that the prince would take such a reasonable view. He had judged the man on the company he kept, namely the magi and nobles like Bellius who supported them. He realised now, that he had done the prince a disservice.

'As for the matter of his training,' the prince went on. 'I am not qualified to judge. I have listened to the reports of his father's tragic downfall, which in my opinion is reason enough for caution.' He paused and Bellius's chin came up once more. 'In this matter I must defer to the Grand Veneratu. It is my understanding that battle mages require a mage to guide them through their training. I leave it to Galen Thrall to decide whether such a guide will be forthcoming.'

The prince had passed judgement and all eyes turned to Galen Thrall.

'Compassionate and wise as ever, your Highness,' said Thrall in a suspiciously gracious tone. 'We have been considering the matter of Master Danté's training since we first learned of his desire to become a battle mage. The role of a guide is no easy task and therefore I took the liberty of putting the matter to the members of the tower. Despite his family history I have no personal objection to his being trained.'

A likely story, thought Falco.

'Unfortunately, however, there is not a single member of the tower who is willing to take on the role of guide to Master Danté. In the absence of a mage to train him, therefore, I suggest he be removed from the Academy of War, where his physical shortcomings would surely be a distraction to the Lanistas and a hindrance to the training of the other cadets.'

He looked at Falco with an air of apology as if the matter was out of his hands. Bellius wore a smug smile of victory and Falco could almost feel the satisfaction radiating from Morgan Saker. Despite being cleared of treason he felt a gut wrenching disappointment. He turned to his left but the emissary did not look at him. His gaze was downcast but Falco could see the tension in his clasped hands as if he were waiting for something.

'Very well then,' said Prince Ludovico. 'Master Danté remains a free man but he will leave the academy forthwith and return...'

'I will train him.'

The words were spoken softly and Falco saw the emissary raise his head, the faint light of satisfaction in his eyes. But he was not looking at Falco. He was staring at Meredith Saker. Still dressed in the robes of a novice, Meredith walked forward to stand before the court.

'I will act as Falco's guide.'

Bellius looked like someone had just punched him in the stomach. Galen Thrall's pale green eyes had taken on the frosty edge of flint. While to Falco's right the fury of Morgan Saker burned like a tangible fire.

Once again Falco felt that strange sense of detachment, as if he were watching the proceedings from far away. Somehow Meredith Saker had found the courage to defy the most powerful mage in all of Wrath. But more than this... he had defied his father.

He met Falco's disbelieving gaze without wavering and the enormity of what he was doing shone in his deep brown eyes.

'He saved my life,' was all he said and Falco felt a sudden tightening in his throat.

Prince Ludovico looked from father to son, an eyebrow raised and an unreadable expression on his face then he leaned back in his chair and turned to Galen Thrall who paused before responding.

'Of course it is only natural that Master Saker might feel a sense of debt, honourable even.'

Falco was amazed by Thrall's self control, the way he maintained his composure even in the face of such blatant defiance.

'But in this instance I must forbid it.'

'You cannot.'

The sudden harsh voice filled the chamber and Falco looked up to see the shrouded figure at the back of the hall getting to its feet.

'The matter of guiding a battle mage is a free and personal choice. He does not need the tower's permission.'

The figure started down the stairs and Falco could see that it was limping and hunched over one side where its left arm was clearly missing. The shadowed figure was Aurelian Cruz.

Thrall's brow lowered and for the first time there was unmistakeable anger in his eyes.

'You dare to interfere in the affairs of the tower?'

'Not interfering,' said Cruz as he hobbled onto the floor. 'Just reminding people of the laws put in place by greater mages than you.'

The words were intended to sting and Falco saw Thrall make a visible effort to restrain himself.

Aurelian's gaze swept around the room. He paused at Falco and gave the emissary a small nod of acknowledgement. He must once have been a tall man, and handsome too perhaps, but that was before the years and trials of battle had marked him. Now his weathered face was notched and scarred like the wooden posts on the training field. Several of his teeth were broken and the skin on the left-hand side of his face was taut with burns. His hair was long, unruly and grey, and yet there was an indefinable dignity about him as if he had faced the very worst of life and had nothing left to prove.

'So,' he continued. 'If this young novice wants to lead the runt to his doom then there's nothing you can do about it. No matter how it might chaff your balls,' he added with obvious glee.

The chamber echoed with silence and the pupils of Galen Thrall's eyes shrank down to tiny black points. His voice was tight with control when he spoke again.

'This is not a matter of permission, but one of safety. You know better than most that the Rite of Assay is not to be taken lightly. More than one promising young life has been lost in the attempt. Besides... there is no evidence that Master Danté has what it takes to be a battle mage.'

Thrall paused, confident that he had now regained control of the situation.

'Aside from the obvious lack of physical strength,' he went on with a contemptuous glance in Falco's direction, 'one would normally expect to see signs of the inner power, especially by his age, but in his case there is no...'

Whoosh!

Galen Thrall was cut off mid sentence as a fireball suddenly burst from Aurelian's hand and streaked across the floor. The terrified constables leapt aside and Falco barely had time to wince before the ball of flame engulfed him. He felt a blast of searing heat and then it was gone.

'This is an outrage!' exclaimed Bellius as the members of the panel started back from the table, upending chairs and spilling goblets of water in their haste.

208

'Oh relax,' growled Aurelian. 'It was only a little one.'

He limped forward and grabbed hold of Falco, hauling him to his feet. Falco's clothes were smoking, his hair was singed and his skin felt red raw but he appeared otherwise unharmed. The chair that he had been sitting in, however, was heavily burned and scorched.

'No evidence?' said Aurelian, repeating Thrall's words. 'That fireball could have killed a normal man. Well, given him some nasty burns at least,' he added with a guilty look in the emissary's direction. 'This boy survived the breath of a dragon and stood against a demon while your magi were shitting their robes. What more evidence do you need?'

He looked at Falco and gave him a shake as if to make sure he was able to stand before letting go of his shirt with a grunt.

'Yes, he might look like a scrawny urchin but make no mistake. The boy has the soul of a battle mage. Only time will tell if he has the strength to see it through.'

'We could refuse to perform the rite,' said Thrall.

'You could,' said Aurelian, a dangerous glint in his ice blue eyes. 'And what would the people say to that, if you refused the final forging of a weapon that could help to save them.'

Galen Thrall hesitated. Even he was not so arrogant as to think he could ignore the will of the people. Indeed, he had worked for many years to change their perception of the magi. He could not afford to throw it away, not when the mage army was so close to proving itself in battle.

'Very well,' he said at last. 'Master Saker will act as Danté's guide, on the condition that it does not interfere with his training as a mage. I will not see his talent wasted on a fool's sense of duty.'

Aurelian answered with a low growl of consent before turning to take a proper look at Falco who shifted uncomfortably beneath the sharp rake of his gaze. He did not appear to be impressed by what he saw and he shook his head as he looked Falco up and down.

'In the mornings you will train with the other cadets,' said Aurelian, staring hard at Falco. 'In the afternoon you will train with me.'

Falco gave him a simple nod, wondering just what he was letting himself in for.

Aurelian swept a last look around the people in the chamber. Finally he settled on the emissary who met his fierce gaze with a faint smile.

'Hah!' laughed Aurelian with another shake of his head. Then, muttering a string of obscenities, he began to limp out of the chamber. He was approaching an exit tunnel when he stopped and looked up towards one of the high entrances behind Falco.

'Your Majesty,' he said with a courteous bow of his head.

Everyone turned to look. There was nothing to be seen in the high dark archway but it was clear that there had been another witness to the proceedings of Falco's trial.

'First hour of the afternoon, Master Danté,' Aurelian's rough voice echoed from the tunnel. 'I'll see you in the crucible.'

And with that he was gone.

'Meredith!?' said Malaki as he, Bryna and the Klingemann brothers huddled round Falco at one of the dining tables in the mess. 'Blades, but that must have taken some balls.'

'What did his father say?' asked Bryna.

'Nothing,' said Falco. 'But you could tell he was fuming.'

'Who is this Meredith?' asked Alex.

'He's the son of Morgan Saker, the senior mage from our town,' said Bryna.

'And do they hate you, like Snidesson?'

Malaki and Bryna exchanged a look.

'Morgan Saker was there when my father died,' said Falco. 'But I think Meredith is different.'

The Klingemann brothers could tell there was a lot more to the story, but Quirren gave a small shake of his head and for once Alex held his curiosity at bay.

'Well it doesn't matter,' said Bryna. 'It's done. They're going to train you.'

'In the crucible!' said Alex, clearly awed by the thought.

'We'll walk up with you tomorrow,' said Malaki, 'when we break for lunch. We'll be back before the afternoon session starts.'

Falco smiled. He would be glad of the moral support. Across the room he saw Jarek cast a glowering look in his direction. The young noble was surrounded by a huddle of his own and it was clear that they too were now familiar with the details of Falco's trial. The smile did not fall from Falco's face but it did take on a grimmer and more determined cast. It seemed that he too had now earned a place at the academy, but something told him that he might live to regret it.

*

'You underestimated him.' Galen Thrall looked at Morgan Saker with the cold dispassion of a snake.

'I didn't know he was going to have the support of a battle mage,' said Saker, pacing back and forth across the polished floor of the Grand Veneratu's chamber.

'Not Danté,' said Thrall. 'You underestimated your son.'

Morgan Saker gave a snarl of suppressed rage. 'It's the emissary,' he said in a fierce whisper. 'He's behind this. He's infected my son with some juvenile sense of nobility.'

'Well, it is done,' said Thrall. 'But do not berate yourself too much. Aurelian Cruz might be there at the start of Danté's training, but we shall be there at the end.'

Morgan Saker ceased his pacing. 'Yes,' he said with sudden conviction. 'Put me on the Torquery for his Rite of Assay. I will break his mind and leave him weeping in the dirt.'

Thrall gave a slow nod of consent. 'We have many here in the tower that could make him crawl.' His smile was veiled and dark. 'And one in particular that will hollow his mind out like a gourd.'

*

210

The chief physician of the mage tower infirmary leaned over to inspect the injured warden.

'Will he live?'

'It is too early to say,' said the surgeon. 'We have sewn up his face but we could not save his eye.'

The chief physician looked at the ragged line of stitching encircling the right side of the warden's face.

'How did Pacatos reach him? I thought they were given strict instructions not to enter his cell.'

'Brother Pacatos did not reach him,' said the surgeon. 'The warden did this to himself.'

*

In the depths of the Clemoncéan mage tower a tortured soul rocked back and forth in the darkest corner of his cell.

'Vino la mine micul meu soim,' said Brother Pacatos, his eyes glazed over with the torpor of Possession. 'Cei frații și toate deliciile lor sunt în așteptare pentru tine.'

Come to me my little Falcon.
The brothers and all their delights are waiting for you.

35
The Crucible

The second day of training began well for Falco. The cadets had woken to the sound of rain on the terracotta roof tiles, but by the time they made their way up to the training field the rain had stopped and the mountains looked unnaturally clear in the warm light of the rising sun. Once again they were kitted out with their weapons and invited to start the day with a climb to the Pike. This time Falco managed a good half mile at a decent pace. It was only when they reached the steeper winding path that he was forced to let Malaki and the others go on ahead. He was still a long way behind the last of the other cadets but today some of them were still eating their breakfast when he stumbled, exhausted back into the tent.

Malaki clapped him on the back and handed him a bowl of hot porridge as he collapsed onto a bench.

Falco nodded his thanks and waited for his breathing to calm before starting to eat.

'I trust you beat Jarek again,' he said, accepting a mug of steaming tea from Quirren.

'Not today,' said the big Illician, taking a seat beside Falco.

Falco looked up but far from looking disappointed Quirren was actually smiling. Alex and Bryna were smiling too. They all seemed to find the fact that Jarek had beaten them highly amusing.

'He was the first one back,' said Bryna, nodding towards the entrance of the tent where Falco could just about make out the figure of Jarek. He was standing outside and clutching the heavy canvas for support. One of his followers went to speak to him but Jarek just waved him away.

'I think the porridge disagreed with him,' said Bryna and they all laughed.

Jarek might have won the race today but he had needed to push himself to the limit and now his dignity was paying the price. Maybe it was this that made him especially vicious when it came to sparring later in the morning.

After a couple of hours general training the cadets were directed to take a seat on the benches and Lanista Deloix came forward with a bag full of small wooden plaques each inscribed with the name a cadet. The cadets then took it in turns to pick out names to see who would fight each other.

Much to Jarek's delight Falco had been beaten twice, first by a young Clemoncéan sword master and then by a thick-set Acheronian youth by the name of Kleitos.

Bryna's first draw was against a tall Illician youth called Kurt Vogler but Vogler fought half-heartedly and the emissary had been forced to intervene.

'Do you think the Possessed will go easy on Mistress Godwin because she is a woman?'

Vogler shook his head.

'Then do not insult her by doing the same.'

The fight had resumed and within a matter of moments Bryna was flat on her back with a bleeding mouth and Vogler's training sword pressed against her neck.

212

'Much better,' said the emissary.

Clearly mortified by what he had done, Vogler reached down to give Bryna a hand up. Flushed with indignation she ran a tongue over her bloody gum.

'I'll have you next time,' she whispered and Vogler smiled.

Jarek was then drawn against a Thraecian spearman by the name of Arakios. Like many of the cadets, sword and shield was not his chosen discipline so it was easy for Jarek to outmatch him. However, he went much further than just beating him. After evading his every attack Jarek finished Arakios off with a flurry of blows which ended with a loud crack as Jarek's sword struck Arakios on the arm with unnecessary force.

The Lanistas frowned at this 'lack of control' but they said nothing as Arakios was led away to the infirmary with a suspected fracture.

Seemingly oblivious to the instructors' disapproval Jarek resumed his seat. Two more bouts were played out before his name was called once more. Wearing an arrogant smirk he moved to the front of the group, waiting for the name of his opponent to be drawn.

'... and Malaki de Vane.'

The smirk disappeared from Jarek's face as Malaki stepped forward to face him.

Falco suddenly found his heart beating faster. He looked across at Bryna who was biting her lip, her sword hand clenched tight against her thigh. There was an air of heightened expectation among the cadets. They all knew of the enmity that existed between these two young men.

'Guard!' said Lanista Deloix and the bout began.

Jarek took the initiative and launched a series of complex attacks but Malaki evaded them with ease. Twice he outmanoeuvred Jarek so effectively that he could have easily landed a blow and yet he refrained. It was clear to everyone watching that Malaki was in control of the bout and yet, before it had the chance to become embarrassing, he feigned an opening and as Jarek lunged forwards Malaki guided him past with his shield before laying his sword across the back of Jarek's neck.

Alex gave a groan of disappointment as if he had been looking forward to seeing Jarek get the thrashing he deserved. Bryna also looked mildly disappointed while Quirren wore a faint smile of satisfaction.

Falco shook his head despairingly. 'You do remember he beat me unconscious,' he muttered as Malaki sat down between him and Bryna.

'Never take away a man's dignity,' said Malaki, quoting the first part of something his father used to say.

I know,' replied Falco. 'And never allow him to take away yours.'

His tone was that of the long-suffering pupil but he looked upon his friend with a deep sense of pride. One of the things he had always loved about Malaki was that he never abused his strength. Yes, he had won more than his fair share of fights but he had never done more than was necessary to prove his point.

As the training continued Falco found himself growing increasingly nervous as it drew closer to the midday break. He felt ravenously hungry and yet he did not feel as if he could face any food. He was glad the others had offered to accompany him up to the crucible. The memory of Aurelian and his fireball was still painfully fresh and he did not relish the thought of stepping into the lion's den alone. However, just before they were about to break for lunch the lanistas called the cadets together. They separated them into two groups, those who were to be trained just as officers, like Bryna and Alex, and the remaining thirteen like Malaki and Quirren, who were hoping to be accepted as knights.

Then Lanista Magnus addressed the potential officers. 'Today you will take your midday meal in the officer's mess along with officers from the main armies,' he told them. 'They wish to meet you before we decide which units you are going to command.'

'Command! Already?' exclaimed Alex, and Lanista Magnus laughed.

'And how else would you expect to learn?'

Suddenly Alex and Bryna looked every bit as anxious as Falco. They bade the others a nervous goodbye before heading back to the barracks to wash and change.

'I didn't know they started command training so quickly,' said Malaki as he, Falco and Quirren sat down to eat in the tent beside the training field.

'Me neither,' said Quirren. 'Perhaps they need to move things on more quickly now the Possessed are so close.'

Falco said little over lunch. He managed only a few mouthfuls of bread and half an apple before Malaki clapped him on the back.

'Come on,' he said. 'It's past midday and you wouldn't want to keep Aurelian Cruz waiting. The next fireball might not be so little!'

Quirren smiled but Falco looked distinctly queasy as they got to their feet. They still had plenty of time but Malaki was right, he did not want to be late. Together they walked out of the tent. They were just starting towards the slope that led up to the crucible when the emissary stepped in front of them.

'And where are you going?'

'We're just going up to the crucible with Falco,' said Malaki. 'We'll be back before the afternoon session starts.'

The emissary shook his head and nodded towards the training field. Turning round the three youths saw a squadron of heavy cavalry horses approaching. The five leading horses were being ridden by knights. The remaining thirteen were riderless but still they followed the leaders in good order. Each of the five knights wore a different coloured surcoat and carried a tall lance from which a pennant of matching colours flew. Of all the emblems rippling in the wind, Falco recognised just one. Shining white, on a field of black, was the mountain insignia of the Adamanti.

The cavalry came to a halt and one of the leaders urged his mount ahead of the rest. He was, without doubt, the most physically impressive man that Falco had ever seen. Tall and muscular with long dark hair he sat astride a magnificent bay coloured stallion. His brow was heavy and his solid jaw was swathed in a thick black beard. His surcoat was a pale silvery blue and the horse head insignia that lay upon his breast was black. He looked down upon the cadets as if they were children, which beside the likes of him, they were.

'The fraternité of knights calls upon those wishing to attempt the épreuve du force to make their presence known,' he called out, his voice a coarse Clemoncéan growl.

Malaki and Quirren looked at each other before turning to look at Falco. It seemed they would all be facing a daunting challenge this day.

'Can't we just...' began Malaki but the emissary shook his head.

'You go now or not at all.'

'Go on,' said Falco. 'I'll be fine.'

Malaki had turned as white as chalk, the red birthmark on the left side of his face standing out more vividly than ever.

'What if I fail?' he said and Falco was surprised to see real fear in his friend's deep brown eyes.

'You won't,' he said with simple conviction and finally Malaki smiled.

'Try not to get beaten up again while we're away.'

'I'll do my best,' replied Falco as he turned to look at Quirren. 'Good luck.'

'And to you,' said Quirren and still they hovered.

'Go,' said Falco. 'They're waiting.'

Falco watched as Malaki, Quirren and eleven other cadets stepped forward, including the huge Beltonian who they now knew to be called Huthgarl. The cadets swung into the saddles of the thirteen riderless horses and the leaders prepared to depart. They gave a respectful nod to the instructors, and then the man wearing the black surcoat of the Adamanti looked over to the emissary and raised his lance in salute. The huge knight in the blue surcoat also looked in their direction. He did not salute, but he acknowledged the emissary's presence with a bow of his head, a gesture that the emissary duly returned.

'Who is that?' asked Falco as the five knights led the cadets away.

'That is Sébastien Cabal,' said the emissary. 'Lord Commander of the Knights of Wrath.'

Falco felt suddenly fearful for his friend and the emissary could sympathise. *He* had met Sébastien Cabal on the tournament field. It was one of the few times in his life he had been beaten in a fight. Smiling at the memory of the epic contest he turned to look at Falco.

'You should be on your way,' he said as the would-be knights disappeared from view. 'You do not want to keep Master Cruz waiting.'

With a faint smile he turned and walked back to the tent.

Falco gave a sigh of resignation. It seemed there would be no moral support for him today after all.

He would enter the crucible alone.

The sky was clear and the sun was shining as Falco approached the curving rim of the crucible. With his heart thumping in his chest he looked down into the great sunken arena but there was no one to be seen, the crucible was empty.

Falco found himself wondering if Aurelian had forgotten or changed his mind, but it was far more likely that he had just not arrived yet. There were, after all, a few more minutes before the bells of the city sounded the first hour of the afternoon.

Steeling his nerves Falco made his way down the sides of the arena until he stood on the sandy floor and still no one appeared. He walked over to one of the four upright pillars and ran his hand over the glossy black stone. In contrast to the scarred walls of the crucible the five-sided pillar was barely marked. There was just a scattering of chips and marks upon its smooth dark surface.

Looking around, Falco felt a reassuring sense of enclosure as the walls of the crucible rose up around him, but then his eyes fell upon the dark archway at the far end of the arena and any feeling of security evaporated. The gaping portal seemed to pull at him and Falco found himself walking towards it. He stopped maybe ten yards short of the threshold and his mind was suddenly filled with whispers as if the passage led to all the terrors he had dreamed of as a child. He felt the urge to back away, to run, but Falco had learned long ago that you cannot escape your dreams. Nightmares are in you, part of you, always waiting for the moment when you close your eyes to sleep.

'Think of nice things,' Fossetta used to say. But thinking of nice things never worked and so with a child's reasoning Falco had done the opposite. He would imagine the worst of all his nightmares and then he would think of ways to defeat them. Only with the image of a shining sword held tight within his mind could he close his eyes to face the terrors of the night. And so Falco did not back away. His green eyes burned and his lip curled in something approaching a snarl. The nightmares had not claimed him as a child and they would not claim him now.

'Not many people have the courage to stand where you stand now.'

Falco started at the sudden voice. He turned to see Aurelian Cruz standing behind him, a fire-blackened sword hanging from a belt around his waist. The old battle mage frowned, looking at him with a wary expression in his eyes. With his single hand he motioned for Falco to come away as if he were a potential suicide standing on the edge of a precipice.

With one last look into the darkness Falco turned away from the archway.

'What is that place?' he asked. 'Where does it lead?'

Aurelian did not answer at first. He drew Falco a short distance away as if even he felt uncomfortable being too close to the tunnel.

'The people of Clemoncé call it L'obscurité, or 'The Darkness', others call it the Labyrinth or the Oubliette. Either way it leads to your fate.' He led Falco to the north side of the crucible where a sword and shield had been laid out and the sun was shining on the lowest tier of steps. 'That's where you will attempt the Rite of Assay.'

Falco looked back at the dark tunnel entrance. Despite his earlier resolve the thought of actually stepping into that impenetrable darkness sent a shiver of fear down his spine.

'So, you're Aquila's boy,' said Aurelian with an appraising eye.

Falco nodded.

'Heaven help us!' muttered the maimed old battle mage, shaking his head and laughing softly.

Falco felt a prickle of embarrassment.

'Oh, don't worry,' said Aurelian when he saw the indignation on Falco's face. 'You've your father's height, and something of his looks.' With a large calloused hand he grabbed Falco's chin and forced him to stand up straight. He nodded as if he approved of Falco's more upright posture. 'Besides, the Chevalier has spoken for you and that's good enough for me.'

Falco did not know what to say. Here was yet another person who seemed to have known his father.

216

'But we're gonna to have to build him up a bit, eh Dwim?' said Aurelian, glancing up to Falco's right.

Following his gaze Falco saw a man sitting half way up the side of the arena, and stretched out on the broad steps beside him was a dragon, its scales a deep iridescent blue. Falco recognised the man as the other 'Crofter' they had seen the other day. And after a moment he recalled the name of Aurelian's dragon, Dwimervane.

The dragon looked at Falco with a kind of guarded curiosity and Falco shifted under its scrutiny but he did not look away.

'So, what can you do?'

Falco looked at Aurelian blankly. He had no idea what he was talking about.

'What can you do?' repeated Aurelian. 'Can you generate heat or fire, move stuff or break things without touching them?'

Falco shook his head, still none the wiser.

'But you have defensive skills?' insisted Aurelian. 'You couldn't have survived that fireball yesterday without being able to defend yourself.'

Again Falco shook his head.

'Balls of a hog!' cursed Aurelian. 'You mean you can cast a protection like that without even realising?'

Falco just shrugged.

'Stand over there,' said Aurelian bad-temperedly.

Not sure what he had done wrong, Falco did as he was told, standing about ten feet away from the annoyed battle mage. Aurelian picked up a handful of gritty sand then without warning he flung it hard at Falco. Falco closed his eyes as the sharp pieces of grit stung his face and hands.

'Defend yourself,' snapped Aurelian, unleashing another fistful of grit.

Raising his hands Falco winced and ducked as Aurelian pelted him again and again then without warning... Whoosh! Instead of grit a fireball streaked towards Falco before exploding around him. Once again Falco felt a burst of intense heat and then it was gone, replaced by the acrid smell of burning hair and scorched clothes.

'Hah!' cried Aurelian as if the whole thing was a bad joke. 'Instinct! Nothing more.' He looked away from Falco, scanning the sides of the crucible as if he were looking for something. 'Now, where the hell is that mage? He's got a cart load of work to do and he's already late!'

'Not late,' said a voice. 'Just observing.'

They all looked up as Meredith Saker suddenly appeared, descending the steps towards them. He gave Falco a nod of acknowledgement before bowing to the two battle mages

'Master Cruz. Master Dusaule.'

'*Dusaule*,' thought Falco, looking at the man sitting beside the dragon. So that was the other Crofter's name. He was tall and broad shouldered with shoulder length brown hair. He acknowledged Meredith's bow with a slow dip of his head, the expression in his eyes wary and suspicious.

Meredith then bowed to the dragon, which responded by tilting its head as if it were surprised to receive such courtesy from one of the magi.

217

'Just 'observing', eh?' said Aurelian with a meaningful look in Dusaule's direction. 'The Chevalier said you had a gift for concealment.'

Meredith said nothing. He was trying to maintain a semblance of composure, not easy when you were in the company of two battle mages and a dragon.

'So maybe you can tell me why this little toe rag can only cast a protection when he thinks his life is in danger.'

Meredith glanced at Falco who seemed completely oblivious to Aurelian's insulting term.

'Instinct, as you say,' said Meredith. 'Falco has never learned to channel his ability. It is only on a subconscious level that any powers have made their presence known.'

Meredith had spent most of the night reading up on the training of a battle mage. It appeared the term 'guide' was quite appropriate. The mage's role was not so much to teach the would-be battle mage, but rather to help them recognise the abilities that they already possessed. Meredith had been watching closely while Aurelian pelted Falco with small stones, but more than this, he had been observing Falco's mind. At first all he had sensed was surprise, pain and mounting irritation but the moment Aurelian summoned his fireball something had stirred in Falco's mind, a dormant energy like a beast quickly roused from slumber. The force had flared to life, suffusing Falco's body as the fireball engulfed him but it was gone the moment the flames disappeared.

'I could cast a basic protection by the age of seven,' said Aurelian. 'By nine I could shatter stones and splinter wood.'

'But Falco has been ill since childhood,' said Meredith. 'He has always perceived himself as weak.' He glanced across at Falco, who conceded the truth of Meredith's words with a shrug. 'The casting of any force requires self-belief, unless it is done by instinct.'

Slowly Aurelian nodded as if he were beginning to understand.

'But why only protection?' he asked.

'Conjuration or fortification would require intent,' replied Meredith.

'What are you talking about?' interrupted Falco, who had never heard these terms.

They all looked at him, realising just how little he knew about the magical arts and the powers of a battle mage.

'These are magi terms,' said Meredith. 'Categories for the different ways that magical force is manifested.' He looked at Falco with a sudden intensity.

Communication

Falco flinched as the word echoed in his mind. He did not 'hear it' exactly. It was more like the thought of the word sounding in his mind.

'A fireball would fall under the category of conjuration,' continued Meredith in a normal voice. 'But it also refers to any tangible force or energy that is created external to the caster. Alteration is the affecting of objects without any visible contact.'

Falco nodded, thinking of the various attacks that Darius had performed against the dragon.

'Fortification refers to anything that strengthens or fortifies the body. A battle mage might use it to resist a blow or absorb the impact when jumping from a height. Resolve is used to resist fear and any assault on the mind.'

Aurelian gave a growl of impatience.

'A battle mage doesn't think in these terms,' he said. 'In a way, everything we do is instinctive. It's just that we can do it at will.' He swung his fist and an arc of bluish energy shot across the crucible before cutting a deep gash in a block of stone on the far wall of the arena. 'If you're to become a battle mage you must learn to do all these things with nothing more than a thought. It takes effort, and doing too much will leave you weak with exhaustion, but there's no time for categories and rules when you're fighting the Possessed.'

He sounded angry and, wandering over to the nearby step, he picked up the sword and shield.

'So, how are you going to help him?' he demanded of Meredith as he handed Falco the sword and shield. 'How are you going to take instinct and transform it into a deliberate act of will? How are you going to save him from certain death?'

With a distinct sense of apprehension Falco gripped the sword and settled the shield on his arm while Meredith shot him an anxious look. He had not expected his 'guidance' to be put to the test so quickly.

'There was a moment,' he said. 'When you summoned the fireball, a flash in Falco's mind. I would get him to focus on that.'

Aurelian seemed unimpressed as he drew his own sword. The blade was notched and discoloured by fire but still it shone with a lethal edge.

'Guard,' said the old battle mage in a voice that was suddenly cold and hard.

Falco felt a sudden rush of nervous energy. Even one-handed, hunched and limping Aurelian made an intimidating opponent. Meredith took a few steps out of harm's way; not at all sure what Aurelian was expecting him to do. Suddenly Aurelian surged forward with an attack that would have killed Falco if he had not blocked it with his shield. Falco staggered under the force of it and struggled to keep his feet.

'What are you going to do, mage?' snarled Aurelian driving Falco back with a series of vicious attacks.

Falco was literally fighting for his life and Meredith was paralysed by a desperate sense of responsibility.

'He's going to die, mage,' gasped Aurelian. 'The Possessed are going tear him apart and rape his soul.' With a savage charge Aurelian knocked Falco over, stamped on his shield arm and kicked the sword from his numb fingers. 'Now what the hell are you going to do?'

His sword came down in a killing stroke and Meredith was certain that Falco was dead. But at the last moment some invisible force knocked the sword from Aurelian's grasp and sent it spinning through the air. It landed with a skittering clang some twenty feet away and a tense silence filled the arena.

Dusaule was on his feet, staring down into the arena. The quiet battle mage seemed unconcerned by the fact that he had just saved Falco's life. Meredith was trembling with shock. Falco was cowering on the floor and Aurelian Cruz was panting with rage. He stepped away from Falco and walked up to Meredith until his face was just inches from the apprentice mage.

'The Rite of Assay is not some country challenge on tournament day,' he hissed. 'It is the attempt to break a man in the hope that he will become unbreakable.'

Meredith tried to back away but Aurelian grabbed his robes.

'The magi skirt the very realms of hell to test the men and women who will stand against the demons of the Possessed. And you can rest assured that Thrall and your father will not spare the rod in the trial of Master Danté. So I will ask you one more time... What are you going to do to prepare him?'

'I don't know,' said Meredith in a quiet voice.

For a moment Aurelian maintained his grip but then his face broke into a craggy smile.

'Finally, a touch of humility,' he said, letting go of Meredith's robes. 'Maybe there's hope for you boys yet.' He turned away and gave a nod of thanks to Dusaule who sat back down beside Dwimervane. He limped over to pick up his sword and wiped off the dust before sliding it back into its scabbard.

Still shaking, Meredith walked over to where Falco was getting to his feet. In age the two of them were now counted as men but here, in the crucible, they stood together like frightened boys.

Aurelian walked towards the steps where Dusaule and Dwimervane had risen from their seats.

'Same time tomorrow,' he said as he walked past Falco and Meredith. 'And maybe next time you'll both be better prepared.' With these 'encouraging' words he climbed out of the arena, the dragon and Dusaule following in his wake.

Falco and Meredith watched until they disappeared over the lip. They looked at each other warily as if they finally realised what they had let themselves in for.

'You don't have to...' began Falco but Meredith raised his hand to cut him off.

'That prickling sensation you felt when he summoned the fireball.'

'That's nothing,' said Falco. 'Just a trill of nerves. I feel something similar with music and stories that move me. Goose bumps, nothing more.'

'No,' said Meredith with certainty. 'That flash. That surge of energy. That's where we shall begin.'

Falco did not know what else to say as, with a bow, Meredith took his leave and began to climb out of the crucible in the direction of the mage tower. Falco was left feeling dazed by everything that had just happened. His arms felt bruised from blocking Aurelian's blows and his legs felt heavy as clay. He took a last look around the great arena then slowly he too climbed the deep steps and started down the hill towards the academy. It was still early and he wondered if he should make his way back to the training field but he was exhausted and he needed to think about what Meredith had said.

That flash. That surge of energy. That's where we shall begin.

Falco knew the sensation Meredith was talking about, that tingling surge that started behind his eyes and swept down through his body, the little death that raised the hairs on his arms and left him feeling cleansed.

He paused on the slopes above the Academy of War. He closed his eyes and tensed his brow as he summoned the feeling in his mind.

Could this really be the beginnings of power?

He opened his eyes and looked at his tingling hands as if seeing them for the first time. Yes, he thought... it could.

36
In All Creation

As the days went on, Falco began to feel that a place at the Academy of War was not so much a prize as an extremely painful punishment. He continued to lose every sparring match in which he was drawn and the physical endurance sessions, which the instructors referred to as 'conditioning', left him feeling shaky and nauseous. And that was before he climbed up to the crucible where Aurelian would thrash him around the arena until he was numb with exhaustion and aching from head to foot. But he *was* making progress. He might not realise it but he was slowly closing the gap between himself and the other cadets. He was also beginning to recognise the sensations in his mind that seemed so obvious to Meredith.

'There!' said Meredith, one afternoon in the crucible, as Falco was attempting to 'resist' the point of the spear that Aurelian was pressing into his chest. 'Now focus on the point of the spear and try to push it away.'

It was a cold and gloomy afternoon with a faint speckle of snow on the air. They had been training for about two hours when Meredith suggested they see if Falco was able to 'fortify' his flesh against the steady pressure of a single point.

'Might be easier than trying to fend off a thousand tiny bits of gravel,' he said.

Aurelian seemed unconvinced but he picked up the spear all the same. He had brought it along to see if Falco was able to deflect it when thrown at him but Meredith feared that he was not ready for such a risky test of his ability. So now Aurelian stood with the spear couched under his arm and the point pressed against Falco's chest.

Eyes closed and concentrating hard, Falco was certain the sharp point was about to sink into his flesh as he felt the pressure from the spear increase. He did not see Aurelian clench his jaw and lean against the spear, his booted feet sliding a little on the gritty floor.

Meredith frowned in appreciation as he saw Falco's power beginning to manifest itself.

'Ah!' gasped Falco, twisting away as he gave up on the attempt and felt the spear cut through his shirt and score the skin of his shoulder. 'It's no good. I just can't do it.'

Aurelian gave a curse as he stumbled forward before catching his balance.

Stepping out of his way Falco put a hand to his bleeding shoulder and looked with confusion at the expression of satisfaction on Meredith's face. Aurelian on the other hand glared at Falco as if he were quite the most exasperating student he had ever had the misfortune to teach.

'Have a look at that shoulder would you, Nicolas,' he said to Dusaule as he made his way back to the steps. 'I'd do it myself but I might be tempted to throttle him.' Shaking his head in disbelief he rubbed the stump of his left arm as if the cold bothered it. 'How he's managed to survive so long is a bloody miracle!'

Dusaule wore a faint smile as he rose from his feet and started smoothly down the steps.

Confused by Aurelian's irritation Falco allowed himself to be led over to the side where Dusaule drew back his shirt and wiped the cut with a clean cloth before laying his hand over the wound. Falco winced then sighed as a sharp tingling sensation ran along the cut before suffusing his shoulder with a deep sense of warmth. The pain faded away and he was reminded of the many times that Simeon had used his own healing powers to tend his various ails. When Dusaule removed his hand the cut had stopped bleeding and the minor wound looked as if it had already begin to heal.

'Thank you,' said Falco, cautiously probing his shoulder.

Dusaule bowed his head and gave Aurelian a small nod before returning to his seat a few steps up the side of the arena. Aurelian's mood however, did not seem to have improved. He sat there mumbling until Dwimervane limped down the steps to sit beside him.

'I've never known someone so ignorant of their potential,' said Aurelian quietly as if the two of them were alone.

The dragon turned its horned head to look at him and Aurelian shifted as if he felt suddenly guilty.

'I know, I know. It's not his fault,' he conceded at last. 'Just damn frustrating that's all.'

Dwimervane briefly rested her head against his shoulder, careful not to let the foot-long curving horns snag on his clothing. Then, somewhat stiffly, she started down the steps, the leading edge of her right wing clipping Aurelian round the back of the head as she passed. He gave a soft curse and Dusaule smiled. The slight knock did not appear to be accidental.

Falco watched as the dragon walked towards him, its blue scales shimmering darkly in the cold grey light. For some reason it seemed unable to stand up to its full height and it approached with a hunched and limping gait, not unlike Aurelian himself. Its wings were deformed and withered, shrunken by burns and thick skeins of scar tissue. The scales on the right side of its body appeared melted and fused and Falco suspected that it was this that prevented the dragon from standing up straight. Even so, Dwimervane stood more than four feet at the shoulder and her great blue head rose well above Falco's own.

She looked down on him with a kind of curious intensity as if she were trying to figure out what kind of creature he was. Her flame yellow eyes shifted to the burns on Falco's neck and raising a foreleg she drew back the neck of his shirt with a sharp adamantine claw. After a brief appraisal her gaze moved back to his face and Falco could read the unspoken question in her eyes.

Did a dragon really do this?

Falco lowered his gaze, his mind filled with guilt. He knew the truth would only bring the dragon pain.

After a moment however, Dwimervane lowered her head and, just as he had with the yellow dragon in Toulwar, Falco pressed his forehead against hers. He closed his eyes and felt again that deep sense of trust, marred only by questions to which he had no answers.

Slowly Dwimervane removed her head and with a last searching look at Falco she approached Meredith who took several steps back as the great beast came closer. Finally he stood his ground and allowed the dragon to observe him,

223

her gaze seeming to delve deep inside his soul. Then once more Dwimervane bowed her head.

Out of the corner of his eye Falco saw Aurelian give Dusaule a sideways glance. It was clear they had never seen her behave this way towards one of the magi before.

'Press your forehead against hers,' said Falco. 'It's how they greet each other.'

He had no idea how he knew this but there was no doubt in his mind that it was true.

Clearly unnerved, Meredith slowly bowed his head until the cool skin of his forehead made contact with the warm scales of the dragon. Falco could see the tension in his body but then he let out a long sigh and relaxed. They came apart and Falco was not surprised to see tears in Meredith's eyes. He seemed embarrassed but Falco gave him a nod of reassurance. He knew the overwhelming sensation of being close to a dragon for the first time.

'Right,' said Aurelian, getting to his feet. 'Now that you've been properly introduced let's talk a bit about dragons.' He limped over and placed a hand on Dwimervane's back. 'You ever met a dragon before? Except for the one at the summoning,' he added quickly.

Meredith shook his head.

'I met Dominic Ginola's dragon in Toulwar,' said Falco.

'And what did you make of her?'

'Beautiful,' said Falco and finally Aurelian smiled.

'Yes,' he said. 'She is.'

Dwimervane looked at each of them in turn, perfectly content to be the focus of their attention.

'Are they all female?' asked Meredith.

'No,' said Aurelian. 'Many are but it makes no difference, male or female, they all fight like devils.'

Once again Falco was entranced. He did not see Dwimervane's injuries and disfigurement. All he saw was her beauty. From the sinuous line of her neck to the lethal spear point at the tip of her tale, from the armoured plates on her chest and shoulders to the perfect tiny scales around her eyes. Her talons were as long as his fingers and her white teeth shone with the lustre of polished metal.

'Is it true their scales are stronger than steel?' he asked.

'Yes,' said Aurelian. 'But they also seem to have some form of fortification. It's very hard to damage a dragon in its prime but if they become exhausted or disheartened they seem more susceptible to injury. It's okay, you can touch her,' he added when he saw Falco reach out then stop.

Falco extended his hand to touch the scales on Dwimervane's shoulder. They felt hard and warm like some kind of glassy metal that has been heated in a fire. There was a slight ridge down the centre of each scale and the edges were almost sharp. As he pressed against her he felt the scales move beneath his hand.

'Here,' said Aurelian. 'Climb onto her. Don't worry she won't bite,' he added with a laugh when Falco hesitated.

Following Aurelian's instructions Falco moved to stand at Dwimervane's shoulder.

'Just swing your leg over as if you were mounting a horse.'

'I thought you used saddles,' said Meredith, still standing a little way back.

'We do,' said Aurelian. 'Although it's more of a riding harness. But you can ride a dragon without one. Look...'

As Falco settled himself onto Dwimervane's back he felt her scales move as if they were moulding themselves to his shape. But more than this they also seemed to grip him slightly as if she were actually holding onto him.

'Trust me,' said Aurelian. 'When you drop into an attack dive for the first time that feeling of being held will be the only thing stopping you from filling your pants.'

'So why do you use a harness?' asked Meredith.

'That grippy thing doesn't work so well on armour,' said Aurelian.

Dwimervane looked round at Falco as if to make sure he was sitting securely then she reared up on her hind legs and flapped her misshapen wings.

Falco felt his heart quicken. The feeling of power beneath him was far greater than any horse he had ever ridden, greater indeed than *anything* he had known before, although something nagged at his memory, a kind of déjà vu suggesting that this had happened before. But the feeling vanished as Dwimervane reached her fullest height and let out a roar that seemed to contradict her damaged form. Then from her jaws a great gout of fire burst forth. It slammed into the stone steps as the sound of her roar echoed around the crucible.

Meredith flinched and staggered back, hands raised against the ferocity of the display but Aurelian laughed.

'She misses the battle field,' he said with obvious pride. He stepped in front of Dwimervane and took her head against his shoulder. 'Showing off, eh old girl?'

Dwimervane gave him a nudge that made him stagger back but he laughed all the more.

'How can they do it?' asked Meredith, slowly mastering his shock. Dwimervane's display had reminded him too keenly of the black dragon in the Castle of the Winds. 'How can they stand in the face of a demon when all other animals flee in terror?'

Aurelian looked at him while Falco climbed down off Dwimervane's back.

'It all comes down to the soul,' said Aurelian in answer to Meredith's question.

He looked up at Dusaule, glanced at Dwimervane then drew his sword before moving to stand before Falco and Meredith.

'In all creation there are but three things that contain a soul... a human, a dragon and the sword of a battle mage.'

He held the blade out level before them.

'It is the strength of a soul that allows it to stand in the presence of evil, a soul forged in fire or tempered by the nightmares of a child. No one knows how dragons are able to resist the fear, but something has prepared them to face the demons of hell, and you can rest assured that it would not have been easy.'

Again he looked at Dwimervane and the dragon returned his gaze as if she understood the words he spoke.

'They are our brothers and our sisters, our salvation and our hope. Without them we are lost.'

Falco heard the truth, and the love, and the sadness in Aurelian's words. He glanced up to find Dusaule staring down at him, the man's handsome face made gaunt by guilt and grief.

'*Our salvation and our hope*,' thought Falco, looking at Dusaule. '*And you were forced to kill one.*'

'But you'll learn about all this,' said Aurelian, blinking as if to clear a certain blurriness from his eyes. 'That's if you manage to learn anything at all,' he added with something of his earlier annoyance.

'Who was it that made your sword?' asked Meredith.

In his reading up on the subject he had learned that the sword of a battle mage is made by a skilled weapon smith but the heat is provided, not by a forge, but by the battle mage himself.

'Same person who's made just about every battle mage sword for the last thirty years,' said Aurelian. 'Antonio Missaglias. Mind you he was little more than an apprentice when he made this.'

He raised his sword again so that the boys could have a closer look. The metal displayed a beautiful pattern, a rippling effect running down the length of the blade. Such patterns were known as the 'serpent in the sword' and were extremely difficult effect to achieve, even for a normal blade.

'He always was a precocious bastard, genius some say, which is just as well. My conjuring has always been a little chaotic to say the least. It's a wonder the metal didn't just explode.'

'I don't understand,' said Falco.

'A battle mage uses their power to heat the blade beyond what a normal forge could achieve,' said Meredith. 'But they must also control the heat and be careful to contain it, otherwise they could destroy the sword completely. It's the only way to produce a blade that can survive the forces that will be channelled through it. A normal blade would be too easily destroyed.'

Falco nodded.

'It helped that we'd known each other since we were little brats like you,' he said. 'Helped him read the metal and match the personality of the sword to the vagaries of my power.'

Falco was intrigued. Aurelian talked about the sword as if it were a living thing. He reached out to touch it and a high resonant note sounded in his mind as if the sword were somehow singing. He drew back his hand in surprise.

'Pah!' exclaimed Aurelian. 'Even my sword knows you're a battle mage.' He gave Falco a good natured shove. 'Come on,' he said. 'Let's work a bit on your footwork before we finish.'

Meredith returned to the lowest step at the side of the arena to watch. Falco had come a long way from being the sickly servant that people had known in Caer Dour. And while he might not yet realise it himself, Meredith could feel the power rising inside of him. But more than this, he thought, as he watched the two of them battle back and forth, Falco was beginning to look like a warrior.

As the two combatants traded blows Meredith's gaze was drawn to one side where Dwimervane was watching the training with a critical eye. He had never experienced anything like 'meeting' a dragon before. It was overwhelming and humbling, so different to the blinding fear he had felt in the presence of the black dragon.

His studies in the tower had started well and he had also found time to learn more about the training of a battle mage. Tonight however, when the Academy of War was sleeping, he would move through to the fifth chamber of the repository where the archives on dragonkind were kept. Somewhere among them, there must surely be an answer as to why black dragons were mad.

37

Dalwhinnies, Full Bonnet &
The Épreuve du Force

Meredith was not the only one to see a difference in Falco. The other cadets were beginning to notice it too. After thirty days of training, Falco almost caught the last of his fellow cadets on the run up to the Pike. The heavy-set Acheronian youth was not the nimblest of figures and was often near the back of the group but when he saw Falco closing on the final sprint to the tent he put on a desperate burst of speed to avoid being beaten. Falco had spent the rest of breakfast retching on an empty stomach, but the expressions on the faces of the other cadets said it all.

The scrawny Valentian could no longer be dismissed.

He was still the weakest of the group and he had more bruises and cuts than the rest of them put together but nothing seemed to deter him. Despite the constant beatings that he received on the training field he seemed to stand a little taller every day. The grip on his wooden sword was now decidedly strong and he took a stance, not like someone who was learning how to fight, but like someone who was remembering that they could.

It was now nearly five weeks since they had begun their training and the cadets began to speculate on when the trainee knights would return.

'The épreuve du force normally lasts for four weeks,' said Alex as they rose from their beds one morning. 'They should be back any time now.'

Alex and Bryna were particularly anxious for their return. Over the weeks they had only caught fleeting glimpses of the would-be knights, running in the mountains or performing endurance exercises on a higher field when the rest of the cadets were heading down to the barracks for dinner. One of the cooks said he had seen them a few miles down the coast wrestling a cart load of heavy rocks across a stretch of muddy sand.

'Cold, wet and completely knackered,' was the way he described them.

Their most recent glimpse had come on an evening four nights ago when the trainee knights thundered towards the stables on horses that looked fit to drop. The trainees looked just as tired but they had been given no time to rest. The stable hands had fresh horses standing ready for each of them and with no more time than it took them to transfer their tack from one horse to another they were off, riding back into the gathering gloom of the night. Falco caught only a quick glimpse of Malaki but he could see that his left forearm was bandaged and bleeding.

So yes, they were worried about their friends but that was not the only thing weighing on the minds of Alex and Bryna as they woke to another day of training. The initial assessment of the cadets was finally over and today the officers-in-training would learn which military units they would be given to command. Some would be regular units getting ready to return to the front while others would be untrained units from the Queen's Irregulars stationed here in Wrath.

'I'm hoping for a company of infantry,' said Alex, pulling on his boots.

Falco gave a groan as he too reached for his boots.

'Are you all right?' asked Bryna.

'I'm fine,' said Falco. He felt as if someone had beaten him up while he was sleeping but he would feel better once he got moving. 'How about you Bryna? What are you hoping for?'

'I don't mind,' said Bryna, 'so long as they're not beginners.'

'Why's that?' asked Alex.

'You should see what we have to teach them,' replied Bryna as they made their way out of the barracks and up towards the training field. 'It's not just range finding and volley fire. There's a technique they call suivez. It means follow,' she added when she saw the blank look on their faces. 'They have suivez cinq and suivez dix - follow five and follow ten. They use it against heavier targets that get too close.'

Falco and Alex looked none the wiser.

'Basically,' said Bryna. 'You work in groups of five or ten, each with a designated 'point'. The idea is that the point chooses a target and the rest of the group then have to hit it at the same time.'

'Sounds like a recipe for disaster,' said Alex.

'It is,' replied Bryna. 'We tried it the other day and I nearly shot Allyster's ear off.'

Falco and Alex laughed.

'I'm not joking!' said Bryna desperately. 'There was blood and everything!'

They walked into the tent beside the training field which was buzzing with a heightened sense of anticipation. A small group of cadets were gathered round Jarek at the far end of the arming tables.

'I don't envy the unit that he gets to command,' muttered Alex as they prepared for the daily run up to the Pike. 'He doesn't listen to a word that anyone else says.'

Falco glanced across at Jarek who appeared to be in a falsely jubilant mood. It seemed that he too was nervous.

The eastern sky was just beginning to lighten as they set out for the Pike but Falco decided not to push it too hard this morning. He wanted to keep something in reserve for sparring. He was determined that today he would at least land a hit. But even taking it easy, the rest of the cadets were only half way through their breakfast as he got back to the tent. Sitting with Bryna and Alex, he ate his fill of bread, bacon and eggs before they made their way out of the tent to sit on the benches.

'Today, at the midday break we'll be announcing the commissions,' said the emissary. 'Until then,' he added, raising his voice to be heard above the murmur of excitement, 'we're going to try something different.'

On the nearby tables the assistants were laying out sets of heavily padded leather armour.

'We're going to try full speed, full contact sparring.'

The cadets looked warily round at each other. The more confident ones seemed excited by the challenge while Falco resigned himself to another painful morning of punishment. The emissary picked up a set of shoulder guards and a helmet. It was similar to the armour they used for normal sparring only more extensive and more heavily padded.

'The leather has been boiled to make it harder,' said the emissary, rapping his knuckles on the rigid surface. 'Also, the face of the helm is covered with this stiff mesh so that not even the point of a sword can get through.'

He turned it round so that the cadets could see the fine dark mesh on the front of the helm then he motioned for one of the cadets to come forward and the assistants kitted him out from head to foot in the bulky leather armour.

'In most combat schools this is simply known as heavy training armour,' continued the emissary. 'But here at the academy we refer to it as 'the full bonnet'.'

The cadets laughed and the young man at the front swung his arms, illustrating the fact that he could still move without restriction.

'We'll be using wooden swords for this exercise,' said the emissary. 'And don't worry, the armour is well capable of protecting you.' He illustrated the point by whacking the armoured cadet on the arm, seemingly without causing any harm.

Each of the cadets was fitted with a suit of armour and they began to warm up, getting used to the way the armour affected their movements. Even though it was still cold Falco found that he was soon sweating. He removed his gauntlets and helmet as the first pairing was drawn in the usual way by picking names out of a sack.

It was thrilling to watch these full speed bouts where nothing was held back. They were quite different from the normal sparring of controlled engagement. The watching cadets winced as the two current fighters beat seven bells out of each other. Even with the protection of the full bonnet there were still a number of nasty bruises and bleeding noses as the sweaty combatants removed their helmets to retake their seats.

Falco found his heart beating faster. The names in the sack were getting fewer and still his name had not been called. Bryna sat beside him, her rich auburn hair matted to her sweaty face and the fierce light of competition in her eyes. She had just done herself proud against a much larger opponent.

'Falco Danté,' said Lanista Deloix, holding up the small plaque of wood bearing Falco's name. 'And Jarek Snidesson.'

A distinct muttering rose up from the cadets. This was the first time these two had been drawn against each other. Many of them laughed and several patted Jarek on his armoured shoulder as he donned his helmet and made his way to the front of the group.

'Kick his ass,' whispered Alex as Falco settled the padded helmet onto his head. He pulled on his gauntlets, armed his shield and picked up the weighted wooden training sword.

Bryna gave Falco a smile and a determined nod. As he walked out to face Jarek she was suddenly struck by how tall he appeared. Gone was the stoop shouldered weakling from Caer Dour, here was a cadet from the Academy of War.

If Falco was simply hoping to score a hit, it was immediately clear to everyone that Jarek saw this as a grudge match. As soon as the instructors gave

230

the command to fight he surged forward with a shield charge that sent Falco reeling backwards. He followed it up with a series of full force blows aimed at Falco's head and neck. Falco managed to block them all, and even tried for an attack on Jarek's leading leg, before Jarek caught him with a low attack that slammed into the back of his thigh. Falco cursed himself for letting Jarek get under his guard and shook his leg to ease the smarting pain. The full bonnet might protect against injury but a blow like that was still sore.

Jarek drew back as the instructors called out the hit and the two of them came back to guard.

The bouts were decided on the best of five hits and Jarek seemed determined to end it quickly. However, when he came in hard with his next attack Falco was ready for him. He sidestepped smoothly and Jarek was forced to twist in a most ungainly way to avoid Falco scoring a hit on his back. He spun round with a vicious backhanded blow that glanced off the rim of Falco's shield and missed his head by a whisker.

'Ooooh!' cried the watching cadets as Jarek regained his balance.

Falco then launched a series of his own attacks but Jarek blocked them with ease before dropping into a low crouch and lunging beneath Falco's shield.

'Hit!' cried Lanista Magnus as the hard thrust slid off Falco's breastplate and dug into the bone of his hip. Ignoring the pain he dropped into a defensive stance.

On the command Jarek tried a low feint before attacking over the top of Falco's shield. However, instead of moving away Falco stepped in close, engaged Jarek's blade with an overhand parry and stabbed down into his chest.

'Hit!' cried Lanista Magnus.

The watching cadets gave a collective gasp of surprise and Alex erupted with an explosive, 'Yes!'

Even though his face was covered, everyone could see that Jarek was fuming. His head had dropped and his shoulders were hunched, not in a submissive way, but in a way that spoke of vengeance.

On the command to fight he came in fast. Falco lifted a leg to avoid a low blow then switched his shield from right to left to block two rapid attacks. He read Jarek's first feint and his second and gave ground before two more vicious swipes. Falco now seemed able to anticipate his attacks and Jarek was getting more and more frustrated.

Once again he turned Jarek and almost scored a hit but then Jarek spun round wildly. Falco ducked beneath the sword but the rim of Jarek's shield slammed into the side of his head, knocking his helmet clean off. The attack sent Falco to his knees. From the corner of his eye he saw Lanista Magnus starting forward, arms raised to stop the fight, but he was too late. Jarek's sword was already swinging towards Falco's unprotected head and it was clear to everyone that his skull was about to be split in two. There was no time for him to raise his sword, no time to block the attack with his shield. But that did not mean that there was no time to stop it.

Faster than a man can blink Falco focussed the energy in his mind. There was a noise like a sudden crack of thunder and Jarek's sword exploded into a cloud of wooden fragments. They drifted around Falco's head and shoulders while Jarek staggered back in shock. Almost in a panic he ripped off his own helmet, staring down at Falco as if he were some kind of monster. But he was not a monster. He was a battle mage and his power was finally coming to life.

The cadets looked on aghast and even the instructors seemed shocked.

Only the emissary seemed unaffected as he stepped between Falco and Jarek. He put a hand on Jarek's arm and looked into his face to make sure he was unhurt but Jarek shook off his hand and stumbled away.

The emissary turned to look down at Falco.

'It's all right,' he said, reaching out a hand to help him up. 'No one's been hurt. Everything is all right.'

Falco was visibly shaking as he slowly got to his feet. There was disbelief and fear in his bright green eyes.

'I only stopped it,' he said. 'I only meant to stop it.'

'And you did,' said the emissary. He could see the tears forming in Falco's eyes and he had a sudden intuition as to what was troubling him.

'I won't become like my father,' said Falco in a low voice. 'I won't become a killer.'

The emissary put a hand on his shoulder.

'I know you won't,' he said, even though he was in no position to offer such assurance.

Falco let out a shuddering breath as Bryna and Alex appeared beside him.

'Is he all right?'

'He's fine,' said the emissary giving Falco a reassuring smile. 'Aurelian's been waiting for something like this to happen. Come on,' he said, leading them towards the tent. 'we'll get something to eat and then it'll be time to announce the commissions.'

Bryna and Alex escorted Falco into the tent while the emissary went to speak with the instructors. They sat him down on a bench and helped him out of the stiff leather armour.

'Thanks,' said Falco as Bryna handed him a cup of water. Sipping the cold clear water he glanced across to where the other cadets were gathered at the far side of the tent. They were talking in low voices and shooting nervous looks in Falco's direction.

'They're frightened,' said Falco.

Bryna just nodded and Alex too seemed more than a little nervous but then he smiled.

'I swear Jarek nearly shat himself,' he said and the tension dissipated as the three of them laughed.

As they watched, Owen, Allyster and several of the other Valentian cadets broke away from the group and made their way over to where Falco was sitting. For a moment they stood in an awkward huddle.

'We knew you'd do it,' said Owen at last. 'Ever since the battle in the mountains... We knew you'd do it.'

Falco felt a quick surge of emotion and gave them a shy nod of thanks.

'That was a good hit,' said Allyster, as they began to move away. 'Over the top of Jarek's shield.'

Falco smiled and presently they were left alone once more.

232

Food was served for the midday break, but although Falco was ravenous he did not feel like eating. He had just stopped something from hitting him with nothing more than the power of his mind. For the first time since the training began he could not wait to get up to the crucible and talk to Aurelian. People were still shooting furtive looks in his direction and he was relieved when Lanistas Magnus and Deloix appeared, each with a scroll of parchment which they pinned to thick posts near the centre of the tent.

There was a great surge as the cadets crowded round to see which military units they would be commanding for the next six months.

Falco remained in his seat as the cadets pressed forward to read the commissions. After a few moments Alex pushed his way out of the press and made his way back to Falco.

'Well? Did you get a company of infantry?' asked Falco.

Alex only nodded, his expression more serious than Falco had ever seen.

'They gave me Die Verbannten,' he said in a slightly stunned voice. 'It means 'The Exiles',' he added but still the name meant little to Falco. 'It's made up of Illician refugees from all the different Leagues, said Alex, sitting heavily beside Falco. 'These are men who have lost everything.'

Falco could see the sense of responsibility settling on his young shoulders like a cloak of lead. He suspected that it was not by chance that the instructors had given this particular company to a young man who greeted each day with a child-like twinkle in his eye.

'What about him?' asked Falco as Jarek moved away from the lists with a fist raised in triumph.

'They gave him a company of Royal Hussars,' said Alex in a distracted voice.

'That sounds a bit unfair,' said Falco. 'Don't see why he should be rewarded with a royal company.'

'You don't understand,' said Alex. 'Our cousin said they award the most difficult units to the most able commanders. The Royal Hussars are already trained. They would only give such a unit to a commander who is lacking in ability.'

Falco nodded slowly. However, it was clear that Jarek was unaware of this convention. He was obviously delighted to be given command of such a high profile company of light cavalry.

The approaching figure of Bryna drew their attention away from Jarek. She walked back to them wearing something of a confused expression. Behind her a number of the other cadets continued to look at her, laughing as if she were the object of a joke.

'Who did you get?' asked Falco as Bryna sat down at the table.

'I don't know, but everyone seems to think it's hilarious,' said Bryna, looking up at the cadets, several of whom were still laughing and glancing in her direction.

'Does the unit have a name?' asked Alex.

'It just said, *Bryna Godwin, Dalwhinnies,*' said Bryna and she scowled as Alex gaped at her in disbelief.

'They've given you the Dalwhinnies!?'

Bryna just nodded.

'What's wrong?' asked Falco. 'Who are the Dalwhinnies?'

'It's a company of archers from the Queen's Irregulars,' said Alex, clearly struggling to stop himself from laughing. 'Imagine two hundred poachers, subordinates, deserters and thieves, all rolling drunk and spoiling for a fight.'

Bryna had been given the task of transforming a mob of dysfunctional miscreants into an effective and disciplined fighting force but then her head tilted to one side as if something had just occurred to her.

'I was trained by a poacher,' she said and the two boys could only look at her and laugh.

The excited discussions about who had been given what soon gave way to more sober questions of what they were expected to do in their new positions of command. The emissary explained that the new commissions would form the basis of a training army, a reduced version of a real army, allowing the cadets to work together, not only in their individual commands but also as part of a greater force.

'As the winter clears you will be sent on a training campaign to another city,' he told them. 'You'll work on everything from military tactics to provisions and logistics, from battlefield triage to the setting up of a full field hospital.

'You'll learn about scouting, communications, map reading, marching rates and strategic deployment, even political etiquette and the management of refugees.' The emissary smiled at their daunted expressions. 'What? Did you think we'd spend the whole year teaching you how to swing a sword?'

As the cadets slowly came to terms with their new positions of responsibility, Falco slipped quietly out of the tent and up towards the crucible. He was desperate to talk to someone who could understand what he had just done, but he was also incredibly nervous. When he reached the rim of the great arena he found Aurelian, Dusaule, Meredith and Dwimervane waiting for him. Feeling deeply self-conscious he made his way down towards them. It was clear they had heard the news of what he had achieved.

Dwimervane and Dusaule sat in their usual place, a little way up the side, while Meredith rose to his seat to join Falco on the sandy floor. Aurelian started forward and, feeling a deep sense of trepidation, Falco crossed the floor to meet him. For a moment the maimed old battle mage just looked at him and Falco felt certain he was in for a scolding but then Aurelian stepped forward, put his large hand round the back of Falco's neck and pulled him into a rough embrace.

Tenderness was the last thing Falco expected to feel from the foul mouthed old battle mage, but tenderness there was.

'Don't worry, lad,' said Aurelian in a low gravelly voice. 'A sword is just a sword. It's how we choose to use it that counts.'

Falco felt a tightness in his throat. He had wondered how he was going to explain what he felt - the fear of knowing he possessed a power that could kill. But there was no need. Aurelian knew. Just like every battle mage that had ever gone before... he knew.

'Now,' said Aurelian, slapping Falco so hard round the side of his head that sparks of light danced in his vision. 'Show me what you can do.'

234

Aurelian drew back and Meredith came forward, ready to sense just what it was that Falco had learned.

'I'm not sure I can do it again,' said Falco as Aurelian stooped to pick up a handful of gritty sand. 'It just kind of...'

He had no time to finish the sentence as Aurelian hurled the handful of sharp grit at his face. Falco flinched in anticipation of the stinging spray but at the same time he decided, 'no'. The small fragments of stone ignited in tiny flares as they struck an invisible barrier that sprang up just inches from his body. A mist of dust filled the air before falling slowly to the ground.

'Hah!' exclaimed Aurelian. 'At last!'

Aurelian looked delighted; Meredith looked stunned, while up on the steps Nicolas Dusaule looked down on Falco with the hint of a sad smile.

'Did you get that?' said Aurelian turning to Meredith. 'Is there enough there to work with?'

Meredith could only nod. It would take a mage several hours to prepare a barrier like that. Falco had done it with barely a thought. But Meredith had been watching closely and although he could not put it into words, he had a sense of what Falco had done. He could see how, with some small adjustments, that force could be manipulated and controlled.

They spent the next two hours testing the limits of Falco's new ability.

'The next step is to shape your defences and project them so that you can use them to protect others,' said Aurelian.

The defensive field that Falco was able to produce seemed to match the contours of his body like an invisible shield sitting a few inches above his skin. Meredith could see how Falco might begin to fashion this barrier into any shape he chose but the subtle changes in the mind were not easy to describe.

'Try to imagine a sphere,' he said. 'A sphere is a natural form of nature. Once you can do that we can work on producing a sphere at a distance.'

Falco nodded but he was too tired to try anything else just now. He was accustomed to physical exhaustion but this mental tiredness was something else entirely.

'It's like anything else,' said Aurelian. 'It'll get stronger with practice.'

He patted him on the back and Falco was surprised at the satisfaction he felt at finally being able to please the cantankerous old veteran.

'We'll leave it there for today. You rest this afternoon and get a good night's sleep. We'll start again tomorrow. Here,' he said when he saw just how exhausted Falco was, 'Nicolas will give you a hand back to the barracks.'

Dusaule appeared at his side and Falco gave a weary nod as the tall Crofter escorted him out of the crucible. Stumbling with fatigue Falco was in something of a daze as they made their way down the slope. He was dimly aware of staggering a couple of times but Dusaule was always there to catch him. He did not remember falling asleep on his feet or Dusaule picking him up and carrying him the last two hundred yards to the barracks before laying him down on his bed.

He woke some time later when the rest of the cadets returned from the afternoon's training. He opened his eyes feeling tired but rested. The cadets were noisy with excitement as they bustled into the sleeping quarters. Still feeling groggy Falco eased himself up and sat on the edge of his bed.

'You look shattered,' said Bryna as she and Alex returned with the others.

'I'm fine,' said Falco, although he could quite happily have gone back to sleep.

'I'm starving,' said Alex. 'Let's see what they've got for dinner.'

Falco nodded getting to his feet and yawning.

'I could eat a horse...'

'Two pigs and a chicken,' said Alex, completing the phrase that had grown up among the cadets, all of whom had noticed an alarming increase in the amount they were eating.

They moved through to the dining hall and Falco leaned his head on his hand, slowly stuffing his face with boiled potatoes, roasted parsnips and braised lamb while Bryna and Alex discussed battlefield orders and the chain of command. The buzz of excitement was slowly giving way to a replete murmur when the door flew open and a cadet burst in.

'The knights are here!' he exclaimed. 'The épreuve du force is over!'

The dining room emptied in something of a stampede as the cadets charged through to the arched entrance of the quad. In the torch-lit darkness they could see a group of figures approaching. They looked filthy, bowed and utterly exhausted. It was raining and cold and the bedraggled knights seemed to have just one thing on their minds, to get to the barracks and bed.

The cadets began to recognise friends amongst the group and running out to meet them they helped them back inside. As they entered the sleeping quarters the cadets wrapped them in blankets and drew them to the fires, pouring hot drinks and hovering in the hope of hearing some account of what they had been through. But the trainee knights were in no fit state to regale them. Some of them simply staggered over to collapse onto their beds, wet clothes and all.

Falco, Alex and Bryna watched anxiously as the last of them returned but there was still no sign of Quirren or Malaki. Then, just as they were about to go in search of Lanista Deloix, another figure appeared out of the night. It was the big Beltonian, Huthgarl and there just behind him was Quirren, but Quirren was not walking alone. Together with a heavily built Acheronian youth they supported another cadet between them. The cadet's arms were draped over their shoulders, his head was bowed and his legs were trailing behind him, stumbling over the muddy ground. His long brown hair was hanging down over his face but then Falco noticed that his left forearm was bound with a wet and dirty bandage.

The cadet being dragged back to the barracks was Malaki.

Bryna must have realised at the same instant because she suddenly ran out into the rain to help bring him in. Alex went too.

As they reached them, Quirren's strength gave out and it was left to Bryna to help the broad shouldered Acheronian get Malaki inside. Despite his own weariness, Falco went out to help Alex with Quirren. The big Illician looked up at them, his stoic face slack with exhaustion.

'We did it,' was all he said.

Falco and Alex each drew an arm across their shoulders and hauled him up to his feet. Then together they staggered through to join the others. Bryna and the

Acheronian had managed to get Malaki onto his bed before turning to enquire about Quirren.

'We did it,' Quirren said again as Falco wrapped a dry towel round his shoulders.

'I... have... no... doubt!' said Alex, tugging hard as he struggled to remove his brother's boots.

Quirren laid a hand on his brother's shoulder and Alex raised his head to look up at him.

'They have chosen me for the Orden Des Schwarzen Adlers,' he said, his voice thick with emotion and disbelief.

Alex ceased pulling at Quirren's boots and rose to hug his brother. 'Father knows,' Falco heard him say, his voice muffled against his brother's shoulder. 'He knows and he is proud.'

Falco turned away as Quirren cried quietly against Alex's shoulder. He had no idea what 'the Orden Des Schwarzen Adlers' meant, only that schwartz was the Illician word for 'dark' or 'black'.

He turned back to find Bryna tending to Malaki. He helped her to remove his wet clothes and went to get him a hot drink while she dried his hair with a towel. Of all the trainee knights Malaki was in the worst shape. He seemed barely conscious as Falco set down a cup of hot coffee beside his bed. Bryna covered him with a warm blanket and stroked his brow as they tried to ascertain if he was all right.

'Tired,' Malaki mumbled like a man on the edge of sleep. 'Just tired.'

At the foot of his bed stood Huthgarl. The large Beltonian was staring down at Malaki with an unreadable expression on his dour looking face. Suddenly a smaller figure appeared beside him.

'I should have known!' spat Jarek Snidesson with vicious glee. 'Should've known the épreuve du force would be too much for a common blacksmith.'

Falco felt his hackles rise as Jarek shook his head in contempt.

'Look at him, our poor little Berry, utterly spent. That's what you get for having ideas above your station.'

Falco saw Bryna start up from the bed, but before she could do anything Huthgarl gave a snarl. Spinning round he wrapped a massive hand around Jarek's throat and slammed him back against one of the sturdy wooden pillars. Jarek gave a strangled cry and pulled at Huthgarl's arm but there was no way he could break that powerful hold. For a moment Huthgarl just stared at Jarek and Falco was worried that he might do serious harm. But finally he relaxed his grip.

'No more,' was all he said and with that he let Jarek fall, retching to the floor. He turned to look at Falco and Bryna, and finally down at Malaki. Then, without another word he turned and walked away.

For a moment Falco watched him leave, wondering just what had happened on the épreuve du force to bring about such a change in the Beltonian's allegiance. He looked down at Jarek, who was slowly getting to his feet, batting away the hands of two of his cronies who were trying to help him up. Jarek's eyes were dark with hatred, made all the hotter by this second humiliation of the day. Falco felt a stab of sympathy but there was nothing to be done. Spite bore its own bitter fruit.

With a sigh of regret he turned back to his friend.

Bryna was still muttering under her breath as she held the cup of hot coffee to Malaki's lips. He sipped slowly and some of the dark liquid ran down his chin. His face was pale with cold and fatigue, and several nasty bruises stood out starkly beneath his skin but slowly he began to revive. He reached up to enclose Bryna's hand with his own, holding the cup to his mouth so that he could drink more deeply.

'Thank you,' he said.

Falco moved to stand beside Bryna as Malaki struggled to focus on their faces. He smiled as if he had woken from a bad dream and a flush of colour returned to his pallid cheeks.

'You survived then,' said Falco.

'No problem,' replied Malaki with a grin.

Bryna gave a sigh of exasperation at the lightness of their tone then raised Malaki's hand to her lips, clearly relieved that there did not appear to be anything seriously wrong. Malaki reached out an arm to pull her closer and she leaned down to kiss him properly.

'You frightened the hell out of me,' she said in a scolding tone and Malaki laughed.

'So, did you pass?' asked Falco and slowly Malaki nodded.

'Only four of us dropped out. The instructors say it's normally more.'

Bryna stuffed another pillow behind him as he struggled to sit up.

'So which order of knights has been foolish enough to sign you up?' said Falco as Malaki had another sip of coffee and took a bite from a piece of fruit cake that had magically appeared on a plate beside his bed. 'Order of the Swan?' he suggested. 'Or the Order du Croissant, perhaps?'

Malaki laughed and shook his head. Falco's crude pronunciation made it clear he meant the curved patisserie and not the 'crescent' for which the order in question was actually named. But then his expression grew more serious.

'Well it can't be the Beltane Heavy Horse,' said Falco. 'There's no way Huthgarl would allow that.'

Again Malaki shook his head and Falco gaped at him in disbelief.

'Don't tell me you've been chosen by the Adamanti!'

'No,' said Malaki, his deep brown eyes shining with disbelief. 'They want me for the Knights of Wrath.'

38
Archives of the Magi

Later that night the first of the winter storms blew in. Clouds of snow swirled around the tall tower of the magi but deep in the bowels of the tower there was no sign of howling wind and pelting hail. Like the depths of a fathomless lake it was calm and unperturbed.

Meredith Saker took another sip of blood red wine and placed the silver cup to one side, careful that it should not spill on the ancient books and scrolls laid out on the black stone table at which he sat. It was well after midnight and apart from the low harmonic drone of distant chanting the repository was quiet. The dark arching catacombs were lit not by torches but by small irregular plates of pale purple onyx, fixed to the wall with black iron spikes. The plates glowed with a faint luminescence, providing just enough light to read by.

Meredith had spent much of the last few weeks in these dark womb-like chambers, setting out the specific aims of his studies. In communication he had developed an idea for connecting mage towers with a live link of communication. Yes, a quintet of skilled mages could project a simple message from one tower to another but this was not the same as holding a conversation. He was convinced his idea could be of immense strategic value in the war against the Possessed.

When it came to history there were numerous things to which he could quite happily dedicate years of study, but for now he had decided to restrict himself to the rise and return of the Possessed.

And finally, even though Galen Thrall had dismissed it, he was determined to learn more about dragonkind. Not only had he always been fascinated by these enigmatic creatures, he was convinced that the madness of black dragons was connected to the Great Possession. If he could find out what made dragons vulnerable to Possession then maybe he could glean some insight into why black dragons were mad. And there were two questions that kept repeating in his mind.

Had the magi known that dragons were susceptible to Possession?

And if so, why did they not warn the people of Wrath?

He knew such questions were controversial but he would not rest until he knew the answers.

Meredith looked up and gave a nod of thanks as one of the archivists placed a new scroll on the table.

'Will you be requiring anything else?' asked the bald-headed man.

'No, thank you,' said Meredith. 'I just want to cross reference the decadal timeline with chronicles from the other kingdoms.'

The archivist gave a disinterested nod and was just moving away when Meredith's eye was drawn to the only other figure in the repository, a figure who had been present ever since Meredith first visited the catacombs four weeks ago.

The old man was sitting in a chair, beside a simple cot laid out near the entrance to the chamber of records. His face was wrinkled like that of a wizened monkey with a fringe of sparse white hair encircling his liver-spotted scalp, and his small rheumy eyes stared into space with a pronounced squint.

Had he known better Meredith might have said he was in a state of conjuration, a trance-like state where the mage's attention was focussed on creating a specific aura or state of mind, but no one could remain in that state for so long and Meredith perceived no hint of a spell being performed.

'Does he live here?' he asked, nodding to the diminutive figure.

'Sometimes,' said the archivist. 'Brother Serulian was a great scholar in his time.'

Meredith nodded slowly. For some reason 'Brother Serulian' made him feel distinctly uncomfortable. The old mage never looked at him, never even acknowledged his presence, but nevertheless, Meredith had the distinct impression that he was being watched. Maybe his father had arranged for the old man to keep an eye on him, watching in case he stepped out of line or tried to study anything of which his father did not approve. Well, he would find out tonight when he went through to the fifth chamber. If his father somehow learned that he was studying dragonkind then Meredith would know that Brother Serulian was a spy.

'Will that be all?'

Meredith looked up at the archivist who was still hovering at the end of the table.

'Yes, thank you.'

The archivist departed, disappearing through the broad archway at the entrance to the chamber. For a moment Meredith continued to stare at Brother Serulian then he turned back to the table and unfurled the scroll that the archivist had brought him. He scanned through the dates on the timeline, checking them against his notes, from the pivotal battle of Erlangaen in 828, through to the Inquisition of Ossanda in 845, when the magi were cleared of withholding information before the Great Possession, which occurred two years earlier.

Twenty minutes passed until, with a soft snort of surprise, Meredith sat back and let the scroll furl back upon itself. The timeline confirmed that he had not missed anything of significance. The Great Possession had taken place in the year 843 Anno Ira (in the Year of Wrath). Naturally, the chronicles of the 84th decade had been among the first he looked at and yet he had learned nothing of any great significance, nothing that he did not already know.

With a sigh of frustration he furled the scroll. Maybe he was wrong. Maybe there simply was nothing more to learn about the Great Possession. Rising from his seat he drained the last of his wine. Then, checking that there was no one else present in the repository, he pushed himself up from the table and moved through to the fifth chamber, where the information on dragonkind was stored. He shuddered slightly as he passed through the vacant gaze of Brother Serulian but the old mage seemed oblivious to his presence. He continued to stare into space through the cataracts in his watery eyes but in his mind there lay the echo of the Grand Veneratu's command.

'The son of Saker must be denied the details of the 84th decade.'
'He must not know the truth.'

Feeling only a vague prickle of disquiet Meredith Saker continued to the fifth chamber to begin his study of dragonkind.

39

Emergence

Deep within the Forsaken Lands an area of tortured rock began to buckle and bulge as something forced its way up from below. The Enlightened set down their tools and gathered round the pit ready to adorn the new arrival in the regalia of war. The surface of the pit cracked open as a shape emerged: powerful shoulders and a monstrous head, bowed by the effort of being born into a new and unfamiliar realm. The demon planted its hands on the sides of the pit and hauled itself free of the molten earth. Its eyes burned with a blood red fire as it struggled to stand on two back-bent legs that seemed to be wreathed in smoke.

Around it the blackened remains of the supplicants hung in the air then one by one they began to descend until they sank into the riven earth. They had served their purpose in guiding the demon through, their suffering a beacon for it to follow. Now the same rift would serve to deliver them from the human world into the greater realms below.

As the last of the supplicants disappeared beneath the shifting crust of rock the transition was complete. The Slayer was now a denizen of this world. Almost immediately the rock began to cool and solidify until all that was left was a tracery of glowing cracks and the smell of scorched rock and burning flesh. But the supplicants were gone. They were not buried in the earth. They were gone. You could dig a thousand feet beneath the pit and never find their bones. They were in a different place now, a place of suffering from which they would never escape. Not unless the Marchio Dolor himself were slain and there was no one in the world with the strength to kill such as he.

Standing eight feet tall the Slayer looked down as the Enlightened moved around it. On the black contorted rock they set down two swords with broad curving blades and sharp wicked points. For a moment the Slayer looked down upon the blades as if it had no use for such crude and simple tools but then it sensed the power and servitude with which they had been made.

The Slayer went down upon one knee and slowly took hold of the blades, one in each enormous fist. While it was bowed low the Enlightened moved around it, laying armoured plates upon its arms, chest and shoulders. Finally one of them lifted the great ridged helmet and settled it on the demon's head. As they stepped back the Slayer bowed its head and closed it eyes and its black flesh began to glow. It glowed like cinders in a fire, rising in temperature until the enchanted steel fused to its foul demonic flesh.

The demon and its protection were one.

Slowly the Slayer rose to its feet. Its massive chest expanded as it breathed the air of the human world. It closed its eyes and the blades weighed in perfect balance at its sides, extensions now, of its black assassin's mind. It had been summoned here for one purpose and one alone.

To kill.

To slay the Defiants and their conceited wyrms.

And it would.

40

Nay Shed a Clout

The trainee knights slept for almost two days after returning from the épreuve du force, and even after that the instructors insisted that they take several more days to rest and recover their strength. None of them seemed to want to speak about their ordeal, which frustrated the curiosity of the other cadets and added to the air of mystery surrounding the infamous selection process.

'Too slow to defend my left side,' was all Malaki would say about the cut on his arm.

But whatever had happened during the trial by force it had formed something of a bond between the would-be knights. Falco would often see them exchange a nod or a handshake and even, occasionally, a laugh. He felt a surprising pang of jealousy that Malaki had undergone such a profound experience without him, but then Falco had his own story to tell.

'Oh, I wish I'd seen that,' said Malaki when he heard about the hit Falco had scored against Jarek.

At first Malaki had been too exhausted to notice much of anything but as he returned to normal he began to notice the changes that had taken place while he and the others were away. Several of the cadets now laughed and joked with Bryna as if, in his absence, they had suddenly become friends.

'Gonna beat you three nil today, Godwin,' said Kurt Vogler one morning as he passed them in the barracks.

'Only if you get a bigger sword,' said Bryna, with a meaningful look and several of the other cadets laughed along with Vogler.

Falco smiled while Malaki just raised his eyebrows in surprise.

'I'll have him one of these days,' said Bryna, sighing as Malaki's eyebrows shot up even higher. 'In a sparring match,' she clarified, whacking Malaki round the head with her gloves.

However, by far the biggest change that Malaki observed was in Falco.

'Are those muscles I see?' he asked in a tone of mock disbelief as Falco drew off the shirt in which he slept.

'More like swelling from all the bruises,' said Falco self-consciously. He was still by far the thinnest of all the cadets but he was secretly pleased that his arms and chest no longer had the skinny appearance of the sickly boy he had always been.

'And I swear you've grown,' said Malaki, blocking Falco's path as he stood up from his bed.

Falco still fell short of Malaki's six-foot-two but not now by much.

'Oomph!'

Malaki hunched over as Falco jabbed him in the solar plexus.

'Out of my way, page,' he said, using the term for an adolescent knight in training.

Malaki swung for him but Falco stepped smartly out of reach. Alex and Quirren laughed while Bryna shook her head and muttered the all too familiar refrain.

'Boys!'

Heading for the showers, Falco glanced back at Malaki with a smile then stopped short as he ran straight into Lanista Deloix. The dark skinned instructor looked at him and for a moment Falco thought he might be in trouble but then the lanista held up a letter.

'From the small town of Lavandier,' he said, handing the letter to Falco.

Falco looked at the folded parchment, bound with string and sealed with a blank press of red wax. He read the writing on the front.

Falco Danté
Academy of War
Wrath

The others crowded round as Lanista Deloix departed.

'Who's it from?' asked Bryna.

'It's from Fossetta,' said Falco as he noted the sender's name on the reverse of the letter.

'Well open it,' said Malaki.

Sitting on the chest at the end of his bed, Falco snapped the seal and discarded the string. His hands shook ever so slightly as he opened the letter and began to read.

To my dearest Falco

I hope this letter finds you well. Indeed, I hope it finds you at all. I did not know where else to send it. And forgive me for not writing sooner but we have been travelling hard, trying to reach a small town called Lavandier before the winter snow comes in. There is talk there of a boy beset by nightmares and of objects being 'damaged' when he is in distress. He will be the fourth child that we have seen since leaving Toulwar but as yet Tobias has only used the word 'Ballymudge' for one of them!

Tobias and I are keeping well and enjoying the chance to see more of this beautiful land. He has embraced the role suggested by the emissary and the responsibility has been good for him. As it turns out Heçamede also decided to accompany us on our journey. Many of these remote villages are without a proper healer and we are both grateful for her company.

From Lavandier (weather permitting) we will continue east, towards the Illician border. It is no surprise, perhaps, that a greater number of 'disturbed children' seem to come from that direction. Even here, in the centre of Clemoncé, the shadow of the Possessed is being felt. I cannot imagine what it must be like, living near the front. Or, yes, perhaps I can.

Anyway. Enough of our adventures. How are things with you?

Heçamede was very encouraged by your recovery in Toulwar. I do so hope you have continued to improve. How is the chest? No sign of the infection returning, I trust. Heçamede says to eat well and breathe deeply. I know Wrath is on the coast but from what I'm told it can still get cold so I don't want to hear that you are going round in nothing but a shirt! Remember...

"Nay shed a clout till oak be out."

Has a decision been made about your training? Don't be disappointed if you are unable to follow in your father's footsteps. You have a good heart and a quick mind. There are many other ways that you can help.

Oh, my dear. There are so many things that I want to ask you. What is Wrath like? And the sea? Have you seen the Queen? Did Malaki and Bryna actually get to meet her? Is the emissary still with you? Does Bellius really have connections with the royal court?

I would love to hear all your news but I'm afraid I can't give you an address to write back too. We rarely stay in one place for long but if we ever do I will try to let you know.

Please give my love to Malaki and Bryna. Not an hour goes past that I do not think about you all.

Farewell for now, my dear. I will write again in the spring.

And remember that whatever happens, and whatever you do. You will always be in my heart.

All my love
Fossetta
(and Tobias)
(and Heçamede)

P.S. Do not worry for our safety. We are being accompanied on our travels by two soldiers from the Toulwarian Royal Chasseurs - a captain by the name of de Roche, and another man who seems to know the forest as if it were his own garden path. I'm not sure of his rank. We know him only as Francois.

They make for pleasant, if quiet, travelling companions. Unlike the two men who drive the cart. They quarrel incessantly (although it has to be said, in the most entertaining way). Tobias, in particular, enjoys their company. I think their good humour reminds him of his father.

Now that really is all
Till spring
Take Care

Malaki and Bryna had been looking over Falco's shoulder but now he stood up from the chest and handed the letter to them so they could read it properly.

'Are you okay?' asked Malaki.

'I'm fine,' said Falco, as he pulled on a clean shirt and trousers. 'Just dawned on me how much I miss her.'

Malaki nodded and Bryna reached out to take his hand. Falco gave them a wan smile and gently squeezed Bryna's hand before heading out to wash before breakfast.

'*She's all right,*' he thought as he crossed the frost covered courtyard. '*And even found time to nag me!*'

Before leaving Caer Dour Falco would never have imagined Fossetta traipsing round the Clemoncéan countryside with armed soldiers to guard her. But why not? She was one of the strongest people he had ever known and he felt sure she would be revelling in the experience. And somehow, just the reminder

244

that there were people like her in the world was deeply reassuring. The cold mist of dawn lingered in the courtyard and Falco smiled as he entered the steamy warmth of the bathhouse.

41

A Passing Shadow

In the Forsaken Lands of Illicia the Slayer watched as the sun rose over the mist covered hills to the east. The humans viewed the sunrise as a symbol of hope, but how then would they explain his presence? He had already killed several creatures, but only the humans offered any sense of satisfaction. The animals were simply sparks of life to be snuffed out, but the humans could be tormented far beyond the ephemeral moment of death. There was something almost divine in the amount of pain they could be made to suffer. The Slayer had relished their anguish but he had been summoned for something more. He had been summoned to travel north to kill the Defiants and wyrms who fought there, souls so arrogant as to believe they could challenge the Faithful.

He rolled his armoured shoulders and the swords in his hands glinted in the morning sun. The light did not concern him but he much preferred the dark and so he would sink beneath the crust of this world and skirt the surface of the infernal plane. Offering up a prayer he opened a gate and disappeared from view. Anyone watching would have seen the demon walk forward, slowly descending into darkness that left a fire-blackened scar upon the earth. And all that could be seen of his passing was a vague shadow that moved across the land.

Now, concealed from any watching eyes, he continued on his journey. Far to the north he could sense one of these great souls and he was eager to claim it as his own. His awareness told him the Defiant was alone, with no wyrm to share the penalty of death. But no matter.

For now he would kill a Defiant. The pleasure of slaying a wyrm would have to wait.

42

Paddy The Feck

The Academy of War was now firmly in the grip of winter and the plateau was covered in the first proper fall of snow. It crunched beneath their boots as they made their way through the darkness and up to the training field.

'So you can actually cast a protection?' said Malaki as they entered the tent.

'Still only round myself,' said Falco. 'But yes.'

Malaki nodded, impressed. There was an odd expression in his eyes that Falco could not quite make out. Then he remembered seeing a similar expression on Balthazak's face the first time Malaki beat his father in a fight. It was a mixture of pride and wariness, the realisation that the balance of power, which had existed for so long, might be about to change.

They ran together as a group that morning. Malaki was still regaining his strength and Falco was continuing to get stronger so an easy pace meant they could stay together. Besides, it was now so dark in the mornings that no one could run full speed up and down the rocky path. It was only beginning to get light as they returned to the tent for breakfast. As the cadets finished eating they became aware of a growing clamour of noise outside. It sounded as if half the Fourth Army was moving past the tent. There was a knowing expression in the eyes of the instructors as one by one the cadets moved outside to see what was going on.

Falco and the others emerged from the tent to see a great number of troops now forming up into ranks on the training field. There were blocks of cavalry, spearmen and infantry armed with sword and shield, along with several units of archers. All together there were almost two thousand men, with a scattering of women, now staring at the open mouthed cadets. The emissary waited until the last of the cadets emerged from the tent before leading them onto the field.

'Academy cadets,' he called out, raising an all embracing arm. 'Meet the army at your command.'

The gathered troops gave a resounding roar, the effect of which was only spoiled by a ragged formation of archers at one end of the field. Their half-hearted cheer, died away long after the main shout had come to a well-coordinated end. Far from seeming embarrassed by their lack of discipline however, the rowdy group continued to mutter and laugh and then the cold still morning was split by a resounding fart that could only have been produced with considerable and deliberate effort.

There was something of an apology in the emissary's smile as a fresh wave of laughter broke out among the group. All the cadets turned to look sympathetically at Bryna who had the horrible feeling that she had just been introduced to the Dalwhinnies.

With this dramatic unveiling concluded, Lanista Magnus stepped forward with a list. As each name was called out, the cadet in question walked forward and the emissary introduced them to their new command. They were all nervous but none more so than Alex Klingemann. He looked pale and Falco wondered if he was going to throw up. When *his* name was called he followed the emissary

247

until he stood before a block of infantry each wearing a black surcoat bearing a design from one of the seven Illician Leagues.

The most senior member of Die Verbannten stepped forward to greet his 'new commander'. His eyes, like the rest of the Exiles, were glazed with trauma and he looked upon Alex with bleak indifference as if it was of little consequence that the academy had chosen a child to lead them.

The emissary began to introduce him but Alex stepped forward before he had a chance. For a moment he met the senior's hollow gaze then he dropped to the ground and prostrated himself, his arms spread wide and his face pressed down into the snow.

'What's he doing?' Bryna whispered to Quirren. Even for Alex, this gesture seemed a little melodramatic.

'It's a display of humility,' said Quirren with a note of surprise in his voice. 'He knows he is not worthy to lead such men. He will only take the position if they accept him.'

The senior member of the Exiles looked down at Alex as if he did not know *what* to do. The gesture seemed to make him distinctly uncomfortable. He looked to the emissary but his uncompromising expression offered no way out. He then glanced round at his fellow Exiles before turning back to Alex. Finally he crouched down and laid his hand on the back of Alex's head. He closed his eyes and his mouth moved as he spoke a few words that no one could hear then he stood back and Alex rose to his feet.

'About time,' he said, rubbing the tip of his nose. 'Thought you were going to leave me down there to freeze.'

The emissary smiled while the senior raised an eyebrow, but then he placed his right hand across his chest and gave Alex a bow. Behind him the rest of unit followed his lead. The Exiles had accepted their young commander and Quirren gave a soft laugh.

'They will teach each other,' was all he said.

A few minutes later it was Bryna who followed the emissary out onto the training field. All the cadets watched her progress and none of them envied the cacophony of laughter, whistles and jeers that accompanied her approach to the Dalwhinnies.

As the emissary came to a stop, the front rank began jostling and nudging each other as if they had not even decided who was going to represent them. Finally a tall dark haired man was singled out and propelled forward. His face was pockmarked and his hair looked like it had been cut with a saw. He smirked as he walked out to meet the emissary, looking back and tossing his chin at the crude comments of support from his comrades.

'He's not the one you have to watch,' said the emissary quietly as the man approached.

He nodded to one side where a broad shouldered man, with two braids at the left temple of his sandy brown hair, was staring at Bryna. His weathered face was grizzled and grim but there was a spark of intelligence in his deep set eyes.

'Patrick Feckler,' whispered the emissary. 'Otherwise known as Paddy the Feck.'

Before he could say any more the pock faced man was standing before them.

'Cadet Bryna Godwin,' said the emissary by way of introduction. 'Now Acting Captain of the Queen's Irregulars, Fifth Company of Archers.'

'Dedric Sayer, at your service,' said the man in a mocking tone, looking Bryna up and down with bare faced appreciation.

'At your service, *Captain*,' said the emissary, his tone hardening.

'At your service, Captain,' repeated Dedric, blushing and casting a sharp look behind at the taunts that followed his capitulation.

Before he turned back, Bryna saw him look to the man known as Paddy the Feck, as if seeking his permission. Patrick Feckler flicked a final glance over Bryna and gave a small nod. Dedric turned back to Bryna then he raised his hand and called out in a loud voice.

'Three cheers for the new captain. Dalwhinnies...'

'HO!' came the resounding reply.

'Dalwhinnies.'

'HO!'

'Dalwhinnies.'

'HO!'

The emissary gave an amused smile while Bryna swallowed hard. She looked utterly terrified.

As the final 'HO!' faded away into more laughter Falco turned to Malaki.

'You worried?'

'No,' said Malaki. 'They're only men. Might take her a while but she'll figure them out.'

Falco was impressed by his friend's confidence.

'Besides,' said Malaki. 'I'll kill any man who so much as lays a finger on her.'

Now that, thought Falco, was a far more honest reply.

After the officer commissions it was the turn of the knights. The emissary came back to stand beside Falco and everyone watched as contingents from six different orders of knighthood cantered through the snow. Dressed in mail and surcoat, and mounted on powerful steeds they made an imposing sight and even the Dalwhinnies seemed subdued by their presence.

Falco recognised the five insignia that he had seen when the trainees set out on the épreuve du force but now he saw an additional design, a black eagle on a field of red. The insignia was clearly of Illician origin and Falco suddenly understood.

Der Orden Des Schwarzen Adlers.

'The Order of the Black Eagle,' he breathed.

'It was our father's order,' said Quirren quietly as they watched the knights form up in front of them, the breath from their horses' nostrils clouding in the cold morning air.

Each of the contingents consisted of two knights and a page who carried a sword sheathed in a scabbard and coiled in a leather belt. One of the knights from each contingent carried the colours of their order and Falco immediately recognised the man bearing the pennant for the Knights of Wrath. It was Sebastien Cabal, the Lord Commander of the order.

The knights bearing the colours remained in the saddle while their fellow knights dismounted. Looking nervous, the pages did likewise. They stood at their knight's shoulder while Lanista Magnus directed the cadets to come forward.

Quirren approached the knight of the Black Eagle. Huthgarl and another cadet by the name of Blaevar approached the knight from the Beltonian Heavy Horse, while two Illician youths moved to stand in front of the Adamanti.

Malaki was the only one to approach the Knights of Wrath.

They came to a halt and then, without further ado, the page passed the sword to the knight who then handed it to the cadet standing before him.

Falco had been expecting some great ceremony or swearing in. He turned to the emissary who was now standing beside him.

'Does this mean they're now knights?'

'No,' said the emissary. 'They are now journeymen, sworn to the order that has accepted them. When they have finished their training they will ride to war with their order. Only after their first battle will they be deemed a knight.'

Falco nodded and looked over at Malaki. The knight standing before him seemed pleased to have inducted Malaki but Sebastien Cabal appeared to be brooding with anger.

'What's the matter with him?' asked Falco, nodding in the Lord Commander's direction.

'Malaki is different,' said the emissary. 'He has already proven himself in battle. He is now considered to be a 'knight in waiting'. He will still complete his training at the academy but if the Knights of Wrath were to call upon him he could ride out with them tomorrow.'

'Why does that bother Lord Cabal?'

'He thinks Malaki is too young and, unlike the other young nobles, he has not been formally trained.'

'So why did they accept him?'

'Oh, the Lord Commander is convinced of his potential. He just doesn't believe that Malaki is ready for war.'

'And is he?'

The emissary pursed his lips.

'We shall see.'

Falco turned back to watch then looked along the edge of the field. He was now the only one of the cadets left and it felt strange to be standing there alone.

'So where does this leave me?' he asked.

'That depends,' said the emissary. 'If all they face are the warriors and beasts of the Possessed then sword and sinew should be enough. But if they face an army with a demon at its head then you might be the only thing that stands between them and an eternity in hell.'

Falco looked into the emissary's hard grey eyes. The young officers in front of them were daunted by the prospect of commanding a few hundred soldiers but that was nothing compared to the responsibility that Falco would bear. The very thought of it was terrifying.

With the inductions complete the 'academy army' dispersed and the cadets came back together, talking excitedly. Most of them had been given some token in recognition of their new commands. Alex had been given a beautiful Illician longsword, Jarek a fine light-footed courser with a dappled grey and white coat, most of the spearmen came away with a Thraecian spear and shield and a short bladed xiphos or curved kopis sword. The archers sported new bows with embossed leather quivers. Bryna, on the other hand walked back to the tent with a small, two-handled drinking cup.

'It's known as a Quaich,' said the emissary. 'A cup of greeting.'

Bryna examined the silver rimmed wooden cup which had a crude elegance to the design.

'They'll expect you to drink with them,' said Alex. 'It's tradition.'

'Drink what?' asked Bryna.

'I'm not sure,' said Alex. 'They keep it to themselves. But it's said to be the finest spirit in all the Seven Kingdoms.'

'Hmm,' said Bryna, hopefully. 'I'm quite partial to spirits.'

They all laughed and Falco looked across at Malaki who was looking down at the sword now lying in his lap. A few inches of the blade showed between the scabbard and the hilt and there, clearly stamped into the steel, was the 'rampant horse' of the Knights of Wrath.

'I can't believe it,' breathed Malaki.

'I can,' said Falco.

Malaki's eyes shone as he looked up at his friends. They were all nodding and smiling. It seemed that Falco spoke for them all.

There was little in the way of training done that morning. The instructors came to sit with the cadets, fielding an endless stream of questions and insecurities. Yes, they would still practise individual skills but their new units would play an increasing role in their training until the cadet army was ready for war.

'And as officers,' said the emissary. 'You will be expected to attend the public strategy meetings in the Chamber of Council. You too,' he added, looking at Falco. 'Battle mages are an integral part of the army.'

Falco glanced up as people turned to look at him. No one doubted the emissary's assertion that Falco was a battle mage. The shock and fear that had been present when he destroyed Jarek's sword had slowly faded. It seemed the cadets had finally realised that Falco was on their side. He might mutter strange and unnerving things in his sleep, and he might have frightening powers that they did not understand, but those powers might one day save their lives. It invoked in Falco a new and unfamiliar feeling, one that only added to the growing sense of responsibility.

The talking went on for the rest of the morning and as the assistants laid out the food for lunch Falco took the opportunity to quietly leave. He grabbed a meat pie, some bread and a handful of fruit and made his way up to the crucible, pushing back his cloak as the clouds began to break and the bright winter sun brought some warmth to the day.

'So they've all got their new playmates have they?' said Aurelian as Falco sat on the crucible steps and took a long drink of water from a copper cup. 'I hear that archer friend of yours got the Dalwhinnies,' he said with a laugh. 'Oh, don't get me wrong,' he added. 'They might be a shower of delinquent bastards but they're also some of the finest archers you're ever likely to see.'

He looked at Falco, noticing his slightly subdued mood.

'Where's Meredith?' asked Falco.

'I asked him not to come today.'

Falco glanced up at Dwimervane and Dusaule, sitting in their normal places a little way up the side of the arena. Dusaule wore a thick woollen cloak while Dwimervane's dark blue scales stood out dramatically against the snow covered steps.

'So, you must be feeling a little left out,' said Aurelian casually.

Wondering what was going on Falco looked around the arena. He shook his head distractedly but it was true, he did feel somewhat left out and a sense of isolation was beginning to form in his mind.

'Don't worry,' said Aurelian. 'It's only natural. Being a battle mage can be a lonely thing. But there are compensations,' he added and Falco caught a twinkle of amusement in his eye. 'That's why I arranged something special for today.'

Falco grew even more suspicious. Normally when Aurelian wanted to 'try something new' it involved a significant amount of pain and discomfort on Falco's part. He watched as Aurelian made his way to the side of the arena. Then, even as the old battle mage nodded up into the sky, Falco felt something falling from the sky. He spun round just in time to see a dragon streaking towards him. Without even thinking he cast a protection around himself to resist the inevitable collision but just at the last moment the dragon pulled out of its dive and swept over his head. As it did so an armoured figure leapt from its back, turned in the air and landed on the ground before him, rolling to absorb the impact before coming back to its feet. The armoured figure drew its sword and dropped into a fighting stance.

Falco had no weapons but still he matched the mystery warrior's pose, his mind coming immediately into sharp focus.

'There!' said Aurelian with obvious delight. 'I told you he was coming on.'

The armoured figure straightened up, sheathed its sword and removed its helm. Long black hair spilled down over the armour on the figure's shoulders.

It was a woman.

She looked at Falco with a penetrating expression in her dark eyes then she stepped forward, put her free hand on his arm and kissed him twice, once on each cheek. She lingered on the second kiss, her cheek resting for a moment against his as she gave him a disarming hug.

'Bienvenue petit frère,' she said.

Her face lit up with a smile and with a final squeeze of Falco's arm she turned to face Aurelian. She took a few steps towards him before launching herself into his embrace. Aurelian staggered back and wrapped his one arm around her as she hugged him tight.

'Steady, girl! You're going to do me a mischief,' he laughed as the hard edges of her armour pressed into the stubbly flesh of his cheek.

Finally she let go of Aurelian and ran up the steps to greet Dusaule and Dwimervane with the same warm abandon.

Falco was only just starting to process the pleasantly intimate greeting when he felt a familiar presence looming over him. In a gust of wind and a flurry of snow, a beautiful amber coloured dragon landed beside him. It folded its wings and looked at Falco with a piercing gaze then it walked over to Aurelian who bowed to press his forehead against the dragon's. The old battle mage raised a hand to the dragon's neck and Falco noticed a number of injuries on its body. Old scars aplenty but also a number of more recent wounds: scorch marks, tears in its wings and deeply scored lines where something had cut through the armour of its scales. But for all this, the dragon did not appear seriously hurt as Aurelian greeted her.

'How are you, my beautiful?' he said.

In reply the dragon nudged him affectionately, pressing the scaly ridge of its muzzle against the damaged side of his torso.

'It's fine,' said Aurelian. 'Just a bit tight in this cold weather.'

For another moment the dragon looked at him. It turned to acknowledge Dusaule and Dwimervane and then it walked towards Falco who bowed his head to greet it.

'Allow me to introduce Nathalie Saigal,' said Aurelian. 'And her dragon, Ciel.'

Falco gave each of them a shallow bow.

'You're taller than I expected,' said Nathalie as she approached Falco once more.

Falco dipped his head self-consciously but he was surprised at how comfortable he felt in her presence. She smiled again as he looked up.

Nathalie Saigal was a woman of some thirty years with an athletic build and a strong face with prominent cheekbones and eyes so dark they were almost black. She appeared lively and genuinely pleased to meet him but Falco also had the sense of deep fatigue as if she was weary from some hard and unrelenting task. The white line of a scar ran from the bridge of her nose to the base of her left ear but, just like her dragon, Nathalie's flesh also bore the marks of more recent violence. Her face and hands were covered with numerous small cuts and grazes. Her right arm was bandaged and there was the shadow of a huge bruise that started at the base of her jaw and disappeared beneath the neck of her breastplate. Nathalie raised an eyebrow at Falco's discreet scrutiny but then she smiled.

'It's good to meet you,' she said with a smooth Clemoncéan accent. 'I never met your father but I don't believe what they say about him. About the end, I mean.'

'It is true,' said Falco. 'He really did kill all those people.'

'Oh, I know,' said Nathalie with a touch of steel in her voice. 'I just don't believe it.'

For a moment Falco looked at her before giving her a nod of understanding.

'So,' said Nathalie, her smile taking on a more challenging cast. 'You'd like to ride a dragon?'

'What... I... No!' stammered Falco looking from Nathalie to the dragon and back again.

They both turned to look at Aurelian who seemed to be suddenly interested in how the clouds were moving across the sky.

'You didn't even tell him?' said Nathalie in an accusing tone. She turned back to Falco. 'He's terrible,' she said with a disapproving frown.

'I didn't want to worry him,' said Aurelian, limping over.

Nathalie gave him a withering look before turning back to Falco.

'So,' she said. 'Would you like to ride a dragon?'

43
Long Forgotten Dreams

Falco gripped with his knees and leaned in close to the dragon's back.

'That's it,' said Nathalie as Falco gripped the ridges at the base of Ciel's neck and laid his forearms on either side of her spine. 'You've ridden before.'

'No,' said Falco. 'Never.'

Nathalie frowned and glanced at Aurelian but Falco did not notice. His heart was pounding at the very thought of what he was about to do. They had adjusted the riding harness to take account of his height and he could feel Ciel's scales gently 'gripping' his forearms.

'Shouldn't I have a strap or belt?' he asked, blushing when both Aurelian and Nathalie laughed. 'What if I fall off?'

'You won't,' said Nathalie.

She moved to stand at Ciel's head.

'Now be gentle with him,' she said as the dragon's horns brushed against her armour.

'How do I tell her where to go?' asked Falco and again the two battle mages laughed.

'You don't,' said Nathalie. 'You decide together.'

Falco gave her an anxious look as if this advice was far from sufficient.

'You'll see what I mean,' Nathalie reassured him. 'The most important thing is just to trust her.'

Falco gave a nervous gulp.

'Try to relax,' said Aurelian. 'You might actually enjoy it.'

They stepped away from Ciel and Falco was readying himself for something to happen when he noticed Dusaule disappearing over the rim of the crucible.

Aurelian followed the line of his gaze.

'Some things are just too painful for him to watch,' said Aurelian and he and Nathalie exchanged a sad look. 'Don't worry,' Aurelian went on. 'It has nothing to do with you.' He waited until he was sure that Falco understood and then he smiled. 'Are you ready?'

Falco gave a stiff nod.

Ciel curved her long neck to look at him and there was something in her deep red eyes that finally began to calm Falco's nerves. Her great head dipped once and then with a surge she started forward. In three great bounds she reached the terraced wall of the crucible. She leapt up, pushed off from the lower steps and spread her wings.

Falco felt as if he had left his stomach on the floor of the arena as they powered up into the sky. It was singularly the most exhilarating, terrifying and wonderful thing he had ever experienced. Eyes clenched and hands aching from the tightness of his grip, he waited as he slowly emerged from the overwhelming barrage of sensations washing over him. From the cold rush of the wind and the reassuring warmth of Ciel's body, to the unbelievable sense of freedom and the great wing-beat surges that carried them higher and higher.

Finally he was able to open his eyes, and much to his surprise he found that he was not afraid. The snow-capped mountains rose up to the north and east, slowly revealing more peaks as they gained in height. Tentatively Falco began to look around. Behind him the sea was a cold winter grey with shades of turquoise along the coast. He looked down and the city of Wrath was laid out beneath him. He could clearly see the outline of the double curtain wall and the harbour bristling with boats. The palace gleamed in a patch of afternoon sunlight and people milled about in the streets like ants. Higher still and Falco tightened his grip as Ciel banked to one side. He found himself looking down on the academy. He could see the square outline of the barracks quads, the long lines of the stables and the numerous other buildings and training fields. Beside one of them stood a large white tent and Falco saw small figures moving around in front of it. He glanced back towards the mountains.

'*It wouldn't take long to reach the Pike like this*,' he thought and suddenly a memory of the pike appeared in his mind, an image of it wreathed in early morning mist.

'Yes,' he breathed and he felt Ciel roll again as she sped towards the mountains.

For a moment the rocky slopes appeared some way off but all of a sudden they seemed to be rushing up to meet them. He felt certain they were about to crash into the mountainside but at the last moment Ciel spread her wings wide and performed a kind of midair pirouette before alighting on the great slab of stone known as the Pike.

Falco was astonished by the gentleness of the landing. There was no jarring thump just a perfectly controlled descent to stillness. He sat there as the cold wind blew through his hair. He could feel the dragon beneath him, her breathing and the slow deep beating of her heart. She moved her head to take in the view and Falco had the strangest feeling that he knew what she was looking at: the flags on the palace... a group of knights perfecting their dressage... the dark tower of the magi, rising like a black spire against the snow covered mountains behind it.

Ciel's gaze lingered on the tower and so did Falco's. More than any other building the tower of the magi looked closed and forbidding, a place of secrets and power.

Falco drew his gaze away and Ciel followed suit as if she, in turn, knew what he was looking at. He looked beyond the city where a three-masted trading schooner was putting out to sea. Falco had never been to sea in a boat. He found the very notion both exciting and frightening. He wondered what it would be like to ride the waves with the salt spray splashing across the deck. With a smile he focussed on the ship and urged Ciel forward. She seemed to know exactly what he had in mind and with a slight leap she dropped from the pike and hugged the rocky slope as she streaked towards the plateau. They sped high over the city and out over the rising swell beyond the harbour wall. They closed on the Schooner quickly and Falco saw the sailors line the rails as the great dragon banked around the vessel in full mastery of the winds upon whose mercy they were carried away.

All trace of anxiety and nerves had long since vanished from Falco's mind and he leaned down over Ciel's warm back using his hands more for balance than clinging on for dear life.

'*Higher,*' he thought. '*Go high and fast.*'

Ciel seemed to register the meaning of his thoughts because she suddenly drew up and climbed rapidly away from the rolling sea. With every beat of her wings Falco felt an incredible surge of power as they drove up into the sky, climbing higher and higher until the ship was just a child's toy on the grey expanse below. The sound of the wind and the feel of cold wet mist across his face suddenly tugged at something in Falco's mind, a memory that had long since been suppressed.

'*We're in the clouds,*' he thought and he suddenly realised he had thought the same thought once before, long ago, almost before he was able to even form the words.

'*We're in the clouds,*' he thought again and in his mind he heard a laugh, deep and soft and just for him. He felt a presence behind him, enclosing him, embracing him, keeping him safe. No words, no face, just a presence - a father showing his son the incomparable wonder of sharing the sky with a dragon.

He *had* done this before, Falco suddenly realised, somewhere in the distant past, before illness, tragedy and loss. He had been here before, known this before.

They burst out from the clouds and Falco felt the warmth of the pale winter sun upon his face. He let go of Ciel's neck and sat up to savour the unbelievable sense of freedom as they cut through the freezing air. His face felt numb and his hands were beginning to stiffen with the cold but he closed his eyes and abandoned himself to trust. At this height he was but a slip away from certain death but he had never felt so safe. He looked down and the world of Wrath was spread out below him like a map. Then in his mind he heard the distant echo of his father's voice.

'*Now, hold tight,*' said the voice and Falco did.

He leaned down close to Ciel's back, grasped the sinewy cords at the base of her neck and felt a reassuring sense of security as the sharp edge of her scales lifted slightly before settling around the contours of his arms. Then the great dragon banked until she was almost inverted and Falco closed his eyes as they fell through the sky, faster than the bird of prey for which he was named.

'This is glory,' thought Falco, filled by the presence of the dragon. 'How could there ever be evil in this?'

*

Far below in the crucible Aurelian and Nathalie saw them emerge from the base of the clouds, diving at full attack speed.

'He *has* done this before,' said Nathalie. 'Ciel would never fly so hard if he had not.'

Beside her Aurelian could only nod.

But they were not the only ones to have witnessed Falco's flight.

*

On the training field the emissary had called the cadets outside to watch.

'Is that Falco?' asked Bryna.

257

The emissary nodded slowly as the great amber dragon tore across the sky above them. Beside them Malaki just smiled. All the other cadets appeared utterly astonished by the sight of him riding a dragon but Malaki had known Falco all his life and he was not surprised. Not surprised at all.

*

From a lofty window of the palace the Queen saw the dragon racing over the city before heading out to sea. She had been surprised when Aurelian asked her permission for Falco to attempt a flight. The old crank was not as insensitive as he would have people believe. He knew the delicate situation that existed between her and the magi. If she was too public in her support of dragons then the magi could use the murderous blacks to call her judgment into question. But she could not bear the thought of turning her back on the great souls who gave the world so much.

'He rides well,' said Cyrano at her shoulder. 'Maybe the Chevalier was right to bring him after all.'

'*Yes*,' thought the Queen, '*Maybe he was.*'

*

From the high balcony outside the Grand Veneratu's chambers, Galen Thrall watched as the dragon climbed towards the clouds, the sun glinting off its burnt orange scales.

'So, there can be no doubt,' he said.

'No,' said Morgan Saker who was standing beside him. 'The son of Danté is a battle mage.'

'How long before he is ready for the Rite?' asked Thrall.

'That depends on how quickly he learns,' replied Morgan. 'Normally it takes a year or more to hone their skills but with this one, who can say?'

'Then tell the brothers to begin their preparations at once,' said Thrall as they watched the dragon emerge from the clouds and drop like a falling star towards the ground. 'Something tells me the son of Aquila Danté will learn quickly and we cannot afford to meet him unprepared.'

*

Falco opened his eyes as they plummeted towards the earth. The speed took his breath away but still he felt no fear. He could see the oval outline of the crucible growing rapidly below them, but it was only as they drew level with the rim that Ciel spread her wings to check the speed of their descent. Falco felt his body press hard against hers as she swept down the side of the crucible and along the floor before rising briefly and coming to a halt just a few yards from Aurelian and Nathalie. They turned their faces away from the blizzard of snow that blew up in the gust of her wings.

The beautiful amber dragon became still and Falco laid his cheek against the warm steely enamel of her scales. He knew now that this was *not* the first time he had flown with a dragon. He had flown with his father when he was barely old enough to remember. In his mind it was dark scales that lay now beneath his hands, scales that shone like the deepest shade of blood, scales that were almost black.

Falco knew that he should move but he found that he could not. He felt that if he moved he would lose this precious memory, like a dream dispelled by

258

waking. Like the memory of his father's last kiss that had sustained him during the demon's assault. Tears ran from his eyes and disappeared between the scales on Ciel's back. But slowly the intensity of the feeling faded, even if the memory did not. Returning to the present he felt embarrassed by this show of naked emotion but then he felt a gentle hand on his shoulder and he opened his eyes to see that Nathalie was crying too. And beyond her there were tears in the eyes of gruff Aurelian Cruz.

They did not know the details of Falco's emotion but they knew the strength of feeling that bonding with a dragon could stir. And above them, looking down through a crack in the rim of the crucible, was Nicolas Dusaule. There were no tears upon his cheeks but in his heart *he* too was crying. And none of them wept so hard as he.

44

The Chamber of Council

Over the next few weeks Falco took three more flights with Ciel, each time going a little further, and each time trying to reach back into his past in the hope of uncovering more memories that might be buried there. It seemed, however, that there were no more revelations to be uncovered but for Falco it was enough to know that the dreamlike images in his mind were true. He would have loved to have flown more but Aurelian explained that Nathalie and Ciel would soon be heading back to the Illician front.

'They're only here for a short while to rest and recover,' Falco told his friends one evening as they sat around a pot-bellied stove in the barracks. 'Nathalie doesn't really speak about it, but it sounds as if things at the front are pretty grim.'

'Maybe we'll find out more tonight,' said Malaki.

The other cadets nodded slowly. Tonight, for the first time, they would be attending a public strategy meeting in the Chamber of Council. Lanista Magnus had also told them that they would hear details of the training campaign that was due to take place in the spring.

'I wonder where they'll be sending us,' said Alex.

'Don't think I'll be going anywhere,' said Bryna disconsolately.

Falco and the others exchanged awkward glances. The instructors had made it quite clear that they would only be allowed on the campaign if their units were able to perform the required battlefield manoeuvres, including the notorious traverser manoeuvre.

All the other cadets were making good progress but Bryna was still struggling to manage the Dalwhinnies. Despite her best efforts they made no more than a pretence of following her orders. It was only when Patrick Feckler gave them a nod that they would finally do as she said and her lack of control was becoming an issue. However, there was no opportunity to discuss it further as Lanista Magnus arrived to escort them down to the public strategy meeting in the city.

'Anyone is allowed to speak,' he told them. 'But I would advise you to hold your tongue unless you have something useful to say. Marshal Breton does not appreciate contributions from the ill informed.'

The cadets muttered in nervous anticipation as they made their way down from the plateau and into the dimly lit streets of the city. Finally they emerged onto the wide paved area surrounding the Chamber of Council and the cadets gazed in awe at the enormous domed building as crowds of people headed towards the entrances.

Lanista Magnus led them to an archway that gave onto a lofty passage, very different to the dark tunnel through which Falco had entered on the day of his hearing. They emerged half way up one side of the terraced seats and were immediately surrounded by a hubbub of noise from hundreds of people talking in low voices.

The cadets filed into a series of rows as everyone began to settle into their seats. Falco sat with his friends while Lanista Magnus took a seat directly behind them. Across the room Falco saw Nathalie sitting with two men in military uniform. A few rows down from her sat a group of magi, including Morgan Saker and Galen Thrall.

Drawing his eyes away from the magi Falco turned his attention back to the huge room which was lit by dozens of brass oil lamps, either fixed to the walls or hung from the ceiling on chains.

The floor of the chamber had been cleared leaving just a single row of ornate chairs to one side. The centre oval space was covered by a large carpet fully thirty feet long and twenty wide. Falco vaguely remembered the carpet from his first visit but on that occasion he had not really appreciated it. From where he was now sitting he could see that it was a map, not just of Clemoncé, but the entire world of Wrath. As he watched, a line of assistants began to roll it back and Falco realised that the carpet was just a covering for the real map that lay beneath, a map of such detail and beauty that it literally took their breath away.

'Look at that!' breathed Bryna in a tone of reverence.

Falco shook his head in wonder. Never in his wildest dreams had he imagined a map like this. Filling the space where the carpet had been was a huge rectangular panel of inlaid marble. The cartographers had used different colours of stone to differentiate land from sea with warm, earthy shades of ochre for the land and a pale rippling grey for the ocean.

The border surrounding the map was defined by an elegant pattern of knot-work inlaid with silver and bronze. The surface was polished to a deep sheen that brought out the rich colours of the stone without detracting from the huge amount of detail that had been worked into the map.

The cadets were enthralled and Falco had the sense that he was back on Ciel, flying high above the world.

'Look,' said Malaki, drawing Falco out of his reverie. 'There's Caer Dour.'

Falco followed the line of his finger until he could see a small black dot denoting the position of their home town in the north of Valentia.

'And there's *our* home city, Reiherstadt,' said Alex. 'In the hills north of Lake Viegal.'

Falco could see the area Alex was meaning, but then he noticed that Reiherstadt lay in the portion of the map that had been painted with some kind of red lacquer. The red area extended across the whole of Ferocia and covered most of Illicia and Beltane. Falco suddenly realised that this red 'shading' marked the area known as the Forsaken Lands, territory that had been lost to the Possessed.

The carpet was finally rolled clear and the assistants departed through a tunnel from which a number of scribes and cartographers now appeared. They carried rolls of parchment and drawing cases with which they could record the details of the meeting. Two of them carried trays filled with small metal ornaments like the pieces of a chess set, while another carried a number of long brass rods that were clearly used as pointers. As they lined up along the near side of the map another man emerged from the tunnel and Falco recognised him as Cyrano, the Queen's advisor.

Dressed as ever in his black chenille doublet and turquoise cloak, he swept the room with his hawk-like gaze. When everything seemed to be in order he stepped back from the archway and the people in the hall rose to their feet. At a prompt from Lanista Magnus the cadets did the same.

Queen Catherine emerged from the tunnel with Prince Ludovico at her side and Falco was reminded of just how striking she was, tall and slender with long dark hair and a face that was both beautiful and strong.

Behind them came a man Falco had never seen before.

'That's Marshal Breton,' whispered Alex, nodding towards the stern looking man with long grey hair and a neatly trimmed moustache and beard. Next came the emissary and a dark haired man with a moustache and beard in the same style as Marshal Breton. 'And that's General Renucci of the Fourth,' said Alex. 'Second in command to the Chevalier.'

Falco looked down at the general but his eye was drawn to the emissary. Looking almost elegant in a tunic of pale grey velvet with his long hair washed and combed, Falco had never seen him looking so well groomed, and yet there remained a distinct shadow of stubble on his jaw.

When the dignitaries were seated the cartographers bowed to the Queen before moving onto the map. Two of them knelt and began to remove the line showing the extent of the Forsaken Lands. Then, referring to a series of smaller maps, they redrew the line and filled in the new area by painting it with the red lacquer. The crimson liquid shrank away from the polished marble to leave a mottled effect which gave the impression of it having been blistered or scorched in a fire. It was a sobering sight to see the advance of the Possessed portrayed so graphically. Only in two areas had the allies held their ground, in the north around the Illician city of Hoffen and in the south around the Beltonian cities of Aengus and Maiden.

'All that, in just a few months,' said Alex. 'Another year and there will be nothing left of Illicia and Beltane.'

Falco glanced across at the two brothers. They were from Illicia but it was clear that even they had not realised just how bad things had become.

With the new 'front line' drawn on the map the cartographers proceeded to lay out the small metal ornaments. Allied armies were represented by small bronze shields, while miniature castles denoted the location of fortified towns.

'The swords mark the location of a battle mage,' explained Lanista Magnus. 'Possessed forces are portrayed by the banners and the demonic figurines mark the location of demons.'

'What about that demon figure in Beltane?' asked Bryna. 'It looks different to the others.'

'We think that's the Enemy's chief lieutenant,' said Lanista Magnus. 'The one they call the Marchio Dolor.'

At the mention of this name Falco felt a prickle of disquiet crawling over his skin. The light in the chamber seemed to dim and in his mind he heard the low demonic voice from his nightmares.

You would never have the courage

You would never have the strength

The extent of Falco's vision seemed to shrink until all he could see was the small bronze figure of the Marchio Dolor. But then his gaze was drawn to the north and Falco frowned as if he had expected to see another distinctive model sitting on the map. A sound pulsed in his ears but he could not tell if it was a demonic growl or just the rush of blood pulsing in his veins.

'Are you all right?'

Malaki's voice drew him back to the present and Falco looked around the room.

The cartographers had finished laying out the pieces and it was clear to all that the armies of Wrath were grossly outnumbered. Stepping back off the map the cartographers bowed to the Queen who then invited Marshal Breton to take the floor.

Moving to the edge of the map the marshal took a long brass rod from one of the cartographers then, without any preamble, he launched into a summary of the strategic position between the allied armies and the forces of the Possessed.

Falco watched with morbid fascination as Marshal Breton outlined the desperate situation of the war. This was the first time he had seen a strategic map like this but even to his eyes the situation looked hopeless. The only thing that seemed odd to him was a strange gap in the forces of the Possessed as if the cartographers had forgotten to place down a figure. He was sure that this would soon be explained but Marshal Breton seemed to be coming to the end of his initial address.

'If the Possessed continue to advance at the same rate they will reach our border within the year,' he concluded.

'What about Acheron and Thraece?' asked someone from across the hall. 'Are they still refusing to join us?

Marshal Breton nodded.

'And what about Valentia?' asked another. 'Will they stand and fight if the Possessed reach their border?'

'We fear not,' said Marshal Breton. 'We now believe that King Vittorio will withdraw his forces to protect Caer Laison.'

'But that would leave the pass of Amaethon completely open,' said General Renucci. 'The Possessed might simply ignore Caer Laison and push straight through into Navaria.'

'That is a danger, yes,' said Marshal Breton.

'That would leave our southern border exposed,' pressed the general. 'Perhaps we should consider reinforcing Navaria?'

'We can't,' said Marshal Breton. 'The treaty with Acheron forbids us from taking an army into Navaria.'

'But Navaria has no army of its own. Tyramimus must realise that they are defenceless.'

'Of course he does,' said the Queen coming to stand beside Marshal Breton. 'That is why the state of Navaria was established in the first place, to provide a buffer between two warring nations.'

'But if the Possessed broke through, the Navarians wouldn't stand a chance.'

'Then let us hope that they do not,' said the Queen smiling at General Renucci's indignation.

Presenting a remarkable sense of calm she also took a pointer from one of the cartographers and proceeded to summarise what the marshal had just told them.

'So, the First Army is currently garrisoned in Hoffen,' she said, pointing to the city in the north of Illicia. 'The Second and the Third are deployed in the south and the Fifth is still recovering and recruiting back to full strength?'

'And the Fourth is now ready for deployment, along with the mage army,' said Marshal Breton.'

The Queen nodded her head in thought. 'That leaves us with the Irregulars and the Légion Du Trône.'

'Which must remain in defence of the capital,' said Marshal Breton as if he suspected what the Queen might be thinking.

'Of course,' said the Queen, somewhat defensively.

'She hates having to stay behind,' said Lanista Magnus quietly. 'Sending others off to war while she remains safely in the capital.'

Using her pointer the Queen drew two lines from Clemoncé to Illicia.

'So, we shall reinforce the city Hoffen with the Fourth and, once it has recovered, the Fifth can move south to shore up the area around Amboss.'

'But that would mean committing all five of the regular armies abroad,' said Prince Ludovico. 'Is it not folly to leave the Kingdom so unprotected?'

'On the contrary,' said the emissary as he too stepped forward. 'Sending armies abroad remains the best way to protect the Kingdom. Our main priority is to halt the advance of the Possessed. And we must convince Acheron and Thraece to join us. Without their strength it is only a matter of time before we fall.'

'Acheron is too arrogant,' said General Renucci. 'And Thraece will never join us. Not while the magi keep King Cleomenes on his deathbed.'

At this Galen Thrall rose from his seat.

'I am quite sure Thraece will join us, once our mage army has had the opportunity to prove itself on the battlefield. They are training mage armies of their own and I am sure these will be successful where conventional armies have failed.'

The military commanders bristled at Thrall's assertion that they had 'failed', but the Queen showed no sign of irritation.

'The mage army will get its chance soon enough,' was all she said. 'In the meantime we will continue to support Illicia and Beltane.' She turned to the emissary. 'When will the Fourth Army be ready to march?'

'Another two or three weeks, Your Majesty,' replied the emissary. 'We're just waiting on the latest reports. If the snowfall in the valleys has not been too great we'll be able to take a direct route to the front.'

'Good,' said the Queen, although Falco sensed her anxiety at the thought of the emissary returning to war. 'And will it still be safe for the cadets to carry out their training campaign later in the season?'

'It should be,' said the emissary. 'We have reports of minor incursions and night raids, but so long as nothing changes in the next few months they should be able to complete the exercise as planned.'

'And have the goals of their campaign been decided?'

'They will be taking supplies and reinforcements to the city of Le Matres,' said the emissary. 'They will then help to build two new bridges over the river Naern before escorting casualties and refugees back to the capital. It should take about two months to complete.'

'Excellent,' said the Queen. 'Now, let us proceed to the orders we need to write.'

The scribes now took up their quills ready to pen the new wave of orders that would be dispatched to the front.

Falco heard Bryna whisper something to Malaki about the training campaign but he was not really listening. He was still waiting for them to address the strange 'gap' to the south of Hoffen, but they never did.

As it became clear that the meeting was coming to a close Falco found himself rising from his seat. The cartographers began to clear the map while the scribes prepared the orders and still Falco stood there. People began to whisper and point. Some of them began to laugh. Lanista Magnus looked at Falco with a raised eyebrow but he made no attempt to sit him down.

'Do you have something to add, cadet?'

Falco's gaze drifted down to Marshal Breton who was now looking up at him. The rest of the people on the floor turned to look at him also. The marshal was clearly irritated and Thrall gave Falco a cold, contemptuous stare. As for the others they merely appeared curious as to what Falco might have to say.

'Well, Master Danté,' said the Queen. 'Do you have something to contribute?'

Falco's mouth went dry as he suddenly realised that everyone in the chamber was now looking at him. He licked his lips.

'I was just wondering about the gap in Illicia.'

'What gap?' said Marshal Breton, looking down at the metal figures that the cartographers had begun to pack away.

'The gap in the forces of the Possessed,' said Falco. 'To the south of Hoffen.'

Marshal Breton frowned as if Falco were talking nonsense but the emissary strode over to the area in question.

'Come and show us,' said the Queen.

Feeling deeply self-conscious Falco made his way out of the row and down the steps leading to the floor. Ignoring the stony looks from Thrall and Marshal Breton he walked out onto the polished marble map.

'Here,' he said. 'There's a gap in the forces of the Possessed.'

'That's not a gap,' said General Renucci. 'Look... there's a Ferocian army here and here with at least two demons in the area.'

'Yes, said Falco. 'But it's one of the few areas where we've had some success. The leader of the Possessed would never allow such victories to go unchallenged. There should be something here.'

Everyone was now staring at him and even the emissary seemed uncertain. Marshal Breton's expression suggested that he had heard enough.

'How long have you been training at the academy?' he asked.

'About three months, my Lord.'

'And how long have you spent studying the movements and strategy of the Possessed.'

Falco bowed his head and Marshal Breton gave a dismissive snort, but the Queen looked up into the seats on the far side of the chamber.

'Battle Mage Saigal,' she said, using the formal title to address Nathalie. 'Do you see anything unusual in the enemy's battle lines?'

Nathalie glanced at Falco before looking back down at the map, her eyes narrowed in thought. Finally she shook her head.

'I would not have noted it myself but I too am surprised that the response has not been stronger in the north.'

The Queen turned back to Falco while Galen Thrall glanced at him with a condescending smile.

'Surely we're not going to take advice from a boy who is not even *trained* as a battle mage,' he said.

'Falco would not have spoken up without reason,' said the emissary but Thrall merely curled his lip in disdain.

'Besides,' said the Queen. 'Was it not Syballian himself who said that battle mages are born and not trained?'

Thrall's pupils shrank with annoyance. It smarted to have the words of the most powerful Veneratu of all time quoted back at him, but he bowed to the Queen and turned away as if Falco's observations were of little consequence.

'Well,' continued the Queen. 'The Illician battle mages Wildegraf Feuerson and Jürgen Focke are in the vicinity. If there is anything untoward in the area I'm sure they will discover it. Besides,' she added, 'the Fourth Army will soon be heading in that direction but we should not be complacent.'

She turned to address the scribes.

'Let it be entered into the records that an irregularity in the enemy lines was noted by battle mage-in-training, Falco Danté.'

Falco swallowed hard as his vague suspicions were entered into the official records. Only time would tell if they had any basis in reality. Glancing round he caught disapproving looks from Marshal Breton and Galen Thrall but then the emissary caught his eye and, while he did not smile, he gave Falco a nod as if to say, 'well done.'

'If there is nothing else,' said the Queen. She glanced around at the people standing on the map but it seemed that no one had anything further to add. 'Then I thank you all for your time and call this public strategy meeting to a close.'

The entire chamber rose to its feet and placed their right hand across their chest in salute then, with a bow to her people, the Queen led the dignitaries back through the tunnel at the far end of the floor.

Falco returned to his friends as the carpet was rolled back into place. The cadets looked at him as if they could not believe how outspoken he had been. Lanista Magnus said nothing at first, although his heavy brow was creased in a frown.

'Sorry,' said Falco. 'I just felt as if I had to say something.'

'Don't apologise,' said Lanista Magnus. 'You will need the courage of your convictions if you are going to lead. Mind you, I thought Galen Thrall was going to pass a stone when the Queen quoted Syballian at him.'

The cadets laughed and together they moved to join the flow of people leaving the chamber. There was much talk and discussion between the cadets as they made their way out. Alex and Quirren were understandably subdued while Malaki was talking to Bryna about the problems she was having with the Dalwhinnies.

'You just have to show them who's in charge,' said Malaki.

'That's the trouble,' said Bryna. 'They know *exactly* who's in charge. Patrick bloody Feckler.'

'Why don't you challenge him to a competition?' suggested Malaki as they emerged onto the plaza. 'If you beat him they might just fall in line.'

'Fat chance of that,' said Bryna. 'Besides, I'm not sure I could beat him. He's a good archer, they all are. It's just that they don't listen to a word I say. In two days time I'm supposed to give a demonstration of suivez cinq, and if we can't perform the traverser manoeuvre we won't be allowed on the training campaign at all.'

Malaki grabbed her shoulders and planted a kiss on the top of her head.

'You'll figure them out,' he said.

Falco smiled but he was not really listening. He was thinking of what Lanista Magnus had said about him being a leader. He had never thought of himself as such. Indeed he found the very notion terrifying. People risking their lives on the strength of his judgement? He did not know how the Queen endured it.

He had only spoken up because he felt that it would have been wrong not to do so. He did not realise that this willingness to step forward and take responsibility was precisely what defined a leader. Had this occurred to him earlier he may well have held his tongue.

45

A Mental Block

The magi were in a dark mood as they returned to the tower. Galen Thrall in particular seemed to be swathed in a cloud of ill temper. Despite his efforts to assert himself the Queen had managed to retain control of the meeting, giving him no opportunity to expand on the virtues of the mage army. For a man like Thrall it was galling to be so efficiently outmanoeuvred. The fact that Falco had been allowed to speak only served to compound his displeasure. As they entered the main reception chamber Thrall gathered the senior mages around him.

'The Queen's lapdog departs in a few weeks' time,' Meredith heard him say. 'We must be ready to give him a lesson in the art of war.'

Meredith arched an eyebrow at Thrall's arrogance, but the words were not meant for him and so he said nothing. Instead he lowered his head and made his way towards the stairs leading down to the archives. He was almost at the top of the spiral staircase when Thrall's voice stopped him in his tracks.

'A moment, Master Saker. If you please.'

Meredith turned to see the Grand Veneratu eyeing him with a disturbingly keen stare. The other mages had begun to disperse and Meredith felt a tremor of unease as he returned to stand before the Worshipful Master of the tower.

'This Danté...' said Thrall, looking at Meredith as if he knew all the hidden secrets of his heart. 'He learns quickly?'

'No, Master,' said Meredith with a shake of his head. 'He learns slowly. But what he does learn he masters quickly.'

'Hmm...' intoned Thrall as if this was not what he wanted to hear. 'And there is still no sign of offensive capability.'

Meredith struggled to conceal his indignation. The Grand Veneratu was clearly keeping an eye on their training sessions.

'No,' he said. 'He is strong but his powers remain purely defensive. When it comes to aggression there is a block in his mind.'

'Have you identified the source?'

Meredith nodded. 'Guilt, shame and fear.'

'Oh?'

'Guilt and shame for what his father did.'

'And fear of the enemy,' suggested Thrall but Meredith shook his head.

'No, Master,' he said. 'Falco fears the Possessed, of course, but that is not the source of the block.'

'Then what is?'

'It is the fear of madness and murder, the fear of turning out like his father.'

Now it was Thrall's turn to nod. 'And will he overcome it?'

'I do not know,' said Meredith. 'He cannot change what happened in the past.'

'Quite,' said Thrall, his waxy green eyes glinting with an edge of ice.

'Will that be all, Master?'

'Yes,' said Thrall. 'I would not wish to keep you from your studies.'

Meredith sensed satisfaction in Thrall's demeanour but there was also a certain wariness lurking behind his outward calm. With a bow he turned once more in the direction of the archives. As he descended the long winding stair he found himself wondering yet again about the magi's opposition to Falco. At some point, in the not too distant future, the magi would attempt to break Falco's resolve in the Rite of Assay and it was his job to make sure he was prepared. But if Falco could not call upon offensive powers then this would leave him at a huge disadvantage. Even if they were never used, the knowledge that such powers were at your disposal provided a powerful psychological crutch. Without it Meredith was certain that Falco would fail.

He spent the rest of the night reading various texts on the history of Wrath and the physiology of dragonkind, but his concentration was broken by an uncomfortable thought that kept surfacing in his mind. It was the fear of letting Falco down.

46

Respect

The cadets were in a reflective mood the following morning. Not only had the strategy meeting given them much to think about but, with the departure of the Fourth Army now imminent, the emissary had announced that today would be his last training session with them. The instructors were also holding a meeting of their own and so the morning session had been concluded early. Most of the cadets took the opportunity for an early lunch while Quirren led several of the trainee knights up to the dressage field to prepare for the afternoon session.

Malaki would have gone with them but Bryna was heading over to the archery ranges to see if she could make any headway with the Dalwhinnies, so he decided to grab some food and go with her. Falco was eager to get up to the crucible but he knew that Bryna would appreciate the moral support so he and Alex went with her too. Reaching the low rise overlooking the archery ranges they spread their cloaks on the cold ground and took out the food they had brought with them.

'I've tried everything,' said Bryna. 'They're completely uncontrollable.'

'Of course they are,' said Alex. 'No one can control the Dalwhinnies. Not unless you're a murdering criminal like Paddy the Feck.'

Malaki and Falco exchanged a worried look. They had never known Bryna so downhearted.

'Well you're early today,' said Malaki. 'Why don't you just go down and start shooting. Maybe some of them will join you.'

'No chance,' said Bryna. 'They never do anything unless Paddy tells them to.'

The others grimaced awkwardly but there was nothing to be done. With a sigh Bryna took up her bow and started down the slope to the ranges. Even from here they could hear the chorus of whistles and laughter that greeted her arrival.

'Think I'd rather face a hoard of Kardakae,' said Alex.

Falco laughed softly but Malaki was watching Bryna intently. It was not easy for him to see her treated in this way. They watched as she tried to engage some of the men in conversation without success. Finally she walked over to one of the ranges and began to shoot.

The Dalwhinnies watched her with a mixture of amusement, indifference and lust. Over to one side they could see the large figure of Patrick Feckler surrounded by a dozen similarly rough-looking individuals. These were men who had carved out their lives in the shadowed quarters of the world: poachers, mercenaries, debt collectors and worse. They were not about to be told what to do by some slip of a girl, no matter how pretty she was or how well she could shoot.

'How's she getting on?'

The boys turned to see the emissary leading his horse, Tapfer, towards them.

'Not well,' said Falco.

Below them Bryna had just finished a round. They saw her collect her arrows before making her way back up towards them. As she drew close they

270

rose to their feet and Malaki offered her a napkin full of food, but Bryna shook her head and turned back to look down at the company of archers that were causing her so much trouble. Now that she had left them the Dalwhinnies began to practice as Paddy walked up to the shooting line.

'They do that just to spite me,' said Bryna and Falco could tell that she was close to tears.

Malaki tried to slip his arm around her waist but Bryna just shrugged him off.

'Have you managed suivez cinq or dix?' asked the emissary.

Bryna shook her head.

'I take it then, that you haven't even begun practicing the traverser.'

Once again Bryna shook her head. The boys looked at each other as an uncomfortable silence settled around them. From below they heard a wave of laughter as Patrick Feckler glanced up towards the small group of people looking down at *his* Dalwhinnies.

'They just don't respect me,' said Bryna.

'And why should they?' asked the emissary and Falco was surprised by the harshness of his tone.

'I...' began Bryna but the emissary cut her off.

'You're just a piece of skirt from a small provincial town. Some of these men have whored girls like you for a living. Do you really expect them to respect you just because you can shoot straight?'

Beside him Bryna shook her head and a single tear ran down her cheek.

Falco glanced at the emissary. He could be a stern man but it was not in his nature to be cruel. He was taking a hard line with Bryna for a reason.

'The Dalwhinnies do not have to respect *you*, Bryna Godwin. But they do have to respect your rank.'

Bryna turned her face to look at the emissary but there was no hint of compromise in his eyes. For a moment she just stared at him and then she smiled. Reaching for Malaki's hand she gave him a light kiss on the lips, an apology for brushing him off a moment ago. Then, slinging her bow across her back she started back down the slope.

A new wave of appreciation rose up from the Dalwhinnies at Bryna's spirited return and her friends watched as she walked into the midst of the rowdy men who parted as she made directly for the large figure of Patrick Feckler.

'Oh blades,' cursed Malaki softly. 'What the hell's she up to now?'

Falco did not know. From where they were standing they could not hear what was being said.

Bryna's heart was thumping in her chest as she made her way up to the man who controlled the Dalwhinnies. Paddy The Feck turned to watch her advance, a look of genuine amusement in his deep set eyes. Bryna walked up until she stood directly in front of him and many of the men laughed to see her slight figure squaring up to Paddy's broad-shoulder bulk.

'This afternoon we will perfect the manoeuvre known as suivez cinq,' said Bryna. 'And tomorrow...'

'Forgive me, little mistress,' interrupted Paddy in an apologetic tone. 'But this afternoon the men will be...'

SLAP!

Bryna smacked Patrick Feckler across the face with all the force she could muster. The big man reeled from the unexpected blow but he smiled a wicked smile as he turned back to look at her.

SLAP!

Another slap, every bit as hard as the first and now Paddy winced at the pain, any trace of amusement gone from his eyes.

'Why, you...'

SLAP!

The Dalwhinnies gave a collective gasp of pure astonishment as Bryna slapped their leader for a third time. She tried for a fourth but Paddy caught her arm in one large calloused fist. His other hand came up, quick and threatening, but Bryna lifted her chin as if she were daring him to strike her. For a moment Paddy's dark gaze burned into Bryna's face with murderous fury, but his hand stalled and he looked suddenly at a loss. He knew the penalty for striking a superior officer and whether he liked it or not, Bryna *was* his superior officer.

A tense silence settled on the scene and still Paddy did not move. Then Dedric Sayer started towards Bryna and there was no mistaking the violence in his eyes. He also knew the penalty for striking an officer, but he was not about to let Bryna humiliate their leader. He would take the lash for Paddy and his standing among the Dalwhinnies would be greatly enhanced.

Striding forward he raised his hand and Bryna flinched in anticipation of the blow but at the last minute Paddy let go of Bryna and punched Sayer in the side of the face. He dropped to the floor like a sack of potatoes and the atmosphere was so thick with shock that you could have cut it with an axe.

Once again silence descended until Bryna broke it with a voice that was surprisingly strong and steady.

'Now,' she said, looking round at the host of dark eyes staring at her. 'This afternoon we are going to master suivez cinq. And tomorrow,' she added, looking at Patrick Feckler and daring him to speak. 'We are going to master suivez dix.'

Unslinging her bow she turned to look at a group of four men standing on the shooting line, the tips of their bows resting casually on their boots.

'You four,' she said, drawing an arrow and nocking it to the string. 'On the command of suivez cinq you will each hit the target I choose.'

One of the men instinctively turned to look at Paddy but quick as a flash Bryna drew her bow and shot an arrow through the man's right boot.

'Don't look at him, damn you!' she cried. 'I am the commander of the Dalwhinnies and by the stars you will look at me!'

The man winced as the arrow nicked the flesh of his calf, but Bryna already had another on the string and it would have been a brave and stupid man who looked away from her then. With a face like thunder she stepped ahead of the four men on the shooting line.

'Suivez cinq!' she called out and shot an arrow into the second target from the left.

Behind her four bowstrings sang and four arrows thudded into the target that Bryna had hit.

'Suivez cinq!' she said again, this time hitting the furthest target to the right.

Behind her there came another collective twang but this time only three of the arrows found their mark. The fourth one had missed the boss completely, but the man who fired it *was* limping on an injured leg with an arrow sticking through his boot.

'Right!' shouted Bryna, rounding on the Dalwhinnies. 'The rest of you split into groups of five and fill the shooting lines. I want every last one of you to be able to perform this before the day is out.'

The Dalwhinnies stared at her, too stunned to move, then...

'Well, what are you waiting for you black hearted bastards?' roared Paddy The Feck. 'You heard the commander. Groups of five, on the line... Go!'

The Dalwhinnies leapt into action and, with a terrible commotion of squabbling, confusion and the odd violent scuffle, they divided themselves into groups of five and began to practice the archery technique known as suivez cinq.

Amidst the confusion and the growing thrum of bowstrings Bryna turned to see Patrick Feckler standing in front of her. The big grizzle-faced man was looking at her with an unreadable expression in his deeply shadowed eyes.

Bryna had been surprised when he added his voice in support of hers but if nothing else, Paddy was a pragmatist. He knew that Bryna had played the one card to which he had no answer. In that moment he had lost his place as first man of the Dalwhinnies. However, with the instincts of a survivor he realised he could still claim the place of second, even if the first man was now a woman.

Face flushed and feeling faint, Bryna waited for him to speak.

'By shite girl, but I bet your father's proud of you.'

Bryna felt a lump rise in her throat.

'My father was killed by a demon in the mountains,' she said. 'But yes. He *was* proud of me.'

For a moment Paddy just looked at her but then he nodded.

'You still got that cup we gave you?'

Bryna dipped her head.

'Then bring it along to the Irregulars' mess tonight and we'll give you a proper Dalwhinnie welcome.'

Bryna gave the smallest of nods and Paddy stepped aside to let her pass.

'*Oh blades,*' she thought as she left the shooting range in search of somewhere to throw up. '*Now they're expecting me to drink with them.*'

As she walked away she heard Paddy's coarse voice ring out as one of the men nearly shot his companion in the back.

'Not like that, Harper, you sheep worrying sodomite! Move your feet if you have to!'

*

Back on the slope Bryna's friends breathed a sigh of relief as it finally became clear that she was not going to get beaten to a pulp. Falco glanced across at Malaki who was staring down at Bryna with a fierce intensity in his eyes. At one point he had been on the verge of charging down to take on the Dalwhinnies single handed, but the emissary held him back.

'Give her a minute,' he said as Bryna slapped Paddy for the second time.

Now they watched as the Dalwhinnies scurried onto the firing line and Bryna faced Paddy before making her way towards the bowyer's workshops where she disappeared behind the low wooden buildings.

'Well you did say she'd figure them out,' said Falco.

Malaki looked at him and shook his head, smiling as the adrenalin slowly leeched out of his body.

'And I thought Paddy the Feck was scary,' said Alex.

The three of them laughed and the emissary laughed with them. He might have given Bryna the secret of how to master the Dalwhinnies but it was Bryna herself who faced down their intimidating leader with two hundred grim faced men at his back. She had shown that when it came to leadership it was not physical strength that was important.

It was strength of character that mattered most.

It was strength of character that earned respect.

47

A Single Touch

Three weeks later, on a cold winter's morning, the Fourth Army departed and it seemed as if the whole of Wrath had turned out to see them off. The city was crowded with civilians as the army marched down from the plateau and made its way along the broad main streets of the city. People watched in respectful silence as the troops filed past and stared in fascination at the column of warrior mages who marched with them. The two forces would continue until they reached The Square of the Nameless Knight. There they would wait for their commanders to join them after a final audience with the Queen, a reminder that they went to war in Her name.

However, before he went to meet the Queen, the commander of the Fourth Army made a point of stopping by the academy barracks to say a personal farewell to the cadets. The emissary spoke encouraging words to Malaki, Bryna, Alex and Quirren and to all the rest but not to Falco, for Falco was not there. He too had been summoned to attend the Queen and he stood with her now as they watched the column of soldiers winding through the city.

'Always such a stirring spectacle,' said the Queen as they stood on the high terrace overlooking the city. 'Both glorious and sad.'

She turned to look at Falco, making no attempt to hide the emotion in her eyes. Beneath her blue cloak and wolf fur mantle the Queen was dressed in armour, a sword hanging from the black horse-head belt that the emissary had made for her. It was quite clear that this was not armour of a ceremonial kind. This was armour designed for battle.

'Absurd, is it not?' said the Queen as she noticed the direction of his gaze. 'As Commander-in-Chief tradition dictates that I dress accordingly, despite the fact that this armour has never known a day of war.'

'There's more than one way to fight a war, Your Majesty,' said Falco and the Queen gave a wry laugh.

'You're beginning to sound like him.' She nodded to one of the riders now making their way up towards the palace, a rider clad in mail and riding a beautiful smoke grey Percheron. Riding beside the emissary was the captain of the mage army, a man called Dagoran Sorn. The emissary wore a surcoat and cloak in the pale blue and turquoise colours of the Queen, while the warrior mage's robes were deep purple over a shirt of close-knit mail.

They caught glimpses of the riders as they made their way through the rising streets towards their parting audience with the Queen. They watched them until they disappeared beneath the outer palace walls and the Queen's gaze moved back to the army.

'They march beyond Le Matres,' she said. 'Towards the city of Hoffen.'

She did not look at him, but Falco understood the anxiety in her voice. So this was why she had wanted to see him. The emissary marched towards the area where he had perceived a gap in the forces of the Possessed. Clemoncé had always prided itself on the quality of its military intelligence and the Queen was tormented by the possibility that she might have missed something, that she might be sending her people into unknown danger.

'Is there nothing more that you can tell me about what you felt in the meeting?'

Falco shook his head. 'It was only a vague sensation,' he said, feeling as if he had somehow let her down. 'I nearly didn't say anything at all.'

The Queen paused for a moment and then she sighed, smiling slightly as if it was unfair to press him for more certainty.

'Is there any word from the Illician battle mages?' asked Falco.

'No. But that's not unusual. It will take some time for Nathalie to find them and even then they might not be free to investigate straight away. Even our great souls cannot be everywhere at once.'

Falco took a discreet sideways glance at the Queen as she gazed down over the city. He could hear the weariness in her voice, the strain of coordinating a war that most people believed they could not win. He took in the clean line of her jaw and the pale expanse of her cheek, the contrast between the soft skin of her throat and the hard edge of her armoured breastplate. A gust of wind blew her dark hair back from her face and for a moment he saw her not as a queen but simply as a woman, strong and beautiful, yet filled with doubt and the terrible fear of letting her people down.

Falco felt a sudden surge of love for her and he knew, in that moment, that he would do anything in his power to help her.

'A gaze like that is enough to make a woman blush, Master Danté,' said the Queen.

Falco turned away, but when the Queen turned to look at him it was not she who blushed, but he. She smiled and Falco was spared any further embarrassment as Cyrano appeared behind them.

'The warrior mage, Dagoran Sorn, and the commander of the Fourth Army, seek an audience with the Throne and the blessing of her Royal Majesty, the Queen.'

The Queen squared her shoulders and lifted her face. Falco saw her take a deep breath and close her eyes as she gathered her courage. To resist the legions of hell was one thing. To say goodbye to the man she loved, in the full knowledge that she might never see him again, that was quite another.

'Thank you, Cyrano.' she said at last.

The Queen's advisor bowed his head and with nothing more than a look he made it clear that Falco's audience was over.

Falco turned to the Queen and bowed.

'Your Majesty,' he said as he waited to be released from her presence.

'Perhaps we might speak again sometime. If your training permits it, of course.'

'I would be honoured,' said Falco, blushing once more.

'Till the next time then,' said the Queen and Falco knew that he had been dismissed.

He walked over to where Cyrano stood at the archway in the palace wall. Beside him were two men. The first was the emissary, the second was a relatively small man with strong hawkish features and dark penetrating eyes. This was the man Galen Thrall had chosen to lead his precious mage army into the fray.

'Lord Sorn,' said Cyrano, inviting the warrior mage to come forward.

Dagoran Sorn gave a stiff bow and allowed the Queen's advisor to lead him forth.

Falco and the emissary watched as the two men made their way towards the Queen who was now standing at the very edge of the terrace, in full view of the people gathered in the streets below.

'Did she ask you about the Possessed?'

Falco glanced at the emissary and nodded.

'Don't be too hard on yourself,' said the emissary. 'Every scout and captain who ever made a report wishes he could tell her more. Anything to ease the strain she bears.'

Now Falco looked at him properly, amazed as ever by the way he saw through to the truth of things.

'Did you get a chance to see the others?'

The emissary nodded.

'Good,' said Falco. 'Alex was convinced you were going to leave without saying goodbye.'

The emissary gave a soft laugh. 'Aurelian tells me you're progressing well.'

'In some ways,' said Falco and the emissary gave a knowing smile.

'He says you're struggling with offensive force.'

'Not struggling, incapable,' said Falco, his tone echoing the dismay he felt at not being able to summon even the smallest magical attack. 'It makes no sense,' he went on. 'Given a sword I'd attack without a second thought.'

'Perhaps it's because you don't associate a sword with murder.'

Falco looked up sharply. Once again the emissary had cut to the chase.

They were silent for a moment as they watched Dagoran Sorn concluding his audience with the Queen.

'I once had to execute a man under my command,' said the emissary. 'A friend who had committed murder in a moment of madness.' He paused. 'Do you know what he said to me as they slipped the noose around his neck?'

Falco just looked at him.

'He said it was easier to die, than to have killed a man and live.'

Falco's eyes welled up because it was true. The fear of committing evil was greater than the fear of evil itself.

'You are not your father, Falco,' said the emissary. 'You are not doomed to share his fate.'

Falco blinked the tears from his eyes. Out on the terrace he suddenly became aware that Cyrano was hovering. Sorn's audience was over. The Queen was waiting on the commander of the Fourth. The emissary gave the Queen's advisor a nod.

'Until we meet again,' he said, offering Falco his hand.

'Do you think we will?'

'In war, who can say?' said the emissary. 'But it's always good to hope.'

He pulled Falco into a rough embrace then with a final smile he walked away to say goodbye to his Queen.

Falco watched as the emissary approached the Queen. Head high and shoulders square, no one would suspect the doubts and fears clutching at his heart. As he reached her he knelt and waited to feel the gentle pressure of her hand upon his head.

Far below them the people watched as the Queen received the commander of the Fourth Army. They watched as she reached out to bestow what blessing she could on the men and women who would march out behind him. Finally she removed her hand and the emissary stood before her. From where he was standing Falco could not hear a word of what was said but the Queen and her emissary spoke for a few minutes while the people of Wrath looked on.

*

Sir William Chevalier felt the full weight of the mail upon his shoulders as he stood to face his Queen. His composure nearly failed him as he raised his eyes to look upon her face, but he knew that they each relied upon the other's strength and so his gaze was steady as he looked into the deep blue eyes of the woman he loved.

*

For what seemed a long time the Queen said nothing but simply let her eyes roam over the emissary's familiar features: the strong and weathered face, the growing number of scars, the stern jaw swathed in its eternal stubble, peppered, as was his shoulder length hair, with an increasing amount of grey. The broken nose, the proud brow, and the eyes... the beautiful stone grey eyes that always reminded her of the sea.

Fully aware that the entire city was watching, the Queen drank in the sight of him. She could not escape the horrible feeling that this might be the last time they saw each other; that he was riding into a shadow from which he might never return. The thought was almost too much and she felt her resolve begin to weaken but, as ever, he was there to steady her.

'The Fourth Army of Clemoncé seeks the blessing of the Throne as we ride out to face the enemies of our realm.'

The stuffy ceremonial words brought the Queen back from the brink and she raised her chin in dignity once more.

'You have it,' she said. 'Ride with the light of our love in your hearts.'

The emissary bowed in acknowledgement and the Queen spoke in a quieter more intimate tone.

'Will there ever come a time, do you think, when we are not bound by the shackles of duty and honour?'

'Duty and honour might dictate of our lives,' said the emissary. 'But my heart remains unbound.'

The Queen gave a sad smile, while inwardly she cursed the forces that prevented them from pronouncing their love for each other. Almost without realising it her hand began to reach out towards his, but at the last moment she reined in her desire for a last parting touch. He was the commander of the Fourth Army, Captain of the Knights Adamant, the Chevalier. She would not embarrass him with such an open display of affection.

'Come back to us, Chevalier.'

'Though all the hordes of hell should stand between us.'

The Queen smiled at the certainty in his tone but she knew that no soldier alive could be so certain of their future.

278

'We've had so little time,' she murmured, her voice finally breaking with emotion. 'No time to share the passing of our lives.'

She lowered her face and a single tear rolled down her cheek.

For a moment the emissary stood there, the very picture of the stoic, immovable knight. But then his hand reached out to find the Queen's, his rough fingers folding around the delicacy of hers. He drew her close, looked into her eyes and then, though Prince Ludovico and all the people of Wrath looked on, he kissed her, just the gentlest touch of his lips to hers, the bristles of his stubble coarse against her skin, every sharp and tiny point a memory to be treasured.

'In a single touch my life entire,' he whispered, his cheek lingering just a breath away from hers.

For a second he felt her fingers tighten around his and then the commander of the Fourth Army turned and walked away, taking the blessing of the Queen down to the men he led to war.

A silence settled over the city, a silence that spoke of twenty thousand equally sad goodbyes: lover to lover, mother to son, and father to confused and frightened child. They promised to be careful. They promised to return. But a soldier cannot keep such promises. He can only hope that they come true.

48

Progress

The departure of the Fourth Army had a marked effect on the cadets. It brought home to them the fact that in a few months' time it would be *them* riding out to face the uncertainty of war. They might survive the first battle but what about the second or the third? How long would it be before they were hacked to pieces or taken by the enemy and delivered into a living hell as one of the Possessed?

Horrifying as it may be, this was the fate that lay in wait for some of them, but their training made it less likely to happen and so they pushed themselves harder than ever. In the mornings they continued to train together, building their stamina and perfecting their skills, while in the afternoon they would work with the units under their command, repeating battlefield drills or studying the elements required to launch a military campaign.

Following the breakthrough with Paddy, Bryna continued to make good progress with the Dalwhinnies and was almost ready to attempt the traverser manoeuvre with cavalry. But she was not the only one making progress. Malaki and Quirren were displaying the qualities of much older and more seasoned men. As individual fighters they were impressive. Mounted on the war horses, gifted to them by their orders, they were beginning to look truly formidable.

In keeping with the Black Eagle's tradition Quirren was given a black Freysian stallion, while Malaki was mounted on a magnificent bay destrier, a war horse bred from the finest courser stock. Over the last few weeks they had been furnished with their armour; custom made suits of plate. Quirren needed an entire suit, from the armoured boots to the distinctive Illician salet, with its double slit visor and reinforced brow. Malaki's own blue-steel armour was as good as anything that Wrath had to offer, so it had simply been adapted although he now wore the intimidating great helm, or heaume, for which the Knights of Wrath were famed.

Truth be told, all the cadets were doing well, but none of them had improved as much as Falco. He had arrived at the academy a tall skinny youth, still recovering from injury, illness and trauma. Now he stood tall and strong, lithe as opposed to stocky but no longer what one might think of as thin. He still suffered from a painful tightness in his chest when he pushed himself to the limit and the burn scars on his neck and shoulder remained tender and raw, but any trace of weakness or frailty had long since vanished.

The emissary's departure left Falco feeling strangely bereft but he also felt clearer in his mind. If he was going to make a difference in the war then it was down to him. Without the emissary he was finding his balance and learning to stand on his own. When the others went to train with their respective units Falco climbed up to the crucible. He was still unable to summon any kind of offensive force, but his repertoire of skills was steadily increasing and he was growing stronger every day.

'Don't worry,' Aurelian told him one afternoon when he failed, yet again, to destroy a clay pot resting on the steps of the arena. 'If ten thousand warriors can stand and fight because you stand with them, then believe me... that will make a difference.'

Falco remembered the way Simeon's presence had steadied the army of Caer Dour in the mountains, allowing them to fight when they would otherwise have thrown down their weapons and fled. But despite knowing this he could not shake off the feeling of failure.

'Come on,' said Aurelian. 'Let's try some combined physical and magical protection. I don't want to blow smoke up your arse but your defences are actually starting to take shape.'

Falco smiled at this backhanded compliment. He knew for a fact that the old battle mage was impressed with his defensive capability. So, pushing his doubts to one side, Falco picked up the sword and shield that no longer felt so heavy in his hands. In terms of physical combat he could now run rings round Aurelian, so Dusaule would often step in to put Falco through his paces. Dusaule never spoke and he showed no appetite for violence but it was quite clear that he was a skilled swordsman.

At times Dwimervane would take on the role of a demon and Aurelian would show Falco how to go about tackling an enemy that might be several times his size. It was one thing to defend yourself against sword and shield, quite another to guard against teeth and claws and fire that could kill you from fifty feet away. At first Dwimervane could slap Falco round the arena like a cat playing with a clumsy mouse, but Falco's skills were developing quickly and his reactions, which had always been limited by the strength of his body, were finally catching up to the speed of his mind.

'That's it,' said Aurelian as Falco took a great paw swipe on his shield and rolled to avoid the full impact of the blow.

He used protection to fend off an attack from Dwimervane's jaws and his shield to block her tail before lunging in quickly to try for a strike behind her left foreleg. But Dwimervane swung her head and smashed him to one side.

'Fortification!' said Aurelian, laughing as Falco was sent sprawling on the cold wet ground. 'You can't afford to get so close without some degree of fortification.'

'You could at least give me a chance,' said Falco, giving Dwimervane a sour look as he got to his feet but the dragon looked at him with disdain. There was no way she was just going to *let* him score a hit. She was far too proud for that.

When it came to casting protection Falco was indeed progressing well. He could now protect himself from most normal attacks and was learning to fortify his body so that even Dwimervane struggled to press him to the ground with one of her mighty paws.

'Remember, it's not just physical strength,' Aurelian would say as Falco strained to stand upright beneath the dragon's massive paw. 'This is your mind, heart and soul. If you start to doubt, your strength will crumble and you will fall.'

Falco remembered the way Simeon had begun to fail under the demon's mental assault. But at least now he knew how Darius had been able to hold the black dragon's jaws at bay in the Castle of the Winds. Falco was doing quite well against Dwimervane but he knew it would be very different against a dragon or a demon that was actually trying to kill him.

Using fortification he could now land safely when jumping from a moving horse, although again, this was a far cry from the aerial acrobatics of leaping from the back of a flying dragon. In addition he had finally learned to cast protection at a distance. The breakthrough had come when Meredith suggested a new way to visualise the task.

'Don't try to surround the target,' he said. 'Just think of a single point and expand it into a sphere.

At first Falco could not envisage a 'single point' but Meredith patiently observed the shifting patterns in his mind until he finally saw what he was looking for.

'There,' he said one afternoon. 'It's almost like a sound, like the first instant of a bell being struck. Focus on that and then expand it to enclose the target.

They practised on a helmet perched on one the fortissite columns some twenty feet away. Falco's job was to protect it while Aurelian knocked it off with a spear. At first Falco only succeeded in dislodging it with the effort of his mind, which Aurelian kept on reminding him was *his* job. But finally he seemed to grasp what Meredith was trying to describe.

A single point and expand it into a sphere

'Try it now,' Meredith told Aurelian as he felt the subtle change in Falco's concentration.

With a grunt Aurelian launched the spear, which flew unerringly towards the helmet, but at the last second it seemed to strike an invisible barrier and shot off to one side. Before it had even stopped skidding along the floor Aurelian sent a fireball hurtling towards the helmet. It exploded around the pillar with tremendous force but still the helmet remained in place and they could all see the way the flames played across the surface of the sphere that Falco had cast around it.

'Good,' said Aurelian. 'That's good.'

As the days lengthened and winter released its grip Falco's skills became ever more impressive. Meredith watched one day as Falco fought against Dusaule and Dwimervane at the same time, his sword and shield a blur, his footwork quick and certain, his every movement a testament to the emerging warrior that had been trapped for so long in the body of a weak and sickly child. There was joy in their sparring and Aurelian laughed out loud as Falco was knocked off his feet only to roll and come back at his assailants with an attack of his own. Every now and then the old battle mage would throw in a surprise attack and Meredith was amazed by the speed with which Falco could repel a fireball or bat aside a barb of glowing light while never breaking the flow of movement in his physical defence.

'Go on, Dwim!' roared Aurelian as the maimed dragon beat Falco down to one knee with a blow from a huge paw. Her other paw swept sideways but Falco switched his shield to block it. The force of the blow drove him back, his feet skidding in the gritty sand but his shield arm did not give way, it was fortified by the redoubtable force of his mind. Falco blocked an attack from Dusaule, rolled beneath another swipe from Dwimervane's tail and even managed to save Meredith from being roasted as Aurelian sent a fireball hurtling in *his* direction.

Meredith cringed as the flames swirled around the protective sphere that Falco had cast around him. He looked at Aurelian with disbelief but the old battle mage just laughed.

'Ah, go on,' he said, dismissing the look of outrage on Meredith's face. 'I was pretty sure he could manage one little fireball.'

Amazed by Aurelian's recklessness Meredith looked back at Falco who was now being driven towards the far end of the crucible by Dusaule and Dwimervane. His stamina still needed work and he looked exhausted. He just about managed to parry an attack from Dusaule but he was too slow to block a back-handed swipe from Dwimervane. The knuckles of the dragon's paw slammed into Falco's side and once again he was sent sprawling on the ground. His sword flew from his grasp and the shield dangled from the strap on his forearm. Meredith watched as he came to a halt just a few feet from the dark archway of L'obscurité.

They all became still as if Falco had fallen at the feet of some dire and dangerous beast. Slowly he got to his feet and Meredith was surprised to see Dusaule step in front of him, as if protecting Falco from whatever might lie in the shadows beyond. Meredith felt a sudden rush of fear looming in his mind and for a moment he thought he could hear a clamour of malevolent whispers issuing from the darkness of the tunnel.

Falco and Dusaule did not move, while to one side Dwimervane also remained still as if she too could sense the unholy presence lurking in the darkness. Meredith's mouth ran dry and he felt an overwhelming desire to back away from the gaping portal. Slowly Aurelian walked up to stand beside Falco and only then did Dusaule step aside.

'I want to do it,' said Falco, breathing heavily from the exertion of the sparring. 'I want to enter.'

The very thought of going into that dark passageway made Meredith feel sick with fear.

'You are not ready,' said Aurelian.

'But the enemy grows stronger every day,' said Falco. 'I have to do something.'

'I know,' said Aurelian. 'But you will gain nothing by dashing your mind on the perils that lie in there.'

'I can do it,' said Falco.

'No!' replied Aurelian and Meredith was surprised by the severity of his tone.

For a moment they stood facing each other and then Aurelian gave a sigh. Taking Falco's arm he led him away from the tunnel and over to the steps at the side of the arena. The others went to follow.

'You can't stop me,' said Falco as they sat down on the lower steps. 'The decision to attempt the rite is mine.'

Aurelian laughed but not in a patronising way. Rather the sound conveyed affection and respect.

'Yes, the decision is yours,' he said. 'But you must decide when you are ready. Not just because you are desperate to *do something*.'

'But my protection is strong,' said Falco. 'You've said as much yourself.'

Again Aurelian laughed. 'It is not only down to protection. You'll need every tool at your disposal to pass the Rite of Assay and as yet, you can't even cast an offensive spell.' He was not criticising. He was just trying to make Falco understand.

'But, surely I'm not expected to 'fight' the magi on the Torquery.'

'No,' said Aurelian. 'But it is their job to oppose you, and you will have to defeat the manifestations that they place in your way.' He paused. 'Just knowing that you *can* attack if you need to offers strength in itself.'

Falco gave a sigh. 'And what if I never achieve offensive abilities?'

'Then for you, it will be more challenging than ever.'

Aurelian shot a concerned glance at Dusaule. The mute Crofter had taken a vow never to use his offensive powers again, but neither of them could imagine attempting the Rite of Assay without at least being in possession of offensive capabilities.

'Do you think I can do it?' asked Falco and now Aurelian smiled.

'I wouldn't be wasting my time on your skinny arse if I didn't.'

He waited until Falco looked up at him, before giving him a nod.

'Listen,' he said, taking a seat beside Falco. 'Tomorrow we'll go and see Antonio at the royal armouries. It's about time we got you measured up for your armour. If he pulls his finger out he could have it finished by the time you get back from the training campaign.'

'But that only gives him about ten weeks,' said Falco. 'Surely he can't produce a complete suit of armour in ten weeks.'

'Pah!' said Aurelian. 'He has more than twenty master armourers lounging about in his workshops. Besides,' he added with a wink, 'I'll speak to the Queen. One word from her and he'd conjure a suit of armour out of thin air.'

'And what about the sword?' asked Falco. 'How is he supposed to create a sword if I can't produce the heat to forge it?'

This time Aurelian looked less certain. Once again he glanced across at Dusaule but the silent Crofter just gave a small shake of his head as if he did not think much of what Aurelian had in mind.

'Well I've been thinking about that,' said Aurelian, scratching the coarse stubble on his jaw. 'I was thinking maybe I could provide the heat and Antonio can do all the hard work.'

'Would that work? I thought you said your conjuration was a bit chaotic.'

Aurelian gave a shrug. 'Got to be worth a try.'

Once again Dusaule shook his head in doubt, while Meredith frowned with uncertainty. Everything he had read about the forging of a battle mage's sword suggested it was a highly skilled and challenging affair. The battle mage and the swordsmith worked in concert to produce a blade that not only matched the physical stature and magical ability of the wielder, but his personality too. The thought of some stranger trying to produce a sword for Falco using Aurelian's volatile powers was sure to end in disaster.

The armour on the other hand was a different matter. It was the magi who designed the intricate patterns that would be etched into the surface of the steel. Arcane designs that allowed the energy of a battle mage to be dispersed without damaging the steel itself.

284

After reading a number of studies on the subject Meredith had made a good start on the designs. He felt confident that he would be able to advise the engraver when the time came. He had now been working with Falco for more than four months, four months of mental observations that gave him a unique insight into the shifting harmonics of his mind. Falco might never develop offensive capabilities but, if he ever did, Meredith was determined that his armour would not let him down.

'Well, that's settled then,' said Aurelian, rubbing his hands together with satisfaction. 'Tomorrow we get you measured up for the armour of a battle mage.'

49

The Last Surviving Witness

The early hours of the following morning found Meredith ensconced once again in the archives of the mage tower. In the amethyst glow of the wall-mounted crystals he sat back from the stone table and tried to ease the tension from his neck and shoulders. He had been studying for hours and his mind was swimming with all that he had learned.

First there had been a series of illustrated books cataloguing the designs incorporated into the armour of battle mages. Meredith had spent a couple of hours working on his own designs and then, on an impulse, he had looked back to see if the designs for Falco's father were contained in the record. Sure enough there were four pages dedicated to the armour of Aquila Danté. Meredith traced the intricate patterns with his finger, nodding as he saw similarities to the designs he had prepared for Falco. The whorls were tighter and the interweaving bands had a more complex structure, but yes, something close to this would serve Falco's powers well.

From this he had moved to a book that proposed several theories on the minds of dragons. The author of this particular work showed that dragons shared a form of collective consciousness. They were not able to 'talk' to each other the way that mages could, but there was certainly some form of connection. But the most interesting section concerned something the author referred to as 'racial memory'.

The author seemed to suggest that dragons could remember things from before they were born, and that this racial memory grew more extensive with age. In other words the older a dragon was, the further back in time it could remember. He even went so far as to suggest that this might be why black dragons went mad, that somehow the memory of Possession could bring about the state of Possession itself. Meredith made a mental note to search out more material on this subject.

After this he had collated his notes on long distance communication. While Falco and the cadets were away on their training campaign he intended to put into practice his ideas for a live link of communication between mage towers.

Meredith had been working with five other mages, two of whom would travel with him to the mage tower in the coastal town of Tempête Havre, fifty miles to the south. The other three would remain here in Wrath. They would establish a mental connection and then they would see how far they could get before the link of communication was broken. Assuming they could maintain their concentration Meredith saw no reason why the mental link should fail. The difficult part came in passing the link from one mage to another. But he was sure it could be done.

Finally he turned to an obscure manuscript containing interviews with survivors of the Great Possession. But once again he found that there was nothing new to be learned. The final chapter concerned a man who was said to be the last surviving witness of the Great Possession itself. However, there were no details about the man's name or what he claimed to have witnessed. Feeling thoroughly disheartened Meredith was actually in the process of closing the manuscript when his attention was drawn to a particular paragraph concerning this particular witness who was questioned during the Inquisition of Ossanda in 851AI.

*"...There remains some confusion over the witness's testimony. However, it is known that he was released by the Inquisition and moved to a tower that was better prepared to treat the symptoms of his distress. The mention of 'confinement' in the transfer order suggests that the witness remained disturbed by the horrors he experienced when the dragons first turned to murder. A more detailed account of his testimony, and an analysis of his mental state, can be found in Sennicio Verde's book entitled, **The Last Surviving Witness**."*

Meredith stared at the title of the work. He was surprised that he had never heard of it before. Turning to the bibliography he ran his finger down the list of books that the author had referenced. If the location of the book was listed as Wrath then it must surely be lost because he had found no sign of it in all his searching. But there was a chance that copies might reside in other mage towers. Finally his finger came to rest and Meredith could only stare at the page. There was the name of the work, the author, and a list of the places where copies of the work were held.

The Last Surviving Witness: Sennicio Verde: Wrath & Le Matres

Le Matres, the city that Falco and the cadets would visit on their training campaign. Meredith's heart was suddenly beating quickly. Here was an account of the Great Possession from someone who had actually survived it. The copy in Wrath had obviously been lost but the copy in Le Matres might still remain.

Meredith's mind raced as he wondered if he might join the cadets on their campaign. Le Matres was much further away than Tempête Havre but distance was not really the issue. His idea should work over two hundred miles as easily as fifty and besides, it would allow him to continue his work with Falco.

He glanced once more at Brother Serulian, perched like a wrinkled mannequin on the edge of his chair. Shaking off the familiar sense of unease Meredith placed the manuscript on the pile ready to go back on the shelves. Thanks to Brother Serulian's skill he had already forgotten the name of the book he had just put down. He had also forgotten most of the information contained within it, but he had not forgotten the title of another book, a book that might yet survive in the mage tower of Le Matres.

Meredith gathered up the notes and sketches he had made for the patterns on Falco's armour. It was late and tomorrow he would need to discuss his change of plans with the mages who were working with him. He could not imagine they would be pleased but they too were eager to see if his idea could work.

As he departed the chamber Meredith passed through the gaze of Brother Serulian but as ever the old man seemed completely oblivious to his presence. His instructions were to make sure Meredith learned nothing of the 84th decade during his time in the archives of Wrath. They made no mention of the 85th decade or works that might exist in the archives of Le Matres, where Meredith Saker might finally learn the truth.

50
The Armour of a Battle Mage

The workshops of Antonio Missaglias lay in the north east quarter of the city where the prevailing winds carried the smoke from the forges into the mountains. Falco and Meredith tried not to get in the way as they waited for Aurelian to return with the master himself.

'Malaki would love this,' said Falco as he savoured the elemental embrace of the royal armoury.

'It's too hot,' replied Meredith, mopping his brow and Falco nodded.

The air felt warm against his face and was filled with a heady mixture of smells that he could actually taste upon his tongue. The earthy aromas of wood-smoke and ore mingled with the sharper tang of metal. There was the distinctive smell of leatherwork and a cloying hint of oil from the quenching baths. The various pumps and bellows gave the impression that the entire building was breathing and the sound of hammer on metal was everywhere, from the rhythmic boom of sledgehammers drawing out a blade, to the lighter prang of peening hammers on bespoke pieces of plate.

It was an environment that Falco found familiar and reassuring. He breathed it in and wiped a bead of sweat from his brow as Aurelian reappeared, weaving his way between the anvils, benches and racks of metal tools. Behind him came another man who did not meet Falco's expectations at all. He had expected a tall and cultured artisan but as they drew closer he could see that Master Missaglias was a hunchback, although Falco could not tell whether he had been born that way or developed the condition from years of bending over an anvil. He was short, almost dwarf-like, with the massive shoulders and soot-blackened skin that one associated with people who spent their entire lives in a forge. His bare arms were thick with scars as was the ruddy skin of his face, but his dark eyes twinkled with a keen intelligence.

'Master Antonio Missaglias, allow me to introduce two of your fellow countrymen, Falco Danté and Meredith Saker.'

Antonio dipped his head and smiled as he saw Falco glancing at a distinctive scar that looked as if he had been hit in the face with a red-hot horseshoe.

'Got that from a warhorse,' he said in the neutral accent of Valentia. 'Think the old fella took issue with my stable manners.'

Falco winced.

'He was only putting me in my place,' said the master with a shrug. 'If he'd meant to hurt me he would have crushed my skull like a melon. So,' he said, looking Falco up and down, 'you're looking for some armour.'

Falco bowed his head, feeling suddenly self conscious.

The master smiled. He made it sound as if they had just popped in to order a new set of arm guards. He cast a searching glance over Falco and then his sharp eyes moved to Meredith.

'You'll be the one designing the surface detail I suppose.'

Meredith dipped his head in acknowledgement. His hand drifted to the leather scroll case hanging at his side which contained the sketches and notes he had been working on the previous night.

'And when would you be needing this armour?' Antonio asked, turning to make his way through the workshop.

'Well, he's joining the cadets on their training campaign,' said Aurelian, falling in beside him. 'So I guess you have about ten or eleven weeks before he gets back.'

The master snorted at Aurelian's confidence in his ability.

'I know we're talking about the armour of a battle mage,' persisted Aurelian. 'But I'm sure, with all your resources...' His voice tailed off as if even he knew it was too much to ask.

Antonio led them down the middle of a long building with work stations on either side. Falco caught the pungent smell of acid and saw pieces of armour being prepared for etching. The noise of the main workshop began to abate as they moved further away. Finally they came to the fitting rooms.

'So what do you think?' asked Aurelian, his earlier confidence giving way to uncertainty as their journey through the workshops reminded him of just how much went in to producing a suit of armour. 'At least you could make a start. It's still going to be some time before Falco can attempt the Rite of Assay.'

Antonio stopped and glanced again at Falco before giving Aurelian a disapproving look. It seemed that he also doubted that Falco was ready to face the challenges of the rite. He turned as one of the fitters approached them.

'This young man is in need of armour,' he said. 'The armour of a battle mage,' he added. 'How soon do you think we could oblige him?'

The fitter bowed his head and smiled politely. He drew a measuring cord from around his neck.

'If the young master would care to follow me.'

Falco glanced at Aurelian who gave an affirmative jerk of his head then, feeling distinctly uncomfortable at being the centre of attention, he followed the man to a fitting area at the far corner of the building. The area was enclosed by curtains and as the man drew them back Falco stopped in his tracks.

There, in the centre of the room, was a suit of dark steel armour arranged on a wooden stand, a suit of half plate and chain with breastplate, armguards and gauntlets on the top half and cuisse, greaves and armoured boots on the lower. Hanging on a separate stand beside it was a metal round-shield and topping it all a barbute helm with its distinctive T-shaped visor that seemed to stare at them in a strangely intimidating way. The armour was clearly not finished but all the main shaping work had been done.

'We kept to the Valentian style,' said Master Missaglias as if he was seeking Falco's approval.

Falco's eyes took in the additional armour on the sword arm and the leading left foot, distinctive features of Valentian armour, but he was too dumbstruck to respond. Behind him Aurelian was quietly laughing.

'When?' asked the amused old battle mage.

'The Queen approached me towards the end of autumn,' said Antonio. 'She said the emissary was bringing a new battle mage to the capital and could I please begin work on a suit of armour.'

'Well, I'll be damned,' muttered Aurelian, shaking his head and moving to inspect the armour more closely.

'It took us a while to prepare the metal and complete the annealing process,' Antonio continued. 'Then once Master Danté arrived we took measurements from the training armour he used at the academy. Finally we took advice from Lanista Magnus on how he thought this particular cadet would develop.' Here he looked again at Falco as if trying to gauge how accurate the lanista's prediction had been. 'We'll need to make some final adjustments, of course, but I think we got it fairly close.'

Behind Falco, Meredith seemed equally impressed by the Queen's subterfuge and foresight. The armour was yet to be properly finished but it was very nearly complete and he found himself wishing he had more time to work on the designs that would be etched into its surface.

'What do you think?' asked Aurelian but Falco could only stare.

Master Missaglias waved over two fitters who were hovering nearby. Meredith and Aurelian were politely ushered out as the two silver haired men came into the room. They relieved Falco of his cloak and sheepskin jacket and began to measure him from head to foot. While one of them held a leather measuring cord up to various parts of Falco's body the other made entries in a book that was already full of notes. And then, stripping Falco down to his shirt and undergarments they began to dress him in the armour, while he stood there, embarrassed and bemused, like a prized bull being prepared for market.

They began with a light quilted hauberk and a pair of leather trousers lined with brushed silk. Over this they laid a shirt of mail, carefully tailored to reduce weight without compromising the areas not covered by plate. Next they helped Falco into a pair of armoured boots and strapped on greaves and cuisse to guard his lower legs and thighs. Over this they fastened the breastplate and back plate, which had two major articulations across the midriff to allow Falco to bend and roll, plus a series of smaller articulations at the neck to prevent the metal from digging into his throat. They strapped layered pauldrons over his shoulders and slipped his hands into gauntlets of leather and finely jointed plate, while his forearms were encased in plate armguards, or the 'lower cannon of vambrace', as the masters of this workshop would say.

Finally they lifted the barbute helm and here Master Missaglias pursed his lips as if the fit of this would show how well they had estimated the dimensions of Falco's body. The fitters did not place the helm on Falco's head but rather handed it to him instead.

'You are not a king,' explained Antonio. 'Tradition has it that a knight should place the helm upon his own head.'

Falco paused and looked down at the cask of steel in his hands. The act of donning this helm suddenly took on a solemn significance, a physical representation of the responsibility he was accepting. But slowly he raised the helm and closed his eyes as he brought it down upon his head. The two fitters drew back as Master Missaglias moved to stand in front of him.

'A little shake,' he said and Falco shook his head from side to side while the master studied the way the helmet moved. 'Hmm,' he droned, clearly unhappy with the fit.

'It feels fine,' said Falco. 'Better than anything I've worn before.'

But the master was not satisfied.

'No,' he said. 'The brow is fine but we'll raise the ridge a little to bring in the sides and increase the occipital curve before the final temper.' He spoke a few quick words to the fitters and a series of notes were duly entered into the book.

'Try the shield,' said Antonio, stepping back as one of the fitters held it up so that Falco could slip his arm into the straps.

The shield was perfectly weighted and Falco finally felt a deep sense of satisfaction surging through him. He had never even seen this armour before, and he certainly did not feel worthy of it, but somehow it felt right. It felt as if it had been made especially for him, which of course, it had.

The fitters turned him to face a full-length mirror and Falco barely recognised the figure staring back at him. Finally they drew back the curtain to allow Aurelian and Meredith back into the room.

Aurelian's gaze was filled with a strange satisfaction while Meredith could only stare.

'What did I tell you?' said Aurelian with an approving smile. 'Out of thin air.'

'It's amazing,' said Falco, flexing his arms and shoulders to test his freedom of movement. 'Feels even lighter than the full bonnet.'

Aurelian gave a snort of laughter while Master Missaglias raised an affronted eyebrow. He had never had someone compare his work to the crude training armour used at the academy before. With a final nod he left Falco in the capable hands of his fitters who would list the modifications that needed to be made to the armour. Falco kept insisting it was fine but the fitters knew that ill-fitting armour could easily cause injury to the wearer, especially one as agile and athletic as a battle mage was required to be. Using a piece of black wax like a tailor's chalk one of them applied a whole series of adjustment marks to Falco's armour, while the other entered the corresponding notes in the book.

While the fitters continued their work Antonio approached Meredith who was still staring at Falco.

'He looks like the power I sense inside,' breathed Meredith.

'I think that is the finest compliment I have ever been paid,' said Antonio and Meredith blushed. He had not meant to speak his thoughts out loud. 'So I take it these are your designs.'

Meredith nodded and put a hand to the scroll case hanging at his side.

Antonio called to a young apprentice who was laying out pieces of armour in a nearby fitting room.

'Go and find Master Dorian in the etching rooms. Ask him to join us if he can spare a few minutes.'

'Yes, master.'

Antonio led Meredith and Aurelian over to a series of drawing tables covered in rolls of parchment and sketches of armour at various stages of completion. He cleared a table and invited Meredith to show him the designs he had been working on. Feeling distinctly nervous Meredith opened the scroll case and began to spread out the pages he had prepared. They kept curling up until Antonio settled the corners with a series of small pewter weights.

'Hmm,' he murmured as he cast his discerning eye over the complex designs. 'Ah, Dorian,' he said as a tall thin man appeared behind them. 'This is Meredith Saker, the mage who is designing the patterns for Master Danté's armour.'

'I'm only an apprentice mage,' said Meredith.

Master Dorian looked at Meredith as if he had no right to correct Master Missaglias. He blinked his small, piercing eyes and drew his fingers over the sharply trimmed beard on his narrow chin.

'May I?'

'Of course,' said Meredith, stepping back to allow the master engraver in to the table.

'Hmm,' said Master Dorian in almost exactly the same tone as Antonio. He pulled a brass rimmed monocle from a pocket in his shirt and leaned in closer to the table, tracing the designs with a long slender finger.

'Interesting,' he said after a thorough inspection. 'Very like his father's.'

Meredith was taken aback to think that this man could see the resemblance without referring directly to the designs of Falco's father.

'Yes,' he said. 'Although I didn't copy them. I only noticed the similarities after deciding on the designs.'

'It is not a criticism, young man,' said Master Dorian. 'Your designs appear perfectly adequate, although it is clearly the first time you have attempted the task.'

Meredith found himself trying to work out whether or not this was a compliment.

Antonio smiled and gave Master Dorian a nod of thanks as he returned to his work.

'So,' said Antonio. 'With the designs for the etching and the list of adjustments we now have everything we need to complete the armour. It'll be ready for Falco when he returns from the campaign. And that just leaves us with the matter of the sword.'

'Ah,' said Aurelian and suddenly it was his turn to look uncomfortable. 'Yes... I was meaning to speak with you about that.'

Once again Master Missaglias raised an eyebrow. He knew Aurelian well enough to know that he was not going to like what he had to say. The old battle mage put his arm around the master's broad hunchback shoulders and led him out of the room.

Meredith was only vaguely aware of them leaving. Across the way he could just make out Falco standing beyond the curtains while the fitters finished their work. Seeing him in the armour had been like seeing him for the first time and Meredith finally began to understand the concerns of Galen Thrall and his father. The armour seemed to suit Falco perfectly, the weight, the style, the design. But more than this, Falco actually looked dangerous and Meredith felt a sudden flash of doubt about trying to help him to unlock his powers.

Was it really such a wise thing to do?

292

What if he did turn against them like his father?

As he watched, the fitters emerged and drew the curtains to give Falco a few minutes alone. Trying to suppress these new misgivings Meredith reminded himself of the instincts that had persuaded him to help Falco in the first place. Reason told him to be wary but instinct told him to trust. He would stay with instinct, for now.

*

Finally alone, Falco stared at the armoured figure in the mirror, a figure that looked strong and intimidating. He had the strangest feeling that he was looking not at himself but at his father and his throat tightened with grief and regret. For a moment he continued to stare but then he looked down at the empty, leather clad palm of his right hand. Master Missaglias was right. He was wearing a suit of armour that few could ever dream of owning.

And, all that was missing was a sword.

51

The Traverser

'I just can't believe you didn't invite me!' said Malaki for about the fifth time since hearing that Falco had been in the workshops of the famous Antonio Missaglias.

'I thought we were just going for a quick visit,' said Falco as they washed after another morning of heavy training. 'Besides, it sounds like you need all the practice you can get in the dressage ring.'

'I only hit the post once,' said Malaki, wiping his face down with a towel.

'Snapped it in half, as I heard,' said Falco, noticing the way Quirren and Alex were trying not to laugh. Even Bryna poked her head round the curtain separating her from the others.

'It's Fidelis,' said Malaki, referring to his bay coloured destrier. 'I swear he's left footed!'

'That's right. Blame the horse,' said Falco, as if he were tired of hearing yet more excuses.

They all laughed and Falco flinched as a wet towel slapped into the side of his face.

'En passant is not easy,' said Quirren, clapping Malaki on the shoulder as he passed. 'Not now that we're doing it at full speed.'

'Exactly,' said Malaki. 'Everything's more difficult when you're doing things at speed...' His voice tailed off as Bryna emerged from behind the curtain, towelling her hair.

The others glanced at each other awkwardly but Bryna just shook her head and threw her wet towel into a nearby bucket. This afternoon the Dalwhinnies would be attempting the traverser manoeuvre with cavalry at speed and Bryna was afraid they would fail and be denied the chance of going on the training campaign.

Tucking her shirt into her trousers she pulled on her sheepskin jacket and walked out of the tent. Malaki grabbed his shirt and went after her, Falco and the Klingemann brothers following in their wake.

'It's going to be all right,' said Malaki, pulling his shirt down over his still damp shoulders. 'You've already done it with infantry and cavalry at a walk.'

'I know,' said Bryna, taking a bread roll from a plate of food on a nearby table. 'But the Whinnies are archers... cavalry makes them nervous. Some of the younger lads are positively terrified of horses.' She took a bite of her roll, the fresh bread steaming in the bright spring sunshine.

'Just reassure them,' said Malaki as Falco, Alex and Quirren took a seat at the table.

'It's all over pretty quickly,' said Alex. 'You just have to get the spacing right and keep the lines straight.'

Bryna raised her eyes skyward as if to say, it's easy for you. The Exiles had successfully completed the exercise several times but they were older and more experienced soldiers. The Dalwhinnies were a mix of ages and volatile personalities, many of whom had difficulty controlling their impulses. She had images of them breaking ranks and getting trampled to death.

'Maybe you could tell the nervous ones not to do it,' suggested Falco.

'But I'm nervous too,' said Bryna. 'It's not easy turning your back on a hoard of galloping horses. Besides,' she added. 'They'd rather die than lose face.'

'You'll do fine,' said Malaki. 'And we still have nearly three weeks before we're due to leave. If you don't manage it today you still have time to try again.'

Bryna tore off another chunk of bread with her teeth and took a swig of water to wash it down. Then, even as they watched, they saw a column of Légion du Trône light cavalry riding up onto the plateau. And then, from the direction of the archery ranges, they saw a motley group of two hundred archers laughing and jostling each other as they approached.

More of the cadets were now emerging from the tent while the assistants began laying out a nearby training field in preparation for the exercise.

'I'd better go and meet them,' said Bryna, forcing down her last mouthful of bread.

Malaki rose from his seat to kiss her.

'Good luck,' he said and the others added their best wishes with a series of nods and awkward smiles.

Looking pale and nervous Bryna fetched her bow and quiver then strode across the field to meet the men under her command. There was no cheering or bravado. The Whinnies knew how much this meant to Bryna, and none of them wanted to look foolish in front of the instructors and the other cadets of the academy.

'She'll be fine,' Falco said to Malaki as they watched the company of cavalry forming up on the training field adjacent to their own. 'If anyone knows how to ride straight it's the Légion du Trône.'

Malaki nodded distractedly and together they made their way over to the side of the field to watch. The lanistas came with them, standing alongside the cadets as the Dalwhinnies moved into position.

'She'll be fine,' said Lanista Magnus. 'She's done a good job with a difficult unit.'

Malaki was grateful for the lanista's words but even he seemed a little on edge. The traverser was simply a dangerous manoeuvre. It was designed to allow one unit of troops to move through another without confusion. History was full of battles that had ended in disaster because units were not able to get into position, armies outflanked and cavalry unable to reach the enemy due to solid blocks of their own infantry getting in their way. It was difficult, but it could be crucial, and so Bryna was determined to get it right.

Conscious of the eyes upon them she walked across the field to meet the distinctive figure of Patrick Feckler.

'How are they doing?'

'Not bad,' said Paddy. 'Laughing and joking, winding each other up. A sure sign that they're nervous.'

Bryna nodded and tried to summon some moisture into her mouth. They had successfully completed the traverser with infantry and cavalry at walking speed, traversing at full gallop was an entirely different proposition. The ground literally shook with the drumming of hooves and the sound of their approach was truly frightening.

On command, the unit to be traversed had to form into ranks leaving gaps for the unit wishing to pass through. The ranks had to be straight and perfectly aligned otherwise it could be disastrous, especially with cavalry at speed. They had worked very hard to get this right but a lot of it still came down to holding one's nerve. As the cavalry approached they were required to turn away and crouch down, heads bowed against the person in front to reduce their profile and limit any chance of injury.

'How're Alnwick and Daniel?' asked Bryna.

'Scared shitless,' said Paddy. 'But they're determined to see it through.'

'Maybe I should just insist they stay out,' said Bryna, looking at two young lads that could not be more than seventeen years old. One of them, Daniel, was what people might refer to as 'simple' but the Dalwhinnies simply accepted him as one of their own. She wandered over to speak with them.

'How are you doing, boys?' she asked as the two young men rested the tips of their bows on their boots.

'Fine and dandy, Captain,' said Alnwick, looking anything but fine.

'Bit scared,' said Daniel, dragging his wavy blonde hair out of his eyes.

'You don't have to do it,' said Bryna. 'You know that, don't you?'

Both boys flushed and averted their eyes. Alnwick looked as if he were about to say something but finally decided against it.

'Bit of fear never hurt anyone,' said Daniel as if he were quoting something the older men had said to him.

Bryna gave them a smile and turned away before it had a chance to slip.

'Keep an eye on them,' she whispered to Paddy. 'And if Alnwick looks like he can't handle it, you keep him out. I don't care if you have to tie him up.'

Paddy glanced back at the two boys before answering.

'They're here by choice,' he said. 'They'll either be all right. Or they won't.'

Bryna glanced at the bear-like figure beside her and wondered if she could ever feel so indifferent. She was only a few years older than the boys but even to her they seemed so young.

'Get the men lined up,' she said. 'We're almost ready to begin.'

Paddy nodded and began to berate the Dalwhinnies into a standard block formation ready for ranged fire. Meanwhile Bryna approached one of the marshals overseeing the exercise.

'Ranged fire at two hundred yards. Ready for the traverser on my command,' said the marshal looking at her with an uncompromising eye. 'On the first clarion the cavalry will advance. The flag will indicate the line of approach.' He held up the red flag he was holding. 'In the event of any problems you have until the second clarion sounds to call off the exercise. After that it will be too late.'

Bryna nodded. If she was not happy with their formation she had a brief opportunity to call the exercise off, at which point marshals would divert the cavalry to the sides of the field. Turning away from the marshal she looked at the Dalwhinnies now standing in a well ordered block. At one end of the field was a line of targeting poles with white rags flapping in the breeze. At the other the horses of the Légion du Trône shifted in the midday sunlight, waiting for the command to traverse at speed. She moved to take up position at the back of the Dalwhinnies, closest to the approaching cavalry. Her position would mark the line upon which the ranks would form up, a position known as 'la point'.

Bryna did not look towards Malaki and the others as she fell into position beside Paddy.

'They're looking good,' said Alex with a note of surprise in his voice.

Falco nodded. The Dalwhinnies had quickly arranged themselves in good order. He glanced at Malaki but *his* attention was firmly fixed on Bryna. Finally the marshal stepped onto the field and raised a stick bearing a red flag. As a single mass the Dalwhinnies fitted their arrows to the string, three strong and calloused fingers taking the strain.

'Draw!'

Even from so far away they could hear Bryna's voice ringing across the field. Unlike many women, whose voices became shrill when raised to shouting, Bryna's voice had a deep resonance that carried well when giving commands.

'Loose!' she cried and two hundred arrows shot from the string. They arced through the air and landed with a collective thud along the line of posts two hundred yards away. They might be nervous around horses but there was nothing wrong with the Dalwhinnies' aim.

They continued to fire at a steady rate until the marshal's flag came down and the first clarion sounded.

'Traverser, sur moi!' cried Bryna.

'Traverser, sur la point,' bellowed Paddy the Feck, reinforcing her command.

To a man the Dalwhinnies lowered their bows and turned to check Bryna's position. She stood at the rear of the block, arms outstretched. She had checked the position of the marshal's flag and now stood with her back to the cavalry, which had suddenly started towards them. The Dalwhinnies had just a few seconds to get into the required formation as the sound of the approaching horses surged towards them like a wave.

The rank closest to Bryna straightened up along the line of her arms and proceeded to space themselves at double interval. From here the files extended away in perfectly straight lines. Bryna felt a quick glow of pride at the speed with which they adopted the new formation.

'About face!' she called and the Dalwhinnies turned their backs on the rapidly approaching cavalry.

'Down and close!' she cried and the entire formation dropped to one knee and leaned in close to the person in front of them, bows laid flat on the ground, heads resting in the small of the next person's back, one hand gripping whatever piece of clothing they could find.

Bryna had a brief moment to check that all was as it should be. The formation was perfect, the channels clear and wide. She gave a nod of satisfaction just as she heard the second clarion call sounding across the field.

'Down!' said Paddy and Bryna felt a strong hand on the back of her neck, forcing her down as he moved to shield her body with his own.

Bryna pressed her forehead into the next man's back and time seemed to stall as the sound of the galloping horses loomed behind them. She smelled leather and sweat and felt the rapid rise and fall of the man's breathing. Glancing up she saw Alnwick in the file to her left and Daniel in the one to her right. Both boys were clearly struggling to stay still as the sound of the cavalry grew ever louder.

Alnwick suddenly lurched forward, trying to make a break for it, but Dedric Sayer dragged him back into line, holding him down with his own body weight.

To the right Bryna saw Daniel shifting nervously, the man behind him trying to calm him with a steady grip.

'*Hold on boys*,' thought Bryna as the ground beneath her shook. '*Just a few seconds more.*'

Bryna clenched her teeth and hunkered down as the first of the horses thundered past. Bits of grass and earth flew up into her face. A sense of panic was rising in her but she knew it was almost over. Risking another glance she looked up towards the boys, catching fleeting glimpses of them between the storm of equine legs and hooves. The man behind Daniel was clearly struggling to keep him calm.

The last of the horses was just passing through when Daniel wrenched his shoulder free and turned to see when it would be over. He did not move very far out of line but it was enough. The edge of a horse's hoof caught him on the side of the head and Bryna winced as a spray of blood burst into the air. The man behind him threw himself over the boy, flattening him to the ground but it was too late. As the last of the horses passed through the lines Bryna broke free of Paddy's grasp and scrambled forward to see if Daniel was all right.

The man lying over him slowly raised himself up and Daniel rolled onto his back. His blond hair was wet with blood and his body twitched as he lay on the churned up turf. Bryna knelt beside him and laid a hand on his cheek.

'Daniel. Can you hear me?' she asked, her voice strained with concern.

Daniel's eyes flickered open.

'I was a bit frightened,' he said, his voice slurred and dreamy. 'Horses,' he added, one side of his face hanging slack and lifeless. 'So big and strong. You don't realise till you see them up close.'

Bryna felt her throat constrict as Daniel's left eye closed, dragged shut by muscles that no longer obeyed his commands. His mouth sagged and he began to drool. He tried to say something else but then his face creased with pain and he began to cry. His body seemed to tighten, his chin shrinking down into his neck. Then he spasmed once, twice and was still, blood pooling in the muddy grass around his head.

Bryna stared at him through a film of tears.

How could this happen?

They were almost finished. They had done it perfectly and they were almost finished.

How could one little slip end like this?

The tragedy of it twisted her guts and it was only when Paddy tried to draw her away that she realised her fists were clenched in Daniel's clothes. The rest of the Dalwhinnies were getting to their feet. Smiles of satisfaction falling from their faces as they realised that something had gone wrong.

'It's Daniel,' Bryna heard them say. 'Young Daniel, dead.'

Young Daniel, dead.

The Dalwhinnies drew back as the marshals arrived along with several assistants carrying a stretcher. The sense of urgency in their movements faded away as they realised that the casualty was dead.

Slowly Bryna stood up and Paddy drew her away.

'I should have kept him out,' she said in a hollow tone. 'I should have kept them both out.'

'It's not your fault,' said Paddy, looking grim but unperturbed. 'I told you. They would either be all right or they would not.'

Bryna stared at him blankly. Somewhere in his words was an arid kind of wisdom. She tried to grasp it but found that she could not. Tears spilled down her cheeks but Paddy just looked at her.

'It does no good to care,' he said. 'It'll only tear you up.'

They watched as the academy assistants carried Daniel away on the stretcher, blood seeping through the pale canvas on which he lay.

'We'll drink to him tonight,' said Paddy. 'And then it'll be done.'

With that he walked away and began to herd the Dalwhinnies back in the direction of the Irregular's barracks. As they moved away Bryna saw Malaki and Falco coming towards her. Her first feeling was one of relief but it was closely followed by guilt. Maybe Paddy was right, maybe it was wrong to care but Bryna could not help it.

She did care.

And it was tearing her up.

*

Despite their best intentions there was nothing that Malaki or anyone else could say to assuage Bryna's guilt. Later that night, in the subdued gloom of the barracks, Falco watched as Malaki and Alex tried their best to comfort her. He stood at the foot of Bryna's bed and now Quirren came to stand beside him.

'It's a shame the emissary isn't here,' said the big Illician. 'He would know what to say.'

Falco nodded.

Quirren had spoken quietly but somehow Bryna heard him.

'And what *would* he say?' she insisted, rising to her feet and coming forward to challenge them.

Quirren looked away uncomfortably but Falco just frowned.

'That would depend on what you decided to do,' he said.

Bryna's chin came up, waiting for him to continue.

'If you were planning to return to the quiet life of a noble woman he would tell you that it's good to grieve for one so young.' Falco did not flinch from the fire that flashed in Bryna's eyes. 'But if you were intending to remain at the academy,' he added, remembering the stern approach the emissary often took, 'he would tell you to stop behaving like the matron of an orphanage and start behaving like a captain of the army.'

For a moment it looked like Bryna might strike him, but then her eyes filled with tears and she lowered her head. Snatching up her sheepskin jacket she pushed past Falco and started out of the room.

'Where are you going?' asked Malaki, rising to his feet.

299

'I'm going to get drunk with the Dalwhinnies,' said Bryna. 'And then it'll be done.'

In the uneasy silence that followed Malaki did not look at Falco. What he had said might be true but Malaki felt angry that Falco had only added to Bryna's pain. Picking up his own jacket he pushed past his friends and followed after Bryna. If she did get drunk it would not be men from the Dalwhinnies who helped her home tonight.

As Malaki left, Alex gave Falco an uneasy smile, while Quirren placed a hand on his shoulder. There were times when it took courage to say what needed to be said.

Falco remained in thought as the two brothers went to get some supper. He had not enjoyed being so hard on Bryna but he felt sure it was the right thing to do. The emissary might have left the academy but his presence and his wisdom still echoed in their hearts.

Over the days that followed Bryna displayed again the strength of character that had won the Dalwhinnies' respect and was soon back to her spirited and bossy self. In a strange way the sad event of Daniel's death brought the cadets closer together. At some point they would all need to deal with the death of people under their command. It was just that Bryna was the first to do so. The marshals determined that Bryna was not to blame for the incident. Furthermore it was judged that the Dalwhinnies had performed the traverser with skill and precision and would be allowed on the training campaign after all.

Winter had now given way to spring and the land was slowly coming back to life. The grass on the plateau appeared greener and even the mountains seemed to take on a warmer hue. In the gardens below the palace the buds were swelling and the orchards were carpeted with wild crocus and small white narcissus. The time of their departure was rapidly approaching and the academy was bustling with activity.

While the cadets continued to train, the workshops were busy preparing all the things they would need. Those cadets commanding units were also required to act as quartermasters, drawing up a list of the provisions their unit would require.

'I thought this was supposed to be a school for combat,' said Alex, looking down at the sheaf of papers in his hand. 'Never thought I'd be spending my time calculating how much flour a unit of two hundred men would get through in a month.'

They all smiled then stopped as Falco struck off in the direction of the crucible.

'I'll see you later,' he said.

'Good luck,' said Bryna.

'Just imagine it's Snidesson's face,' said Malaki.

Falco laughed and waved as he continued on his way. They all knew he was struggling to produce any kind of offensive force. Aurelian continued to insist that the most important thing was his ability to shield people from the fear. But what good would that be if he could not stop a demon from rampaging across the battlefield.

Pausing at the rim of the crucible he gave a bitter laugh.

300

Stop a rampaging demon... Hah!

Falco now bore little resemblance to the feeble youth that had woken up in the infirmary of Toulwar. But the idea that he might *ever* be able to stop a rampaging demon struck him as an outrageous conceit. He remembered the terrifying power of the creature that had torn through the ranks of Caer Dour's warriors in the mountains. How could anyone hope to stop something like that?

'Are you coming down or what?!'

The irritated cry echoed around the crucible and Falco looked down to see Aurelian staring up at him with Meredith, Dusaule and Dwimervane close by as ever. On the broad steps at the far end of the arena were a number of large clay urns laid out as targets. It seemed that Aurelian for one had not given up on his offensive capabilities.

Putting aside his doubts Falco started down the terraced sides of the crucible. During their time in Wrath, Malaki, Bryna and Meredith had all shown the depth of their character. It was time for Falco to show the depth of his own.

52
The Elemental Weakness of Steel

In the Forsaken Lands of Illicia a group of riders fled from the terrifying presence of a demon. The Slayer gave no thought to the men fleeing through the trees. Instead it looked into the Defiant's eyes as he hung in the air, impaled on one of the demon's great curving blades. Even now the man displayed no fear, only pain and regret at the failure of his defeat.

The Slayer gave a sudden thrust and the Defiant coughed out a bloody gasp as the point of the blade emerged through the armour on his back. At first the metal had resisted its blows and the Slayer had been surprised by the strength of faith that denied its weapons, but as the Defiant grew weaker so the armour showed its elemental weakness, no match for steel forged by the Enlightened.

Even now, in the grip of an agonising death, the Defiant did not capitulate and the Slayer found itself wondering how long it would take to break such faith and claim his soul. But that was not its mission. The Slayer's assignment was simply to kill and with this, it was content. It might have severed the Defiant's head or thrust higher to cleave his heart but instead the demon simply held him up and watched him as he died. As the last breath went out of his body, the Slayer flung the 'great soul' down beside the horse that was cloven from breastbone to saddle, two piles of meat, now barely distinguishable in death.

With the Defiant's blood still steaming on its blade the Slayer turned again to the northwest where another Defiant was entering the sphere of its awareness. Striding into shadow once more it sank beneath the surface of the world and moved on.

*

Far to the south, in the Forsaken Lands of Beltane, the Marchio Dolor closed his eyes in appreciation of the creature his prayers had called forth. It was a rare demon that could defeat a battle mage in single combat, but now such a creature was roaming in the north. Now he could focus all his energy on Vercincallidus, the man they called the Serthian Wolf. The Beltonian general offered little in the way of a challenge but there was always a degree of satisfaction in laying low the proud.

Part III

RAGE

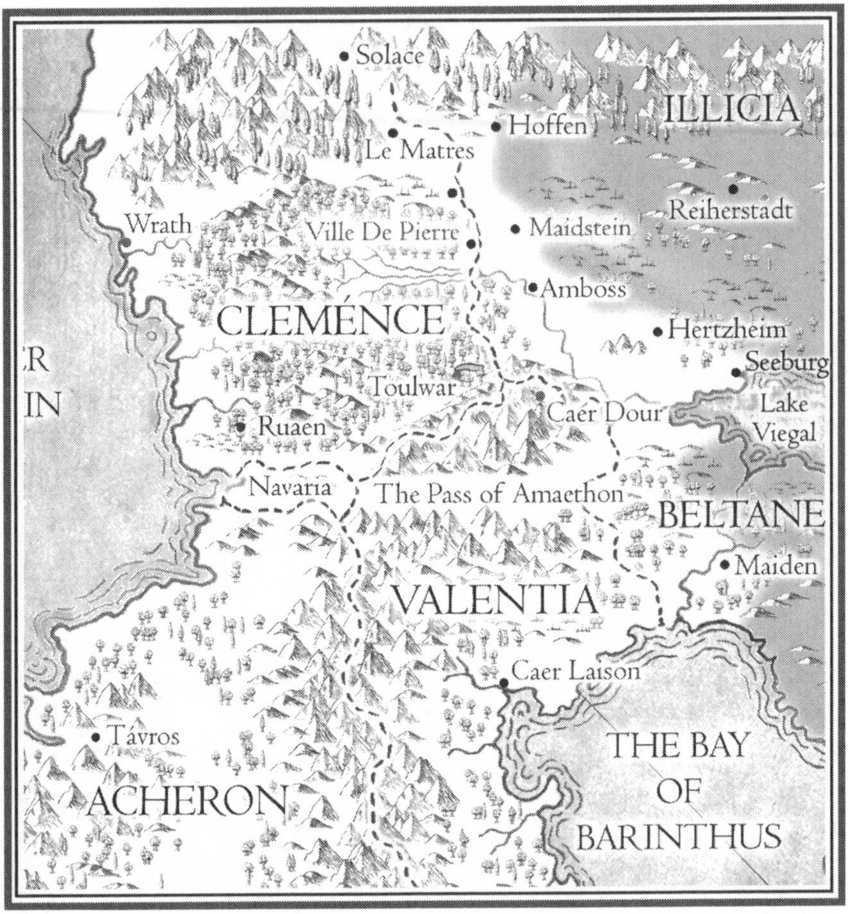

53

Convergence

Despite Aurelian's persistence and Meredith's patience, Falco failed to make any progress with regard to magical attacks. But while he struggled with offensive capabilities he continued to improve in others. As the training campaign approached they began to focus on healing, something for which Falco had a natural affinity. Nicolas was particularly skilled in this respect and would often accompany them on their visits to the academy's infirmary.

'It's mostly fairly minor injuries,' explained the chief physician as Falco laid his hands on the broken leg of a stable hand who had taken a kick from horse. 'Sprains, minor wounds and broken bones, like this.'

The chief physician was no stranger to the healing powers of a battle mage and was always pleased to see Dusaule walk into his infirmary.

'The ability to relieve pain is a wonderful gift,' he went on. 'But people do not die from pain. Constricted breathing, bleeding, shock and infection... These are the things that kill.'

Falco closed his eyes and focussed on the injury he could feel inside the man's leg. He could not perceive the precise details, but he was able to form a sense of it.

'Don't try to heal the specific injury,' said Meredith, standing over him. 'Just infuse the body so it can heal itself.' Beside him Dusaule gave a nod of agreement while the man lying on the bed first winced at the sudden sensation of tingling heat, then sighed as the pain in his leg subsided. He looked at Falco in astonishment.

'Merci, jeune maître,' he said in the language of Clemoncé. 'Thank you, young master.'

Falco smiled and stood back as two of the attendants came forward to splint and bind the man's leg. It was not mended yet but it would heal much more quickly thanks to Falco's intervention.

'In the same way you can stop bleeding, stabilize internal systems and prevent the putrefaction of a wound,' continued Meredith. 'But such accelerated healing is not achieved without a cost. Treating serious injuries can leave a battle mage exhausted.'

Falco nodded his understanding as they moved down the ward to see who else they could help. A detachment from the Royal Corps of Physicians would be joining the cadets on the training campaign and they would be relieved to know that they could call on the services of a battle mage, even a battle mage in training who was still discovering the extent of his skills.

On the eve of the cadets' departure Aurelian presented Falco with armour, sword and shield for the campaign.

'It'll do well enough,' said the old battle mage, adjusting the pauldrons on Falco's shoulders. 'It's a long way from Antonio's standards but the quality's not bad.'

Falco tried on the helm before taking up the Valentian round-shield and sword.

'The sword wouldn't survive the magical energy of a battle mage,' said Aurelian. 'But as you can't heat so much as a bowl of soup that shouldn't be a problem. Besides,' he added. 'It's a training campaign. I'm not really sure why you need a sword at all.'

'Thank you,' said Falco, testing his movement in the armour. The helmet was an open faced barbute and Aurelian had found a pair of armoured cavalry boots in Falco's size. It was well made, but it felt crude and uncomfortable after the bespoke armour that Master Missaglias was working on.

'Remember,' said Aurelian, as Falco prepared to leave. 'The soldiers of an army might not feel comfortable in your presence. Do not take it personally. Men have always feared what they do not understand. They'll whisper and talk behind your back. Their laughter and singing will cease as you walk by. But make no mistake. If you do encounter the Possessed, then every man and woman in the army will look to you for guidance. Do you understand?'

For a moment Falco just stared at the grim faced old battle mage and the armour on his shoulders felt suddenly heavy, but finally he nodded.

'Then good luck,' said Aurelian. 'And try not to make a fool of yourself.'

The cadet army departed on a cold spring morning with a thin layer of mist hanging over the dew laden grass. In contrast to the departure of the Fourth, they got underway with little in the way of fanfare. A solitary horn sounded the traditional salute as the cadets led their units down from the plateau. They did not pass through the city. Instead they followed a broad road that led down from the plateau before turning inland towards the Ford of Garr.

As they passed behind the city they could just make out a distant figure standing on the eastern terrace of the palace. It was too far away to be certain but they knew it was the Queen. Many of the cadets raised arms or weapons in salute but Falco just stared. He remembered the Queen's anxiety during their last meeting. He knew she was haunted by uncertainty and questions to which she had no answers.

Could Beltane survive against the armies of the Marchio Dolor?

Would Valentia stand fast or leave the way open to the defenceless state of Navaria?

Was there something they had overlooked in Illicia?

And if so... had she sent the emissary to his death?

Finally Falco drew his eyes away from the distant figure. They were embarking on a training exercise that would take them within a few miles of the front. They were not expected to engage the enemy, but Falco was determined to keep his mind open to anything that could help the Queen. If there was any way he could glean something of the enemy's mind, he would.

Not having a unit to command, Falco rode with Malaki and the other knights-in-training, each of whom wore a mail shirt and carried a lance in addition to the longswords hanging from their belts. The rest of their armour was stowed in their saddle bags. In this army they now comprised a unit in their own right, a unit that was currently under the command of one Malaki de Vane.

One might have expected the other young knights to be jealous of Malaki's appointment but it seemed the cadets were growing in maturity as well as the skills of war. Not for the first time Falco found himself thinking that bravado and posturing were born of fear and insecurity. As the young warriors of the academy gained in ability they seemed less inclined to jostle and boast. Even Jarek had grown less obnoxious. He still disliked Falco, that was clear, but he no longer went out of his way to be nasty or unpleasant.

Looking up the line, Falco could see the young nobleman riding at the head of his company of Royal Hussars, immaculately dressed in light plate and a turquoise cloak. Behind Jarek's cavalry, came the sombre-clad unit of the Exiles. The well disciplined unit marched in time. However, their young commander kept switching legs and throwing them out of step. He made it look accidental but Falco and the others knew that it was not.

'It's just nerves,' said Falco, laughing as the ranks behind Alex struggled to get back in step.

'If only it were,' said Quirren disapprovingly.

Alex repeated his intermittent 'joke' until the senior member of the Exiles caught his eye with a steely glower. Alex bowed his head and the Exiles marched smoothly on.

'He shows no respect,' said Quirren but Falco noticed the senior member give one of his comrades a sideways glance. These were bereaved and hollow men. Like Quirren, they despaired of Alex's frivolity but at the same time, Falco was certain they exchanged a smile. And when, a few hundred yards on, the Exiles stumbled again as Alex dropped another step, there was a ripple of restrained laughter among the ranks of Die Verbannten.

'Hopeless!' said Quirren but Falco and Malaki only smiled.

Behind them was yet more laughter but this was anything but restrained and glancing back they could see the untidy ranks of the Dalwhinnies.

'At least we're not marching behind them!' said Malaki.

Falco laughed, as did several of the nearby knights. The pungency of the Dalwhinnies was already famous throughout the army, especially after a night of heavy drinking. Falco could just make out Bryna's distinctive red hair as she rode at the head of her unit. Now kitted out with light armour, blue padded gambesons and turquoise travelling cloaks the Dalwhinnies resembled a real fighting unit, but as Dedric Sayer was fond of saying.

'You can't make a silk shirt from a sow's arse!'

The cadet army was strung out in a line of two thousand troops plus wagons and carts loaded with supplies for the city of Le Matres. Escorting the army, and dressed in robes of silver-grey, were the assessors and temporary commanders who formed the chain of command. As the campaign went on they would pass more and more responsibility to the cadets, until the army was entirely under their command.

At the back of the column rode three figures in the purple robes of the magi. As the day wore on Falco dropped back to ride with Meredith who acknowledged his presence with a nod while the other two mages did not seem to notice him. One appeared to be dozing in the saddle, while the other just stared straight ahead as if he were in some kind of trance.

'He's concentrating,' explained Meredith when he saw Falco watching the man. 'His mind is connected to a mage back in Wrath, one of the other three helping me with this experiment.'

'So I could speak to someone in the tower from here?'

'Not directly,' replied Meredith. 'But your words could be relayed to him.'

Falco nodded in appreciation. 'So if he loses concentration the link will be lost?'

'That's right.' Meredith's expression conveyed the difficulty of the challenge he had set himself.

'And what happens when he falls asleep,' asked Falco.

'When *he* gets tired one of us will take over,' said Meredith. 'He will transfer the link to us.'

Again Falco nodded, impressed by the magi's ability to maintain such a demanding state of mind. They rode in silence for a while and Falco was surprised by how comfortable he now felt in Meredith's presence. Quite a contrast to the fear and anxiety he felt in the presence of Meredith's father.

'Have you made any progress with the exercises I set you?' asked Meredith. He had been trying to teach Falco how to generate heat and channel it through an object like a sword.

'I can feel the energy building, but it fades away as soon as I try to channel it,' replied Falco. 'The truth is it frightens me. It's like there's a monster inside of me that mustn't be set free.'

Meredith looked up until their eyes met.

'We are the sons of our fathers, Falco. But we are not them.'

Falco returned his gaze. It had never occurred to him that Meredith might fear turning out like his father, just as he feared succumbing to madness, like his own. He gave the apprentice mage a nod and they rode on in companionable silence until it was time for Meredith to take over the communications link.

'I'll look for you this evening,' he said. 'We'll do some work on moving objects at a distance.'

Falco nodded. He could now move objects and draw them towards himself from a short distance. Even from twenty feet away he could make a sword drag across the ground until he was able to bend down and pick it up. Aurelian himself could not achieve such a feat, but Meredith was convinced that Falco could do more.

'Till later then,' said Falco.

Meredith bowed his head but his expression was already growing more distant as he focussed his mind on a man who was now more than ten miles behind them in the mage tower of Wrath.

The army continued at a steady pace. The windswept hills of the coast gave way to woodland and Falco was reminded of the journey that had brought them to Wrath. The trees were just coming into leaf and the setting sun made them glow a bright green as the army stopped for the night on the wide floor of a river valley. Making camp seemed to take far longer than was necessary and the assessors appeared less than impressed. The more experienced troops fell into their routines easily enough but to everyone's surprise it was the Dalwhinnies who were eating and drinking first.

308

'I just let them get on with it,' said Bryna when Alex asked her how she had managed it.

Over the days that followed they made good progress. They adapted quickly to the new routines and were soon making and striking camp with the calm efficiency of seasoned campaigners.

Meredith continued to find time to work on Falco's magical abilities but still he failed to show any signs of the breakthrough they were hoping for. Ten days into the campaign Falco and his friends were sitting together when one of the camp runners appeared with a bundle of letters from Wrath. Falco watched as several of the cadets were handed letters then, to his surprise, the runner approached him.

'This arrived at the academy a few days after you left,' he said, handing Falco a letter.

Falco immediately recognised the handwriting. 'It's from Fossetta,' he said with a word of thanks to the runner.

'What does it say?' asked Bryna.

She and Malaki moved closer as Falco began to read, and even Alex leaned over Falco's shoulder to look. Letters from home were a rare and precious thing and all the cadets drew strength from being reminded of why they were at the academy in the first place.

My dearest Falco

If my last letter reached you then hopefully this will too. I am writing to tell you that we are heading to the province of Tourienne, and will be staying in the region for several weeks, so we finally have a chance to receive a letter (if you feel inclined to send one). There are a number of children in the area that we need to see, so we will be using the town of Daston as a base. The mayor of the town has kindly offered to receive correspondence on our behalf so you can address any letters to...

Fossetta Pieroni
Care of, Maire Philippe Decazes
Destan
Tourienne

Winter has now passed and we are moving steadily east. As we draw closer to the border we are having to be especially vigilant. Twice, in the night, we have encountered the Possessed. Once, a lone Sciritae appeared at the edge of our camp. It did nothing, only stared in the most unsettling manner, and faded into nothingness when Captain de Roche moved to attack it. Then again, when maybe a dozen Sciritae and a large beast attacked the village we were staying in.

The villagers managed to defend themselves but it took eight men with boar spears to bring down the creature (or bestiarum, as the people in the village called it). Several of the men were injured and one would have died were it not for Heçamede's swift intervention.

Apparently this was not the first such attack and the people live in constant fear. However, despite the danger, Tobias is determined to go on, but if these attacks grow more frequent we may be forced to restrict our search to areas that are still beyond the enemy's reach.

But enough of our woes. How are you? I am desperate to hear that you are all safe and well, so please write back if you can.

With love always
Fossetta

'Daston,' said Alex, leaning over Falco's shoulder. 'That's only a few miles from Le Matres, is it not?'

'Maybe we'll get a chance to see her,' said Malaki and Falco found his heart surging at the thought.

'Best not to get too excited,' he said.

'But we might,' said Bryna.

'Who is this?' asked Huthgarl for they were all curious to know.

'It's the woman who raised me,' said Falco, feeling his throat constrict.

'Then you must go to see her, if you can,' said the big Beltonian.

All the cadets nodded, sharing in this link to the things they had left behind when life was simpler and the world seemed a much smaller place.

'Yes,' said Falco. 'I will.'

Later that night Falco found himself lying awake, thinking of the strange coincidence of fate that found them all travelling to the same place. But then he realised that it was not fate, or coincidence, it was the Possessed. Tobias and Fossetta, Nathalie and the emissary, and now himself along with the cadets, all heading to the area where the Possessed pressed them most closely, to where they were needed most.

Further south there would be other convergences heading to the endangered cities of Illicia and Beltane, the people of Wrath doing whatever they could to slow the relentless advance of the enemy. It was easy to feel overwhelmed and hopeless but then Falco's jaw bunched and his green eyes shone in the darkness. If those other convergences were anything like the one that moved towards Le Matres then surely there was still hope.

Comforted by the thought, and lifted by the slender possibility of seeing Fossetta, Tobias and Heçamede, Falco drifted off to sleep.

54
The Tale of Jürgen Focke

A hundred miles to the east the emissary stirred in his sleep. Raising his head he wondered what it was that had roused him.

Nothing...

Just the normal sounds of a camp at rest, scattered snoring, the flap of canvas, the low voices of those on watch and the sound of horses chomping at their feed nets.

All seemed quiet but the emissary could not be too careful. The Fourth Army was now at the Illician front and he never drifted too far from wakefulness. Outside the tent Tapfer gave a soft snort and the emissary lay back down to sleep. The smoke grey Percheron was not alarmed. There was nothing to fear just now.

He grasped the horse head pendant that hung around his neck and nestled his head into the sheepskin pad that served as a pillow against his saddle. They were all more watchful than normal. Twice in the last few days they had been set upon by small forces of Possessed. Small groups of Sciritae appearing out of the darkness with the occasional bestiarum and blindfolded Toxitae firing black arrows into their midst. Not a threat to the army itself but enough to sow fear and disturb their sleep.

Only on one occasion had they fought an actual battle but it was a small Possessed force and they had defeated it quickly. So quickly in fact that the warrior mages had not been required to fight, something that did not sit well with their commander, Dagoran Sorn. The commander of the mage army was desperate to prove himself, desperate to be able to report back to Galen Thrall that the mage army had been a success.

The man seemed almost afraid of failure whereas the emissary's greatest fear was that of meeting a demon on the battlefield. Veterans of the war might resist the fear for a while but no one could fight for long in the presence of a demon, not without a battle mage.

Trying to calm his fears he closed his eyes. Nathalie had met them twice on the journey. Apparently there was only one demon in the area and she had promised to return before it became a threat to the Fourth Army. The emissary was grateful for her reassurance but he also knew she was worried. She had still not been able to locate the Illician battle mages, Wildegraf or Jürgen. She had heard reports that Wildegraf was investigating rumours to the south. Even now she was heading in that direction to seek him out, after which she would meet the emissary south of Hoffen ready to face the demon that was closing on that area.

Comforted by the fact that she would be returning soon the emissary allowed his thoughts to fall away then, still clasping the horse head pendant to his breast, he fell back into a shallow and watchful sleep.

*

Fifty miles southeast of the emissary's position Nathalie looked down on the midnight world as Ciel alighted on a craggy ridge of rock. It was too dark to see much of anything but she could sense that something was wrong. Wildegraf was not where he was supposed to be, and now she had heard that Jürgen Focke had gone missing.

But it was too late to continue the search tonight. They would wait until sunrise before going on. She had promised to meet the emissary south of Hoffen but she did not want to give up the search until she had spoken to Wildegraf and confirmed that there was nothing behind the suspicions Falco had voiced in the Chamber of Council.

Nathalie hoped that Falco was mistaken, but something told her he was not. The Queen shared her concerns, but one way or another, they needed to know. But for now it was time to rest and so they moved down to a sheltered ledge where Nathalie curled up beneath the embracing canopy of Ciel's wing, the dragon's scales warm against her back.

*

In the mage tower of Wrath, Galen Thrall looked down into the chamber of discourse where the three mages helping Meredith were now ensconced. One was deep in meditation, sitting on a stone chair at the centre of the chamber. Another was asleep on a simple cot, while the third sat at a wooden table to eat a late supper. None of them had left the chamber during the last eleven days, nor would they until the experiment was concluded or ended in failure.

'Are they still in contact?' asked Thrall in a soft voice that did not carry.

'Yes,' said Morgan Saker who was standing beside him. 'The link remains unbroken.'

The pupils of Thrall's waxy green eyes narrowed.

'Impressive,' he said. 'Your son's idea might work after all.'

Morgan Saker gave a demure bow.

'And you are sure he will notify us of any developments.'

'He knows his duty,' said Saker. 'If Danté makes any progress with offensive capabilities he will tell us.'

'And the mage army?'

'Rest assured. If Meredith learns anything of the mage army's success we will know about it instantly.'

'Good,' said Thrall and the pupils of his eyes glinted like tiny beads of coal. 'There can be no delay. As soon as we have confirmation of the mage army's success we can move against the Queen. With Ludovico on the throne we will be one step closer to seizing power.'

*

The Queen stood at the window of her chambers looking, not out to sea, but inland to the east. Somewhere out there her subjects were marching into mortal danger but still she envied them. Better to face a thousand black swords than the shadowy manoeuvrings of those who sought to depose her.

She knew that Thrall waited only to hear of the mage army's success before staging his coup. He would voice his regret and pronounce his loyalty, but finally he would have the leverage he needed and she would have no option but to accept Prince Ludovico's hand in marriage. For the sake of her people she would accede and they would never know the depth of her sorrow. She would bury her feelings and devote herself to the union that could save them.

The night air felt suddenly cold and unforgiving and the Queen shivered. For a brief embittered moment she found herself hoping the mage army would fail, but the thought filled her with shame and a tear rolled down her cheek. She

312

would do anything to save her people. If that meant submitting to Thrall, and surrendering her personal happiness, then so be it.

With all the will she could muster she sent her love out into the world, to the emissary and the armies of Clemoncé, to the cadets in all their youthful determination, to the battle mages and dragons in their unthinkable struggle and finally to the warrior mages who marched in the Grand Veneratu's name.

Were they not men also?

Were they not her subjects too?

Finally her thoughts came to rest on young Master Danté. By now he would be very much closer to the front and she wondered if he had sensed anything more. There was still no word from Nathalie, and the Queen wondered if she had managed to find Wildegraf or Jürgen. The Illician battle mages had been fighting in that area for years. If anything was amiss then they would surely know about it.

Saving her final thought for her beloved Chevalier, the Queen turned from the balcony to seek the brief respite of a few hours sleep. Maybe tomorrow would bring the news that all was well, and there was nothing new to fear.

*

The night passed, and the sun rose, and in the Forsaken Lands of Illicia the battle mage Wildegraf Feuerson listened patiently as the riders told their tale. They spoke in broken fragments of fear and shock and shame. How they had gone to look for family members trapped in the Forsaken Lands. How they had been scouring the woods when a shadow came upon them, a shadow of all-consuming fear that disgorged a demon of lethal strength and steel. Thrown from their horses they would have died had another figure not burst from the trees, a warrior on a horse... a battle mage.

'He charged but the demon cut the horse from under him,' one of the traumatised men told Wildegraf. 'He attacked with fire and sword but it wasn't enough. The demon was unhurt.'

'He screamed at us to run.'

'We ran.'

'Mounted our horses and ran.'

'There was nothing we could do.'

'He told us to run.'

'There was nothing we could do.'

Wildegraf frowned at their stumbling account. It was true that there was nothing they could have done, but still they would carry the guilt for the rest of their lives.

'Where was this?' he asked them.

'In the Keiler Valley,' they said. 'About four days south.'

Wildegraf thanked them and gave them directions to the city of Hoffen where he knew they would be safe. Then as the men watched, he returned to his dragon, Berylian, who was just visible between the trees. The dragon's emerald green scales shimmered in the dim light of the forest and the soldiers eyed it warily as they mounted their horses once more. The dragon was undeniably powerful but it did not terrify them as the demon had. Rather it brought on a feeling of awe and respect.

Wildegraf was deep in thought as Berylian returned to the clearing where they could gain the sky. From their brief description he believed the soldiers spoke of Jürgen Focke, the only other battle mage in the area. Jürgen's summoning had gone unanswered, but that had not prevented him from making a huge contribution to the war. The chances of him coming across the soldiers by chance was slim, far more likely that he was searching for the demon that attacked them.

But Wildegraf was concerned. The soldiers' account held worrying clues about the nature of this demon. It was not uncommon for them to cloak themselves in shadow, but he was surprised to hear that this demon shook off a battle mage attack without harm. Jürgen might not have been blessed with a dragon but he was anything but weak. As Berylian readied himself for flight, Wildegraf feared the worst. Why had Jürgen not returned to help the soldiers after his fight with the demon?

Berylian turned his head and the images that swirled in his mind were dire.

'Yes, my friend,' said Wildegraf. 'I fear you are right.'

He gripped the riding harness as Berylian launched himself into the air. If this demon had killed Jürgen single handed then it was more dangerous than any they had yet encountered. He laid a reassuring hand on Berylian's powerful neck. They would look for this demon but they could not afford to be away for long. The armies around Hoffen needed their protection. But if this demon was something new then Wildegraf needed to find it. And find it quickly.

The emerald green dragon soared up into the sky and disappeared into the clouds. The Keiler Valley was not so far for a dragon but the rugged hills were clothed in ancient forest. If this demon was concealing its presence it would not be easy to find, but find it they would. And if Jürgen had indeed fallen, then the least they could do was avenge his death.

55

The Trials of Leadership

The weather remained largely fair and the cadet army made good progress through the wooded heartland of Clemoncé. The campaign presented numerous issues for the cadets to deal with but, shortly after passing through one small town, Bryna was faced with a disciplinary matter of a more serious kind. One of her men had been caught stealing from a local house. Most of the camp was oblivious to the misdemeanour, but the Dalwhinnies were notably subdued as the guilty man was brought before their captain.

'What do you think she'll do?' asked Falco as he and Malaki watched from one side of the proceedings.

'Don't know,' said Malaki. 'But she's absolutely fuming. Wouldn't be surprised if she swung the whip herself.'

Bryna was aware that everyone was watching, but she could barely look at the man standing at the centre of the clearing. Beside her Patrick Feckler held a many stranded leather whip known as a starter.

'What should I do?' murmured Bryna and Paddy gave a shrug.

'You could order two hundred lashes or more,' he said as the dejected man stood there with his head bowed. 'Less than a hundred and the men'll think you haven't the stomach for proper discipline.'

'Proper discipline,' said Bryna, giving Paddy a look of disgust.

'Men like this need a firm hand,' said Paddy. 'They feel more comfortable if they know where they stand.'

Bryna gave a snort of derision. She glanced over towards Falco and Malaki, but then her gaze slid across to one of the assessors who was also watching from a discreet distance. Finally Bryna waved the man forward.

'Why?' she asked.

The man glanced up, clearly mortified at being the centre of such adverse attention. 'The house was empty. I didn't think no one would notice, mistress.'

'Captain,' Paddy corrected him.

'Captain,' repeated the man, knuckling his forehead in some semblance of a salute.

Bryna glared at the man, furious at being placed in such a position. She had seen men flogged before and had no wish to relive the experience. She paused in thought before speaking again.

'Where are you from?' she asked at last.

'Verinae,' said the man. 'A small town near the border with Valentia.'

'Then to Verinae you shall return,' said Bryna.

The man looked at her, confused. 'I don't understand.'

'This is an archery unit of the Queen's Irregulars,' said Bryna, her face now a blank dispassionate mask. 'I have no use for thieves.'

'But mistress, I mean, Captain...' said the man.

He took a step forward but Paddy stopped him with a hand on his chest. Bryna ignored him completely.

'Give him enough food and supplies for the journey,' she said and with that she turned her back on the man and strode out of the camp.

The man watched her go with something like despair in his eyes and even the Dalwhinnies looked shocked. Bryna's cold dismissal had struck them more brutally than any strand of the lash. Across the way the assessor raised an appraising eyebrow, while Falco and Malaki watched Bryna disappear into the gloom of the surrounding trees.

'That will have cut her deeply,' said Malaki.

Falco nodded, but he also felt sorry for the guilty man. He knew from experience that few things cut more deeply than shame.

The following day Bryna chose to ride with Falco and Malaki. She was unusually subdued and rode in silence until she noticed that Patrick Feckler was not at the head of the Dalwhinnies, where she had left him. With a muttered curse she rode back to see where he was. Falco and Malaki gave each other a look before going to follow her. They found Paddy at the rear of the column, speaking to one of the Dalwhinnies who was walking beside another man who was clearly struggling to keep up. Paddy was remonstrating with the Dalwhinnie, and as they drew closer, they could hear what was being said.

'I told you to put him in the wagon and keep him hidden!' growled Paddy.

'Stubborn bastard insists on walking,' replied the man.

'What's going on here?' asked Bryna as she drew up beside Paddy.

Paddy gave the man a 'now see what you've done' look as Bryna spotted the man that was walking, or rather 'stumbling' behind the wagon. His head was bowed and the back of his shirt was dark with blood at various stages of drying. Falco recognised the man instantly but it took Bryna a moment to realise what was going on. Finally the truth dawned on her.

'I thought I told you to send him home,' she said to Paddy in a hard accusing tone.

'Quite so, Captain,' said Paddy, glancing at the other Dalwhinnie to hold his tongue. 'That was Jean Bonnot, the thief. I sent him away with my boot in his arse. This, on the other hand, is Jean Bonnot, an archer of the Queen's Irregulars.'

The man in question staggered as Paddy slapped him on the shoulder, his face was chalky white and dripping with sweat. They could all see that he was on the verge of passing out.

Bryna flushed with fury but Paddy did not flinch. She seemed about to say something but then her gaze came to rest on the pitiful figure of Jean Bonnot. The man's back had been whipped to a mass of raw and bloody flesh. Such a beating would normally put a man in the infirmary for a week, but here he was, refusing even to ride in the wagon. He had chosen to take the lash rather than be cast out of the Dalwhinnies in shame.

Bryna's eyes filled with tears.

'Well it looks like Monsieur Bonnot has hurt his back,' she said, her voice somewhat tight and husky. 'You will take care that it does not become infected.'

'Aye, Captain,' said Paddy, touching a finger to his brow.

'And throw him in the wagon until he can keep up with the other men.'

'Aye, Captain.'

Bryna gave her second in command a nod that confirmed the matter was ended then, with nothing left to be said, she turned to Falco and Malaki.

'I'll see you later,' she said and with that she urged her horse back up the column.

The Dalwhinnies watched warily as she overtook them. To a man they knew what had taken place and they wondered how their captain would respond to such blatant defiance of her orders. But finally Bryna reined in her horse and resumed her position at the head of her unit. The Dalwhinnies breathed a sigh of relief and allowed themselves a satisfied smile.

Falco and Malaki also breathed a sigh of relief. It would be easy to lose control over a unit as wild as the Dalwhinnies, but it appeared that the spell Bryna had cast over these rough hewn men was stronger than ever.

Later in the day Falco was riding with Malaki and the other knights when he noticed three riders closing on the main road from a path that came in from the side. The two at the rear appeared to be boys of about fifteen while the rider leading the group was a large man on a war horse similar to Malaki's destrier and sure enough, his surcoat displayed a black horse's head on a field of silver blue, the colours of the Knights of Wrath.

Catching Malaki's attention, Falco nodded over towards the approaching knight. They watched as he joined the main column of the army and approached one of the temporary commanders. A brief exchange took place and the commander turned in the saddle to point back towards the trainee knights. The knight and his squires moved to one side until Malaki and the others drew level then he nodded the squires to the back of the group and fell in beside Malaki.

The man was tall and broad shouldered but Falco noticed a freshly healed scar running from the man's nose to his left ear. He also recognised the gaunt shadow on the man's cheeks and the way the bones of his face stood out beneath his pale skin. Here was a man recovering from illness and injury.

'La force, l'honneur et la foi,' said the knight.

'Strength, honour and faith,' replied Malaki, honoured that the man should use the order's motto as if he were greeting a fellow knight.

As the knight joined them, Falco dropped back a little to allow Malaki some space, and for a while they rode on in silence.

'So you're the cause of the Lord Commander's deliberation?'

Malaki turned sharply, amazed that anyone outside of the Academy of War should know who he was. 'It was never my intention,' he began but the knight raised a hand to stall any further explanation.

'Sir Garnier, of Ledorne,' said the knight leaning across to offer his hand and glancing at the bright red birthmark on Malaki's face.

'Malaki de Vane, of Caer Dour'

The knight nodded as if he already knew the name. 'And this is your training campaign, from the academy?'

'Yes,' said Malaki. 'To the city of Le Matres.'

'And from there?'

Malaki looked at him, confused.

'Will you be returning to Wrath or travelling south with the order?'

'I will return to Wrath,' said Malaki, surprised that the knight would even suggest leaving the academy before his training was complete. 'I still have much to learn.'

'We need every possible sword,' said the knight. There was a faint note of disapproval in his voice as if he could not understand why a knight would turn from such an opportunity to join the fight. 'The Lord Commander is mustering the third chapter to the south of Le Matres. I would be happy to have you ride with me.'

'But the Lord Commander might not accept me,' said Malaki, thrown by the prospect of actually riding to war.

'With my sponsorship, he would,' said the knight.

Malaki glanced at the man as the full force of the proposition struck him. Was he ready to leave his friends and ride with the Knights of Wrath? Would they consider him a coward if he did not?

Falco had caught the gist of what was being said and he too was shaken by the prospect of them going their separate ways, but he decided not to say anything. It was for Malaki to make such a decision for himself.

As the afternoon lengthened a scout worked his way down the line, informing the commanders that they still had a little way to go before stopping for the night.

'There's a series of meadows two miles beyond the next village,' the scout told Malaki. 'We'll be making camp there.'

Malaki nodded and the scout moved on to the next unit.

The light was fading as they caught sight of the village ahead of them, a scattering of maybe fifty houses nestled against a bend in the river.

'Looks like it'll be dry tonight,' said Malaki as the army skirted the village.

Falco nodded but he was not really listening. A cold prickle of foreboding raised the hairs on his neck and his gaze moved to the edge of the clearing where the shadows beneath the trees were growing steadily deeper. He could not shake off the feeling that something of malice was moving among them. Malaki tensed as he noticed the intensity in Falco's gaze but then he relaxed as a procession of about a hundred villagers came into view. Many of them carried torches as they emerged from the trees, moving at an easy pace back towards the village.

'Looks like a wedding party,' said Malaki.

With an effort Falco focussed his mind on the line of villagers winding their way back towards their homes before night fell completely. Near the front was a young woman in a long dress of cream and yellow with spring flowers in her hair. Around her people chattered and laughed and children chased each other around the adults. The soldiers of the cadet army smiled to see such a happy occasion, looking wistfully at the inviting houses of the village, but not for them, a soft bed and a warm hearth tonight. They would be spending another damp night under the canopy of the sky.

At the sight of the villagers Falco began to relax, but then he noticed how some of the men at the back of the group were looking back nervously into the trees. One or two held swords or spears but all looked anxious and afraid.

Without even realising, Falco moved out of the column and towards the villagers while the army marched on.

'What is it?' asked Malaki, riding over to join him.

'Stop the column,' said Falco.

For a moment Malaki thought Falco was joking, but he recognised this particular tone of voice. The tone that was ageless and strong and spoke of things that normal people could not possibly understand. He looked at the line of revellers then he too noticed the men looking back into the trees.

Turning in the saddle he gave the command to halt. Those within ear shot stopped accordingly while those further on simply continued along the road and disappeared from view. Alex's Exiles and Jarek's unit of Royal Hussars were close enough to stop, but Jarek looked irritated at being held up on Malaki's command. He urged his horse towards them to see what was going on. Alex followed in his wake as Sir Garnier rode over to join them.

'What's the matter? Why have we stopped?' asked the knight but Falco said nothing. The feeling in his mind was reaching a critical pitch as if a piece of fabric were being stretched to the point of tearing.

'There,' said Falco, pointing to the fringe of trees from which the wedding procession had emerged. The shadows beneath the trees seemed darker than the fading light could account for.

'I don't see anything,' said Jarek but they could all feel the tension now.

Suddenly a dart shot out from the trees and one of the revellers fell to the ground with a black arrow in his back.

'La possédé!' screamed one of the villagers and chaos ensued as a group of about sixty Sciritae burst from the trees and went tearing after the villagers who fled in terror towards their homes. Behind the Sciritae came dozens of dark archers swathed in black rags with a piece of dark cloth bound across their eyes.

'Toxitae,' breathed Sir Garnier.

'Knights, to me!' cried Malaki and the trainee knights started forward, each now couching the spear they had been holding at rest.

'No!' said Falco, seeing how quickly the Possessed were closing on the villagers. 'They'll be in amongst the houses by the time you reach them.' He turned to Jarek. 'The Hussars would be better in the tight spaces.'

Malaki looked annoyed and Sir Garnier gave Falco a sharp censorious look. For a second Jarek stared at Falco, torn between the satisfaction of having his unit's skills recognised and the rancour of taking an order from Falco. But then...

'Hussars,' he cried. 'First form with me. Second form swing left to engage the archers.'

Jarek trotted forward as fifty of the Hussars formed up behind him.

'Charge!' he cried and the light horses sprang forward while the other half of his unit approached the Toxitae in a curving attack that made them less susceptible to being hit by arrows.

The Sciritae were closing quickly and two more of the villagers fell to black arrows before they reached the cover of the buildings.

'Bryna!' cried Falco but Bryna had already brought the Dalwhinnies forward.

They jogged down, formed into ranks and began firing at the black swathed figures of the Toxitae. The range was quite far but the Dalwhinnies aim was true and as the Toxitae began to fall so Bryna advanced.

'Stay with them,' Falco said to Malaki. 'There's something more than foot soldiers abroad this night.'

319

Malaki gave a grim nod and with a series of short commands he divided his knights into two groups to guard the archers' flanks. Falco could tell he was smarting at being overlooked in favour of Jarek, but now was not the time for complaints or recriminations.

Drawing his sword Falco advanced with the knights as the sound of fighting broke out in the village. The screams of the villagers mingled with the clash of steel and the neighing and scuffle of horses, but Falco had been right to send Jarek. In the tight confines of the village the Hussar's lighter mounts and exceptional horsemanship proved their worth, dodging frightened villagers and cutting down the Sciritae who snarled and raged at the fast and powerful horse soldiers.

The sounds of fighting faded away as the Hussars cleared the last of the Possessed from the village, but still the Dalwhinnies remained in formation, standing in the open space between the houses and the tree line of the forest. Alex had formed his infantry into a defensive line ready to advance or hold against any further attacks.

Jarek's second form of Hussars finished off the last of the Toxitae before heading back towards the Dalwhinnies. One of the men had an arrow through his arm and he swayed in the saddle, while another had been thrown when his horse took an arrow in the shoulder but these were the only casualties. The unseated man was now back in the saddle and trying to calm his injured mount as the Hussars retreated.

As the fighting ended the villagers moved towards the secure position established by the Exiles and the Dalwhinnies, while Jarek's hussars searched the village for any remaining Sciritae. The tension was beginning to dissipate but Falco continued to stare into the trees where the shadows still appeared unnaturally dark, and suddenly he realised it was not a shadow but a breach in the fabric of the world. And then he felt them coming... large and powerful and fast.

'Bestiarum!' he cried. 'Stand ready!'

Even as he spoke two huge shapes burst out of the darkness with a third one close behind.

They looked like great black bulls forged from the embers of a fire except that their limbs were muscular, with claws instead of hooves, and their heads were more like a bear or some kind of hellish ape. Teeth flashed and eyes glared and everything happened so quickly.

Two of the beasts charged straight for the Dalwhinnies who had begun to lose formation. A few hurried shots were fired off, but they were not enough to stop such heavy opponents. Falco felt a surge of energy rising within him but the violence of it was terrifying and it vanished like the ghost of something dark that lurked inside of him. It seemed as if the bestiarum would tear into the Dalwhinnies, but Malaki and his knights were well positioned to meet such an attack. Their warhorses were bred for their power and could spring from standing into a full attack with a burst of explosive force. With a cry they charged forward to engage the beasts.

Huthgarl struck the first with a lance thrust that entered the creature's neck and drove deep into its chest while Malaki's spear took the second in the shoulder causing the hideous creature to pitch forward exposing its ribs to the lance of Quirren Klingemann.

With their momentum checked the first two beasts were quickly dispatched. However, the third beast went not for the Dalwhinnies but directly for the group of villagers that had been moving towards the Exiles. Some of them began to run but others just huddled together, transfixed as the creature bore down upon them. The powerful beast was about to tear into the villagers when a shout went up from the right flank of the Dalwhinnies.

'Suivez dix!'

Dedric Sayer loosed his arrow and not ten, but twelve others followed its course. The range was close and the arrows struck the beast in the hindquarters with a collective thump that sent it sprawling sideways. With a snarl it regained its balance but its back leg was dragging and before it could make another move Sir Garnier struck it in the face with his sword as he galloped swiftly past.

The terrified villagers held onto each other as the beast thrashed around not twenty feet from them, but a few more arrows from the Dalwhinnies and a final spear thrust from one of the knights soon brought an end to the raging beast's death throes. The three huge corpses lay like heaps of glowing ashes, their bodies slowly breaking up and blowing away on the wind to leave behind only a blackened skeleton with massive teeth and claws.

The night became suddenly quiet and was only disturbed by the panting breath of horses and the muted sounds of distress as the villagers tried to calm their children. The strange curtain of darkness faded from beneath the trees and the sense of danger receded in Falco's mind.

There would be no more visitations from the Possessed tonight.

From the road came a rising clamour as those from further up or further down the column surged forward to see what had happened. It was only then that Falco realised the entire encounter had lasted only a few short minutes. Four of the villagers lay dead, with at least a dozen more injured. Several of Jarek's Hussars were wounded and a number of the Dalwhinnies had been hit by Toxitae arrows but the volume of their swearing was an indication that none were seriously hurt.

Now the commanders took control, setting up a defensive perimeter and organising a thorough search of the surrounding area. After some discussion it was agreed that the villagers would sleep with the army tonight and after gathering a few belongings they were escorted to the rear of the column where space was found for them in the wagons.

A subdued calm settled on the clearing and it was almost surreal to hear the ordinary sounds of the night slowly returning to the world: wind in the trees, the distant babble of the river and the mournful hoot of an owl. Children were crying and the injured moaned as Falco and the army medics did what they could to ease their suffering. Falco had just 'cleansed' the entry wound of a Toxitae arrow when one of the assessors addressed him.

'Falco Danté,' said the man in a stern tone. 'You will follow me.'

Falco wanted to stay and help the injured, but then he noticed that Bryna, Malaki, Jarek and Alex were also standing ready to go with the assessor. To one side, Sir Garnier watched them with an unreadable expression in his eyes, his gaze moving from Malaki to Falco and back again. Quickly washing his hands, Falco followed the assessor who took them to the command tent where they were questioned about the incident that had just taken place.

'And what was it that made you call the column to a halt?' asked one of the assessors.

'Just a feeling,' said Falco. 'I could feel something in the trees.'

'The scouts saw nothing when they passed through,' insisted one of the commanders.

'There was nothing there when the scouts passed through,' said Falco.

'Then where did the Possessed come from? Did they cross the river?'

Falco shook his head. 'They just appeared,' he said. 'They came out of the shadows as if the darkness led to another place.'

The assessors looked at each other nervously. They had all heard stories of the Possessed appearing out of nowhere.

'Then it seems that we are fortunate,' said the spokesman finally. 'For if the army had moved on just a little further the villagers would have been dead before we could have come to their aid.'

Falco accepted this acknowledgement, but in his heart he felt guilty that he had not read the warning signs more quickly. Had he done so, the four deceased villagers might still be alive. But at least he now recognised the strange darkness from which the Possessed could emerge. He would not make the same mistake again.

After a thorough analysis of events it was judged that the cadets had acted with exemplary speed and judgement. The Hussars in particular were singled out for the skill and efficiency with which they had cleared the village.

Jarek simply bowed his head in a rare display of modesty, but as the assessors dismissed them he glanced at Falco and the expression in his eyes was filled with a complex array of emotions. There were the after effects of fear and excitement, pride and satisfaction at the praise he had received, but there was also a strange sense of conflict. It was Falco who had favoured his unit over the knights, and it was Falco who had instinctively taken command of the situation. Something told Jarek that this was worthy of respect, but somehow he could not bring himself to acknowledge it.

Falco gave a sigh as Jarek moved off to rejoin the Hussars.

'I wouldn't expect a thank you from that one,' said Malaki.

'And I wouldn't expect a Knight of Wrath to be ordered about by a man who hasn't even passed his own rite of trial.'

The disapproving voice came from Sir Garnier and Malaki stopped as he stood face to face with the senior member of his order.

'Why would you let your decision to attack be overruled?' asked Sir Garnier. 'Do you have so little faith in your knights?'

Malaki's face flushed red. For a moment Falco did not know if he would retort with anger or submit before the knight's unbending gaze. Finally he replied with the calm dignity for which he was known.

'You speak in ignorance, my Lord,' said Malaki and Sir Garnier's eyebrow arched at such insubordination. 'If you knew Falco as I do, you would not need to ask.'

Sir Garnier's face settled into a hard expression but there was a condescending smile on his lips.

'The Lord Commander was right,' he said. 'You are not ready to ride to war with us. Above all else you must have faith in your brothers.'

'Falco *is* my brother,' said Malaki and Bryna's eyes fair shone with pride.

Sir Garnier stared at Malaki for a moment more. His smile broadened as if he was amused by the naivety of Malaki's words.

'Farewell, Malaki de Vane,' said the knight. 'I'm sure one day you will be ready to ride with the Knights of Wrath.'

'La force, l'honneur et la foi,' said Malaki, refusing to be dismissed so easily.

'Strength, honour and faith,' said the knight and the smile had gone from his lips as he bowed his head.

Sir Garnier walked away and the friends continued back to the area where their units were now encamped. As they drew close to the Dalwhinnies, Patrick Feckler came forward to meet them.

'Any problems?' he asked.

'No,' said Bryna. 'Just talking things through. Where's Dedric? I want to congratulate him on stopping that beast.'

Paddy gave a wry smile and some of the nearby Dalwhinnies laughed. 'He's over there in the woods, crying like a baby.'

Bryna looked concerned but Paddy shook his head.

'Don't you worry. Some of the villagers came over to thank him for saving their lives. Hugged him and brought him gifts. Made quite a fuss, eh lads?' Paddy exchanged another mischievous grin with the Dalwhinnies but Bryna still looked confused.

'You could be brute'n nasty to Dedric Sayer for a year and he'd never bat an eye,' said Paddy. 'But kindness and gratitude... Well, that's something he's never had to deal with before.'

Bryna gazed into the trees.

'Just leave him,' said Paddy. 'He'll be right.'

A few of the men came forward with food and drink and they sat together talking quietly about the battle that had just taken place, but Falco noticed the hushed comments and the way many of the men looked at him when they thought he wasn't looking. None of *them* had sensed the evil emerging from the darkness. None of *them* had such an awareness of the Possessed.

'Don't worry about them,' said Malaki, handing Falco a skewer of seared venison chunks. 'They don't understand how you knew, but they're glad that you did.'

Falco gave him a dubious look.

'It's true,' said Malaki, tearing a chunk of meat from his own skewer. 'Some of the other units are asking if you can ride with them tomorrow.'

Falco glanced up at two men who had been speaking in lowered tones. One of them looked away, embarrassed at being caught out, but the other offered a tight-lipped smile and gave Falco a nod of acknowledgement. Falco was reminded of Aurelian's words.

Make no mistake. If you do encounter the Possessed, then every man and woman in the army will look to you for guidance.

He wondered at the way he had taken command when the Possessed broke through. It had seemed so natural. But he also noticed the way it rankled with Jarek and Sir Garnier, and even Malaki.

'You were right,' said Malaki suddenly.

'What?'

'You were right to send Jarek into the village.'

Malaki picked a stringy piece of meat from between his teeth. And Falco smiled.

56

Le Matres, Hunting &
The Commander of the Fourth

Two days south of the city of Hoffen, the command tent of the Fourth Army was charged with tension. Since arriving on the front they had fought a number of small engagements but now two larger Possessed armies were closing on their position and there was also a demon army moving up from the south.

I don't understand,' said one of the younger officers. 'I thought this area was fairly secure.'

'Something's happened to the south,' said the emissary. 'Both Jürgen and Wildegraf are now missing and we won't know why until Nathalie returns.'

He looked down at the campaign map. If they acted quickly they could defeat the two Possessed armies before they could come together into a larger and more dangerous force. But if they were joined by the demon that was moving up from the south then the Fourth Army would have no way of stopping them.

The emissary's contemplation was suddenly broken as Dagoran Sorn slammed his hand down onto the map.

'Enough of this waiting! We need to attack!'

The parchment around his hand began to darken with the pent up magical energy that suffused his flesh. The commander of the mage army was growing increasingly impatient. The battles they had fought thus far had been over quickly and the magi had not had the opportunity to demonstrate their skills.

'We know where the enemy is. We should attack now before the two forces have a chance to join together!'

'We will,' said the emissary.

'Then what are we waiting for?' demanded Sorn.

'We cannot attack until the scouts have returned,' said General Renucci. 'We cannot plan a battle until we know what we face.'

'But we know what we face,' said Sorn. 'We face the Possessed and unless we stop them they will reach the Clemoncéan border within months.'

'I have been fighting the Possessed for twenty years,' said General Renucci between clenched teeth. 'I refuse to be lectured by a pompous mystic who's never known a day of battle.'

He raised his eyes to glare at Sorn who matched his anger with cold contempt.

'We are all aware of the threat we are facing,' said the emissary. 'And I commend Lord Sorn for his eagerness to join the fight.'

Despite the emissary's calming presence the tension between General Renucci and Sorn persisted while the other officers shifted uneasily. They had never known such discord in the command tent of the Fourth.

Looking down at the map the emissary breathed a heavy sigh.

'Lord Sorn is right. We need to engage the Possessed armies before they have the chance to combine. But we must be careful and we will not attack until the scouts return.' Sorn's mouth took on a sour twist while General Renucci gave a satisfied sniff of concurrence. 'And whatever happens we cannot allow them to join up with the demon army that is approaching from the south. Until Nathalie returns we have no way of stopping a demon.'

'*We* could stop it,' said Sorn, raising his chin to meet the disbelieving looks of the other officers.

General Renucci was about to voice their collective incredulity when the emissary spoke.

'Have you ever faced a demon, my Lord?'

'We have been trained to face them,' said Sorn, deftly avoiding a direct answer.

The emissary gave a sigh. They had all heard stories of the mage warrior training. How each of them had been submitted to mental assaults designed to harden their minds against evil. But there was an expression in the eyes of those who had faced a demon. It was an expression of utter hopelessness, the realisation that the sum of all one's courage was simply not enough. For all his pride and arrogance, such an expression was absent from the eyes of Dagoran Sorn.

'No,' said the emissary and Sorn's indignation flared anew. 'We will attack the Possessed armies to the east but then we must wait for Nathalie.'

Sorn glared at the emissary, enraged that he seemed to value one battle mage over *his* force of a thousand warrior mages. He already felt it beneath him to take orders from a simple soldier, but his force had been placed under the emissary's command and would remain so until such time as the magi could prove their boasts. With nothing more to be said he gave a stiff bow and swept from the command tent with two of his purple cloaked warriors at his heels.

'He'll change his tune,' muttered General Renucci. 'Once he's faced a real Possessed army. He'll not be so eager then.'

The emissary remained in the command tent as the officers took their leave. He shared General Renucci's annoyance but he also understood Sorn's impatience. Sorn was eager to report their success back to Galen Thrall and he saw the emissary's caution as a deliberate attempt to delay the inevitable. However, despite the threat they posed to the Queen, the emissary was determined to give the magi a fair opportunity to prove themselves. But he would not risk the Fourth Army to do it.

*

The following day, and sixty miles to the south, Wildegraf Feuerson and his dragon, Berylian, were soaring over the wooded hills of Illicia. Banking suddenly the great green dragon circled back as if he had detected some sign of their quarry. Wildegraf leaned low over the dragon's back, staring down into the trees. For a moment he was certain that there was something down there, but now he sensed nothing. After a few wing beats of hovering flight they moved on.

*

Far below, the Slayer drew back into its cloak of darkness as the wyrm hovered over the forest, the Defiant clinging to its scaly back. He knew they could sense his presence, as he sensed theirs. He also knew that they could not see him. If they could they would have already attacked. For a moment the Slayer considered letting the shadow fall and roaring out a challenge, but no. He could feel their power and he did not want to risk an encounter without the element of surprise. Better to wait until they came to ground and then to strike from darkness. After all - the darkness was a powerful weapon to have at one's command.

*

The city of Le Matres was built around the confluence of two rivers with a great castle sitting on a low hill at its centre. As the cadet army drew closer the trees gave way and the land opened out into a wide valley looking east towards the border with Illicia. A substantial curtain wall encircled the city, but even from here the cadets could see the makeshift camps of refugees spreading out onto the plain.

'I guess that's who we'll be escorting back to Wrath,' said Malaki.

Falco nodded, daunted by the sheer number of people who needed their help.

The cadet army made camp within sight of the city and when morning came they began the task of distributing supplies and preparing to start work on the bridges they had been sent here to build.

With all the units busy, Falco found himself at a bit of a loss, so as the sun climbed into a hazy sky he rode into Le Matres and followed a cobbled street that led up to the castle. Leaving his horse at the stables in the courtyard, he climbed a series of stone stairways onto the battlements. The elevated position gave an expansive view of the surrounding territory and his thoughts flashed back to the great map in the Chamber of Council.

Back then, the city of Le Matres had been nothing more than a small black disk circled in brass. Now he was standing high above the city and he began to get a true sense of the world in which they lived. To the northeast lay the Illician city of Hoffen, and Falco found his thoughts drifting to the emissary and the soldiers of the Fourth Army. He wondered if they were safe and he felt guilty that he was here doing nothing while they risked their lives to hold the Possessed at bay.

Once they returned to Wrath Falco was determined that this would change.

*

Just thirty miles to the east of Le Matres, the morning sun was shining through a thin layer of cloud. The Fourth Army had moved into position shortly after sunrise and now the emissary and his officers looked down from a low rise as the Possessed appeared in the valley.

Dagoran Sorn seemed contemptuous of the forces ranged against them. He gave the impression that his mage warriors could defeat them alone. General Renucci had reacted with predictable scorn but the emissary was still determined to give them a fair chance. He had placed the mage army on the right flank with three thousand of his most experienced troops. The rest of the Fourth Army was arranged across the valley ready to bring their full force to bear.

They needed to break the Possessed quickly so that they could redeploy and be ready to meet the second army that was already closing on their position. The emissary knew his own men were up to the task, but he was not so sure about the magi. They looked like warriors and trained like warriors, but he trusted the courage of ordinary men. He was yet to be convinced by the mage warriors' conceited sense of superiority.

327

Drawing his thoughts back from the magi the emissary turned to General Renucci.

'Have the scouts made their final count?'

'A little over ten thousand,' said General Renucci. 'With no more than a hundred bestiarum.'

'And the second force?'

'A similar size, and about five hours away.'

The emissary nodded. He had some twenty thousand troops at his command plus the thousand warriors of the mage army. Their greater numbers gave them a definite advantage but, in battle, nothing could be taken for granted. The important thing was to defeat the Possessed quickly without sustaining too many losses.

'Gentlemen, to your places,' he said and with a salute the officers returned to the units under their command.'

The emissary turned to the waiting signalmen.

'Sound the parati.'

The two signalmen raised their horns and blew the call to stand ready, and the signal was immediately taken up by other musicians and relayed across the battlefield.

The emissary watched as the black mass of the Possessed advanced towards them. Looking up he saw the shapes of two dark angels hovering high in the sky, a sure sign that the demon army to the south was getting closer. He drew the horse head pendant from beneath his breastplate and kissed it before tucking it away and drawing down the bellows visor of his helm. He was the Commander of Clemoncé's Fourth Army but in battle he wore the Illician armour of the Adamanti and now he drew his sword as he waited for the battle to begin.

57

The Slayer

Wildegraf kept low to the rocks as he looked down from the escarpment while Berylian shifted uneasily beside him.

'Easy, my friend. I feel it too.'

Together the battle mage and the dragon gazed down, trying to detect any sign of the creature they had been hunting. Their search had brought them back towards the city of Hoffen but they were still within the Forsaken Lands and not a bird sang nor beast stirred beneath the trees. Even the animals of the wild seemed to know the land was doomed. Just twenty miles from here the armies of Illicia and Clemoncé were trying to hold the Possessed at bay, but they were grossly outnumbered and every month saw them being pushed further and further back.

Wildegraf clenched his fist in frustration. He and Berylian were needed there, at the front. He could not afford to spend much longer searching for the demon that had killed Jürgen.

They had found the battle mage's corpse beside the cloven body of his horse. Rather than leave them to rot, Berylian had cremated them where they lay and Wildegraf drove Jürgen's sword into the mound of glowing ashes, a token to mark the place where a great man had fallen.

But they had found no sign of the demon that slew him. It was not until this morning that they caught a definite hint of something, a sense of malice that left a faint trail of darkness as it moved across the land. Even now they were not certain of what they had found, but Wildegraf felt sure it was the demon. He sensed its presence but this was no minor duke. Only a demon of great power could shield itself from the concentrated vision of a battle mage.

He let out the breath he had been holding. If the demon *had* been down there it was gone now. Slowly they backed away from the cliff. Behind them the escarpment was level for a hundred yards before rising up a further series of cliffs. Wildegraf replaced his helm and slung his shield across his back. He was just reaching for the riding harness when he felt it, the presence of darkness on the escarpment behind them. Berylian gave a growl. He had sensed it too.

Peering through the visor of his helm Wildegraf frowned. He shrugged the shield from his back and reached for his sword. At first there was nothing to be seen but then, some sixty yards away, the grass and scrub started to wither as if burned by intense heat. Berylian tensed as the patch of scorched earth began to grow, extending towards them with the speed of a charging bull. The battle mage barely had time to couch his shield and draw his sword before the demon was upon them. It burst from the blackened earth, launching a vicious attack with two large curving blades. Wildegraf ducked beneath one, while Berylian recoiled from the other. The dragon did well to avoid a fatal blow as the enchanted blade opened a shallow cut along his ribs.

Wildegraf stole a moment of stillness to focus on their attacker. The demon was about eight feet tall with powerful shoulders and strong back-bent legs that were wreathed in smoke. Its head, arms and upper torso were covered in heavy armour with two curving swords held tight within its fists. It was smaller than most of the demons they had faced but also more powerful. And now Wildegraf knew why Jürgen had fallen. This was no ordinary demon, this was an assassin, a Slayer.

But there was no time for further consideration as the demon continued its attack and Wildegraf found himself blocking a series of powerful blows. Then, as Berylian lunged with his jaws, Wildegraf launched a magical attack that should have been enough to stop the Slayer in its tracks, but the glowing harpoon of light deflected off the demon's armour. Wildegraf attacked with his sword but somehow the Slayer managed to dodge it.

'Its fast!' thought Wildegraf as Berylian closed from the other side. 'Too fast!'

The dragon attacked with his steel hard talons, but the demon countered with its vicious blades and Berylian was fortunate not to lose a limb. Wildegraf sent a searing arc of energy at the back of the Slayer's legs but the demon merely stumbled and whirled about with a mighty downward blow that would have split a normal knight in two. Again Wildegraf raised his shield and fortified his arm but with each crushing attack his protection was growing less. He shot a bolt of energy into the Slayer's midriff causing the demon's strike to go wide. The Slayer drew back for another attack when a familiar sensation warned Wildegraf that Berylian was about to attack with fire.

With an instinctive reflex the battle mage surrounded himself in a protective sphere but the demon must have sensed it too and with that same astonishing speed it turned to face the fiery attack. Berylian's flames slammed into its head and shoulders but the Slayer was protected by its unholy armour and Wildegraf watched in horror as it thrust one of its blades through the writhing jet of flame.

'NO!' he cried as the demon's blade sank into the base of Berylian's neck.

The flames vanished and Berylian reared back. The sword had cut through nerves and tendons above the dragon's shoulder and his left forelimb dragged as he shifted to avoid a second thrust.

Lunging forward Wildegraf struck the Slayer in the small of the back, an attack of passion that finally did some damage, but the Slayer turned and Wildegraf was sent reeling as one of its swords hacked into his shield. Fortification saved his life but it was not enough and the battle mage felt warm blood coursing down his arm. Gritting his teeth against the pain he launched several attacks of his own but the demon parried them all until it was ready to strike back.

The Slayer broke Wildegraf's leg with a savage kick then drove him to his knees with a punch that caved in the left-hand side of his helm. Finally an upward cut threw the battle mage onto his back and he lay there coughing up blood in the echoing confines of his helm.

Fighting to remain conscious Wildegraf rolled onto his side. His shield arm and his right leg were broken and the Slayer's upward strike had sliced deep into his chest. But still he turned to see.

Through the mangled slits in his visor he saw the Slayer striding towards Berylian who backed away, limping on the injured leg that would no longer take his weight. He saw the demon reel as the mighty green dragon landed a heavy blow but it was not enough to stop it. The scene explode in flames as Berylian attacked with fire once more but again the demon hunkered down to ride out the storm. There followed a brutal exchange of blows and for a moment Wildegraf thought Berylian might prevail but then an arc of blood went flying from one of the Slayer's curving blades.

As his vision began to fade Wildegraf saw Berylian slump to one side, his wings flapping awkwardly as the demon stood over him. It tore at Wildegraf's heart to see his brother-in-arms at the mercy of such a fiend, but his own body was broken and there was nothing he could do to stop it. They had underestimated this Slayer and paid the ultimate price, but far worse was the fact that they could no longer warn their friends. The armies of Queen Catherine were fighting in this area and they had no way of knowing about the instrument of death that was come upon them.

The Slayer dragged Berylian over towards the cliff before returning for the battle mage. Wildegraf looked up as the demon loomed over him. With unwavering faith he gazed into the Slayer's hot inhuman eyes but instead of murder he saw cruelty and guile and he knew that he and Berylian would not be allowed to die just yet. The Slayer would make them suffer and use their pain as a beacon to draw yet more great souls within reach of its blades, and then it would kill again.

As the Slayer reached for him Wildegraf tried to send his thoughts out into the world.

'Beware! My beloved people and fellow Souls.

The enemy has a new weapon.

Beware!'

58
The Failings of Normal Men

The air above the valley shimmered with the unearthly heat of the Possessed but without a demon in their midst the emissary knew he could defeat them.

The enemy had come on with predictable ferocity, but the soldiers of the Fourth had faced them many times before and they held formation as their archers broke the first wave of attacks. Hundreds of lightly armoured Sciritae fell in those first few volleys but hundreds more leapt over them in a relentless surge of hatred. Only the most serious of injuries would stop the Possessed. Pain meant nothing to them and the only fear they felt was the fear of failing their master. The soldiers of the Fourth were ready for such mindless violence and they met it with courage, discipline and skill, but now the Possessed swept round to the right flank and it was Sorn's warrior mages who stood in their path.

'Now we'll see,' said General Renucci.

Feeling an unnerving degree of tension the emissary watched as the Possessed streamed towards the magi, but before the leading Sciritae could attack they were cut down by a blinding volley of magical attacks. Hundreds of glowing blue shafts speared into the Possessed, as effective as any unit of archers. And even when the Possessed did reach them the warrior mages did not yield. Fighting with sword and shield they put on a fine display of skill.

'They seem to be holding,' said General Renucci, sounding almost disappointed.

The emissary nodded but he could see the tension in the magi's ranks. The warriors in the front were fighting well but many had already moved out of line and the ranks were beginning to lose cohesion. For a regular unit of swordsmen this could prove disastrous, but the magi were not regular swordsmen. Their magic infused blades seemed to slice right through the bronze-steel armour of the Sciritae and they were supported by hundreds of magical attacks from their brothers in the ranks behind.

Satisfaction and annoyance vied for position in the emissary's mind as he turned his attention back to the rest of the battle. The centre was holding firm and the left flank had already begun its advance, ready to envelop the Possessed.

Satisfied that the main part of the battle was under control, the emissary turned back to the magi. In addition to the Sciritae, a large unit of heavily armoured Kardakae were now approaching them and the emissary wondered how they would deal with this more powerful threat. Galen Thrall's mage army had finally been given the chance to prove itself.

As the heavy shock troops advanced the emissary could see Sorn giving orders for his men to redress the ranks. The warrior mages reacted with impressive discipline, overlapping their shields and bracing for the inevitable impact. Then, at the last minute several bestiarum came charging through the Possessed. They leapt clear over the front ranks of warrior mages and immediately began tearing into the magi.

Watching anxiously, the emissary moved forward to get a better view.

'Isolate, contain, dispatch!' he breathed, repeating the infantry mantra for confronting bestiarum.

Then, even as the magi struggled to contain the raging beasts, more than six hundred Kardakae attacked their front ranks.

For a second it appeared as if the mage army would collapse and the emissary feared the worst. But then a collective burst of light exploded from the magi as they unleashed a huge magical attack. The sound of the attack rolled across the valley like thunder and the first ranks of Kardakae were literally torn apart.

'By the heavens and all the stars that fall,' intoned General Renucci.

The emissary was equally stunned by the force of the magi's attack but his thoughts went immediately to the Queen who was waiting to hear if the mage army's success would seal her fate.

'*Oh, my love,*' thought the emissary. '*Steel your heart, for Thrall's boasts were not in vain.*'

It seemed the magi were right. They *could* offer something that might save them all. For a moment the emissary was paralysed by the consequences of what this meant for himself and the Queen, for their chances of ever being together. As soon as he heard the news, Galen Thrall would call for a vote of no confidence in the Queen and insist that she accept the 'support' of Prince Ludovico as King.

The anguish of the thought wrung at the emissary's heart, but then he noticed the bodies of numerous magi that had also been blasted along with the Kardakae. He saw that two of the bestiarum had not yet been killed and that the remaining ranks of Kardakae had already recovered and were pressing forward once more. He waited for the magi to unleash a second attack and press home their advantage, but no such attack materialised. Instead the mage army began to give ground, stumbling backwards and breaking the formation of the troops behind them.

'They're folding!' said General Renucci aghast.

For a moment longer the emissary looked down upon the magi as the entire right flank of the army began to give way. Far from enveloping the Possessed it was *their* flank that was about to be turned. He swept a quick glance over the battlefield. If they drew back, and consolidated the centre, they could still win the battle but not before the second Possessed army arrived. Steeling his mind against the urge to fight on he made the inevitable decision.

'Sound the retreat!'

'We can still defeat them!' cried General Renucci.

'But not in time. And not without heavy casualties. Now, sound the retreat!'

General Renucci seemed about to protest again but he too could see that the collapse of the mage army had changed everything. The magi had gone from being a unit of great potential to a liability that had cost them the battle. Baring his teeth in frustration he ordered the signalmen to sound the retreat.

As the horn blasts echoed across the valley the emissary watched anxiously as the army struggled to check its momentum and fall back. Disengaging from battle was one of the most dangerous things an army could do but the soldiers of the Fourth were able to hold formation as they backed away.

Sensing weakness the Possessed rushed to follow them but the emissary used archers and sweeping cavalry charges to prevent them from closing and slowly a gap began to open up between the two forces. They had managed to avert disaster but they had lost the initiative and now there was no way they could prevent the two Possessed armies from joining up.

The truth was that they could probably defeat even this larger force but the cost would be too high. The emissary would need reinforcements if he was going to keep his army intact. As soon as they were out of the valley he would send a rider to Hoffen. And once the reinforcements arrived he would turn and fight again.

And as for the approaching demon, well... they could only hope that Nathalie returned in time.

*

Flying high over the forested valleys of Illicia, Nathalie winced as they felt it again, the soundless echoes of a soul in torment. After finding no sign of Wildegraf they had finally decided to give up the search and return to the emissary, and even now they would arrive later than they had planned. But there it was again, an overwhelming sense of agony that drew them back for one last look.

'I don't know,' whispered Nathalie in response to the questioning thoughts of her dragon.

Ciel's mind was filled with disturbing images of fear and terrible pain while to Nathalie's mind it had sounded almost like a scream. Somebody somewhere was suffering. But this was not only the sound of a human in pain; a dragon was in anguish too.

'Don't worry, my love,' breathed Nathalie. 'Whoever it is, we'll help them.'

Making a small adjustment to the direction of their flight the battle mage and her dragon flew on. They would free these souls from whatever torment they were enduring and then they would return to the emissary with all possible speed.

*

In contrast to General Renucci's fury the emissary felt a distinct sense of pity towards Dagoran Sorn. It appeared that for all their impressive powers the magi had succumbed to the failings of normal men. In their fear and excitement they had unleashed all their power in one explosive outburst, just like any inexperienced soldier who expends all their energy in the first few minutes of battle.

'And how long before you can use these offensive spells again?' asked the emissary as they held a quick meeting around a field table laid out with maps.

'Several hours of meditation are needed for a single attack,' said Sorn. 'But it takes weeks to build up the stores of energy required for a battle.'

General Renucci gave a snort of contempt and even the emissary could not contain his frustration.

'Then I will not keep you from your preparations,' he said in a clipped and censorious tone.

With a stiff bow Dagoran Sorn returned to the broken ranks of his army and the ravages of his own shattered ego.

They had finally succeeded in putting some distance between themselves and the enemy but the two Possessed armies had now joined up and they were being pursued by a force that was roughly the same size as their own.

334

'We could still defeat them,' said Captain Salien, a veteran of the war against the Possessed.

'Yes, we could,' said the emissary. 'But we cannot afford to break the Fourth Army in the process. Another eight thousand troops from Hoffen will give us the advantage and reduce our casualties.'

'But we have to destroy the Possessed army now before the demon arrives!'

'And we will,' said the emissary. 'As soon as the reinforcements arrive from Hoffen.'

'The reinforcements aren't coming!'

They all turned as a travel weary scout came stumbling towards them, his face pale with the news he bore.

'My Lord,' said the scout, giving the emissary a hasty bow. 'Marshal Vitrion sends his apologies. The garrison at Hoffen has been called away to prevent an incursion to the north. It will be more than a week before they can come to our aid.'

The emissary closed his eyes while the other commanders all began to speak at once.

'We must retreat to the city.'

'Are you mad?' said General Renucci. 'We can't lead a demon army to a city without a battle mage. Walls alone won't keep it out!'

'Then we have no choice but to attack the Possessed before the demon arrives!'

'And lose half the army!'

'At least we'd keep them from joining with the demon. Better a demon with a handful of troops than a demon with an army of twenty thousand.'

As the officers continued to wrangle, the emissary looked down at the map. General Renucci was right. They could not lead a demon army to an unprotected city. Somehow they needed to lead the Possessed away from Hoffen and give Nathalie time to return. He was still confident that she would get back to them but if she did not then the city of Hoffen and this whole area could be lost.

No. There had to be another way.

The emissary's finger began to trace a line on the map, a line that followed a new valley leading away from Hoffen, a valley that led in the direction of Le Matres. Suddenly a thought occurred to him that might just give them a chance. The officers ceased their heated debates as the emissary turned to one of the dispatch riders waiting nearby.

'Ride to Le Matres,' he said. 'There you will find a garrison of three thousand plus the cadet army from the Academy of War.' He ignored the gasps of disbelief from several of his officers.

Were they now expecting cadets to fight with them?

'Tell them to ride out immediately and to meet us in this valley, somewhere here.' The emissary tapped an area on the map with his finger. 'And tell them to bring Falco Danté.'

'Danté!' exclaimed General Renucci and the other officers looked at them uncertainly.

'He's strong,' said the emissary. 'Stronger than he looks.'

'But he's not fully trained!' said General Renucci.

'No,' said the emissary. 'But if the demon reaches us before we can destroy the Possessed then he might just give us a chance.'

59

Daston

In Le Matres the supplies were distributed, the bridge work had begun and a census was being drawn up of the refugees they would be escorting back to Wrath. While the cadets were busy with the practicalities Falco spent some final time with Meredith. So far the communication experiment had proven to be a success but the master of Le Matres' mage tower seemed reluctant to grant Meredith an audience.

'They're feeling a little put out,' he explained. 'They don't appreciate an upstart like me telling them how things could be improved.'

Falco smiled in sympathy. Meredith was clearly pleased at his achievement but he also looked drained by the effort.

'I take it you'll return to Wrath once you convince them.'

Meredith nodded. 'It'll take a few days to teach them how to transfer the awareness. And I have some research to carry out while I'm here. But yes. I will be returning to Wrath.'

'Good,' said Falco. 'I'll be needing your help when we get back.'

Meredith looked at him but said nothing. He knew Falco was thinking about the Rite of Assay, but like Aurelian, Meredith knew he was not ready.

'Are you going to see Fossetta?'

'We're not even sure if she'll be there,' said Falco. 'But Daston's only about twenty miles away so we're certainly going to try.'

Meredith gave a slow nod. He wondered what it must be like to have people you cared about like that.

Falco and Malaki were going to head off in the morning but Bryna could not leave just now. A number of fights had broken out between the Dalwhinnies and members of the local militia. It seemed that Bryna's men now objected to being labelled as poachers and cutpurses.

In the grey light of the following morning she stood by and watched as Falco and Malaki saddled their horses.

'I'll try to come over in a day or two,' she said. 'Just as soon as I can convince Patrick Feckler that beating up the locals is not the best way to convince people of one's honour.'

They all laughed and Malaki gave Bryna a long lingering kiss.

'Take care,' she told them.

'You too,' said Malaki and with that they set off into the misty drizzle that clung to the surrounding hills like smoke.

The path took them along an old drover's road that wound between the hills and it was late afternoon when they finally arrived in the forest town of Daston. The inhabitants eyed them warily as they followed the main road into the centre. The people of Daston were used to strangers moving through the town. Most were fearful refugees fleeing from the advance of the Possessed, but not these two young warriors. There was nothing fearful about them.

A gaggle of children began to follow them until they stopped to water their horses outside a blacksmith's forge.

'That's a handsome beast you have there, my Lord,' said the smith, wiping his hands on a rag as he emerged from the forge.

'That he is,' said Malaki, patting Fidelis's neck. 'But I'm not a lord, only a knight in training.'

The smith gave Malaki a discerning look that seemed to say, 'If you say so.'

'Can I be of service?' he asked casting a similarly appraising gaze over Falco.

'We're looking for a friend of ours,' said Falco. 'A woman by the name of Fossetta Pieroni. We understand the mayor might know a way of reaching her.'

'Aye, he might,' said the smith. 'But so do I.' He took a few steps into the street and nodded down the road towards a large building that had the appearance of an inn. 'Mesdames Pieroni and Asclepios are guests at The Oak Leaf.'

Falco's heart was suddenly racing. For some bizarre reason he felt nervous.

'But you'll not find them there just now" said the smith. 'They'll be back later,' he added, noticing the disappointment on Falco's face. 'They're away up the valley visiting Old Dame Casta.'

Falco's face lifted. He had hardly dared to believe that Fossetta would actually be here.

'And young Master Merryweather is with them too,' said the smith, clearly pleased at being able to offer good news. 'They'll be back before sundown.' His expression darkened. 'Not wise to stay out beyond sundown.'

'Thank you,' said Falco.

'You're welcome,' said the smith. 'It's been good to have a proper healer in town.' He stepped aside as they drew their horses back from the water trough. 'You can wait for them in The Leaf, if you like. Madame Beaujon won't mind. Get yourself something to eat and a bed too, if you've a mind.'

With another word of thanks they took their leave and made their way down the road to the inn. The Oak Leaf was a large two storey building which had the look of a fine establishment that had recently fallen on hard times. Leaving their horses in the care of a young stable hand, Falco and Malaki ducked under the low frame of the inn's front door. The interior of The Oak Leaf was surprisingly homely with just a few patrons who stopped talking as the armed youngsters approached.

'Can I help you?' asked a stout woman behind the bar who they took to be Madam Beaujon.

'We understand Fossetta Pieroni is boarding here,' said Falco. 'We'd like to wait for her, if that's all right.'

'Friends of hers are you?'

Falco nodded. 'Do you know when she might be back?'

'Shouldn't be late,' said Madam Beaujon, rinsing her hands in a stone basin before stepping out from behind the bar to greet them. 'Valentians, eh?' This was more of a statement than a question. 'Come through to the courtyard and we'll get you some food.' She ushered them through to an open courtyard laid out with tables and chairs. 'You'd not be from Caer Dour, would you?' she asked.

'Yes, we are,' said Falco and there was a knowing look in the landlady's eyes.

An elderly man appeared through a doorway and began crossing the courtyard with a slow arthritic gait.

'Albert,' said Madam Beaujon, and the elderly man teetered to a stop. 'Would you mind fetching some food for our guests?'

'I suppose so,' said the man, without so much as turning his head.

'And some wine too...'

'If I have to,' he drawled in the tone of a long suffering servant.

Madam Beaujon made no apology for his lacklustre service. Indeed the smile on her lips conveyed a distinct fondness for the old man. Clearly resisting the temptation to ply her new guests with questions she took her leave and returned to the bar.

It was some time before Albert reappeared, and it took a further two trips before they were both provided with wine and food. Replete and rested they sat back in their chairs.

'What are we going to do now?' asked Malaki. 'We could take a walk round the town.'

'Think I'll just wait here,' said Falco.

There was no way he was going to leave, not when Fossetta could appear at any time. Malaki simply shrugged his shoulders, shifted down into his chair and within the space of a minute he was asleep.

60

Defiants

Ciel spotted it first. A strange mass of green and black near some cliffs at the edge of a steep escarpment. It was from here that the sense of torment was emanating. Knowing that something truly horrible had happened they circled the area at a great height before slowly beginning their descent. As they came lower Ciel's sharper eyes began to pick out the details.

'Oh my heart!' gasped Nathalie as she realised that the green mass was a dragon and the black shadow splashed across it was blood.

'Wildegraf!' she choked as she finally recognised the body of the Illician battle mage sprawled, no, stretched across the body of his dragon.

Ciel's landing was decidedly shaky as the full impact of what they were seeing dawned upon them. Someone, or something, had mutilated and then 'displayed' the bodies of Wildegraf and his dragon Berylian. The dragon had been pinned to the rock by Wildegraf's sword. Its body was contorted and bent and somehow secured to Wildegraf's wrists and ankles, stretching his body as savagely as any torturer's rack. The battle mage's armour lay strewn across the ground and one of Berylian's horns protruded from the bloody flesh of his belly.

Whatever foul sadistic fiend had done this had turned each of them into an instrument of torment for the other.

Looking round for any sign of danger, Nathalie slipped from Ciel's back, arming her shield and drawing her sword as she did so. Whatever had done this might still be in the area. Ciel knew this too and the dragon scented the air warily as they slowly advanced.

Nathalie could not believe that either Wildegraf or Berylian were still alive but this was one of the unholy powers of the Possessed, to keep someone alive beyond the limits of normal suffering. They could see that great ribbons of Berylian's skin had been peeled from the dragon's flesh and used as bindings to tie the battle mage's wrists and ankles. Both of Wildegraf's shoulders were dislocated, the joints misshapen and discoloured by bruising. The left side of his face was a mass of scabs and the blood that seeped from the puncture wound in his abdomen was black. It ran like oil down the pale skin of his torso.

It was a sickening truth that Nathalie had seen torture like this before, but never against a battle mage, never against a dragon. Only a demon of great power could have done such a thing.

She knew there was nothing they could do to save them. All they could do was end their suffering and bring them some peace. While Ciel kept watch for any sign of danger Nathalie sheathed her sword and reached out her hand to release the two great souls from torment.

*

Through a thin veil of ethereal rock the Slayer watched as the Defiant came closer to the cliffs, drawn to help her fallen comrade by the weakness of compassion. So arrogant, so easy to manipulate. It was almost a disappointment to have caught her so easily. Just a few more steps and he would kill her with a single blow.

*

Wildegraf's mind was filled with pain and it was all he could do not to give in to the screaming sense of panic that threatened to overwhelm him. But then he felt a presence descending towards him. It was a presence of strength that gave him hope. At first he thought it was just a dream or a trick of his tormented mind, but then he recognised the aura of a kindred soul... two souls, one human, one dragon, descending towards them with love and compassion flowing from their hearts.

He almost wept with the joy of it, but then he remembered the Slayer lurking nearby, waiting for them to walk into the jaws of its trap. He sensed the demon's anticipation as his fellow souls came closer, landing a short distance away and approaching with caution. The Slayer was hidden, they would not see it! Taken by surprise they would suffer the same fate as he.

'*Go back!*' thought Wildegraf, struggling to bring the words to his dry and broken lips. The frustration of not being able to warn them was worse than all the pain and a single tear ran from the corner of his eye.

'*Go back!*'

*

'*Closer!*' thought the Slayer, gripping its blades. '*Just a little closer.*'

*

Nathalie's heart ached with pity as she saw the tear run from Wildegraf's eye.

'*Heavens help him, but he knows we're here.*'

Still watching for any sign of danger she moved a step closer and now Wildegraf turned a swollen bloodshot eye upon her. His cracked lips moved but no sound would emerge. Nathalie was about to move a little closer when finally the battle mage spoke.

'Flee,' said Wildegraf in the rasping voice of a corpse.

Nathalie froze. She had never dreamed to hear such fear in the voice of a battle mage.

'Flee!' repeated Wildegraf but it was too late.

Even as Nathalie began to back away, the Slayer burst from its concealment in the cliffs. The first strike from one of its large curved blades would have severed Nathalie's neck, but Wildegraf's warning gave her just enough time to duck behind her shield. Even so the blow knocked her off balance and she rolled backwards before coming to her feet. But the Slayer was quicker and Nathalie barely had time to raise her sword before another blow threatened to open her chest. Head, knee and belly, the Slayer's attacks came with blinding speed and it was only sheer reflex that saved Nathalie from disaster, but then the demon kicked her in the thigh with an obsidian hoof and Nathalie stumbled on a leg that had suddenly gone numb.

She would have died had it not been for Ciel. The amber dragon threw herself at the Slayer and caught its right arm in her powerful jaws. The Slayer roared in pain but its armour denied the worst of the dragon's teeth and Ciel was forced to let go as the demon's other blade scythed towards her neck. She arched back from the stroke and struck down with a taloned paw but again the armour of the Enlightened protected the demon from harm.

Ignoring the damage to her knee and hip Nathalie got to her feet, her mind blazing with fury at what this creature had done. Swiftly summoning her power she brought her sword and shield together and shot a spearhead of glowing light directly at the Slayer's chest. Even Ciel recoiled from the intensity of the attack but in the next instant Nathalie understood the fear in Wildegraf's bloodshot eye. The powerful attack would have severely wounded a normal demon but the Slayer's armour absorbed the damage leaving the demon with little more than a blackened flesh wound over its ribs.

If anything, the attack only drove the Slayer into a more dangerous frenzy. It attacked with whirling blades and an arc of burning brimstone that Nathalie only just managed to block with a shield of iridescent light.

Taking a step to the left she staggered on her injured leg and the demon was on her instantly. She took one blow on her shield and parried another with her sword, but a third struck her a glancing blow on her helm and she reeled from the impact as she felt warm blood running down her neck. Behind her she felt a sudden explosion of heat as Ciel blasted the Slayer with fire, but somehow it remained unharmed and with chilling clarity she realised they could not defeat it.

'Ciel!' cried Nathalie. 'Run!'

Responding instantly to Nathalie's command, Ciel cut off the stream of fire, but even as the dragon turned to run the Slayer struck out with one of its swords. The curving blade missed the dragon's neck but it hacked into the leading edge of Ciel's right wing. The dragon snarled in pain and the Slayer aimed another blow but then Nathalie blasted it in the face with a fireball.

Hampered by their injuries, Nathalie and Ciel raced for the edge of the cliff, but the Slayer shook off the last writhing coils of flame and started after them. For all its size the demon was incredibly fast and it would have caught them, but an invisible force took hold of its legs and brought it crashing down.

The demon sprawled on the ground as Nathalie and Ciel leapt from the escarpment and disappeared from view, but a moment later they reappeared with Nathalie hanging precariously from the riding harness on the dragon's back.

The Slayer's mind flared white with fury as it saw its quarry escaping. But even as it watched it saw the dragon bank to the side and crash into the trees, its right wing had been damaged and it could no longer fly properly. There would be no swift escape for the female Defiant and her wyrm, and the Slayer would follow them until they had no more strength to flee.

The knowledge that they would not escape took the heat out of the demon's frustration. Soon it would begin the hunt, but first it would deal with the one who had tripped it, the one who it *thought* had been emasculated and broken.

*

With his sight fading Wildegraf saw the Slayer turn back towards him. It had taken the last of all his strength to bring the demon down, but Nathalie and Ciel had got away. That was all that mattered. Now they could raise the alarm and his fellow battle mages would have time to prepare for this new and powerful foe. Wildegraf knew the demon would make him pay a terrible price for his interference but he did not care. It was not for naught that the enemy called them Defiants.

61

Flight

Nathalie clung to the riding harness as they whipped through the treetops. Her shield made it difficult to hold on with both hands and she thought she might fall, but then Ciel had swung beneath her and she was able to pull herself into the saddle. But even now they were not safe. Ciel's wing was injured and Nathalie could sense her searing pain as the dragon struggled to control their descent. Nathalie tried to fortify both their bodies as they plunged through the trees and crashed into the forest floor.

Wincing from the force of the impact Nathalie got to her feet, spitting out dirt and pine needles as she fought to clear her head. Ciel was standing to one side, her scaled brow gathered in pain as her right wing hung lower than the left. Nathalie immediately rushed round to see what was wrong, glancing up through the trees to see if there was any sign of pursuit.

A quick investigation revealed that the main bone of Ciel's wing had been damaged. The Slayer's blade had bit into the scales and fractured the bone beneath.

'Can you fly?' asked Nathalie, trying to keep the desperate need out of her voice.

Ciel gave a sigh and the dejected angle of her head spoke volumes, but still she nudged Nathalie with her great head, urging her to get into the saddle.

Nathalie almost wept at her dragon's courage. She could feel her pain but they needed speed.

'Just a moment,' she said to Ciel and, looking up towards the escarpment she started back through the trees.

Falling through the air she had let go of her sword as she reached for the riding harness and now she could feel it lying at the base of the escarpment. She was certain that the Slayer would come after them but the sword of a battle mage was like a part of them. To leave it behind would be like abandoning a friend.

Emerging from the trees she caught sight of the sword among the rocks. She started towards it but then she heard a demonic roar from the top of the escarpment and she knew she had no time. Focussing her mind she reached out and the blade dislodged a rock before flying through the air and into her hand. Despite a growing sense of fear and panic, the feel of the sword brought a certain calm. But then the silhouette of an armoured demon appeared at the edge of escarpment and she knew the hunt was on.

Limping on her own injured leg she started back to Ciel. The amber dragon was waiting for her. She too had heard the Slayer's roar.

With a final backward glance Nathalie sheathed her sword and climbed into the saddle. As she felt Ciel prepare for flight she tried to channel her healing powers into the dragon's wing. There was no time for anything more.

Tears flowed inside her helm as Nathalie whispered words of encouragement against Ciel's amber neck.

'Fly, my love,' she breathed. 'As hard and fast as you can. Just fly.'

62
Old Times

In the sheltered courtyard of The Oak Leaf, Falco was dozing in his chair. He was not sure what it was that roused him but sitting up he caught the sound of people entering the inn. He heard furniture being moved and then he heard Madam Beaujon's voice.

'My apologies, Master Merryweather,' said the landlady. 'I should have known better than to leave that there.'

His heart suddenly pounding, Falco reached across to whack Malaki on the knee.

'What was that for?' asked Malaki, blinking in the late afternoon light.

Falco did not reply. In the dark interior of the inn he caught sight of an armed soldier pushing a young man in a wheeled chair.

'Evening, Madam Pieroni,' said Madam Beaujon. 'And how is Dame Casta these days.'

'Not well,' said a voice that was intimately familiar to Falco. 'But Heçamede was able to help her, I think. And I'm sure the company did her some good.'

It appeared the group was about to head into the parlour when Madam Beaujon called them back.

'You might want to take a look in the courtyard before you settle down for supper,' she said with a knowing suggestion in her tone. 'There's a couple of young men waiting to see you.'

'Is that so?' said Fossetta in the no nonsense tone of someone who expected to be asked a favour. Would it be someone whose child or nephew was having nightmares or yet more people who needed Heçamede's help?

Falco began to smile as he heard footsteps coming towards them. Finally Fossetta appeared, undoing the cords of a travelling cloak as she looked expectantly around the courtyard. For an instant her eyes passed over the two young soldiers without recognition, but then she looked back at Falco and the angle of her head shifted subtly as she focussed on his face. Then suddenly her cloak fell to the floor and she raised her hands to her mouth.

Falco was about to speak when Fossetta suddenly turned away, her eyes filled with tears. Falco felt suddenly awkward as if he had somehow hurt her feelings, but then the young man in the chair wheeled himself forward.

'Ballymudge!' said Tobias with undisguised delight and now it was Falco who choked on his tears.

The crippled boy smiled warmly and Falco moved forward to grasp his trembling hand.

'Hello Tobias,' said Falco. 'Hello Heçamede,' he added as the healer stepped out into the courtyard.

'Well met, Master Danté,' said the healer, her dark Thraecian eyes shining with warmth. 'Master de Vane,' she added, smiling at Malaki who had now also come forward.

With an encouraging smile Heçamede nodded Falco towards Fossetta.

'Hello Fossetta,' he said.

Finally the housekeeper raised her eyes and with a sudden rush of emotion she gathered him into her arms.

'You could have written to let me know you were coming,' she said, when finally they could speak.

'I didn't think,' said Falco huskily.

'Well, no. You never do!' she scolded and now Falco smiled. That was the Fossetta he knew and loved.

With much sniffing and wiping of eyes Fossetta let go of Falco to give Malaki an equally emotional embrace. Then moving into the light of the courtyard she stepped back to look at them properly.

'I can't believe it,' she said, drinking in the sight of Falco. 'I almost didn't recognise you. And then for just a second I thought I was looking at your father. Except for your eyes,' she added stroking his cheek. 'You've your mother's eyes.'

Falco also had to accommodate some changes in Fossetta's appearance. She had lost weight for a start and the skin of her face was weathered from all the travelling, but she looked well.

'Let's sit down,' said Fossetta, although she kept Falco standing for a moment longer as she struggled to reconcile the sickly youth she had known with the strong young man who now stood before her. His shoulders were broad and his chest was deep and his arms looked like he had been working the land for the last eight months. His dark hair was thick and healthy and even his neck looked strong and muscular. And as for Malaki... well he had always been big and strong but now he looked positively intimidating.

'Heaven's larder!' she exclaimed as they sank into chairs at the centre of the courtyard. 'What on earth do they feed you on in Wrath?'

They all laughed and suddenly the words began to flow.

'Where had they come from?'

'How long would they be staying?'

'How were Bryna and the emissary and the other young people from Caer Dour?'

They wanted to know everything: the Academy of War and their training, the city of Wrath and the ocean that lay beside it. And the Queen! Fossetta could not get over the fact that they had actually met the Queen.

'I thought she'd just wave at you as you entered the academy!'

Tobias wanted to hear about the dragons and seemed to be particularly taken with Falco's description of Aurelian and Dwimervane.

Fossetta introduced the two soldiers from Toulwar who had been accompanying them on their travels, Captain Reynald de Roche and Lieutenant Francois de Lacy of the Toulwarian Royal Chasseurs.

The two men bowed with military formality but remained at a discreet distance so the old friends could reacquaint themselves properly.

The talking continued with barely a pause until Madam Beaujon invited them to move into the parlour where it was warmer and food had been laid out for them. They sat around the fire taking it in turns to ask questions and share their experiences.

'And what about your search?' asked Falco when the conversation came round to the reason they were travelling the land in the first place. 'You mentioned one Ballymudge in your letter.'

'We found a'other one,' said Tobias. 'Bu' he mi' not make it.'

Falco nodded slowly. He had disturbingly vivid memories of his own ordeal as a child, nightmare visions that almost tore his mind apart until he learned how to survive them.

'But enough of such difficult things,' said Fossetta. 'Tell us of your achievements, something to cheer us up.'

'I can tell you about the night Bryna got drunk with the Dalwhinnies,' said Malaki with a mischievous smile.

'Mistress Godwin?' said Heçamede. 'Surely not!'

Neither she nor Fossetta had heard of the notorious archery unit, but Falco noticed the way Francois and Captain de Roche suddenly leaned a little closer to listen. It was clear that they at least had heard of the infamous Dalwhinnies.

'Yes,' said Malaki. 'Threw up all over me, she did.' And with that he launched into the tale.

As the evening wore on two other men came in to join them, greeting Tobias with an exchange of foul mouthed banter that would have made even Dedric Sayer proud.

'Allow me to introduce Pierre Laffite and Louis Macaire,' said Fossetta with a disapproving glare. 'Wagon drivers extraordinaire,' she added with practised sarcasm.

'Pleasure!' said the two men, turning to Falco with disarming smiles

'Blades and buggery!' said Pierre as he looked up at Malaki's face. 'But that's some birthmark you've got there!'

'I thought the midwife was supposed to smack the baby's arse!' said Louis Macaire and the two men exploded in self congratulatory laughter.

Malaki raised an indignant eyebrow but Falco could not help laughing and even Fossetta raised a hand to conceal a smile. And that was that. It seemed that these two men could match any of the Dalwhinnies' antics and the rest of the night was spent in carefree conversation and laughter such as Falco had rarely known.

They talked long into the night and after that they went to sleep in real beds. Falco smiled as his head sank into the deep feather pillow. They could only stay for a day or two, but it was enough to know that tomorrow he would wake up and have breakfast with people he had known all his life.

As he drifted off to sleep he imagined that he was sleeping in his old room in Simeon's villa. He imagined that life was simple and the only thing he needed to worry about was making sure he did not forget his master's wine. He could almost hear Simeon's voice, chastising him over some minor misdeed in that deep tone of authority that also managed to convey an underlying sense of affection. He could almost convince himself that this, most normal of scenarios, was true.

And oh, but by the stars, he wished it were.

63

The Call To Arms

Back at Le Matres, Bryna was sorting the Dalwhinnies into work details when the signalmen sounded the call to arms. Having arranged an escort with two of the local scouts, she had been hoping to set off for Daston once the Whinnies were on their way, but now everyone stopped what they were doing and looked back towards the camp. At first they thought it must be a mistake or a drill, but then they noticed the commotion around the command tent and the fact that the red battle flag had been raised. This was no drill and Bryna suddenly found herself running back towards the camp.

'What's going on?' asked Patrick Feckler as he fell in beside her.

'No idea,' said Bryna as they reached the Dalwhinnies' tents. 'But have the men fall in. I want them armed and ready to deploy in ten minutes.'

Paddy frowned. He had seen enough of the world to know trouble when he saw it and the tension now spreading through the camp was certainly not a training exercise. This was an actual mobilization. He barked a few commands and smacked a few heads to get the men moving then he ducked into the tent he shared with Dedric and ten others. All around, men were cursing and falling over each other as they exchanged work clothes for armour.

Paddy was quicker than most. With hands that were used to working under pressure, he donned his armour, belted on his sword, grabbed his bow, campaign pack and helmet and left the tent, stuffing a few last minute things in his pack as he went.

'Get the men lined up,' said Bryna as Paddy emerged from the tent. 'I'm going to see what's happened.'

The entire cadet army was scrambling to fall in as Bryna made her way towards the command tent. The commanders were now gathered outside along with a number of the other cadets. They were speaking with a rider who was clearly exhausted from a long ride.

'What is it?' asked Bryna. 'What's happened?'

'It's the Chevalier,' said Alex as the cadets moved closer to the centre of discussion. 'He's leading a Possessed army away from Hoffen and he needs our help?'

'Why does he need our help?' asked Huthgarl as several of the knights in training joined them.

'There's a demon moving up from the south. He needs to destroy the Possessed army before the demon arrives.'

'Is the Possessed army so large?' asked Quirren.

'Large enough,' said the commander. 'But Battle Mage Saigal has still not returned from the south. If the Chevalier cannot defeat the Possessed quickly then the Fourth could be destroyed when the demon arrives.'

'Great heavens!' breathed Bryna.

She could not decide which prospect was harder to contemplate, losing the entire Fourth Army or losing the emissary.

The commanders led them over to a field table where a large map had been laid out.

'The Chevalier is retreating along this valley with the Possessed army in pursuit.' He traced the line of the valley with his finger. 'The demon army is closing from the south, somewhere around here.'

Bryna could clearly see that the emissary was in danger of being cut off and attacked on both sides.

'The Chevalier wants us to join him as quickly as possible. As soon as we arrive he will turn and together we can destroy the Possessed army quickly.'

'Why doesn't he just retreat to Hoffen?' asked Jarek, who had now joined them.

'The garrison has been called away and there are no battle mages to support them,' said the commander. 'He cannot lead a demon army to a city full of people.'

'And what about the demon?' asked Huthgarl. 'How are we supposed to stop it without a battle mage?'

The commanders exchanged another nervous look.

'Where is Master Danté?'

'He's in Daston,' said Bryna. 'With Malaki.'

The commanders looked stricken by the news.

'You said he could go,' said Bryna. 'They left yesterday.'

'How far is Daston?' asked one of the commanders.

'About twenty miles.'

'Then we must send for Master Danté, with all speed.'

'But he's not a battle mage!' objected Jarek. 'He can't even summon a magical attack.'

'But his presence might allow us to fight,' said the commander. 'Without a battle mage we would crumble before the demon.'

Jarek looked less than convinced. He had not yet experienced the debilitating fear that a demon cast over a battlefield.

'They won't know where to go!' said Bryna, thinking of Malaki and Falco.

'We will wait for them,' said Huthgarl, speaking for the rest of the knights in training.

'We'll send a rider to bring them back,' added Quirren. 'And then we'll join you at the point of attack.' He stabbed a finger at the location where the emissary was hoping to engage the Possessed.

'So be it,' said the commander. 'Send for Master Danté. But the army marches within the hour.'

64

Master Danté

After the joyous meeting of the previous night the morning brought with it a more sobering mood and Falco knew this visit to Daston was only a temporary diversion. So it was with a distinct sense of impending sadness that he enjoyed their time together. They ate breakfast and went for a walk in the woods before returning to the inn for the tea and cheese scones that Madam Beaujon had laid out for them.

'Bryna should be here later,' said Malaki. 'She was hoping to come with a couple of the local scouts.'

'That'll be lovely,' said Fossetta. 'She was always such a spirited young thing. I'm not surprised she got the measure of those Dalminnies.'

Falco and Malaki just grinned. They had given up trying to correct Fossetta on the name of Bryna's unit. As the morning wore on the two Toulwarian officers became more involved in the conversation. They were keenly interested in everything Falco and Malaki could tell them about the world. Toulwar had seemed a long way from the war and the two men had been eager to do something that made a difference. It was only during these conversations that Falco learned that it was *they* who had found the message from Caer Dour and sent the battle mage Dominic Ginola to find them in the mountains. Once again he found it strange how the threads of people's lives became intertwined.

After lunch Falco agreed to accompany Heçamede and Fossetta on a visit to a man who had broken his ribs in a tree felling accident.

'I've given him some drafts to help with the pain but with an injury like this there's always the risk of infection. If there's any way you could help...'

After so many years of being in the healer's care it felt odd that she should be asking for his help, but he was more than happy to do what he could. So, leaving Tobias at the inn, they followed a small track up into the hills. They'd only been gone an hour when a rider came racing into town. He pulled up sharply outside the Oak Leaf and leaping from the saddle he marched inside.

'I'm looking for a man by the name of Danté!' he gasped to a startled Madam Beaujon.

*

The emissary waited until the latest rearguard detachment reappeared in the valley. As the force of four hundred cavalry came into view he was reminded of the flight from the town of Caer Dour. All his life he had been giving ground to the Possessed. His own town of birth lay more than two hundred miles to the east, now deep within the Forsaken Lands, a distant memory of a life that no longer seemed real.

As the cavalry came closer he gave a slow nod of satisfaction. Only a handful of the saddles were empty.

'How far?' he asked as the captain of the detachment approached.

'Still about two miles, my Lord,' said the exhausted man. 'I don't think we can hope for anything more.'

The emissary narrowed his eyes. The Possessed were close but at least they weren't gaining. If the Fourth maintained their current pace they should be able to reach the place where the cadet army could join them. It would mean marching through the night but come tomorrow they would turn and fight.

As the next rearguard force prepared to depart the emissary found his gaze turning to the sky, desperately hoping to see the distinctive shape of Nathalie's dragon descending through the clouds, but no. All he saw was the occasional glimpse of a dark angel shadowing their movements from above. The demon was steadily closing from the south and the timing of this battle would be crucial.

He suddenly felt the full weight of the responsibility on his shoulders. The lives of twenty thousand men and women depended on the decisions he had made. He was risking everything on the strength of a young man he had known for less than a year.

Was it right of him to do so?

Was it fair?

The answer to both questions was, no. But the truth was he had no other choice.

*

Ten miles east of Le Matres the cadet army was crossing a series of shallow rivers with the city's garrison struggling to match their pace. As they climbed back onto the heath covered moor Bryna could not resist another look back in the direction of the city. She knew the rider would only now be reaching Daston, but she could not help looking for some sign that Falco and Malaki were following on behind them. She tried to calculate when they might arrive and realised with a wrench that it would not be before nightfall. Falco and Malaki would need to travel the twenty miles back to Le Matres before setting out to follow them.

Bryna looked out over the plain. There was no change in the scenery but she knew that in crossing these rivers they had just passed into the Kingdom of Illicia. From here it was about eighteen miles to the valley where they hoped to meet the emissary, but the road was little more than a rough track in the peaty soil, quickly turned to black mud by the passage of the army. Their progress was slow and the commanders had decided that they would rest for several hours during the darkest hours of the night. Come the morning they would travel the final few miles to the battle site.

Looking back Bryna could see the muddy trail of their passing, snaking over the hills towards Le Matres. At least Falco and Malaki would have no trouble following their path.

*

Falco sensed the urgency of the rider's thoughts even before they heard the sound of hooves scrabbling up the stony track.

They had just emerged from the forester's cottage where Falco had been able to help the man who was now breathing deeply rather than wincing at every shallow breath.

'Amazing,' said Heçamede. 'And I thought Master le Roy had a gift for healing.'

Malaki was suitably impressed and Fossetta smiled with pride but Falco was not paying attention. He was staring down the track as the rider came into view.

350

'Something's wrong,' he said as the rider urged his horse up the last turn of the path.

'Danté!' cried the breathless man. 'Are you Falco Danté?'

'I am.'

'You must come at once,' gasped the man. 'The Commander of the Fourth Army has sent for you.'

65

Into The Night

It was getting dark by the time Falco and Malaki came within sight of Le Matres. They both felt the need for haste but Malaki insisted that they keep to campaign pace.

'We've a long way to go,' he said. 'And this way is quicker in the long run.'

Despite his anxiety Falco trusted Malaki's knowledge. The knights had been extensively trained in cavalry speed and endurance. They could drive harder and get a change of horses in Le Matres, but there was no way Malaki was going to ride into battle on a horse other than Fidelis. The two of them had become extremely close and such a relationship with a trained war horse was a powerful combination. So they literally had to rein in their desire for haste and hope that they could reach the site of the battle in time. Malaki could not bear the thought of not being there to support Bryna and the others, but Falco knew why the emissary had asked for him to come.

'He's hoping I can shield them from the effects of the demon,' he had explained as they said a hurried farewell to Fossetta and Heçamede.

'And can you?' asked Fossetta, clearly terrified by the very notion of such a thing.

'I don't know,' said Falco. 'But if I can the army might still be able to fight.'

'I thought Nathalie was supposed to be with them,' whispered Malaki as they readied the horses.

'Something must have happened,' said Falco and his blood ran cold at the thought. It must have been something truly desperate for Nathalie to leave the Fourth Army unprotected.

As he turned to say goodbye he feared the effect that such a desperate summons might have on Fossetta, but he had forgotten the redoubtable strength of Simeon's housekeeper.

'Go and help your friends,' was all she said and with a final kiss Falco and Malaki swung into the saddle.

'Apologise to Tobias for us,' said Falco.

'He'll understand,' said Fossetta. 'Now go!'

As they rode towards Le Matres the meeting in Daston began to feel like a dream. But if it was a dream then it had been a good one and whatever lay ahead Falco would draw strength from it. He tried to keep the images in his mind as they continued along the winding forest path. Emerging into the valley of Le Matres they were met by Huthgarl and the other knights-in-training, all dressed in campaign mail with their battle armour carefully stowed in the bags behind their saddles.

'We've been waiting for you,' said Quirren as they fell in beside Falco and Malaki.

They handed them food and water, and Quirren had brought the rest of Malaki's armour in two large saddle bags. Falco had worn his armour out of habit, but Malaki had ridden to Daston wearing only his mail shirt and armoured boots. Eating as they rode, they skirted the city while the knights gave them a brief summary of events.

'The cadet army marched out this morning,' said Huthgarl. 'If we ride through the night we should be able to catch them up before the battle begins.'

Falco and Malaki nodded but then their attention was drawn ahead where the road to Illicia cut off across the moors. Gathered at the intersection was another group of mounted figures, five knights dressed in mail, each accompanied by two squires with more than a dozen riderless horses shifting nervously beside them.

'That's Sir Garnier,' said Malaki as he recognised the knight they had met on their journey to Le Matres.

'And that's Lord Cabal,' said Quirren, his tone filled with surprise and awe.

'Well met,' said Sir Garnier as the knights-in-training approached.

'My Lord,' said Huthgarl, and the others bowed in deference to the Knights of Wrath.

Malaki bowed too but his face was burning with mortification. By now Lord Cabal would have heard about the skirmish in the forest and he could not imagine that his actions would have improved the Lord Commander's opinion of him.

'We were heading south when we heard news of the Chevalier's plight,' said Sir Garnier. 'We would like to ride with you.'

Falco glanced up at the imposing figure of Sebastien Cabal. He remembered the tension between the emissary and the Lord Commander.

'We'd be honoured,' said Quirren and Sir Garnier bowed but Falco noticed the way Lord Cabal's gaze lingered on Malaki. He had considered Malaki too young to be formally accepted into the Knights of Wrath and his expression made it clear that he had not change his mind.

'We've brought spare horses,' said Sir Garnier. 'It will make it easier for our own mounts as we ride through the night.'

Huthgarl nodded and they quickly transferred to the spare horses. Then, with each of them trailing their own horse on a tether they headed off across the moors. The light began to fade and the night closed in around them until they seemed to be riding in a grey world of unchanging shadow. There were no landmarks by which to gauge their progress but the cadet army had left a wide trail in the dark earth and it was this that they followed into the gathering night.

353

66
Haste

Nathalie tumbled into the heather as Ciel came to ground once more. Dawn was breaking over the rugged moors of Illicia but the grey light did little to raise her spirits. Regaining her feet she walked back to Ciel and tried to comfort her dragon as best she could.

'It's all right,' she said, placing her hands on the leading edge of Ciel's wing. 'We're almost there.'

Closing her eyes Nathalie did what she could to ease the pain and mend the damaged bone. Given time it would heal quickly but time was the one thing they did not have. Even now she kept glancing back, looking for any sign of the Slayer's pursuit. Ciel could manage no more than a mile or two of flight before the pain in her wing became too great. If she tried to push it further the fractured bone could break and then they would never be able to warn their friends about the terrible demon that came after them.

Even now she knew that at some point she would have to turn and face the Slayer. She put some weight on her damaged leg and cursed in frustration. Even at full strength the Slayer had managed to defeat her, but then she had been taken unawares. Now she knew the lethal power of her adversary and she would raise the pitch of her own attack to meet it.

With a nudge of her great horned head Ciel indicated that she was ready to try again. They climbed a low crag and turned into the light wind for extra lift then Nathalie climbed into the riding harness as Ciel spread her flame coloured wings. The dragon's body trembled with the pain as she flapped her wings to gain them some height and Nathalie almost wept at the effort of will such a feat required. But they were flying again and the morning mist was cold against her face as they flew north to warn the emissary.

*

The Slayer let out a growl of annoyance as it felt the Defiant rise into the air and slip away once more. The demon knew the dragon was injured and it was surprised by the wyrm's speed. It should have cut more deeply and severed the wing completely but the wyrm's scales were as strong as steel, protecting it even from the blades of the Enlightened. But no matter. The Slayer could feel their exhaustion and pain. The chase would not go on for long. And now it could feel one of the Faithful moving ahead of it, a duke of moderate power. It could feel the demon's appetite and anticipation. Just like The Slayer, it was moving in for the kill.

*

Standing in the early morning mist the emissary tried not to show his concern as he dismissed the exhausted scout. She was one of several scouts keeping track of the demon that was moving up from the south and the news she delivered was grim. The demon had increased its pace and now he would be forced to engage the Possessed before the reinforcements from Le Matres arrived to help them.

'Maybe we should have retreated to Hoffen after all,' said General Renucci.

'No,' said the emissary. 'We would have found ourselves holed up in the city with a demon army at the gates. At least this way we buy them time to bring a battle mage down from the north.'

'And still no word from Nathalie?'

'None,' said the emissary. 'We must proceed on the basis that she will not be here to help us.'

General Renucci's face was pale in the early morning light. Like the emissary he had learned to cope with the fear of fighting the Possessed, but the fear of a demon was not something that a normal man could learn to overcome.

'Have the scouts found us a new place to fight?'

General Renucci gave a sigh of resignation.

'Five miles along the valley,' he said. 'There's a rise in the ground that we could use to our advantage.'

'Good,' said the emissary. 'Then we will make our stand there.'

*

Bryna felt sick with fatigue as they pushed on further into Illicia. As an officer she was entitled to ride but her mount was tired and she needed to know how the Dalwhinnies were feeling and so she led her horse by the reins. The army had rested during the darkest part of the night, but no one slept and the anxiety of waiting was every bit as exhausting as tramping through the boggy ground. Doing her best not to let her tiredness show Bryna looked up as Paddy returned from speaking to one of the scouts.

'Well?' she asked.

'Another four miles,' said her dour looking second in command.

Like many of the hard-bitten Dalwhinnies Paddy seemed largely unaffected by the difficult march. The only sign that he might be struggling was an air of ill temper that seemed to hang about him like a cloud.

'Any sign of the Fourth?'

'Not yet. But they can't be far away.'

Bryna's voice dropped to a whisper.

'And the demon?'

'Closer than we thought,' said Paddy, looking round to make sure none of the men could hear them. 'Can't see us finishing a battle before it arrives.'

Bryna felt a surge of panic clutching at her heart. She remembered the debilitating fear of the demon in the mountains, washing over the people of Caer Dour like a hot shadow of despair.

'Is the fear as bad as they say?' asked Paddy.

Bryna said nothing but the expression in her eyes filled Patrick Feckler with dread.

*

Falco's body was numb from lack of sleep and being in the saddle for so many hours. The route over the bleak moors had not been easy and when the moon set they had been forced to walk through the cold wet blackness. The trail had disappeared in the darkness so they proceeded by the light of two burning torches held by those in the front. Slowly the smothering gloom began to lift and they could make out the path once more. Shortly after dawn they came across the site where the cadet army had made camp. By the residual heat of the camp fires they guessed the army was now just two or three hours ahead of them. They rode on for a few more miles until the heath covered moors gave way to low rocky hills. Along the way the piles of dung were now still steaming slightly in the cold morning air.

'We're getting close,' said Sir Garnier as they reached the summit of a stony hill.

Falco and the others were eager to continue, but the knights insisted that they stop and eat before going on.

'You will need your strength,' said one of the knights when Malaki refused to eat.

He felt that they were wasting time but finally he took the food and forced it down his throat. Taking a swig of water he started towards his horse, the other knights-in-training following his lead.

'Wait!' the voice of Sebastien Cabal brought them all to a halt.

'We will arm ourselves here,' said the Lord Commander and they all realised what this meant. It meant they were now in hostile territory and could come upon the enemy at any time.

Without another word the squires began removing items of armour from the saddle bags. In the grey light of morning the knights were quickly decked in additional layers of plate, transforming them from mail wearing cavalry soldiers into the formidable ironclad warriors renowned throughout the world.

The scene was like some ancient ritual, which indeed it was, a ceremony of preparation going back to the very dawn of war. Not having squires of their own the knights-in-training helped each other. Falco had been wearing his armour throughout the training campaign so he helped Malaki to don the blue steel armour that had been made by his father. It was a strangely intimate experience and, as he tightened the last buckles and straps, he looked into his friend's eyes.

'We'll find them,' he said. 'We'll get there in time.'

Malaki did not reply but his deep brown eyes burned with determination as they turned their attention to the horses.

Being part of a training campaign the academy horses had not been equipped with armour but Quirren and the others had managed to secure some from the armouries in Le Matres and so the horses too were quickly fitted with armour that would help to protect them.

The whole process took far less time than Falco had expected and within a matter of minutes the war horses were ready and they stood there shifting and snorting in nervous anticipation. These were animals bred and trained for war. They knew what was coming and their blood was rising to meet it.

Finally the knights strapped their helmets to their saddles and climbed onto their mounts. Lances, which had been bundled together and carried by the squires, were now untied and handed round, one to each knight. Falco watched as Malaki swung up onto Fidelis' back and took a lance from one of the squires. There was little now to distinguish the cadets from the Knights of Wrath. They may not be many in number but the strength of their presence was profound.

Climbing onto his own horse Falco unstrapped his shield and slipped his arm into the straps. Then he took up the reins and swung round ready to depart.

'La force, l'honneur et la foi,' said Lord Cabal.

'Strength, honour and faith,' the knights replied and with that they went on.

As they continued they came across a group of soldiers who had fallen behind the cadet army, men suffering from injury or exhaustion, unable to keep up with the rest of the army. As the knights appeared they stepped back from the track, pointing in the direction that the cadet army had gone.

'That way,' said one of the men. 'No more than two hours ahead of you.'

'Just two hours ahead,' thought Falco. They were almost at the site where the Fourth Army planned to make its stand. The cadet army must be there already and now they too would definitely arrive in time to play their part in the battle.

*

Bryna looked down into the valley where the Fourth Army was supposed to be but there was no sign of them or the Possessed army that pursued them. Her heart was instantly filled with doubt. Had they come to the wrong location or had the Fourth Army already been overtaken? The answer to both questions came almost immediately in the form of a rider making his way up the side of the valley towards them.

'What news?' asked one of the commanders as the man gained the higher ground.

The man was clearly exhausted and he took several deep breaths before speaking.

'The demon army comes on more quickly than we thought,' said the man. 'The Chevalier was forced to engage them sooner than he had planned.'

'How far?' demanded the commander.

'Another four miles to the west.'

The commander muttered a curse but then he called to the signalmen.

'Sound the call to march. Pace and a half.'

There was a groan of complaint from the already footsore soldiers, but they fell back into line and prepared to move out.

'Do you think Falco and the others are coming?' said Kurt Vogler and the fear in the cadets' eyes was painfully clear. They had all heard stories of what it was like to face a demon.

The question was put to Bryna but it was Alex who answered.

'They'll be here,' he said, with not the faintest trace of doubt in his voice.

The cadets nodded in agreement although their expressions were far less certain than Alex Klingemann's. Unsettled by their fear, Bryna rode back to the Dalwhinnies who moaned and cursed at being made to march on.

'That's enough whinging, you gutless worms!' growled Paddy. 'Now, one last push and we can show the poxy twangers of the Fourth how real archers fight.'

The men were too tired for anything more than a few half hearted cheers, but they shuffled back into line and matched the pace that was set for them.

'Four miles,' thought Bryna.

Just four more miles and they would be charging into battle. As the army moved on she glanced back down towards the moors, looking for any sign of Falco and Malaki. Like Alex, she had no doubt that they were coming. The only question was whether they would get here in time.

67

The Fourth Army

The emissary looked around as the battle raged before him. He had a difficult decision to make. The Possessed had attacked with a frenzied energy, while the soldiers of the Fourth met them with the dogged resilience of people who were fighting for their lives. The emissary knew they were exhausted, but he also knew they would hold. Unfortunately, holding was not enough.

Not for the first time he turned to look up the valley hoping to see some sign of the reinforcements from Le Matres but there was nothing to be seen and he could not afford to count on their arrival. This left him with two choices. He could be patient and conserve his troops or he could go on the offensive and throw caution to the wind. That would end the battle sooner, but it would also be far more costly in terms of casualties. However, if they were still fighting when the demon arrived then the Fourth Army would be annihilated.

The emissary looked to the right where the infantry were fighting to contain the hordes of Sciritae. While on the left, General Renucci was using archery salvos and cavalry charges to prevent the Possessed from coming around their flank.

At the centre the massed ranks of spearmen prevented the Possessed from driving forward while his cavalry and heavy infantry dealt with any blocks of Kardakae that managed to break through. Even the mage warriors were contributing to the fight. Now split up into small groups, and distributed throughout the army, many were able to use magical attacks to support the regular troops who fought beside them.

But it was not enough.

Winning the battle this way would take too long and he could wait no longer for the reinforcements to arrive. Knowing he had no other choice he made the decision to advance.

Turning to the signalmen he was about to issue the order for 'Repulsus', meaning to repel or drive back, but then he noticed something against the skyline of the ridge to the left, a fringe of dark shapes that spread and grew deeper as he watched. The fringe resolved into human figures and the banners that fluttered in the breeze bore the turquoise and blue of Clemoncé. The cadet army had arrived with the garrison from Le Matres. Five thousand troops ready to fall on the Possessed from the high ground at the side of the valley.

The emissary felt a great rush of elation as a chorus of horn blasts rang out.

Impetus!

Impetus!

The reinforcements from Le Matres were sounding the attack.

*

Bryna's mouth felt dry as dust as she stood at the head of the Dalwhinnies waiting for the order to attack. Coming upon the battle in full spate the commanders had wasted no time in moving them into position just below the line of the ridge overlooking the valley. They waited until the whole force was in place before giving the order to advance. In near silence they had crested the ridge and looked down into the valley.

'By the shades but you can feel the heat of them,' said Patrick Feckler as the infernal heat of the Possessed rose up towards them.

For many of the soldiers, and most of the cadets, this was their first sight of a Possessed army and it filled them with dread. They saw the Possessed stabbing and clawing at the soldiers of the Fourth, fighting with a mindless violence that was truly terrifying. The battlefield was littered with bodies from both sides and they could see injured men being trampled underfoot or trying to crawl back behind the safety of their lines. By contrast the Possessed appeared undeterred by injury.

'Does nothing stop them?' breathed Dedric Sayer.

'They can be stopped,' said Bryna, remembering what Old Man Reese had said to her in the mountains. 'You just have to keep on shooting.'

Patrick Feckler glanced at Bryna, an inscrutable expression in his deep-set eyes. In his wildest imaginings he never dreamed that he would take courage from some slip of a girl that was young enough to be his daughter.

Hearts thumping and limbs trembling with adrenaline the Dalwhinnies watched as the signalmen came forward. The call for '*Impetus*' rang out and the reinforcements from Le Matres charged down the grassy slopes.

The emissary wasted no time in adding his orders to those now driving the reinforcements into the valley. The soldiers of the Fourth Army gave a great shout as their own signalmen sounded the order for Impetus. From somewhere deep inside they found the strength to push forward.

At the centre the spearmen broke their defensive formation and brought their spears to 'charge', deep ranks of long spears now driving forward in a wall of vicious stabbing points.

To the right the swordsmen locked their shields together and braced themselves for the crush that would drive them forward, forcing the Sciritae back into their own heaving ranks. As the Possessed stumbled back the shield wall opened and swords flashed out in perfectly drilled co-ordination before the shields came together once more.

Close... push... open... attack.

Close... push... open... attack.

At first the progress was slow, but as the front ranks of Sciritae were cut down so the swordsmen advanced in a savage line of rhythmic lethality.

On the left flank General Renucci gave up the task of containing the Possessed and directed his cavalry into attack formations with the most heavily armoured warriors at the front. Lances were couched and lines dressed, and even before the reinforcements arrived the general led a charge that drove deep into the main body of the Possessed. He did not worry about being engulfed because the entire left flank was pushing forward with him and the reinforcements were coming on behind.

The Possessed were slowly being encircled and for all their ferocity it was now only a matter of time before they were overcome.

Bryna's orders were to occupy a slight promontory to the right, behind the main body of spearmen. From there they could cover both the centre and the left flank of the battle. Glancing to her left she saw the dark surcoats of the Exiles streaming down the hillside with Alex at their head, and outstripping them all were the spritely horses of Jarek's Royal Hussars.

Jarek Snidesson felt sick with fear but he was still haunted by the fact that he and his father had left the people of Caer Dour in the mountains. Such an act had justified the contempt people felt towards his family and he was determined to prove that he did not need Falco Danté or any other supposed 'battle mage' to give him courage in the face of the enemy. And so he led his cavalry on, letting the heat of battle sweep away the fear of what might happen if he were unhorsed and taken by the Possessed.

Bryna could almost sense the determination with which Jarek drove his horse down the hillside. But the attack was bravely made and so she forgave him any trace of hubris. In fact a great surge of pride swept through her as she saw the cadets coming into their own, but the battle was far from over. There were still thousands of Possessed who feared neither injury nor death. They would never collapse and run as a regular army might. They would need to be destroyed to the last.

Reaching the promontory the Dalwhinnies moved into position. Every one of them had a war quiver containing sixty four arrows and they each carried a second sheaf for when the first was spent. Placing the bundle of spare arrows at her feet Bryna glanced back to make sure the Dalwhinnies were in formation. Then looking down at the battle she searched for an area where the Fourth's advance was being stalled.

'Thirty yards ahead of the nearest phalanx of spear!' she cried. 'Ten shafts, standard rate!'

Among the seething ranks of Sciritae they could all see a block of Kardakae that was refusing to give ground.

'Ready your bows!' bellowed Patrick Feckler, his coarse voice cutting through the deafening clamour of battle.

'Nock!'

'Mark!'

'Draw!'

There was a collective 'creak' of tight strings and straining wood then...

'Loose!' cried Bryna and two hundred arrows leapt from the bow.

'Loose!' cried Bryna, for the men had already set a second arrow to the string.

There was no need to call the order again. The Dalwhinnies fired to the rate at which they had been trained. There was something almost theatrical about the synchronised rhythm of their movements, barely pausing at full draw before letting go with a collective thrum that shook the air.

In a series of regular waves two thousand arrows stabbed down into the block of dark warriors and although arrows alone were not enough to stop the Kardakae it was enough to weaken their position and allow the spearmen to drive forward once more.

With a grim nod Bryna looked around for her next target.

*

There was an expression of fierce pride in the emissary's eyes as he watched the cadet army charging the Possessed. They must have had a difficult march to get here so quickly, but the weariness did not show and, as he looked round the valley, he knew they could now defeat the Possessed and quickly.

Calling up his reserves he decided to throw them into the fray. He would move his own archers forward to match the steady advance of the spears and send his swordsmen to relieve the right flank where the men were starting to tire. And as for the cavalry he would lead them himself He would take them up the southern slope of the valley ready to fall upon the enemy's rear.

But even as he turned to issue his orders he knew that something was wrong. The troops behind him appeared hesitant and slow to respond to his orders. They showed no sign of relief that the reinforcements from Le Matres had arrived. Instead their faces were filled with fear. Many were looking behind them to a point where this valley was joined by another coming up from the south.

The emissary turned his horse, his brow gathering into a deep frown of foreboding. Then he saw it... a single dark angel emerging from between the hills so that it could see down the valley towards them.

The soldiers of the reserves saw it too and then they began to back away as armoured shapes emerged from the southern valley behind the emissary's army.

Sciritae... hundreds of them.

And now he felt it... a terrifying presence, like the poisoned vapour that seeps into a dream, turning a normal scene into a nightmare. More dark figures came streaming into the valley and in a sudden flash of black despair the emissary knew that they were out of time.

The demon was upon them.

*

Jarek did not know what had happened. All he knew was that one minute he was confident of being able to master his fear and the next he was not. The day was not bright, but it seemed as if an intangible cloud was spreading across the sun and the valley behind the emissary's army appeared darker than it had before. Glancing up from the battle he tried to see what might account for this change in his perceptions.

More Possessed had appeared in the valley, but far worse was the sense that something else was approaching, something that dwarfed the courage in his heart, something he could never hope to oppose.

A sudden rush of movement brought him back to his immediate surroundings.

'Have a care, my Lord!' called one of the older hussars as his horse smashed aside two Sciritae that were closing on Jarek.

'Darkness is coming!' cried Jarek.

'Just hold for as long as you can,' shouted the seasoned hussar, hacking desperately at the Sciritae who were now pressing forward more strongly than ever.

Jarek knew he could not resist such fear for long, but he was of the noble house of Snidesson and while he could fight, he would. Knowing he was close to panic he slashed down at the Possessed warriors that were trying to kill him, but he felt hot liquid running down the inside of his thigh and his weakness made him feel sick with shame. He had heard about the terrible fear that went before a demon but he had never understood such tales. Until now.

361

*

The fear came on like a dark intangible mist, washing over the emissary's reserves and spreading out over the army until the very pitch of battle changed. Optimism and valour were suddenly replaced by doubt and uncertainty. The emissary watched as two columns of Kardakae followed the Sciritae into the valley behind them and then the demon appeared, huge and black and horned and hot, a totem of fear and despair.

Almost twice the height of a man it stood, its powerful body sculpted from dark and cindered flesh. Its massive head was ridged and angular with downward curving horns and a heavy thrusting jaw with teeth protruding like blackened points of steel. The familiar back-bent legs were short but its arms were long and the fingers on its hands ended in claws that could rip through armour and tear a man in two.

Looking down, the emissary saw that it was carrying something in its fist. It took him a moment to realise it was one of the scouts he had sent to track the demon's movements. The demon held the man by one ankle leaving his head and arms to drag and bump along the ground. The emissary could only hope that he was dead but at least this explained why he had not been warned of the demon's imminent arrival.

For a moment the demon paused to look at the emissary. It raised the scout's body like a taunt before dropping it with an air of contempt. The demon's small eyes flared and the emissary felt the first cracks in the foundations of his courage. He had no choice now but to accept that Nathalie was lost and there was no sign of Falco among the reinforcements from Le Matres. And without a battle mage they were doomed. They might struggle on for an hour or two but wherever the demon came, so death would follow.

Held by the demon's searing gaze he was suddenly filled with the fear that *he* could be transformed into one of the Possessed. He had a sudden vision of himself cleaving through the palace guards in Wrath until he reached the Queen and then of cutting her down until she was all blood and ribboned flesh, begging for mercy while he gloried in her agony and the utter desecration of their love.

With an effort the emissary tore his gaze away from the demon.

Tears blurred his eyes as he tried to expunge the images of horror from his mind. He told himself that such a thing could never happen, but he knew for a fact that it could. If the Possessed took him then he would be remade in *their* image, robbed of all humanity with only the faintest vestige of his former self allowed to persist because it would add to his everlasting torment.

Determined to keep the fear at bay for as long as possible the emissary clenched his jaw and tried to think what he should do. Strong leadership was what they needed now otherwise half the army would throw down their weapons and plead for mercy that would never come.

More possessed warriors were emerging into the valley and they would soon be fighting on both sides. There was no way they could win and the only thing he could do was to try and save some of the men and women who were now caught in the valley. He would form two lines of battle, one to the east and one to the west. And while these held he would try to evacuate as many as

362

possible up the sides of the valley to the north. Some of them might even make it back to Hoffen or Le Matres.

With the decision made he gave the order for the reserves to form a defensive line to their rear.

At the centre of the army the advance of the spearmen ground to a halt and their tight formation began to lose cohesion as they glanced behind them, desperate to see what it was that had made them so afraid. On the right flank the swordsmen were suddenly aware of how exhausted they were. Their line became ragged and the Sciritae attacked through gaps in the shield wall that had not been there before. Archers stopped shooting and the whole army was gripped by an overwhelming urge to run.

Bryna saw the effect of the fear passing over the army like an insidious wave of uncertainty. Around her the Dalwhinnies began to mutter and curse. Many of these men had done terrible things in their lives and guilt was like an open door to the evil of the Possessed.

Beside her, Patrick Feckler looked like a cornered animal. His normally ruddy complexion was pale and his deep set eyes looked hostile and guarded. The instinct to survive was making its presence known and Bryna knew that now, at this moment, Paddy would commit murder if it might help him survive.

She was far from immune to the fear herself, but she knew it would only get worse as the demon drew closer. Down the slope she could see the emissary forming a new line of defence to his rear. Knowing she only had moments before the Dalwhinnies broke and fled she barked the order to advance. Paddy shot her a feral look and for a moment she thought he might refuse, but then a sense of recognition returned to his gaze.

'Come on you limp shafted bastards!' he roared. 'A few more shots before you turn tail and run.'

There was a smattering of nervous laughter. Surely they could manage a few more shots. Bryna offered Paddy a look of thanks but he just shrugged.

'We're fucked anyway,' he muttered. 'Might as well go down fighting.'

Bryna gave him a nod and the closest thing to a smile she could muster. Then she led the Dalwhinnies down to a point where they could support the emissary's lines of defence. She reached for an arrow but her hand was trembling so much that she could not fit it to the string.

'Don't let them take me, Paddy,' she whispered as the tears of fear began to flow. 'Promise you won't let them take me.'

'Don't worry lass,' said Patrick Feckler. 'Yours'll not be the first throat I've cut.'

*

The emissary felt the fear like a multitude of hooks clawing at his guts. He felt the guilt of a commander who has led his soldiers to their deaths and winced as the hooks found purchase in his soul.

'*At least we didn't lead the demon to the children of Hoffen,*' he thought and some of the hooks tore free.

He knew the ways of the enemy. Guilt, grief, pain and despair, these were the tools of its dominion. He knew he could not resist the fear forever. Like every

363

man and woman in the valley it would claim him in the end. But not without a fight.

He felt a great welling of pride as the soldiers of the Fourth resisted the fear and came together to form two battle lines. Up on the slope he saw the dishevelled unit of the Dalwhinnies. Even in uniform they managed to look scruffy and unkempt, but they held formation as they moved into position to support him. And at their head the diminutive figure of Bryna Godwin, her auburn hair tied back in a braid. At that moment he wished with all his heart that he had never sent for the reinforcements from Le Matres. And the hooks of guilt snagged a little deeper in his soul.

Biting down his regrets he raised his sword and gave the order for his archers to loose.

The vanguard of the demon's force was already in range and scores of Sciritae fell under the ragged volley that flew from shaking bows. The demon's army was not a large force, perhaps no more than a thousand Possessed, but with the demon among them it might as well have been twenty. Behind him the emissary heard the crunching impact of the revitalised Possessed slamming into the main body of the Fourth.

So this was the place where he would die.

Well, so be it. He was a member of the Knights Adamant, the Queen's emissary. He would show the enemy how such a warrior met his death.

The simple acceptance of his fate brought with it a certain calm and he could almost feel the fear lifting from his mind, but then he noticed that the untidy block of swordsmen were dressing their ranks once more, overlapping their shields ready to meet the Sciritae streaming towards them. The archers, which only a moment ago had appeared on the edge of panic, now seemed steadier and even the cavalry had regained their composure, their horses no longer shying from a fear they did not understand. Behind him he heard a concerted shout as the spearmen tried to reassert themselves over the pressing ranks of the Possessed.

No. It was not his imagination. The fear was definitely lifting from his mind and that could mean only one thing...

The emissary turned to scan the ridge to the south, convinced that Nathalie had finally returned but there was no sign of her or her amber coloured dragon. His gaze swung to the north ridge but all he could see was a small group of riders silhouetted against the sky. From the look of them they appeared to be knights but one, a somewhat slighter figure, stood forward from the rest and the emissary almost wept with relief.

Danté.

68

The Greatest of These

Falco looked down at the army now hemmed in on either side by the Possessed; twenty thousand souls, floundering in a storm of fear. For a moment he was overwhelmed by the sheer volume of it but then he closed his eyes and reached out to embrace them. In his mind he drew them close then he opened his eyes and looked down upon the source of the fear and his green eyes burned as his gaze found that of the demon.

'*No,*' he thought, '*If you want to get to them. You will have to come through me.*'

On the floor of the valley the demon stopped to look at him, its heavy brow lowered as it tried to reconcile the strength of this Defiant's will with the image of the adolescent gazing down at him from a horse. For a moment something like humour surfaced in its mind.

Were the Faithful now to be opposed by children?

Falco could feel the heat of the demon's scorn but the strength of a battle mage came not from a belief in victory, but from the act of defiance itself. Reaching across his body he drew his sword and looked down the smooth slope towards the demon.

'No!' said Lord Cabal as he saw what Falco intended to do. 'You have no offensive abilities and we cannot afford to lose you.'

'The Lord Commander is right,' said Sir Garnier. 'You cannot waste your life in confronting the demon. You must shield the army while we try to save as many as we can.'

The look that Falco turned upon them was implacable and dangerous. This was his responsibility, the very reason he was alive. The Lord Commander held his gaze, surprised to see such a challenge in the eyes of one so young.

'But what about those in the front ranks?' asked Huthgarl. 'There's no way they can disengage.'

'They must hold the Possessed while those in the centre retreat up the sides of the valley,' said Sir Garnier. 'And *we* will charge any Possessed that try to cut them off.'

'But our friends are in the front ranks,' said Quirren. Both the Exiles and the Dalwhinnies were among the front lines of the battle. 'You can't expect us to abandon them.'

'The Chevalier is also in the front ranks,' said Lord Cabal, still staring at Falco. 'He would not expect us to risk the entire army just to save him. Now come. We must act swiftly.'

The Knights of Wrath quickly donned their helms and Falco turned to Malaki, but if he had been hoping for some gesture of support he was disappointed. Malaki's eyes were as dark and hard as Falco had ever seen them, his jaw set with unthinkable resolve.

'They are right,' he said, his voice hollow and distant. 'You have no offensive powers and we cannot afford to lose you.'

Falco just stared at him while Lord Cabal gave a stern nod of approval. The Knights of Wrath swung their horses about, ready to ride to the point where the main part of the besieged army might just be able to retreat out of the valley. Looking desperately torn, the knights-in-training began to follow, all except Malaki and Quirren.

'Quickly!' barked Sir Garnier but Malaki made no move to follow. Instead he turned his horse away and moved a few steps off the path. With Fidelis now facing down into the valley he turned to Falco.

'Can you protect me?' he asked and the fear of what he was about to do swam in his deep brown eyes.

Falco wanted to scream, '*No! It should be me!*' but he knew that if *he* died then the entire army would be destroyed and reborn into the ranks of the Possessed. So instead he gave his friend a nod.

'Always,' he said and Malaki actually smiled before settling the great-helm onto his head. Then he armed his shield and couched his lance.

Without a word Quirren fell in beside him and then Huthgarl and the rest of the young knights from the academy.

'What are you doing!?' cried Sir Garnier when he saw the direction of their charge. 'You cannot charge a demon. No knight has ever brought down a demon!'

'If the demon isn't killed then our friends will die,' said Quirren.

Malaki said nothing. This was not an act of bravery. He simply had no choice. There was no way in the world he could leave Bryna down there to die. For a second he turned to look at the Knights of Wrath, his helmeted gaze settling on the huge figure of Lord Cabal. He gave the Lord Commander an almost imperceptible bow of respect then he turned to look down into the valley where the demon had now started towards them, a line of black armoured Kardakae moving ahead of it.

'Huthgarl,' said Malaki. 'You take point with the others in chevron to forge a path for Quirren and myself.'

The big Beltonian gave a nod and moved into position.

'Quirren, you draw the demon with en passant to the left and leave the final attack for me.'

Quirren just stared straight ahead.

'This is madness!' cried Sir Garnier but the knights-in-training were beyond such remonstrations.

'For our friends and for the Queen,' said Malaki.

'For our friends and for the Queen,' said the others and with that they started forward.

The slope leading down into the valley was fairly smooth with just a few rocks and patches of heath along the line of their attack.

Fighting against a terrible feeling of inadequacy Falco dismounted from his horse and moved to a flat edge of rock overlooking the valley. He watched the young knights as they quickly descended the steeper slope before the side of the valley levelled out. Glancing to the left he saw the battle raging as fiercely as ever. He could not afford to relax the shield of faith he had spread across the army, but as the knights closed the distance the demon began to focus its malice on the V-shaped formation that was now charging towards it. The weight of its spite was like a physical force and Falco began to wonder if he *could* protect

366

Malaki in the face of so much power. Dropping to one knee on the flat edge of rock he closed his eyes as Sir Garnier voiced the collective doubt of the Knights of Wrath.

'It cannot be done!'

Falco heard the conviction in the knight's words but he quashed all doubts as he tried to shield his friends from the fear that was threatening to rip them from the saddle.

On the slope below Malaki felt like they were charging headlong into an inferno that would sear the flesh from their bones. Every instinct screamed at him to stop, to veer away and flee, but he simply refused to listen. Twenty yards ahead he could see Huthgarl and the others struggling to hold formation. It was only the unwavering sense of Falco's presence that allowed them to drive on into the fear.

Fighting to keep his focus Malaki stared at the demon which seemed to be growing in size as they galloped towards it. There was not the faintest trace of concern in the creature's bearing. Rather it hunched forward relishing the pleasure of claiming such strong young souls. In front of it the line of Kardakae braced for the impact of the charging knights, but even these powerful warriors were not enough to stop Huthgarl and the others. They slammed into the Kardakae at full charge, smashing a great hole in their line before wheeling round to engage with swords and their horses' battle shod hooves.

As the way ahead was opened Malaki saw Quirren adjust his course. At this speed there was no margin for error and Quirren would have to be careful not to be caught within the demon's long and powerful reach. Somehow, amid the raging storm of hatred, Quirren managed to maintain his composure. Spear point lowered and shield raised he charged the demon, disguising his feint until the last possible moment. The demon got ready to deliver a blow that would fell both horse and rider but then Quirren yanked the reins to one side and his horse almost lost its footing as it fought to respond to his command.

Veering to the left, Quirren leaned away from the demon's lethal attack but he could not avoid the blow completely. The demon's talons caught his horse as it sped past, gouging four deep gashes in the black Freysian's rump. The blow sent the horse skidding sideways and Quirren was thrown from the saddle.

Malaki had no chance to see what became of him, but for now that did not matter. The feint had worked and the demon had no time to recover before Malaki was upon it.

Time seemed to hang on a heartbeat as the demon turned back to confront its second attacker, its face contorted with rage as it balled one massive fist. Malaki saw the red hot fist driving towards him but he also saw the hollow in the demon's arm pit. An instant before the demon struck him he leaned into his lance and drove the spear point into the demon's flesh. The collision was so forceful that Malaki was snatched from the saddle. For a moment his right arm and shoulder screamed with pain but then he hit the ground and the breath was punched from his lungs. His helmet rolled free and his entire body thrummed, his ears ringing so loudly that all the commotion of the battle was reduced to a distant fuzzy roar.

Stunned by the fall Malaki struggled to get his bearings. He tried to push himself up but his body felt numb and lifeless. He blinked and shook his head, trying to clear his vision. For a moment he thought he might have killed the demon but then a huge shadow loomed over him and he knew that he had not.

Malaki's sight cleared and he looked up into the burning eyes of the demon. The heat of its body was greater than any blacksmith's forge and Malaki's face was beaded with sweat. Looking down at him the demon reached under its left arm and with a snarl of pain it drew out the foot-long tip of Malaki's lance. The point had driven deep but failed to find its mortal heart. The ringing in Malaki's ears grew louder as he realised that he had failed. He saw the demon drop the point of his lance and look down on him in triumph and then it raised a massive hoof to kill him.

A drumming sound suddenly impeded upon Malaki's thoughts, but he could not tell if it was the rush of blood in his ears or the sound of approaching hooves. He tried to conjure an image of Bryna in his mind but all he could see was the shape of her lips, the blue of her eyes and a stray curl of auburn hair.

'VÉRITÉ!'

The shout was accompanied by a rush of movement and Malaki flinched as a bay coloured horse flashed before his eyes. Looking up he saw the demon rear back as a spear glanced off its black obsidian skin.

'VÉRITÉ!'

The demon recovered quickly as a second lance bit into its shoulder before tearing free but this time it lashed out and the knight who had attacked was struck from his horse by a blow that crushed his breastplate and broke his spine.

'VÉRITÉ!' cried a third voice but the demon avoided the attack and swung again and a second Knight of Wrath died before he hit the ground.

But then another knight cried out his challenge and Malaki had never heard such force in a human voice before.

'EN 'VÉRITÉ!'

Lord Cabal's destrier was in mid air when he drove his lance into the demon's mighty chest. Despite the fact that he had been required to leap over one of his fallen comrades, the Lord Commander's poise and commitment to the charge were absolute as he thrust his spear-point home. The force of the attack snapped his lance and dislocated his shoulder as both horse and rider were sent tumbling to the ground.

The demon gave a great roar, part pain and part disbelief that any such attack could pierce its flesh. It looked down at the shaft of smouldering wood protruding from its chest, but then another lance speared into its belly. The great beast hunched forward and a final attack drove deep into the base of its neck. Dark mercurial blood gushed forth and the demon slumped to the ground.

Malaki thought he must be dreaming as he saw the towering figure of the demon brought down. A great weariness came over him and his vision began to fade. He felt hands lifting him and dragging him across the ground. He heard the tumultuous sound of battle and the ring of steel on steel but none of it mattered. His brothers fought beside him and there was no longer any need for him to be afraid.

On the hillside above him Falco let out a great breath as the demon was slain. He felt utterly drained but the impossible had been accomplished. Together they had killed a demon. Rising to his feet he looked down into the valley. Below him the knights were now retreating in a defensive group, dragging Malaki and two other injured comrades with them. Most of the knights-in-training were still in the saddle but they were greatly outnumbered by the black-armoured Kardakae.

To the left Falco saw the emissary's forces pushing towards them, but they would not arrive in time to save them. One additional sword might not be enough to make a difference but then again it might. Shaking off the leaden weight of fatigue Falco moved quickly to his horse. He might not have any offensive magical abilities but for now that did not matter. The time had come for him to fight.

The knights retreated slowly up the side of the hillside, fighting to prevent the Kardakae from surrounding them. In their midst they struggled to protect Malaki, Lord Cabal and another knight who was unable to defend himself. They fought with unrivalled skill but even the Knights of Wrath could not hold against so many Kardakae and it was only a matter of time before they were overcome. But then Falco entered the fray, driving between the Kardakae and the beleaguered knights.

As he reached the centre of their line he leapt from the saddle to land in front of the huge dark warriors. With sword and shield in hand he settled into a fighting stance and the Kardakae paused as if they sensed something of the entity that now stood before them. The brief respite gave the knights the chance to rally before the Kardakae surged forward once more, but then a hail of arrows rained down into their midst, followed quickly by another and another. And then came the sound of approaching horses.

Falco glanced across to the left, to where the emissary's cavalry was now charging towards them. A little further up the slope the Dalwhinnies stopped shooting, but they had achieved their goal in stalling the Kardakae's advance. As the sound of approaching horses grew louder Falco turned back to the dark warriors facing him. The battle was far from over, but finally he was fighting the enemy, and he was content. He remembered the first time he had faced a warrior of the Possessed. Then he had been unable to defeat a single injured Sciritae, now he traded blows with Kardakae and what he lacked in physical strength he more than made up for with the fortification of his mind.

In a matter of moments Falco killed his first Kardakae but he was surprised by the lack of satisfaction that it gave him. As the armoured body collapsed before him he felt only sadness. This warrior had once been a man, probably a knight like those who fought alongside Falco. He had not chosen to turn against humanity, he had been appropriated, corrupted, possessed.

As Falco engaged the next armour-clad warrior he was suddenly struck by the tragedy that had befallen humankind, a tragedy that required him to kill.

For a while the battle continued to rage, but once again the tide had turned against the Possessed and there was nothing now to turn it back. Time passed and Falco's limbs were trembling with exhaustion but the Kardakae had been broken and the main body of the Possessed army was now being corralled at the centre of the valley. The battle was won and as the danger lessened Falco dropped out of the line and went in search of Malaki. Further up the slopes he could see where the injured knights had gathered, finally able to rest in safety. Falco came upon Lord Cabal first and immediately went to see what he could do to help, but the Lord Commander just waved him away.

'Go and see to your friend,' he said as two of the knights prepared to reset his dislocated shoulder.

The great knight was bleeding and pale, but his eyes were resolute as he prepared for the pain of what was about to happen. Falco would come back to treat him later but for now he continued to the point where Quirren had just laid Malaki back against a bank of grass after struggling to remove his armour. The young Ilician's face and neck were covered with blood from a shallow head wound but all his concern was focussed on Malaki.

'It's his arm and shoulder,' said Quirren. 'And ribs too, I think.'

Falco dropped down beside his friend who was hovering on the edge of consciousness. Closing his eyes he placed his hands on Malaki's arm and shoulder, trying to assess the damage the way Meredith had shown him. His main fear was of internal injury and the possibility that Malaki might slip into shock, but the strength of Malaki's heartbeat dispelled that particular concern.

'I could feel you with me,' said Malaki, opening his eyes. His face was pale and beaded with sweat. 'Right to the end. I knew you were there.'

'Never could trust you to do anything by yourself,' said Falco and Malaki smiled.

Falco smiled too but then he opened his mind to the damage in Malaki's body. His upper arm and collar bone were broken but fortunately his shoulder joint was intact. He had four cracked ribs and a decent concussion but apart from that it was mostly bruising and strained ligaments. Nothing snapped or badly torn, thank the stars. Opening his eyes Falco turned to Quirren.

'Take his arm like this and lean back with a steady pressure until I tell you to stop.'

Quirren nodded and Malaki gasped through gritted teeth as the two pieces of bone in his upper arm ground against each other. As Falco felt them come back into alignment he sent a wave of healing energy into Malaki's body. The power was perhaps more intense than he had intended and Malaki swore as his arm burned with a tingling fire.

'All right. You can let go,' said Falco and Quirren slowly released his hold.

Malaki let out a deep sigh and settled back against the damp grass, but Falco would not let him rest just yet. For another ten minutes he bent over Malaki's injuries, suffusing them with all the healing power he could until he was confident that they would quickly heal.

Finally satisfied, he was about to turn to Quirren's injuries when a shadow fell across them and he looked up to see Lord Cabal standing over them. His right arm was strapped across his chest and his pale skin contrasted sharply against his dark beard and blood-matted hair. Even injured he remained a grim and imposing figure. Beside him Sir Garnier held the Lord Commander's great-helm.

Lord Cabal looked down at Falco who, after a moment's pause, moved aside to let him approach Malaki. The great knight dropped to one knee, wincing from the pain in his damaged shoulder. For a moment he looked down at Malaki, taking in the extent of his injuries, then he raised his gaze to look him in the eye. Pale and exhausted Malaki stared back and for a while the two just looked at each other.

From his bearing Falco could tell nothing of the Lord Commander's mood. All he knew was there was not the least trace of contrition in Malaki's eyes. He had disobeyed the most senior member of his order and his entire future as a knight hung in the balance. But given the choice he would do the same thing again.

Finally Lord Cabal spoke.

'How did you know your friend could protect us?' he asked.

'I didn't,' said Malaki. 'But I believed he could.'

For a moment the Lord Commander held Malaki's eye then he nodded slowly and a fierce smile sharpened his gaze.

'Strength, honour and faith,' he said. 'But the greatest of these is faith.'

With these words the Lord Commander turned to take his great-helm from Sir Garnier. Still down on one knee he placed the helm on the ground and looked again at Malaki.

'This was your victory,' he said. 'It was you who led the charge for lesser knights to follow.'

Malaki tried to protest but the Lord Commander waved him to silence. With his one good hand he reached out and gently turned Malaki's face to better see the bright red birthmark which stood out vividly against his pallid skin.

'Did they tease you as a child?' he asked.

Malaki lowered his eyes in embarrassment.

'No one will ever tease you again.'

With that the Lord Commander reached up to his own injured head. He pushed aside the dressing and opened the wound until his hand was slick with blood then he looked down and spread the crimson vitality over the left 'cheek' of his great-helm. Studying the effect he looked back at Malaki's face and nodded in satisfaction. Then taking a sword from Sir Garnier he laid it first on Malaki's right shoulder and then on his left. The sword was returned and in its place Lord Cabal held a horse-head pendant on a pale blue ribbon which he now slipped over Malaki's head.

'Welcome to the Knights of Wrath, Sir Malaki.'

69

A Grievous Wound

It was early evening before the last of the Possessed were dispatched and the emissary went in search of Falco. He found him in the field hospital that had now been set up a little further along the valley. Falco was helping the physicians as they moved from one injured soldier to the next. He looked tired but he refused to rest while so many people groaned in pain.

'That will do for now,' the emissary told the physician as he appeared before them. 'You will have to manage without Master Danté for a while.'

The physicians were clearly reluctant to let Falco go, but there were hundreds of wounded and there was no way that Falco could see to them all. He had done enough and it was time for him to rest. With a bow they continued on their way and the emissary turned to Falco.

'By the stars but it's good to see you,' he said, placing a hand on Falco's shoulder.

Falco lowered his eyes self-consciously.

'I'm sorry I took so long,' he said. 'I was in Daston.'

For a moment the emissary just looked at him as if he was joking, but then he shook his head and laughed. Falco looked more uncomfortable than ever but the emissary smiled and held his eye.

'Simeon would have been proud of you today,' he said and this time Falco dipped his head to hide a sudden swell of tears. 'Come. Let's go and find your friends.'

They found Malaki at the far edge of the field hospital, sitting with Bryna, Alex, Quirren and Huthgarl. All the young knights sported some kind of injury but none of them were as bad as Malaki. His broken arm had now been bound and splinted to protect it until it was properly healed. Despite Falco's healing it was still painful and Malaki gave a stifled gasp as Bryna leaned in to kiss him for what must have been the hundredth time. When she had first found him she had been unable to speak. She had simply buried her face against his chest and cried while Patrick Feckler and several of the other Dalwhinnies looked on. They had all seen Malaki and the other cadet knights charging the demon.

Paddy said nothing, only giving Malaki a nod that somehow managed to convey respect.

'By the shades but you've got some balls,' said one of the others.

'He'd need 'em, goin' out with her,' muttered Dedric, earning himself a swift elbow in the stomach from Paddy.

As ever, the Dalwhinnies managed to ease the tension and everyone laughed as Paddy and the others took their leave. Now the friends sat up straight as Falco and the emissary came over to join them. A short distance away they saw Lord Cabal speaking to one of his fellow knights. The knight's great helm sat at the end of his makeshift bed and they could all see that the left hand side of the helm had been smeared with blood.

'I see the Knights of Wrath are now wearing colour on their great-helms,' said the emissary and Malaki blushed. It seemed that the entire order had followed Lord Cabal's example and bloodied the left cheek of their helms. In this way they would honour Malaki's part in bringing down a demon.

'Twenty years a knight and I have never seen the like,' said the emissary. He might have said more but one of the scouts came riding towards them and there was a sense of urgency in the way he drove his horse.

'My Lord!' said the man as the emissary moved out of the field hospital to speak with him. 'Someone approaches from the south.'

Weary as he was the emissary was suddenly tense and alert.

'Friend or foe?' he asked, looking in the direction that the scout was pointing.

'My Lord,' said the man as if he could not quite believe what he was saying. 'It is Battle Mage Saigal.'

'Thank the stars!' said the emissary, his voice flooded with relief, for he honestly thought that she was dead. 'Show me!'

The others had also come forward and now they went with the emissary as he followed the scout.

'There, my Lord,' said the man and now they could see Nathalie working her way towards them with Ciel beside her.

'Ciel's injured,' said Falco and the emissary nodded. They could all see the dragon's limping gait and the unnatural way she was holding one of her wings.

The emissary began to hurry forward and Falco went with him. He was clearly elated, but Falco was suddenly filled with a dark premonition of danger. He sensed Nathalie's anxiety before they heard the tension in her voice.

'What are you doing here?' she exclaimed. 'You cannot stay here. You have to leave!'

The emissary's relief turned to concern as they saw the state of Nathalie and Ciel. Both were exhausted and covered in dirt and grime.

'You have to go!' said Nathalie as she reached them.

'It's all right,' said the emissary. 'The demon was defeated, the Possessed have been destroyed.'

But Nathalie shook her head. 'No!' she said. 'You must leave!' Here she turned to look back the way she had come as if she expected to see another Possessed army emerging into the valley. 'You must divide the army into smaller forces. Send them by different routes back to Hoffen and Le Matres. Send for more battle mages...'

The emissary cast Falco a look of deep concern. Nathalie seemed almost delirious and appeared to be making no sense. He turned to look at the scout.

'Could we have overlooked another force?'

'I do not believe so, my Lord,' said the scout but his conviction was suddenly tinged with doubt. It was a bold scout who would contest the assertion of a battle mage.

They began to escort Nathalie back towards the camp, but both she and Ciel kept looking backwards and Falco felt a bead of fear trickle down his spine. What could possibly instil such anxiety in a battle mage and her dragon?

They were still some way from the field hospital when Ciel stopped. The great amber dragon turned and lowered her head, an ominous growl rising in her chest. Nathalie had turned too and now Falco could also sense the presence of something approaching. The three of them were staring at the same point on the hillside as if they could see something that was invisible to normal eyes.

'You must go,' said Nathalie in a cold disturbing tone. 'It is here.'

'Look at the grass on the hillside,' said Alex. 'It's turning black.'

Sure enough there was a patch of scorched earth that seemed to be extending towards them and now they could all feel the unmistakable presence of a demon, that soul clenching fear that made even the bravest man feel like a lost and terrified child.

'We killed one demon,' said Quirren. 'We can kill another.'

'No,' said Nathalie. 'This one is beyond us.'

'Surely together...' began the emissary but she cut him off.

'I cannot defeat it, Chevalier,' she said and the certainty in her voice chilled the emissary to the bone. 'But I will try to hold it as long as I can.'

For a moment the emissary could not move. The thought of leaving her alone to face the demon was unthinkable, but he could see from her eyes that he had no choice. If Nathalie and Ciel could not defeat this demon then his only choice was to get his troops as far away from the danger as he could.

'Back to the camp,' he said. 'All of you, quickly!'

He began to physically push them back towards the army.

'We cannot leave them,' said Falco.

'But we cannot help them either,' said the emissary. 'Now come. You must shield the army while we make our escape.'

With great reluctance they began to stumble back towards the camp, each of them looking back as the area of blackened heath spread towards them as if driven on by a swift and burning wind.

As they retreated so Nathalie went out to meet the approaching darkness, Ciel walking calmly at her side.

Reaching the camp, Falco looked back at her, a small figure going out to meet her doom. Close by the emissary was calling out orders.

'Up! Up!' he cried. 'Get these men up and ready to move.'

The men looked at him as if he was mad but they could tell by the urgency in his voice that he was serious. They could also feel the resurgent fear of the approaching demon. Men driven to the limits of their endurance were now forced to rouse themselves once more.

The emissary saw a signalman and called him over.

'Sound the call to rally and retreat. Double time!' he snapped when the man paused in confusion.

Had they not just won the battle?

But he paused for only a moment before lifting the horn to his lips and the call sounded across the valley like a cruel and ill-timed joke.

The emissary looked around as the wounded soldiers in the field hospital struggled to respond. They were helped onto horses and carts or hauled across the shoulders of more able men, but at least they were starting to move.

The sounds of activity echoed in Falco's ears. Around him the army was rousing itself in a collective state of fear and confusion, all moving away from the small figure who stood with her dragon as the darkness surged towards them. Beside him his friends were mounting horses and two orderlies were helping

Malaki onto Fidelis. Quirren handed Falco his helmet and the reins of his horse before climbing into the saddle of his own injured mount. Bryna too had mounted a horse and Alex had left to rejoin the Exiles, while across the battlefield Jarek Snidesson had lost the ability to act. The fear that he had thought banished was now swelling in his mind once more, hotter and blacker than ever.

'*Not again!*' he thought. '*Heavens help us, not again!*'

The veteran hussars drew their young commander away as they joined the retreat, the entire army now making its way up the northern slopes of the valley. And still Falco did not move. He sat on his horse while his friends moved away.

'Falco!' called the emissary. 'We need you.'

But Falco could not turn away from the figures of Nathalie and Ciel. Beyond them the blackened earth was now splitting apart as something unholy emerged into the fading light of day.

The Slayer had arrived.

The soldiers of the Fourth Army began to retreat in earnest as the demon appeared and ripples of panic spread throughout their ranks. Falco could feel their fear and he tried to protect them but he was unable to concentrate. He could not shake off the sense that he was abandoning Nathalie and Ciel.

'Falco, come on!' cried Bryna and without any prompting Falco's horse turned to follow the others.

Almost in a dream Falco was borne away while behind him a shower of cindered earth fell from the demon's armoured form. The Slayer stepped up into the world and settled its gaze on the Defiant and the wyrm who stood before it. They had tried to escape and they had failed, but even now they showed no fear and the Slayer felt a thrill of ecstasy in anticipation of their deaths.

*

Nathalie watched as the Slayer rose up from the earth. She looked into the eyes of death and for a moment she was almost overcome with despair. Somehow she had known they could not escape, and now she had led the demon here, to the emissary and the soldiers of the Fourth. She knew the guilt could consume her, but she also knew she did not have very long to live and so she levelled her sword and raised her shield.

Beside her she felt Ciel tense as the dragon also prepared to fight.

*

Falco felt as if he were moving through a thick unyielding fog. Sounds and sensations seemed distant and indistinct. They were moving away from the threat and the fear, but somehow it felt wrong. As the army continued to retreat Falco drew on the reins and brought his horse to a halt. He turned and looked back once more as the dragon and the battle mage were suddenly engulfed by fire.

*

Nathalie had not been expecting this assassin to use Baëlfire, but still she managed to conjure a wall of protection before the hellish flames could devour her flesh. Ciel reacted too, lunging to one side as the Slayer unleashed the ferocious storm of dark fire.

The moment the flames subsided Nathalie struck back with an attack of her own. A lance of white light speared towards the Slayer but was deflected by the armour of the Enlightened. At the same time Ciel sent a torrent of flame at the demon and as it faded Nathalie struck at the demon with her sword. Her blade swept beneath the Slayer's guard and scored a shallow wound in the exposed flesh of the demon's hip.

The Slayer retreated as Ciel joined the fight raking her steel hard talons across the demon's armoured helm. For a moment they tried to press their advantage but then the Slayer struck back and Ciel was required to twist violently to avoid a blow that almost severed her neck. At the same time the Slayer levelled a blow that would have broken Nathalie's shield arm had she not fortified her body to absorb the attack. Even so she was thrown off balance, spinning quickly so as not to offer her back to the Slayer's lethal blades.

The Slayer now attacked in earnest and only their skill and speed prevented Nathalie and Ciel from being cut down. But they could not resist such ferocity for long and when the Slayer hammered a sword pommel into the side of Nathalie's helm it seemed the end had come. Her legs buckled and she slumped insensible to the ground.

Nathalie would surely have died had Ciel not launched herself at the demon. The amber dragon leapt onto the Slayer's armoured shoulders trying to grapple its powerful arms. For a moment it seemed the Slayer might lose its footing but then it stabbed one of its blades over its shoulder, cutting deep into the upper part of Ciel's left foreleg. The dragon lost her grip and tumbled backwards, growling in pain as she rolled over on her injured wing. However, despite the pain she came quickly to her feet and moved to stand over the inert figure of Nathalie as the Slayer turned to face her.

The demon looked as strong as ever and there was murder in its eyes as it bowed its head and flexed its muscular arms. The moment of victory had arrived and even the mighty wyrm seemed to know that the end had come as it stood like a pathetically loyal hound over the unconscious body of its master.

So much for the great souls of this the charnel world.

The sharp sword points lifted as the Slayer gripped its blades and came on. But hardly had it taken a step when a dark shape came surging towards it. A horse with a rider, charging from nowhere, and the Slayer frowned as it recognised the distinctive glare of another Defiant's soul. With a flash of its searing gaze it stopped the horse in its tracks and the beast went down in a mass of fear and flailing hooves but the rider had already begun to dismount.

Pushing up onto the saddle he leapt from the horse, and the Slayer reeled as this new Defiant kicked it full in the face of its high ridged helm. Surprised by the force of this attack the Slayer turned to face this new opponent and as it did so it almost smiled. This new Defiant was young and untried and devoid of any power that could harm it. With an air of utter contempt the Slayer moved to end its life.

*

Even as the army scrambled up the side of the valley Falco had watched as Nathalie and Ciel did battle with the Slayer. At one point he thought they might win but then he saw Nathalie collapse, felled by a massive blow to the side of her helm.

With no conscious thought Falco dug his heels into his horse's flanks and charged down the valley towards them. As if from a great distance he watched

Ciel wrestle with the demon before it stabbed back over its shoulder and Ciel lost her grip and tumbled backwards. The Slayer started towards Nathalie but Ciel recovered quickly and moved to stand over Nathalie's prone and lifeless form.

The wind was rushing in Falco's ears as he drove his horse at full gallop towards them. He had no thought as to what he would do when he reached them, only that he could not allow them to stand alone. He was almost upon them when the demon sensed his presence and turned towards him. The focussed will of the Slayer slammed into them and Falco's horse simply collapsed in terror but Falco had already been preparing to dismount, just as he had practised so many times in the Crucible. Even as his horse fell, Falco leapt through the air, kicking the demon in the face before hitting the ground and rolling to his feet.

Sword drawn and shield raised he turned to face the Slayer.

The demon paused for just a moment and Falco felt the force if its contempt but then it surged forward. It attacked with dismissive savagery as if it intended to kill him with two swift cuts but Falco dodged the first attack and deflected the second with his shield. He even managed to slash at the back of the Slayer's wrist, but it felt like he had struck a statue of solid bronze and his sword made no impression at all.

The Slayer's eyes flared as Falco avoided its first two attacks. Bringing more focus to bear it launched a more sustained assault but still Falco managed to dodge, block or parry each attack. Realising that it had underestimated this new opponent the Slayer tensed in readiness for all-out fury but at that moment Ciel attacked from the rear.

The dragon caught the Slayer's right arm in her jaws and tried to pull it backwards but the Slayer turned quickly and struck out with the sword in its left hand. Ciel was forced to let go before the blade bit into her chest. Arching back she avoided the blow but when she tried to attack, her left foreleg gave way. Her head dropped low and the Slayer delivered a savage kick that caught her squarely on the side of the head stunning the great dragon who collapsed to the ground close to the body of the still unconscious Nathalie. The Slayer turned back to Falco and it was clear that this time there would be no holding back.

Still Falco held his ground. He might not have the offensive ability to harm the Slayer but his defence was strong. He would be a rock on which the Slayer's violence could break. So let it come. If this was to be a battle of wills then let it come. Let it test the limits of its unholy might against the strength of *this* Defiant's faith.

Somehow the Slayer sensed Falco's challenge and its eyes glowed with satisfaction. As it started forward Falco tensed his mind and a great surge of tingling energy swept through his body. For a moment he felt transformed by its power but then the demon hit him. With terrifying force it unleashed blows from sword and fist and crushing hooves. The brutality was like nothing Falco had imagined and he knew that for all his defensive strength he could not hold out for long.

He took a kick in the thigh that would have broken the leg of a cart horse. He ducked beneath a great scything attack and fortified his shield arm to absorb the impact from a blow that shook his body like a sledgehammer. His arm was undamaged but the Slayer's curved blade cut a deep gash into the metal of his shield.

Already drained by the day's exertions it was all Falco could do to resist the Slayer's attacks, much less launch any of his own. He blocked and parried and twisted out of harm's way, and when he could not avoid a blow he blocked it with the fortification of his mind. But the Slayer's violence seemed inexhaustible and Falco's strength began to fail.

A heavy downward strike cut away half of his shield and Falco felt blood running down his arm. A dizzying strike glanced off his helm and another sent a numbing pain through his shoulder but still Falco eluded that lethal blow and the Slayer was becoming increasingly frustrated.

Realising the end was near Falco made one last great effort and ducking beneath an attack he struck at the Slayer with all his remaining strength. His sword found an area of exposed skin but this blade had not come from the forge of Master Missaglias, it was not a battle mage's sword and the steel shattered as it struck the demon's unyielding flesh. Falco was left with just a few inches of glowing steel so when he turned to block the next attack he had no sword to meet it. The Slayer's curved blade caught him in the side of the head, knocking off his helm and filling his vision with stars. Falco fell to his knees and struggled to remain conscious but then he spat out a mouthful of blood and raised his face to look at the demon standing over him.

The Slayer looked down at him, its great chest heaving with exertion. This young Defiant was beaten despite the fire that continued to burn in his bright green eyes.

Knowing he was about to pass out Falco looked into the small hot eyes of the Slayer and hell-be-damned but if he did not smile. It was not a smile of mirth. It was a smile of disdain, the smile of a man who was not afraid to meet his end. And for all its murderous strength it gave the Slayer pause. This was no ordinary Defiant that knelt before it. This was a soul of dark and dangerous strength and it could not be allowed to live.

Falco lifted his chin as the Slayer raised his sword to kill, but even as the curved blade came down a bolt of blue energy punched into the demon's fist and its strike went wide. The demon's eyes blazed with fury as it turned to see where this latest attack had come from and then it roared with pain as Nathalie sent a tight ball of fire into the base of its neck. The fireball was no bigger than a fist but it burned with a furious heat and rather than exploding it bored into the Slayer's flesh.

Emerging from unconsciousness Nathalie had been horrified to see Falco battling the demon. He was being pounded and beaten and hammered and yet somehow he remained alive. Nathalie's body burned with pain and fatigue but she could not bear to see Falco die and so, determined to protect him, she staggered forward, her helmet gone, her face begrimed and bloody. In her right hand she trailed her sword across the ground while her left hand was thrust forward as she struggled to drive the fireball deeper into the Slayer's body.

The Slayer tried to claw the writhing ball of flame from its flesh but it could not. Roaring with pain it realised that the only way to stop it was to kill the female Defiant once and for all. It surged forward but hardly managed a step before it was engulfed by dragon fire. Taken by surprise once more it hunkered down then reeled as Ciel struck it a mighty blow with the talons of her undamaged right paw. The Slayer's helm took most of the damage but one of the dragon's claws scored a deep cut beneath the demon's left eye. Dark silvery blood welled up and the Slayer blinked and staggered back as it struggled to clear its vision and still the small fireball burned at the base of its neck. It managed to block a sword strike from Nathalie but now Ciel was closing again, limping and wounded but still dangerous.

The Slayer began to back away and although it looked like Nathalie might collapse at any moment she continued to push forward. Finally she relinquished her grip on the fireball and swung her sword to send a glowing arc of light scything towards the retreating demon. The Slayer tried to block it with its enchanted blades but a small piece got past its defences and cut a deep gash in its side, finally a grievous wound to threaten the hellish fiend.

With a sense of furious disbelief the Slayer realised it had lost the initiative and was now in very real danger of being defeated by this bitch Defiant and her wyrm. Both would surely have died had it not been for the untested Defiant. But the Slayer had underestimated the youngling and now the tables had turned. If it were going to survive it needed to withdraw.

With a roar of frustration the Slayer drew up a wall of Baëlfire, and as its opponents shied from the terrible heat, the demon tore a rift in the fabric of reality and stepped down into the underworld where it could sear its wounds and regain its strength. The Slayer would suffer terribly for its defeat, but it would endure its penance until it was stronger and more powerful than ever. And then it would return for vengeance.

Nathalie gave a cry of frustration as she saw the Slayer escaping. They had failed to kill it and she knew with dreadful certainty that it would return. But such horror was for another day. Today they had prevailed and for that they must be grateful.

Feeling utterly spent she turned to see Ciel approaching the hunched figure of Falco. Nathalie could scarcely believe that he was alive at all. Struggling over to him she laid a gentle hand on Falco's blood matted hair. At first she feared that he was lost, but then slowly he straightened up to look at her. Even now his green eyes held a distant and dangerous light and Nathalie wondered if he had given too much in opposing the Slayer, but slowly his gaze came into focus and he returned to them. He seemed confused and surprised to see her alive. A tear ran down his face and Nathalie wiped it away with the armoured thumb of her gauntlet.

'Welcome back, little brother,' she said.

*

Far to the south, in the Forsaken Lands of Beltane, the Marchio Dolor scorched the earth with the force of his displeasure. Not only had another demon been slain but now the Slayer had been forced to retreat. The Marchio could almost sense its fury and shame, shame that would drive it deep into the flames of hell where its flesh and its weapons would be further tempered until they rivalled the Marchio's own. For a moment he considered leaving Beltane to journey north, but then he smiled for he could feel the Slayer's eagerness to return, its hunger for revenge.

Besides... the Serthian Wolf was still proving troublesome. No. First he would destroy Vercincallidus and then he would go north to visit the same slaughter on the people of Clemoncé. Till then let the Slayer suffer the agony of its disgrace and pity the Defiant that meets it when it is finally reborn into the world.

70

On a Late Spring Evening

In the mage tower of Le Matres Meredith Saker had finally finished teaching the resident magi how to transfer the live link of communication. Earlier in the day a dispatch rider had arrived in the city with news of the Fourth Army's victory and Meredith found it ironic that the first time the link was used was to inform Galen Thrall of the mage army's collapse on the battlefield.

With his experiment successfully concluded he was free to begin his search for the book he had come here to find. However, the archives of Le Matres were not catalogued with the same rigour as those in Wrath and after several hours searching he was beginning to realise that finding 'The Last Surviving Witness' might not be as easy as he had hoped. He looked for someone to help him, but it was getting late and the only person remaining in the archives was an old mage who was clearly ready for his bed.

'If you could wait until morning,' said the aging archivist. 'Brother Ignatius will be able to tell you if we have it or not. He knows every book and scroll down to the last scrap of faded parchment.'

Meredith gave a sigh of frustration.

'And what time will Brother Ignatius be here?'

'Early,' said the old man, stifling a yawn. 'Unless he's transcribing documents. In which case he'll be working in one of the tower's south facing rooms. He needs the light for that kind of work.'

'Very well,' said Meredith. 'In the meantime could you tell me if you have a section on dragonkind?'

'We most certainly do!' said the old mage with an affronted air. 'End of the north aisle on the left hand wall.'

'Thank you,' said Meredith and the old man gave him a curt nod before turning to leave.

Now alone in the archives, Meredith went to the end of the north aisle where he found a small section dedicated to the study of dragons. Most were copies or variations of works he had already seen in Wrath, but a few were new to him and he removed two that looked intriguing. Moving back to the main chamber he sat down at a table and began to read. The first work was an interesting study on the anatomy of dragons, while the second supported the notion that dragons possessed a racial memory which grew more extensive with age, allowing them to remember things that happened many years before they were born.

Meredith knew that battle mages experienced some form of mental link with their dragons and a dreadful thought occurred to him. If a dragon could be affected by the memory of Possession then perhaps a battle mage could be too. Was it possible that Falco's father had not gone mad, but had in fact become Possessed through the mental bond he shared with his dragon?

After weeks of intense concentration Meredith was not prepared for a long night of study. Still reading about dragons he fell asleep and his dreams were all of fire and black scales and a dark haired man crying out in murderous rage.

He woke to feel himself being gently shaken by the old archivist that he had spoken to the previous night. The man's face took on a look of disgust and Meredith realised he had been drooling in his sleep. He drew the sleeve of his robe across his mouth and tried to blink the tiredness from his eyes.

'I see you've been reading about dragons,' said a slightly younger man with stark white hair and disturbingly dark eyebrows.

'Er, yes,' said Meredith, his head feeling thick and fuzzy.

'A fascinating topic but I understand there's another book you are looking for.'

Meredith realised that this must be Brother Ignatius, the only mage who seemed to know how the archives of Le Matres were arranged.

'Yes,' said Meredith getting to his feet. 'It's a book called 'The Last Surviving Witness' by a mage called Sennicio Verde. Do you know it?'

'I should do,' said Brother Ignatius. 'Brother Verde was after all a member of this tower.'

Meredith's heart leapt at this news. Finally he might learn something new about the Great Possession.

'Do you have a copy?' he asked, trying to keep the desperation out of his voice. 'The records list two copies but the one in Wrath no longer exists.'

'I believe we do,' said Brother Ignatius.

Now fully awake Meredith followed him as he walked off down the aisles.

'As I recall it was placed under 'afflictions of the mind' and not with the chronicles of the time as one might expect.'

'You've read it?' asked Meredith his hopes rising still further.

'No,' said Brother Ignatius. 'I prefer my history a little more believable.'

They stopped in a small alcove stacked to the ceiling with books and scrolls.

'Let me see,' said the archivist, bending down to trace the books in the bottom right hand corner. 'Vanier... Vaughn... Veilleux... hmm!' The tone of his 'hmm' was not encouraging. With a groan he straightened up and stared at the shelf as if he could not understand why it was not there. 'Strange,' he said. 'I don't remember anyone taking it out.'

Meredith's shoulders slumped with disappointment. He bowed his head and rubbed his tired eyes.

'I am sorry, young master,' said Brother Ignatius. 'It seems the book you are looking for is no longer present in the archives of Le Matres.'

'Could it have been removed for study?' asked Meredith. 'Is there any way you could trace it?'

'I do not believe so. There is no record of it being removed and so no one to approach about its whereabouts.'

Meredith's disappointment was painfully apparent and Brother Ignatius seemed embarrassed by his inability to produce the book. He began to offer another apology but Meredith just turned away, muttering some dejected thanks.

'You could always ask Brother Verde himself.'

Meredith stopped in his tracks.

'What did you say?'

'I said you could always ask Brother Verde himself, although you might not get much by way of an answer.'

'He's still alive?' asked Meredith. 'I thought this was supposed to be a firsthand account from a survivor of the Great Possession.'

Brother Ignatius raised a sceptical eyebrow. 'I understand that is the book's claim, yes.'

'But the Great Possession took place more than four hundred years ago. How can anyone alive have spoken to someone who survived it?'

'As I say,' said Brother Ignatius. 'I prefer my history a little more believable.'

Meredith did not know how it could be possible, but if the author *was* still alive then maybe he could talk to him. That would be even better than reading the book itself.

'Is he still in the tower?' he asked but Brother Ignatius shook his head.

'Alas, no. Brother Verde's mind began to fail more than a year since. He was removed to the tower of Solace, a retreat in the north where the elderly and infirm can be properly cared for.'

'Is he still there? At the retreat, I mean?'

'I believe so. At least, I don't remember hearing any news of his demise.'

Meredith's eyes were suddenly burning with renewed purpose, all trace of weariness gone.

'How far is it to this retreat?'

'About a week,' said Brother Ignatius. 'There's a small road that leads into the mountains.'

Meredith muttered his thanks but he was already making plans. He would wait for the Fourth Army to return but then he would go. He could not miss the opportunity to speak to someone who knew so much about the Great Possession, even if they were four hundred years old.

*

It was another two days before the Fourth Army arrived back in Le Matres, battered and bloodied but ultimately victorious. The city was already overcrowded with refugees but the people did their best to accommodate the exhausted army. An estate on the outskirts was made available to them and it was here that many of the wounded were also housed, including Falco who was given a room in the villa overlooking the river. The healers of Le Matres seemed to think that Falco would recover more quickly if he were left alone, a view not shared by Fossetta who, along with Heçamede and Tobias, had arrived in the city the previous day.

'He has been through a great ordeal,' said the senior healer. 'He needs rest and recuperation.'

'Nonsense!' said Fossetta. 'What he needs is his friends.'

The healer was clearly not accustomed to having his decisions challenged but finally he gave way.

'Just be certain not to overtax him.'

And so, rather than being a quiet haven of convalescence, Falco's room began to resemble the cadet barracks back at the academy. Over the next couple of days Fossetta could often be seen sitting in the corner, quietly embroidering a pearl coloured garment, while the youngsters sat around talking. And Tobias would also spend time with them, just sitting and listening to what was being said.

Falco still bore the marks of numerous injuries but the cuts and grazes were healing and the bruises had faded from an ugly purple to a less alarming shade of green. He remained quieter and more pensive than normal, but he was recovering well and he laughed now as Alex commented on the state of his helm, which the people of Le Matres had laid out with the rest of his armour, as if it were something other than damaged and useless scrap.

'I mean look at it!' said Alex, holding up the helm so that everyone could see the sharp dent where the Slayer's blade had finally struck Falco down. 'How the hell does anyone survive a blow like that? It's ridiculous!' His tone of irritation made everyone in the room smile.

'I always said Falco had a thick head,' said Bryna and people laughed again, even Fossetta who seemed delighted by the way Bryna now joined in with the boys' banter.

It was a relief to hear some of the old joviality coming back into the conversation. After the battle even Alex had been quiet and withdrawn. They had lost eight of their fellow cadets, including Kurt Vogler, Bryna's frequent sparring partner.

However, they all knew that Alex's humour was an attempt to distract them from the trauma of what had happened and the uncertainty of what lay ahead. Many of the cadets had voiced a desire to remain at the front rather than returning to the academy. However, the emissary had spoken of a special task he wanted them to perform and later that evening he revealed his plans as they sat in Falco's room.

'I need you to return to Wrath,' he told them. 'We're redeploying our forces along the front but we are now more stretched than ever. We need more troops.'

'What is it you want us to do?' asked Quirren.

'I want you to return to Wrath and get the Queen's Irregulars ready for battle.'

'I thought you said they weren't very good,' said Malaki.

'Excuse me!' said Bryna indignantly. 'The Dalwhinnies are from the Irregulars, don't forget!'

'Precisely,' said the emissary. 'They just need the proper leadership.'

'You want *us* to train the Irregulars?' said Malaki.

'I do,' said the emissary. 'But Lanista Magnus and the other instructors will help. I don't know how long you will have, but I want you to turn the Irregulars into a fighting force that can make a contribution to the war.' He paused, looking at Malaki, Quirren and Huthgarl. 'And I would like you three to relieve the current leaders of their command.' His expression suggested that this might prove easier said than done.

'Does the Queen not command them?' asked Bryna.

'In name,' said the emissary. 'But in reality they languish under the authority of two thugs that make Patrick Feckler look like a pillar of the community.' His tone held a contempt they had not heard in his voice before. 'General Connard Forbier and Major Viktor Gazon are the official commanders,

384

although the authenticity of their ranks is dubious to say the least. They've created a cosy life for themselves and getting them to give it up will not be easy, but I will write to Master Cyrano. If you need money to persuade them he will make sure you have what you need.'

The expressions on their faces made it clear what they thought of bribing soldiers who were supposed to be loyal to the Queen.

'Be careful,' said the emissary. 'They are not nice men and they surround themselves with equally unpleasant followers.'

They assured the emissary that they would not let him down and the conversation turned to other things, including the matter of escorting the refugees back to the capital.

'I can't wait for the refugees,' said Falco.

'I understand,' said the emissary. 'Why don't you ride ahead with Malaki, Quirren and Huthgarl? The others can follow in their own time. But none of you can tarry. We need the Irregulars as soon as possible. So return to Wrath and wait for orders from Marshal Breton. If you are lucky you might have a few weeks to prepare them for war.'

And so it was settled. Falco and the three knights would ride quickly back to Wrath, while Bryna, Alex and the other cadets would follow with the refugees from Le Matres. With this decided they talked quietly for a while and the emissary explained that the battle mages had been redistributed along the front to account for the deaths of Jürgen and Wildegraf. It would be some time before Ciel could fly again but Nathalie had assured Falco that she would be all right.

'Never underestimate the resilience of dragons,' she had said.

Finally the emissary stood up to take his leave and the others took this as their cue to do the same. There was a murmur of goodbyes and the emissary was about to leave when Falco nudged Malaki.

'Have you asked him yet?'

'Asked me what?' said the emissary as Huthgarl, Alex and Quirren left the room. However, on hearing the question, Alex's head reappeared round the door, grinning widely until Quirren pulled him away, bumping his head on the door frame as he went.

The emissary hovered and Malaki looked tongue tied while Bryna stood behind him and Falco shook his head in despair at their bashfulness.

'They want to know if you'll marry them,' said Falco and the smile that came over the emissary's face was more complex and poignant than any they had seen before.

'It would be my honour and my pleasure,' said the emissary his grey eyes shining.

Malaki gave him a nod of thanks while Bryna came forward to kiss him lightly on the cheek. Falco smiled and from outside the door they heard Alex Klingemann's voice.

'Finally!' he exclaimed, his voice fading away into the villa. 'I was beginning to think I'd die of old age before you two tied the knot.'

They all smiled and then Bryna spoke.

'We came so close to losing each other.'

'There's no need to explain,' said the emissary. 'Have you someone to give you away?'

Malaki shook his head as if he could not believe who she had chosen. Patrick Feckler had not cried since he was a grubby and ill-treated child. But this simple request from Bryna had found a chink in his calloused heart and brought a tear to his deep set eyes.

The emissary smiled as he guessed who Bryna had chosen.

'Tomorrow evening?' he suggested. 'Before we go our separate ways.'

Bryna and Malaki nodded and with a shallow bow the emissary left the room. The others followed shortly after and Falco was just turning back his bed when there was a knock on his door. It was Meredith Saker and it was clear that he had something on his mind.

'Is everything all right?' asked Falco, gesturing him into the room.

Meredith declined the invitation to enter and hovered outside the door shifting uncomfortably.

'I'm afraid I won't be able to return with you to Wrath.'

Falco just stared at him. He had been hoping that Meredith would help him prepare for the Rite of Assay.

'But I thought you'd finished your experiment,' he said, unable to conceal his disappointment.

'I have,' said Meredith. 'But I've just learned of something that means I cannot return just yet.'

'Is it really that important?'

'I believe so.'

'Then you must attend to it,' said Falco making an effort to keep his disappointment in check.

'I am sorry,' said Meredith. 'I will try to get back in time, if I can.'

'It's all right. Aurelian and Dusaule will be there to help me.'

'Thank you,' said Meredith. He turned to leave then paused. 'If my father is on the Torquery he will try to stop you with fire.'

For a second Falco's eyes narrowed, but then a dark smile spread across his face.

'I know how to deal with fire,' he said and now it was Meredith's turn to smile.

As Meredith disappeared from view Falco found himself wondering how it was that a man could turn out so different to his father. He wondered if it might be the same for him, but somehow he knew that it was not. Somewhere deep inside he could feel the heat of his father's legacy, a heat that had the potential to devour him and deliver his soul into the hands of the Possessed. Maybe his subconscious was right to keep such power entombed.

The following day saw the cadets busily preparing for the return to Wrath, while Meredith Saker set out on a new journey, heading north to the mage retreat of Solace. Falco wondered what could possibly be so important, but as the day wore on he found his thoughts converging on the event that was planned for the evening.

As the sun grew lower in the sky Falco walked with Malaki down towards the manicured lawn where Patrick Feckler had prepared a simple scene. At one end of the lawn a circle of grass had been marked out with flowers strewn upon the grass. The Dalwhinnies had been busy and it seemed that not a plant on the estate had been spared. If it bore a flower it had met with a Dalwhinnie knife. And they were all present, the Dalwhinnies, the surviving cadets and many from the Fourth Army itself. All come to share in a moment of joy amidst the ever present horror of war.

Blushing furiously Malaki allowed Falco to lead him to the circle of flowers where he stood looking awkward and self conscious. He was dressed in a tailored shirt, embroidered with Valentian knotwork, and a pair of fine leather trousers, the seams of which bore subtle stitching of the same design. He looked handsome and even Alex could not think of anything witty or insulting to say.

To one side Tobias sat with the two Chasseur soldiers and the wagon drivers that had brought them over from Daston. Then Fossetta appeared with Heçamede, and with them came Bryna on the arm of Patrick Feckler. She was dressed in a beautiful gown of pearl white silk, delicately embroidered in coloured thread to match the patterns on Malaki's shirt. With flowers in her deep red hair and a flush of nervous excitement on her cheeks she looked stunning, a point not wasted on the Dalwhinnies who met her arrival with a chorus of crude comments and whistles. Finally the emissary appeared, dressed in a pair of fine black trousers and a beautiful doublet of quilted grey silk. As the raucous greeting continued Patrick Feckler tried to calm things down.

'Quiet! You lecherous dogs!' he roared. 'Let's get started or there'll be no time for drinking!'

'Aye, but not too much for the big fella,' shouted one man. 'Or there'll be no testing his spurtle tonight!'

'Bollocks!' cried another. 'They've been shaggin each other for months.'

Fossetta scowled disapprovingly but Messrs Laffite and Macaire roared with laughter along with the Dalwhinnies and the cadets who had been witness to Malaki and Bryna's growing relationship.

In the end it only took the emissary to raise a hand for the gathered throng to come to order. Smiling indulgently he brought the two young people together amid the circle of flowers and then with quiet solemnity he performed a simple ceremony in which he bound their hands together with a strip of plain white cloth. And so, on a late spring evening, Bryna Godwin and Malaki de Vane were married.

As the bond was made Falco came forward with two silver rings that Patrick Feckler had somehow procured, and with the symbol of eternity adorning their hands Malaki and Bryna exchanged the gifts that they had agreed upon.

Malaki gave Bryna a new quiver filled with arrows, while Bryna gave him a new scabbard for his sword. There was silence as she shouldered her quiver and Malaki fastened the sword about his waist, tokens of the lives they had chosen and the weapons of war that defined them.

Finally they turned to face each other.

'In the quiet of the night,' said Malaki.

'And in the raging heat of battle,' said Bryna.

'I will love you,' they said together and more than one Dalwhinnie snorted back a tear.

There was a moment of stillness in which Falco did not know if he had lost a brother or gained a sister. Either way it did not matter. In the face of so much suffering and fear, this was something good.

'Right!' cried Dedric Sayer. 'Let's get pissed!'

The party raged long into the night and even the emissary got drunk, finally succumbing to an arm wrestling challenge from Paddy. The two men fought a mighty contest over a wooden table that was not up to the task and as they both collapsed to the floor Falco joined in the laughter, spilling a glass of beer down his front in the process. He was just wiping it away when he turned to see Jarek Snidesson standing beside him.

'I think her father would have approved,' said Jarek.

'So do I,' said Falco, wondering why Jarek had chosen this moment to speak to him.

They stood in awkward silence until Jarek spoke again.

'How can you do it?' he asked.

Falco shook his head, uncomprehending.

'The demons,' said Jarek. 'They are like nothing I ever imagined. How can you...'

'I don't know,' said Falco. 'All I know is that I can.'

For a long moment Jarek simply stared at him.

'I'm sorry,' he said, his voice cracking with emotion. 'For everything... I... I never understood.'

With this simple gesture an entire lifetime of unpleasantness was washed away.

Falco felt his own throat tighten. He did not trust himself to speak. Instead he held out his hand.

As Jarek moved away Falco turned back to watch Malaki and Bryna trying to extricate themselves from two hundred Dalwhinnies, each of whom seemed to think that they too were entitled to kiss the bride. In the end Patrick Feckler started laying about with a huge leather tankard and the happy couple were able to make their escape. Falco smiled but then his thoughts grew sombre. Tomorrow they would begin the journey back to Wrath and he would face a new series of trials, some of which were every bit as terrifying as facing the Slayer.

The forging of a sword, the Rite of Assay and the summoning of a dragon.

These were the things that would define *his* place in the world. But all that was for another time. Tonight his two best friends had got married and Falco was content.

71

The Serthian Wolf

The Beltonian general Vercincallidus looked down from the ridge as his Heavy Horse smashed through the last line of Kardakae before continuing down the valley to safety. Behind them the remnants of the Possessed army swung about, searching for victims to satisfy their boundless appetite for death. But there would be no more death today. Not for the Sons of Eldur. Six hundred of his blessed warriors already lay dead, but they had died bravely and would be welcomed into the Halls of Hugrekki tonight.

The general had already withdrawn his infantry. Now he raised his hand and a sigh rose up around the valley as a thousand poplar shafts drew back against a thousand bows of elm. The Possessed snarled and raged, surging forward but the general lowered his hand and a cloud of arrows shot down into the remaining ranks of the enemy. The longbows loosed and loosed again until only a few heavily armoured Kardakae remained, and then even these powerful warriors were destroyed by a final charge of Beltonian Heavy Horse. Another Possessed army destroyed by the great Vercincallidus, the man they called the Serthian Wolf.

He did not wait to clear the field. He did not even pause to bury his own dead. Their bodies would provide food for the crows but their souls were safe, and that was all that mattered, that and the fact that they had thwarted the enemy once more.

But he could not wait. Another Possessed army was advancing on their position, but this army was led by a demon and Vercincallidus would never confront such a force without the support of a battle mage. Instead he would seek out a target of *his* choosing. His scouts had already identified a suitable force, an army of four thousand Possessed just thirty miles east. This would take them further into the Forsaken Lands, but the general had learned to make these border lands his own.

As the army moved out, Vercincallidus turned to the blacksmith standing beside him. He threw back his wolf-skin cloak and drew up his sleeve, baring an arm that was covered with circular marks branded into the skin, each one representing a Possessed army that he had destroyed. The blacksmith raised the branding iron that glowed in the fading light of dusk. He glanced at his commander and waited for the familiar nod before pressing the red hot iron into the general's flesh. The smell that rose up was a sickly combination of roasting meat and burning hair, but Vercincallidus uttered not a sound. He ground his teeth against the pain and offered it up as a prayer for those who had given their lives this day.

Then, mounting his beautiful silver-dapple gelding he raised his mutilated arm to wave the army on. He might not be able to face the demon now closing on their position, but somewhere to the east there was a Possessed force that they *could* attack. This would be the next target of Vercincallidus, the next army to feel the teeth of the Serthian Wolf.

*

The Marchio Dolor bowed his head as the dark angel gave its report. It was not spoken. It came in the form of broken images playing across his mind... leagues of empty plains and scorched forests, hills shot through with rivers choked and poisoned with the bodies of the dead, the landscape of the Forsaken Lands. He saw armies of the Faithful moving through the land, rendered small by the height at which the angel flew.

Lower now, towards a dark stain that lay upon the land, closer still and he could make out the corpses of several thousand Possessed, their flesh rotting on blackened bones, their souls departed and drawn below where the price of their failure would be paid in full. No sign of the great Vercincallidus and his army. They had fled the scene, but even the most careful army leaves a trail and one of his fellow demons was already moving east to intercept him.

Good, thought the Marchio Dolor. He would keep his own army moving south and call upon another Duke to bring its forces north. Together they would herd the Serthian Wolf until he had nowhere else to run.

72

Diplomacy

As the emissary had suggested, Quirren and Huthgarl would accompany Falco and Malaki on the journey back to Wrath. In these dangerous times a group of four would offer greater security and Falco had no objections so long as it did not slow them down. And so, in a scene reminiscent of the departure from Toulwar they said their farewells, leaving Bryna and the rest of the cadets to follow with the refugees from Le Matres. Tobias would continue his search with Fossetta and Heçamede but not so close to the front. They would move back into the heartland of Clemoncé where the danger was not yet so pressing.

'We'll work our way back to the capital,' was the way Fossetta had put it. 'Perhaps we'll see you there.'

Falco had nodded and kissed them all, gaining strength from seeing them again, even if it had been for just a short while. And with that they had set off through the forested heartland of Clemoncé. Each trailing a spare horse, they had maintained a steady pace and in little more than a week they were drawing near to the city. They decided to stop at an inn overlooking the Ford of Garr. Then in the evening they rode on to the city to take a look at the Irregulars before deciding how best to approach the task that the emissary had set for them.

The Irregulars' camp was like a ramshackle settlement on the outskirts of the city, a sprawling mass of tents and temporary wooden structures. They came across a group of boys playing on a rope swing and asked them if they knew General Forbier and Major Gazon. The boys nodded and, in exchange for two small coins, led them to a low hill overlooking the camp.

'There,' said one of the boys, pointing out two individuals who had clearly just returned from a hunting trip. Both were large men, but they left others to clean and prepare their kills while they washed in copper basins before reclining in chairs with what appeared to be glasses of wine.

'Who's the third man?' asked Huthgarl, looking at another man who was clearly directing the work.

'That's Sergeant Hickey,' said the boy. 'He does the general's bidding.'

'They look like mercenaries,' said Quirren and the others nodded. These men certainly did not look like disciplined soldiers.

'Right,' said Malaki. 'We'll write to them tonight and meet with them tomorrow as planned.'

Huthgarl and Quirren nodded while Falco looked on, intrigued. They had not discussed their plans with him.

'Don't you worry about it,' was all Malaki would say. 'This is our task. You just focus on the Crucible and getting ready for the Rite.'

Back at the tavern the three conspirators had composed two letters to be delivered by courier before the end of the day. One was to the instructors at the academy, advising them of their arrival. The other was to the current commanders of the Queen's Irregulars 'asking' them to gather the army on the academy training grounds at the tenth hour of the following morning. A dispatch from the emissary had already been sent informing them that the cadets would be arriving to assume command, while a further note had been sent to Master

Cyrano, warning him that a discreet sum of money might be required to facilitate the 'retirement' of certain military officers.

They still refused to tell Falco what they had planned, but at least they allowed him to read the letter.

'Well, it's to the point,' he said, somewhat dubiously.

'Precisely,' said Malaki. 'They've already had notification from the emissary and that should be enough in itself. We'll see what they have to say for themselves tomorrow.'

The letter was duly delivered and if they could have heard the string of expletives issuing from the commanders' quarters they would have realised that the emissary's concerns about their intransigence had been fully justified.

The young knights spent the rest of the evening cleaning their armour. They had now proven themselves in battle and before leaving Le Matres they had each been presented with a cloak, surcoat and lance pennant bearing the colours of the orders to which they now belonged. For Malaki a black horse head on a field of pale blue, Quirren bore the Black Eagle on red, while for Huthgarl it was a vibrant ochre with the single black flame of the Beltonian Heavy Horse. They would be wearing their colours tomorrow when they went to speak with the Irregulars' commanders.

The following day they rose early and ate a good breakfast before crossing the ford and riding down to the city. Skirting the double curtain wall they avoided the crowds and made their way round to the road that led up onto the plateau. Falco had been given some new armour before they set out for Wrath, but he felt decidedly underdressed beside the resplendent figures of Malaki, Quirren and Huthgarl. As they began the climb they saw a rider at the rim of the plateau. He noted their approach before galloping away.

'Well I guess they know we're on the way,' said Quirren, a faint hint of nerves in his voice.

However, Malaki looked as calm as you like, helm and shield strapped to his saddle, and the pale blue pennant flying from the point of his lance. His expression was resolute, the birthmark on his face muted by the grey light of a cloudy morning. Cresting the rise they could see that the army of the Queen's Irregulars was gathered on the training fields just as their letter had requested, but it was not until they gained another rise that they appreciated just what a force it was.

'It must be eight thousand strong,' muttered Huthgarl looking at the disorderly ranks. 'And to think they've been lying here in Wrath doing nothing.'

'It's a desperate leader that sends an untrained army to war,' said Quirren.

Malaki said nothing. His gaze was on the three men standing ahead of the army. They looked completely assured of their position as the young knights rode towards them.

Falco allowed the others to go ahead of him. As Malaki had said, this was their task. But from the expression on their faces it was clear that General Forbier and Major Gazon had received Malaki's letter and Falco suspected it was going to take more than a little bribery to dislodge them from the positions of power they enjoyed.

Twenty yards from the two leaders Malaki, Quirren and Huthgarl dismounted and the man known as Forbier turned to face his army.

'Men and women of the Irregulars,' he bellowed. 'You must be wondering why you have been mustered here this morning. Have you been chosen for a prestigious place at the Academy of War?'

There was a chorus of mocking laughter.

'No!' said Forbier and he allowed the laughter to die down. 'Have you been ordered to march out by the Queen, in whose name we serve?'

This brought a chorus of cheers but there were many among the gathered host that seemed less than comfortable at the mention of the Queen.

'No!' said Forbier again. 'We are here because an *Illician* nobleman thinks the *Clemoncéan* Irregulars would do better under the command of boys!'

The laughter returned but it was no longer quite so enthusiastic. The soldiers of the army were looking at the three young knights now approaching their leaders. Despite what the general said they certainly did not look like boys.

General Forbier turned away from his army and walked forwards. He was a big man, as were Major Gazon and Sergeant Hickey, the burly individual who 'did the general's bidding'. Quirren was right, they looked like hardened mercenaries and none more so than General Connard Forbier himself. Wearing half plate and split-skirted cavalry mail he approached Malaki with a heavy shouldered swagger, his hand resting casually on the hilt of his sword. Beside him came Major Gazon, looking every bit as dangerous. They watched the three young knights approach with feral amusement in their eyes.

'Look here!' sneered General Forbier, taking note of the design on Malaki's surcoat. 'This one fancies himself a Knight of Wrath!'

Many among the ranks laughed, but as Malaki came close General Forbier's voice dropped to a menacing whisper.

'So you're the cocksure bastard who thinks he can... ungh!

Malaki kicked him squarely in the testicles, his foot driving up through the split in his mail shirt. As the general bent forward in pain Malaki caught hold of his head, his forearm clenched tight across the groaning man's throat.

With a curse Major Cazan moved to draw his sword but Huthgarl felled him with a punch that broke his nose and laid him flat out on the grass. Taken by surprise Sergeant Hickey reached for his own weapon only to find Quirren Klingemann's sword point at his throat.

'Move and you bleed,' said Quirren and Sergeant Hickey was still.

Still holding General Forbier in front of him Malaki turned to address the army who looked on in stunned silence.

'Soldiers of the Queen's Irregulars,' he said. 'My name is Sir Malaki de Vane of the Knights of Wrath and I am here to offer you a choice.' General Forbier began to struggle as the pain in his groin was eclipsed by the desperate need to breathe but still Malaki refused to let him go.

'You can either waste your lives following men like this,' Malaki leaned back on his hold and General Forbier rose up on his tip toes. 'Or you can follow a soldier's calling and honour the Queen, whose name you bear.' He paused as eight thousand soldiers shifted to get a better view of what was taking place.

'You have a chance to make a difference and take some pride in what you do. It will not be easy and many of you will die. But those who survive will be able to look their loved ones in the eye and not feel ashamed when people ask to which army you belong.'

Finally he let General Forbier fall at his feet.

'So what will it be?' he called out, his voice echoing across the training grounds. 'Will you fight? Or will you remain the butt of every soldier's joke, with so little dignity that you would follow a man like this.'

He looked down at Forbier and a wave of disquiet swept through the army of the Irregulars. Not all of them had heard, but the question was quickly passed through the ranks. This knight with the birthmark face was serious. He was actually asking them to make a choice.

'What gives you the right?' asked a man from a block of soldiers that had the same mercenary look as the commanders. 'What makes you think you can come here and start throwing your weight around?'

He began to walk forward and forty similarly disgruntled men moved with him.

'You attack the General and the Major, when they thought you were here to talk.' The mood was turning ugly and this block of soldiers was beginning to look like a mob. 'We know you ain't gonna start killing people, so how's about we give *you* a good kicking and then we'll see how cocky you are.'

The men continued to advance and Malaki stood his ground as if he were ready to take them all on. Sergeant Hickey began to laugh, but then the block of mercenaries stopped. They looked suddenly uncertain and afraid. Malaki thought perhaps that Quirren's blade or Huthgarl's great size had made them think again but behind him Falco turned in the saddle and smiled. Walking up the slope behind them was Lanista Magnus and Lanista Deloix with twenty more instructors from the Academy of War. Gone were the instructor's black surcoats with their white horse head motif. They were dressed in the armour of the soldiers that they were and their faces were grim as they came to stand beside their students.

'I'm glad to see that the academy lessons on diplomacy didn't go to waste,' said Lanista Magnus.

Malaki looked a little sheepish and Lanista Magnus smiled.

'Welcome back to Wrath, Sir Malaki.'

Together they looked at the angry mob that had suddenly come to a stop. Even with the instructors, Malaki and his friends were still heavily outnumbered but they exuded an intimidating confidence that the thugs and bullies could never hope to match.

And so, with a little moral support, Malaki explained to the Queen's Irregulars that from today they would be following the orders of the academy's newly graduated cadets, the rest of whom would be arriving in a few days' time. General Forbier and Major Gazon were duly relieved of duty, as was Sergeant Hickey and a number of officers with close ties to the commanders.

Over the next few nights some four hundred 'soldiers' would quietly leave the capital, deciding that they were not comfortable with the new state of affairs, but most simply accepted it as yet another twist of fate in their often chequered lives. But there were also many who felt a great thrill of excitement to think that they might finally be part of an army that was worthy of its name.

This was why they had joined the Irregulars in the first place; naive or troubled young men and women without the skill or training to pass muster for a regular army, but still with a desire to fight for their Queen. Well now they were to be given the chance. As Malaki had suggested it was not going to be easy and a good number would surely die but what were such things beside a life that actually meant something.

Still sitting on his horse Falco smiled as he watched Malaki and the others begin to impose some order on the stunned ranks of the Irregulars. This day was not turning out the way any of them had expected. He thought back to the way Bryna had mastered the Dalwhinnies and thought that she and Malaki were indeed a perfect match.

Leaving his friends to their new duties he turned his horse towards the slope leading up to the Crucible. They had all returned with challenges awaiting them. Malaki and the others had made a good start in meeting theirs. It was time for Falco to face his own.

*

Looking down from the mage tower Galen Thrall watched as Falco made his way up to the Crucible before veering off towards the short row of cottages where the two defunct battle mages lived.

'He has returned to attempt the Rite?' he asked, the small pupils of his waxy green eyes following Falco with the intensity of a hawk.

'I believe so,' said Morgan Saker beside him.

'Are we prepared?'

'We are.'

'And still no sign of offensive capabilities?'

'No,' said Saker. 'Although the reports suggest that his defences are particularly strong.'

'Do not worry,' said Thrall. 'Together you have more than enough strength to crush him. Besides,' he added, the pupils of his eyes shrinking further still. 'Brother Pacatos will begin his assault before the young falcon is even aware that he is under attack.'

Morgan Saker cast a sideways glance at the Grand Veneratu. Despite spending the last few months preparing for Falco's Rite of Assay he still had not met Brother Pacatos.

He did not question the Grand Veneratu's judgement, but the Rite of Assay was not to be taken lightly. The amount of magical energy being stored up in preparation could be a hazard to anyone involved.

Putting aside his doubts he watched as Falco rode towards the small row of cottages overlooking the plateau. He still believed that it was dangerous to let Aquila Dante's son become a fully fledged battle mage and he was determined to stop him, but not knowing the full details of the Torquery made him uneasy. Back in Caer Dour he had been the veneratu of his own tower. He was not accustomed to being kept in the dark.

*

395

Falco found Aurelian in the Crofters' cottage where he lived with Nicolas Dusaule. They sat beside the stove as he told them everything that had happened since he left on the training campaign. It seemed that some news had already reached the capital so Aurelian knew something of what had taken place. He knew about the Possessed attack on the village, the failure of the mage army and Malaki's charge against the demon. He also knew that an especially dangerous demon had killed Wildegraf and Jürgen and almost Nathalie too. But he did not know the details and he listened in grim silence as Falco described the Slayer and the single-minded focus of its violence.

'It was summoned specifically to kill battle mages,' said Aurelian when Falco had finished. 'Is this what you sensed during the strategy meeting?'

'I think what I sensed was the gap waiting to be filled by it,' said Falco and Aurelian nodded.

'And when you fought it, you're certain you didn't feel the stirring of any fire? Not even when things became so desperate?'

Falco shook his head. He knew Aurelian had been hoping that his offensive powers might be unlocked if the need to survive became so great.

'No matter,' he said, although Falco could sense his disappointment. 'You defied the demon and saved the lives of Nathalie and Ciel. We must all be grateful for that.'

Falco appreciated the words of encouragement, but the fact remained that without the ability to harm the demons of the Possessed he would always be on the defensive, avoiding confrontation. This was one reason why he was determined to complete his training. If he could succeed and summon a dragon then at least together they could mount some kind of attack. Unless the dragon he summoned turned out to be black in which case Falco would have to add the killing of a dragon to the shadows that stalked his soul.

'So,' said Aurelian. 'You're determined to attempt the Rite?'

'I am,' said Falco and there was not the merest hint of compromise in his eyes.

Aurelian gave a sigh of resignation.

'Then I will send a note of your intentions to Thrall.'

'Can he refuse?'

'No,' said Aurelian. 'It's merely a formality. He will confirm that all the preparations are in place and provide a list of the mages on the Torquery, but ultimately the decision is yours.'

Falco nodded, relieved. He could not imagine being denied the Rite now that he had made up his mind.

'Then I suppose we'd better see about getting you a sword.'

*

Nearly a hundred miles northwest of Le Matres Meredith Saker was drawing close to the magi retreat of Solace. The journey had taken him longer than he expected but now they could see it, perched on the far side of the valley with snow capped mountains rising behind. Surrounded by gardens and open woodlands it looked the very picture of tranquillity, but Meredith felt anything but tranquil. His mind was full of questions and tomorrow he might finally get some answers.

396

73

Sinner

The following morning Falco ate breakfast with Malaki, Quirren and Huthgarl before going up to meet Aurelian. The other cadets would be arriving in a few days but the young knights were determined to make a start on the Irregulars.

'There's a lot of work to be done,' said Malaki. 'And no time to waste.'

Falco admired their enthusiasm. He felt much the same way himself. Bidding them good luck he made his way up to meet Aurelian. Today they were going to speak with Master Missaglias about the forging of Falco's sword. He found the one armed battle mage waiting for him outside the cottage. He was sitting in the early morning sunlight with Dwimervane stretched out along the wall beside him.

'Just heard from the tower,' he said, shaking out the grainy dregs from his morning cup of coffee. 'Thrall will meet us in the Crucible this afternoon to formerly endorse your Rite.'

Falco felt a sudden rush of uncertainty and Aurelian clapped him on the shoulder.

'Don't worry,' he said. 'Only a fool would *not* be nervous,' and with that they made their way down from the plateau.

The workshops were already busy with noise as they entered. An assistant led them through to the fitting room where they were met by the hunchbacked master himself. The artisans had now completed their work and Falco stood in awe as Antonio drew back the curtain. The armour was there on its stand, as it had been the first time he saw it, but now it was finished and lined with leather and quilted silk. The surface was covered with the finely etched patterns that Meredith had designed and the steel was now polished to a dark satin sheen. Falco had seen gaudier and more impressive looking suits of armour before, but never one like this, never one that married so perfectly the elements of function and form.

'Beautiful,' breathed Aurelian but Falco was too entranced to speak.

Fortunately Antonio took his silence as a sign of approval and his scarred face softened with an immodest smile. Falco tried the armour on and sure enough it fitted even better than it had the first time he had worn it.

'Hopefully there'll be no more of this,' said Aurelian, pointing to a fading bruise at the base Falco's neck where the edge of the breastplate he had worn for the training campaign had dug into his flesh.

'Sometimes I think the armour causes more damage than it deflects.'

Falco had numerous other marks on his body, caused by the less than perfect armour, but he could not agree with Antonio. He remembered the impressive dent in his helm and was thankful for the protection even this armour had provided.

'So,' said Aurelian as Falco finished getting dressed. 'Have you had a chance to think about the sword?'

A troubled look crept over Antonio's face and he led them through to the forge at the far end of the workshops.

'I have the steel,' he said, indicating a number of rectangular billets each embossed with a stamp certifying that the metal was of the rare quality required for a battle mage's sword. 'But I'm still not sure about the idea of a third party supplying the heat.' He turned to Falco. 'You still have no fire of your own?'

Falco shook his head and the master frowned.

'Perhaps if I knew you better or we had that young mage who designed the patterns for your armour.'

'What difference would that make?' asked Falco and Aurelian motioned for him to sit down on a block of fire blackened wood.

'A smith gets used to the way metal behaves,' said Antonio. 'The heat, the colour, the way it feels beneath the hammer. Skill can take you so far but there's a point when only instinct can guide you.' He paused and Falco could hear the soft crackle of cinders from the forge. 'Making any decent sword requires skill, but the sword of a battle mage is more than just sharpened steel. It is the manifestation of faith, and it is intimately matched to the personality of the battle mage who will wield it. I could make a sword to match your physical stature but I don't know you well enough to match it to your soul.'

'But will you attempt it?' asked Aurelian. 'I've asked Dusaule and he is also willing to help.'

Still Antonio seemed unconvinced.

'Nicolas might provide an element of control,' he conceded. 'But I fear that if we get it wrong then the sword will fail, either here in the forge or during some critical exchange with the enemy.'

'But will you do it?'

For a while the master remained silent in thought.

'Come back in the morning,' he said at last. 'There's someone I would like to talk to before I give you an answer.'

As they left the workshops Aurelian could see the disappointment and uncertainty on Falco's face.

'Come on,' he said. 'Nicolas and Dwim will be waiting for us in the Crucible. We'll get in some training before Thrall arrives. And try not to worry,' he added. 'I've never known Antonio to give up on a challenge. If he can think of a way to make you a sword, he will.'

Heading back up to the Crucible they spent the next few hours testing Falco's skills and trying to anticipate what the mages on the Torquery might throw at him.

'Some will try to stop you with pain,' said Aurelian as they took a break to eat some food. 'Others will use cold or fire, or sheer mental force.'

Falco dunked a piece of bread in a cup of soup that Dusaule had brought to the Crucible. The silent battle mage was now sitting in his usual place with Dwimervane and for a moment Falco felt as if he had never been away.

'There's normally an element of animaré,' Aurelian went on. 'And trust me... it feels very weird to fight a suit of armour with no one inside.'

'I've not heard of that before,' said Falco. 'Surely that could be useful on the battle field.'

'Fat chance!' scoffed Aurelian. 'It takes the magi months to prepare for just a few minutes of combat.'

'At least that doesn't sound too dangerous?' said Falco and Aurelian almost choked on his soup.

'It's the Rite of Assay!' he cried. 'Of course it's bloody dangerous! One strike from an animaré's icy blade and you'll wish they'd hit you with steel. Two will send you to your knees. Three or four and the magi will have to carry you out of the labyrinth.'

Falco hung his head and Aurelian took pity.

'Their goal is to try and stop you,' he said. 'And a part of that is the threat of actual harm.'

'Has anyone ever died?' asked Falco and there was an uncomfortable silence as Aurelian glanced up at Nicolas before he spoke again.

'You can always concede,' he said. 'The magi will do everything they can to stop you but it is not their intention to kill. Just call out, *cedo* and the magi will desist. Even to think it will be enough to stop them.'

The prospect of submitting to the magi brought an edge of steel to Falco's gaze.

'But it's the fear that will be your greatest challenge,' said Aurelian.

Falco frowned. Surely no fear generated by the magi could compare with that experienced in the presence of a demon.

'It is not the fear of burning alive or being disembowelled that will stop you,' said Aurelian. 'It's not even the fear of failure, which for many battle mages is particularly great. It's the fear we take in with us. The darkness in there is black with the stench of it, the secret fears of every battle mage that ever trod its ways.'

Falco followed his gaze to the dark portal at the far end of the Crucible. And even from here he could sense the creeping whispers of terror that waited for him in the labyrinthine depths of L'obscurité. He felt a strange sense of vertigo as if he were being drawn towards the darkness but then he looked up as he sensed the approach of several magi.

'Ah... Here he is! The greasy haired tosser!' muttered Aurelian as a group of purple clad figures appeared at the edge of the Crucible.

Falco recognised Thrall from the hearing in the Chamber of Council. He was the most powerful mage in all of Wrath and yet Falco was more affected by the sight of the man beside him. He felt a familiar wave of disquiet sweep through his body as Morgan Saker descended the broad steps of the training arena. With them came two other magi in their dark purple robes.

As the magi came down so Dusaule and Dwimervane withdrew leaving Falco and Aurelian to face the magi delegation alone. Falco found himself staring at Galen Thrall. He was not a man of great stature and his hair certainly did appear greasy. And yet, despite his slender pale-skinned body, Falco could sense the great reserves of power held within, like a dangerous animal lurking beneath the milky surface of a calm subterranean pool.

Thrall did not once look at him, but Falco knew that he was being studied and appraised. The sensation made his skin crawl and he found himself moving towards Aurelian.

'I'm not sure the two of you have been properly introduced,' said Aurelian, turning from Thrall to Falco and back again. 'Galen Thrall... Falco Danté. Falco Danté... Galen Thrall, Grand Veneratu and Worshipful Master of the Magi.'

For the first time Thrall's gaze met his and Falco was struck by the unnaturally small size of the pupils in his pale green eyes.

'So,' said Aurelian. 'Do you have the names of the magi against whom this young man will test his strength?'

Falco glanced at Morgan Saker and, from the look of satisfaction in his dark eyes, it was clear that his name was among those chosen by Thrall.

*

In the mage retreat of Solace, Meredith Saker sat on the terrace waiting for the orderlies to see if Brother Verde was feeling well enough for a visitor.

'Some days are better than others,' they had told him.

The retreat was bright and picturesque but the residents left Meredith feeling far from serene. Many were just old and suffering from the diminished capacity of age, but others were clearly disturbed. One white haired old mage seemed particularly intrigued by his arrival and followed him out onto the terrace. The man seemed uncertain as to whether to engage Meredith in conversation and merely hovered nearby muttering half sentences as if he were talking to the wall.

'It's the alkaloids, you see. Very dangerous. Poisons everywhere.'

Meredith gave a sigh of relief as two mages appeared, pushing a withered old man in a wheeled chair.

'Come now, Brother Dinas,' said one of the mages, leading the white haired man away. 'Why don't you show me all the lethal plants we have in the garden.'

The second mage gave Meredith an indulgent smile and he was suddenly struck by their compassion. The towers of the magi were invariably cold austere places and Meredith had often wondered if mages possessed such qualities at all. He found it deeply satisfying to know that at least some of them did. He watched now as the orderly leaned in to speak with the old man in the wheeled chair who sat looking disorientated while running his fingers along an old scar that ran from the corner of his mouth to the base of his ear.

'Brother Verde... this is the man we just spoke of, Lord Saker. He has come to ask you about your writing. But only for a short while,' he added turning to Meredith. 'He gets breathless and easily tired.'

Meredith gave a nod of understanding and adjusted his chair to face the old scholar.

'Thank you for agreeing to speak to me,' he said.

'Writing,' said Brother Verde brightly, 'I used to write books.' His speech was a little marred by the scar that tugged at the side of his mouth.

'That's right,' said Meredith. 'It's one of your books I'd like to ask you about.'

'History!' said Brother Verde. 'It's all there, you know, in history. From the first kings of Thraece to the Treaty of Wrath. Did you know...'

The orderly put a hand on Brother Verde's arm.

'Lord Saker would like to ask you about one book in particular.'

'Oh?' said Brother Verde. 'The Unification of The Tribes, perhaps? The Fall of Protégia? The Viemann Heresy...'

His words fell over each other as he listed the books he had written.

'It's a book called 'The Last Surviving Witness',' said Meredith and Brother Verde looked suddenly lost.

Gone was the enthusiasm for a lifetime of study, instantly replaced by a welling of emotions that played across his face: confusion, sadness, suspicion and fear. Meredith was shocked by the dramatic change and had no wish to cause the old mage distress but he desperately needed some answers.

'The book is supposed to be a firsthand account from someone who witnessed the Great Possession,' he said. 'But that event took place over four hundred years ago.' He paused, trying to catch Brother Verde's eye, but the old mage refused to look at him. Beside them the orderly began to look concerned. 'Is it a story passed down through time?' asked Meredith. 'Could there be a mistake in the records?'

Brother Verde suddenly fixed him with a vehement eye.

'A mistake!' he spat. He raised a quavering hand to the scar on his cheek. 'Is this a mistake?'

'But that would make the witness four hundred years old,' said Meredith trying to get Brother Verde to accept something that was clearly impossible, but the old monk simply held his eye.

'Evil does not die,' he said. 'The witness was a bad man, a powerful man. Even death refused to claim him.'

Meredith found himself backing away as a shadow seemed to fill the room and Brother Verde began to cry.

'Sinner!' he said and Meredith felt the fear oozing like sweat from the old man's pores. 'Sinner...' he sobbed again, his thick knuckled fingers clawing at his cheek. 'Sinner...'

'That's enough,' said the orderly, pulling Brother Verde's chair away from Meredith. 'We don't want a repeat of what happened last year.' He waved the second carer over.

'What happened?'

'He was calm when he first came to us,' said the carer as the second orderly tried to reassure the distressed old man. 'Then one night, just as winter was setting in, he started weeping uncontrollably... He said the sinner had awoken.'

'Nothing else?' asked Meredith.

'No,' said the orderly. 'Just that... The sinner has awoken. Just that and the weeping.'

Meredith looked down at the old mage, the tears streaming down his face. Despite his frailty the orderly was struggling to contain him, but then suddenly the old man became still. His eyes took on a blank and distant expression and suddenly the room was filled with a voice, but it was not the voice of an old man it was a voice of deep and unsettling power.

'*Vino la mine micul meu şoim, Cei fraţii şi toate deliciile lor sunt în aşteptare pentru tine,*' said the voice and with a terrible feeling of dread Meredith realised he had heard this voice before.

'I'm sorry,' said the orderly. 'He has done this before. We believe it is the language of the enemy but no one here can speak it.'

But Meredith had studied the language of Ferocia and he knew what the old man had just said.

'Come to me my little falcon
The brothers and all their delights are waiting for you.'

Meredith closed his eyes as he realised the truth.

'*Sinner*,' the old man had said.

In the language of Ferocia the word for sinner was pacatos.

Brother Pacatos, the mad old mage locked away beneath the mage tower of Wrath *was* the last surviving witness of the Great Possession.

*

Falco stood to one side as Aurelian looked at the names of the mages who would be on the Torquery.

'Of course the mage who helped to train the battle mage should really be here,' said Thrall, his eyes angling back towards Morgan Saker.

'Well he isn't,' said Aurelian. 'So you will have to deal with me.' He glanced down the list. He had heard of most of the names on the list, but there were two that were unfamiliar.

'Brother Daedalus?' he asked. 'I've not heard of him before.'

Ah, yes,' said Thrall. 'He is one of our youngest members.'

'And Brother Pacatos?'

The pupils of Thralls eyes shrank to tiny points of darkness and a smile crept across his face.

'Let's just say that he is one of our oldest.'

74

The Sword of a Battle Mage

Falco's mind was filled with new anxieties as they returned to the workshop the following day. After the meeting with the magi the Rite of Assay now seemed more intimidating than ever. Thrall would not be on the Torquery himself but Morgan Saker was a mage of formidable knowledge and power. The prospect of facing half a dozen mages of similar stature was truly daunting, but Falco tried to push all this to the back of his mind as they entered the gloaming warmth of the forge.

Master Missaglias was alone but there were several large men standing in the adjacent tool room as if *they* were waiting to use the forge. Falco's hopes dipped and the ambiguous expression on Antonio's face did little to raise them. Aurelian too looked more than a little apprehensive as he asked the question once more.

'All right,' he said. 'Enough stalling. Will you make him a sword or not?'

'I will not,' said Antonio and Falco's heart sank.

Aurelian flushed with indignation but Antonio held up a hand and turned to Falco.

'If you had your own fire I would do it without hesitation,' he said. 'But without it I cannot take the chance. I simply don't know you well enough.' He paused. 'But there's a blacksmith here who does.'

Master Missaglias turned to the large men who were now emerging from the tool room. Falco had never seen the first two before but he had known the third man since he was a child. He had the broad shoulders of a blacksmith, and the strong hands of a blacksmith, and a bright red birthmark down the side of his face.

Falco felt his eyes brim with tears.

'As if I don't have enough to do!' said Malaki.

Aurelian muttered a curse while Falco seemed embarrassed by his emotional reaction, but Antonio Missaglias only smiled. The making of a sword *should* be an emotional experience and he remembered a verse his own master had often quoted during his apprenticeship.

Some say oil and some say blood
Some say the temper of the years
But there's no blade stronger
Ever forged by man
Than a sword that's quenched in tears

*

Meredith had not even stopped for food before setting off on the return journey to Le Matres. If he could get back to the city he could use the communication link to send a message, warning Falco not to attempt the Rite of Assay until he returned. He would not reveal the tower's secret, not until he had given Thrall the chance to explain why he had kept Brother Pacatos 'confined' in the Capital's tower, although Meredith had his suspicions.

He was kept secret because he knew the truth of what happened during the Great Possession, and he was confined because he was insane, driven mad by what he had witnessed on that terrible day. And now Meredith was convinced the magi had lied. They *had* known that dragons were susceptible to Possession. They had known this could lead to disaster and yet, in their obsessive lust for power they had said nothing. Their silence had condemned an entire generation of battle mages and scores of magi to death at the claws of dragons driven mad by Possession.

Meredith could only imagine what the people would do if they ever learned the truth. There would be riots and murder and ruin. But for now his thoughts were only for Falco. He must not attempt the Rite with a mage like Brother Pacatos on the Torquery. Meredith was fairly sure his father would not wish for Falco's death, but he could not say the same for Thrall. And so he rode with reckless haste for the city of Le Matres.

*

Falco spent the first day in the forge watching Malaki work on the design with the other craftsmen who would be helping to make his sword. He watched him now as he sat with the master responsible for creating the sword's hilt. Falco smiled as Malaki took the man's pen and made several adjustments to the sketch he had prepared.

'The blade will be shorter and the handle longer,' he said. 'So you can reduce the size of the pommel. Also the quillons need to be curved and the design should be simpler, more subtle. So you don't see it all at once.'

A less confident man might have taken offense but the master simply took back his pen and made several new sketches.

'That's it,' said Malaki, glancing at Falco as if to see how well the design would suit his friend. 'That's perfect.'

Falco was intrigued and eager to see the design but he did not want to intrude. The sword they were making was for him, but the making of it was Malaki's responsibility and he had now been consulted on everything from engraving and polishing to binding and leatherwork. Even the workshop's gold and silversmiths had asked if their services would be required but Malaki had declined. There would be no exotic inlays on the sword of Falco Danté. Indeed most of the master craftsmen had left the forge with modest demands upon their skill. Balance and strength were the two things that Malaki was most concerned with.

And so, even on the first day, a great deal of progress was made. Working alone it could take a master swordsmith several months to finish a complex piece but Antonio had placed the resources of his entire workshop at Malaki's disposal and he assured Falco that, if everything went well, his sword would be ready in little more than a week.

Falco and Aurelian would remain in the workshop with Malaki until the forging of the sword was finished. Antonio had cleared a space and made up three cots where they could sleep. It was noisy and smelly but it allowed them to share in the experience.

The following day they had begun in earnest and Falco watched the sledgehammers fall in a rhythmic cycle of blows as the two large smiths laboured

404

to draw out the blade. Standing before them, and guiding the lengthening block of steel, was Malaki, back bent and hands clenched around the rod which had been welded to the specially prepared billet.

Master Missaglias had insisted that Malaki choose the block of steel from which the sword would be forged.

'It all begins with the steel,' he said. 'This is where we start to match the character of the blade to the character of the man.'

'Will we be folding it?' asked Malaki, referring to the technique where the metal was hammered out and folded to produce thousands of layers within the finished blade. Such a technique was said to produce a weapon of exceptional strength but the master had shaken his head.

'Folding helps to even-out the flaws in poor quality steel. It does nothing to increase the strength.'

'So which would I choose?'

'That's up to you,' said Antonio laying the heavy billets out on the bench, each of which was stamped with the master's mark of quality. 'This is the hardest but also quite difficult to work. While this has the greatest flexibility but won't take an edge quite so well. They are all of equal quality and most of it comes down to the final treatment. It all depends on what you are looking for in a blade.'

'What about this one?' asked Malaki and Antonio raised an eyebrow.

'That combines the best qualities of all the rest. But it's also a capricious bastard. If you get it wrong it will explode in your face and even at the end it can shatter in the final quenching. But if you get it right...'

Malaki paused in thought. He had made a number of swords back in his father's forge, but that was the problem. He knew enough to know just how little he knew.

'If you could guide me...'

'But of course,' replied the master.

So now Falco watched as the glowing rectangular billet grew longer and thinner under the relentless pounding of heavy hammers. Falco had been surprised when they used the forge to heat the metal.

'I thought *you* were going to supply the heat,' he said, turning to Aurelian who was sitting beside him.

'That comes later,' said Aurelian. 'For now the heat of the forge is more than sufficient.'

It took all day to draw out the blade and by the end of it Falco's ears were ringing from the noise and Malaki was exhausted, his back aching and his hands numb from gripping the steel.

The following day the heavy hammers were not required and Malaki spent the time slowly shaping the emerging blade. The day was warm and Falco watched the sweat dripping from his face but Malaki stopped only to eat and drink, constantly examining the blade for line and thickness. Antonio was never far away and Malaki would often seek his opinion.

'Cherry red for normal steel...' he said as the rough blade rested in the forge. 'But for this alloy you need to go a shade or two hotter... There!' he said. 'You see that flush? That will normalise the steel and release any stresses that might be building up.'

Malaki allowed the blade to cool in the air before heating it again and continuing to shape it with the hammer. By the end of the day he was happy with the shape. He had now drawn in the shoulder, extended the tang and shaped the point. As the late spring sky began to darken he coated the blade in a special clay before bringing it back up to a heat that would allow the elements in the steel to properly combine.

'What's the clay for?' asked Falco as they stared into the scalding heat of the forge.

'The Beltonians call it onæling,' said Malaki. 'It stops the blade from cooling down too quickly. This way the metal will be soft enough to grind into the final shape.'

'I thought a sword was supposed to be hard.'

'It will be,' said Malaki, laughing at Falco's ignorance. 'But that comes in the final heating. For now we need to be able to file it down and make sure the balance is right.'

'Do you two washer-women plan on sleeping at all tonight?' came Aurelian's bad tempered voice.

Malaki and Falco exchanged an amused look.

'He's right,' said Malaki. 'There's nothing more to be done for now. It'll need the best part of a day to cool.'

So Falco lay down to sleep, listening to the faint ticks and pops as the encased blade slowly gave up its heat.

*

It was dark when Meredith arrived in Le Matres but he wasted no time in heading straight for the mage tower. However, when he got there he was dismayed to find that the communication link with Wrath was no longer in place.

'What do you mean it was broken?' he said, his temper frayed by tension and fatigue.

'A stomach upset, I believe,' said the tower's veneratu. 'The mage in contact with Wrath had tried to maintain the link but he succumbed to a bout of vomiting and the connection was lost. I am sorry,' he said although Meredith failed to detect any real sincerity in his tone. The master of the Le Matres tower had never shown any enthusiasm for his idea, but Meredith was determined to get a message through to Wrath.

'No matter,' he snapped. 'Summon a quintet to the chamber of discourse. I need to send a message to the capital about a forthcoming Rite of Assay.'

'Forgive me, young master,' said the veneratu. 'But I cannot assemble a quintet tonight. Indeed, not for several days.'

Meredith stared at the man, trying to determine if he was being deliberately obstructive.

'All the magi trained for such a task were called to Hoffen. To help convey orders down the newly established front. They should be back within the week.'

'*A week!*' thought Meredith. He could be back in Wrath himself in a week. By which time Falco might have already attempted the Rite of Assay.

406

Taking a breath he tried to clear his thoughts... It was too late to set out tonight but the sun would be rising early and if he pushed hard and changed horses at the staging posts he could certainly do it in a week. Bidding the veneratu a terse goodnight he went in search of a bath and a bed. He was already weary and aching but tomorrow, at first light, he would set out again.

*

The veneratu of the Le Matres mage tower waited until Meredith was gone before descending to a secret chamber at the base of the tower, a chamber that was now guarded by two mages with orders to deny any but those authorised to enter. They stood aside as the veneratu approached. He entered quietly so as not to disturb the mage who was currently in contact with Wrath.

'I have a message for Grand Veneratu Thrall,' he said.

The mage closed his eyes as he conveyed the message then opened them before speaking.

'A moment,' he said. 'Lord Thrall would hear this message for himself.'

There followed several minutes during which the veneratu shifted uneasily. He was already uncomfortable using this new form of communication and now he would be using it to address the Worshipful Master of the Clemoncéan magi. But the orders had been unambiguous.

The apprentice mage Saker must not know of the link's continuing existence.

His movements, thoughts and intentions must be conveyed to Wrath without delay.

Suddenly the mage in the centre of the chamber spoke and there was no mistaking the authority in his voice.

'You have word of Saker?'

'Yes, my Lord,' said the veneratu, trying to accommodate the pause in conversation as his words were conveyed across so many miles. 'He has returned from his venture and wishes to send a message to the capital.'

'Do you know what he learned in Solace?'

'No, my Lord. But he said something about a forthcoming Rite of Assay. I believe he intends to prevent it. He is setting out for the capital at first light.'

There was a longer than normal pause and the veneratu wondered if Thrall was still present but then the mage before him spoke again.

'You have done well. You will inform us when Saker is on his way.'

'Yes, my Lord,' said the Veneratu and with that the conversation was over.

*

In the mage tower of Wrath, Thrall turned to Morgan Saker.

'I see your son has inherited his father's persistence.'

'He has been influenced by the undisciplined minds of common folk,' said Saker. 'This would not have happened if I had been able to complete his training in the mage tower of Caer Dour.'

Thrall gave a transparent smile at Saker's excuses.

'It matters not,' he said. 'He believes the link is broken and will need to ride back to the capital. We must therefore make sure the Rite takes place before his return.'

'Do you know what he might have learned in Solace?' asked Saker.

407

'No,' said Thrall. 'But I suspect it is something to do with the Great Possession and we all know the events of that time must never be made public.'

Morgan Saker nodded but there was a disquiet in his eyes that was not present in Thrall's. Despite their collusion in keeping the secret, most magi bore some degree of shame for what happened on that terrible day. Regardless of his hard and ruthless heart, Morgan Saker certainly did while Thrall, it seemed, did not. He wore a cold smile as if Saker's doubts were a weakness he did not share.

They had done what they needed to do.

The magi would always do what they needed to do.

*

It would take all day for the blade to cool and the onæling process to be complete. So while Malaki went to supervise the other elements of the sword Falco and Aurelian walked up to the Crucible to get in some training.

Aurelian was amazed by the way that Falco had grown. His defences had always been good but now his control was confident and assured. He was also more serious, more focussed, as if he finally understood just how important it was for him to succeed, whether he had fire of his own or not.

They had just finished an intensive session and Nicolas was spitting grit from his mouth after Falco had sent him sprawling in the dirt but Aurelian just laughed.

'You know what, old friend,' he said, patting his fellow Crofter on the back. 'By Thrall's withered plums, I think he might do it!'

Laying down his training sword and shield Falco smiled at Aurelian's irreverent compliment, but it was time for them to go. Taking their leave of Nicolas and Dwim they made their way back down to the forge. It was now late afternoon and Malaki was just about to break the blade out of the clay. A few taps on the anvil revealed a slender piece of black metal. It was still warm but not too hot to handle and Malaki wasted no time in taking it through to another part or the workshop filled with numerous files, whetstones and grinding wheels.

Under the watchful eye of Antonio, he then began the final shaping of the blade.

'Slow and steady,' said the master. 'It's a lot easier to take it off than it is to put it back on.'

Malaki remembered his father saying much the same thing but the grinding wheels made the laborious task far quicker than filing it all by hand. Even so, his right leg soon felt numb and shaky from working the treadle that drove the spinning disks of stone. The noise was relentless and the air was filled with the taste and smell of hot metal and cooling oil, but slowly the black surface was ground away to reveal the bright face of the steel beneath.

As the shaping continued Malaki moved to more specialised stones for grinding the bevels and cutting in the fuller, a broad groove running down the length of the blade. The fuller was designed to reduce weight without compromising strength. It was *not* to 'let the blood out' or to prevent the blade being 'trapped' in the body of an enemy, as some people continued to believe.

It took two days to finish the shaping, during which time Bryna and the rest of the cadets arrived back in Wrath. Having learned what was going on, Bryna immediately went to see Malaki in the workshops, although her reaction was not perhaps as warm as he might have hoped.

'Ugh! You're filthy!' she said as Malaki gathered her into his arms and silenced her with a kiss. 'And you stink too!' she added as she emerged from his embrace.

Malaki smiled and tried to wipe a smudge of oily dust from her cheek but his hands were equally dirty and he only succeeded in making it worse.

'Enough!' said Bryna, pushing him away. 'I'll see you in a few days. When you've had a bath!' she gave him a disapproving glare, but her eyes were shining and her cheeks were flushed. 'Master Missaglias,' she said by way of introduction as she turned to go.

'My lady,' said Antonio with a bow and they watched as she left the forge, the curls in her auburn hair bouncing as she went. 'Never known a smith with a wife like *that*!' said Antonio with a meaningful smile.

'They should count themselves lucky,' said Malaki and Antonio laughed although it was patently clear that he adored her.

And with that they returned to their work. The shaping was painstaking and slow, and Malaki did the final stages by hand but finally it was done and Antonio leaned over to inspect his work.

'I think you're just about there,' said the master with a smile of amusement on his scarred face. The work might not be up to the normal standard of his workshop but he was confident Malaki's father would not be turning in his grave.

'I think it needs a little more off the tip,' said Malaki but Antonio just laughed and clapped him on the back.

'Have courage,' he said. 'You cannot put it off forever.'

Malaki gave a sigh and ran a rag down the blade to wipe away the final layer of dust.

'You've done a good job,' said the master. 'Now it's time to have some faith.'

Malaki gave a nod and Falco looked up as Dusaule entered the workshop. For now the work of normal smithing was done. It was time to temper the blade in the forge of a battle mage's fire.

Antonio led them back to the forge where a kind of bench had now been set up in the centre of the room. Mounted on two great anvils the bench was covered in a large black-and-white cow skin. Antonio drew back the skin to reveal a slab of smooth dark stone, five feet long and about a foot wide, the surface shining like mirrored smoke.

'Fortissite,' he said. 'The only thing that magical force can't damage.'

Falco reached out to touch it and despite its dark glassy surface it actually felt warm.

Beside the forge three large ceramic tubes had been set upright in a wooden frame. Each was filled with a different liquid and Antonio explained their uses to Malaki who was still holding the newly shaped blade.

'Acid to remove any grease or impurities... Water to remove the acid... And oil for the final quenching.'

Pointing to the last tube his expression took on a more meaningful look. After all Malaki's hard work this was the stage when it could all go wrong. Even

409

if it survived Aurelian's chaotic fire the blade could still shatter when it was finally quenched in oil.

Using a pair of tongs Malaki picked up the blade by the tang and lowered it into the bath of acid, just a quick dip to burn off any impurities without harming the metal. Next he transferred it to the water and let it drip dry before laying it down the centre of the fortissite slab.

Now Antonio leaned in close.

'The blade will be heated beyond the limit of any forge,' he said as he explained this final part in the process. 'At this heat the metal would normally disintegrate, but there's something about the energy that holds it together. Aurelian will heat the blade until Falco feels it is enough.'

'How will I know?' asked Falco.

'The metal will start to sing,' said Aurelian. 'Somewhere deep inside of you it will resonate. When you recognise the note, you will know. That's if I can control the heat,' he added with a less than certain grimace.

Antonio turned to Malaki and for the first time there was genuine tension in his voice.

'The fortissite will absorb the heat,' he said. 'Much quicker than you might imagine. After only a few minutes the blade will return to normal forge heat and then you must be ready. You know the colours of a differential temper... bruise blue down the centre, sun-kissed wheat along the edge. The moment you see it you must act. But have a care. You will only get one chance.'

'And what if I've made a mistake with the sword?' asked Malaki.

'If the sword doesn't match the man then it will either explode or shatter in the oil,' said Antonio. 'But you made it with Falco in mind, did you not?'

Malaki nodded.

'Then I guess we'll find out just how well you know your friend.'

Malaki's jaw set with resolution and Antonio gave him a smile. This then was the responsibility of those who would forge a battle mage's sword.

Antonio turned to Aurelian and the one armed battle mage came forward with Dusaule at his side. Feeling dizzy with nerves Falco stood too. Malaki moved to the head of the fortissite, a large pair of metal tongs held ready in his hand. Antonio stood at his shoulder while, just outside the room, several of the workshop's master craftsmen looked on. The forging of a battle mage's sword was a rare and special event. It offered them a further glimpse into the endless mysteries of steel, mysteries that normal men could never hope to understand.

*

Outside the forge, in the pale shadows of an early summer's night, stood a mage who was trained to hear the song of a magically heated sword. He was there to report on the outcome of the forging and Grand Veneratu Thrall was keen for it to be a success. He was insistent that the Rite should go ahead without delay. And so the magi waited for the sword to be completed, at which point they would take possession of the blade and remove it to L'obscurité where it would be placed at the centre of the labyrinth as a goal to aim for, a prize to be won, a statement that the magi held the power for which the battle mages strove.

*

Falco watched as the metal began to glow, a dull red that grew deeper and brighter until it became orange then yellow. Glancing to one side he saw the effort and concentration on Aurelian's face as he tried to maintain a steadily increasing level of heat. This was very different to the explosive conjuration of a fireball. This required control and restraint, two qualities for which Aurelian was not renowned. But he was doing his best and beside him Nicolas Dusaule was concentrating too. Together they channelled their power into the blade and from yellow the steel rose to white. And still they drove it hotter.

Eyes half shut against the brightness Falco returned his focus to the blade. Aurelian had spoken of the metal beginning to sing and now he could almost hear it... a sound, like the ring of steel but continuous and faint as if it were coming from some great distance deep within the blade. The sound grew louder until it really was like a musical note, a high ringing note that was strangely beautiful, beautiful and yet not quite right.

'Hotter,' said Falco and he felt Aurelian redouble his efforts to raise the heat higher. He became aware of people watching him, waiting for him to say, 'yes, that's it.' He was still not sure exactly what Aurelian meant about him 'recognising' the note but some instinct told him they still had some way to go.

Standing at the end of the fortissite table Malaki was shielding his eyes from the intense heat of the blade, his face dripping with sweat.

'More,' said Falco and from the corner of his eye he saw Aurelian shoot him an anxious glance as he struggled to sustain the flow of energy.

'Nicolas!' he gasped.

Nicolas Dusaule had made a vow never again to use his powers for destructive violence and for a moment he frowned in indecision, but perhaps this was something he could do and so, even as he tried to smooth out the fluctuations in Aurelian's fitful power, so he added his own. And the blade brightened to a blinding, incandescent white.

'More,' said Falco as the note within the steel rose until it was more akin to a scream.

'Falco!' said Antonio and the master was actually backing away from the blade but Malaki held his ground.

'It... will not... take much more,' gasped Aurelian through clenched teeth.

'Higher,' said Falco and now all his thoughts were on the sword.

The note began to remind him of something, but still it was not quite right.

'Higher,' he breathed and the note rose to an impossible pitch before suddenly, it disappeared. It had gone beyond the point of hearing and become a kind of silence, a silence filled with loss and grief and guilt and fear. But also something more. For somewhere, in this place of endless space, the silence echoed with faith and hope and love.

In all creation there are but three things that contain a soul
A human, a dragon, and the sword of a battle mage

'There...' breathed Falco and Aurelian sank to his knees. Malaki and Antonio were shielding their eyes from the scalding light but slowly it began to fade. The black fortissite had taken on a ruddy glow and the colour of the blade receded from silver white to searing yellow. Antonio stepped to one side and Malaki brought up his tongs, edging forward ready to grasp the cooling blade.

The point and the edges cooled most quickly, while the thicker steel down the centre of the blade was slower to give up its heat, but slowly the colour faded until the centre was a bluish shade of purple, while the tip and edges shone with a faint golden hue.

Bruise blue and sun-kissed wheat.

Without hesitation Malaki grasped the tang of the blade, lifted it high and plunged it into the oil-filled quenching bath. The liquid bubbled and flames leapt up but Malaki did not waver as he moved the blade slowly in the cooling oil. He had no way of knowing how long to leave it or whether, even now, the stresses would be too great and the blade would shatter, but Malaki had grown up in a forge and somehow the instincts of the father had been passed down to the son.

Just a few seconds more and he drew it forth, black with scale and dripping dark oil, he laid it down on the warm edge of the forge. It was not pretty but it was straight and true and had survived a baptism of fire that would have destroyed any normal blade.

But this was not any normal blade.

It was the sword of a battle mage and its forging was complete.

*

On hearing the news Galen Thrall wasted no time in arranging the Rite. At daybreak the following morning a messenger arrived from the tower.

'Two days!' cried Aurelian. 'He's having a laugh!'

But the messenger from the tower insisted that Grand Veneratu Thrall was *not* joking and the Rite would take place at sunset in two days' time. Aurelian was clearly furious but Falco just turned to Malaki.

'Can you do it? Can you finish the sword in two days?'

Malaki looked uncertain but Antonio pursed his lips.

'It might not be the most perfect job. And we might not get much sleep. But yes, we can do it.'

And so began the final grinding, polishing and sharpening of Falco's sword, and with only two days left to prepare Falco and Aurelian left the workshop to spend their time in the Crucible.

Meanwhile, at a wayside inn not three days from Wrath, Meredith Saker ate an early breakfast before climbing back into the saddle for another day of punishing travel. Still concerned that he might arrive too late he did a quick mental calculation. Falco would have returned to the capital shortly before he had arrived in Solace, which was now almost two weeks ago. Knowing Falco, he would have immediately insisted that they prepare for the Rite, which meant forging a sword. Meredith was not sure if it was even possible to make a battle mage's sword in two weeks.

Surely not. But even so, he would not linger or slacken his pace. He could not take the chance of Falco attempting the Rite with a mage like Brother Pacatos on the Torquery.

Two days later and Falco had just finished a last minute training session. It was the afternoon of the Rite and Aurelian had been focussing not so much on his protection or fighting skills but on the dangers that lay within.

'The greatest threat will come from your own doubts and fears,' said Aurelian. 'Down there, in the darkness such things are magnified and laid bare.'

Staring at the dark archway at the far end of the Crucible Falco could well believe it, but they had done everything they could for now. They were just gathering up their things when an apprentice from the workshop appeared to inform them that the sword was finished.

'What's the matter?' said Aurelian when the apprentice hovered, looking uncomfortable.

'It's the magi,' he said. 'They have already taken the sword.'

Falco frowned but Aurelian just shook his head.

'Bloody Thrall!' he said. 'He doesn't want you touching the sword before the Rite.'

'Why not?'

'I suspect it's because he thinks it might unlock your powers.'

'And could it?'

'It might or it might not,' said Aurelian. 'But either way your sword now lies at the heart of the Labyrinth and the only way to reach it is to overcome the obstacles that the magi have placed in your path.'

75

The Rite of Assay

Assay: from the Clemoncéan *assaier* meaning 'to test'

It was sunset and the Crucible was filled with a pale dusky light. The clear blue sky was darkening but the moon was now rising above the mountains.

'That's good,' said Aurelian, handing Falco his barbute helm. 'Always better if there's some light when you emerge.'

Falco could hear the anxiety in his voice, the effort to remain positive, but he was not really listening. His mind was focussed on the dark archway at the end of the arena.

Dressed in the armour of Antonio Missaglias Falco looked lithe and formidable, the dark metal shimmering with the arcane patterns etched into its surface. He put on his helm and took up his shield which was now embossed with the subtle design of a dragon, the insignia of Valentia. Antonio had also given him a sword. It was a sword of good quality but it was not *his* sword, not the sword of a battle mage. Even so, Falco was glad to have it. He loosened it in the scabbard then stiffened as he sensed the approaching magi. He looked up just as Thrall and two other magi appeared over the lip of the Crucible.

'About time!' muttered Aurelian as they made their way down into the arena.

Flanked by two senior mages, Thrall appeared calm and assured as they took their places on the lower steps. Aurelian gave them a curt nod of acknowledgement and Thrall inclined his head, a faint smile on his narrow lips. The smile made Aurelian nervous and he looked to the other side of the arena, where Dusaule and Dwimervane sat like spectators at some poorly attended games. Everything was now in place and the mage sitting to Thrall's right rose to his feet.

'Let the aspirant step forward,' he called out in a voice that echoed around the arena.

Falco looked up at Aurelian who gave him a grim nod of reassurance.

'We'll be here when you come out.'

Without a word Falco dipped his head and walked to the centre of the arena where the magi spokesman looked down at him with cold dispassion.

'Falco Danté,' he began. 'We are here tonight to complete your training as a battle mage, to see if you have the strength to protect the armies of Wrath from all the burning might of the enemy. Pain, guilt, anguish and fear, these are the weapons with which the enemy will try to strike you down. And so it is with these that you shall be tested. If you succeed then we will know that we can place our trust in you, that you are worthy of the title, *battle mage*.

'Do you accept this challenge?'

Falco stared up through the T-shaped visor of his helm.

'I do.'

'And do you attempt the Rite of Assay by your own free will?'

'I do.'

'Then may the light have mercy on your soul.'

The spokesman waited for some acknowledgment, but Falco did not bow or salute them. Instead he only stared. The spokesman bridled with indignation but Thrall's smile only broadened. He wondered if the young pretender would be so bold when he was dragged weeping and broken from the labyrinth.

Cedo

Falco heard the word as if Thrall had spoken directly into his mind, but he had no intention of conceding, no intention of even thinking the word. With a mental swipe he cast out the word and the smile dropped from Thrall's face. Then, in a further gesture of defiance he drew his sword before turning away, his heart quickening as he walked towards the gaping archway at the end of the Crucible. For a moment he paused before the bare unguarded threshold then he stepped forward into the place they called L'obscurité.

The darkness engulfed Falco like a close pressing fog, but slowly the blackness receded as the way was lit by a series of irregular crystal plaques, fixed at intervals to the walls with black iron spikes. The plaques gave off a pale green light and he could now see that he was in a passageway formed from close fitting blocks of stone. It was dim and thick with shadows but he was glad of even the meanest light.

Outside the fear had been unsettling, now it was almost overwhelming and Falco felt a powerful urge to step back into the Crucible or even just to turn around, to prove to himself that the entrance was still there behind him. But the magi's spokesman had been right. He had chosen this path. He would not turn away at the first hint of horror.

Shield raised and sword at the ready he walked forward, fifty feet... a hundred. The sound of his breathing echoed off the walls as did the wary tread of his boots against the gritty flagstones of the floor. The air was cold and damp and filled with the musty smell of a tomb. He had only been in a matter of minutes but he could already feel the haunted miasma of this place closing around his mind, the foul demonic whispers and the sense that he was not alone, that there was something there, hovering behind him or lurking just beyond the edge of his vision.

At first it was just fleeting sounds, some of which seemed to emanate from a distance while others sounded so close that he flinched from the sudden proximity. But as he moved deeper the whispers became more distinct, speaking in a language he did not understand. The words were alien but the malice behind them was not. Falco tried to ignore them. He told himself they could not harm him but he knew in his heart that they could.

He passed openings and alcoves filled with shadow and at each one he expected something hideous to come screaming out. These empty voids began to play on his mind, as did the patches of darkness that lay between the widely spaced plaques. Had he fire, he could have illuminated the darkness and eased his fears, but without it he could only steel his mind and press on. A little further and he reached a junction, the passage heading to left and right. He needed to choose which way to go but both ways faded quickly into blackness. There was no way to differentiate one way from the other. But for some reason Falco found

415

himself being drawn to the passage on his right. He had no way to be certain, only the vaguest sense that it was this way that led to his sword.

He started forward and for the first time he felt the opposing presence of the magi. It was as if the labyrinth suddenly saw him, as if the whispers knew the darkest secrets of his heart. The sensation made him feel vulnerable and exposed but this was only the start of their opposition and so Falco clenched his jaw and continued.

Guided by nothing more than the vaguest sense of intuition he wound his way through the labyrinth while the whispers grew louder and more insistent. He began to glance back as if he could hear something following him. He tried to tell himself that it was all in his imagination, but as he proceeded down a long passageway he stopped.

Slowly he turned around. There was something in the passageway behind him. The whispers receded as if they too were awed by its presence. It was there, in the dark space between one green crystal and the next. Straining his eyes for any hint of what it might be Falco readied his sword and shield then tensed as a screaming shape loomed towards him. It grew larger and louder until the noise filled the entire passage and then it stalled, becoming silent and still the moment before it reached him.

Heart pounding Falco leaned back from the disturbing presence, the light too dim to make out anything more than an unsettling and indistinct shadow. He started as he felt something brush against his cheek. The touch was light, almost negligible and he wondered how it could reach him through the metal of his helm. Shocked at how terrifying such an innocuous touch could be he began to back away but then the presence let out a low sound, half human, half demonic growl. The light from the crystal plaques suddenly dimmed, subdued by a smothering cloak of evil.

In near total darkness Falco felt something sharp snag in the soft skin of his neck. It pierced his flesh and began to tear. With a cry he reared back and swung his sword but the blade met with nothing until it struck the stones of the tunnel wall. A flash of sparks illuminated a terrifying hooded figure and Falco stumbled back in fear. But the hooded wraith followed and he gasped as he felt two sharp points beneath his left arm and a hot stabbing pain in the crease of his groin. He gasped as the invisible claws gouged deep into his flesh then cried out as they tore free.

In desperation he swung both sword and shield but all to no effect. Something began to claw at his throat and Falco started run. He stumbled blindly down sparse-lit ways, pursued by an angry spirit that cared nothing for armour, sword or strength. Falco had no way of fighting it, no way to banish it with light or fire. Instead he could only flee.

Outside in the Crucible Thrall's smile had returned. He did not know the details of what was taking place but he could sense the first cracks in the pretender's resolve. Cracks that could now be exploited and driven wider until his mind shattered like a frost-riven rock.

Across the arena Aurelian was gripped by concern. He could see the satisfaction on Thrall's face. He knew of Falco's acrimonious history with

416

Morgan Saker, but he could not understand Thrall's vindictive determination to see him fail. The magi always went to great lengths to test a battle mage, but he had never known it to become so personal. All he could think was that the magi had some way of knowing that Falco would turn against them, just as his father had done before him. Aurelian did not believe that this would be the case, but he could not rule out such a possibility. After all, if it could happen to Aquila Danté it could happen to anyone.

But whatever lay in the future one thing was certain. Down there in the labyrinth Falco was now beset.

Falco had lost all sense of time and space. He was trapped in a world of nightmare where he could no longer distinguish what was real from what was not. He had fled the sadistic wraith until he emerged into a chamber lit once more with a ghostly light from the green crystal plaques on the wall. In the centre of the room was a figure clad in steel and armed with sword and shield, it stood like a sentinel barring his way. But the figure was not human. Its body was formed from smoke, swirling beneath a skin of shimmering blue energy.

It was an animaré, a conjuration of the magi, real armour brought to life upon an effigy of magical force. It radiated a sense of power and Falco realised that this was no clumsy marionette. The magi controlling it knew how to fight, but he had spent the last seven months training with the likes of Malaki and Quirren. He had fought the black armoured Kardakae and the twin bladed Slayer. He had become the warrior his early years had promised, something no mage could ever hope to match.

Casting a fearful glance back towards the archway, Falco tried to calm his breathing as he moved into the room and dropped into a fighting stance. Here, at least, was an enemy he knew how to fight. Poised and balanced, he was ready for the attack but even so the speed of it took him by surprise. The animaré was fast and it fought with a precision he had never encountered before, but it was also predictable and slowly Falco began to take the upper hand. He blocked a well-timed cut and parried a series of perfectly executed thrusts before launching a counter attack of his own. He forced an opening and was about to deliver a killing strike when the animaré suddenly turned into Alex. Falco almost sprained his wrist as he fought to pull his stroke.

How could Alex suddenly be here and why had he wanted to kill him?

Guilt and confusion suddenly clouded Falco's mind, made him question why he was fighting. The hesitation cost him dearly and he reeled from an attack that glanced off his helm as the face of the animaré returned to a featureless mask of shimmering energy. The fight continued and Falco regained his composure, but each time he was about to deliver a decisive blow the animaré would transform into a person he knew: Malaki, Bryna, Dusaule. The illusions were utterly convincing and any normal person would have been undone by confusion and guilt. But a battle mage is used to the lies of the enemy and they are subtler and crueller than anything the magi could devise. For all its perfection Falco began to recognise the magi's deception for what it was.

Despite this, it still took all his determination to deal the fatal blow and he felt a terrible stab of remorse as his sword bit down into the sun weathered neck of the emissary. A part of him knew it was not real but the dreamlike sense of guilt refused to fade - one more burden for him to carry through the soul sapping darkness of the labyrinth.

At the far end of the room another archway beckoned and Falco forced himself to walk through it, on into the haunted pathways where unseen nightmares were waiting to tear at his sanity. The next time he emerged he was stumbling with fear and the searing pain of countless illusory wounds. He staggered from the labyrinth into a room that glowed with the flickering light of fire. Trembling with the strain he struggled to clear the latest flood of horrific images from his mind as he tried to take in his surroundings.

The room was maybe fifty feet long and twenty wide. Flames rose up from the bare flagstones, covering the floor like some infernal maze. Falco thought he could see a way through, but as he moved into the room the flames flared as if they were reacting to his presence, as if somehow they knew him. He suddenly remembered something Meredith had said?

'If my father is on the Torquery he will try to stop you with fire.'

Falco had no doubt that the next mind to stand in his way was that of Morgan Saker.

Sheathing his sword he started forward, weaving his way between the flames as he focussed on reaching the archway at the far end of the room, but the heat soon became unbearable and he was forced to summon a protective wall around his body. There were no longer any gaps between the flames and he found himself pushing through walls of fire. Beneath his armour he was dripping with sweat and the hot air scalded his throat and lungs. His defence was strong and he knew that he could make it, but then he noticed a smell on the searing air. It was the smell of burning pinewood and Falco was instantly transported back to the last time he had smelled that acrid scent.

He was a boy of about five years old and standing in the burning ruins of his home. His eyes and throat stung from the smoke but he was too numbed by grief to care. They had told him his father was dead. He did not want to believe them but a part of him knew that it was true. Racing home he found their villa in flames. He charged inside but the house was empty and in the blazing inferno the young Falco realised he was now totally alone.

Of all the things that could happen in his life this was surely the worst, to lose the strong embrace of the man he loved. The man who took him to ride on dragons and taught him how to hold a sword. The man who laughed with him and chastised him and told him stories of a woman he had never met, a woman who had lived just long enough to hold her son. Even in death the woman loved him, or so the man had told him. But now the man was gone. His father was dead. And who now could make him believe that *she* had ever been real?

Falco let out a cry of anguish as the flames of grief curled around his heart. Fire now filled the room and the tears on his cheeks evaporated almost as soon as they were shed.

But no.

He was no longer that little boy trapped in a burning building. He had survived that grief and lived with that grief. He would not let it destroy him now, but the flames felt like a physical barrier and Falco realised he was pushing

418

against the current of Morgan Saker's mind. The mage's will was as strong as ever and Falco was not sure he could overcome it, but he raised his shield and forced himself on until Morgan Saker struck him with yet more memories bound together by a twisted thread of fire.

Darius burning as he pushed forward to kill the dragon.

Darius burning as he and the dragon fell to their deaths.

The smell of a forge's fire and the tragic death of Malaki's father.

Simeon kneeling before the flames of Baëlfire, another soul that he had failed to save.

Falco fell to his knees and the flames reached for him anew. His leather trousers started to smoulder and the skin on his face blistered as his resolve began to crumble in the face of all his guilt.

'*Cedo...*'

The voice of Morgan Saker came to him through the conflagration.

'*Simply concede and it will all be over.*'

Morgan Saker had been utterly ruthless in his preparations, certain that no human being could endure the trial he had prepared, especially one he knew as well as Falco. But he had erred in one crucial detail. You cannot defeat a battle mage by reminding him of the things he loves. You can torment him and cause him pain, but the memory of such things will only make him stronger.

Gathering his strength Falco climbed to his feet and stared into the fire that surrounded him. He drew a breath and the flames seemed to suck in around him, but then he closed his eyes and let the tingling sensation of power surge through his body. Like a dying star it shrank to his core before rebounding back in a shockwave of energy. The flames were suddenly extinguished and in a nearby chamber Morgan Saker sank to his knees as the sum of all his power was snuffed out by a boy he had always thought of as weak.

As the tingling sensation dissipated Falco opened his eyes. It took a moment for him to remember where he was and another for his eyes to adjust to the dim green light of the crystals on the walls. His scalded skin felt raw and his entire body shook from the trauma of the flames. The aftershocks of grief reverberated through his mind but he had no time for sadness and regret. Every minute he spent in this hellish place he grew weaker and so he drove himself on, back into the unforgiving tunnels of the labyrinth where all the horrors from his childhood dreams were waiting for him.

There were the demons, and the shades, and the vile sadistic children with their misshapen faces and glazed white eyes. There were the crawling things and the gnawing things and the worms that bored beneath his skin, and finally the mad old woman with the slime-black hair and the insane glint in the empty sockets of her eyes. They came to feast on his beleaguered soul and Falco was powerless to stop them. The fire of a battle mage could have dispelled them, but Falco had no such powers, and so he could only stagger on as they tore at him with teeth and claws and scything blades that filled his body with mind numbing pain.

Saturated with fear and delirious with fatigue, Falco was nearing the end of his strength. Stumbling in the darkness he lost his footing and dropped his sword. The straps of his shield twisted around his arm as he scrambled backwards, unable to get to his feet as the mad old woman loomed out of the darkness. She did not walk, but crawled, on swollen knees and arthritic knuckles, she crawled, coming on with unnatural speed.

In mindless panic Falco backed away, shuffling awkwardly as the terrifying figure advanced, her skeletal nose gathered in a snarl like the corpse of an unrepentant witch. Just a few more feet and she would be on him. Just a few more feet and those black decaying teeth would sink into his neck while she clawed at his face with nails that would break off in his flesh like foul rotting splinters.

Fuelled by desperation Falco fled, but still she closed him down, scrabbling and clawing to reach him. Knowing he could no longer escape Falco had no choice but to concede, but even as the word began to form in his mind, he emerged into the open space of yet another room. Back in the passageway the apparitions of torment hovered in the darkness and even the whispers faded to the edge of hearing. Falco felt suddenly frightened to turn around. What could possibly be so terrible as to give such horrors pause? Finally he found the courage and when at last he turned he almost wept with relief.

He had entered a circular chamber, the walls of which curved away into darkness and there, lying in a pool of pale light at the centre of the room, was his sword, the sword his friend had made for him, the sword that sang in silence, the sword that had burned forever in his soul.

*

The moon was riding high when Meredith finally arrived at the mage tower of Wrath. Despite his weariness he climbed the steps and made his way directly to Thrall's personal chambers only to find the door closed. Raising his hand he began to bang on the dark polished wood.

'What's going on here?' asked a passing mage, shocked to see an apprentice pounding on the Master's door.

'I need to speak with the Grand Veneratu.'

'He is not here,' said the mage. 'The Worshipful Master is attending the Rite of Assay in the Crucible.'

Meredith knew it. 'The magi on the Torquery,' he snapped, advancing on the mage. 'Who are they?'

'It is not my place to know such things!' said the mage backing away.

With a gasp of irritation Meredith turned to leave the tower then checked himself. There was a quicker way to learn what he needed to know. Leaving the senior mage gaping at his disrespect he hurried down to the cells of contemplation where he had first encountered brother Pacatos.

Emerging from the winding stairwell Meredith saw no sign of the wardens who watched over the troubled mage. Hurrying down the long corridor he was filled with a terrible sense of foreboding. He half expected to hear that dreadful voice filling the air around him, but there was only silence. Even before he reached the endmost cell Meredith knew it would be empty. Brother Pacatos was gone and with a cold feeling of dread Meredith knew precisely where he would be.

*

420

Falco had never seen the finished sword but he recognised it instantly. A beautifully proportioned Valentian bastard sword with a handle designed for one hand or two. The blade was too short for a fencing match but ideal for those who fought with sword and shield, the weight and taper perfectly matched to a simple hilt of steel, cast and chased in the subtle likeness of dragons. No garish showpiece this, no flamboyant expression of wealth and power. This was the sword of a battle mage. The strength and power lay within.

The sight of the sword filled Falco with hope, but he tried to hold his excitement in check. Surely it could not be as simple as it appeared.

Coming to his knees he withdrew his arm from the twisted strap of his shield. He reached out with his perception, trying to detect the final barrier that lay between him and his goal. All he could sense was a simple field of energy holding his sword in place, nothing insurmountable, just enough to prevent him from using his powers to retrieve it. He would need to take the sword with his hand. But that was it. There was nothing else in the way and this was just as well for he did not think he had the strength to overcome another challenge.

Climbing to his feet Falco started forward. And then he felt it. The sword was not the only thing in this room. In the darkness beyond it there was something else. And now, with its presence unmasked, the entity revealed itself. Ten feet beyond the sword, a cold light illuminated a man sitting in a stone chair, a man ravaged not by age but by the relentless passage of time.

Dressed in the filthy robes of a mage, his bare arms were grey and disfigured with open sores and bruise-like shadows of purple and black. His lips were thin and shrunken, revealing the decaying stumps of broken teeth. Wisps of hair clung to his scalp, the translucent skin covered with tar coloured spots and a tracery of dark capillaries as if the blood in his veins had been replaced by ink. Falco might have taken him for a corpse, were it not for the light of malice in his milk white eyes.

'Salutări tineri Falcon, Bun venit la moarte,' intoned the man and Falco stared at him in horror and suspicion. This apparition of death spoke in a language that made Falco's skin crawl, but his sword was almost in reach and it would take more than a mad old mage to stop him now. But Falco did not appreciate the nature of the creature sitting before him.

Born more than four hundred years ago, he was once a senior researcher at the remote mage tower of Ossanda. He was the last surviving witness to the Great Possession. His mind had been broken by the events of that terrible day, although there are those who say he had ever been drawn to darkness.

His true name was lost in the swirling mists of time. Now he was known only by the name that his depravity had earned him. A name drawn from the ancient language of the enemy. They called him Pacatos... Sinner.

Oblivious to all of this Falco started towards his sword, but he had barely taken a step when he was struck down by the force of the Sinner's mind. The power of Brother Pacatos flooded his thoughts with a terrible sense of corruption. It felt as if something vile had just forced its way into his skull and Falco felt an overwhelming urge to tear it out. Pushing the helmet from his head he gouged his nails into the flesh beneath his right eye and the wizened old mage began to

421

laugh, not the wheezing death rattle that one might have expected, but a deep guttural laugh that reverberated around the room.

Falco felt blood running down his cheek but a part of him understood the nature of this new attack. Self harm was a particularly cruel weapon of the enemy. Convince a person that they are worthless or defiled and they could inflict the most horrific injuries upon themselves. With an immense effort of will Falco lowered his hands and struggled to his feet.

Beyond the sword the mad old mage frowned with displeasure, surprised that any single person could withstand the full force of his compulsion. Even the stone-hearted wardens of the tower attended him in threes and even then it was sometimes not enough to restrain him. His frown turned to one of determination and he raised a mummified finger to point directly at Falco's heart.

Once again Falco collapsed to his knees as the blood in his veins was replaced by some kind of foul burning excrement. Pulling off his gauntlets he stared in horror as the veins on the back of his hands turned black. He tried to get to his feet but his legs felt numb and heavy and would no longer hold his weight. Falling forward he began to crawl as a tracery of black veins stretched up his neck and spread beneath the pale skin of his face.

Fear coursed through Falco's mind as the inky poison bled into the small capillaries of his eyes. His breath became shallow and his heart lurched as the corruption choked his veins. His stomach heaved and he coughed up a great gout of stinking black vomit, the bilious fluid scouring his nose and throat. Finally the world around him began to disappear as his eyes clouded over with thick grey cataracts.

But still he crawled.

Lost in anguish he crawled towards the only light that still existed in his mind. Not because he had any hope of salvation, but because it was all that he *could* do. After all that he had been through it was not the cruel designs of the magi that had brought him down, it was the unholy power of the last surviving witness. The other magi on the Torquery had merely tried to break him, tried to force him to concede. There would be no such clemency here. Brother Pacatos would never allow him to surrender. Falco could cry 'cedo' until his lungs burst but it would not save him now.

Falco's body was being consumed from within, his mind slowly being eclipsed by evil. He should have curled into a wailing ball of despair, but still he crawled and beyond his sword Brother Pacatos spat out a dry cadaverous curse. There was nothing left of this Defiant's resolve and yet somehow he remained. Leaning forward in his chair the living corpse gave a hissing snarl and redoubled his efforts, but still Falco inched towards his sword.

The Sinner's snarl became a consumptive roar and the very walls of the labyrinth began to shake. Dust billowed and chunks of masonry broke free, flying through the air to strike at Falco. Most bounced harmlessly off his armour but one gave a dull 'clock' as it struck him in the head. He slumped as the rock rendered him momentarily senseless. He had no strength to summon a defence and more blows hammered into his body but he was now barely an arm's length from his sword. With a trembling hand he began to reach out. But even as he did so he felt an invisible force clutching at his throat.

Ahead of him Brother Pacatos reached out a skeletal hand and began to squeeze. Whatever happened he could not allow this Defiant to claim his sword. To Falco the sword sang with the silent song of faith, but to a sinner it sang with the promise of redemption, and to those lost in darkness there was nothing more terrifying, to face what they had become and to breathe life back into the withered clinker of their soul. No torment of hell could ever be worse than this and so, with all his vitriolic might the mad old mage tried to crush the life from Falco. Four hundred years of insanity, anguish and blind psychotic rage. He disgorged it all.

Behind the cataracts on his eyes Falco's vision began to fade. A new kind of darkness was encroaching on his mind, one from which he would never return. Beyond the realm of normal suffering Falco was finally spent. But then his fingers closed around the hilt of a sword, a sword he had never held before and yet had known for all his life.

It was a thing of metal, base, unliving and yet it gave him strength.

The mad old mage seemed to sense the faint glimmer of hope and raised his attack to crush it. The renewed assault was like a scream that tore at Falco's sanity and the only thing to stand against it was the silent singing of a sword. He gripped the handle of his sword and the crusted cataracts faded from his eyes. He dragged himself up to his knees and set the sword upright with its point stabbing into the floor. He pressed his face to the steel hilt and felt the burning ichor draining from his veins. His arms shook with exertion as he summoned every last shred of will to oppose the ancient mind that was trying to destroy him.

The battle rose to a soul rending intensity and both contestants knew that this was now a fight to the death. Whoever failed first would be dashed on the rocks of defeat, their minds shattered beyond all hope of repair.

Falco knew he had to fight but a part of him no longer cared. The world no longer seemed to exist. He was lost in a timeless void somewhere between the silence and the scream.

*

The Crucible was flooded with the pale light of the moon. It was now almost two hours since Falco had entered the labyrinth and Aurelian was growing increasingly concerned. It was not unusual for a Rite to last so long but he could not shake off the feeling that something had gone wrong. From the expression on his face Dusaule shared his concerns and even Dwimervane seemed anxious. The dragon was staring at the archway, a low growl sounding in her chest. Aurelian laid his hand on her shoulder.

'It's all right. He'll be out soon.'

Despite the growing sense of unease, he refused to believe that Falco would fail. He might not have offensive capabilities but he had the strongest defence that Aurelian had ever known and he did not believe that any mage was strong enough to overcome that. But then a figure appeared over the lip of the Crucible. It was Meredith, and even from a distance Aurelian could sense the mortal fear surging through his mind.

With a feeling of dread Aurelian turned back to look at the archway. All hope had suddenly vanished. Somewhere down there in the labyrinth Falco had

423

been overcome. As if to confirm the fact there was a sudden pulse of energy from somewhere deep underground and a great cloud of dust rolled out of the archway.

A stillness settled on the arena and all eyes were fixed on the gaping maw of the entrance. The minutes stretched and the archway was filled with deep shadow cast by the light of the silver moon. Ten minutes past, twenty, and neither word nor breath was heard in the arena until suddenly...

There was something there in the tunnel, but it was impossible to say if it was Falco or the labyrinth wardens dragging out the senseless body of a young man who had not been up to the task. But then a figure appeared, a figure that shone with the unmistakable glint of steel. Like a man waking from a dream Falco emerged into the moonlight. His helmet, shield and gauntlets were gone, but in his hand he held a sword. Swaying with weariness he took a few halting steps before turning to face the magi. With the last of his strength he raised his sword like a victorious gladiator but then his legs gave way and he collapsed flat on his face on the shifting gravel of the Crucible.

Thrall's displeasure was like a palpable force but it did not matter. Falco had walked the pathways of the oubliette. He had faced all that the magi could throw at him, and survived. He had passed the Rite of Assay. And whether it went unanswered, or conjured a lethal black, he had won the right to a summoning.

76

For What You Will Become

Dusaule carried Falco to the Crofters' cottage where he and Aurelian removed his armour and bathed his tormented skin before taking it in turns to infuse his body with waves of healing energy. While they worked, Meredith went to find Malaki and Bryna who then sat with Falco while the two battle mages went to retrieve Falco's gauntlets, shield and helm from the Labyrinth.

'Will they be all right?' asked Bryna.

'They'll be fine,' said Meredith. 'There are no magi to stand in their way but it won't be easy. That place is thick with the echoes of nightmare.'

Almost an hour later Aurelian and Dusaule returned. Both looked pale and strained but they had found the armour that Falco had left behind. They had also found the belt and scabbard for his sword, beautifully crafted from ebony leather with polished steel fittings.

Malaki sheathed the sword and laid it beside Falco on the bed, then he and Dusaule set about cleaning Falco's armour which was filthy with dirt and soot and blood. While they worked Aurelian moved to speak with Meredith. He remembered seeing the fear on his face when he arrived at the Crucible and wanted to know what it was that had made him so afraid. Meredith told him everything he knew about Brother Pacatos and his efforts to find out exactly what had happened during the Great Possession.

'Bloody Thrall!' cursed Aurelian as Meredith finished. 'How could he allow an insane mage to take part in the Rite!' He clenched his fist in anger, his brow gathered in thought. 'And what about you?' he asked. 'Do *you* think this Pacatos could be four hundred years old?'

'It's impossible,' said Meredith. 'But I'm certain he knows something about the Great Possession.'

'Is there really more to know?' said Aurelian. He sounded distinctly weary of the topic. 'So the magi made a mistake, or kept the knowledge to themselves. What does it matter? It's all ancient history now.'

Meredith had not expected to hear such indifference from the old battle mage but he was not surprised. Despite their wariness and suspicion, most people simply accepted the magi with all their secrecy and jostling for power. But Meredith was about to become one of them. He would soon be making vows of loyalty and secrecy, vows that simply could not be broken. He could not allow himself to be bound by such constraints, not while he harboured so much doubt.

'You be careful,' said Aurelian, guessing at the rebellious nature of Meredith's thoughts. 'The magi won't thank you for dredging up the past.'

'I know,' said Meredith, rising from his chair. 'But it's something I have to do.'

Aurelian shook his head.

'Well I need to dig out a clean shirt,' he said. 'The Queen asked me to tell her when the Rite was over. She was hoping to speak with Falco and will be anxious to hear that he's all right.'

Meredith was suddenly struck by the dramatic changes that had taken place in their lives. Less than a year ago they had been little more than boys, their horizons limited to the petty squabbles of a small provincial town. Now *he* was about to question the most powerful Mage in the world while the Queen of Wrath was waiting to speak to someone who, for most of his life, had been thought of as nothing more than a weak and sickly servant.

He glanced up at Malaki and Bryna. They too had come into their own.

'We'll tell him you were here,' said Bryna, and Meredith gave a nod of thanks as he left the cottage and turned in the direction of the mage tower.

Now that the Rite was over he felt the full weight of the fatigue that he had been holding at bay for days. He was desperate to confront Thrall but he would need his wits about him. He would not risk it when his mind was fogged by the need for sleep. Suppressing a wave of impatience he made his way to his own chambers and drank a large glass of vermillion wine before lying down to sleep.

It was late morning when Falco woke. His mouth and throat felt raw and his entire body ached but his mind was clear. Wincing with pain he raised himself up on one elbow and blinked the sleep from his eyes as he gazed around the dimly lit room. He was in the Crofters' cottage.

Beside the bed, Bryna and Malaki were dozing in a chair, Bryna sitting on her husband's lap. Falco stared at them, struggling to reconcile their presence with the terrible visions he had endured in the labyrinth. He looked at them again as if to convince himself that they were really here, that he had not hurt or betrayed them as the whispers would have had him believe.

'You're alive then!'

Falco looked up to see Aurelian walking towards him. The old battle mage helped him sit up and handed him a cup of water. He sipped at the cool liquid and his stomach growled with a healthy pang of hunger. Lowering the cup he settled back against the pillows.

'How do you feel?' asked Aurelian.

A shadow passed over Falco's gaze and he paused before answering.

'Unsettled,' he said.

'I should bloody well think so!' said Aurelian, snorting at the understatement. Moving to the side of the room he drew back the curtains and opened two small windows in the cottage wall. A cool salt-laden breeze freshened the room and the light of an early summer's day made the cottage seem warm and homely.

Beside them Malaki and Bryna stirred in the chair.

'You're awake,' said Bryna, easing the stiffness from her back as she came to sit beside Falco on the bed.

'And not looking quite so dreadful,' added Malaki.

Falco smiled at his friends then rolled his eyes as Aurelian pulled back the blanket to examine his injuries. The bruising, bites and welts were all much improved and most of the cuts had closed nicely, including two which had required a couple of catgut stitches.

'You'll live,' said Aurelian, clearly satisfied by the way Falco's body was recovering. He moved through to the kitchen area where a pot of soup was simmering on the stove.

Malaki and Bryna knew better than to ask Falco about his ordeal, instead they told him about the progress they were making with the Irregulars.

'They're coming on surprisingly well,' concluded Bryna. 'Which is just as well because Marshal Breton has just sent orders for us to march within the week.'

They waited for Falco to express his surprise at this sudden change of plans but his gaze was turned inwards.

'At least you'll be here for the summoning,' was all he said.

'Surely you're not planning to attempt it so soon,' said Malaki.

'The Possessed won't wait,' said Falco, his tone dark and deadly serious. 'Besides,' he added more lightly. 'If the summoning isn't successful then I can ride out with you and the Irregulars.'

Malaki and Bryna exchanged a concerned glance, but they knew it would be impossible to change his mind.

'Well, I'm going back to the barracks for a bath,' said Bryna.

Rising to her feet she leaned down and kissed Falco on the forehead. 'I'm glad you're all right,' she told him. 'But take it easy. Just imagine what Fossetta would say.'

Falco smiled and gave her a nod but there was no concession in his eyes.

As Bryna left, Falco's eyes moved to the side of the room where his armour was now laid out on a bench, his shield hanging on the wall above it.

'Aurelian and Dusaule went to get the pieces you left in the labyrinth,' said Malaki and Falco could not suppress a shudder at the mere mention of the place that had almost broken him. His eyes moved down and his hand came to rest on the sword lying on the bed beside him, now sheathed in its custom-made scabbard. Lifting it onto his lap he drew a few inches of the blade, his gaze shadowed by the memory of reaching for the sword the previous night.

'I would have died if it wasn't for this,' he said and Malaki paused at the grim certainty in his voice.

'It's a little heavy right now. But it's right for what you will become.'

'It's perfect,' said Falco.

'You're welcome,' said Malaki and the two shared a look that only life-long friends could understand.

'Well... when I say perfect,' said Falco. 'I mean not bad for a country blacksmith who took seven attempts to make his first nail.'

Malaki laughed, shaking his head at the memory of those first failed attempts to copy his father.

'Right,' he said, stifling a yawn. 'I need to get back to the Irregulars.'

Falco nodded but Malaki hesitated before leaving.

'Don't rush into the summoning, Falco,' he said. 'You know, better than anyone, how dangerous it could be.'

Falco just stared at him, and Malaki recognised the stubborn intensity in his eyes.

'Just make sure you're ready.'

'I will,' said Falco.

'Oh,' said Malaki pausing at the door. 'Meredith was here last night. He sat with you for a while.'

Falco raised an eyebrow in surprise.

'I didn't expect him to be back so soon.'

'Seems he hurried back,' said Malaki. 'He was concerned about one of the mages in the Rite. He seemed worried, but I guess everything turned out all right.'

In the filtered light of the cottage Falco's gaze darkened. He remembered the overwhelming sense of evil he had felt in the presence of the last mage he had faced, the one who spoke in a strange and disturbing tongue.

'I'll see you later,' said Malaki and with a wave to Aurelian, he left.

Falco could see Aurelian standing at the stove but in his mind he was transported back to the central chamber of the labyrinth, the room that had echoed with a voice of evil.

Salutări tineri Falcon. Bun venit la moarte

Falco did not understand the language but somehow he understood the meaning of the words.

Welcome young Falcon. Welcome to your death.

He shook the memory from his head as Aurelian handed him a bowl of soup and a wooden spoon. With an age-weary groan the old battle mage settled in the chair while Falco set about demolishing the hot and wholesome broth.

'He's right, you know,' said Aurelian as Falco tipped the bowl to scoop up the last of his soup. 'You shouldn't attempt the summoning until you're ready.'

'I can't wait,' said Falco and Aurelian breathed a sigh of resignation.

'Well maybe you should attend to this before you get your head bitten off by a dragon.'

Reaching into his jerkin he drew forth a folded piece of cream coloured parchment, tied with turquoise ribbon and embossed with the royal crest.

Falco put down his empty soup bowl and wiped his hands before taking the note and starting to read.

Dear Master Danté

I am very much relieved to hear that you have survived your ordeal without any lasting harm. I understand that you will need time to rest and recover your strength. I also understand that you will soon have other matters to attend to, but I wonder if you could spare a few minutes to offer me your council.

I have always valued the advice of our battle mages and your recent experiences at the Illician front could prove invaluable.

I will send a messenger each day at noon. When you are feeling stronger, simply give your reply to her and, if you are able, then a time will be arranged.

With kind regards

Queen Catherine de Sage

Aurelian laughed at Falco's stunned expression.

'She's asking *me* if I might have the time to speak with *her!*'

'Well what do you expect?' said Aurelian with a smile. 'You're a battle mage now. Kings and generals, and every frightened scoundrel in the ranks will look to you for guidance.'

Falco leaned back against the pillows. Aurelian was right. Having completed the Rite of Assay he was now, officially, a battle mage. But to Falco's mind he was not there yet. Before he could accept the title for himself there was one last thing he needed to do.

*

Meredith slept-in far longer than he intended and it was early afternoon before he had bathed and dressed in clean robes, ready to confront Thrall. Determined not to be swayed or deterred he made his way down to the Grand Veneratu's chambers only to find his way barred by two mages guarding the door. They eyed him warily and he was about to demand entry when the door opened and Galen Thrall stood in the doorway, a faint smile of amusement on his lips. At a gesture the two guards stood back and Meredith was invited to enter. He followed Thrall, who stepped up onto the low dais bearing his chair, before turning to face him. Tense with anger Meredith was ready for any kind of reaction from Thrall, any reaction, that is, save praise.

'Well done, Lord Saker,' said Thrall, flattering Meredith with the title normally reserved for a fully fledged mage. 'It seems you discharged your duty as guide to Master Danté with distinction.'

Thrall's reaction took the heat out of Meredith's anger and left him feeling confused and irritated.

'Thank you, my Lord,' he heard himself say. 'But I'm afraid I can claim little credit for Falco's success.'

'Oh, but you are too modest. But for your guidance and skill I am quite sure he would have failed.'

'Not at all, My Lord. In fact I'm surprised he survived at all with a mage like Brother Pacatos on the Torquery.'

Thrall's smile faltered and the pupils in his waxy green eyes shrank as he looked at Meredith with a sterner gaze.

'Is there something you wish to say to me, Master Saker?'

Meredith steeled himself. Now that it came to it the thought of openly questioning the Grand Veneratu did not come easily.

'I wish to know why you put Brother Pacatos on the Torquery,' he managed with renewed determination. 'I want to know who he is, why he is here in the tower of Wrath and the nature of the illness that troubles him.'

'Is that all?' returned Thrall, his smile now firmly back in place.

'No,' said Meredith. 'I also wish to speak with Brother Pacatos myself.'

At this Thrall's face creased with regret.

'I'm afraid that will not be possible.'

Meredith was about to ask why but Thrall raised a hand to forestall him.

'Brother Pacatos is a linguist and historian from the mage tower of Le Matres. However, he also suffers from delusions of grandeur and the belief that he has been alive for centuries. He is here in this tower because we are best equipped to care for his needs and I put him on the Torquery because I felt that he would provide the greatest challenge to Master Danté's attempt.'

Meredith was burning to ask if he really was the last surviving witness to the Great Possession but that would betray the true nature of his interest.

'As to you speaking to Brother Pacatos yourself...'

Meredith's eyes narrowed in suspicion.

'It seems Brother Pacatos was not as strong as I had believed. Opposing Master Danté proved more than he could bear.'

'He's dead!'

'Not yet,' said Thrall. 'He is being cared for in the infirmary, but the end is not far off and he should not be disturbed.'

'But I need to talk to him.'

'I'm afraid I can't allow that,' said Thrall as if he only had the stricken mage's welfare in mind. 'Brother Pacatos is a venerable member of our order. He should be allowed to spend what time remains to him in peace.'

Thrall's gaze slid past Meredith as the two guards now re-entered the chamber and moved to stand at his shoulder. Both had stunning spells held ready in their minds and Meredith took the opportunity to memorise the pattern of thought required for such a spell.

'Now, if you will excuse me,' said Thrall. 'I have a summoning to prepare for.'

Thrall was clearly not enamoured by the thought and it was quite obvious that he held Meredith accountable. If anything went wrong with the summoning then a large part of the blame would rest with Saker's son.

Meredith's stomach was knotted in frustration, but still he refused to accept defeat. Casting a wary glance at the two guards, he drew a veil across his thoughts to prevent Thrall from guessing his intentions.

'My Lord,' he said with a respectful bow. 'I am sorry to have disturbed you.'

'Not at all,' said Thrall. His tone was benevolent but his eyes narrowed as he sensed the barrier Meredith had placed around his thoughts.

Meredith waited until the doors to Thrall's chamber closed before turning in the direction of the infirmary. He knew that Brother Pacatos would be guarded and inaccessible, but he needed to confirm his presence and assess the measures that Thrall had put in place to isolate him. He had no idea how long the mad old mage was expected to live or whether he would be capable of answering questions, but Meredith was determined to try.

Climbing to the infirmary on the south side of the tower he found that the entire corridor had been cordoned off, with four stern looking wardens standing guard at the entrance.

'Can we help you?' asked one of the men.

Meredith paused, as he checked for any wards or spells that might prevent him from entering the corridor.

'I was looking for my father,' he said at last. 'Morgan Saker. He was one of the mages on last night's Torquery.'

'Lord Saker is recovering in his own chambers,' said the man, the suspicion on his face lessening slightly.

'Thank you,' said Meredith, relieved to find that there were no other obstacles. Apart from four imposing and steely minded wardens.

As he made his way down the winding stone stairs he felt a sudden stab of guilt. He had lied about visiting his father, but the truth was that he had avoided doing exactly that. He should have gone to visit him, to see if he was all right

430

after trying to stop Falco, but he could not bring himself to do so. He was now convinced that the magi had lied to the people of Wrath and that meant that his father had lied too. He was the veneratu of a mage tower. There was no way he was not privy to the secrets of the magi, whatever those secrets might turn out to be.

Feeling a disturbing mixture of anger, betrayal and disloyalty Meredith made his way back to his chambers. He could not allow his personal feelings to distract him from finding the truth. He did not know how long he had before Brother Pacatos passed away. It was time to start preparing the spells he would need to get past the wardens guarding him. He could only hope that the mad old mage did not die before he was ready.

*

After another day of rest Falco was feeling much stronger, so when the Queen's messenger arrived at noon it was agreed that he would meet her the following evening in the Chamber of Council. A message had also arrived from Galen Thrall. The earliest the magi would be ready for a summoning would be two days from now.

'The Grand Veneratu insists that we should be properly prepared,' said the messenger from the tower.

'I'll bet he does,' muttered Aurelian.

And so it was settled. Tomorrow evening Falco would go and speak with the Queen, and the following night he would climb into the mountains in an attempt to summon a dragon. He was still physically and mentally drained from the demands of the Rite but he simply refused to be deterred. He resumed his training and Aurelian and Dusaule continued to aid his recovery with their healing powers. But as the time of the summoning drew closer Dusaule grew more distant and reserved.

'Don't worry,' Aurelian told Falco. 'The thought of a summoning brings back painful memories. That's all.'

Falco completely understood. He too had felt the power and majesty of a black dragon but he had also witnessed their blind hatred and murderous violence. If a black dragon did answer his call then he was fully prepared to do what was required.

The following evening, as the cool shadows of twilight filled the city streets, Falco made his way down from the plateau for his meeting with the Queen. The atmosphere in the capital was a strange mixture of calm with an underlying current of anxiety and fear. The number of refugees now camped in the surrounding area was putting a huge strain on the city's resources and the endless tales of woe made the front feel far closer than it actually was. The people of Wrath were beginning to feel the effects of the war and for the first time they began to realise that the destruction that had driven the refugees here, might one day be visited upon them.

Dressed once more in the armour of Antonio Missaglias, Falco noticed the way people looked at him as he rode through the city. Some bowed in respect while others raised their hands in blessing. They did not see a young man, recently grown into adulthood. They saw a battle mage and Falco was both humbled and daunted by the faith they had in his ability to save them.

Emerging into the paved plaza surrounding the Chamber he was met by two palace guards who escorted him into the building. The enormous domed chamber was lit by more than a dozen great oil lamps, their shiny brass cowls designed to fill the space with a warm yellow light. With a bow the guards left him in the centre of the floor and Falco gazed around. With no people crowding the terraced seats the huge building looked bigger than ever. The carpet had been rolled back and the great marble map was covered once more with the pewter figures that had been used during the public strategy meeting.

Swallowing with nervous anticipation, Falco looked around the empty chamber but then his eyes focussed on one of the unlit side entrances. Someone was watching him.

'Uncanny, the way a battle mage can do that,' said the Queen as she emerged from the darkness of the tunnel.

Falco immediately offered a hasty bow but the Queen waved aside such formality.

'Thank you for coming, Master Danté. I know that you have other things on your mind.'

'Not at all, Your Majesty,' said Falco. 'It is an honour and a pleasure.'

'Please,' said the Queen. 'If we must use titles then let it be, my Lady.'

'Yes, my Lady.'

'Better,' said the Queen with a smile. 'I had hoped to speak to you when you returned from the front but I didn't want to disrupt your preparations for the Rite.'

Falco bowed his head in appreciation and the Queen cast a critical eye over the armour that she had commissioned in the autumn.

'I see the skills of Master Missaglias have not diminished with age.'

Falco blushed, mortified that he had not even thanked her for this princely gift.

'Yes, thank you, my Lady,' he mumbled. 'It is far more than I ever dreamed.'

The Queen smiled at his discomfiture.

'The least I could do,' she said as if she had commissioned nothing more than a new pair of riding gloves.

Releasing Falco from her gaze she turned away to look at the pewter figures strategically placed on the map. The layout had changed since the public meeting and the situation looked worse than ever. She walked slowly over the map, following the line of the front and pausing wherever a concentration of pieces indicated that the fighting was particularly fierce.

As she moved slowly across the floor Falco could not help but look at her, long dark hair worn loose but for a silver ribbon holding it back from her face, her smooth skin radiant in the golden glow of the oil lamps. She wore a long gown of dusky peach silk, bound at the waist with the emissary's belt, the silver horse-head buckle bright against the black braided leather. About her shoulders was a cloak of emerald green, the crushed velvet of which seemed to cast shadows and highlights over her form. Once again he was struck by the captivating duality of her presence, the symbol of her as the Queen and the simple beauty of her as a woman.

'It appears there is nothing we can do to stop them,' said the Queen and Falco moved onto the map, the spell of watching her broken.

'We seem to be holding here,' he said, looking down at a group of figures in Beltane.

'Ah, yes,' said the Queen, coming to stand beside him, 'Vercincallidus. As cunning a general as ever there was. Somehow he has managed to outmanoeuvre the enemy for years, but see here.' She gestured towards the largest demon figure on the map. 'It appears the Marchio Dolor is moving against him and I can't help thinking that time is running out for the Serthian Wolf.' She gave a heavy sigh. 'But let us hope that I am wrong.'

Falco gazed at the figure representing the demon known as the Marquis of Pain, and sure enough, it had definitely moved towards the area where Vercincallidus played his deadly game of cat and mouse with the armies of the Possessed.

'And what of the situation further north?' asked the Queen taking a few strides up the map towards the cities of Hoffen and Le Matres. 'Do you still get the sense of something amiss?'

Falco followed her and looked down at the enemy lines.

'Not like before,' he said. 'Our forces look thinly stretched and the demon that attacked Nathalie isn't dead, but I don't see anything that suggests it is about to return.'

The Queen was clearly relieved.

'I understand that Nathalie would have been killed by the demon assassin, if you hadn't intervened.'

Falco bowed his head self-consciously.

'And the entire Fourth Army would have been lost if you and the cadet knights had not arrived when you did.'

Shifting awkwardly, Falco did not know what to say. He had done what he *had* to do. It had never been a matter of choice.

'We are in your debt, Battle Mage Danté,' said the Queen. She seemed to derive a deep pleasure from using Falco's official title, but she could see that such praise made him uncomfortable.

'Has there been any word from Nathalie or the emissary?' asked Falco, trying to change the subject.

'Nothing for a week or so,' said the Queen. 'Nathalie and Ciel are currently stationed in Hoffen. They are both still recovering, but their presence is a great comfort to the troops now housed in the city. And as for the emissary...'

She paused and the catch in her breath did not go unnoticed.

'Following your victory with the Fourth he has been able to establish a new front, but more demon armies are emerging from the Forsaken Lands. The Possessed are now pushing towards the city of Amboss and Marshal Breton has just sent orders for the Fourth Army to move south.

She tried to make it sound as if this were just another battle report, but Falco could hear the anxiety in her voice.

'He'll be all right,' said Falco. 'If anyone can survive a campaign, it's the emissary. I've never known anyone like him.'

433

'Nor me,' said the Queen. Her eyes glistened but she smiled at the kindness of Falco's words. 'You should have seen him when he first came to Wrath, so young and serious, filled with grief and desperate to fight. My Father recognised his potential but he also knew that men who bore such grief rarely lived long in battle. They would often seek out death in the hope of finding peace. And so he forbade the young Chevalier from returning to the front and appointed him as my tutor, my instructor in the art of war.'

She raised her eyes and smiled.

'He wasn't happy with the appointment, of course, but even then he was a man of honour and he performed his duty well. He taught me how to fight and how to wage war; how to deal with kings who thought me a girl and how to speak to normal people who could only ever see me as a Queen. All the things my father had been trying to teach me for years. But somehow, hearing it from this sad and serious young man was different. And in return... I taught him how to smile again.'

She paused, staring across the map as if she were looking back across the years.

'I had no idea that we were falling in love. Not until the day of my betrothal to Prince Philip, the day the Chevalier told me he was returning to war.'

The Queen's smile was beautiful and sad.

'Have you ever known love, Master Danté?'

'No, my Lady. Not in the way you mean it.'

'But you shall...' The Queen's tone was hopeful but Falco shook his head.

'I have friends that I love, but I don't think I could ever share my soul. It would not be fair.'

'Are the dreams of a battle mage really so terrible?'

Falco did not reply. The darkness in his gaze was answer enough.

'Then you have my pity. For your sacrifice is far greater than mine.'

For a moment they held each other's gaze.

'But, come now,' said the Queen. 'Let us look at the world and see what can be done, for I refuse to believe that we are yet beyond hope.'

Falco moved to stand beside her and together they looked down at the map. Growing up in a small mountain town he could never have imagined such an intimate meeting with the world's most powerful monarch. At the same time he was amazed at how comfortable he felt in her presence. Despite his youth and lack of experience the Queen spoke to him as if he were an equal. She shared her concerns over the fate of Beltane and Illicia and asked his opinion on the potential collapse of Valentia.

'Do you think King Vittorio will stand?' she asked as they looked at two demon figures threatening the eastern border of Valentia.

Falco shook his head.

'No,' he said. 'He will abandon the north and withdraw his forces to defend the south.'

'And what of the two demon armies gathered on his border?'

'They will go west,' said Falco without any trace of doubt. 'They will try to reach the coast, driving a wedge between the kingdoms that still stand against them.'

'And what then of Navaria?' asked the Queen.

Falco did not answer. The outcome of such an attack against an unguarded state was obvious.

'Yes,' said the Queen as if she had read Falco's thoughts. 'It will fall. And the Possessed will sit upon both our borders.' She gave a sigh and her gaze shifted to the great expanse of Acheron. 'If only the Bull could be roused to fight,' she breathed and Falco was certain that she had not intended him to hear.

For another while they discussed the fate of the world and Falco was surprised by the sense he was able to form of the enemy's intentions and movements. It was as if the Possessed were an animal that he understood, or a forest fire driven on by winds and appetites that he could somehow comprehend, and the wave of destruction did indeed seem unstoppable. If only Acheron and Thraece could be persuaded to join the fight.

'There is always the chance that they will join us,' said the Queen as they contemplated the two great kingdoms to the south. 'The failure of Thrall's mage army has undermined the position of the Thraecian magi but there is little that can be done while King Cleomenes remains under their control.'

For a moment more she stared at the map before lifting her head and offering him a smile.

'But come now...' she moved to take his arm. 'I have already taken up too much of your time. You need rest and time to gather your strength.' Gently she led Falco off the map where one of the palace guards was waiting to escort him from the chamber.

'Thank you for sharing your thoughts, Master Danté,' said the Queen as Falco prepared to leave.

'My deepest pleasure, my Lady.'

The Queen smiled at his courtesy.

'May the dragon you summon be strong and bright,' she said.

Falco nodded his thanks and offered a final bow. It would be amazing to think he might summon a brightly coloured dragon like Ciel, but his heart told him not to hope for too much.

For Falco, the day of the summoning passed in something of a haze. He did not know if his mind was clouded by the aftershocks of the Rite or the apprehension of what he was about to do. Aurelian was still concerned that it was too soon but Falco would not be deterred. As the afternoon wore on he joined Malaki and the other cadets in the barracks for a final meal, although he ate little and said less. Most of the cadets were in awe of what Falco was about to attempt, but Malaki and Bryna knew what had happened the last time he attended a summoning. They could barely imagine what he must be feeling now.

As Falco got up to leave, the cadets became silent. They might not appreciate the significance of this summoning but they had all experienced what his presence could mean on the battlefield, and so they wished him well. Even Jarek Snidesson gave him a nod of acknowledgement. Huthgarl, Quirren and Alex came round the table to embrace him and Bryna kissed his cheek before Falco turned to Malaki who clasped his hand before pulling him into a tight embrace.

'We'll be here when you return,' he said.

Falco could find no words to say. His mind was retreating into a guarded space somewhere deep inside of him, a dark place where emotions were dulled and the contrast between hope and fear was almost bearable. Feeling strangely detached he left the barracks and made his way back up to the cottage where Aurelian was waiting for him with two horses saddled and ready.

Despite his initial objections Falco had finally agreed to let Aurelian accompany him to the summoning. Without offensive powers even the sword that Malaki had made would struggle to cleave a dragon's scales. If the worst *did* happen then he would need someone to infuse the blade with energy and Falco could not bear the thought of leaving this to the magi.

'Are you ready?' asked Aurelian and Falco gave him a nod.

Dusaule was nowhere to be seen but Dwimervane was there, standing a little way back, so as not to frighten the horses. The dragon's blue scales were noticeably darker than when Falco had first met her. She looked at him with a curious intensity but there was no judgement in her flame yellow eyes. To normal dragons the madness of the blacks was a sad and shameful mystery, but their violence and hatred was undeniable and so they must be stopped.

Falco could sense the conflict in Dwimervane's mind but there was a hint of darkness too, like clouds on the distant horizon. At some point, in the not too distant future, she too would turn black and Aurelian would be faced with an unthinkable proposition.

Guessing something of his thoughts Aurelian placed a hand on Falco's shoulder.

'Summon with a true heart and I'm quite sure it will be answered in kind,' said the old battle mage and Falco's resolve almost wavered.

Aurelian's kindness cut through his defences and vapours of doubt began to rise in his mind. He thought of Dusaule, his spirit broken by the guilt of what he had done. Could *he* be about to suffer the same fate?

No.

It was a black dragon that had killed Darius, and a black dragon that had led to his father's death. If a black dragon answered his call tonight, he would kill it.

Hunter and Hunted

In the dusky wilds of Beltane, Vercincallidus frowned as the scout finished her report. It seemed the demon she had been sent to watch was much closer than they thought.

'It moves with a purpose,' she said. 'It knows we are here. The enemy bends his will towards us.'

Vercincallidus said nothing as he looked across at the Ferocian army now hemmed in against the river. This latest Possessed force was beaten, but it would take time to finish them off and time was the one thing he did not have.

The general's lip curled in frustration.

This was the third time in the last few weeks that he had been forced to call off an attack before the enemy was annihilated. The scout was right, this was not happening by chance, this was the result of a coordinated campaign. Most demons were predictable and thus fairly easy to avoid. Some were cunning but this recent turn of events spoke of much greater control. There had been rumours of a powerful demon moving towards them, a demon the Illicians referred to as the Marchio Dolor. Vercincallidus feared no man that walked the earth but the thought of such a demon filled his bowels with ice. He clenched his fists, refusing to allow such fears a foothold in his mind. For now he had the lives of ten thousand warriors to save.

Turning away from the scout he surveyed the field as he considered his options. At the start of the battle he had used the river to his advantage but now it cut off the quickest line of retreat. His only other option was to retreat north through the gully, but he needed a way to hold the Possessed back while the army made their escape.

With his decision made, Vercincallidus turned to his aide-de-camp.

'Sound the call for the Revered,' he said. 'I need three hundred to hold the gully while we retreat onto the plateau.'

The aide gave his commander a grim nod and turned to the nearest musician who raised his carnyx to summon the volunteers who would lay down their lives for the sake of the army and the general who led them. For five years Vercincallidus had used his skill to outwit the demons and hunt the Possessed, but now the enemy's chief lieutenant was moving against him and he realised that it was he who was now being hunted.

Meanwhile in the northwest of Illicia, near the newly established front line, an area of green heathland started to wither as something in the netherworld began to stir. In the merciless fires of hell the Slayer had completed its penance. Skin burned to blackened cinders, and twin blades glowing white with infernal heat, it began its slow ascension, up through the many planes of hell. Soon it would be reborn into the world of men and the only thought in its hateful mind was vengeance.

Answers

Meredith watched as the summoning party left the tower. Mounted on horses they headed for the winding path leading up into the mountains. There were still three hours until sunset, but Thrall would want to make sure everything was in place before Falco and Aurelian arrived. Meredith waited until the Grand Veneratu disappeared from view before turning away from the window.

It would have been foolish to try to speak with Brother Pacatos while Thrall was still in the tower, but now he would be away for several hours and Meredith would never get a better chance.

Returning to his chambers he spent a few minutes meditating in final preparation then, clearing his mind of all distractions, he made his way to the stairs leading to the infirmary. With his heart beating wildly in his chest he focussed his mind and began to weave a complex cloak of concealment around himself. Even his father acknowledged his gift for concealment. Now it was time to put that gift to the test.

The world seemed to recede and the sound of his own breathing changed as Meredith was cocooned in a muffled shell of magical force, his movements slow and deliberate as he climbed the few remaining steps to the infirmary. As he emerged onto the landing he could see the four wardens standing guard, rigid and vigilant. Fortunately there appeared to be just enough room for a person to pass between them. Hardly daring to breathe he started forward then stopped as one of the men looked directly at him. Had the man seen something? Heard something?

Meredith paused and the warden's gaze moved on. He remained undetected and slowly he continued his approach. He knew that the challenge would grow more difficult the closer he got. In addition to sight and sound he would need to mask his own body odour and somehow account for the movements in the air that might otherwise betray his presence. But his preparations had been thorough and he conducted his passing with a skill beyond his years.

Numbed by the sheer force of concentration Meredith moved past the four wardens and into the main corridor. Careful not to let his concealment slip he began to check each of the rooms, but then he sensed the presence of the man he had come to speak with, a dark unsettling presence that seemed to dim and flare like the guttering flame of a candle and Meredith knew he had come in the very nick of time.

The old mage was indeed dying and Meredith could only hope that he was still capable of answering his questions. As he turned into the room it was clear that he need not have worried. Brother Pacatos was shackled to a bed halfway down the room. Propped up on pillows and dressed in a soiled white bed shirt, the ancient mage was looking directly at him. His eyes were clouded with cataracts, but it was obvious that he could see Meredith as clear as day.

Moving into the room Meredith took a moment to conjure a magical seal over the doorway so they could speak in private before turning back to the bedridden monk.

'Ah, fiul lui Saker. Vin să pună întrebări despre cel trecut,' wheezed Brother Pacatos in the ancient language of Ferocia.

Ah, the son of Saker. Here to ask questions about the past.

Meredith froze. Not only could Pacatos see him he also knew why he was here. For the first time Meredith felt a surge of doubt. A small muscle twitched at the corner of his right eye and he raised a hand to scratch a faint itching beneath the skin of his temple. Just being in the presence of 'The Sinner' was unnerving, but there was no way he was going to be deterred now. Meredith had a basic grasp of Ferocian, but he would struggle to voice his questions in that tongue.

'În comun, dacă vă rog,' he said.

In common, if you please.

'As you wish,' said Brother Pacatos, switching to the universal language of Wrath.

His skin was a sickly translucent grey, mottled with black contusions and weeping with open sores. The veins beneath his skin were threaded black and his withered lips were cracked and shrunken. His uneven breathing issued with a dry rattle, filling the air with a nauseating stench. Meredith could not disguise his revulsion but Brother Pacatos just smiled.

'Ask away, Son of Saker,' he said, his words punctuated by unpleasant rasping breaths.

'What is your name?' said Meredith, raising a hand to his temple as the itching became more insistent.

'They call me Pacatos. That will suffice.'

'How old are you?' asked Meredith and Brother Pacatos smiled, revealing a mouth filled with the blackened stumps of rotten teeth.

'You know how old I am.'

'Then it's true,' said Meredith. 'You were alive at the time of the Great Possession.'

Brother Pacatos gave a wheezing snort as if he found the description amusing.

'What happened?' asked Meredith. 'Why did the magi not tell people that dragons were susceptible to Possession.'

Brother Pacatos began to laugh, a deep guttural laugh that seemed to claw at Meredith's mind.

'Why!' he demanded. 'Why did they not warn us?'

'Because it is not true,' said Pacatos and now his clouded eyes took on a disturbing directness.

'What do you mean?' asked Meredith. 'I know it's true. They lied about it then and they are still lying about it now.'

'You are wrong,' said Pacatos. 'None of it is true.'

'What are you saying?' said Meredith as he felt a sickening fear leeching into his mind. 'Are you saying there was no such thing as the Great Possession?'

At this Brother Pacatos began to choke on his laughter and Meredith raised a hand to his head. The itch had become a gnawing pain and he was suddenly convinced that there was something moving beneath the skin of his right temple.

'Ah, my poor little Saker,' gasped Pacatos. 'The secrets of the magi... are eating away at you, and you don't even know... what they are.'

His tone was thick with mockery and Meredith could stand it no more. Starting forward he grabbed the dying mage's bed shirt.

439

'Just tell me!' he cried then recoiled as the pain in his head suddenly intensified.

'You already know the truth,' wheezed Pacatos as Meredith clasped his hand to the side of his head. 'You have read it a dozen times and more.'

'You're lying,' breathed Meredith. 'I haven't...'

Meredith could not complete the sentence. The pain in his head made it difficult to concentrate and his stomach heaved as his mind was overcome by a growing sense of corruption. Something foul was seeping into his body, poisoning his blood. And now he was convinced that something was writhing beneath the skin of his temple. The nails on his right hand gouged into his skin and blood trickled down his cheek.

'Your eyes were open but you did not see,' said Pacatos as Meredith staggered back and stumbled to one knee. 'You turned the pages... but still the words of the past were wasted on you. Your ears... stopped up... by Brother Serulian's guile.'

Even close to death the force of Brother Pacatos's malice was too much for Meredith. Collapsing forward he began to crawl away as a series of images flashed through his mind. Images of himself bent over the table in the archives of the magi, his finger tracing the words of a manuscript. But the words were blurred and indistinct and he did not recognise the text from which he read, did not even remember reading it.

Your ears stopped up by Brother Serulian's guile

These words echoed in Meredith's mind as he tried to escape the befouling touch of the Sinner's presence. Could it be true? Could he really have read the truth without realising?

The answer was a resounding 'yes' but such conviction was now beyond him. What remained of his reason could think only of getting away and still he tried to claw the burrowing creatures from out his skull. Behind him Brother Pacatos laughed a drowning laugh, the scorn and vitriol gurgled in his throat as the decayed membranes of his lungs ruptured and stinking black ichor spilled down his chin. Even as he died, this vessel of evil was determined to take one last soul down with him to hell.

'You have failed, Saker,' he coughed. 'Just as the Falcon will fail.

'He shall summon darkness.

'And slay darkness.

'And the shame of murder shall damn his soul!'

Blind and helpless Meredith crawled away. His nails now scraped against the wet bone of his skull as he clawed the flesh from the side of his face. It was only by sheer will that he managed to reach the doorway and breach the seal that he had set in place.

The four wardens responded instantly. Charging down the corridor they ignored the young mage crawling from the room. Magical energy exploded around Meredith as the wardens unleashed spells to subdue Pacatos, but their power was not required. After four hundred years of hateful beating the Sinner's heart finally burst. The man known as Brother Pacatos, the last surviving witness of the Great Possession, was dead.

440

Meredith felt the vile images receding from his mind. The side of his head now burned with a terrible pain but somehow he was able to get to his feet. His right hand was dripping with blood but he wiped it on his robes before raising it again to try and staunch the flow of blood running down his neck. Still dazed and disorientated he made it to the end of the corridor and started towards the stairs.

A novice appeared on the landing carrying a tray of food and drinks for the wardens, but the tray slipped from his grasp as he recoiled from the bloody apparition weaving towards him.

Meredith ignored him.

There was only one thing on his mind, to get down to the archives and find the manuscripts that had been hidden from him. He encountered several more magi and some of them tried to help him but Meredith just pushed his way past, stumbling down the stairs while they stared after him in shock. Finally he reached the archives and one of the librarians moved to prevent him from entering.

'What's going on here?' said the man. 'You can't come in here like that!'

But Meredith shoved him back against the wall, leaving a bloody handprint on his robes. He moved through to the chamber where he had studied and sure enough Brother Serulian was still in his chair, still staring into space as if he never moved from the spot. As ever, the wrinkled old mage did not respond to his presence but Meredith did not care. Raising his hand he cast the stunning spell that he had learned from Thrall's guards and Brother Serulian slumped forward, falling from his chair to lie sprawled across the library floor.

Feeling dizzy and breathless Meredith stood for a moment and looked down at the stone table as if seeing it for the first time. Squinting from the pain that lanced through his temple he began to scan the shelves of history texts. His gaze immediately alighted on several manuscripts he had not noticed before. Ignoring the state of his bloody hands he snatched the books from the shelves and tucked them under his arm before moving through to the fifth chamber where the texts on dragonkind were kept. Once again he noticed a number of works that he had previously overlooked, but as he pulled them from the shelves his mind flickered with dreamlike images of having read the books before.

Laden with as many as he could carry he moved back through and deposited them on the table. The librarian reappeared with a senior archivist in tow, but one flash of the dire expression in Meredith's eyes and both men retreated in fear.

Meredith turned to his books.

With the confounding veil lifted from his mind a strange sense of familiarity returned as he flicked over pages and unfurled scrolls. Blood dripped from his face and his hands smeared the manuscripts with red as he rediscovered passages that he knew were there, his eyes moving with manic rapidity across the page.

As he read, his mind began to recall other books and other threads of discourse: the magi's growing resentment of the battle mages and the influence they wielded in circles of power. There was a passage that spoke of an 'opportunity' now that the Possessed were no longer a threat. He remembered the note of caution and deception in the voices of the past. There was discussion and disagreement but all doubt and opposition was swept aside by the burning vision of Syballian the Prophet, the Grand Veneratu of the time.

Meredith blazed through the texts, a ferocious anger rising in his chest. There were historical accounts and records of the communication between various mage towers. There was a thesis on the 'madness and memory of dragons' and more recently there were references to people that Meredith knew. His hands were shaking as he scanned the words, his gaze flitting from one accursed book to the next. But as he read his eyes narrowed and a frown gathered upon his brow. Finally he could bear it no more and the pages beneath his hands grew black as the parchment began to smoulder, scorched by a rising tide of fury. In utter dismay Meredith squeezed his eyes shut as the truth tore at his heart. But then the final words of Brother Pacatos returned to him.

He shall summon darkness
And slay darkness
And the shame of murder shall damn his soul

Scattering burned pages about the room Meredith swept from the archives and ran in the direction of the stables. He was in great pain and the right side of his face was a mess of torn flesh and congealed blood but his mind was startlingly clear.

The summoning must not be allowed to go ahead.

Falco must be stopped.

*

It took Falco and Aurelian about two hours to reach the point where the twisting mountain path became too difficult for the horses. The animals were breathing heavily from the climb but they had gained some considerable height and both the plateau and the city now lay far below them. The night remained fair and clear but the air was cold and the wind whipped about them, whistling against the hard edges of Falco's armour.

To one side of the path there was an area of rocky ground where more than a dozen horses stood tethered to a rusty metal chain that was fixed to the cliffs. They shifted nervously as Falco and Aurelian dismounted and tied their own horses beside those of the magi.

Falco had just removed his shield and helm from his saddle when Aurelian nodded towards the way ahead. Turning round, he saw two magi, standing like sentinels on either side of the path.

'The Grand Veneratu is waiting for you,' said one of the men.

Giving them a wary glance Falco armed his shield and carried his helm as he and Aurelian continued up the path. It climbed for another twenty minutes before weaving its way through a towering landscape of fractured rocks and jagged boulders. Finally they crested the ridge and Falco found himself looking down into a vast space that seemed to have been chiselled from the mountainside.

Just like Caer Dour's Castle of the Winds the crags rose up around a flat expanse of bare rock that looked out over a yawning space of nothing. On three sides the dragon stone was surrounded by cliffs but the fourth side was open towards the sea. Here in the mountains they were several miles from the coast but such was the height, and the sheer vertical drop, that the ocean seemed to be right there below them.

Bathed in the warm light of the setting sun it was a beautiful and awe-inspiring sight. Such a view would normally inspire Falco with memories of home, but now his heart was racing for another reason. He felt lightheaded and breathless as all the horrific memories of Darius's summoning came rushing back. For a moment he almost backed away but then his uncertainty was checked by the force of his resolve.

He was here to summon a dragon. And despite the years of illness and frailty it felt as if his whole life had been leading to this point. He could not choose what kind of creature would answer his call and there was always the chance that, like Simeon, his call could go unanswered. But he would not shy away from his destiny.

Falco's breathing calmed as he regained his composure and together he and Aurelian started down a series of steps leading to the dragon stone. As they descended, Falco became aware of the magi.

'Can you see them?' asked Aurelian and Falco nodded.

Thirteen magi, each one standing on a ledge carved out of the cliffs surrounding the dragon stone. Two of the men were warrior mages, dressed for battle and primed with deadly spells. They were all shrouded in magic to conceal their presence from a dragon, but the two battle mages could see them well enough.

As Falco looked more closely he noticed that each of these ledges was protected by a standing stone of fortissite set into the rock. If the summoning went awry the magi could shelter behind these indestructible columns of stone. As they reached the flat expanse of rock, Galen Thrall stepped out from behind an ten foot shard of fortissite at the back of the dragon stone.

'Well met, my lords,' he said. 'Your timing is impeccable.' He glanced towards the horizon where the sun was about to set.

Aurelian looked at the glowing band of clouds on the horizon, but Falco just stared at Thrall. The Grand Veneratu was positively thrumming with stored energy and his waxy green eyes were filled with resentment. He had tried to prevent Falco from being trained in the first place and had done his utmost to stop him during the Rite of Assay, but even Thrall could not suppress a degree of anticipation over what was about to happen.

'We have reserved a place for the summoner's second,' said Thrall, raising an arm to indicate a ledge for Aurelian.

'And what about concealment?' asked Aurelian and Thrall smiled.

The powers of a battle mage were many, but the subtlety required to conceal one's presence was a skill that only the magi had learned to master.

'Don't worry,' said Thrall. 'We will hide you from the gaze of ptero draconis.'

Aurelian's expression made it clear that he did not trust Thrall, but they had no choice. Turning to Falco he placed a hand on his shoulder.

'With a true heart,' he said and Falco gave him a nod.

Aurelian climbed the rocks to take his place on the ledge overlooking the dragon stone while Thrall swept his gaze round the cliffs as each of the magi confirmed their readiness. Finally he turned to look at Falco.

'Whenever you're ready, Master Danté.'

Falco gave a slight bow and with a last look in Aurelian's direction he walked to the very edge of the dragon stone. With his helm still under his arm he gazed down at the great sweep of land below him. The cliff dropped for more than a thousand feet before the tumbling slopes of the mountain levelled out towards the coast. The sun was now lost behind the veil of clouds on the horizon, but apart from that the sky was clear. For a moment Falco breathed in the cold mountain air as the wind whipped his long dark hair about his face. He felt the reassuring weight of the armour on his shoulders and the comforting presence of Malaki's sword at his waist.

He was Falco Danté, son of Aquila and Eleanora Danté, here as a battle mage to summon a dragon. Falco could barely comprehend the magnitude of what he was about to do and yet he was at peace.

Sweeping the hair back from his face he donned his helmet and moved to the centre of the open space. Then dropping to one knee he placed his armoured fist against the stone. Gathering all the power he possessed he closed his eyes and felt the tingling sensation of power surge down from the crown of his head. For just a moment he held it tight. And then he let it go.

Boom!

The very mountain shook with a great compression of the air as the silent call travelled out into the void.

Boom!

Again a pulse of energy that stunned the watching magi with its force.

Boom!

Like the rolling of silent thunder the echoes of Falco's third and final call reverberated around the cliffs. Slowly he rose to his feet. The ethereal bell of his soul had been tolled and the next few minutes would bear witness, either to the culmination of his heart's desire or the folly of his doom.

But for good or ill the act was done.

A dragon had been summoned and all they could do now was wait to see if the call would be answered.

*

Meredith ignored the pain as he raced up the tortuous mountain path. His horse cried out as its hooves skidded on the loose stones but he hauled on the reins and drove it on. The horse's nostrils flared and its eyes rolled as it fought to obey the commands of this fierce master who smelled of blood.

Reaching the end of the bridle way Meredith slipped from the saddle, but as he tried to continue two magi stepped forward to block his advance.

'The summoning is underway,' said one.

'We cannot allow you to pass,' said the other.

Without breaking stride Meredith stunned one of the magi and caused the other to double over with a pulse of energy that punched into his stomach and left him groaning on the ground. Without another glance Meredith strode past the two men and started on the last part of the climb, but he was too late.

444

On the dragon stone Falco stared out to sea where a dark shape could now been seen in the bright sky to the west. Already too big to be mistaken for a bird, the shape grew larger and more distinct until there could be no doubt.

Falco's call had been answered.

79

Darkness Falls

The air around the dragon stone was alive with anticipation and the pent up energy of the magi. Aurelian stared into the twilight sky, desperately searching for some sign of colour in the silhouette of the rapidly approaching dragon.

'Please,' he breathed. 'Please.'

He knew the magi were prepared for the worst, but he could not bear the thought of Falco being forced to slay a dragon. In the sky there was a sudden flash of light and one of the magi called out.

'Yellow! I saw a flash of yellow!'

Aurelian's heart soared but then he looked down at Falco and all his hopes were dashed. Falco had settled into a fighting stance. Moving back from the centre of the dragon stone he drew his sword and raised it up in the way they had agreed. It was the signal for Aurelian to infuse the blade with energy.

The old battle mage felt a sense of desolation as he opened his mind and channelled his power into the sword.

What, in the name of all things, was he going to say to Dwim?

*

Even before the deceptive flash of light Falco knew the dragon was black. Just as he had known at Darius's summoning. He felt it in his soul and his heart ached with a burning sense of regret. The creature flying towards them should have been his life's companion, his brother-in-arms, but the dragon he had summoned was black, with a black and murderous heart. The dark shape drew closer and closer, and just as before Falco caught glimpses of the dragon's mind.

Confusion... suspicion... hatred...

Why had it come to this hope-forsaken place?

Where was the brother who had summoned it?

Looking down upon the summoning stone the dragon hung in the air, its mighty wings beating back and forth to hold it aloft. It was uncertain and cautious but not afraid. Along the coast it had seen thousands of humans, swarming like ants around the stone walls of a city, but there was nothing here, only the wind and the rocks and the vast expanse of air.

So why was it here?

Slowly the dragon came lower until, with exquisite control, it landed on the flat area of stone. Behind it the cliff plunged a thousand feet to the rocks and scree of the mountain's slopes, while before it thirteen magi began to weave a subtle web of power. And still the dragon was oblivious.

Hidden by the concealing powers of the magi Falco gazed in wonder at the creature before him: the steel hard plates and shimmering scales rippling over a muscular body of flesh and blood, the horned head and lethal jaws, the fierce intelligence burning in eyes of fire and molten gold. It was the very embodiment of obsidian might.

Hardly daring to breathe Falco blinked his eyes as the boundary between his own thoughts and those of the dragon remained blurred. Once again he felt surging waves of empathy and compassion, but he hardened his heart and closed his mind to such things. It was just such weakness that had led to the death of

Darius and the destruction of his home. It was just such weakness that had diminished a great warrior like Nicolas Dusaule.

Falco knew that given the chance the dragon would destroy them all. The last time he had encountered such a beast he had been powerless to stop the killing but now he was a battle mage and he would not let it happen again.

Holding his stance he waited for the dragon to come closer, his sword humming with the force of Aurelian's power. Just a few more seconds and it would be done. He could feel the magi's net drawing tighter. Soon the dragon would sense it too and the moment it tried to react, it would die.

*

Galen Thrall watched with morbid fascination as the magnificent animal came to rest on the dragon stone. Over the years he had attended four summonings but this was the first time that a black dragon had answered the call. And all the stories were true.

Here was a creature of beauty and power, the oldest and strongest of all dragonkind. It was not especially large but there was something about its bearing, something deeply impressive and utterly terrifying.

As the dragon took another step forward Thrall felt the magi follow its progress, drawing their magical net tighter, ready to hold it down while Danté and the warrior mages dispatched it. But then the dragon seemed to sense that something was wrong. Its nostrils scented the air and its spear pointed tale began to weave back and forth. Its posture changed as it tensed in the face of an unseen threat, but it was too late. The magi's web of confinement was in place.

With a concerted effort eleven magi used their power to pull the dragon down while Falco lunged forward to strike. Thrall smiled as an arc of bright red blood sprayed onto the dragon stone.

*

Falco was astonished by the speed with which the dragon reacted. Despite the coils of restraining force it reared back and his blow merely inflicted a shallow cut to its long and powerful neck. The dragon stumbled as if under a great weight, its wings hampered by the invisible net of energy. But its tail remained free and Falco was forced to block a deadly strike as the blade-like point struck hard against his shield.

From the left, one of the warrior mages shot a bolt of energy that scored a deep gash across the dragon's ribs. It twisted violently and the attack of the second warrior mage went wide, blasting a jagged hole in the surface of the summoning stone. The dragon responded by exhaling a sudden gout of fire that would have killed one of the warrior mages who was too slow in casting his defensive spell. Fortunately Falco could now cast such spells with the speed of thought and the man merely flinched as the dragon's fire slammed into the protective sphere that surrounded him.

The dragon was struggling to remain on its feet but the spell of concealment had been broken and now it could see its tormentors. Staggering round it raked the cliffs with a sustained stream of fire and two of the magi were forced to duck behind their slabs of fortissite.

These two had now lost concentration but the nine that remained were more than enough to contain the dragon. Thrall had taken no chances with the

447

summoning of Falco Danté. Despite Falco's apparent determination, the Grand Veneratu had prepared a killing spell of his own. So powerful was this spell that Thrall's mind burned with the effort of holding it in check. As he watched the dragon being forced to the ground he realised that he might not need his lethal spell after all, but he would not relinquish it until he was certain the dragon was dead.

He watched as Falco deflected another tail strike and drove through a storm of fire to bring his blade within reach of the dragon's neck. The mighty creature was no longer able to raise its head but still it roared its fury and struggled to rise.

Thrall was tense with anticipation and the pupils of his eyes shrank to tiny beads of night. In truth he had doubted that Falco would have the resolve to kill a dragon, but once again this young battle mage surprised him. Thrall smiled as Falco blocked a lethal attack from one of the warrior mages. It seemed that Danté was finally taking responsibility. The young battle mage was determined to end this failed summoning himself.

*

Aurelian could scarcely bring himself to watch as Falco closed in on the subdued dragon. The old battle mage was weeping openly and for the first time he understood the true horror of the deed that had robbed Dusaule of his faith.

But all the tales were true.

Although he could not perceive it as strongly as Falco, he too could sense the dragon's mind. It wanted to kill them and so they had no choice but to kill it first, despite the fact that it would surely break their hearts.

Looking down at the great dragon he could only watch as Falco raised his sword and fortified his arm to deliver the coup de grâce.

*

Doubt screamed in Falco's mind. Pain wrung his soul and beat like futile fists upon the wall of steel he had placed around his heart.

'Wrong!' The feelings bellowed at him. *'This is wrong!'*

But Falco refused to listen. Once before he had allowed himself to be swayed by the voice of compassion and his weakness had cost them dear. But Falco was no longer weak, no longer prey to the foolish naivety of youth.

Through the T-shaped visor of his helm he looked down at the mighty beast, still struggling against the invisible cords that bound it. He looked down into the golden eyes that still blazed with fury. There was no sense of defeat or entreaty in the dragon's eyes. It looked at him with loathing and inextinguishable rage.

To his right one of the warrior mages unleashed a bolt of energy that would have killed the dragon, but with a contemptuous swipe of his mind Falco smacked it aside.

It was he who had summoned this agent of death.

It was he who would now see it dead.

His sword rang with Aurelian's power as he raised it high.

Black dragons are the enemy of humankind.

Black dragons are mad!

'Falco! No!'

448

A normal voice would never have been enough to stay Falco's hand, but Meredith's cry burst into his mind like a thunderclap. The force of it made him stagger, left him dazed. But then he looked up to where Meredith stood, staring down upon the dragon stone, and now it was Falco's eyes that blazed with fury.

It had taken all his strength to overcome his instinct to spare the dragon. He would never forgive Meredith for forcing him to face this burden a second time.

'Don't do it!' cried Meredith in a normal voice as he made his way down the steps towards them. The apprentice mage was sweating and pale and covered in blood, but his voice was clear. 'They lied to us,' he said, his eyes sweeping the cliffs to take in the magi.

'Silence!' cried Thrall and Meredith stumbled as a pulse of mental energy thumped into his mind. 'No one is permitted on the dragon stone once a summoning has begun!'

Falco's green eyes burned as he stared up at Meredith. He resented any doubt over what he had to do, but Meredith's voice rang with a desperate note of truth. Again he glanced down at the dragon and the certainty in his stance wavered.

'Let him speak!' bellowed Aurelian and Meredith came lower until he was almost level with the stone.

He glanced at the prostrate dragon and tried to ignore the heat of Thrall's furious gaze. All his thoughts were directed at Falco.

'The Great Possession is a lie,' he said. 'None of it is true.'

Falco might have been carved from stone as Meredith's gaze moved to Galen Thrall.

'It was not the dragons who were Possessed. It was the magi.'

The Grand Veneratu's lipid eyes fixed Meredith with the promise of retribution. To think that one of their own would betray them to the dull minded fools who swore their allegiance to the thrones. The young Saker was just weeks from completing his apprenticeship, just weeks from swearing oaths of unbreakable loyalty to the magi. But until then he was free to flap his treacherous tongue.

With no outward sign Thrall passed new instructions to the magi and the warrior mages surrounding the stone. And as Meredith continued, he allowed the killing spell, that he had held in check, to rise closer to the surface of his mind.

Meanwhile Falco stared at Meredith as if he did not understand the words he had just spoken.

'It's the dragons, Falco,' said Meredith, trying to penetrate the wall of cold dispassion that Falco had built around his heart. 'It's the dragons that know the truth.' Reaching the dragon stone he gazed down at the magnificent creature still straining against its bonds. 'They do not teach each other history as we do,' said Meredith. 'They experience it. As they age their memories reach further back in time. It is only as they turn black that they are old enough to recall the time of the Great Possession.'

Meredith's eyes filled with tears.

'Black dragons do not hate us because they are mad,' he told Falco. 'They hate us because they remember.'

Falco blinked and shook his head as images began to form in his mind.

'The magi killed them, Falco,' said Meredith. 'They killed them all.'

With his shield still strapped to his arm Falco raised a hand to his head. His mind was suddenly burning with indescribable anger.

He saw a place in the mountains, like a great bowl carved out of the earth. Dark clouds boiled in the sky and the wind howled as hundreds of magi appeared upon the surrounding rocks. Bodies lay upon the ground. Nineteen warriors dressed in armour. Nineteen battle mages. Dead. Not a mark on their bodies, except for a dark discolouration about their lips.

Falco reeled from a storm of memories that were not his own.

Fire and lightning exploded all around him as magical force scorched the air, leaving the burned scent of death upon the wind. His dragon kin fought back, but they were stunned by grief and shock. They fought back and killed by the score but the magi were too many, too well prepared and too consumed by the certainty of minds Possessed, minds that had been led to murder by the poisonous guile of Syballian the Prophet.

Falco almost buckled beneath the weight of emotion as Thrall's voice echoed round the dragon stone, his words thick with contempt.

'What's done is done!' he cried. 'It makes no difference. Their hatred for us will never die.' His gaze fell on the trapped and helpless dragon. 'They will kill us, unless we kill them first.'

Falco heard the insanity in the Grand Veneratu's voice, a madness to eclipse anything in the dragon's mind. But his own mind was struggling to comprehend the magnitude of Meredith's words. An indescribable act of murder, perpetrated in secret and covered over with four hundred years of lies.

Slowly he sheathed his sword.

These lies had been sold to kings and queens and cost them fully half the world, but Falco could think of nothing beyond his own enduring pain. His words were quiet as he voiced the question that Meredith had dreaded to hear.

'And my father?'

Meredith's heart was wracked with shame at the part his own father had played in the death of Aquila Danté.

'He grew too close to his dragon,' said Meredith. 'He learned too much.' Meredith knew the hurt that these words would cause, but there was one more thing that Falco needed to hear.

'Simeon didn't know,' he said and he could only hope that Falco could still hear him.

Simeon didn't know

The words echoed in Falco's head like the curse of long dead ghosts.

Simeon didn't know

Simeon le Roy, the man who had raised him, forced to kill his greatest friend because of the magi's lies. In the vacuum of his soul Falco felt all the years of torment and condemnation come rushing back to consume him, tearing at his mind and rending his heart.

All his life he had dreaded the thought of turning out like his father: a madman, a murderer. But it was all a lie.

Simeon didn't know

On the dragon stone of Wrath Falco Danté clenched his fists. He clenched his fists and the tingling sensation of power swept through his body. He clenched his fists and the tingling sensation in his mind turned to an ominous hum. The hum became a whine and the bonds around the dragon began to fail as Falco's fury leached out into the world.

'What are you doing!' cried Thrall as the magi's web of power was torn apart by the force of Falco's ire.

Falco clenched his fists and the dragon began to rise.

'You fool!' cried Thrall. 'You will kill us all.'

But Falco had passed beyond such petty concerns. A maelstrom of treachery, death and incalculable loss burned in his mind. If death was coming then let it come. They deserved no less.

Falco clenched his fists and the dragon was free.

'Kill it!' cried Thrall. 'Kill it now!' and thirteen magi unleashed their deadly spells.

But Falco had made his position clear. There would be no killing here tonight. Wielding his shield and his empty hand he swept aside the magi's attacks or blocked them with the protective force of his mind. But even his defensive skills were not enough to counter all the attacks and the dragon roared as several bolts of magical force blasted scales from its body.

Reaching out with his mind Falco grabbed one of the warrior mages and yanked him sideways, slamming his head into the fortissite column beside which he stood. He spun round and contained the second warrior mage in a sphere of energy just as the man unleashed a spell of his own. The man let out a scream as the fire of his own spell exploded around him.

The rest of the magi continued to fire off spells, but they were far less potent and the dragon was now free to vent some fury of its own. With a bound it leapt into the air and flooded one of the magi ledges with a storm of ferocious fire. The two men would surely have died had not a dome of magical force sprung up around them. The dragon's head whipped round, searching for the source of this new interfering player and its gaze fell upon the one-armed figure of Aurelian Cruz.

Eyes red with tears Aurelian looked up into the eyes of the dragon that was about to kill him. After what he had learned he did not have the heart to protect himself.

Falco looked up as the dragon reared above Aurelian. He saw it draw a breath.

'NO!' he cried and with a great effort of will he snatched the dragon from the sky.

The summoning stone shook as the mighty dragon came crashing down. With the speed of a giant cat it regained its feet, spun round and struck Falco a mighty blow that drove him to his knees. A second blow sent him flying back and a strike from its tail drew blood as it found a gap in his armour. Two ineffectual attacks from the magi distracted the dragon but a blast of dragon fire sent them scurrying for cover.

Dazed by the attacks Falco struggled to his feet as the dragon turned back to face him. He refused to draw his sword, refused to raise his shield or summon any kind of magical defence.

They had killed the dragons, their greatest allies, their fellow souls.

He might be only one man, cast adrift on the churning swells of grief. But he was human. And to fight now would make him complicit in the crime that had broken the bond between their two great races.

As the dragon reared above him Falco lowered his arms and raised his head. There was no excuse or plea for mercy in the bleak desolation of his gaze, only shame and sadness and the unquenchable fire of regret.

The dragon paused.

Nothing, in all its sable years, had challenged the animosity that it felt for humankind. There had been no doubt, no mitigation, no quarter near conceived. But still it paused. In its own mind it now saw images that it had never known before. Images from a dragon that might once have been red and of the soul that fought beside it. It felt the emotion of *human* fury at what had been done, not just to his dragon kin, but also to the great souls in human form. He saw the dragon and the man go out to face a new battle, to reconcile the present and the past. It was a battle that failed, and as the dragon and the man passed into darkness the image was replaced by that of a small boy, standing in the burnt out ruins of his home.

Wings spread and talons poised, the dragon paused as he looked down upon the mirror of his soul.

*

On a ledge above the dragon stone, concealed by a tall column of fortissite, Galen Thrall muttered the words of a spell that would see this dragon dead. He filled it with all his power and all his hateful spite. Then he closed his waxy green eyes, drew a breath and prepared to strike.

*

Lost in a world of pain Falco looked up into the golden eyes of the dragon. He was ready for the final blow, but then the dragon paused. Memories of his father swirled through his mind, intertwined with those of his dragon, impossible now to tell them apart. For a moment he felt the smallest hint of hope, a slender bridge that might lead them back from the brink of disaster. But then he felt the surge of Galen Thrall's will and the forming of his murderous spell.

With a roar of primal rage Falco spun round and thrust out his hand as a life's worth of pent up energy burst free in a sheet of blinding flame. It parted the air and severed the column of fortissite behind which Thrall had finalised his spell. But the Grand Veneratu never uttered the final word of release. The guillotine of light struck him in the chest, scything through ribs, lungs and spine. His lifeless body tumbled into view, the pupils in his waxy green eyes now fixed, never to narrow in malice again.

Above him the column of fortissite remained upright, the only substance that magical force cannot damage, sliced clean through by the power of an orphan's rage.

Silence descended on the dragon stone as the truth of what had just happened sank in.

452

The Worshipful Master of the magi was dead.

All eyes turned to look at Falco, but only the dragon watched him.

The dragon watched as Falco's mind cleared and he slowly became aware of what he had done. The fear of turning out like his father had kept his power locked away. His entire life had been scarred by the stigma of madness and murder, but now he knew that this perception was untrue. His father had never been a murderer and had only killed in self defence.

But what of him?

Could he have blocked the Grand Veneratu's spell?

Or had he lashed out in anger?

Killed in anger?

And what was that, if it was not murder?

All eyes were fixed on Falco, but only the dragon watched him. The dragon watched him as the realisation dawned in his mind, as remorse bloomed like an all consuming star in his breast. After all his fears and inhibitions, Falco had finally unlocked his power, only to become what his father never was. And he could not bear it.

'Falco! No!'

Meredith called out and Aurelian tried to stop him with mental force, but they were both too late. With the conviction of the damned Falco sprinted across the dragon stone and leapt into the consoling arms of death.

454

Part IV

REDEMPTION

Solace

Hoffen

ILLICIA

Le Matres

Wrath

Ville De Pierre

Maidstein

Reiherstadt

Amboss

CLEMÉNCE

Hertzheim

Seeburg

Toulwar

Caer Dour

Lake
Viegal

Ruaen

Navaria

The Pass of Amaethon

BELTANE

Maiden

VALENTIA

Caer Laison

Tavros

THE BAY
OF
BARINTHUS

ACHERON

R
IN

80

Great Chief

'No!' cried Aurelian as Falco disappeared from view.

But as quickly as Falco vanished over the edge of the dragon stone so he was followed by a winged streak of night.

While everyone else had been looking at Falco, the dragon had watched him. It had watched as the storm of emotions tore through his mind until there was nothing left but blind, unbearable remorse. It was just such naked emotion that had stayed the dragon's hand, cut through its own madness and the vengeful mist of hate. It was just such emotion that had saved the dragon's life. And now the vessel of that emotion had leapt to his death.

Even as Falco started to run the dragon moved to follow. It was still confused and burning with rage, but finally it recognised the brother who had summoned it, the brother who had saved it from the magic users' bonds and killed the master who would surely have slain it.

As Falco leapt from the summoning stone the dragon leapt after him. Turning in the air it gave a mighty sweep of its wings, accelerating towards the figure that was plummeting towards the rocks below. With no time for a second beat the dragon tucked in its wings, tightened its scales and cut through the air with the speed of a stooping hawk. The wind whistled over its streamlined body as the mountain loomed below it.

A hundred feet from the jagged rocks the dragon broke out of its dive and snatched the armoured body from the air. There was no time for gentleness. It gripped the figure by the shoulder, forcing its talons through the gaps in his armour then it spread its wings to arrest their descent. But it was too late to avoid an outcrop of grass and rocky shale.

Throwing up a shower of rocky soil Falco's body clipped the outcrop as the dragon struggled to find some purchase on the air. Rolling to one side it swung Falco away from a ridge of solid rock, but this left it with no room to manoeuvre as it plunged towards the mountain's slopes. As the ground rushed up to meet it the dragon turned onto its back and gathered Falco's inert form against its chest.

The mighty beast skidded into a bank of scree, ploughing a rough furrow with the hard mass of its body before coming to rest in a mounded crater, shrouded in a cloud of gritty dust.

*

Aurelian and Meredith stared down in horror as the dragon turned in the air, curled into a ball and smashed into the rocky slopes of the mountain. A great cloud of grey dust burst into the air, obscuring the site of the impact. With their hearts frozen in their chests they waited for the dust to clear.

A thousand feet below them, the twilight wind tugged at the cloud of dust and carried it away across the valley. As the view cleared they saw the dark shape of the dragon rise from the ground. For a moment it looked down at something before lowering its head and mantling its wings like an eagle protecting its kill. But then it shifted its position and turned its head to look at them. For a moment it gazed up at the two humans as if it were memorising their faces with its aquiline sight. Then it spread its wings and surged into the sky.

It was too far away for Aurelian and Meredith to make out much more than an outline, but as the dragon rose into the air they were certain that it was holding something close against its chest. It gained height quickly then angled north away from the city. They watched it for a few more seconds before it disappeared behind an arm of the mountain. And suddenly the wide expanse of sky was empty.

Before they could speak or even try to absorb what had just happened they heard movement behind them. Turning round they saw the magi standing on the dragon stone, shocked and scared and dangerous.

'The Grand Veneratu is dead,' said one of the men.

'Danté killed him,' said another.

'You betrayed us,' said a third, his eyes focussed on Meredith.

On a nearby ledge one of the warrior mages struggled down onto the stone. His clothes were black and his flesh was burned from the fire of his own spell. He needed medical attention but the magi seemed unable to focus on anything beyond Thrall's death and Meredith's revelations.

'You cannot tell anyone,' said the other warrior mage. 'You would put your brothers at risk.'

'The magi are no brothers of mine,' said Meredith. He spoke through gritted teeth and the atmosphere on the dragon stone darkened beyond the limits of the encroaching night.

The magi formed a line in front of them and the unharmed warrior mage levelled his sword.

'Enough!' cried Aurelian and a fierce ball of fire sprang up around his fist. His face was streaked with tears and his voice was coarse with the strain of all that had happened and all that he had learned. 'We are leaving now,' he told them. 'It would be a mistake to try to prevent us.'

The magi recoiled in the face of Aurelian's anger, and with a shove of his armless shoulder he urged Meredith forwards, the fireball still writhing around his fist. As they reached the rough steps leading away from the dragon stone Meredith stumbled, the strain of this terrible night was finally taking its toll.

'What have I done?' he asked as the adrenaline leached away and the ramifications of his actions began to dawn on his mind.

'You have uncovered the truth and saved the lives of two great souls,' said Aurelian taking Meredith's weight as the young man stumbled.

'But Thrall...'

'The Grand Veneratu was lost long before tonight,' said Aurelian as the full extent of the magi's corruption became suddenly clear. The power of Possession had not died with Syballian the prophet. It had endured like a shadow in the minds of the magi ever since. It explained their enduring animosity towards the battle mages and the dragons who bore them. It explained their reluctance to support the thrones in the war against the Possessed. And it explained the vague distrust that the people had always felt towards the magi. For all the battle mages' insight they had underestimated the instincts of common folk.

'But where will we go,' said Meredith, as if the thought had just occurred to him. 'I can't go back to the tower... I can't face my father.'

458

'Don't worry,' said Aurelian as they descended towards the horses. 'I know where we can go.'

'But where?' cried Meredith, a note of hysteria creeping into his voice. 'Where can we go that they cannot reach us?'

'We'll go to the Queen,' said Aurelian. 'She will know what to do.'

'And may the heavens preserve her,' thought Aurelian as he struggled to get Meredith onto a horse.

The Queen bore the troubles of the entire world upon her shoulders and now he was about to bring chaos to her door.

*

The Queen looked down at the young man now sleeping in her bed, the pearl white pillow on which he lay stained dark with his blood.

'Will he be all right?' she asked as Aurelian stood back from the bed.

'It's hard to say. He has borne a great deal and now he has cut himself adrift from everything he knew.'

'Not everything, I hope,' said the Queen and Aurelian tilted his head in concession.

He remembered the awkward beginnings of friendship that Meredith had begun to establish with Falco, Malaki and Bryna, and he knew that Dwimervane had always liked the apprentice mage. Meredith had surely severed his ties with his father and the magi, but he was not entirely without friends.

They looked down at his pale face, horribly disfigured by the wounds that Brother Pacatos had caused him to inflict upon himself. The court physician had done what he could to repair the torn flap of skin but Meredith would bear an ugly scar for the rest of his days.

There were a few seconds of silence before the Queen spoke again.

'And you still think that Falco is alive?'

Aurelian gave a thoughtful nod. 'I believe so,' he said. 'The dragon definitely tried to save him.'

'But where will it take him?'

'Somewhere safe,' said Aurelian, thinking of the times that Dwimervane had carried *him* away from danger.

'What about you? Are you sure you will be safe at the cottage?'

'The magi have more to worry about than one old battle mage,' said Aurelian. 'They'll be too busy thinking of ways to justify their deceit.'

'And Nicolas?'

Aurelian shook his head at the thought of telling Dusaule. How do you tell a man that there was no justification for the deed that broke his heart?

'I should go,' he said, his voice filled with a deep weariness. 'Falco's friends will be wondering why we haven't returned.'

With a bow he left the room and the Queen stared after him until the door re-opened and Cyrano came back into the room. The Queen's advisor had been horrified when she gave the order to take the injured man to her chambers, but now that they had learned the truth he could think of no safer place for the apprentice mage. Still struggling to process the ramifications of all that they had learned he made his way over to stand beside the Queen.

'What will you do?' he asked.

'I don't know,' said the Queen and Cyrano gave her a sideways glance.

He had been amazed by the cold calm with which she had listened to Meredith's tale, but he knew that she burned with fury too. And now the impossible question of how to proceed lay with her.

'I wish the Chevalier were here,' said the Queen. 'He would know what to do.'

Cyrano could hear the desperate loneliness in her voice.

'Perhaps it's better he is not,' he said. 'Else I fear we would still be collecting magi bodies from the foot of the dragon stone.'

Here the Queen actually smiled at her advisor's dark humour.

'Perhaps you are right,' she said.

'You still think we should tell the people?' asked Cyrano and the Queen nodded.

'They have a right to know the truth.'

'There will be trouble.'

'What!' snapped the Queen. 'More trouble than four hundred years of spiteful opposition: of slaying innocent dragons and emasculating battle mages who might have saved us?'

Cyrano bowed his head. Like her, he could barely comprehend the enormity of this deceit, but he did not see how sacking the towers and lynching hundreds of magi would help them in the war against the Possessed.

The Queen's anger was written in the tight lines of her face. However, behind the physical reaction Cyrano could see her mind working furiously to think of a solution. He knew she would not act in haste, but he needed to know what she intended to do and how much additional security might be required in the city.

'So will you tell them,' he persisted.

'No,' said the Queen and here she looked down at Meredith. 'I will not tell them. He will,'

'You can't be serious,' said Cyrano but the Queen's eyes had taken on a fierce glint and there was no indication that she spoke in jest.

'Do you know the meaning of his name?' she asked and Cyrano just looked at her. 'Meredith,' she mused. 'From an old Valentian tongue. It means great chief.'

Cyrano turned back to look at the young man asleep on the bed.

'If the magi are going to survive this they will need a new spokesman,' continued the Queen as if the idea was gathering weight in her mind. 'Someone the people can actually trust. And I can think of no one better than the one man who had the courage to lay bare their lies.'

Cyrano was shocked at the very idea, but then he recalled what the Queen had said about the Chevalier and he shook his head despairingly.

'*Yes*,' he thought. '*This was precisely the kind of solution that Sir William would suggest.*'

81

Reconciled

Falco became aware of pain in his right shoulder and left arm. His helmet and been pushed askew and the muscles in his neck protested as he turned his head to straighten it. Blinking to clear his vision he tried to take in his surroundings. It was night time and he was lying on bare, slate-coloured rock that shone with the faint glow of moonlight. He tried to shift round but his entire body ached. He felt as if he had taken a beating and had the vague sense that he had lost consciousness. His thoughts and memories felt fuzzy and indistinct. The last thing he remembered was riding into the mountains with Aurelian.

Inching round he saw that his left arm was still hooked in the straps of his shield, twisted at an awkward angle. With a gasp of pain he adjusted his position and finally succeeded in pulling his arm free. Easing off his gauntlet he tried to move his fingers. They felt stiff and numb but they opened and closed easily enough. It seemed that nothing was broken.

Shifting again he winced as pain lanced through his right shoulder. He slipped his hand beneath his armour and felt the sticky wetness of blood.

Removing his other gauntlet he reached up and fumbled with the strap of his helmet. Slipping the buckle he pushed it from his head and the night air felt cold against his sweat damp hair. The left side of his face ached as if from a heavy blow and he reached up gingerly to probe his nose and cheekbone. Again, nothing appeared to be broken but there was more blood around his mouth and nose. With a lightheaded breath he pushed his long hair back from his face and stared out over a remote mountain landscape. He was high in the mountains, very high. Pushing up from the ground he struggled to his knees then froze.

He was not alone.

With a rush of adrenaline Falco leapt to his feet and drew his sword, the pain in his right shoulder flaring at the sudden movement. There, not ten feet in front of him, was a mighty black dragon. Like an avatar of darkness it stared down at him with eyes the colour of molten gold.

And now everything came rushing back.

The unbearable hope and the desperate fear of what might come to pass at his summoning. The determination to send out a pure and honest call and the excruciating wait to see what, if anything, would answer. The screaming disappointment when he sensed the colour black. The deception, the violence, and then the revelations that had struck him to the core.

The sadness, the despair.

And the unbearable fury that had driven him to kill.

With a cry of anguish Falco let the sword fall from his grasp. He had tried to end the pain but he had failed. Falling to his knees he bowed his head and wept. He wept for the dragons and he wept for his father, he wept for Darius and Simeon and for all those who had paid the price for the magi's lies.

Finally he wept for himself and he wished with all his heart that the dragon would kill him. But then he sensed movement and felt the gentle pressure of something pressing against his head.

He was not the only one who wept.

Falco felt an overwhelming rush of feeling as the dragon laid its horned head against his. All the emotions that tore at his heart were mirrored in the dragon's mind. There was no way to distinguish one from the other. Slowly the tumult died away until all that was left was a sadness. Just a few hours ago they had each sought the other's death, both acted with hate in their hearts. But long before they had ever met their fates had been entwined and now, high in the mountains of northern Clemoncé, these two great souls were reconciled.

Slowly the dragon drew back. It raised its head and closed its eyes and then Falco staggered as from a great compression of the air, a silent clap of thunder that echoed through his mind. Finally he understood that the summoning of a dragon was not just the tolling of some ethereal bell, it was a pledge.

My life,

My strength,

My soul, I cleave to thee.

Falco had sent his message out into the world and now a dragon had answered.

Boom!

*

In the mountains of Illicia a wild man cowered in the haunted darkness of his cave.

In the olive groves of Thraece a healer woke, sweating and breathless, from a deep and troubled sleep.

And on the rugged coast of Beltane a fisherman stared out to sea as the unforgiving waves of the past bore down upon his soul.

*

In a distant land, far beyond the Endless Sea, the dragon's reply was also heard.

And three that never answered did.

82

Sidian

The clear night gave way to a wet morning and the city of Wrath steamed as shafts of sunlight shone through the breaking cloud. Cyrano stood with the Queen at the eastern balcony of her chambers. He had just come from the royal pigeonnier where a message had arrived from their contacts in Valentia. It contained pressing news but the advisor kept the small piece of parchment hidden in his hand. Now was not the time to deliver such a message. Warily he glanced at the Queen who stood beside him, eyes narrowed, jaw set and hair dampened by the morning showers, she stared out over a city shrouded in smoke.

No one knew how the riots began. Some said that magi appeared in the night, spreading rumours of the Grand Veneratu's murder, others that a crazed old man had wandered into the city, naked and covered in ashes, and shouting about treachery and lies. People spoke of how the magi had come to remove him and injured two women who had tried to intervene. But however they began, by the time the ninth bell of the morning sounded, there were more than a dozen people dead and numerous buildings alight, sending dark clouds of smoke billowing up into the sky.

'Is it spreading?' asked the Queen.

'No,' said Cyrano. 'It is still largely confined to the eastern quarter, but the city guard is standing ready to intervene.'

'Not without my order,' said the Queen and Cyrano could hear the controlled anger in her voice.

He was no longer surprised by the calm clarity with which she dealt with such things. A more nervous leader might have already sent in the troops, but they both remembered one of her father's tenets when it came to civil unrest.

Do not feed the fire

For now the mob's anger was directed towards the magi and those businesses in the eastern quarter who dealt with them: the apothecaries and alchemists, the clothiers, scribes and bookbinders. If the soldiers went in now that anger could quickly switch to city officials, store masters and anyone else who might be deemed responsible for the hardships the people were suffering.

'Do they know the truth?' asked the Queen.

'Various versions and rumours seem to be circulating,' replied Cyrano. 'But they know they have been betrayed.'

'This is all my fault.'

They turned to see Meredith emerge onto the balcony. His robes had been washed and dried and he wore them now as he made his way to stand beside them. He looked pale and distressed, his eyes hollow, and a blood stained dressing bound to the side of his head.

'What have I done?'

'What was necessary,' replied the Queen.

There was a knock on the Queen's chamber door and presently a captain of the Palace Guard appeared. He waited just inside the room until Cyrano moved to speak with him.

'What is it?' asked the Queen.

'The attacks in the city have stopped,' said Cyrano. 'But the people are now massing outside the eastern gate. They intend to march on the tower.'

The Queen turned to look back over the city, to where the road wound up onto the plateau. She could not see the area immediately beyond the wall, but she could imagine the unruly throng slowly building up the courage to storm the mysterious tower of the magi.

Lowering her brow in determination she turned away from the balcony.

'Fetch my horse,' she told Cyrano as she swept back into the room. 'Louisa,' she went on, addressing her lady-in-waiting who emerged with two other maids from the adjoining parlour. 'Riding breeches, shirt and jerkin.' Louisa gave a white-faced nod and ushered the two maids into the Queen's dressing room. Finally the Queen turned to the captain of the Palace Guard. 'Have ten of your men meet us in the courtyard,' she commanded.

'You can't go down there!' protested Cyrano.

'We can't send in the army,' said the Queen. 'You know what will happen if we do.'

The concern was chiselled into Cyrano's face, but he remembered the famine of twenty years ago, when the city guard had tried to prevent people from looting the grain stores.

'I'm coming with you,' said Meredith.

'No!' said Cyrano and the captain together, but Meredith would not be deterred.

'This is my doing,' he said. 'You must give me the chance to make amends.'

For a moment the Queen simply stared at him.

'So be it,' she said and turned to continue on her way. 'Have a horse brought for Lord Saker.'

'Your Majesty!' cried Cyrano.

'They will tear him from the saddle!' said the captain.

'Not while he is under *my* protection, they will not!' bellowed the Queen and both men stood back in shock. For a moment her eyes blazed but then she drew a breath and spoke more calmly. 'We spoke of him leading a change, did we not?'

'Yes,' said Cyrano. 'To head a commission or lead an inquiry. Not to face down an angry mob!'

'We cannot always choose the time and place of our battles,' said the Queen and Cyrano felt the corners of the concealed note pressing into the palm of his hand. 'Now. Horses, gentlemen. As quick as you please!' And with that the doors to her dressing room closed.

In a matter of minutes ten mounted palace guard were waiting in the courtyard with the Queen's own horse, a beautiful black stallion by the name of Souverain. There was also a spare mount for Meredith. The captain had furnished him with a blue guard's cloak to hide his magi robes.

'This way he might make it through the city,' said the captain and the Queen gave him a nod of acknowledgement before swinging lightly into the saddle.

She was now dressed in riding boots, leather breeches, a white blouse and a dark leather jerkin cinched at the waist by the emissary's black belt, from which hung her sword. Over this she wore a turquoise cloak emblazoned with the white

464

horse-head insignia. It was not the most elegant of outfits but no one would mistake their Queen.

The palace gates were swung open and with military precision the Queen's guard matched her pace as she trotted out of the courtyard and down the road that led into the city. The streets were narrow and filled with worried looking people, but the troops held formation as they escorted the Queen towards the eastern gate and the road that led up to the plateau. However, as they passed through the double curtain wall it was clear that they were too late. The main body of the crowd had now disappeared over the lip of the plateau. They would be at the tower before the Queen could reach them.

*

Morgan Saker stood with several of the tower's most senior magi as the crowds appeared. The balcony was high and the doors to the tower were strong, but they had not been designed to withstand a siege.

'How many warriors do we have in the tower,' asked one of the men beside him.

'Enough to scatter this rabble,' said another.

They spoke with customary arrogance, but this tone was not echoed by the majority of the magi in the tower. Most appeared shaken and overwrought with doubt. News of the Grand Veneratu's death had struck them deeply, but it had also fractured the cloak of certainty beneath which they had lived their lives.

For four hundred years they had kept a terrible secret. Now that secret had been uncovered and it was as if a veil had been lifted from their minds. For the first time they felt complicit in the crime and the justifications for keeping it secret seemed empty and meaningless. Many were openly chastising themselves or gathered together in fearful groups, while others discussed ways to defend the magi against the judgement that would surely come.

As Morgan Saker looked out from the tower he realised that this judgment was now upon them.

*

At the Crofters' cottage Aurelian looked down as a great host of people streamed over the plateau.

'They're heading for the tower,' he said to Dwimervane who was standing beside him.

Telling her and Dusaule the night's dreadful news had been a heart rending experience. Dwimervane was clearly unsettled but Aurelian was concerned about Dusaule. He had stumbled from the cottage and disappeared into the night. Aurelian was desperately worried for his friend, but then he saw a column of palace guard riding up onto the plateau.

'That's the Queen!' he said in disbelief. 'She's going to try and intervene!'

'Surely she must know how dangerous and unpredictable situations like this could be?'

'Come on,' he said, hurrying along the slope that swept round towards the tower. 'Looks like she might need some help.'

With only the slightest hesitation Dwimervane moved to follow him. In the years to come she might well succumb to anger and madness, but for now her

465

instinct was to protect humankind at all costs, even if that meant protecting them from each other.

*

On the outskirts of the Irregulars' camp Falco's friends watched as the mob swept towards the tower with all the aggression of an advancing army.

'Looks like the people have discovered the truth?' said Alex and Malaki nodded.

Aurelian had come to speak with them in the night and they were still reeling from the news, although they were less concerned with the magi's treachery than with what had become of Falco.

'I'm sure he's alive,' was all Aurelian had been able to say.

Now Bryna stepped forward as a troop of palace guard appeared on the plateau.

'That's the Queen,' she said as she caught sight of the horse-head motif on one of the riders' cloaks.

'Looks like they could do with some support,' said Quirren.

Malaki gave a grim nod and turned to Bryna and Alex.

'Keep a close eye on the Irregulars,' he said as he moved to where the horses were tethered. 'The last thing we want is them being caught up in any trouble.'

Untying his horse he called over to Huthgarl and five of the other cadet knights who were standing nearby. Within moments they were mounted and riding parallel to the Queen who was struggling to make headway through the milling throng.

'She'll never get ahead of them,' called out Quirren as it became clear that the crowd would reach the tower before the Queen.

'Just be ready to help if things get out of hand,' said Malaki.

*

Falco woke to the light of day but the sky above him was black. The air was cold but he felt warm as if he had slept with his back to a fire. Pushing himself up from the ground he groaned at the stiffness in his body then blinked as the black canopy drew back and clouds appeared in the sky. Realisation finally dawned and he watched as the dragon folded its wings and moved back along the ledge, watching him intently.

Moving slowly Falco eased himself up and sat on a knee-high slab of rock. He had no idea how long he had slept but it appeared to be well into morning. As he slowly got his bearings he recalled dreamlike images of the previous night. He remembered the summoning, and the leap into nothingness, before coming round in the presence of the dragon.

He remembered the dragon's powerful call, like an echo of his own, and then a time of cautious discovery as they became accustomed to each other's presence. But as the tumult of emotions finally subsided, Falco had been overcome by a deep weariness and an irresistible urge to sleep.

Using his shield for a pillow he had simply curled up on the bare ground just a few feet from the dragon. Earlier in the night they had tried to kill each other, but as Falco had closed his eyes, he was not troubled by the merest shred of doubt that he was safe.

466

For its part the dragon had simply watched him, as if trying to fathom the contrasting sense of power and vulnerability. In all its years it had never known such strength in one so young. *He* was among the strongest of all his kind and yet he felt no disparity between himself and the human soul with which he had been twinned.

As the night wore on it had started to rain and the dragon had moved to lie beside Falco, spreading a great black wing to shelter him while he slept. The aftershocks of rage still thrummed in its veins, but the madness had passed and he realised that a new chapter had opened in the legend of his life. The dragon now knew that he had come to this land to fight the ancient foe and he was content to know that this human would fight beside him.

Now they sat together on a craggy mountain ridge and as the fuzziness of sleep cleared away, Falco's eyes focussed on the dragon. It was one thing to encounter such a creature in the charged excitement of a summoning. It was quite another to see it in the clear light of morning. Like something sculpted from black volcanic rock it watched him, its head moving slightly, fierce golden eyes slowly blinking, chest rising and falling, and breath steaming in the cold mountain air.

Falco's gaze took in the black scales and armoured plates, the smooth leathery wings and the huge claws, resting against the stone. His eyes travelled over the long spear-pointed tail and powerful body. He saw crimson patches of exposed flesh where the dragon's scales had been damaged by the mage warriors' attacks. Then his eyes came to rest on the cut in the dragon's neck, the cut that *he* had inflicted.

Slowly he got to his feet and the dragon tensed as he moved towards it.

'It's all right,' said Falco, wincing from a sudden pain in his shoulder as he raised his hand.

The dragon seemed wary but held its ground as Falco approached.

A sense of remorse swept through Falco's mind as he remembered striking at the dragon's neck. Slowly he reached out a hand and the dragon reared back, but Falco turned to look up into its hot golden eyes.

'It's all right,' he said again and the dragon's posture seemed to relax just a little.

Extending his arm he ran his hand over the shallow cut and the dragon let out a low growl of suppressed pain as the wound was suffused by waves of healing energy. The dragon's lip curled and Falco caught a glimpse of steel hard teeth as the intense tingling sensation faded from its flesh. Over time the damaged scales would slowly be replaced but for now the cut was closed as if it had been healing for several days.

Moving slowly Falco tended the other injuries inflicted by the magi before stepping back to sit on the rocks. His own body still throbbed with pain and he struggled to remove his shoulder guards and chest armour so that he could begin to treat himself. He already knew there was nothing broken, but there was a nasty gouge down the back of his shoulder and a puncture wound in the flesh where his chest and shoulder met. He did not remember how he had acquired these injuries, but fortunately they were not too serious.

467

Placing his left hand over each wound in turn he ground his teeth as he imbued his own body with curative power. This definitely helped and as the sense of tingling fire faded away he found the pain greatly reduced although, as with the dragon, it would be some days before the wounds were properly healed.

Falco drew a deep breath and took a minute to take in their surroundings. The rain had now stopped, the clouds were lifting and he could see that they were high up in the mountains. The dragon must have caught him as he fell and carried him here.

Glancing again at the impressive creature he rose to his feet and moved to a hollow in the rocks that was filled with water. He washed his hands and splashed water on his face and winced as he worked his battered body back into his armour. On the rocks nearby were his shield, gauntlets, helmet and sword. He retrieved each in turn and the dragon watched him as he covered his body in armour once more.

Slowly the dragon rose to its feet and moved towards him, watching as Falco fastened the chin strap of his helm. The dragon loomed over him then bent its head to examine Falco more closely, sniffing at the steel helmet and armour.

'Yes,' said Falco, feeling strangely self conscious. 'We can take our armour off.'

He stumbled back a step as the dragon tested one of its horns against his chest; the sound was more like metal on metal than steel against something organic. Once again he reached out to place a hand on the dragon's jet black scales.

'*Like obsidian*,' he thought and the dragon drew back to look at him.

Falco found images of the black volcanic rock flashing through his mind and he felt the dragon's curiosity as something like a name began to form. He had the sudden insight that dragon's did not use names for each other. Such things were purely a human need.

'It's what we do,' said Falco, surprised at how natural it felt for him to be addressing a dragon. 'I'll have to call you something,' he mused and the dragon stared at him as if it had some understanding of what he was trying to say. 'I mean... what would you call me?' he asked.

Of course the dragon did not answer in words. Instead Falco's mind was suddenly filled with a swift burst of emotions and images. The experience left him reeling from its force. It would be impossible to express it effectively, but if it could be translated into human words it might be rendered as, *He That Burns With Grief.*

Falco bowed his head in humility.

'For us, names gain strength and meaning as we come to know a person,' he said and the dragon looked down at him with a proud and wary expression.

Falco gazed at the dragon's shining black scales and the obsidian sheen of the horns that curved out from its head.

'Sidian,' he said softly as if testing the way the word sounded when spoken aloud. 'Yes. That will do,' he added and the dragon angled its head. The haughty expression on its face softening ever so slightly as it deigned to accept so crude a thing as a name.

Falco smiled as if they had finally been introduced, but then the dragon stiffened and turned its head, its nostrils flaring as it scented something on the air. Falco turned to follow the direction of its gaze. Veils of mist and low cloud still drifted across the mountains but through the gaps they could see the city of Wrath in the distance. For a moment Falco saw nothing amiss, but then he noticed the plumes of smoke rising up from the landward side of the city.

There was no way he could know for certain but instinct told him that the fires had something to do with the magi and the secret they had kept from the people. There was trouble afoot and it was time for him to return to the city.

He looked out over the impassable terrain that lay before him and wondered how on earth he was going to get down. Then slowly he turned to look at the dragon standing beside him. With a sudden sense of anticipation he found himself wondering if a black dragon could fly as well as a younger dragon like Ciel.

Sidian gave him a distinctly affronted look as images of an amber dragon and sunset skies played across his mind. Angling his body towards Falco he lowered his wing and looked at him expectantly.

Falco swallowed a sense of nervousness, his heart suddenly hammering in his chest. Easing the stiffness from his body he slipped his arm through the shoulder strap on his shield and slung it across his back then using a rock for a boost he climbed onto Sidian's back.

The black dragon was a little bigger than Ciel but still its body was only about the size of a slender horse. Falco tucked his knees below the membrane of the dragon's wings and felt the roll of its muscular shoulders as it walked to the top of the ridge. For a moment he stared down at the steep crags dropping away below them then Sidian spread his wings and turned his head to look back at him. Leaning forward Falco squeezed with his knees and gripped the ridges at the base of Sidian's neck. The dragon's scales seemed to shift beneath him, moulding themselves to the contours of his body.

Just as they were about to go Falco felt the dragon hesitate, its body tense, its claws digging into the rocks and suddenly he understood. They were about to fly down to a city full of people, full of humans.

'It's all right,' said Falco. 'Not all humans are like the magi. And not all magi are like Galen Thrall.'

An image of Thrall appeared in his mind and with it came a hot flash of anger, but the sense of his words seemed to reach the great black dragon and Falco tensed as Sidian dropped back on his haunches. Then he felt a stomach clenching lurch as the dragon kicked off from the ridge and dropped like a stone before spreading his wings and soaring away from the jagged cliffs. They streaked down into the steep sided corrie and swept over a turquoise tarn before the land fell away in a series of inaccessible cliffs and tumbling waterfalls.

The wind roared in Falco's ears, muffled only slightly by the padding in his helm. His eyes watered and his breath seemed to catch in his throat, but slowly he became accustomed to the exhilarating speed. Far below, the crags and hills went past in a blur as they descended quickly towards the city.

As they drew closer he could see the mass of people swarming towards the mage tower. Even as he watched he saw distant figures appear on the steps of the tower. A few seconds later a bright ball of flame shot out towards the advancing crowd, but it only served to spur it on. The reality of what was about to happen was horribly clear and Falco knew that once the violence began it would be impossible to stop.

'*Faster,*' he thought, and with two rapid wing beats Sidian drove them on at ever greater speed.

*

Leading the knights up to a higher level of the plateau Malaki watched as the black gates of the tower opened and a line of warrior mages emerged onto the steps. He doubted that the magi would attack the people, but in such volatile circumstances it was impossible to be sure. Then, even as he tried to convince himself that they would not be so foolish, one of the warrior mages sent a ball of fire streaking from his hand. The attack struck the ground and exploded several yards ahead of the advancing mob. It was clearly intended to deter the angry crowd, but it had exactly the opposite effect. With a cry of outrage the people charged forward. Two more fireballs shot forth, but this time a number of civilians were thrown aside in showers of dirt and flame.

Sweeping around the blasts the people in the front ranks surged forwards and Malaki suddenly realised that the mage tower was about to be overrun. More warrior mages emerged from the tower and it was clear that hundreds of people were about to die but then a ripple of fear ran through the crowd and people started pointing upwards.

Malaki felt the hairs on the back of his neck stand on end as a shadow swept across the sky. Glancing up he felt his heart quicken as a great black shape swooped down into the space between the tower and the wild advancing throng. The front ranks of the mob stumbled to a terrified halt as a huge black dragon landed before them. It reared up and spread its wings, staring down at them with a fierce, imperious gaze. And on its back was a rider clad in the unmistakable armour of Antonio Missaglias.

83

Le Cœur Noir

Falco stared out through the T-shaped visor in his helm. He could see the fear on the faces of the people as they stared in awe at the mighty black dragon. His own heart was racing after the incredible descent from the mountains and he could feel the tension in Sidian's body at being so close to a multitude of beings that he had hated for so long. Making an effort to calm his own breathing Falco tried to reassure Sidian that he had nothing to fear from the hordes of people now standing before them.

The humans behind them, however, were a different matter and Falco turned to sweep his gaze over the warrior mages gathered on the steps of the tower. He could feel their fear and the nervous spikes of power as spells hovered on the edge of release. With newfound control he allowed his own power to rise in his breast, and such was the force of its dark luminescence that the warrior mages literally staggered back in dread.

Falco's gaze moved up to the magi gathered at the windows and balconies above them, the flesh of their faces blanched with shock. These men could meditate for a week and never match the power that he could unleash in a heartbeat. From his earliest memories Falco had been afraid of the magi, but now he had come of age and there was nothing left to fear from the shadow-hearted men in purple robes.

Something drew his attention and Falco's eyes alighted on the familiar face of Morgan Saker. His eyes were as black and implacable as ever, but the sense of utter conviction was gone. There was a crack in the Veneratu's gaze and Falco knew he would spend the rest of his days riven by doubt and inescapable guilt.

'That's him!' cried a mage to Saker's right, a bald-headed man with a series of runes tattooed down the side of his face. Leaning over the balcony he stabbed a finger directly at Falco. 'That's the man who killed the Grand Veneratu! Little wonder a black dragon answered *his* black heart!'

'Black heart!' echoed a different mage.

'Murderer!' shouted another.

'Shame!' cried a fourth and several magi took up the cry of murder but then another voice echoed back from the walls of the tower.

'Shame?' cried Meredith as the Queen's retinue finally broke through to the front of the crowd. 'You talk of shame!'

From her own black mount the Queen watched as Meredith slid down from his horse and turned towards the tower. With an impatient gesture he pulled off the palace guard's cloak and threw it to the ground. A murmur of disquiet ran through the crowd at the sight of a mage within their reach, but by now they had all noted the presence of the Queen. For many of these common folk this was the first time they had seen their monarch up close and a ripple of whispers spread through the crowd as angry shouts were replaced by an expectant hush.

Meredith's face was as pale as the bandages wrapped around his head and he wavered slightly as he stumbled forward, but his voice was clear as he looked up into the collective face of the magi.

'Traitor!' called one of the magi, leaning from a window and Meredith turned to look at him.

'You have the nerve to call *me* traitor,' he said. 'Are you really so blind to the wrong you have done.'

'Kill them!' called out a voice from the crowd and Meredith felt the mob's anger surge like a wave about to break upon the tower.

'They don't deserve to live,' cried another voice.

'They betrayed us all.'

'They deserve to die.'

'Kill them!'

The calls for retribution were gaining in voice and number.

'You have no right to judge us!' came the defiant cry from one of the magi.

'No?' queried Meredith, and behind him the Queen raised a hand to quieten the crowd. 'What about the thousands of people camped around the city,' Meredith went on. 'The bereaved families, driven from their homes because we lacked the strength to stop the Possessed?'

Up on the balcony the mage's mouth drew a thin tight line, his chin sinking back into the folds of his neck as he gazed down at Meredith, unrepentant, arrogant to the last.

'What about the battle mages whose dragons you have slain. Great souls betrayed and broken to protect your lies. What about them? Do they have a right to judge?'

'Kill them!' came the now familiar refrain.

'Drag them out. Burn it down. Hang them all.'

The ugly violence of the mob was beginning to rise once more and several magi ducked back from windows as stones began to smack and shatter against the dark walls of the tower.

'No,' said Meredith his voice now quiet. 'Death and vengeance will only serve the enemy's designs.'

'We cannot leave them,' said an elderly man from nearby. 'We cannot trust them.'

'Then we shall bind them,' said Meredith and his voice had the dire tone of an executioner. 'The magi are sworn to ancient bonds, oaths of unbreakable loyalty.' His eyes were filled with such a dark light as to give even his father pause. 'We shall forge a new oath. Not to the magi and the person of the Grand Veneratu, but to the people of Wrath, to *their* safety and solace.'

'And what if we refuse to swear such an oath?' asked the bald man with the rune decorated face. His words were directed to Meredith, but it was the Queen who answered.

'Then you will be exiled to the Forsaken Lands, where you can throw yourselves upon the mercy of the Possessed whose mission you have served for the past four hundred years.'

'We would never serve the Possessed,' said one of the magi, an old man with white hair and a kindly face.

'And yet you have,' said the Queen and if they had doubted the certainty in Meredith's voice then the cold dispassion of her tone left them in no doubt. This would not be the first time she had sentenced someone to death. And if the magi

472

failed to swear an oath to the people of Wrath she would do precisely as she had said.

'And what about him?' asked the rune-faced mage. 'What about the black hearted devil who killed the Grand Veneratu? What punishment will the Throne of Wrath visit upon him?'

The Queen gave a sigh and turned to look at Falco who still sat astride the great black dragon. The plateau was embraced by silence as the people waited to hear what she would say.

'As I understand it,' she began. 'The Grand Veneratu was himself about to commit murder when he was struck down. Battle Mage Danté was acting in defence of his dragon.'

'And what about the hellish beast? You cannot leave a creature like that free to roam the world! It's too dangerous... Something needs to be done!'

'Yes it does,' said the Queen and, turning away from the tower, she guided her horse towards the mighty black dragon.

As they drew closer Souverain began to shy away and the people watched as the Queen dismounted to close the final few yards on foot. This was the closest she had ever been to a dragon and her heart was thudding in her chest as her vision was filled by the terrible beauty of the creature before her. Everything she had ever heard about black dragons spoke of violence, hatred and death and it was not easy to go against such preconceptions, but she was the Queen of Wrath and the magi were right... something needed to be done.

Staring into the fierce golden eyes the Queen advanced until it could have taken her head with a single bite. For a moment she paused, overwhelmed by the dragon's sheer presence. She thought of all the black dragons that had been slain at the behest of the magi, a crime of such proportions that she could barely comprehend it.

Sidian looked down at her with an austere and quizzical expression as if he were trying to reconcile the vulnerable human body with the strength of the will he sensed within.

The Queen held the dragon with her gaze and her deep blue eyes swam with tears.

'Forgive us,' she breathed and with that she swept back her cloak and dropped to one knee, head bowed in obeisance.

*

Falco looked down at the kneeling figure of the Queen. Beneath him he could feel Sidian's rapidly beating heart and he waited to see what the dragon would do. For a moment Falco thought he might take flight and retreat from this unsettling scene but then, in the front row of the crowd, the old man who had spoken out followed the Queen's example as he too knelt before the dragon.

And that was that.

Like a field of wheat bowing before a gust of wind the gesture spread throughout the crowd as two thousand people dropped to one knee and offered up their regret for the wrong that had been done to dragonkind.

Falco's heart swelled with emotion and he could feel the powerful effect this display of remorse was having on Sidian. Seeing movement near the tower he turned as several of the warrior mages put down their swords and dropped to

473

their knees. More followed their example until only two remained on their feet, while at the balconies and windows of the tower many of the magi closed their eyes and bowed their heads as the realisation of what they had done began to dawn in their minds.

*

Sounds seemed to echo strangely in the Queen's ears as she waited to see what the dragon would do. She was fairly sure that it would not attack her but she could not be certain. Suddenly she sensed movement and heard the faint sigh of the dragon's scales moving against each other. A shadow loomed over her and she tensed, but then she held her breath and froze as the dragon laid its forehead gently against hers.

Catherine de Sage closed her eyes as she felt the warmth of the dragon through the steel hard plates on its skull. She could feel its breath on her face, and she caught the vaguely spiced smell of earth and heated metal. She had met kings and princes and warriors of great renown, but she had never experienced anything like being in the presence of a dragon. She had been born into an ancient and royal family but never in her life had she felt so humble.

As the dragon withdrew its head she looked up in wonder. So this was what it felt like to meet a dragon.

*

Falco watched as Sidian slowly lifted his head, still looking down at the woman kneeling before him. He knew what each was feeling and almost smiled at the similarity in their reactions, armoured scales or soft pale flesh, it was the soul within that mattered.

Together he and Sidian gazed out over the sea of people bowed before them.

Over to the right, on the slopes leading down to the Crofters' cottage, he could see Aurelian and Dwimervane and for a moment Sidian's gaze lingered on the crippled blue dragon. While, away to the left, Falco now saw the familiar figures of Malaki and Quirren, with Huthgarl and several of the other cadet knights.

As he felt Sidian begin to shift beneath him, Falco gave his friend a nod and saw Malaki dip his head in response. Then he gripped the ridges at the base of Sidian's neck and squeezed his knees against the dragon's flanks. It was time for them to leave.

The Queen came to her feet and held Falco's gaze as the great black dragon slowly backed away. Looking into her deep blue eyes Falco felt as captivated as ever and he laid his right hand across his chest in salute, a gesture of respect and loyalty that the Queen returned.

Reaching a clear space, Sidian spread his wings. Sinking back onto his haunches he reached his pinions high and with a powerful spring he launched himself skyward, drawing his wings sharply downwards as he propelled them both into the air.

The Queen staggered back as the downdraft beat against her face. She blinked her eyes and squinted up as the dragon climbed higher and higher, lofting twenty feet with each mighty wing beat. Behind her the people began to get to their feet. Their gasps turning to mutterings of awe and amazement, and then the

474

old man from the front of the crowd whispered something in the language of Clemoncé.

'Cœur noir,' he murmured, echoing the derisive description one of the magi had used for Falco. But now, as the people watched the black dragon and its dark rider rise above them, the name seemed deeply appropriate. The man had spoken to himself but not so quietly that those around him had not heard. Beside him a woman repeated the words.

'Le Cœur Noir,' she said, and the name spread like a mantra through the crowd.

'Le Cœur Noir,' they murmured.

The Black Heart

*

On the slopes leading up from the Crofters' cottage Aurelian and Dwimervane watched as Falco and his dragon disappeared into the clouds. Their hearts had ached as they saw the people offer up their collective sorrow, while on the opposite slopes Malaki and the cadet knights were joined by a man they recognised as the Queen's advisor.

'Well,' said Cyrano as he pulled up on a horse beside them. 'It looks like we might not be needed after all.'

Malaki glanced over his shoulder where a hundred city guard cavalry were shifting nervously as they waited to hear if they would be deployed. Cyrano had kept the troops below the brow of the slope and now, with a sigh of deep relief, he gave the order for them to retire. He had respected the Queen's foolhardy decision to handle the situation in her own way, but he would have been remiss in his duties if he had not taken steps to guard against a more unfortunate turn of events. With a bow he took his leave and Malaki and the others turned back to the sky where Falco had now disappeared from view.

'I remember the night you arrived in the barracks,' said Huthgarl in his strong Beltonian accent. 'I couldn't wait to fight you. But I felt insulted by *his* presence - that we should have to share a room with one so weak.' He gave a deep snort, laughing at his own folly.

'Did you know what he would become?' asked Quirren.

'No, and yes,' said Malaki. 'For most of my life I thought he would die before his twenty first birthday.' He paused, thinking of the disease that had blighted the major part of Falco's life. 'But I always knew he was different.'

'Aldrei vanmeta a Valentian,' said Huthgarl in his native tongue.

Malaki looked at him in confusion but Quirren just laughed.

'Never underestimate a Valentian,' he translated. 'We say the same in Illicia. Although I think the real phrase is, never underestimate the stupidity of a Valentian,' he added, and the others smiled at his attempt to make a joke.

'I'll be sure to tell Bryna you said that,' said Malaki but Quirren shrugged off the threat.

'I'll just tell her it was something Alex said.'

'And she'd believe you,' laughed Malaki and together the young knights rode back down to the Irregulars.

*

475

Later that afternoon the Queen stood at her balcony once more, watching the smoke over the city slowly fade as the fires were brought under control.

'Things are beginning to settle down,' said Cyrano as the last of the officials were escorted from the audience room and the Queen's chambers were once again her own.

The Queen said nothing, only giving her advisor a sideways look and raising a hand to her dry and aching throat. The last few hours had been spent trying to minimise the effects of the riots and discussing how to stop others from taking advantage of the heightened sense of anxiety. Sixteen people were now confirmed dead and despite the tentative peace that had been achieved the anger and reprisals reverberated through a city that was already feeling the strain of the rapidly encroaching war.

Moving to a side table Cyrano poured the Queen a glass of honey and lemon water from a silver rimmed decanter. He came to stand beside her and she took the glass with a grateful nod before looking up towards the mountains where Falco and his dragon had disappeared.

'And to think I almost declined the emissary's request to train him,' she mused, sipping her drink.

'Maybe it would have been better if you had,' said Cyrano and the Queen half turned towards him, an eyebrow arched in surprise.

'This news will spread to every city in the land and not every tower will be so lucky. It's bad enough that we should have the Possessed on our doorstep without such troubles weakening our cities from within.'

'The magi can send word quicker than any dockside gossip,' said the Queen. 'They will have a chance to prepare themselves. And Master Saker has already begun work on a magically binding oath.'

'Even so,' said Cyrano. 'There will be trouble, and there will be death, and you will not always be able to prevent it.'

'I know,' replied the Queen sounding suddenly weary.

Cyrano gave a nod and for a while they stood in silence.

'Well?' said the Queen as her advisor was about to excuse himself. 'Are you going to show me the note that's burning a hole in your pocket or not?'

Cyrano put a hand to his doublet pocket where he had secreted the brief message from Valentia. He would rather the Queen had a good night's sleep before reading it. Slowly now he withdrew the crumpled rectangle of parchment. Placing it in her hand he took two steps back to afford her a modicum of privacy then watched as she unfolded the note and began to read.

For a moment she just held it in her slender fingers, the corners trembling ever so slightly, and then she folded the note and crumpled it in her fist. Cyrano's heart went out to her. The Irregulars were desperately needed at the front, their numbers essential to support the armies of Marshal Breton and the emissary. He could only imagine what she must be feeling, knowing that she could no longer allow them to leave, no longer send them to aid her Chevalier.

Finally the Queen spoke and Cyrano had never heard such detached and steely determination in her voice before.

'You will not mention this to anyone until the Irregulars have departed the city,' she said.

'But Your Majesty!'

'On your honour, Cyrano!' said the Queen, turning a stone cold gaze upon her advisor. 'Not until the army of the Irregulars are on their way.'

Cyrano began to protest but he could see that it was pointless.

'As you command,' he said at last, though every instinct told him that what she had in mind was a mistake.

Torn between obedience and safeguarding his charge, he waited for her to dismiss him. All it took was a slight raising of her chin and with a bow Cyrano moved towards the door. Outside her chambers the two palace guards stood to attention but he did not even acknowledge their presence. In his mind he saw again the message that had arrived this morning. The ramifications of which now filled him with dread.

Valentia has withdrawn its forces
Demon armies have entered the Pass of Amaethon
Navaria will fall within a month
Southern border now under imminent threat
Recommend Ruaen be reinforced with all possible speed

The writer of the note clearly did not know that there were no armies left to reinforce the southern city of Ruaen. Only the Irregulars remained and in a matter of days they would be heading east. The only other force of any size was the Legion du Trône, the Commander of which was none other than the Queen herself.

Cyrano paused at the head of the stairs. The Queen had always hated sending others off to fight her wars and now it seemed she had a legitimate excuse to lead a campaign of her own. Cyrano remembered the promise he had made to her father... to keep her safe. For nearly twenty years he had kept his promise but now he feared that he might fail.

How could he save the most powerful woman in the world from herself?

477

84

Unexpected Threats

Following the departure of the Irregulars the Queen waited just four days before calling an emergency meeting of the district's most powerful nobles. The Chamber of Council was far from full, but there were still more than a hundred men and women seated on the terraced steps, each with a small retinue of personnel from their estates. The magi's fall from grace had significantly weakened the position of those who opposed the Queen but even so, they were not about to let plans to leave the capital unprotected go unchallenged.

'The sole purpose of the Legion du Trône is to protect the capital of Clemoncé, not the capital of Navaria,' said Lord Brosse a middle aged man with silver hair and a club foot.

His comments raised a chorus of agreement and the Queen waited for the noise to subside before continuing.

'And what if the best way to protect the capital is to march to the aid of Navaria?' she asked.

'How can you even suggest such a thing?' asked an elderly count whose flamboyant robes reflected his incredible wealth. Clutching at a gold mounted walking stick he hauled himself to his feet. 'Thanks to your policy of intervention, all of Clemoncé's armies are now committed abroad. And what have they achieved? Nothing,' he added, when no one else seemed inclined to answer. 'We sacrifice our soldiers in other people's lands and still the enemy draws closer. Rumour has it that Hoffen and Le Matres will be the next to fall. And what then?' he asked. 'Voisier? Ville de Pierre? Toulwar?'

'No,' said the Queen. 'If we do not act, the next city to fall will be Ruaen.'

Behind her the officers of the Legion du Trône looked on with grave expressions. To them the thought of one of their own cities falling to the Possessed while they remained safe in the capital was unthinkable, but the nobleman in the fancy robes remained unconvinced.

'Nonsense,' he said. 'You said yourself that the demon armies in the Pass of Amaethon are not large.'

The Queen sighed. Could these people really be so ignorant and naive? Without turning she addressed one of the officers standing behind her.

'Colonel Laville. Would you be so kind as to educate the Comte du Savere in the ways of the enemy?'

With a stiff bow Colonel Laville stepped forward, a chiselled featured man of middle years. His hair was streaked with grey but his thick eyebrows and groomed moustache were black. He made no attempt to hide the contempt in his ebony eyes as he addressed the count.

'The two demon armies currently moving through the Pass of Amaethon *are* relatively small, with only about fourteen thousand troops between them. But Navaria has no army of its own. Fully half of the state's population lives in the capital city of Sophia, which has a garrison of just one thousand troops. When they are defeated most of them will be reborn as Possessed.'

The Comte du Savere pursed his lips. An additional eight hundred Possessed did not sound too threatening but Colonel Laville had not finished.

'The garrison might only be a thousand, but the city of Sophia has a population of almost sixty-thousand,' he went on. 'If Navaria falls, and it will fall, then many of its citizens will also be subsumed. We estimate the army that crosses our border could be forty thousand strong.'

The nobles looked at him as if they could not quite believe what he was saying.

'The provincial army at Ruaen will not be able to resist them and the demon army that moves north will have grown by another twenty thousand benighted souls.'

The Queen stared around the chamber and few escaped the touch of her granite gaze. 'Dumonté and the Porte du Château will be the next to fall. And with them a thousand farms and vineyards, razed and ruined as our beloved country becomes part of the Forsaken Lands.'

Finally she took a breath and her eyes were filled with grim determination.

'The truth is this,' she said at length. 'If the Legion du Trône is to protect the capital then it must ride out now. If we wait for the Possessed to come to us then we are lost.'

'But danger might come from another direction,' said a softly spoken nobleman to the Queen's right.'

'Yes, it might,' conceded the Queen. 'But other armies are fighting to prevent that. We cannot hide behind our walls, waiting for the threat of future years. We must address the danger that threatens us now.'

'We should recall the armies from Illicia and Beltane,' said a dark haired man with a ducal crest hanging from a gold chain about his neck. 'The army of the Irregulars departed only days hence. Why were they allowed to march east when we knew of this danger to the south?'

The duke's tone was accusing and he turned to the Queen's right, looking to Prince Ludovico for support. But the Prince remained unmoved, sitting forward with one hand resting on his velvet clad thigh while the fingers of his other hand stroked his chin in thought.

The medallion-wearing duke seemed momentarily thrown by the Prince's unwillingness to support what he clearly saw as common sense, but the Queen just gave a weary sigh. These men had no idea of the enemy's strength, no idea of the horror and the struggle that had been raging at the front for decades.

'And what about the demons?' persisted the duke. 'If I am not mistaken, the last battle mage in the city departed with the Irregulars. Would Her Majesty care to explain how she intends to fight demon armies without the support of a battle mage?'

'She will have the support of two!' came a gruff and angry voice from the higher seats of the chamber.

Everyone turned to look as Aurelian and Dusaule stood up from their seats.

It had been late evening on the day of the Irregular's departure when the Queen herself arrived at the cottage to speak with them. Dusaule had only just returned from his tormented wanderings and Aurelian had wondered if it would send him back out into the night. But the silent Crofter had only listened as the Queen outlined her plans to save the Navarian capital. Aurelian needed no persuasion but Dusaule seemed uncertain.

479

'I wouldn't expect you to fight,' said the Queen, aware of the vow he had sworn. 'But with your protection and Aurelian's fire...'

The Queen's voice faded away. She had no wish to add to Dusaule's suffering. However, after a few moments of shadowed thought Dusaule had answered her with a simple nod.

Now the two men stood before the astonished gaze of the gathered nobles.

'What?' said a sour faced man with oiled hair and shiny skin. 'Are we to trust the safety of the Legion to a cripple and a mute?'

Aurelian stared at the man as he would an obnoxious drunk who had just pissed on his boot. There was no need for a show of power, the force of his contempt was enough.

'Battle Mages Cruz and Dusaule have agreed to accompany us, and we are grateful for their protection,' said the Queen. 'The latest intelligence suggests the two Possessed armies are moving separately. If we engage them one at a time...'

'Enough!' blustered the medallion duke. 'This is madness! We must recall our armies from foreign lands and task *them* with the defence of our realm.' He paused. 'No,' he continued and here he had the temerity to wag his finger at the Queen. 'We cannot allow you to deploy the Legion while other options remain.'

'You mistake me, sir,' said the Queen and behind her Cyrano tensed as he recognised the steely tone in her voice. 'I did not call this meeting to ask for your permission.' The Queen threw back her cloak to reveal the armoured breastplate she wore beneath.' Her hand moved to the pommel of her sword as she turned to face the man who dared to think he could command the Queen of Wrath. 'I called this meeting to tell you that I am taking the Legion south and to ask Prince Ludovico if he would do me the honour of governing the city in my stead.'

There was a collective gasp of astonishment and Prince Ludovico sat up straight, his face filled with surprise and confusion. Eyes narrowed, he looked down as the Queen turned towards him.

'I offer no promise or concession, my Lord,' she said as the Prince's gaze flicked to the black sword belt at her waist. 'You must know by now that our houses will never be joined.'

The Prince's jaw bunched. His face flushed and the chamber echoed with disapproval at the Queen's public renunciation of the second most powerful person in the kingdom.

'Forgive me, my Lord,' said the Queen. 'But my heart is already cleaved, first to the people of Wrath and then to the Chevalier, whom I can no longer deny.'

The Prince's dark eyes were hot with mortification and for a moment it appeared he might refuse, but the Queen did not release him from her gaze.

'So, my Prince,' she asked again. 'Will you be the steward of this city and care for the people in my absence? For I know you love them too.'

For the longest time the prince just stared at the Queen but then, quietly.

'I will.'

The Queen's chest heaved with a great breath, part relief, part gratitude, and part fear of the path she had chosen. For a moment she could not find her voice, but then she swept an all embracing arm around the room.

'All hail the Prince of Wrath,' she said and the nobles echoed her words as if under some kind of spell.

'Hail the Prince of Wrath.'

Still frowning from a barrage of emotions Prince Ludovico rose to his feet and bowed to the Queen who returned the gesture with genuine respect.

'Master Cyrano will supervise your investiture,' she said, and the Queen's advisor stepped forward.

From his outward composure no one would suspect the anguish tearing at Cyrano's heart; the effort of will it required to release the Queen from his charge and not scream at these 'nobles' to lead the army in her place. But the Legion was sworn to the Throne of Wrath and she was the Throne personified.

'Colonel Laville,' said the Queen as she turned to address her second in command. 'The Legion will be ready to march at dawn.'

'Yes, Your Majesty,' said the veteran knight.

And with that the Queen disappeared into the tunnel leading from the floor.

Above her, Aurelian led Dusaule into one of the stairwells leading from the upper levels of the chamber. Like the nobles, he too thought the Queen's plan was madness, but it was also their only option. Falco and the Irregulars were needed at the front. Besides, like the Queen, he too felt the strain on his honour - that others marched into danger while he remained safe in the Crofters' cottage. Even Dwimervane, with all her scars and injuries had let out an ominous growl of anticipation at the thought of facing the enemy once more.

In the morning the Legion du Trône would march to war and the Crofters would march with them.

*

More than two hundred miles to the east, the emissary scanned the sky for any sign of the enemy's spies. Since leaving Hoffen their progress had been dogged by attacks from small forces of Possessed, emerging from nowhere to strike at his unsuspecting troops. For an allied army in the Forsaken Lands, such surprise attacks were to be expected, but they were always worse when the army had been scouted by a dark angel and so they marched with one eye on the sky looking for the telltale shape of the winged demons that might herald an attack.

On this occasion the sky was clear and the emissary watched as the Fourth Army wound its way over the rocky moors of eastern Illicia. They were now ten days south of Hoffen and the emissary's thoughts turned to what they would find when they reached the city of Amboss. The area around Amboss had been subject to a sustained assault and there were even reports that small forces and minor demons had managed to slip through the allies defences and cross the border into Clemoncé.

So far any breaches were thought to be small, but this was why Marshal Breton had called them south, to strengthen their position around the city while they still could. Once the area was secure the marshal intended to drive south-east, keeping the supply routes to Beltane open and preventing the Possessed from encircling the north coast of Lake Viegal.

By all accounts, the remaining strongholds in Beltane were still holding, thanks largely to the success of Vercincallidus. His hit-and-run tactics had allowed him to wear down the Possessed armies, a strategy the emissary had now

481

employed in the north. The biggest problem was the lack of battle mages and the emissary found himself wondering how Falco had faired on his return to Wrath.

Had he passed the Rite of Assay?

Had he summoned a dragon?

By now the Irregulars should be on *their* way to Amboss, but it was too much to hope that Falco was coming with them. Surely he could not complete his training in just a few short weeks. No. They must play their hand and not wish for cards they did not have. His one consolation was that Hoffen and Le Matres were standing firm, which meant the northern routes into Clemoncé were secure. The Possessed would not strike for the capital while these defensive strongholds still remained intact. The Queen was safe, for now.

The emissary's gaze was pensive as the lines of spear and swordsmen marched past. He was painfully aware that all of Clemoncé's armies were now committed abroad. And it was just as well that its borders were safe, for he dreaded to think what the Queen might do if her beloved kingdom came under threat.

He shuddered as a cloud passed over the sun then urged Tapfer forward, his grey eyes ever vigilant as the Fourth Army snaked across the land. There were no reports of Possessed armies in the area, but in these dangerous times they could not afford to be complacent. They must all be prepared to react to a threat, no matter how unexpected, or from which direction it may come.

85
Pain, Pain and Eternal Pain

Vercincallidus looked out from the low crags as the enemy came into view. It was late afternoon and the breeze was cool but the air above the Possessed shimmered and boiled as if it were noon on the hottest of summer days. The host of dark warriors swept into the valley and he knew that a similar force was now closing on their position from the rear. After years of outwitting the enemy he had finally been cornered, but even now he looked for a way to escape.

Rather than being hemmed in on both sides he would try to punch through this first Possessed army before the second could attack him from the rear. This was a tactic he had used many times before, but both of the armies now closing on his position were led by demons. Normally he would avoid a demon army at all costs, but today the Sons of Eldur were not alone.

Vercincallidus turned to look at the man mounted on the deep crimson dragon beside him. Forged from a Beltonian alloy, his plate and lamellar armour had the lustre of antique bronze. His helmet was of a traditional design with nose and cheek guards and reinforced bands around the eyes. His sword was also of a tribal design and his shield was embossed with the boar motif of the Gullinbursti tribe.

Vercincallidus had resisted sending for a battle mage for he knew how badly they were needed elsewhere, but if his army was going to survive this day it would need the protection that a great soul could provide. Over the years he had seen this man kill several demons but today was different. The entity that drove the Possessed towards them was something that neither of them had encountered before.

Trying to ignore a growing sense of uncertainty Vercincallidus brought his thoughts back to the battle at hand. He had arranged his forces in the most aggressive formation possible. Their only hope was to kill the demon and break free before the second Possessed force arrived.

He cast his gaze over his army, nine thousand of the finest troops in all of Beltane. Over the past few years they had faced the Possessed dozens of times, but now their general was filled with doubt and they could feel the garrotte of fear tightening around their throats. Baring his teeth Vercincallidus snarled at his weakness, but then his bowels turned to water as the demon appeared from a gully in a low line of cliffs.

Clad in dark armour it was smaller than most of the demons he had seen, and walked like a man on two human legs, but the power of it was like nothing he had felt before. The general had seen towering behemoths that could crush a horse's ribcage in their fists, and others that could bite an armoured knight in two. But he had never witnessed anything with the force of presence that this demon possessed. He felt the shock of it ripple through his army and thought for a moment that they would fold, but then he felt the will of the man beside him. It was like a shield of steel before the fragile vessel of his soul and Vercincallidus breathed a sigh of relief as the battle mage spread his cloak of faith over the army.

Now they could stand.

Now they could fight.

Beside him the battle mage drew his sword as the dragon readied itself for flight. Looking down he saw the demon stop and lock eyes with the man who thought to oppose it. The crimson dragon shifted uneasily, rearing to fight but the battle mage held it in check and Vercincallidus knew he was trying to gauge the strength of his enemy, probing for weaknesses, trying to determine something of its nature.

The general turned to look down at the enemy and to his horror the demon's attention shifted to him. The force of its scrutiny was excruciating but he could not look away. The world seemed to recede as the demon held him with its infernal gaze and a sound began to rise up on the edge of hearing, like a distant cacophony of screams and pitiful cries. The sound grew louder until it filled his mind and then suddenly it was gone, replaced by an ominous silence. And into the silence there came a deep voice that spoke to him in the language of the tribes.

'*Verkir, verkir og eilíft verkir,*' said the voice and the fear clutched once more at the general's bowels.

'Do not listen to it,' said the man beside him and Vercincallidus returned to the world around him. 'No fate is set in stone,' continued the battle mage as the dragon took two steps back from the crags. 'The enemy tries to weaken us with his lies. But we will not listen.'

The battle mage hunkered down, gripping the straps of the riding harness with his shield hand. He turned to look down at Vercincallidus, his dark eyes burning through the spectacled visor of his helm.

'For the Tribe of One,' he said, invoking the mythical tribe that had once united all the people of Beltane.

'For the Tribe of One,' echoed Vercincallidus and with that the great red dragon bounded forward and leapt from the crags.

The general watched as the red dragon swept down the valley, the battle mage leaning low against its back. They attacked as a single entity and Vercincallidus was certain that nothing could withstand such an attack but then he remembered the words that had echoed in his mind and suddenly he knew the name of the demon they faced.

The Illicians called it the Marchio Dolor, a name in the language of ancient Protégia. Here then was the enemy's chief lieutenant.

The Marchio Dolor.

The Marquis of Pain.

*

The Marchio Dolor watched with scornful amusement as the wyrm leaped from the crags and swept down the valley towards him, the Defiant leaning low against its back, shield ready and sword pointing directly towards him. The Marchio could feel their strength and the power building inside them but he did not flinch. Instead he drew his sword and settled into a solid stance to meet them. He raised the shield armour on his left arm and readied the massive sword in his right hand.

The sword was in the style of a Ferocian machaira, a single edged weapon with a heavy forward-curving blade. Like his armour the steel of the sword was dark and shot through with a filigree of veins that glowed as the Marchio clenched his armoured fist.

It was a long time since he had killed a Defiant. He would savour the moment well.

*

Even as the dragon streaked down the valley, Vercincallidus unleashed his troops and nine thousand warriors charged towards the Possessed. The valley shook with the drumming of hooves and the braying sound of the carnyx war trumpets. A storm of arrows flew towards the massed ranks of Sciritae but the battle mage and the dragon would be the first to strike.

The Marchio Dolor braced himself and hunched forward as a lance of searing blue light burst from the battle mage's sword. It speared towards him but the lethal barb was deflected by the shield armour on his left arm. The attack scored a deep gouge but failed to penetrate the enchanted steel.

Before he could launch an attack of his own the Marchio Dolor was engulfed in flame as the dragon hit him with a jet of ferocious fire. The dragon's flames burned hot but the Marchio was protected by a thousand years of devotion. His eyes blazed with fury as the flames died away and the dragon came in for the kill, jaws gaping and talons outstretched.

However, a moment before the dragon struck the Marchio surged forward and swung his sword, delivering a blow that cut deep into the dragon's chest. Still, one of the dragon's claws caught a patch of exposed skin and tore a gash in his neck but the Marchio barely felt it as the mortally wounded dragon came crashing down.

As the dragon went down the battle mage had leapt from its back and the Marchio turned as the man rolled on the ground before coming quickly to his feet. With no trace of hesitation he charged forward, unleashing a fireball as he came, but the Marchio smacked the ball of flame aside and aimed a blow with his sword to cut the man in two. Ducking low the battle mage avoided the killing strike and sent forth a pulse of energy that knocked the Marchio's sword from his grasp.

Sensing victory the battle mage moved in for the kill but once again the demon was too quick. Blocking the attack he lunged forward and grabbed the man by the throat. Lifting him from his feet the Marchio forced him backwards and the battle mage dropped his sword as the demon unleashed his own infernal power. Baëlfire surged down his arm to engulf the battle mage's head and shoulders. He tried to fortify his body but the Marchio's power was too great. His tribal helmet began to glow and his flesh began to burn as the demon slammed his body into a wall of rock, and such was the heat of his fury that the face of the stone outcrop began to crack and melt. Still growling with rage the Marchio began to pray as he pressed the battle mage back against the tortured rock.

Too far gone to make any sound, the battle mage beat at the Marchio's arm, arcs of blue energy leaping from his hands as he tried to focus his power through the agony that enveloped him. But it was no use. The demon's prayers were too powerful, his strength too great. The wall of stone was now glowing red as the Marchio Dolor forced the battle mage into the wall of molten rock. Still the man tried to resist but there was nothing he could do and slowly the magma closed

485

around him, the demon forcing him deeper until just his hands and armoured boots remained in the open air, twitching and straining in spasms of unimaginable pain.

Finally the Marchio released his grip and drew forth his arm, the molten rock dripping from his armour and his dark unearthly skin. He might not be able to claim the soul of this Defiant but he could make certain that he suffered. The demon's unholy power would keep the man alive as the rock slowly cooled around him. The battle mage would suffer a tortured death of suffocating immolation, tormented by the fact that he had failed.

His hand still glowing from the heat, the Marchio Dolor moved to retrieve his sword then he turned in the direction of the dragon. The demon's blade had cut deeply and blood spilled from a gaping wound in the dragon's chest but still it prepared to fight. Its eyes burned with defiance even though it knew that victory was impossible. This demon was simply beyond their power to defeat.

As the battle mage was overcome, the full weight of the demon's malice filled the valley and Vercincallidus watched as his army began to fold. The fear beat against him like a scorching wind and he knew that he would not be able to resist it for long, but while something of his will remained he would fight. Drawing on his last reserves of courage he drew his sword and called forth his honour guard of Beltonian Heavy Horse.

Their only chance now was to die before the fear claimed them. Only by virtue of a warrior's death could they evade Possession and enter the halls of Hugrekki. The warriors around him knew this too but he could see the fear swimming in their eyes.

'The Tribe of One,' he cried and the men of his guard replied in kind.

Descending a rocky bank, the general led his men in a final charge. They attacked where the enemy was at its strongest, the quicker to meet their end, but the demon saw their intention and with a sweep of his mind he commanded his minions to take them alive. He would not allow the Serthian Wolf the easy escape of death.

For a while the Sons of Eldur fought on, but even these battle hardened veterans could not resist the fear for long and soon the valley was filled with the wails of their despair. As the last of any fighting died away they were corralled into a single group on the valley floor: the living, the dead, the dying - a pitiful mass of terrified humanity. Surrounded by the warriors of the Possessed they watched in terror as the Marchio Dolor stepped forward. Bowing his demonic head he raised his arms as if to embrace them. But there was no fondness in this gesture, only dark prayers of subjugation.

A great moan of horror rose up as the defeated army was surrounded by a wall of Baëlfire. And then they were crying out and crawling over each other as the flames spread slowly inwards until at last they were all consumed.

Dragged from his horse, beaten, bound and helpless, Vercincallidus wept as his brave warriors were baptised in the flames of Hell. The valley echoed to the sound of their screams and they seemed to go on for an eternity until finally the flames died away and the Beltonian warriors were reborn. All trace of their humanity had been expunged and even their Beltonian armour had been reformed in the mould of Ferocian steel.

Through unbearable pain the pledge of their devotion had been secured, the heat of their armour a constant reminder of the punishment that awaited any who should fail. Such was the fate that had befallen the Sons of Eldur, and such was the fate that now awaited their general.

Vercincallidus shook with terror as the Marchio Dolor turned towards him. He knew that he was doomed, but he was a man of the Vísunduri Tribe and he was determined to resist for as long as possible. The Marchio Dolor seemed to sense his resistance and something like amusement crept into his burning gaze. Even now the last of the Beltonian army was emerging from the sacred flames. It was time for their general to join them.

Kneeling before the demon Vercincallidus flinched as the Marchio Dolor reached down and placed one massive hand on either side of his helm. His breathing came in terrified snorts and flecks of spittle flew from his clenched teeth as he prepared to resist with every fibre of his being.

The Marchio Dolor offered up a prayer and the general's head was engulfed in Baëlfire.

Vercincallidus was no stranger to pain and yet his resolve lasted less than a heartbeat before he gave himself unconditionally to darkness. In his worst nightmares he had never imagined pain like this, but finally his screams gave way to a guttural snarl and his eyes were seared white as he became Possessed.

The Marchio looked down at his new general and his eyes narrowed in approval. He had not reshaped the Wolf's armour. Rather he had left it in the tribal style so that the people of Beltane might recognise the man who now moved against them. How ironic that King Osric's kingdom should fall to the very man that he hoped would save it.

Still trembling with the agony of revelation Vercincallidus climbed to his feet. It was late evening and the sun was setting behind the hills, but come the morning he would lead his army out once more. Only minutes before he would have gladly died to save the lives of his people. Now he relished the suffering he was about to visit upon them. In the deepest recess of his soul, the thing that had once been human wept tears that would never flow. The Serthian Wolf was about to tear the throat out of the kingdom that he loved and the people of Beltane would learn the cost of their resistance.

Verkir, verkir og eilíft verkir.

Pain, pain and eternal pain.

Such is the promise of the Possessed.

*

Even as Vercincallidus was being inducted to the Possessed so the assassin that the Marchio had summoned was preparing to re-enter the world.

Far to the north, near the Illician city of Hoffen, an area of green heathland had now been reduced to a layer of white ash lying like snow on the black bedrock. As the sun sank towards the horizon the rock began to glow and split apart as something forced its way up from below. The assassin had wandered far in its atonement, but its penance was almost over. Soon the Slayer would be reborn.

86

A Sense of Foreboding

Falco's dreams had been troubled of late. The Irregulars were now more than two weeks out of Wrath and travelling through a series of canyons carved by the passage of three fast flowing rivers. Soon the deep valleys would open out onto a rocky plain where the rivers came together before spilling over an escarpment known as La Grande Cascade. The escarpment marked the border with Illicia and from there it was just thirty miles to the city of Amboss where the Irregulars would join the allied forces under the command of Marshal Breton.

In just six days' time Marshal Breton was due to hold his monthly strategy meeting and the Irregulars were hoping to reach the city in time to attend. They still had some way to go but they were making good progress. If they kept up their current pace they should reach the Illician city with a few days to spare.

Tonight they were camped along the banks of the Tonnerre, the most northerly of the three rivers, and the noise of the rushing water echoed off the white cliffs with a sound like distant thunder. It was approaching dusk and hundreds of camp fires were springing up along the bank as the army settled down for the night, but around one such campfire there was a second source of light.

Falco stared at the ethereal fire surrounding his right hand. He relaxed his mind and the flames died away leaving his armoured gauntlet completely undamaged. With ever increasing control he allowed the tingling sensation of power to flow down his arm and the fire returned hovering around his hand as the flame of a candle hovers around the wick without actually touching it.

'Does it hurt?' asked Malaki as he placed a steaming bowl of venison stew on the rock beside him.

'No,' said Falco distractedly. He was still fascinated by his emerging powers, but slowly he became aware that the others were also watching him. 'Sorry,' he said with a self conscious smile as the flames disappeared from his hand.

'Don't apologise,' said Alex. 'Starting the camp fire has never been so easy.'

The others laughed but it *was* quite unnerving, the way Falco could ignite even the dampest firewood with his mysterious powers. They all remembered the first night he had tried, when the carefully laid stack of wood had been blasted apart sending them all diving for cover as a shower of burning sticks rained down across the clearing. But Falco's control had improved greatly. Not only could he now produce a fireball that would make even Aurelian proud, he was also learning to shape his power and 'tune' it to different levels of intensity. It was like trying to master a new weapon or musical instrument and Falco tried to remember what Aurelian had told him before he departed with the Irregulars.

'Don't think about it too much,' the old battle mage had said. 'Just trust your instincts and the fire will follow.'

Falco missed the reassuring presence of his cantankerous friend. He remembered the night when he had brought Sidian down to the Crucible to meet him and Dwimervane. Aurelian had been awed and emotional, but Dwimervane appeared distressed and confused. She understood the revelations they had learned at the summoning, but hearing of a crime is not the same as experiencing it and her racial memory did not yet reach back far enough for her to witness the magi's betrayal for herself.

With Falco's help Sidian had been able to master his feelings, but soon Dwimervane would also turn black and there was no telling how she would handle the grief and the hate and the rage? The blue dragon was still subdued when Falco came to say goodbye. Pressing his forehead to hers, he had tried to reassure her.

'Don't worry,' said Aurelian. 'She's a sensitive old mare but she's got a heart of steel.'

Falco found it surprisingly hard to say goodbye and he remembered the last words of advice that Aurelian had given him.

'You've been through a lot in these last few months so take time to recover. Stay with the army and don't be tempted to fly on ahead.'

Falco simply nodded his understanding.

'Learn to master your power,' Aurelian told him. 'Trust Sidian. And don't lose faith. Whatever happens... don't lose faith.'

Falco remembered Simeon saying exactly the same thing in what seemed like another life. He felt a sudden wave of nostalgia and was grateful for the company of his friends on the march to the front. Their command duties now meant that they seldom ate all together so this was a rare treat. Picking up his bowl of stew Falco listened as they exchanged light-hearted insults, banal, inconsequential comments that somehow bound them together.

To one side Alex suddenly started as something sploshed into his own bowl, sending a spatter of hot stew into his face.

'What the!' he spluttered, fishing out a small pine cone from his bowl before looking up to see where it had come from.

Across the fire Huthgarl did his best to look innocent until Quirren started laughing, at which point the big Beltonian began to snigger like a boy of half his age.

'A fine shot,' said Quirren and Huthgarl gave a modest shrug.

It was an entirely childish thing to do but also quite funny and Alex's indignation only made it worse.

'Oh, very mature!' he said, and coming from Alex this made it funnier than ever.

Malaki and Bryna joined in the laughter and Falco too. It felt good to be with his friends and turning away from the fire he gazed into the trees where Sidian was lying on a low outcrop of rock.

When they first set out from Wrath Falco had kept the dragon away from the army but Sidian seemed to sense that Falco still needed the company of his friends and so they would often come down to the edge of camp so that Falco could spend time with Malaki and Bryna, and whoever else was gathered round the fire. The dragon was still wary of humans but he was also curious. He seemed fascinated by the sheer variety to be found in humankind and would often study those brave enough to come close, every bit as interested in them as they were in him.

489

But Sidian was not the only curiosity that people came to view. They also came to see the 'Knight of the Crimson Helm' and to see for themselves the bright red birthmark that covered the left side of his face. They did not come to tease or taunt, they came in respect and awe.

'That's him,' they could sometimes be heard to whisper. 'He's the one who killed a demon.'

No one seemed concerned by the fact that it was Lord Cabal, and not Malaki, who had struck the crucial blow. They were merely satisfied with seeing his face, as if they could somehow share in his achievement or absorb something of the courage he possessed.

For his part Malaki could have done without the attention, but this was quite difficult as his face constantly betrayed him, and even his helmet now bore the symbol of the victory that he and the Knights of Wrath had achieved.

One day, while he had been training the Irregulars at the academy, his great-helm had mysteriously gone missing from the barracks. No amount of searching had revealed its whereabouts. It was not until the next morning that the helm reappeared on the chest at the foot of Malaki's bed. Only now the left 'cheek' of the helm had been expertly coated with a shining layer of crimson enamel. Beside the newly decorated helm lay a small piece of parchment.

By order of the Queen, to remind her subjects that with strength, honour and faith nothing is impossible.
A. Missaglias

So Malaki had no choice but to endure the burden of fame as best he could. And it was no bad thing that the Irregulars had a hero and a dragon-mounted battle mage to accompany them on their march to the front.

With every day that passed the sense of danger grew stronger and there were always new stories of woe from the refugees that they passed along the way. Some even spoke of a strange demon that had broken through the allied defences near Amboss. Thankfully the Irregulars had only encountered small forces of Possessed and a few bestiarum that emerged from shadowed rents in the fabric of the world. On each of these occasions Falco had sensed the impending attack and the damage had been contained, but the very threat of such unexpected violence kept them on edge and the army was clearly nervous as they settled down for the night.

'I wonder how many we'll lose tonight,' said Quirren as the mood around the fire became more subdued.

'I don't know,' replied Malaki. 'But I'm not surprised. Some of them are just boys.'

'Says the veteran campaigner,' said Bryna, giving him a shove with her shoulder as they sat together on a crate of supplies.

'You know what I mean,' said Malaki, shaking golden liquid from his hand as Bryna's shove spilled the tankard of honeyed ale he was holding. 'I saw two boys the other day that couldn't have been more than fifteen.'

They all nodded, sobered by the thought of such young people facing the horrors of war.

490

'But it's not the youngsters leaving,' said Alex. 'It's the older men who have some idea of what we're marching into.'

It was true. Every night they lost a few more to the steadily increasing sense of fear. They melted away under cover of darkness and come daylight they would simply join the endless stream of refugees travelling the road in the opposite direction.

'It's not happening with the Dalwhinnies,' said Bryna. 'Seems like hardly a day goes by without a new group of bowmen asking to join.'

Somehow the reputation of the Dalwhinnies had reached even the most rural parts of the kingdom and many a wayward 'hunter' was eager to give up a life of dubious practise in order to join the Queen's Fifth Company of Archers.

'How do you decide if they're up to it?' asked Quirren.

'I don't,' said Bryna. 'I simply ask if they can be trusted then I leave it up to Paddy. If they can shoot he licks them into shape, and if they can't then he puts them to work in the field kitchen.'

'And a fine job they're doing too,' said Alex mopping up the last of his stew with a piece of bread. 'Even if they are all thieves and poachers!' He added, deliberately raising his voice so that several of the nearby Dalwhinnies could hear him as they sat together preparing a batch of goose feather fletchings.

Bryna glanced up with an air of amused anticipation. Alex was now a well known character and taunting the Dalwhinnies had become one of his favourite pastimes.

'Better check your snares, Fred,' said one of the men without turning from his work. 'I can hear a wee coney squealing.'

'Nah,' replied one of the other men. 'That's one of them boys from the poncey fighting school.'

'Aye, the one with not a hair on his chin.'

'Nor his arse, neither.'

'Uppity gobshite!' was their final word and with a shared smile of victory they went back to preparing their feathers.

The cadets laughed and none more so than Alex who was clearly delighted by their insults.

'They're not all criminals,' laughed Bryna. 'Some of them just want to fight for the Queen.'

The light-hearted mood died away as quickly as it had begun. Bryna's reference to the Queen raised another issue that weighed heavy on their hearts.

'She must be at the Navarian border by now,' said Malaki as they bowed their heads in thought.

They had been well into their journey before word of the Queen's expedition reached them. The cadets wanted to turn back immediately but the older commanders disagreed.

'No,' said Lanista Magnus. 'There's a reason why she didn't tell us before we left, a reason why it's taken so long for the news to reach us.'

'She wanted to make sure we couldn't turn back,' said Bryna.

'Precisely,' said Lanista Magnus. 'She knew that if we were in Wrath the pressure for us to march south would have been overwhelming and Marshal Breton would be denied his reinforcements.'

'But to lead the army herself...' said Alex.

'She's commander in chief,' said Lanista Magnus. 'In spirit as much as rank.'

'But to think of her placing herself in such danger,' said Malaki.

'She has the Legion, and she has Aurelian Cruz,' said Lanista Magnus. 'And I for one would not want to face him in anger.'

The cadets responded with nervous laughter, glancing at Falco who knew Aurelian better than any of them. He agreed that, even old and one armed, Aurelian would prove a formidable foe.

Falco also felt the urge to go to the Queen's aid and, unlike the army, he might have been able to find her in time, but he knew that Lanista Magnus was right. The Queen wished them to continue to the front, but more than this he felt that it would be a mistake for him to turn back. He could not say why, he just had a growing sense of impending danger and somehow he must be ready to meet it.

An awkward silence had settled as they realised there was nothing they could do. Now they sat around the fire wondering what might be happening in the south.

'Do you think she'll enter Navaria without permission?' asked Quirren.

'To do so would be an act of war,' said Huthgarl.

The treaty between Clemoncé and Acheron forbade either kingdom from deploying troops in Navaria without explicit permission from the other.

'Whatever happens it'll be some time before we hear the news,' said Malaki.

'That's true,' said Alex. 'No point worrying about things we can't do anything about.' It was a surprise to hear Alex taking such a philosophical view. 'Well, I'd better go and see to the Exiles,' he said, rising from his seat and rinsing his bowl in a nearby water butt. 'We're manning the riverside pickets tonight.' And with that he bade them all goodnight and made his way off into the camp.

'And I've got some things to sort out with the Dalwhinnies,' said Bryna.

Malaki also made to stand up but Quirren waved him back down.

'Huthgarl and I will see to the horses. You finish your drink.'

Malaki raised a hand in thanks and took another swig of ale. As the others moved away he came to sit closer to Falco. The sky above them was still blue but down here on the valley floor it was getting dark and Malaki could just make out the dark shape of Sidian lying beneath the trees a short distance away.

'Do *you* think the Queen will cross the Navarian border?' he asked.

'Of course she will,' replied Falco. 'There's no way she would just sit there and let Navaria fall.'

Malaki nodded his agreement.

'And how about you? Do you still think you should have gone to find her?'

'I don't know. I feel like I'm being pulled in different directions.'

'Well Aurelian told you to take it easy and it's been good to have you with us. The surprise attacks from the Possessed would have been far more damaging if you hadn't been here.'

Falco shrugged.

'Besides,' continued Malaki. 'We'll be at the front soon and I'm sure Marshal Breton will have a long list of demons for you to attack.'

Falco gave a grim laugh but he still seemed troubled.

'Are you sleeping any better?'

'You tell me,' said Falco and Malaki smiled at the tone of embarrassment in his voice. All the cadets knew about his nocturnal struggles, but his dreams seemed to be growing more intense as they got closer to the front.

'Well, you were muttering for a while again last night,' said Malaki, trying not to make him feel too guilty.

'Did I say anything in particular?'

'Nothing that made much sense,' said Malaki, remembering the way he and Bryna had watched Falco murmuring in his sleep.

'So what was it?' asked Falco with a sense of foreboding.

Malaki shook his head as if to dismiss it but Falco would not let him get away with being so evasive.

'Just the same old stuff,' said Malaki. 'Darkness is coming... darkness in the earth, darkness in the deep, darkness on the hills.'

Falco felt a prickle of disquiet crawl up his spine.

'The hills?' he repeated. 'You're sure I said darkness on the hills?'

'Not sure,' said Malaki. 'But yes, I think so.'

Falco bowed his head in thought.

'What does it mean?' asked Malaki.

'I don't know. But Simeon and Fossetta said I used to talk about three hills when I was younger.'

'Is it a good thing?'

Falco shook his head and shrugged in frustration. There were times when he remembered his dreams with terrifying clarity but there were other dreams that seemed to be wreathed in shadow. All he knew was that darkness was indeed coming.

'I don't know,' he said at last. 'Maybe things will seem clearer when we reach the front.'

Ever since the summoning Falco had experienced a growing sense of apprehension. At first he thought it was simply a case of getting closer to the enemy, but this was something different. He could sense the armies of the Possessed to the east, like dark clouds on the horizon. But there were also other nodes of fear and despair. There was one to the north, in the inaccessible mountains of Illicia, another far to the southeast on the remote Beltonian coast. And a third, so far south that it could only be in Thraece.

The Possessed had not even reached these areas but one thing was certain, darkness was descending upon them and those who dwelt in its shadow were cowering in fear, afraid of something worse than the mere prospect of death.

Falco could make little sense of the feelings that dominated his dreams and Malaki watched with concern as he wrestled with the doubt and uncertainty. It was one thing to train a person in the skills of combat or the use of magical powers, but how do you train them to interpret the shifting shadows and treacherous mind of the enemy.

Malaki leaned across and placed a strong hand on the back of Falco's neck.

'Don't be too hard on yourself,' he said. 'Just think what you've achieved. I'm sure your father would have been...'

Malaki was unable to finish the sentence as Falco suddenly sat up straight. All trace of uncertainty gone. His green eyes blazed as he turned to the east, where the river flowed towards Illicia.

'What is it?' asked Malaki as they both rose to their feet. 'Possessed? Bestiarum?'

'No,' said Falco. 'Something else.'

Even as they stared into the trees they heard the sound of approaching horses. Two riders came into view, one from the camp's patrol, the other was one of the scouts that rode ahead of the army.

'What is it?' asked Malaki as the riders careered into the clearing.

'A dark angel,' said the scout, breathless and afraid.

'Which way?' demanded Malaki.

The scout twisted in the saddle to point back the way he had come.

'Down river,' he gasped. 'About five miles.'

If a dark angel spotted the army the Possessed attacks would be greatly increased. These winged creatures were the eyes and ears of the enemy and most armies had no choice but to suffer their scrutiny. But on this occasion the Irregulars were accompanied by someone who could intercept a creature of the air and keep the enemy ignorant of their movements.

With a nod of acknowledgement Malaki turned back to his friend but Falco was already running.

87

Darkness Reborn

Pulling on his helmet Falco sprinted through the trees, Sidian running parallel to him until they converged in a clearing. Falco ran up a ledge of moss covered rock and leapt onto the dragon's back. Sidian took one stride... two and launched himself into the air, branches snapping as he ploughed through the surrounding trees.

As they climbed clear of the canopy Falco reached out with his perception but he could not yet feel the distinctive signature of the creature. Being a lesser demon, the dark angel would not radiate the same force of presence as its greater brethren, but if he got close enough Falco should be able to sense it.

Rising into the twilight sky they sped east, following the course of the turquoise river. The walls of the canyon went by in a blur, towering cliffs of white rock, green fern and stunted mountain pine. The air was cold and clear with just a few veils of evening mist to obscure the view.

The wind whistled against the hard edges of Falco's armour and sighed over Sidian's black scales. Through the T-shaped visor of his helm Falco scanned the sky ahead of them, looking for the silhouette of a creature with bat like wings and the demonic body of a withered human. For the first two miles there was nothing but then Falco began to sense a shadow in the air. It was still some way off and higher, several hundred feet higher than the tree clad tops of the canyon.

Knowing that the evening light could betray their presence he kept Sidian low, using the darker landscape of the canyon to conceal their approach. They continued on and Falco could sense the fierce intensity of Sidian's gaze and suddenly there it was, captured by the superior clarity of the dragon's vision.

For Falco it was a strange experience to 'see' something that was still beyond the reach of his own inadequate eyes. He shook his head as his mind reeled from a sense of vertigo, but slowly he became accustomed to it, and as the dark shape grew larger Sidian's view faded away and his own vision returned to the fore.

The dark angel was a mere five hundred yards away when Sidian broke from cover and surged up towards it. It spotted the dragon almost immediately and after a momentary pause it turned in the air to flee. With a hiss of hatred it flapped its wings and made off with surprising speed, but it was being pursued by a larger and far more powerful creature of the air and there was little hope of escape. Its only chance would be to drop down and try to lose its pursuers in the maze of smaller gullies and chasms that connected the main canyons carved by the rivers.

Even as they watched, the dark angel angled its wings and dived towards one such gully. Falco was still confident they could catch it before it entered the narrow defile, but then he saw it turn to the right and let out a piercing shriek. At first he thought it nothing more than a gesture of contempt but then, away to the right, he saw a flurry of movement. Turning his head he saw another winged shadow hanging in the air.

There was not one dark angel, but two.

Sidian was still driving forwards but if they stayed with the first they might well lose sight of the second. Without even thinking Falco reached out his hand and a ball of fire shot over Sidian's head. It streaked through the air, growing larger until it engulfed the first dark angel some sixty yards ahead of them. At the same time Sidian banked to the right as their entwined minds switched their attention to the second.

Behind them there came an unearthly scream as the first dark angel was engulfed in flames. The membranes of its wings were burned away, causing it to plunge earthwards, its screams suddenly cut off as it crashed into the trees and tumbled rocks below.

Falco and Sidian now focused entirely on the second dark angel, which seemed determined to avoid the fate of its companion. It too was flying towards a smaller gully in the canyon wall, but when Falco sent forth another fireball it jinked sideways, dodging the mass of flames which continued on its way before causing a small landslide as it punched into the unstable rock of the canyon wall.

Sidian adjusted course to stay with the demonic scout, which continued its evasive flight, dodging this way and that. Falco sent forth a tighter bolt of energy that shot through the air much faster than the two fireballs. It looked like it might strike the dark angel squarely, but at the last instant the demon pulled hard to the left and the bolt of energy merely burned a fist sized hole in the leathery membrane of its wing.

The emaciated creature was almost at the mouth of the gully but Sidian was closing fast. Falco was about to try for another attack but then he was forced to hold on tight as Sidian put on a sudden burst of speed. The dark angel tried to drop beneath them as they surged towards it, but Sidian reached out with his right foreleg and caught the creature in his talons. The dark angel let out a hissing shriek that was quickly silenced as Sidian broke its neck before casting the limp body aside.

Falco felt a rush of relief as the enemy's eyes were blinded but this was suddenly eclipsed by the realisation that they were about to crash into the cliffs. Sidian was going too fast, the white walls of the canyon too close. Closing his eyes Falco braced himself for the impact, but then the air was driven from his lungs and he was pressed hard against Sidian's ridged back as the dragon spread his wings to their fullest extent.

Falco almost passed out from the force of their deceleration, but he hung on tight as Sidian struck the vertical wall of the cliffs. For a moment the dragon's talons gouged into the crumbling rock and Falco was sure they were about to fall, but then Sidian pushed away from the cliff and suddenly they were soaring through the air once more.

Falco was grateful for the cold wind on his face and neck. His skin was covered in a sheen of sweat and he drew deep breaths as his body fought to regain its equilibrium. The adrenaline of the chase and the experience of almost passing out had left him feeling decidedly shaky. He felt a wave of concern from Sidian and placed a reassuring hand on the dragon's neck.

'I'm fine,' he said and Sidian's concern faded away. It was replaced by a sensation of gentle mockery. There was no language in the communication between himself and Sidian, but the dragon's thoughts were clear.

'Yes,' said Falco. 'I suppose I am a puny human.'

As his mind cleared he reached out with his perception to see if he could sense any more servants of the enemy. There were no more dark angels in the area, but he frowned as he sensed a shadow to the south east. It was diffuse, like a Possessed force, but there was definitely some kind of demon within it. Could this be the strange demon that the refugees had spoken of?

He would need to investigate and Sidian began to veer in the shadow's direction when Falco sensed someone watching them from below.

Sidian pulled up sharply, hovering in the air as they stared down into the dusk veiled trees below. The shadows on the canyon floor were now deep and impenetrable but there was definitely someone there. Slowly Sidian began to descend and as he did so Falco's fears were allayed. Whoever was watching them was human.

Down they went until Sidian's wings clipped leaves and branches and they landed on the valley floor.

'Don't be afraid,' said Falco as they came to rest.

Cowering in the shadow of a twisted oak tree was another human scout, although it was clear that he was not from the Irregulars. The man's horse was trembling with fear but remained silent as it had been trained. The man was trying to reassure it, holding the frightened animal's head against his shoulder.

'It's all right.' said Falco as he swung down from Sidian's back. 'We're with the Queen's Irregulars, heading for Amboss.'

The man's eyes remained fearful and wary. His gaze flicked past Falco to take in the black dragon standing behind him. Falco glanced backwards.

'Don't worry. He's a friend. You can trust him as you would any dragon.'

The man did not seem particularly reassured by this but Falco removed his helm and finally the man seemed to relax. In his armour Falco struck an intimidating figure and the man was clearly relieved to see a young man behind the helm of dark steel. His eyes took in Falco's angular face with its green eyes and long dark hair before moving back to Sidian.

'Draconis noir,' he said and Falco smiled at the tone of disbelief.

Slowly the man nodded and finally he seemed convinced that this imposing warrior and his dragon were not here to kill him. He let out a deep breath as if this were the first time he had relaxed in days.

'Soren Forestier,' he said by way of introduction. 'Deep scout from Ville de Pierre.'

'Falco Danté, from...' Falco paused. 'From Wrath.'

'Valentian?'

'Yes.'

The scout raised his eyes to the sky.

'You killed the dark angels?'

Falco nodded. The man had the strongest Clemoncéan accent that he had ever heard and it was clear that he was not accustomed to speaking in the common language of Wrath.

'And you?'

'I wait for them to go,' said Soren. 'Need to report the presence of a Geôlier to the south.'

'Geôlier?' queried Falco.

'Erm... gaoler,' said the man, translating the word into its common form. 'A minor duke with a skirt of pain.'

Falco nodded as the man confirmed what he had sensed to the south, although he frowned at this strange description. He had never heard of a gaoler before.

'Is it travelling with a force... an army?'

'Yes,' said Soren. 'Small army. Maybe four hundred. But they move through a different valley. They follow les Argenté Fleuve, the Silver River.' He made a gesture with his hands to illustrate the river that flowed parallel to the Tonnerre.

Falco paused in thought. Four hundred Possessed was not so large a force but it *was* led by a demon, even if it was of some obscure kind. He and the Irregulars could certainly handle it but that would delay their arrival at the front. Besides, there might not even be a path between the two river canyons. He would discuss the matter with Lanista Magnus and the other commanders. For now he turned back to the scout.

'The Irregulars are camped a few miles upriver,' he said. 'Can you tell us how we might reach this gaoler?'

'Of course, my lord,' said Soren.

Falco was about to reply when he tensed. A black shadow of fear had suddenly passed across his soul.

'Is everything all right?' asked the scout as he saw the sudden tension in Falco's eyes.

'Yes,' said Falco, trying to mask his discomfort. The feeling of impending danger had suddenly flared in his mind as a distant rumble of thunder might herald the arrival of a storm. Turning away from the scout he replaced his helm and returned to Sidian 'I'll head back now and tell the Irregulars you're coming,' he said as he leapt onto the dragon's back. 'Just follow the river and you will find us.'

Soren nodded and held tight to his horse's reins as Sidian sprang into the air.

As they rose clear of valley Falco reached out with his mind. The sky was now a deep shade of blue as night fell across the eastern massive and the deep canyons were like dark chasms in the surface of the world. The air was cold and Falco's eyes watered as he searched for the source of his disquiet.

'I'm not sure,' he said in answer to Sidian's questioning thoughts. 'But yes... Somewhere far to the north.'

Adjusting the pressure of his knees he turned Sidian back in the direction of the Irregular's camp and together they scythed through the rapidly cooling air.

*

Twenty miles south west of Hoffen, an area of fractured rock shifted like the surface of a volcanic pool. The surface began to bulge upwards as a dark shape emerged from below like some infernal golem. Higher the shape rose until it stepped from the pool, its back-bent legs wreathed in smoke and its great hooves glowing with heat.

The demon rolled its shoulders and the clinging magma slipped from a body clad in dark armour with powerful arms, cinder black skin and two curved blades, one in each massive fist.

As the rock beneath it began to cool the demon opened its mouth and let out a searing hiss. Slowly the heat of hell faded from its body and it stood once more in the charnel world of men. It opened its blood red eyes and looked to the west. There, in the confines of a human city, was a Defiant and its wyrm. They were surrounded by troops and thick walls of stone but none of that mattered. The demon would tear apart the city and kill a thousand souls to reach them. It would spend the night in prayer but then, with the rising of the sun, they would die.

Flexing its arms the demon raised its curved blades then it threw back its head and roared its challenge to the night.

*

The force of the challenge struck Falco's mind so hard that he almost fell from Sidian's back. He slipped sideways and would have fallen but Sidian stalled in the air and shifted beneath him to balance his weight. Slowly the resonance of evil faded away but as Falco's thoughts ran clear they were dominated by a single realisation.

The Slayer had returned.

It was there to the north. Falco could sense it. But more than this he could sense something of its intentions. The Slayer had already chosen a target and its appetite for death had not diminished in its absence. It was going to kill a battle mage and a dragon and there was nothing they could do to stop it.

Suddenly the various threads of responsibility pulling at Falco died away, the Queen's peril, the armies at the front, even his friends and the Irregulars. They were all eclipsed by the need to stop the Slayer. When last abroad it had killed two battle mages and a dragon, a terrible loss for which they were still paying the price. They could not afford to lose any more to its curved and merciless swords.

Blind to all other considerations, Falco and Sidian turned north. The demon was close to its target, Falco could feel its anticipation. They would have to fly far and fast and hope that they could arrive in time. He did not stop to think that Malaki and the others would wonder what had happened to him. All he knew was that the Slayer must be stopped.

88

Hard Decisions

It was almost midnight by the time the Irregular Commanders agreed that they could wait no longer for Falco to return. It was now several hours since the scout from Ville de Pierre had arrived in the camp and a meeting had been hastily convened. The scout told the commanders that Falco had killed the dark angels. He also told them about the gaoler and the small force of Possessed moving through the canyon that ran parallel to their own. The Irregulars were not in any danger from this demon, but their own scouts had just reported that a group of refugees were also travelling along this route and would soon be overtaken by the Possessed.

'We have to do something to help them,' said Alex but Lanista Magnus shook his head.

'We can't confront a demon without Falco.'

'Something must have happened,' said Malaki. 'He wouldn't disappear without good reason.

'Maybe he went to check on the Possessed force,' suggested Bryna.

'But Soren says he was heading straight back here,' said Lanista Magnus.

'Maybe he's hurt,' said one of the commanders who had led the cadet army during the training campaign.

'Not likely!' snorted Alex. 'Have you seen what he's riding lately?'

Many smiled at Alex's tone but they could not deny the concern they felt at Falco's sudden disappearance.

'No. We have to proceed on the basis that he might not be back for some time,' said Lanista Magnus. 'Which means we must decide for ourselves what to do about this 'gaoler' and the refugees in its path.'

The scout from Ville de Pierre had marked the gaoler's position on the map and they could all see that is was dangerously close to the refugees that moved ahead of it. These people were from Illicia and the Illician cadets were especially keen to help them.

'They are moving through here,' said Quirren, indicating the valley formed by Les Argenté Fleuve, the river that ran parallel to the Tonnerre. 'The river doesn't divide or diverge. There is only one route for the people to follow and so it's only a matter of time before the demon catches up with them.'

'We cannot risk an encounter with a gaoler,' repeated Lanista Magnus. 'Not without Falco or another battle mage.'

The older commanders had heard of these particular demons. They scoured the land for victims that were either particularly strong or filled with deep feeling: powerful warriors, parents, children, lovers - anyone who could be made to experience a greater amount of suffering. They did not kill or possess them, they took them alive and bound their tortured bodies into bags made from chains. These bundles of human suffering were then attached to the gaoler's belt, trailing after the demon like reservoirs of devotion that could be delivered to a greater demon, or used for some unholy purpose of the Possessed.

The thought of leaving the refugees to the mercy of such a fiend was too horrible to contemplate, but they could not risk the entire army to save a hundred refugees.

'It makes little difference,' said Lanista Deloix. 'We would need to go back thirty miles to find a road that connects the two valleys.'

'There are smaller routes,' said the Irregular's scout and the man from Ville de Pierre nodded in agreement. 'Narrow gullies. Hard to find and prone to rock falls but passable with care. There is one such path just a few miles downriver.'

Lanista Magnus looked round at the eager faces of the cadets. They now shared the responsibility of commanding an army, but the cadets were too young to know that many a force had been led to disaster by the naivety of good intentions. He glanced at Lanista Deloix before Malaki directed a question to the scouts.

'The walls of this route, they are unstable, you say?'

'They are, my Lord,' replied the scout.

'They could be made to collapse?'

'I should imagine so.'

Malaki nodded and Quirren smiled as he guessed what Malaki was thinking.

'We could send a small force with a scout to guide them,' said Malaki. 'If it is safe to do so we could direct the refugees to safety and collapse the gully behind them.'

'We cannot risk a demon coming close to the army,' said one of the older commanders.

'We won't,' said Malaki and for all his youth no one doubted the strength of his resolve. 'If the refugees cannot be brought to safety then we will collapse the gully and return.'

Malaki's use of the word 'we' was not lost on the cadets.

'The Exiles will help,' said Alex. 'There may be people known to them among the refugees.'

Malaki nodded.

'And the Dalwhinnies will guard the mouth of the gully,' said Bryna. 'In case any of the Possessed should break through.'

Around the command tent there was a general murmur of agreement. The finer details were yet to be decided but the outline of a plan was formed. They would send a scout to rendezvous with the refugees and guide them towards the gully that connected the two canyons. There they would be met by a small force to bring them safely through. Not enough to oppose the Possessed, just enough to fend off a forward scouting party. Finally Malaki turned to one of the aide-de-camps standing nearby.

'Find the captain of the engineers,' he said. 'Tell him to find twenty men with experience of quarrying or mining. Have them gather hammers, picks and prising bars and meet us at the eastern end of the camp in one hour.'

With a nervous nod the young boy raced away and the commanders began to disperse. As Malaki made to leave the tent Lanista Magnus caught his arm.

'This is a risky move,' he said. 'Sometimes it requires more strength to avoid the enemy than it does to attack.'

'We can't just abandon them because Falco isn't here,' said Malaki. 'We have to try.'

'Yes,' said the Lanista, a grim expression on his scarred face. 'We do.'

*

All through the night Falco flew north, only stopping to let Sidian rest or to check the direction of their flight. After the force of the initial challenge the sense of the Slayer's location had faded and Falco needed to concentrate hard to discern just where in the world it had re-emerged. But as they continued north it became clear that the Slayer had returned to the place where Nathalie had driven it from the world. North and slightly east they flew, straight towards the Illician city of Hoffen and Falco wondered if Nathalie was still in the city, if she too had sensed the demon's return and was, even now, preparing to meet the Slayer's might once more.

Falco could not believe that the Slayer had grown weaker in its absence. He had no idea if he would have the power to damage it. All he knew was that Nathalie, or whichever battle mage now lay in its path, must not face it alone.

As the eastern sky began to lighten, he leaned down over Sidian's back and flew on.

*

In the city of Hoffen an injured battle mage rose from his sickbed and limped out onto the crenulated walls of the citadel. The sun was rising behind a bank of cloud and he narrowed his eyes against the brightness of the light. With his left arm in a sling he struggled over to the wall as a young man in healer's robes emerged from the tower behind him.

'My lord!' protested the healer. 'The chief physician said you were not to put weight on your leg. I was to make sure you stayed in bed.'

The healer spoke the truth but the battle mage waved him away. With a worried frown the young man went to find someone who could talk some sense into their strong willed patient, but the battle mage barely noticed his departure. Despite the healing draft they had given him, his sleep had been troubled but now, as he walked out onto the battlements, he realised that the shadow in the night had not been a dream. There really was something out there in the wilds.

A gap in the clouds allowed the sun's light to fall across the man's pale face and he raised his good hand to shield his eyes, wincing at the sudden pain that pulsed in his temples. Perhaps the young healer was right, maybe it was too early for him to be up. Leaning on the wall he let out a sigh as the pain subsided then he glanced to one side as a tiger-striped dragon emerged from the canvas shelter that the healers had erected for it. With its left foreleg held up against its body the dragon limped across the open space. There was an air of concern in its gaze as it came to stand beside him.

'You don't look so good yourself,' replied the battle mage casting his eyes over the dragon's injured body.

Like him, the dragon displayed a number of recently acquired wounds, including one to its left foreleg that prevented the dragon from walking properly. There were burn marks on its wings and a deep gash to the wing muscles on its chest, but the dragon simply curled its lip and gave a dismissive snort.

502

With a grim smile the battle mage placed his hand on the dragon's neck and together they stared out over the mist shrouded moors, each trying to perceive what it was that had disturbed their sleep. The dragon's scaled brows drew down over its vibrant orange eyes and a low growl rumbled in its throat.

'Yes,' murmured the battle mage. 'There's definitely something out there.'

The battle mage's name was Lysander Müller, a man of thirty-four from a rural town in the heartland of Illicia. It was now eleven years since his hometown had been overtaken by the Possessed, eleven years since his parents and sister had died in despair while he was away completing his training at the mage tower of Vaidas.

The pain of that loss still burned in his heart but he tried to console himself with thoughts of all the lives he had saved since then. Only last week he and Feurig had brought eight hundred people back to the safety of Hoffen. Like so many remote communities they had been cut off by the rapid advance of the Possessed.

It had taken twelve days, and some fierce fighting, to bring them out of the Forsaken Lands, but finally they had made it. However, the fighting had taken its toll and there was no way they could return to the front just yet. Lysander had worried about the gap their absence would leave, but Nathalie Saigal had insisted that she and Ciel would cover his region while he recovered. They too had been injured in a recent confrontation, but they had recovered well and there had been little evidence of Ciel's damaged wing as the dragon flew out of the city.

That was four days ago and Lysander knew that they would now be back in the thick of it, flying from one battle to the next, slowly exhausting the strength they regained in a few weeks' rest. Now it was his turn to recover and the frustration was worse than the pain. Their injuries were slowly healing but it would still be several weeks before they could return to the front. But now, gazing out across the moors, Lysander had the terrible feeling that the enemy was coming to them. Beside him Feurig began to snarl.

'I don't know,' said Lysander as the dragon gave him a questioning look. 'I've never felt its like before.'

Out there, in the morning mist they could feel the presence of a demon. Normally the enemy's minions would avoid a confrontation with a battle mage, but this one seemed to be getting closer and Lysander's eyes narrowed as he remembered the fearless assassin that Nathalie had spoken of.

The noise of the tower door opening broke the battle mage's thoughts and he turned to see the chief physician striding onto the battlements while the young healer hovered in the doorway.

'I thought I told you to stay in bed!' said the physician, a white haired man with a stern face and a keen eye. 'How do you expect your leg to heal if you...' The chief physician was clearly angry, but his scolding was brought to a halt by a bellowing roar that broke over the city.

Lysander turned back to the battlements and he did not need a dragon's sight to see the dark shape emerging from the mist not half a mile from the city's walls. His brow gathered and he gave a heavy sigh as he looked down upon the assassin that Nathalie had described.

'Fetch my armour.'

503

'What!' cried the physician. 'Your armour isn't repaired and your wounds are barely closed. You're in no condition to fight!'

The chief physician's voice was shrill with fear and the junior healer was now cowering in the doorway. Even as the morning mist lifted from the moors so a dreadful fear settled over the city. From the watch towers the alarm bells began to ring. They were designed to bring the city to arms, but Lysander Müller could feel the strength of the demon that had come upon them and to him the bells were like the tolling of doom.

*

The Slayer drew a breath as its challenge rolled out over the city. It was now so close that it could see the Defiant and the wyrm standing on the wall of the citadel. It was clear that both were badly injured and the Slayer felt a pang of disappointment that the satisfaction of this victory should be diminished by their weakness. But then it heard the alarm bells, the screams and the cries of panic rising up from the city. The Defiant and the wyrm might offer little gratification but a city of twelve thousand souls would provide some consolation. The first day of its return to the charnel world would not be without reward.

*

Flying low over the misty moors Falco could just make out the vague shape of a city in the distance. With no sleep and little rest both he and Sidian were exhausted but they would not let up now. They could both feel the tension mounting ahead of them, the fear in the city and the sadistic anticipation of the Slayer. Suddenly a distant roar disturbed the morning stillness. And then the far off sound of tolling bells. The city of Hoffen was going to fall and two great souls were about to die.

89

Mina

Malaki and the members of the rescue party slept little during the night. They had left the army shortly after the meeting and huddled under campaign blankets through the darkest part of the night. By sunrise they were in position. It had taken several hours to traverse the narrow gully and another two for the quarrymen to scale the cliffs and prepare them for a controlled collapse. The scouts had not been lying when they said the walls of the canyon were unstable and there had been several occasions when they needed to stop and take cover as loose rocks clattered down into the gully.

'How the hell did they find this route?' whispered Alex.

'They're scouts,' replied Bryna. 'It pays to know every twist and turn of the land.'

After some discussion it had been agreed that Bryna would bring a small contingent of Dalwhinnies into the gully, rather than waiting back at the entrance. Another scout had come forward to say that he knew routes leading to the summit of the crags where the archers could get a good vantage point without being vulnerable to attack. So Bryna and the Dalwhinnies climbed up to the lofty heights where they could cover the retreat of the people on the ground.

All in all the rescue party numbered almost a hundred. Malaki, Quirren and Huthgarl led a score of heavy infantry. Alex had brought a small company of Exiles and then there were Bryna's Dalwhinnies. The rest were sturdy, callus-handed men, bearing ropes, climbing spikes and various quarrying tools. They looked nervous but resolved, for they knew that lives might depend on the skills they had to offer.

But now, as the sky above the canyon began to lighten, they were ready.

The gully joined the main canyon at a wide space where a shallow tributary ran through an area of scrubby woodland and weathered rock formations. On either side of the canyon floor there were dense banks of heather, braken and birch trees that concealed the entrance. All they needed to do was guide the refugees into the gully and retreat before the Possessed arrived. With luck their escape route would be overlooked, but if necessary the quarrymen were now ready to block it just a short way back into the gully.

Malaki glanced to one side where Alex's Exiles were hunkered down behind a series of rock buttresses. Their black surcoats blended with the deep shadows and these sombre men had a natural capacity for remaining quiet and calm.

Glancing up, Malaki could see no sign of the Dalwhinnies who were now in place on top of the cliffs. He was glad they were out of danger, although he did not envy them having to traverse the overgrown summits of the surrounding crags which were riven with cracks and crevasses.

'Psst!'

The small noise caught his attention and Malaki looked down to see Quirren pointing across the open space where a scout was making his way up the shallow river towards them.

'He looks nervous,' said Quirren and Malaki nodded.

The man was constantly turning in the saddle to look back the way he had come. As he drew closer Malaki stood out from his hiding place and gave a short whistle. The man saw him immediately and quickly crossed the canyon floor.

'What news?'

'The people are close, my Lord. But the enemy is not far behind.'

'Have they been spotted? Are the Possessed pursuing them?'

'Not pursuing,' said the scout. 'But it won't be long before the people are overtaken.'

'Can they reach us before the Possessed?'

'Yes, my Lord. They are pushing hard but some of the children are struggling.'

Malaki bit down on his anxiety.

'Go back to them,' he said. 'Bring them to us quickly and maybe we can disappear before the Possessed arrive.'

The scout gave a determined nod and urged his horse back down the canyon.

'This is going to be close,' said Huthgarl as they watched him disappear.

Malaki gave a thoughtful nod. Turning back towards the gully he was relieved to see that it was almost invisible, hidden by undergrowth and a convenient fold in the cliffs. So long as they did not leave a clear trail they should be okay.

The minutes stretched out and the tension mounted but presently they could hear people approaching. The sound of shuffling footsteps, the crying of an infant and the occasional cough echoed off the canyon walls.

'Here they come,' said Quirren as the refugees appeared around a bend in the canyon.

Throwing caution to the wind the three of them moved into the open and waved the people forward.

'Come on!' they hissed. 'This way!'

The people spotted them and surged towards the gully that might see them safe.

'So many!' said Alex, who had come to stand beside them.

'Where's the scout?' asked Huthgarl.

'Probably checking on the Possessed,' said Malaki.

'By the stars, but those scouts have some courage,' said Quirren and they all nodded.

It was one thing to stand and fight in the ranks of an army. Quite another to roam the countryside alone, tracking the enemy and gathering information, while trying all the while to avoid discovery and capture.

'Alex,' said Malaki as the first of the refugees approached. 'Have the Exiles guide them through in small groups.'

Alex nodded and began to move away.

'Keep them calm but keep them moving.'

'Hot soup and warm blankets,' said Alex with a smile.

'Exactly,' said Malaki.

Quirren looked at his brother with fondness as Alex met the first of the refugees.

506

'Grüße madam,' said Alex. 'Dies weise für die heiße suppe und warme decken.'

The woman's face cracked with emotion at the sound of such kind words spoken in her native tongue. Taking Alex's hand she kissed it warmly before ushering her children to follow this young soldier in the shining armour and black surcoat. At his command, more of the Exiles emerged from cover to bring their countrymen into the safety of the gully. They spoke to them in calming tones, resisting the urge to ask questions about where they had come from and who they might know. Such things could wait until the danger had passed.

Slowly the line of refugees came on, but Malaki could now see that they were quite strung out with some of the oldest and youngest bringing up the rear. As the last few dozen came into view the canyon was filled with the sound of approaching hooves. Suddenly the scout appeared, riding fast. He did not shout but his frantic waving made the situation clear.

The Possessed were coming.

His arrival caused a wave of panic and many of the refugees immediately ran for cover on either side of the canyon.

'No!' hissed Malaki. 'This way! Quickly!'

In the ensuing chaos the remaining Exiles darted out into the canyon. Sensitivity and gentleness were put aside as they herded, bullied and dragged the terrified refugees towards the entrance to the gully.

Cursing the frightened cries Malaki caught the scout's reins as his horse skidded to a halt.

'How far?'

'They are upon us, my Lord!' said the scout and sure enough Malaki could now feel the familiar sensation of an approaching demon.

Immediately he felt his mind begin to cloud over with fear, but this was not the first time Malaki had encountered a demon, and the experience offered a small measure of protection. The same was true for many of the Exiles and it was only their stoicism that allowed them to keep control of the situation.

Finally the last of the refugees were escorted into the gully and Malaki could hear the Exiles calling for quiet. Some of the men were sweeping the ground with twiggy branches, trying to obliterate the signs of their passing.

As the commotion passed the gentle gurgle of the shallow river could once again be heard. Malaki and Quirren were the last to seek cover. They stood in the open as the unmistakable sound of clanking armour and marching feet echoed up the canyon towards them.

'Time to go,' said Quirren and Malaki heartily agreed.

Slinging their shields across their backs they moved back towards the gully. Any moment now the Possessed would appear around the bend just two hundred yards down river. They had just reached the trees when a fearful cry broke the stillness.

'Mina!'

A woman emerged from the gully with one of the Exiles trying to restrain her.

'Mina!' she cried again.

'Hush, sister!' hissed the man from Alex's unit. 'They are all through. We will find her in the gully.'

But the woman would not be calmed. She shook off his arm and ran towards the canyon until Malaki stopped her.

'My daughter!' she cried. 'She was with the little ones. I thought they were ahead of us but they are not!'

Malaki's blood ran cold as he realised there might still be children in the canyon. The noise of the approaching Possessed was now louder than ever and there was no time to search. Together he and Quirren whipped round, scanning the trees on the far side of the canyon for any sign of someone hiding. For a moment there was nothing and then...

'There!' said Quirren and sure enough they could make out the partially obscured faces of several children peering out from the trees.

'Mina!' cried the woman, trying to break free of Malaki's grasp.

The Possessed sounded impossibly close and they could all feel the gathering fear of the demon advancing towards them. There was no time to do anything but run.

'Quirren! No!'

As Malaki dragged the woman back towards the gully Quirren ran in the opposite direction. Even dressed in armour he crossed the canyon quickly and charged into the trees just as the first of the Possessed appeared round the bend in the river.

Hiding in the bushes at the mouth of the gully Malaki clung to the struggling woman. Across the way he saw Quirren moving the children back into the deeper cover at the base of the cliffs. As the canyon filled with the sound of the approaching force Malaki retreated into the gully. Around him the faces of Exiles and refugees were white with horror. Huthgarl had put on his helmet and was preparing to fight.

'We must save them!'

'We can't,' hissed Malaki.

For a moment the big Beltonian just stood there looking at Malaki as if *he* were the enemy. People glanced from one to the other, their eyes wide with shock. They desperately wanted to help the children but they could all feel the fear tightening around their hearts. Suddenly Alex reappeared from the gully, pushing his way through the closely packed refugees. His face was set like stone and he made to draw his sword but Huthgarl grabbed him round the chest and held him fast.

'I'm sorry,' said Huthgarl, his voice breaking with emotion. 'Malaki is right. There is nothing we can do.'

'But it's Quirren!' snarled Alex. For a moment he struggled violently but there was no way he could break the larger man's hold. Presently he became still and pressed his face against the cold steel of Huthgarl's armour.

'Go!' said Malaki and slowly they began to move.

The truth of the situation had finally dawned and with a feeling of despair they began to make their way back along the narrow gully, Alex stumbling ahead of Huthgarl, his face white and slack with disbelief. The woman in Malaki's arms was now limp and weeping inconsolably and Malaki felt like the cruellest person alive as he dragged her along.

'I'm sorry,' he repeated over and over. 'I'm sorry.'

Behind him he could hear the sound of the Possessed approaching the mouth of the gully. The noise grew fainter with every twist and turn and it appeared that they had been overlooked, but then a figure appeared in the gully behind Malaki. For a brief moment he thought it might be Quirren. But it was not. It was the rotting half corpse of an armoured Sciritae.

'Huthgarl!' cried Malaki as the Sciritae suddenly charged towards him.

Malaki thrust the woman ahead of him and tried to draw his sword, shrugging his shield from its shoulder strap as he did so, but he stumbled over a clump of loose rocks and lost his footing. The Possessed warrior was on him instantly, its vicious kopis sword slashing down. Malaki raised his arm to ward off the blow but then Huthgarl leapt over him, shoulder charging the Sciritae against the rocks before killing it with a single stroke that clove its breastplate half in two.

More Possessed poured into the gully and several steel tipped javelins deflected off rocks as a number of Peltae appeared. These skirmishers were fast and lightly armoured, but behind them came a thick press of Sciritae.

Malaki got to his feet as a number of Exiles moved past him. At various points the gully widened and narrowed. Sometimes it was wide enough for five men to fight abreast, at others Huthgarl himself was enough to bar the way. This was a place that called for close quarter fighting and so the Exiles came into their own, their overlapping shields provided an impenetrable barrier and their stabbing swords exacted a heavy price for the Possessed who came after them. They gave ground slowly, allowing the refugees and other troops to move on behind them.

The gully was now thick with Possessed but they could not bring their numbers to bear and for a while it seemed like there was no way they could break through, but then the deep defile seemed to grow more oppressive and Malaki realised that the demon had moved into the gully. The Exiles began to glance backwards as the fear swept over them, looking for an opportunity to flee and as their concentration was broken so they began to fall. Stabbing swords and javelins found gaps in the shield wall and Malaki saw one man fall with a javelin through the base of his neck. The man was not killed and he screamed as he fell to the ground and was trampled underfoot by the mass of Sciritae that pressed them slowly backwards.

'They are starting to fail!' cried Huthgarl above the echoing din of combat and Malaki knew he spoke the truth.

As the demon came closer so the defence would crumble and the gully would turn into a channel of death. Glancing up at the cliffs Malaki saw arrows stabbing down into the Possessed. The Dalwhinnies were doing their job but soon they too would be overcome by the fear of the demon. Even as he watched, Malaki saw a gout of dark fire and molten rock blasting upwards from some point further down the gully. The stream of glowing shrapnel tore into the crags and two bodies came tumbling down in a hail of falling stone and shredded vegetation.

'Malaki!' cried Huthgarl.

'Just a little further,' Malaki called back.

They were almost at the point where the avalanche had been set up. If they triggered it too soon then they too would be crushed or cut off on the wrong side of the fall.

They had chosen a point where the walls were close together and almost sheer. The location had been marked with thick lines of chalk and soot but as they fought their way backwards Malaki became confused and disorientated. The fear was slowly mounting and he was finding it increasingly difficult to think.

'Malaki!' shouted Huthgarl once more and Malaki could hear the strain in his voice.

Behind him the refugees were now in full flight and even a number of the Exiles were turning their backs to run. If they did not stop the Possessed soon then they would be overrun but Malaki could see no sign of the marks they had made on the rocks. With the wings of panic beating at his mind he searched the rocks, trying to remember the distinctive features that marked the two extremes of the collapse. The Possessed could feel their growing panic and were pressing harder when Malaki suddenly spotted an anvil shaped formation in the cliffs to his right.

They had already passed the point of the avalanche and in a sudden flash of dread he wondered if the quarrymen were still in place. They too would be feeling the effects of the fear and might well have abandoned their position on the cliffs.

'NOW!' cried Malaki. 'DO IT NOW!'

For several heart-stopping seconds nothing happened and Malaki was certain they were lost but then a series of ominous cracks reverberated through the gully. There was a moment's pause and then the world disappeared in a storm of choking dust and deafening noise. The ground shook and rocks tumbled down around them, clanging off shoulder, back and helm. Had they not been armoured then many of the Exiles would surely have been killed, but as it was they merely stumbled and flinched, coughing and blinking as the dust filled their eyes and throats.

From out the roiling clouds the Possessed emerged, battered and bleeding but still hungry for their blood. Stunned and half blinded by the avalanche the Exiles did their best to defend themselves but they were in no condition to fight. Somehow they managed to kill the first rush of Sciritae and then, to their great relief, the assault was over. No more Ferocian warriors emerged from the choking fog and as the dust began to settle they could see that the gully had been completely blocked. They could still feel the oppressive fear of the demon but now the effect was dulled by a thousand tons of rock.

In the numbing stillness, with rocks and stones still tumbling down around him, Malaki stood like a limestone statue. His hair was matted and his face was pale, the tracks of his tears leaving streaks in the death mask of his face.

More than two hundred refugees had been saved from the torment of the Possessed and they had lost only a handful of soldiers in the attempt. The balance of life was firmly in their favour but Malaki's heart was broken. He could not think of all the lives they had saved. All he could think of was the souls they had left behind.

*

Quirren moved the children further back as the Possessed poured into the canyon. His heart was hammering in his chest and his hand was shaking as he motioned for them to be still.

'Are they going to find us?'

He turned to see a young girl who could not have been more than thirteen. In the thick shadows of the undergrowth he could barely see the other four children that he had hoped to save. Only their eyes, bright and fearful, showed clearly in the dark.

'No,' he whispered. 'They're not going to find us.'

The girl just stared and he knew she did not believe him. In addition to the terrifying sound of the Possessed they could all feel the overwhelming fear of the approaching demon. One of the younger boys was clearly paralysed by fear. He stood, stiff and trembling as the fear mounted, but then it lessened slightly as if the demon's attention had been drawn away.

Quirren moved a step forward so that he could see through a gap in the bushes. He saw a massive figure, fully nine feet tall, with long limbs, corded muscles and leathery ash-white skin. It was clearly humanoid in form, but far bigger and more horrible than any human that walked the earth. The nails on its hands were like chisels and its head was like the heavy browed wood trolls that Quirren remembered from the myths and fairytales of his childhood. Its black eyes were like hollow pits of darkness, and about its waist it wore a steel belt from which trailed a series of long chains.

Quirren could not see what lay at the end of the chains but he could hear heavy objects bumping and dragging along the ground, accompanied by muffled cries like the choking sobs of people in pain.

He was immensely grateful that the demon did not look in their direction. Instead it turned away and headed towards the gully down which Malaki and the others had fled. Likewise the Possessed seemed to be focussed on that side of the canyon and for the first time he thought they might actually be overlooked.

For several minutes the entire Possessed force was focussed on the gully and Quirren could hear the sound of fighting. The sounds of battle slowly drew away and he wondered if the rescue force might be overcome, but then the canyon shook with a rumbling boom and a great cloud of dust burst out from the gully.

Quirren felt a rush of satisfaction as he realised that the avalanche had been triggered and the gully blocked. However, the feeling of victory was quickly followed by the realisation that they were now completely cut off. For a moment he wondered if the demon might have been caught in the landslide, buried under many tons of rock, but then he felt the unholy presence moving back towards them.

As the fear started to mount once more some of the children began to cry. There was still a chance that they might remain undiscovered, but as Quirren continued to watch he saw a black robed Toxitae turn in their direction. The blindfolded archer seemed to be staring directly at their hiding place. Its head

511

tilted to one side as if it was not certain of what it sensed, but then it let out a hissing snarl and put a black feathered arrow to its bow.

Slowly the entire Possessed force turned towards them and Quirren knew that they were lost. Beside him stood the young girl who had spoken out. Quirren turned to look at her, trying desperately to quash the images of what was about to happen. He felt a surge of panic at the hopelessness of their situation, but then the girl looked down at the dagger hanging from his belt.

'Are you going to save us?' she asked and Quirren could only weep in the face of her courage.

The tightness in his throat would not allow him to speak but he gave her a nod and the girl turned away. Quietly she gathered the children into a line and turned them to face the cliffs.

'It's all right,' she told the youngest boy. 'The Knight of the Black Eagle is going to save us.'

As he drew his dagger the girl turned towards him and Quirren almost collapsed at the childlike trust in her eyes.

'What is your name, little sister?'

'Mina,' said the girl and with that she turned away.

Moving to stand behind her he kissed the top of her head and felt her body shudder with a terrified sob. Behind him he could hear the Possessed approaching and for pity's sake he could not fail them now.

Heart screaming and vision blurred with tears Quirren Klingemann sent the children of Illicia to a place where the Possessed would never find them. Then he drew his sword, armed his shield and turned to fight.

90

Hoffen

As it turned out there had been no time to fetch Lysander's armour. Indeed he barely had time to don a pair of leather trousers and force his feet into his armoured boots. Sweeping up his sword from a table at the side of the room he had limped from his chambers and made his way as quickly as possible to the battlements overlooking the approach to Hoffen. There he was met by Major Dahler of the city guard who narrowed his eyes at the sight of the great Lysander Müller still dressed in his nightshirt.

Lysander gave no thought to the state of his clothes but he accepted a heater shield from one of the major's men. Working his arm into the straps, he glanced down to the open courtyard behind the gates where Feurig had taken up his own position. Behind him dozens of civilians were milling about, unsure of what to do and glancing warily at the tiger-striped dragon that stood like a sentinel facing the fortified entrance.

'We need to get these people out of here,' said Lysander as more soldiers appeared on the walls.

Major Dahler gave a stiff nod as his men moved into position. Two hundred archers lined the walls and crowned the guard towers that flanked the main entrance to the city. Meanwhile, a similar number of spearmen and foot knights now arrived in the courtyard behind the gates. Like the civilians, they too stared at the great dragon standing before them, but at a command from Major Dahler they began to herd the people out of harm's way. Then suddenly a horn sounded the call of an enemy approaching.

Feeling lightheaded and weak Lysander turned to look down from the battlements.

Beyond the gates a cobbled road curved down from the walls of the city. The road levelled out as it reached the moors and there, just on the edge of the rolling heathland, was the demon that Nathalie had called the Slayer.

At around eight feet tall it was smaller than Lysander had expected and was approaching at a steady and menacing walk. Its back-bent legs appeared to be wreathed in smoke and its muscular body was covered in armour. In each hand it carried a huge curving blade and the burning light in its red eyes held not the slightest trace of uncertainty. It knew there was nothing in the city of Hoffen to challenge it.

Despite his injuries and the deep weariness in his bones Lysander's mind flared at the Slayer's conceit. Even in peak condition he and Feurig might not have been able to defeat it, but still they would strive to teach this demon some humility. Wearing a frown of determination Lysander drew his sword and flexed his mind to shield the soldiers with a cloak of faith. Beside him Major Dahler's archers drew their bows and the battle mage tried to imbue each sharp point with something of the power he possessed.

As the demon came closer Major Dahler gave the order to loose and the demon hunched forward as a storm of arrows converged on its unearthly form. Shafts snapped and sharp points skipped off its armour but a few of the energised

513

points managed to pierce the Slayer's charred skin. Dark blood bubbled and hissed from a dozen shallow wounds and Lysander looked down in satisfaction.

First blood went to the men of Hoffen.

The Slayer sensed their satisfaction and its eyes narrowed to livid slits as it resumed its advance. The pace of its strides was growing quicker as the archers raised their bows once more, but the Slayer did not allow them a second attack. With a sweep of a blade it sent an arc of brimstone screaming towards the battlements. The hellish attack tore through the crenulated walls and more than a dozen defenders were killed. As the rest the archers dived for cover the demon began to run, surging up the slope towards the tunnel that led through the walls of the city.

'Brace for charge!' cried Lysander, but hardly had he spoken when the battlements shook as the Slayer struck the gates.

The gates of Hoffen were more than a foot thick and bound in iron. They buckled, and cracks appeared in the wooden beams holding them shut, but they withstood the Slayer's initial charge.

A terrifying roar echoed off the surrounding buildings as the Slayer voiced its frustration but then it began its assault in earnest, the heat of its rage steadily growing until the wood began to smoulder and the wrought iron bands glowed red with heat. The Slayer's blades took great chucks out of the doors, hacking through both timber and iron. The kicks from its hooves were like the blows of a battering ram until, with terrifying brutality, it literally tore the gates of Hoffen apart.

Its final assault was delivered with an explosive burst of energy and the soldiers in the courtyard recoiled as the doors were blasted open. Splinters of wood and fragments of glowing iron flew through the air and several foot soldiers were struck down while others ducked behind their shields. This was an opponent that they could not hope to oppose.

In the midst of this storm stood Feurig, and as the air cleared the dragon raised its head to look at the Slayer. Like a murderous shadow the demon stood in the darkness of the tunnel. Even its outline looked sinister and its eyes glowed with a fierce red light as it suddenly charged forward.

From above the gate Lysander watched as the Slayer burst from the tunnel, blades swinging as it came in for the kill. Feurig met its advance with a blast of dragon fire, but the demon was protected by its reborn faith. Forging its way through the fiery torrent it struck at the dragon and Feurig might well have been killed if Lysander had not attacked from above.

A bolt of blue energy punched into the demon's shoulder and it spun round as Lysander limped down into the courtyard. Once again the Slayer was facing two powerful opponents but they were both hampered by injury and both were about to die.

It was only by protecting each other that Lysander and Feurig were able to survive even the first flurry of attacks. As soon as the Slayer closed on one, the other would attack it from behind, but they were growing weaker with each exchange and it would only be a matter of time before the Slayer drove one of its attacks home.

Even now Lysander was defending desperately as the Slayer forced him backwards. As he retreated so Feurig lunged in to strike at the demon's back. The Slayer immediately spun to attack him and the dragon tried to withdraw but his injured leg gave way leaving his neck exposed to the Slayer's curved swords. Twisting aside, the dragon managed to avoid one scything blade but then the demon reversed the attack and struck him a powerful blow with the mace-like pommel of its sword. The blow caught Feurig on the side of the head and the mighty dragon was struck senseless. He collapsed to the ground and would have died had Lysander not thrown himself forward to engage the Slayer.

The battle mage sent a bolt of energy into the Slayer's side then ducked beneath a sweeping attack that would have removed his head. He thrust his sword towards a gap in the demon's armour but his own injured leg would not bear the weight of his lunge. He stumbled and almost fell, but even before he hit the ground the Slayer kicked him in the face with a massive black hoof. A moment of fortification saved his face from being smashed to a pulp but even so, Lysander was thrown onto his back, spitting blood as his vision became crowded with darkness. Stunned and barely conscious he looked up as the demon loomed over him.

The Slayer flexed its arms and rolled its head as both its opponents were subdued. With the Defiant hovering on the edge of consciousness the cloak of his protection faded away leaving Major Dahler and the soldiers exposed to the full force of the demon's presence. To a man, the will went out of them, their courage shrivelling up like a naked heart in the embers of a fire. They were lost, and soon the Slayer would claim them, but first it would end the two 'great souls' that it had just defeated. With an air of consummation it approached the Defiant who lay dazed and helpless on the ground.

Lysander Müller looked into the burning eyes of the Slayer and saw the great curved sword rise up like an executioner's axe. Even as it began to fall he spat his defiance into the mind of the Slayer. As if from a great distance he heard the whine of a sword whistling through the air, but instead of pain and cleaving death he heard the crackling buzz of metal striking magical force.

Struggling to remain conscious Lysander saw a great black shape falling upon them. He knew it could only be the shadow of death and yet somehow it felt like the dark hand of deliverance.

*

Through Sidian's superior vision Falco saw the blur of arrows as the Slayer moved up the sloping approach to Hoffen. He saw the gate towers destroyed by a burning arc of hellstone and then he saw the Slayer disappear into the tunnel that ran through the thick defensive wall. Still a mile from the city he heard a crunching boom as the Slayer broke through into the city. Then, as his vision returned to the perspective of his own eyes, he saw flashes of fire beyond the ruin of Hoffen's gates.

The Slayer had breached the walls and his murderous work had begun.

The prospect of failure drove all thoughts of fear from Falco's mind. Beyond the walls two great souls were doing battle with darkness. After flying through the night Falco could not bear to think that they had now arrived too late. There was no need to convey his anxiety to Sidian. The dragon's fears were the

515

same. He could feel one of his own kind struggling beyond the walls, standing together with the mirror of *its* soul.

With a great surge of effort Sidian ignored the pain of his tired muscles and forced them on through the unforgiving air. As they neared the city he raised the angle of their flight so that they could descend more sharply into the space behind the walls, the space where their brothers were now so close to death.

*

Time stretched into a sublime moment of devotion. The Slayer offered up a prayer of offering as it raised one of its huge blades high above its head. Even now the Defiant stared up at it with fire in his fading gaze. The man's strength infuriated the Slayer and it pressed even more energy into the power of its strike. The sword whistled down and the Slayer wished that the moment of victory could last forever, but then the blade struck a wall of invisible force. The impact sent a shock wave up the Slayer's arm and he bellowed in pain as the sinew of his mortal flesh was strained to breaking point. Surely the Defiant was too far gone to produce so strong a shield.

The brief confusion lasted only an instant as the Slayer sensed another presence falling from the sky. He looked up to see a black wyrm plummeting towards him, and on its back the accursed brightness of another Defiant. From the wyrm's mouth came a stream of dragon fire, hotter than any the Slayer had felt before. The fierce flames blinded the demon. It lashed out wildly but then it felt the wyrm's talons clamp around its shoulder.

As the dragon came down it turned in the air, spilling the rider from its back and launching the Slayer across the courtyard. The demon smashed into the stables, snapping timbers and demolishing the stone-built walls, while the dragon crashed down into the courtyard. Its rider attempted to control his fall but their descent had been reckless and headlong, with little thought for what might happen at the moment of impact.

Foot knights and spearmen were scattered and Lysander languished in stunned disbelief as the new combatants found their feet.

*

Falco landed heavily as he was thrown from Sidian's back. There had been no time to plan their attack, no time to think about anything else except deflecting the Slayer's blade. Reaching out with his mind, Falco had blocked the demon's strike, maintaining the shield as Sidian covered the demon in fire. The great black dragon had caught hold of the Slayer and used his momentum to literally throw the demon across the courtyard. In the same instant they all crashed to the ground. In the next, they all rose to their feet.

Still clutching its blades the Slayer pushed aside rubble and fallen beams as it stepped out of the ruined stables. At the opposite side of the courtyard Sidian had regained his feet after reducing a hay cart to matchwood, while across the way Falco had slammed into the side of a building. Such a collision should have resulted in broken bones, but Falco had suffused his body with protective energy and felt merely stiff and bruised as he got to his feet and turned to face the Slayer.

*

516

Regaining the courtyard the Slayer's eyes burned as it looked upon these new opponents. The wyrm's strength was patently clear, but the reserves of this new Defiant were not so easy to fathom. The Slayer paused...

Had they met before?

The demon had the strangest feeling that they had. And then, slowly, recognition began to dawn. Could it be? Was this the child who had opposed it before the female Defiant forced it from the world?

The Slayer looked at the armoured figure standing before it. The appearance was different but the stench of its aura was the same. And yet not. The last time they had met this Defiant had been all raw emotion and damaged potential. Now it radiated a force of presence that the Slayer had never thought to encounter in the charnel world. Here was a soul that had survived the fires of grief and guilt, of doubt and despair. The Slayer tried to reconcile the boy it had almost killed with the man who now stood before it. A thousand years might have passed and still they would not account for the change in this Defiant's will.

The Slayer's eyes narrowed in satisfaction. Here then were two adversaries that might test the mettle of its hell-forged blades. The demon relished the prospect of such a fight, confident in its own infernal strength. It had not the slightest doubt that it would win.

Until the Defiant drew his sword.

*

Falco felt the full force of its gaze as the Slayer stepped out from the ruins of the stable. The demon moved with self assured power and its confidence was terrifying. Feeling suitably intimidated Falco shrugged his shield from its shoulder strap and settled it on his arm. He felt daunted, inadequate and completely over matched.

Until he drew his sword.

The Slayer's blades had been forged by the Enlightened and tempered in the fires of hell, but Falco's sword rang with the silent note of friendship, loss and love.

Finally comprehending the true danger of its adversary, the Slayer levelled its curving blades and attacked.

Although he was ready for it, the speed of the Slayer's attack took Falco by surprise with savage blows to head, body, neck and groin. Even his academy training was not enough and it was only by instinct that Falco was able to block and parry the lethal blur of steel. As the demon pressed forward he gave ground, retreating rapidly until he was pressed back against a wall.

With Falco's movement now restricted the Slayer pressed home its advantage, but Falco took one strike on his shield and ducked beneath a second. The Slayer's blade gouged into the stone wall behind him and Falco took the opportunity to slip free, but the Slayer yanked its blade from the stone and whirled to meet him.

Around the courtyard foot knights and spearmen emerged from their stupor and struggled to drag their comrades clear of the fighting. They had managed to pull Lysander out of danger while Sidian had pulled the insensible Feurig clear of the fray.

517

Meanwhile Falco danced and weaved as the Slayer tried to cut him down. Over the last year his skill had reached its full potential but even this was not enough to evade the whirling blades of the Slayer and on several occasions it was only fortification and the quality of his armour that prevented a severed limb or neck. Memories of their previous encounter came flooding back and Falco suddenly realised that he could not win. At least he could not win alone.

Unleashing yet another lethal barrage of attacks the Slayer suddenly stumbled as something heavy struck it from behind. Having dragged Feurig clear Sidian now joined the fight. The talons of his right paw inflicted three parallel cuts to the back of the Slayer's leg, but then the black dragon was forced to rear back, flapping his wings as the demon whipped round, its curved blades slicing at the dragon's chest.

Trying to take advantage of the distraction, Falco lunged forwards to attack but he was forced to dodge aside as the Slayer wheeled about once more. It seemed impossible to find an opening in the demon's guard and it was only a matter of time before one of those great curving blades found its mark.

Sidian attacked again, his talons making a horrible sound as they screeched off the Slayer's armour. Kicking Falco in the thigh the Slayer spun round and Sidian let out a roar as he took a glancing blow on his left foreleg. Shards of dragon scales flew across the courtyard and deep red blood spattered down upon the cobblestones as the Slayer turned back to its human opponent, but this time Falco infused his sword with searing energy and then let it fly in an arc of incandescent light. This was an attack the Slayer could not block and the arc of energy burned a glowing line of damage in both armour and blackened skin alike.

The attack sent the demon into a frenzy and Falco was driven onto the defensive once more. Sidian tried to attack from the rear but the Slayer seemed to anticipate the move and with blinding speed it turned its violence upon the dragon. Despite facing two opponents it was the Slayer that maintained the initiative and Falco tasted blood as one of the Slayer's blades slammed into the side of his helm. Fortification saved him from critical harm but still the strike left him momentarily dazed. A follow up attack might have proven more serious had Sidian not caught the demon's arm in his jaws even as it was about to strike.

Fire burst from the dragon's mouth and the Slayer roared as its arm burned while still locked in the dragon's teeth. Wrenching its arm down it stabbed at the dragon's neck with its other blade and Sidian had no choice but to relinquish his hold. The dragon tried to back away but the Slayer lashed out once more. Sidian avoided one attack and jerked his body back from another, but then a third blow whipped towards his head and he was not quick enough to avoid it. He managed to turn his head away from the cut but even so the Slayer's blade drew a nasty gash across his face.

Sidian blinked through a film of blood as the Slayer loomed once more but then Falco struck it a heavy blow across its back. Protected by its armour the Slayer turned back to kill the Defiant once and for all but its intentions were foiled as Falco unleashed a fireball that struck the slayer full in the face. The demon snarled and struck out wildly but finally Falco and Sidian were learning how to fight together.

As Falco brought up his shield and parried a blow, so Sidian attacked once more. He delivered a claw-strike to the demon's legs before leaping back from a vicious counterattack as the Slayer's blades tried to open the dragon's chest.

Falco was beginning to tire and his chest burned with the exertion of the fight. Knowing he could not sustain this level of exertion for much longer he began to pour energy into the cold steel of his sword.

Even as the Slayer turned back towards him he continued to imbue his sword with all the power he could muster. He blocked with his shield and dodged the demon's blows as best he could, knowing his fortification would be diminished while he focussed so much power into Malaki's blade. An ordinary sword could never have contained so much energy. Even another battle mage's blade could not have withstood so much, but Falco's sword had been tempered with the heat of not one, but two battle mages and so it could withstand the forces now building within it.

*

Across the courtyard Lysander Müller frowned through the haze of his concussion as he sensed the energy building in the young warrior's sword. Never before had he heard such a note in a battle mage's blade. It was both beautiful and terrifying and he wondered at the soul that could conjure such a concentration of magical force.

To his blurred vision the fight had been like some titanic struggle between legends of old. There was the black dragon, the demonic whirlwind and the dark warrior, apparently vulnerable in his youth and naivety. But as the fight wore on Lysander realised that this battle mage was anything but weak. He was simply inexperienced and as the fog of injury began to clear he realised that this was the first time these two great souls had fought together. The timing of their attacks was clumsy and uncoordinated, but they were learning fast.

A combination of luck and natural talent had saved them from the Slayer's blades thus far, but now he could see that they were tiring. Adrenaline and exertion were taking their toll and it would not be long before the Slayer's blades ended the fight. But now the young battle mage was raising the stakes.

Focussing so much energy into his blade meant reducing his fortification and there were several times when he was only saved by the quality of his dark armour, but finally the note in his sword passed into a kind of silence. Then, just at that very moment, the young battle mage dropped his guard. Maybe it was an error of judgement or maybe it was simply exhaustion, but either way it was a fatal mistake and the Slayer was quick to take advantage. With frightening speed the Slayer's curved blade stabbed towards the battle mage's throat.

*

Falco was not sure if he could maintain the flow of energy into his blade. In both body and mind he had never felt so weary, but he refused to let up. If they were going to defeat the Slayer it would require all his strength, anything less simply would not be enough. And so he poured his soul into Malaki's sword, trusting that the blade would be strong enough to contain it. Finally the singing of the steel disappeared into silence just as the Slayer turned back towards him. Without a second thought Falco lowered his guard and the Slayer's blade leapt instantly for his throat.

519

Malaki or Quirren would never have fallen for such an obvious feint, but the Slayer had not trained at the Academy of War and so it did not recognise the danger until it was too late. At the last possible moment Falco twisted out of the way and brought his sword whipping round in an arc that severed the Slayer's weapon at the hilt. The blade went cart wheeling through the air but even as the Slayer growled in frustration his second sword scythed towards Falco's head. Falco had no strength left to fortify his helm against the attack and it would surely have killed him had Sidian not chosen that precise moment to land a massive blow on the Slayer's neck.

The blow knocked the demon to one side and instead of carving into Falco's helm the Slayer's blade simply left a deep gouge in the engraved steel. Bellowing in fury the Slayer kicked Falco between his legs and he collapsed at the demon's feet. A second kick broke his collar bone and he slumped forward, his neck exposed to the Slayer's remaining blade. The curved sword began to fall but Sidian grappled the Slayer from behind.

Quick as a striking snake the Slayer twisted in the dragon's grasp and stabbed out with its sword. The sharp point slipped between the armoured plates on his chest and Sidian let out a hiss of pain, grabbing at the Slayer's arm as he fought to prevent the point of the blade sinking closer to his heart.

Growling through jagged teeth the Slayer grabbed the dragon round the back of his neck and flooded his blade with the searing heat of hell. Then, snarling with exertion, he tried to press the point further into the dragon's chest. For all his strength Sidian knew he could not match the demon's unholy might. In desperation he opened his mouth and breathed a stream of fire into the Slayer's face.

Not even during its recent penance had the demon known such agony. The cinder black flesh of its face began to peel away but still it refused to relinquish its hold. As his flames subsided Sidian felt the Slayer's blade inching towards his heart. The dragon knew that he was close to death but then the demon stiffened and the strength went out of his powerful limbs.

Still reeling from the vicious kicks Falco had struggled up from his knees. In front of him Sidian was wrestling with the Slayer and he could see that the demon had him in an embrace of death. Falco shied away as a jet of fire streamed out from Sidian's jaws, but still the Slayer held on. Limping from the sickening pain in his groin Falco stumbled forward and, even as Sidian's flames died away, he struck.

With a final effort of will Falco infused his blade with magical force and thrust it deep into the Slayer's armoured back. The armour of the Enlightened was strong but it was no match for Falco's sword. The glowing blade sank almost to the hilt and the strength went out of the Slayer's limbs. Still spitting hot bile into Sidian's face the demon slumped forward and the dragon was able to twist free of the blade that was embedded in his chest.

The Slayer's eyes glowed with a furious light but Falco sent a final pulse of energy flowing through his sword and finally the livid hatred faded from the Slayer's gaze. The muscular body went limp and a final searing breath escaped its sharp-toothed maw. Sidian moved to one side and the demon's armoured body collapsed to the floor.

As the assassin fell so Falco withdrew his sword and sank to his knees. Both he and Sidian were utterly spent and they could only stare in disbelief as the Slayer's corpse slowly cooled beside them.

*

Far to the south, in the Forsaken Lands of Beltane, the Marchio Dolor stopped in his tracks and turned his burning gaze to the north. Someone had achieved the unthinkable. Someone had slain the Slayer. A ripple of disquiet spread through the Possessed as they sensed their commander's rising fury. The entire army ground to a halt while the Marchio's attention lingered in the north.

A Defiant and a wyrm had killed his assassin and the shame of this defeat resonated through the upper planes of hell. At so great a distance he could discern little of the Defiant's identity and yet he had the sense that this particular soul had troubled them before. Its origins were shrouded and indistinct and yet it possessed the unmistakable stench of Clemoncé, that accursed Kingdom, with its accursed queen. Even now, when victory was so close, the bitch queen managed to stall their advance.

Still staring north the Marchio Dolor slowly turned until his body faced the direction of his gaze. He was just two days away from crushing King Osric in the mighty stronghold of Aengus, but no... He would leave the humbling of the Beltonian King in the capable hands of his new general. Vercincallidus would lay waste to Aengus and deliver the soul of Osric Goudicca unto darkness.

The Marchio would go north to deal with Clemoncé himself. The mewling sow and her fawning Defiants had frustrated the Faithful for long enough. It was time to crush their resistance once and for all.

Dropping to one knee the Marchio Dolor thrust his fists into the earth and began to pray. He prayed until the underworld thrummed with his rage, until he held the attention of every demon that moved within the Forsaken Lands of Illicia. And then he gave his orders.

'Move west,' he told them. 'Forget the pockets of resistance and forego the pleasures of torment. Turn your thoughts to Clemoncé and bring your legions west.'

To those demons in the north of Beltane, and to all the gaolers and reapers collecting souls along the border, he told them to cease their incursions and meet him at the western edge of the 'great lake'. There he would gather such an army as would sweep across Clemoncé like a plague. He would drive through the heartland to Wrath itself, where he would crush Queen Catherine's throat with his own two hands and claim her soul as his own.

And to the people of Clemoncé he sent a message.

Your time of grace is over.

I am coming.

91

The Cost of Defiance

Malaki could not tell what had stunned him more. Was it the impact of the avalanche or the thought of leaving Quirren and the children behind? Either way he was struggling to come to terms with what had just happened. As they stumbled along the gully it was the older men of the Exiles who coped with the trauma best. Somehow *they* were able to operate through the anguish and the wailing cries of the refugees, while Malaki and Huthgarl merely followed after them in a cocoon of numbness.

They had barely gone a hundred yards before the Dalwhinnies came careering down the crumbling slopes to join them. After witnessing the avalanche they had abandoned their lofty position and come down to join the rescue party.

'What happened?' asked Bryna as she saw the terrible expression on Malaki's face.

Malaki could not answer. He could not even bring himself to hold his wife.

'Did you not see?' asked Huthgarl and Bryna shook her head.

'We withdrew when the fear became a threat.'

Looking through the mix of soldiers and refugees she tried to see if someone was missing. Then suddenly she caught sight of Alex and felt a stab of pain in the pit of her stomach.

"Quirren?' she gasped and Huthgarl bowed his head.

As Bryna clasped a hand to her mouth Alex moved towards the rough path that led up to the cliffs.

'It's not safe,' said Patrick Feckler. He reached out a restraining hand but Alex pushed past him and started up the path.

Bryna's eyes were filled with tears as she watched Alex scrambling up the route down which the Dalwhinnies had just come. She started to call him back but then Malaki moved past her, following after Alex.

'Malaki, wait!' she said. 'It's too dangerous!' But then Huthgarl also started up the path.

'We have to see what became of him,' said the big Beltonian.

'There's nothing you can do!' cried Bryna. 'There's no way down on the other side.'

She looked imploringly at Paddy but the grizzled man simply shrugged.

'Past caring,' was all he said.

Bryna gave a gasp of exasperation and started after them with Paddy following close behind.

*

Quirren's arms were aching with exertion and the ground around him was littered with the bodies of Sciritae. Emerging from the bushes he had killed the Toxitae that had discovered them and then he had stood in the middle of the shallow river as more Ferocian warriors came to cut him down. They failed.

Quirren was a tall and powerful man from the kingdom of Illicia. Already skilled before arriving in Wrath his abilities had now been honed and hardened. He would show the Possessed how such a warrior could fight.

The Sciritae had attacked in twos and threes and he had defeated them with ease, but as the clouds of dust dissipated Quirren saw the white skinned demon emerge from the gully.

He felt a deep sense of relief at having saved the children from its malice, but this offered little comfort beside the fear that was now reaching an unbearable pitch in his mind. His only hope was to die quickly and so he picked out a group of heavily armoured Kardakae and made directly for them. With luck they would kill him before the demon could claim his soul.

Maybe he should have dropped his guard and offered his throat but Quirren was a warrior at heart and it was not in his nature to go down without a fight. Surrounded by three of the dark warriors he fought with heroic strength, cutting down the Kardakae as if they were mannequins on the academy training field. But as the first three fell so more came forward and these were now forewarned of his skill.

They came in hard and it was only a matter of time before Quirren succumbed. He killed one more before another struck him a savage blow in the side of his knee. A second blow glanced off his shoulder pauldron and grazed his skull, but then a guttural command echoed through the canyon and the dark warriors stepped back from Quirren who stood there, breathing heavily and struggling to stay on his feet.

With a sickening sense of despair he looked up to see the white-skinned demon walking towards him. Tall and powerful it strode forward, dragging its train of misery through the rocks and icy water of the shallow river. Its vaguely human face was misshapen and its black eyes looked at Quirren with unsettling interest.

The Gaoler had seen the way this young warrior fought. Far too good a soul to waste. But the Gaoler's train was full. Twelve chains trailed from the iron belt about its waist. At the end of each the tortured remains of a human being kept alive by the unholy power of the Possessed. Held in a state of permanent agony, they were reservoirs of devotion, stores of suffering to be used by the Faithful.

With a low growl the gaoler gave the Kardakae an order. They rushed forward and Quirren no longer had the will to fight. He was quickly disarmed and then they stripped him of his armour until he stood there, helpless and paralysed by fear.

Slowly the gaoler drew in one of the tethers on his belt. The body at the end of it was beyond recognition, just a mass of raw flesh and dark congealed blood. This was the first soul that this gaoler had claimed on this current excursion. It was almost beyond his ability to keep it alive. Driven insane by the constant pain the pitiful soul had passed the peak of its usefulness. Only in the fiery pits of hell could its suffering be renewed and so the gaoler held it up and the corded muscles in its arm bunched as it sent its infernal energy coursing through the iron links that encased it.

Formed from a net of chains the bag suddenly flared as the human remains were consumed by fire until nothing remained but white ash and a sticky residue that clung to the chains like tar. The person that had been bound into the bag was gone.

In some corner of his mind Quirren might have imagined a distant wail of despair as the tortured soul was delivered into hell. The bag that it had occupied was now empty and Quirren began to tremble with fear. Unable to move he closed his eyes as members of the Possessed came forward, not warriors but half naked humans with pale skin and milk white eyes. Some carried heavy steel hammers, others chisels and tongs as might be found in a blacksmith's forge. Standing more than six feet tall Quirren was far too big to fit into the chain bag. He would need to be broken before he could be bound.

As the first of the 'body-breakers' raised his hammer so an arrow thudded into Quirren's chest. Just inches from his heart, it might have killed him, had the gaoler not reached out a gnarled fist to hold him up. The demon's power would not permit the demise of Quirren's flesh and any hope of a quick death was cruelly quashed.

Held up by the Gaoler's will Quirren swayed on his feet like a marionette, groaning through clenched teeth at the pain of the arrow protruding from his chest. Meanwhile the demon looked up to see where the arrow had come from. It could not see them, but it could sense the humans hiding in the bushes that crowned the cliffs overlooking the canyon. It had thought it too much trouble to scale the landslide and pursue those that had fled through the gully, but now it could feel the strength of the watching souls. Maybe it would be worth it after all. He would add a few more prime trophies to his belt before delivering his catch to the Marchio Dolor.

With a dismissive snort he signalled for the hammers to begin their work.

*

Up on the cliffs Quirren's friends watched in anguish as he was stripped of his armour. They had witnessed the last minutes of his fight against the Kardakae, but it was painfully clear that there was nothing they could do. In the end it was Malaki who had broken the horrified silence.

'You have to kill him,' he said, turning to Bryna.

Bryna had looked at him in disbelief, but she knew that he spoke the truth. Hardly able to see through her tears she had nocked an arrow and taken aim. But it was not Bryna's arrow but Paddy's that had struck Quirren in the chest. Bryna's arms had been shaking too violently and her arrow had struck the stony river bed two feet to his right, while the arrow of Patrick Feckler had taken the young man cleanly in the chest. Horrific as it was they all felt a sense of relief as Quirren staggered, but then the demon intervened and any hope of a clean death was crushed.

Now they watched in dismay as Quirren was literally broken by the Possessed. The sight was too much for Huthgarl and Bryna, both of whom brought up the contents of their stomachs, while Malaki and Paddy fought to restrain Alex from leaping from the cliffs.

'But he's still alive!' the younger brother cried. 'He's still alive.'

Weeping in despair they dragged him back and Malaki thought his cries might have gone unnoticed but then the demon's attention switched to *them* and he knew that they were discovered. As Paddy wrestled Alex back the way they had come Malaki looked down one last time. The Possessed were stuffing

524

Quirren's broken body into the loose chain bag and Malaki felt a terrible surge of panic at the thought of what Quirren must be going through.

Finally the half naked Possessed bent in close. There was a brief glow of light as the bag was closed with red hot rivets and then their work was done. Pleased with its new acquisition the gaoler stepped forward until Quirren's chain fanned out with the rest of its sadistic skirt.

Malaki was about to turn away when the demon raised its face to look at him. At the same time Huthgarl appeared beside him.

'We should go,' said the big Beltonian.

Malaki knew that Huthgarl was right although it felt like they were abandoning Quirren all over again.

'We must track it,' he said. His voice sounded hollow and distant. 'We must track the demon until Falco returns.'

'No need,' said Huthgarl. 'Look! The demon is coming for us.'

With a flash of dread Malaki saw that he was right. Even now the demon was heading towards the gully. It would tear its way through the landslide and hunt them down.

'We must go!' said Huthgarl and Malaki could hear the rising panic in his voice.

The fear wafted up towards them like a scorching wind but just as they were about to turn away the demon stopped. It stood in the middle of the shallow river, its head cocked to one side as if listening.

Far to the north Falco had just killed the Slayer and far to the south the Marchio Dolor had reacted with fury. Thrusting his hands into the earth he had sent out his orders, some of which applied to the demon now standing in the canyon. To all the gaolers and reapers collecting souls along the border he had said this...

'Forsake your current incursions and meet me at the western edge of the great lake.'

To ignore such an order was unthinkable and so the gaoler had turned away from the bright souls that cowered on the cliffs. Had it wished to travel by the normal means it would have headed back down the canyon, but the urgency in the Marchio's command had been clear and so the demon opened a rift in the fabric of reality and stepped down onto the swifter byways of the underworld.

To Malaki and Huthgarl it seemed as if a dark cleft had opened in the world and the demon had simply disappeared into it. One minute it was there and the next it was gone. For a moment the Possessed just milled about as if confused by the gaoler's sudden disappearance but then, in the absence of a guiding mind, they turned west, following the canyon towards the distant glow of human life in the heart of Clemoncé.

Up on the cliffs Malaki felt a great wave of relief at the gaoler's departure. But this was quickly followed by an overwhelming sense of dismay. The gaoler had departed from the world, but it had taken Quirren with it. There was no way they could track it now, no way they could save their friend from his torment. The thought was too much for Malaki and he simply fell to his knees in shock. It had been his idea to try to save the refugees, his idea to risk getting close to a demon when they all knew how dangerous it could be. Such guilt was enough to drive a person mad and it took all of Malaki's strength to hold the despair at bay.

Wordless and numbed by grief they made their way down from the crags where they were met by members of the Exiles who had stayed back to wait for them.

Finally they caught up with the Irregulars but Malaki and the others were deaf to the cries of joy and relief as people recognised faces among the refugees they had saved. All they wanted to do was hide away, but the older commanders insisted on hearing a full report. They listened with grim faces to the account of the expedition and narrowed their eyes in disbelief as Patrick Feckler gave a brief account of Quirren's demise. Of all those who witnessed the event, only Paddy could bring himself to speak of it.

Despite the fact that so many people had been saved, the youngsters could not bear to hear the venture described as a success. As the meeting was concluded Lanista Magnus came over to speak with Malaki. He laid his hand on the younger man's broad back.

'We always knew we were going to lose people,' he said.

Malaki did not reply. If anything his head drooped even lower but then a cold voice caused him to look up.

'This wouldn't have happened if Falco was here.'

They looked up to see Alex standing beside them. His face was gaunt, his eyes glazed with trauma. Gone was any trace of the light-hearted joker and there was a distinct note of blame in his voice. They still did not know why Falco had disappeared but it was clear that Alex held him accountable. Malaki struggled not to let this idea gain a foothold in his mind. But it was true. If Falco had been with them, they would have been able to confront the demon, and Quirren would not now be lost.

In the night that followed Malaki and Bryna lay in each other's arms.

'We cannot let it destroy us,' said Bryna, her voice low and cracked from too much crying.

'But it was my idea to go.'

Bryna lifted Malaki's chin and stared into his deep brown eyes.

'Enough!' she said, and Malaki was surprised by the harshness of her tone. 'Guilt is just another one of the enemy's weapons. Isn't that what they taught us at the academy?' She paused and her eyes glistened in the darkness. 'In all my life I have never seen you flinch from a weapon.'

'But this is diff...'

'No. It is not.' And here she reached up to wipe the tears from Malaki's face. 'The guilt and the grief is an attack. And we must have the strength to meet it.'

Finally some semblance of resolve appeared in Malaki's hollow gaze and he gave the smallest of nods.

For a while they just held each other close. And then Malaki spoke again.

'I wonder what *did* happen to Falco,' he said.

'I don't know,' said Bryna. 'But he will need you when he returns.'

Malaki frowned until Bryna explained.

'He is the only one who *could* have done anything to stop what happened today. Imagine how he's going to feel when he returns to find that Quirren was taken because he wasn't here to stop it.'

Malaki squeezed his eyes shut, trying to block out the thought. He was anxious to know what had become of Falco and eager for his return, but now he dreaded the thought of telling him what had become of Quirren. Trying to remember what it felt like to be strong, Malaki drew Bryna close and tried not to think about what had happened. He failed. And when sleep did at last come, his dreams were haunted by the sound of snapping bone and the agonised moans of a soul that wanted to die.

*

Meanwhile, in the city of Hoffen, Falco was also struggling to sleep. Exhausted and stiff with pain he lay on a makeshift cot in the corner of Lysander's room while Sidian lay outside on the rooftop terrace. The older man had helped the healers tend to Falco's injuries. He had used his own power to set the broken collar bone and grimaced in sympathy when the healers placed an icepack in Falco's groin.

Falco was grateful for the help but he was eager to return to the south. 'I need to get back to my friends.'

'I understand,' said Lysander. 'And Marshal Breton will be expecting you in Amboss.'

He was clearly fascinated by Falco and brimming with questions, but he knew that now was not the time. He had heard the rumours of the black dragon causing havoc in Wrath, but these vague stories had not prepared him for the revelations that he and Feurig were now trying to comprehend.

'But stay a few days,' he added. 'Take some time to recover, at least.'

Falco reluctantly agreed. In truth he had little choice. Both he and Sidian were far too drained to fly. The dragon had also required healing. The stab wound in his chest had come dangerously close to being mortal and Sidian had roared in pain as Falco cauterized the deep injury with a fierce burst of healing energy. The slash on his face had required a number of silver staples and the scar now mirrored the deep gouge in the steel of Falco's helm. They were both lucky just to be alive.

They had defeated one of the enemy's most powerful agents and Falco expected to feel some sense of satisfaction but he did not. If anything the sense of impending doom was stronger than ever. And there had been something else, just moments after the Slayer had died - a burst of fury that seemed to resonate through the earth at his feet.

'Did you feel it?' he asked Lysander when the healers had finally departed.

'Yes,' said Lysander. 'It is not unusual to feel a flare of outrage after slaying a demon, only never as strongly as this. We have struck the enemy a heavy blow but we have also drawn their attention.'

'And do you also feel the shadows of fear?' said Falco. He was hoping that the older man might be able to explain the uncomfortable feelings that had been growing in his mind, but Lysander just frowned in confusion.

'Shadows of fear?' he repeated, shaking his head. 'I feel the fear of the people, but you speak of something different...'

527

Falco nodded, feeling suddenly uncomfortable.

'Darkness in the earth?' he suggested but Lysander's frown only deepened. 'Darkness in the deep...' added Falco, desperately hoping for some sign of recognition. 'Darkness on the hills?'

Lysander felt a prickle of unease crawling up his spine but he shook his head. He could sense the force of Falco's vision but could offer no explanation as to its source.

Falco lowered his eyes in disappointment. To him the sense of approaching darkness was almost overpowering and he had hoped that another battle mage might be able to provide some answers, but it was clear that Lysander had not experienced anything like the feelings Falco described.

'Try to get some sleep,' said Lysander. 'If I see Nathalie or one of the others I will ask *them* about this darkness.'

Falco nodded but he did not hold out much hope. He looked down at the bed the healers had made up for him and paused. The bed looked comfortable enough, and yet.

'The healers can move it onto the terrace if you want to sleep beside Sidian.'

It was as if Lysander had read his mind.

'I just seem to sleep better for some reason,' said Falco and Lysander gave a dark smile.

'They keep the nightmares at bay, don't they?'

Falco could only nod. All his life he had been tormented by nightmares but he had never felt as safe as when he closed his eyes to sleep beside the black dragon that had answered his call.

Sidian raised his head as the healers helped Falco down to the terrace. He watched as they laid out the makeshift bed before departing with a bow. Falco offered his thanks and gave a faint groan of pain as he lowered himself gingerly onto the mattress.

'Yes,' he said in answer to a thought from Sidian. 'I prefer a cold terrace and your heavy breathing to the soft crackle of a cosy fire.'

The dragon raised a scaled brow at his sarcasm and Falco winced as he worked his way under the quilted blanket.

'We'll stay a couple of nights,' he said as he laid his head on the pillow. 'But then we head back south.'

Sidian's expression appeared thoughtful as images of flying south played through his mind. He caught flashes of maps that Falco had looked at and saw the faces of Malaki, Bryna and the other humans from the army they had left. He gave a low rumble of agreement and laid his head down on the paved floor of the terrace.

Falco now took it for granted that Sidian understood what he was saying and it seemed entirely natural to see his own thoughts echoed in the dragon's mind.

He was looking forward to seeing his friends but the thought of what might happen when they reached Amboss brought him little comfort. It was likely that he and the Irregulars would be posted to different areas of the front. Even so, he was eager to see them and there was also the chance of seeing the emissary again.

He too should have arrived in Amboss by now. Falco smiled at the prospect but thoughts of the emissary inevitably lead to thoughts of the Queen and there was no peace in thinking of her expedition into Navaria. The thought of her riding into battle made Falco's guts twist with anxiety.

'*At least she has Aurelian and Dusaule with her,*' he thought and Sidian half opened a golden eye.

'Yes, and Dwimervane,' added Falco as an image of the scarred blue dragon appeared in his mind.

Falco smiled and Sidian closed his eye. With an effort he put aside his concerns for Aurelian and the Queen. In a few days he would be back with his friends. Comforted by the thought he finally gave in to the foggy tug of sleep, oblivious to the fact that one of those friends had been taken by the enemy.

While *he* lay down in relative comfort, so Quirren spent the night in agony, just as he would spend every night and every day until the demon that took him was slain. But Falco was ignorant of his suffering and so, at last, he slept.

92

Pride Before the Fall

The landscape of southern Clemoncé was lush and green with craggy hills and open woodland. The roads of this rural area were not ideal for an army on the march but the Legion du Trône had made good progress on its journey from the capital. They had spent the night camped in a broad valley, the silvery leaves of poplar trees clapping gently in the breeze. But even as the sun rose the soldiers of the Legion had risen from their blankets to continue on their way. Two hours later they reached the north bank of the river Castanea and the Queen called her army to a halt.

The river was shallow and not particularly wide but it marked the southern extent of her domain. Beyond this modest watercourse lay the independent state of Navaria. The territory was a demilitarised zone and leading an armed force onto its soil was considered an act of war. It was for this reason that the Queen had sent two diplomatic messengers to King Tyramimus advising him of the two Possessed armies and asking for permission to enter Navaria with a Clemoncéan army.

The first messenger had already come back empty-handed and now the second had returned and still there was no word from the Lord High Protector of Acheron. Apparently the king was 'outside the normal channels of communication' and could not be contacted. The Queen suspected this was some strategic ploy to force her into taking action that he could then use against her. But this was no time for political manoeuvring. Her scouts reported that the first demon army was less than a day's march from Sophia and the second would soon be closing from the south.

'Damn the great oaf!' she cursed as the messenger delivered his report.

'We could always divert the demon armies south,' said Aurelian, sitting on his own horse beside her. 'Lead them into Acheron... That might get the great bullock's attention.'

The Queen did not respond to Aurelian's dark humour. In truth she had expected nothing less from a man as arrogant and stubborn as Tyramimus.

Aurelian glanced across to Dusaule but his mute friend seemed unconcerned. Ever since Falco's summoning he had appeared even more detached, as if he had moved beyond the limits of caring. He returned Aurelian's gaze before turning to look back across the river. Either they would continue or not. It did not matter to him.

For Queen Catherine the decision was surprisingly simple. She was Clemoncé's monarch but she had never seen the other nations as 'foreign' simply because they lived on the other side of a line on a map. To her they were all people of Wrath.

With not a glimmer of hesitation she raised her hand and led her army across the river. They had a day to reach the city of Sophia before it was overtaken by the enemy. If that meant offending the sensibilities of the great Tyramimus then so be it. Let him declare war. If they did not stop the Possessed then they were doomed in any case.

As the Queen led six thousand troops across the river Aurelian looked to the right where a dark blue shape followed their progress, moving parallel to the army but keeping her distance so as not to spook the horses.

With her damaged body and tight scar tissue the journey had not been easy for Dwimervane but she ignored the pain as she kept pace with the army. Like him she could sense the dark shadow of the enemy and she yearned to oppose them. Aurelian could feel her anticipation and it matched his own. Despite their injuries they were warriors both. Whatever the challenge that might lie ahead they would face it together.

*

On the opposite side of Navaria the army of King Tyramimus gathered on a broad hill as they waited for the enemy to come into view. Clad in traditional muscle armour, the king looked the very image of regal might. His sun-bronzed skin shone with vigour and his teeth looked startlingly white through the black swathe of his beard. Sitting astride his slate grey warhorse he gave a snort of derision as the dispatch rider conveyed the latest diplomatic message from Queen Catherine of Clemoncé.

Tyramimus shook his head at the Queen's folly. Poor Catherine was as insufferably polite as her father. A demon army threatened her southern border and still she 'asked' for his permission to enter Navaria. He had shown no such consideration in bringing his own army north. He had crossed into the neutral state without a second thought and would deal with these invaders as he saw fit. He certainly would not ask for permission from a leader whose own kingdom was on the brink of collapse.

'My Lord!'

The king's thoughts were suddenly interrupted as the battle mage beside him pointed to the far side of the valley where a black flag had been raised against the early morning sky.

The Possessed were approaching.

Trying to calm his rapidly beating heart Tyramimus urged his mount forward. The initial reports had spoken of fourteen thousand Possessed divided into one large and one smaller force, and each with a demon marching at their head. One of the armies had taken a direct route towards Sophia while the other had swung south. Tyramimus had sent out scouts to assess the enemy numbers before deciding which force to engage.

The scouts from Sophia were yet to return but it did not matter. The force in front of them numbered more than eight thousand so that was the one he had chosen to attack. He would leave the smaller force for Queen Catherine, for he had no doubt that she would enter Navaria with or without his permission.

Pleased by his own magnanimity the king sat up straight in the saddle as a ripple of disquiet moved through his army. They could all feel the unnerving sense of something approaching and Tyramimus clenched his jaw as a tide of doubt rose up around his heart. Half a mile down the valley the mist began to dissipate as a dark mass of troops came into view. This was the first time Tyramimus had seen a Possessed force and the sight of it sickened him.

Though dark and lacking in elegance, the Ferocian armour resembled that of his own glorious troops. Thousands of Sciritae with hoplite helm, round-shield and plate cuirass, and dark blocks of more heavily armoured Kardakae and all carrying weapons that would not look out of place among the armies of Acheron or Thraece. But it was not the rank and file of the enemy that chilled the great king's marrow. It was the massive creature that marched at their head, a thing of nightmare and legend, a demon.

Tyramimus was ashamed of the fear that flooded his mind. For a moment he was worried that the army would perceive his weakness. Fortunately there was someone present who could spare the great king's pride. Like a bastion of indomitable will the battle mage looked down upon the massive foe and took the fear upon himself. Tyramimus was not lacking in courage but the fear that swept up the valley was simply beyond the ability of any normal man to bear. Wiping the sweat from his palm he reached across his body to draw his ivory handled kopis sword.

'We will wait until they reach the crossing,' he said, intending to attack the Ferocian force as they exposed their flank.

'That will not be possible, my Lord,' said the battle mage as the demon stopped and raised its head to look directly at them. 'As I sense its presence, so it senses mine,' he explained.

Tyramimus shuddered to think of such an intimate link with these monsters of hell.

'We will tackle the demon and the bestiarum,' said the battle mage, referring to his storm blue dragon. 'If his Majesty can prevent us from being overrun...'

The muscles in the king's jaw bunched with determination.

'You will not be overrun,' he said and he was proud of the certainty in his voice.

Feeling a newfound sense of calm he raised his sword and a chorus of salpinx war trumpets sounded the piercing call for étoimoi, *stand ready*. Beside him the great dragon shifted in anticipation as they waited for the enemy to move into position. They would hold until the Possessed reached the foot of the hill and then the army of King Tyramimus would attack.

*

Pausing on the narrow drovers' road the Queen frowned as she received the latest report on the whereabouts of King Tyramimus. Far from being tucked away in some palatial retreat, the Acheronian king had led an army of his own to confront the Possessed in Navaria. However, he had chosen to attack the force that swung close to his border, while her scouts reported that the other Possessed army was closing on Sophia more quickly than they had thought.

'How far do we have to go?' asked the Queen.

'Eighteen miles,' replied the scout. 'But the road is not easy.'

The Queen turned to Colonel Laville.

'Can we do it? Can we reach Sophia before the Possessed?'

The Colonel's eyes narrowed at the challenge. A further eighteen miles over difficult terrain would not be easy. And at the end of it they would be required to fight a battle. But the Legion spent its time training for such challenges and so Colonel Laville gave the Queen a decisive nod.

'Then let us be about it,' she said.

With that she urged her black stallion forward, the fifty knights of her personal guard falling in behind her. She ignored the penetrating gaze of Aurelian Cruz who was beginning to suspect that she intended to lead the charge into battle herself.

'Don't be absurd,' she had told him but Aurelian was far from convinced.

Ever since the young Chevalier had taken up his post as military advisor, the Queen had taken her lessons with deadly seriousness. She could ride as well as any man and was skilled with lance, sword and bow. She might not have the brute strength of a trained soldier but she had the soul of a knight. Her armour bore all the hallmarks of the Missaglias workshop and Aurelian could not help thinking that she intended to put it to the test.

*

Tyramimus's heart was still beating rapidly but his face was flushed with the exhilaration of victory. He felt no pain as the royal surgeon stitched up the gash on his forehead. The day was theirs.

Cutting the catgut thread with a small knife, the surgeon pressed a turmeric dressing to his scalp and bound it before fixing the bandage with an expert knot. The king gave him a nod of thanks and rose to calm his horse which stood trembling at the edge of the battlefield, the fresh scent of carnage thick in its nostrils. The animal's legs bore numerous cuts and a flap of skin hung from its right shoulder but still it gave a snort of recognition as the King laid a hand on its sweat-soaked neck. The battle was won but the injured animal offered visible evidence of the challenge they had overcome.

Tyramimus had fought in several battles but never against the Possessed and their heedless ferocity had come as a brutal shock. The Acheronian soldiers were accustomed to armies that fought in formation, armies whose morale could be broken, but not the Possessed. Injury only drove them to greater heights of fury and many an Acheronian soldier had died by underestimating what it took to put one of the Possessed down.

Even the battle mage's dragon had been injured and would need several hours of healing before it was able to fly again. But finally it was over. The remaining Possessed were being slaughtered and a fire was raging over the demon's corpse, an attempt, the men said, to prevent its hateful spirit from returning to the world.

His heart swelled with pride, but as the lust of battle faded away Tyramimus began to reflect on what it had taken to defeat this enemy. His army had outnumbered the Possessed and still it had taken all their strength to prevail. For the first time the Acheronian king had some insight into what the other kingdoms had been facing and the realisation had a sobering effect. He had called them weak because of the territory they had ceded to the Possessed, but they had been fighting this enemy for decades and now he wondered that anything of Illicia or Beltane remained at all.

Before he could dwell on such matters any further his attention was drawn by one of his officers.

'My Lord,' said the man, pointing towards the northwest slope of the valley. 'The scout from Sophia has returned.'

533

Wiping the residue of blood from his left eye Tyramimus stepped forward as the rider approached. The man's face was white with shock at the state of the king's army.

'What news from Sophia?' asked Tyramimus, irritated by the man's reaction. 'Has the Queen reached the city?'

Drawing his eyes away from the battlefield the man shook his head.

'No, my Lord. The last reports suggested she was still a day's ride away.'

'But she will get there before the Possessed?' pressed Tyramimus.

'If she can reach the city before sunset,' said the scout. 'But her arrival will be in vain.'

'Nonsense, man!' said Tyramimus. 'She leads the Legion du Trône. And the garrison at Sophia will surely help.'

'But the Possessed army, my Lord.'

'What of it?' snapped Tyramimus. 'We have dealt with the larger of the two armies. She has six thousand elite troops to deal with the smaller force.'

The man's face blanched and Tyramimus was filled with a horrible sense of foreboding.

'My Lord,' said the scout and he paused to wet his lips. 'The Possessed armies must have grown on their passage through Valentia. The army you defeated here was the smaller of the two.'

Tyramimus felt the earth shift beneath his feet as he turned to the northwest. Twenty miles in that direction lay the Navarian capital of Sophia, a city which, despite its claims of independence, he considered to be his own. He had thought the city would be safe; that he had faced the greater danger in confronting the Possessed army that ventured south. Now he learned that he was wrong.

Shame surged through the king's heart, shame and bitter regret. Thoughts whirling he turned away, casting his eyes over the army that was now resting on the slopes of the valley. Some searched the battlefield for any who might still be alive, while the officers organised work parties to bury the dead.

Tyramimus glanced at the sky before turning back to the northwest. His troops were exhausted but there was still the best part of an hour before midday.

'Twenty miles,' he thought.

If she can reach the city before sunset, the scout had said.

His jaw clenched with grim resolve, King Tyramimus turned to a nearby officer.

'Give the signal for the army to fall in and prepare to march.'

'But the men are exhausted, my Lord. They need time to recover.'

'They are soldiers of Acheron!' bellowed Tyramimus. 'They will do what is required of them! And right now their king requires them to march.'

'To where?'

'To Sophia,' said King Tyramimus. 'To the aid of Queen Catherine of Wrath.'

*

The Queen looked down upon the beautiful city of Sophia and her heart almost quailed in despair. The walled city sat at the head of a broad valley, its terraced streets rising steeply to the magnificent Hall of Stars and the pointed towers of the Consul's Palace. To the west the sun was setting, its warm light

534

contrasting starkly with the black clouds of a storm that was approaching from the west. The city glowed in a nimbus of golden light but a shadow on the land mirrored the dark clouds in the sky and like the weather it too was steadily encroaching upon the city. The vanguard of the Possessed was less than a mile from the city walls.

But for the sound of jangling tack and the sporadic whinnying of nervous horses the Queen's army stood in silence until Colonel Laville offered a perfect example of military pragmatism.

'Their numbers have grown,' was all he said.

The Queen did not answer. She was trying to calm her breathing, which was suddenly too shallow, too short. The Possessed army was far larger than they had expected and suddenly the mighty Legion du Trône seemed small and inadequate.

Apart from the occasional captured warrior this was the first time the Queen had laid eyes on the Possessed and the sight of it filled her with dread. They moved with horrible certainty, confident that nothing could come between them and the prize of sixty thousand souls.

'It is not too late to withdraw.'

Colonel Laville was required to point out strategic options but the Queen could hear the reluctance in his voice. Even outnumbered as they were, the commander of the Legion was ready to face the enemy. His courage shamed the Queen.

'We could retreat to Ruaen,' said another of her officers. 'Call in reinforcements and make a new stand there.'

The prospect of retreating offered an overwhelming sense of relief and the Queen was on the brink of giving the order. But then her thoughts returned to the people of Sophia. The mothers and daughters, the fathers and sons, the soldiers and city officials who knew there was nothing *they* could do to save their city. The garrison numbered barely a thousand while a Ferocian army of more than ten thousand moved towards the city.

She could retreat and gather a larger army at Ruaen. Perhaps that would be the prudent thing to do. Temptation tugged at the Queen like a physical force. It would be so easy to give in. But she was the daughter of King Philip the Commoner. She could no more abandon the people of Sophia than a mother her child.

As if in a dream the Queen urged Souverain forward and every man in the Legion felt a terrible conflict in their hearts, the urge to follow her into battle vying with the instinct to protect their Queen. She was a woman, like their sisters and wives, but she was also their Commander In Chief.

Urging her mount a few lengths forward the Queen drew her sword and the air was filled with a symphony of steel as six thousand knights drew theirs in turn. Trained war horses shifted, stamped and snorted as they recognised the tension that comes before a charge.

The Queen's heart was filled with a terrible fear and she could not shake off the feeling that the enemy was coming for her alone. The Possessed were now so close that she could see the great shape of the demon moving in their midst. The fear was so strong that it was all she could do not to break down and cry but then she felt another presence beside her. It was a presence she had known for many years and yet she had never really appreciated just how strong it was.

'It knows I'm here,' she said, her eyes fearful beneath the raised visor of her helm.

'That's just the way it feels,' said Aurelian. 'It knows we are at our weakest when we think only of ourselves.'

The Queen gave a barely discernible nod. If that was the case then she had an entire nation of souls that could come to her aid. She would think of all those she loved, and one in particular, one who had faced this fear countless times. Through the leather of her gauntlet the Queen traced the horse-head buckle on the belt about her waist. She would think of her Chevalier and try to match the courage he had shown throughout the years.

'Leave the demon to me and Dwimervane,' said Aurelian and the Queen shuddered at the thought of facing such a foe.

'We need to hit them hard,' said Colonel Laville. 'Make the most of our heavy cavalry.'

The Queen gave a nod of agreement.

'If you're quick you could hit them while they're still on the flood plain.'

'And we could form a defensive line along the edge of the higher ground,' said Aurelian, indicating a rise in the land that followed the curving edge of the flood plain.

'That would make it difficult for them to encircle us, but that won't stop the vanguard from reaching the city,' said Colonel Laville.

'Leave the vanguard to me,' said the Queen.

Colonel Laville was about to object but the Queen cut him off.

'Captain Ney. Captain Geraldi,' she called out. 'You will ride with me to secure the city walls.'

The two captains bowed their heads. Each of them led a squadron of a hundred knights. Even with the Queen's honour guard that would still leave them outnumbered more than four-to-one, but the Queen knew she could ask for no more. Colonel Laville would need every possible sword and spear if he were to stop the main body of the Possessed.

Without risking a look in Aurelian's direction she addressed Colonel Laville.

'May the light shine upon your blades.'

'And yours,' said the colonel and they could all hear the strain in his voice.

As the Queen turned her horse towards the city Aurelian looked over to Dusaule.

'*Go with her*,' he said with a simple jerk of his chin.

Dusaule's eyes were dark and unreadable but he dipped his head in acknowledgement. Ever since the night of Falco's summoning he had avoided all contact with Dwimervane, but now he turned to face the dragon. Aurelian knew she did not blame the silent Crofter for what he had done but Dusaule was too consumed by guilt and grief to see it. With a barely discernible bow he lowered his eyes and turned to follow the Queen.

Aurelian watched as she began her descent towards the city while Colonel Laville led the rest of the army to engage the main body of the Possessed. The heavy cavalry went ahead of the rest. If they timed it right they could strike a heavy blow before the demon came to the fore. Once that happened it would be down to himself and Dwimervane to stop it.

The old battle mage felt the familiar weight of responsibility settle upon his shoulders but he was ready for it. He had languished too long in the cosy backwaters of Wrath. One arm be-damned, this was where he belonged, facing down the enemy on the battlefields of the world.

Sensing his determination Dwimervane let out a low growl as the Legion began its advance. No time now to think about the Queen. The main body of Ferocian troops lay before them plus a demon that could render even the Legion's courage obsolete. But Aurelian had spent many years protecting soldiers from such fear and despite his damaged body his faith was as strong as ever.

Holding the Legion safe within his grasp he went with the army as they moved to engage the Possessed.

*

Cantering down the slope the Queen's mind was retreating to a place that all soldiers must find if they are to face the spectre of death. As the vanguard of the Possessed closed on the city she raised her sword. She did not have the booming voice of a parade ground sergeant but still her words rose above the drumming of hooves as she raised the tempo of their charge.

'For Navaria!' she cried but the Knights of Wrath had a war cry of their own.

'For the Queen!' they bellowed and for all her fear, the Queen's heart soared as she led her brothers into battle.

*

On the walls of the city the people of Sophia looked up in disbelief as the Queen's army appeared on the hillside. Until now they had thought themselves lost to the black army approaching from the east. Now they wept as they watched the Queen herself riding to their aid. It was some small mercy that only the oldest soldiers of the city could see that even her great heart might not be enough to save them.

537

93

The Battle of Navaria

Into the valley of Sophia rode the Queen of Wrath, her knights strung out beside her in a thundering wall of steel. For a moment all her thoughts were drowned out by the overwhelming sound of hoof beats. Raised up in her stirrups the Queen crouched low over Souverain's back, her sword arm pointing down and back, the reins in her shield hand gripping the pommel of her saddle for balance.

Now, just two hundred yards from the Possessed, they were still one beat short of full attack speed but the Queen would hold back that final burst of acceleration until the last possible moment. Already the ground beneath her swept past in a blur and she felt almost as if she were flying. The wind streamed through the slits in her helm, cooling the sheen of sweat on her face. Her breath seemed to ebb and flow in slow motion, the rhythm of her horse a rolling cadence rather than the headlong charge that it actually was, the world drawing a breath before it was plunged to chaos.

To her right was the rising outline of the city, the towers glowing in the light of the evening sun. Away to her left there was a great looming shadow, the main body of the Ferocian force. And straight ahead, the vanguard of the Possessed, a mass of Sciritae and Kardakae that still seemed intent on capturing the city. They were almost at the walls and the first bestiarum was closing rapidly on the gate. So massive was the bison like creature that Sophia's gate must surely fail and then the Possessed would flood the streets of the city. The knights had just moments to strike before it was too late.

'EN VÉRITÉ!' cried the Queen and two hundred and fifty war horses leapt forward anew as they raised their charge to the full.

Only now did the Possessed seem to notice them and with disturbing single-mindedness they swung about to meet the new threat storming down the hill. Many of the Possessed ran towards the oncoming knights but most formed up into deep ranks, close packed and braced for the powerful attack. It was clear that they had some idea of the damage such a cavalry charge could inflict.

The second bestiarum also noticed the Queen's charge and its clawed feet threw up clods of earth as it changed its course to drive headlong at the approaching horses. However, the first bestiarum was too intent on the gate to notice anything else and the Queen muttered a curse as the beast held to its course.

Through the restricted vision of her helm she caught only fleeting glimpses of the black shape powering towards the gate. A volley of arrows shot down from the walls as the city's defenders tried to stop it but the defence was poorly co-ordinated and ineffective and the beast slammed into the gate with a boom that reverberated across the field.

Even in the midst of her charge the Queen flinched at the sound, but there was no time to see if the gates of Sophia had held. The remaining distance to the Possessed had closed in a rush and she braced herself for the impact.

More than a hundred Sciritae were streaming towards them but the Knights of Wrath simply rode them down and they disappeared beneath a wall of churning hooves. The Queen saw one Possessed warrior raise its sword to attack her but a twitch of her reins and the Sciritae was smashed aside by the steel peytral on Souverain's chest. Black blood spattered the Queen's armour but any thoughts of disgust were swept away as they struck the main body of the vanguard.

For an instant the Queen marked the centre of a bristling line of spears and then the world seemed to explode in a deafening crunch of steel and mangled flesh. Their charge was a savage wave of death and the Knights of Wrath rode it deep into the Possessed. Horses screamed and lances splintered but the wave rolled on and the Queen went with it. Her legs felt battered and bruised from all the glancing blows and collisions. Three times she was almost unhorsed, but somehow she held on and as the charge finally ground to halt she struggled to get her bearings in the maelstrom that raged around her.

This was the first time she had been in the thick of battle and the avalanche of sensations was almost too much for her. The noise was deafening and the violence so fast and brutal that she was in danger of freezing completely. She suddenly realised that the knights around her were shielding her from the enemy. Her inactivity was putting them at risk and with a flush of shame she recalled one of the emissary's lessons on mounted combat.

'Movement and aggression, not bloody dressage!' he had roared in frustration, forgetting that he spoke to his sovereign and not to some slow witted knight in training.

Remembering the indignation she had felt at his tone, the Queen took up her reins and drove Souverain into a group of Sciritae that had surrounded a nearby knight. Finally her mind came into focus and she felt the reassuring weight of the sword in her hand.

'I'll give him bloody aggression,' she thought as she began to strike at the Possessed, not the delicate blows of a woman who wore the finest dresses of the royal court, but rather the blows a mother might unleash on a killer who thought to harm her child. Savage blows that clove armour and cut deep into putrefying flesh.

All at once the Queen felt at one with the warriors around her. They were still hugely outnumbered, but they had dealt the vanguard a heavy blow and she began to believe they might prevail. Then, just thirty yards to her left, a horse was suddenly thrown into the air, its rider tumbling from the saddle before disappearing into a mass of stabbing Sciritae. A second knight was smashed aside and even several of the Possessed were sent flying as the bestiarum came into view.

Tall as a draught horse and more heavily muscled than a prize winning bull the bestiarum forged a direct path towards the Queen as if it could smell her royal blood. Two knights moved to intervene but the beast barely broke its stride as it powered past them.

And then it was upon her.

Helpless and transfixed, the Queen felt a flash of terror as Souverain reared up beneath her. The massive creature seemed to fill her entire vision as it charged in for the kill, but then it simply stopped. One of its horns snapped and its face distorted as it struck the wall of force that Nicolas Dusaule had placed in its path. So close was the impact that the Queen felt a percussive blast of air as the

539

enormous beast struck the invisible barrier and slumped to the ground where it was finally dispatched by a dozen stabbing lances.

Heart pounding she turned to Dusaule, but the Silent Crofter simply looked down at the beast with the same emotionless expression he had worn throughout the journey south. He raised his eyes to look at the Queen and she could see a trickle of blood running from his nose, the only evidence of the effort it had required to stop such a titanic creature in its tracks.

With this brief exchange Dusaule turned back to the battle and once again they were fighting for their lives. The momentum of their charge had been spent and the enemy's greater numbers were beginning to tell. The Knights of Wrath fought like champions, but the Possessed were simply too many.

With Souverain turning and kicking beneath her the Queen killed two more Possessed, but then she felt a sickening pain in her left knee and glanced down to see a Sciritae drawing back for a second attack. She killed the creature with a stab to the face and tried not to faint as she felt the blood running down her leg. With a growing sense of panic she swept her gaze over the battle. For all their strength her knights were beginning to fall as they were overwhelmed by the enemy. The pain in her leg made her head swim and for a moment she thought she might fall from Souverain's back but then she heard the sound of horns coming from the city.

Looking up she saw a column of troops moving down from the city gates. The garrison of Sophia was coming to their aid.

Despite the first bestiarum's mighty charge the gates of Sophia had refused to yield. They had buckled and cracked but the Queen's arrival had prevented the Possessed from breaching the city. The Navarian defenders had finally succeeded in killing the beast and now it was they who rode out to help the Queen. Arrows rained down among the Possessed and light cavalry charged from the direction of the city. They did not have the strength or training of the Knights of Wrath, but it was enough to tip the balance.

With a renewed effort the Queen's knights were able to break free and they moved up the hillside to regroup. With military discipline they reformed the line and were about to charge back into the fray when Captain Geraldi noticed the Queen's leg.

'You're injured!'

'It's nothing,' said the Queen, although the horrible pain in her knee told her otherwise.

'Your Majesty has done enough to satisfy her honour,' said Captain Geraldi but the Queen was having none of it.

'This is not about honour!' she snapped. 'Now, break out the new lances and prepare to move down the valley.'

The captain should have known better than to patronise their commander in chief but his motives were honourable and so the Queen continued in a gentler tone.

'Sophia's garrison can deal with what's left of the vanguard. Now we must do what we can to help Colonel Laville.'

The Captain gave a stern nod as the squires began to distribute new lances to the knights, their young faces pale and determined. In no time at all the knights were ready to move out. They had lost sixty of their original number, including Captain Ney, and a further twelve were too badly injured to continue, but that still saw nearly a hundred and eighty knights moving down the valley where the Legion du Trône was trying to hold back the main body of the Possessed army.

'They're still holding the higher ground,' said Captain Geraldi as they looked down from the slopes. 'Although it looks like the Possessed are breaking through on the left flank.'

'Then that's where we'll hit them,' said the Queen.

And without any further argument she led her knights back into battle.

*

Down on the front line Aurelian blocked a Sciritae's low attack and kicked the creature in the face as it tried to scramble up the bank towards him. Turning to his left he used a concentrated pulse of energy to punch aside a Kardakae that was about kill one of the swordsmen who fought beside him, while to his right Dwimervane struck down anything that was foolish enough to come within her reach.

All along the edge of the bluff the soldiers of the Legion were fighting to prevent the Possessed from bringing their greater numbers to bear. They fought with strength and courage but it was only the lay of the land that prevented them from being overrun.

Still shielding the Queen's army with his cloak of faith, Aurelian muttered a curse as he saw the Possessed surging across the river on their left. If the enemy managed to get around their flanks then the Legion's advantage would be lost.

Closer by, Aurelian saw a group of some two hundred Toxitae moving to the front of the seething horde, their eyes bound with black and bloody rags. It was said that these blind archers were able to target a human soul and that their eyes had been taken to remove all earthly distractions. Whatever the case, the way they were able to hit their mark was truly chilling.

Aurelian watched as hundreds of black arrows stabbed up at the defenders. The attack broke the line of defence and the Possessed rushed in to fill the gap. Hundreds of Sciritae charged up the rise, scrambling over the mounds of dark bodies that lined the base of the bluff. The attack might well have proven successful had Aurelian not sent a fireball screaming into their midst. This was not like the small fireballs he had used in Falco's training, this was an elemental burst of fury that blasted a hole in the ranks of the Possessed. Dark bodies flew in all directions and the momentum of the attack was broken. Aurelian scattered the Toxitae with a second blast of fire, giving the Legion the time they needed to reform their defensive line.

As the fireballs dissipated, Aurelian's head swam and he took a deep breath to steady himself. He had forgotten how much energy it required to launch a truly damaging attack. But it also felt good to flex his powers and he could feel his strength surging to the fore as his soul remembered what it had been born to do. With the battle raging around him he turned back to the main body of the Possessed and locked eyes with the demon.

As the Legion moved into position the Possessed had surged forward but the demon had stopped, allowing the dark army to simply flow around it. It seemed almost wary, but Aurelian had never known a demon hesitate like this

541

before. They were normally so arrogant, so self assured. Caution like this was uncharacteristic and it gave him cause for concern. For a while he thought it might have been trying to summon another demon, but now the towering figure was surging towards them, a huge bestiarum keeping pace beside it.

Dwimervane had already killed one of these massive creatures. The terrible beast had ploughed through the Possessed before launching itself at the soldiers on the edge of the bluff. Infantry were trained to give ground before bestiarum, surrounding the huge creatures before attacking them from all sides. However, to give ground in this situation would have left the way open to the Possessed so the soldiers had tried to hold their ground. Eight had died before Dwimervane reached them. The bestiarum actually had a man in its jaws as Dwimervane attacked. With one paw she landed a blow on the beast's shoulder, her talons leaving four deep gashes in its blackened hide.

The bestiarum dropped the soldier and spun round to confront her, its wicked horns slashing towards the dragon's chest. Dwimervane lurched backwards but the scar tissue on her body restricted her movement and the tip of a horn tore into her shoulder. With a roar of pain she grabbed the creature's other horn and forced its head upwards while her tail whipped forward to stab at its side. The bestiarum reared up to grapple with the dragon but she flipped it over onto its back and drove one of her own horns deep into its ravening face. The beast let out a horrible sound and tried to rise, but Dwimervane opened her mouth and killed it with a blast of dragon fire that stripped the flesh from its hideous skull.

The bestiarum's body went slack as it slumped back against the scorched earth, a cloud of noxious smoke rising up from its twitching corpse. Then Dwimervane heaved it over the edge of the bluff and moved aside, allowing the soldiers to close the breach. They did so with wary respect. They had all seen Dwimervane limping along as she followed the army south, but none of them had ever seen a dragon fight in battle and the sight was more than a little unnerving.

After that, Aurelian and the dragon had fought together at the centre, providing an immovable point that steadied the entire line. But now the demon was moving to the front of its army and the bestiarum that came with it was much larger than the one that Dwimervane had just killed. The sound of battle seemed to fade away as Aurelian watched the huge shapes striding towards them. There was no uncertainty in the demon's movement now.

'I know,' he said as Dwimervane growled beside him. 'We'll take them together.'

*

The demon looked up at the Defiant, standing with its wyrm at the edge of the rise. The other 'great soul' was further up the valley near the city, but he was of little consequence, his mind crippled, as it was, by guilt.

The sudden appearance of this army had come as a surprise and the demon had paused as it sensed the presence of the wyrm and not one, but two Defiants. The Faithful had flowed around it while it tried to gauge the strength of its opponents. One was old and physically diminished while the other had been neutered by grief. Even the dragon was a limping shadow of what it might once have been.

542

But still, they were dangerous and the demon held back while it reached into the nether planes of hell for aid. It was not powerful enough to summon another demon, but it had sufficient devotion to drag another bestiarum onto this earthly plane, and this fell creature was more powerful than any of those that currently walked the field. Even now the demon could feel the beast rising towards them. All that was needed was a final prayer to bring it crashing into the world. But the demon would wait. It would choose its moment to unleash this hidden hound of hell.

Secure in the knowledge that it now had more than enough strength to defeat its opponents, the demon came on.

*

Colonel Laville muttered a curse as he watched his left flank begin to crumble. The Possessed army was just too large and he could not afford to divert any more troops from the centre. He had already committed his reserves to shore up the right flank and now the demon was making its move. The Legion's defensive position was slowly being overwhelmed and he simply did not have the numbers to go on the offensive.

Had he known that the army of King Tyramimus was now less than four miles away he would have raced for Sophia and placed his back against the walls of the city.

But he did not.

The Possessed were coming round his left flank and it seemed like there was nothing he could do to prevent his force from being encircled, but then he noticed a line of lance pennants streaming down the valley to his left. For a moment he thought it was one of his own cavalry units moving out of position, but then he noticed the royal banner flying in their midst and his heart soared.

Somehow the Queen had managed to defeat the vanguard of the Possessed and now she was riding back down the valley to join them. Even from here he could see that her numbers were greatly diminished but still, it might just be enough to secure the left flank and push the Possessed back across the river. If nothing else, it might buy them another hour.

Feeling a great swell of emotion he brought his attention back to the main battle and led his cavalry over to the right where more than a hundred Sciritae had broken through onto the higher ground. His knights charged into the Possessed, cutting them down before they could do too much damage. Then suddenly the twilight was split asunder as the demon unleashed a great gout of dark fire that carved out a hole in the centre of his line.

The sound of screaming filled the air and the acrid smell of burning flesh assaulted his nostrils as Colonel Laville watched men staggering away from the location of the attack, an attack that was centred on Aurelian Cruz and the blue dragon called Dwimervane.

Surely nothing could survive such an explosion of hell-spawned fire.

*

Aurelian only had enough strength to protect the three soldiers fighting closest to himself and Dwimervane. The rest were simply engulfed in a storm of Baëlfire. The screams were horrible to hear, but Aurelian shut them out as he concentrated on resisting the fire that was trying to consume their souls. Even

543

within his sphere of protection the heat was almost intolerable and the air scorched his lungs with every painful breath. But as the dark fire faded away he unleashed an attack of his own. His skin was raw and soaked with sweat, his grey hair singed and smoking, but his eyes were fierce as he straightened up.

Summoning his power he swung his sword and sent a curving blade of light scything towards the demon. The blade cut clean through several Possessed, but the demon had just enough time to summon a dark shadow of protection. Even so, Aurelian's attack was so strong that it clove the darkness and burned a glowing line of agony from the demon's right hip to its left shoulder, cutting across the palm of one outstretched hand. The creature bellowed in fury then it lowered its head and charged. Beside it the bestiarum also broke into a loping run and together the two behemoths stormed their way towards the bluff.

Aurelian's face was set like stone as he watched them come. He gripped his sword and even felt the muscles in his left shoulder tense as if he could still feel the weight of the shield he used to wear.

Barging Possessed warriors aside the demon surged up the bluff towards him, the bestiarum beside it clearing the rise in a single bound as it closed on Dwimervane. The hellish monsters looked unassailable, but this was not the first time Aurelian Cruz and Dwimervane had faced such beasts and neither man nor dragon flinched as the two great souls prepared to fight.

*

The Queen's charge was enough to secure the Legion's left flank and, as the Possessed were pushed back into the river, she finally agreed to move back from the front line.

'I will charge again if I see the need,' she told Captain Geraldi.

'I know you will, my Queen,' replied the Captain and with that she had moved behind the centre with Dusaule and ten knights from her honour guard.

They retreated onto the higher ground where units of cavalry were fighting to contain small groups of Possessed that had managed to break through. The Legion was stretched out in a line along the edge of the bluff, but the line was growing thinner and it would not be long before it collapsed completely.

As they came to a halt the Queen suddenly swayed in the saddle as a wave of pain and exhaustion swept through her. The movement did not go unnoticed and Dusaule dismounted to see what he could do to help, but before he could apply his healing powers their attention was drawn to the centre of the battle where Aurelian and Dwimervane were fighting the Demon and the last of the bestiarum.

Above the jostling ranks of the Legion they could see flashes of light and bursts of fire. Bodies flew through the air and the rest of the battle seemed calm compared to the tempest that raged at its heart.

'They're getting closer,' breathed the Queen and it was true.

Aurelian and Dwimervane were still fighting but they were being pushed back. And as they retreated so the Possessed surged onto the higher ground, driving a wedge into the heart of the Queen's army and splitting the Legion in two.

Suddenly the Queen's location no longer seemed safe. One of the knights insisted that they escort her to the city, but the Queen was not listening. She and

Dusaule were watching as the storm of violence drew closer. They were now so close that the combatants were visible through the thinning ranks of the Legion. They could all see their outlines, but only Dusaule could sense their minds.

The bestiarum - all brute strength and animal might.

The demon - malice incarnate and raging with fury at being so opposed.

Dwimervane - powerful and true, with the heart of a summer storm.

And Aurelian - shining with a light that belied his ravaged body and ill-tempered tongue.

But there was something else, something hidden.

With a sudden flush of dread Dusaule realised that the demon had a final card to play.

Taking a step forward he raised his shield and drew his sword. Then, with the frown deepening upon his brow Dusaule advanced, pushing his way through the thinning ranks of the soldiers. The battling titans were now dangerously close and the Queen's knights formed a defensive line in front of her.

The rest of the battle seemed to fade away as Dusaule focussed all his attention on the demon, but try as he might he could not discern the nature of the attack that it was holding in check. Ahead of him Aurelian was struggling to hold the demon at bay. Dusaule saw him dodge a great claw swipe and blast off a quick fireball but then the demon struck him in the chest with a heavy blow that left him dazed and vulnerable. The demon drew back its fist and Aurelian would have died if Dwimervane had not lunged forward, clamping the demon's arm in her jaws before it could deliver a fatal blow. However, the instinct to protect Aurelian left her exposed and the dragon gave a grunt of pain as the bestiarum thrust one of its curved horns into her belly.

Dwimervane was thrown onto her side and she let out a terrible roar as she felt the horn tear free. With blood gushing from her side she tried to rise, but the bestiarum attacked again, driving a horn deep into the dragon's chest.

Dusaule's mind screamed as he saw the beautiful blue dragon go down. And with this burst of emotion the demon was suddenly aware of his presence. Realising that it was now facing two Defiants, the demon started to pray. Dusaule pushed forward, but even as he broke through the last of the soldiers he realised he was too late.

Something was coming up from below.

*

Aurelian felt his ribs crack as the demon struck him in the chest. Through bleary eyes he saw Dwimervane grab the demon's arm in her jaws only to be struck down by the bestiarum. He tried to come to her aid, but the demon blocked his way and he could only watch as the beast drove a sharp horn into Dwimervane's chest.

'NO!' screamed Aurelian as he sensed the mortal wound.

Blazing with fury he struck the demon with a bolt of primal force that sent the towering creature to its knees then, ignoring the pain in his chest, he surged forward. The demon reached out to grab him, but Aurelian stepped in close and drove his sword into the base of the demon's neck. Light flared around the battle mage's blade and cracks spread through the demon's dark magmatic skin. With a roar of agony the demon clamped his massive hands over Aurelian's shoulders.

Baëlfire spread down its arms as it tried to prise the human free, but Aurelian refused to be moved. He flooded his body with fortification and channelled all his remaining strength into the blade of his sword.

*

Dusaule was too late to prevent the fatal attack on Dwimervane, but even as the bestiarum drew back he struck it in the side. His sword was not suffused with power but something of his emotion must have leached into the blade because it cut deep into the beast's left shoulder.

With an unholy roar the beast turned its violence on Dusaule, but the silent Crofter was transported. He blocked the beast's ravening maw with his shield and drew two heavy cuts across its chest. The bestiarum staggered as muscle and sinew were severed. Using the strength of its back legs it powered forward, but Dusaule side-stepped the charge and struck the bestiarum full in the face with his sword. The creature's lower jaw swung loose and Dusaule finished it with a thrust that pierced its heart.

The massive beast collapsed and Dusaule turned to see Aurelian engulfed in a writhing mass of Baëlfire. The demon was on its knees, its hands gripping the battle mage as the two combatants glared into each other's eyes. Trying to resist the screaming conflagration Aurelian leaned against his sword, but his strength was beginning to fail and the flames of hell were taking hold in his hair and clothes.

Moving towards them Dusaule used all his strength to protect his friend from the flames. Aurelian had beaten the demon. It was dying. But now it looked like the one armed battle mage would die with it. The vortex of Baëlfire now engulfed them both and Dusaule felt the terrible heat of it upon his face. Aurelian's power was all but spent and the only thing that prevented him from being consumed was the strength of Dusaule's love.

Caught in a storm of hellfire Aurelian's vision began to fade.

Dwimervane was dead and it was time for him to join her.

Even as Aurelian drifted towards oblivion Dusaule pushed into the flames to strike the demon from behind. His blade clove through the demon's neck, and the Baëlfire suddenly flared as the demon arched its back in pain. With all his energy focussed on protecting Aurelian, Dusaule had nothing left to protect himself. Even as the demon died so the dark flames burned away his clothes and reduced his face to a bloody mask of glistening flesh. The muscles and tendons in his sword arm were laid bare as he stood there, twitching and trembling in unspeakable pain. But he would not complain.

Finally, here was a penance to match the pain he felt inside. Swaying in agony Dusaule was waiting for death to claim him when the earth behind him bucked and broke apart. The demon's dying prayer was suddenly answered as another massive bestiarum burst out of the ground.

In a haze of agony Dusaule saw the beast explode from the earth. Like a monstrous hound, with cinder black skin and a thick mane of wiry hair, the beast looked round for something to kill. And its glowing eyes settled on the Queen.

Soldiers scattered before it and the only ones to hold their ground were the ten knights of the Queen's honour guard. Two charged forward but the beast killed them both as it drove directly for the Queen. The others fought to hold it

546

back but the beast was too strong and with a dreadful revelation Dusaule realised he could not allow himself to die just yet.

Stumbling forward he started towards the Queen but his burned legs would not move quickly enough. The world seemed to tilt and his sword slipped from his fire-scourged hand. Dusaule knew he was not going to get there in time. The beast tore through the knights as if they were children on village ponies and then it reached for the Queen.

Dusaule watched as Souverain reared up, driving his steel shod hooves into the bestiarum's face but the beast barely seemed to notice the blows. It felled the warhorse with a slash to the chest and caught the Queen's sword arm in its crushing jaws.

Dusaule accepted the pain in his body. He accepted the pain in his heart. He had killed something of grace and beauty and he did not deserve to live. On the night of that murder he had sworn never again to use his powers for violence and even now he would not have used them to save his own soul. But he would use them to save his Queen.

Reaching deep inside he tried to find the withered spark of fire that he hoped still burned within him. For a moment he thought it might have gone, snuffed out at last by the crushing weight of guilt. But then, in the vast emptiness of his soul he found it.

He called to it.

And it answered him.

*

The Queen watched in horror as the beast exploded out of the earth. Soldiers scattered and even her knights were smashed aside as the bestiarum tore its way towards her. There would be no wall of invisible force to stop such a monster now. She had seen both Aurelian and Dusaule disappear in the final blast of the demon's fire.

The last of her knights were rent aside and Souverain reared up as the beast leapt towards her. The stallion's brave attack had little effect and the horse screamed as the beast's talons slashed deep into his chest. Even as Souverain fell the Queen tried to attack but the beast's jaws closed over her sword arm, crushing the armour of Antonio Missaglias as it tore her from the saddle. She hit the ground hard with the beast looming over her, its teeth still locked on her arm then it shook its massive head and tore the arm away from her body.

The Queen's body shook with a great convulsion as her arm was bitten off, leaving only a short stump of broken bone and ragged flesh. Black shapes swam before her eyes and the world seemed to echo strangely as the blood gushed from the gaping wound. Not satisfied with an arm, the beast clawed at her body, tearing the armour from her right leg and snapping the horse-head belt from around her waist. Hot saliva dripped from the beast's jaws as its teeth reached for her face but then it disappeared in a flash of blinding light.

*

So strong was Dusaule's burst of power that it blasted the bestiarum away from the Queen. The massive beast spun round, its ribs laid bare by a great smoking hole in its side. It turned its baleful gaze on this new attacker and charged towards him.

The silent Crofter watched it come, his mind burning with the force of his own power. With frightening speed, the bestiarum leapt towards him, lips drawn back over jagged teeth.

Twenty yards...

Ten...

And then Dusaule killed it.

Raising his hand he struck it in the chest with a beam of fearsome light. The beast seemed to hang in the air as the fire illuminated its body from within, its bones showing dark through the shredded membrane of its skin. The remains of the creature ground to a halt at Dusaule's feet, now little more than a mound of charred bone and smoking flesh.

Dusaule gave it not another thought. All his mind was focussed on the Queen and the life that was running out of her. On tortured legs he started forward, desperate to reach her before she was lost to darkness. But the blood was flowing too quickly, pulsing from her body with every fatal beat of her heart.

The silent Crofter struggled on, but his body had exhausted the last of its strength. Stumbling over the uneven ground he fell forward, his raw face pressed against the earth, his breath coming and going with a pained wheezing rasp. His body could go no further and so he reached out with the force of his mind, using all his power to keep the Queen on this side of the eternal veil.

*

The Queen could feel the life seeping out of her. It was as if she hovered over a great sea of darkness and she felt an overwhelming urge to sleep. She had heard sailors talk of the drowning sleep of death and she was certain that if she gave in now she would slip beneath the surface of the dark waters never to return. She felt her heart beginning to slow and her mind was suddenly filled with panic.

'No!' she pleaded in the dream-world of her mind. 'I can't leave. I can't...'

But it was not the fear of dying that caused her so much distress. It was the fear of the emissary's grief. How could he face the enemy if he knew that she was lost? It would destroy him, just as it would destroy her if she were ever to lose him.

'Please,' she sobbed but the power calling her to sleep was too great.

She tried to picture the Chevalier's face, tried to remember the last moment they had shared on the high terrace of the palace. But the image was receding. She could no longer feel the touch of his fingers, the brush of his lips or the harsh stubble of his jaw against her cheek. He was fading and even the grey steel of his eyes seemed to blur with the looming sea of death.

'I'm sorry, my love,' breathed the Queen. 'I'm sorry.'

As if from a great distance she could hear the sound of battle still raging around her but the sound was giving way to silence. For a moment she thought she heard the braying sound of Acheronian war trumpets but that was surely an illusion, a cruel trick of her failing mind.

Tears of regret ran down her face.

Then her heart beat once.

Twice.

And...

548

94

A Token of Love and Loss

The arrival of the Acheronian army marked the end of the Possessed and as the last of the fighting died away so an eerie silence settled over the valley. News of the Queen's demise had now reached Sophia and a single bell began to toll, slow and mournful, from some tall tower in the city. The dark storm clouds still hovered to the east and the light began to fade as day gave way to night.

Down on the battlefield a tent had now been erected over the great souls that had fallen. In one compartment lay Aurelian and Dusaule, both alive but with their fates uncertain. In the other compartment lay Dwimervane, her scarred body curled with her wings folded as if in sleep. And beside the dragon, on a makeshift bier, lay the Queen, her slender body covered with a simple sheet of pure white linen. In each compartment were two knights standing guard over the unconscious, the dying, and the dead. The two knights in the Queen's compartment looked straight ahead as Colonel Laville entered with King Tyramimus.

Moving to one side of the Queen's bier Colonel Laville lifted the top edge of the sheet and drew it back so that King Tyramimus could look upon her face.

The great King felt a gut wrenching spasm at the sight of the chalk-white mask. It was almost twenty years since he had last laid eyes on the Queen, but he could still see the features of the fiery little princess in the face of the beautiful woman before him. His heart burned with grief and tears of shame rolled down his cheeks before disappearing into the black mass of his beard. With great tenderness he laid his hand against the cool skin of the Queen's face.

'Forgive me,' he breathed, shamed by the courage and leadership this woman had shown. Then the king leaned in close and his voice dropped to a fierce and vengeful whisper. 'Rest in peace, my Queen, and be assured that the Great Bull has finally heard your voice. I promise you that Clemoncé will not fall, not while one Acheronian warrior remains alive. It is time to raise our arm, and clench our fist, and let the hammer fall.'

The king's tears were hot and bitter as he placed a kiss on Queen Catherine's brow.

'How did it happen?' he asked as he straightened up and removed his hand.

'A bestiarum,' said Colonel Laville. 'Even as the demon was slain.' His own voice was hoarse with grief. With trembling hands he replaced the linen sheet as Tyramimus moved to the side of the tent where the Queen's armour and sword had been laid out on a table.

Tyramimus ran his fingers over the bloody and battered armour, finally coming to rest on the black sword belt with its silver buckle in the shape of a horse's head. The leather strands were torn and snapped but the king lifted it with great care as a new sadness dawned in his mind. He had heard of the tokens of mourning that the Queen wore to stall the advances of Prince Ludovico, tokens given to her by the man they called the Chevalier. Tyramimus had always thought it a gesture of naive sentimentality, but the Chevalier's name was known even in Acheron and the king could not bear the thought of such a man hearing of the Queen's death through the chattering gossip of the army.

Still holding the belt he turned as the Acheronian battle mage entered the compartment. The man's name was Anaximander and he had been doing what he could to help Aurelian and Dusaule.

'Were you able to help them?' asked Tyramimus.

'Master Cruz has endured much but his mind is strong. He will wake in time,' said Anaximander, his voice thick with his Acheronian accent. 'As for Master Dusaule... I do not know how he is still alive.'

Tyramimus gave a grim nod. He too had been shocked by the horrible extent of Dusaule's burns.

'Could he not be made more comfortable in the city?' he asked.

'Perhaps,' said Colonel Laville. 'But any attempt to move him seems to cause him great distress,'

'Something binds him to this world,' said Anaximander. 'But whatever it is, he will not suffer for long.'

Even as he spoke there came a choking sound from the other compartment. The three men moved through and Anaximander went immediately to Dusaule's side as the dying man was gripped by a series of convulsions.

'Even now he fights for something,' said the battle mage as he tried to use his powers to ease Dusaule's suffering. But slowly the life went out of the Silent Crofter's body and with a last spasm he slumped back onto the blood soaked bed. A final breath issued from his blistered lips and he was gone.

'Thank the stars,' said Colonel Laville, his tone heavy with both sadness and relief. 'For many years he endured life as one of the Disavowed. Now, at least, he is at peace.'

Anaximander frowned as he stood up from Dusaule. So this battle mage had been forced to kill the dragon that answered his summoning. Anaximander could not imagine the strength it would require to live with such an act. This explained some of the torment he had sensed in Dusaule's mind.

With nothing left for them to do the three men made their way out of the tent. Tyramimus was still holding the black horse head belt and he bent his head to look at it as they stood in the cool night air.

'The Chevalier deserves to know,' he said.

'The news will break him,' said Colonel Laville.

'Even so, he has a right.'

Despite his reservations, Colonel Laville gave a slow nod of agreement and Tyramimus turned to Anaximander.

'Take this,' he said, folding the broken belt into the battle mage's hands. 'Find the man they call the Chevalier and tell him the people of Acheron share in his grief.'

'Where will I find him?'

'Last we heard he was in the city of Hoffen,' said Colonel Laville.

Anaximander gave a nod and tucked the belt into a leather pouch at his waist.

'With your leave, my King,' he said and with a bow he turned to his dragon who was standing in the dark close by.

King Tyramimus and Colonel Laville watched as the battle mage swung up onto the dragon's back and turned the mighty creature to the northeast. The dragon took three quickening strides and leapt into the air and within seconds it had disappeared into the night carrying a token of love and loss that was sure to break the emissary's heart.

'May he find the strength,' said King Tyramimus.

'May we all,' said Colonel Laville, for now he had the unthinkable task of returning to Wrath with news of the Queen's death.

*

At twenty-four Jeran de Foix was the youngest knight in the Queen's personal guard. Riding into battle with the Queen had been the greatest honour of his life. Standing vigil at her deathbed was the saddest and also the hardest duty he had ever been required to perform.

He stood in silence as Colonel Laville escorted King Tyramimus into the tent, and was deeply moved by the force of the Acheronian king's pledge. He had remained, unflinching, when they moved through at the sound of Dusaule's final tortured moments. Jeran remembered the sense of horror he had felt upon seeing the poor man's injuries and was glad that his suffering was now at an end.

However, as the Silent Crofter finally passed away, Jeran was sure he had seen the Queen's death shroud lift a fraction and fall in the flickering lamplight. He looked again, mindful of the fact that it was unseemly for his eyes to linger on her covered form.

There was nothing, and Jeran felt a shudder of supernatural disquiet as if the Queen's spirit had made some gesture from beyond the veil. Getting a grip of his imagination he averted his eyes, but just as he was looking away he noticed a bloom of crimson on the white linen coverlet, a stain of red where the cloth hung down over the Queen's mutilated arm. As he watched he saw the stain suddenly swell, almost as if fresh blood was pumping from the wound.

For a moment Jeran simply stared at the growing shadow, then he remembered something he had learned in triage training.

Corpses do not bleed.

95

Reunited & Torn Apart

Falco stayed just two nights in Hoffen before he and Sidian headed south, but even before they left it was clear that something was wrong. Reports started coming in that the pattern of the enemy's movements had changed. It was too early to reach any firm conclusions, but Falco felt sure it had something to do with the death of the Slayer.

What was it Lysander had said?

'We have struck the enemy a heavy blow but we have also drawn their attention.'

Whatever the case, he could not tarry any longer. He had left his friends without a word and was eager to get back to them. Besides, he was still hoping to make it in time for the strategy meeting in Amboss. So, with a final farewell to Lysander and Feurig they had flown south. Their journey north had been a desperate race that pushed Sidian's endurance to the limit. Now they made their way south at a more normal pace but even then Falco felt Sidian tense with pain each time he responded to a sudden shift in the wind.

'How's the chest?' he asked as they soared above the rolling hills of Illicia.

Sidian's pride dismissed any notion of discomfort but he could not conceal a quick memory of Falco's attempt to treat the wound inflicted by the Slayer.

'I had to make sure the healing went deep,' said Falco.

Sidian's injuries were still mending so they rested frequently and spent the first night on the outskirts of an Illician town some twenty miles north east of Ville de Pierre, but even here the reports were the same. The enemy was foregoing all other distractions and pushing west towards Clemoncé. This worrying development did nothing to alleviate the growing sense of danger that had now reached fever pitch in Falco's mind. He knew that something dark was getting closer, but what it was he could not say.

Sidian looked at him as if to say, 'there's nothing to fear', but Falco was unconvinced.

All he knew was that his dreams were filled with dark caves, buried secrets and crashing waves of guilt.

By noon the following day they had reached the river Türkis, the single river that emerged from the confluence of Le Grande Cascade. Following the river would lead them to Amboss and it was not long before the bulwarked city came into view. From their lofty vantage point they could see the anvil shape of the craggy hill around which the walled city was built.

Amboss was easily as large as Wrath and was currently surrounded by a number of military encampments, the canvas tents laid out in precise rows and blocks. As Sidian descended through the lower layers of cloud they could see that the camps were swarming with activity. Their approach was quickly noted and people began pointing upwards while others emerged from tents to watch the black dragon descending towards them.

Dropping lower Falco could make out numerous unfamiliar banners and flags, but then he saw one camp flying the light blue and turquoise colours of

Clemoncé. He smiled in satisfaction as he recognised the flag of the Queen's Irregulars.

Banking round, Falco brought Sidian down on a low hummock at the edge of the camp. Having grown accustomed to Sidian's presence, the Irregulars had no reservations about coming forward, but the troops from the neighbouring camp were careful to keep their distance. By now every soldier at the front had heard the story of the black dragon that had arrived in Wrath but even so, the thought of getting too close went against everything they had been told about such creatures.

Stiff from several hours flying Falco removed his helm and strapped it to the riding harness before climbing down from Sidian's back. He ducked as the black dragon folded his wings then smiled as he saw Malaki, Bryna and Huthgarl working their way through the crowd of Irregulars. But even as he moved towards them the smile faded from his face. Something was wrong.

'What is it?' he asked as Bryna embraced him and Malaki clasped his hand.

His heart was suddenly filled with apprehension and he saw Malaki glance back towards the Irregulars where several of the Exiles were standing. Through the milling crowds Falco thought he saw Alex disappearing behind the white wall of a tent, head bowed and shoulders slumped.

'Where's Quirren?' he asked and the look that passed between Malaki and Bryna filled him with dread.

'Let's find somewhere we can talk,' said Malaki.

'No,' said Falco. 'Tell me now. Where's Quirren?'

'He was taken by a demon,' whispered Malaki, and now the Irregulars turned away. They all knew the story of what had happened.

'When?' asked Falco and Malaki shot Huthgarl a worried glance before answering.

'The morning after you left,' he said and Falco felt the ground shift beneath his feet. He remembered the demon he had sensed after he and Sidian had killed the two dark angels. What was it the Clemoncéan scout had called it, a 'geôlier'. But the demon had been miles away, in a different canyon.

'How?'

Malaki had hoped to be able to speak with Falco in private but it was clear that he was going nowhere until he heard what they had to say, so Malaki led him over to a stand of rocks where they could sit and talk.

Falco sat in silence as Malaki described the events of that fateful morning. His voice wavered several times as he described the final moments of Quirren's capture.

Falco could not move.

They broke his body and stuffed him into a bag made from chains.

He was still alive.

The demon vanished.

Just walked into a shadow of darkness and vanished.

He was still alive.

Falco's mind was ablaze.

'Falco!' said Bryna but he did not hear her voice. He was now standing before them, eyes tight shut and gauntleted hands clenched into fists.

553

'Falco! Stop it!' cried Bryna and Falco opened his eyes to see that his hands were surrounded by a fierce blue fire that crackled and danced over the steel on his arms. They could feel the heat of it, the barely constrained fury of it.

Slowly Falco let the power leach from his body while his friends just stared at him in shock.

'He'd still be here if you hadn't left us,' said a voice and they all turned to see Alex standing just a few yards away, his eyes red rimmed and bleak.

Falco said nothing. The words 'I'm sorry' seemed meaningless and hollow.

'You shouldn't have left us.'

'I didn't kn...' began Falco but Alex raised a black gauntleted hand.

'You shouldn't have left us,' he said again and with that he turned his back on them and walked away.

Falco just stood there as the guilt mounted in his chest. There was a sound in his ears like the thrum of angry bees, throbbing and pulsing to the beat of his heart. Darius... Balthazak... Sir Gerallt... Merryweather... Simeon... All lost and now Quirren, taken not because he did not have the power to stop it, but simply because he was not there.

The angry hum grew louder in Falco's mind until it began to resonate with the unholy drone of his nightmares. And deep within that unsettling growl there were words.

You would never have the courage
You would never have the faith

Falco clenched his fists. He squeezed his eyes shut and suddenly the hum and the demonic growling were gone. Turning on the spot he strode towards Sidian who had watched the exchange with an expression of concern on his scaled brow.

'Where are you going?' asked Malaki although he already knew what Falco was thinking. 'Falco, you can't!' he cried as Falco approached Sidian. 'You'll never find him!'

Falco was deaf to reason and when Malaki put a hand on his shoulder he shook it off, but as he closed on Sidian the black dragon began to back away. He moved to the dragon's side but Sidian shifted round, angling his body to prevent Falco from reaching the straps on the riding harness.

'What are you doing?' hissed Falco but Sidian only looked at him. The dragon's golden eyes were narrowed, his posture unyielding.

'But he's still alive,' said Falco and Sidian flinched as an image of Quirren's face appeared in his mind. 'He's in pain,' whispered Falco and his voice began to crack. He stopped trying to advance on Sidian and the two faced each other while Malaki, Bryna and Huthgarl looked on.

Sidian's gaze did not waver, but the angle of his head changed in a way that conveyed understanding. Falco's mind was suddenly filled with images of rolling hills and wilderness, endless miles of uncharted territory, empty of anything that matched the gaoler's description. He recalled the faint trace they had caught of the demon before they left to confront the Slayer and it was clear that Sidian was trying to convey the impossibility of finding this particular demon in the vast expanse of the Forsaken Lands.

'I have to try,' said Falco.

554

Sidian's eyes narrowed a little more and his thoughts moved to the army of the Irregulars and all the times that he and Falco had saved them from surprise attacks by the Possessed. Falco's mind was then filled with images of what had happened to Quirren only now it was Malaki and then Bryna being broken and tortured.

The message from Sidian's thoughts was clear... How many more would suffer if they left to pursue a demon they might never find?

'But it's my fault,' said Falco and here Sidian loomed over Falco, teeth bared and snarling. His ebony claws tensed against the rock and Falco's mind was suddenly slammed by images of the Possessed, the bestiarum, the Slayer and even the maniacal light in the eyes of Galen Thrall. It was *not* his fault but theirs and the dragon would have none of this human self pity.

Finally Falco took a breath and looked up. Sidian was right. It was the demons and their minions who were responsible, not those who failed to stop them. There was no denying the fact that he had not been there when Quirren needed him most, and so he could not absolve himself completely. But somehow he must be stronger than his guilt or the enemy would use it to destroy him.

Finally a sense of approval emanated from Sidian's mind and the dragon inclined his head in something like a bow. For a moment they held each other's gaze then together they turned as they sensed someone approaching. It was Lanista Magnus.

'Have you two sorted out your differences?'

Falco's silence was answer enough.

'Then come,' said the senior instructor. 'The Irregular commanders need to know what it was that drew you away in such haste.'

With a last glance in Sidian's direction Falco allowed himself to be led away. He exchanged a brief look with his friends who were clearly relieved to see him returned to his senses. He had accepted the folly of hunting for a demon that he might never find, but he had also made himself a promise. If ever he caught the faintest trace of this gaoler then nothing would prevent him from seeking it out.

The Irregular commanders listened in silence as Falco relayed all that had happened since he left them, from killing the two dark angels, to the death of the Slayer.

'And you're sure it was the same demon that attacked Nathalie?' asked one of the commanders who had taken part in the cadet training campaign. 'The same one that killed Jürgen and Wildegraf?'

Falco nodded.

'Then you have done us all a great service. The great souls in the north are stretched as it is. To lose any more would have been disastrous.'

The other commanders nodded in agreement. Many of them remembered the black assassin that had almost killed Nathalie. Their need for an explanation had been satisfied and slowly they began to disperse.

'Will you be joining us for tonight's strategy meeting?'

Falco looked up to see Lanista Magnus standing beside him. He felt exhausted but he gave the lanista a nod.

'Good,' said Lanista Magnus. 'Sir William was hoping you would be able to make it.'

Falco's eyes flicked up at the mention of the emissary.

'There was a letter waiting for us when we arrived,' he explained. 'Apparently Marshal Breton has him scouring the area to the east. Although I suspect that's just an excuse to keep him away from the meeting,' he continued, for it was well known that Marshal Breton felt challenged by the emissary's presence. 'He was hoping to be able to make it himself, but I'm sure he will be relieved to know that you will be there, even if he cannot.'

Falco was disappointed by this news. He knew the chance was slim, but he had been hoping to see the emissary. Lanista Magnus seemed to read his thoughts and he offered Falco a smile of encouragement.

'Welcome back, Master Danté,' he said then, sweeping his gaze over Malaki and Bryna, he gave them a grim smile before leaving the tent.

'Come on,' said Malaki as the last of the commanders left the tent. 'Let's find you something to eat, and then you can get cleaned up before tonight's meeting.'

Food was the last thing on Falco's mind, but he got up to follow his friends all the same. He rose from his seat and then stopped as Huthgarl hovered beside him.

'You know he saved the children,' said the big Beltonian and Falco felt his throat burn at the pain in Huthgarl's voice. 'He might have fallen but he saved the children first.'

Everyone now understood why Falco had been drawn away in such haste, but this understanding could not change what had happened. Somewhere in the world their friend was enduring horrific pain and the thought was almost too much to bear.

'We will find him,' said Falco and the look of hope in Huthgarl's eyes pierced him to the core.

Huthgarl gave a stoic nod and Malaki and Bryna did the same. It was a simple gesture, but to the four friends it felt like a solemn pact. With a final look of shared conviction Malaki led the way out of the tent and Falco moved to follow them but then he stopped.

Beyond the thin white wall of the tent he felt the tormented presence of Alex Klingemann move slowly away. Falco did not know if the healing powers of a battle mage extended to wounds of the spirit, but he summoned all the faith he could muster and hoped with all his heart that Alex could feel something of its warmth.

96

The Son of Aquila Danté

The council hall of Amboss was basically a large debating chamber, a lofty rectangular building with a vaulted ceiling and tiered seats facing each other across an expanse of tiled floor. Tall windows of stained glass were interspersed with huge tapestries depicting key scenes from the city's troubled past. Wall-mounted braziers lined the walls and hung from beams in the ceiling. In normal life the hall was used for all manner of civic meetings, but tonight it was hosting a council of war and the noisy clamour of conversation was accompanied by the clank and jangle of armour.

'It's like market day in Wrath, but with swords,' said Malaki as he, Falco, Bryna and Huthgarl entered the hall.

The room was crowded with military commanders from both Illicia and Clemoncé with dozens of aides, messengers and scribes in attendance. As newcomers to the front they had hoped to enter the hall quietly, presuming that their presence would be of little consequence to these experienced commanders. However, as soon as they entered the hall people began to turn and look in their direction.

It reminded Falco of the night they walked into the barracks at the Academy of War. But now it was not a weakling, a woman and a lowly blacksmith who were the focus of attention. It was the battle mage who had summoned a black dragon, the famous Knight of the Crimson Helm and the female archer who, though she knew it not, was now being referred to as the Mistress of the Rogues. And finally a young Beltonian knight who, despite his relative youth, was easily the largest man in the room.

Not likely that such a group would gain their seats unnoticed.

For his part, Falco met the appraising eyes without flinching, but then he recognised the stern face of Marshal Breton and he felt a tremor of disquiet as the marshal fixed him with a stony gaze. At their last such a meeting he had embarrassed Clemoncé's most senior commander and it was clear that Marshal Breton had not forgotten. For a moment more the marshal's eyes lingered on Falco before he withdrew his gaze and turned his attention back to the men gathered around him, one of whom Falco recognised as Dominic Ginola, the battle mage who had saved the people of Caer Dour in the mountains.

Unlike Marshal Breton there was no hostility in the battle mage's eyes, although he frowned as he gave Falco a nod of acknowledgement. He tried to hide it but he was clearly astonished by the change that had taken place in Falco, and troubled by the secrets that had come to light during his summoning. But there was no time for reintroductions and Dominic turned back to Marshal Breton as the people in the room returned to their conversations.

The four newcomers continued towards the left-hand-side where Lanista Magnus and several of the other Irregular commanders were now seated just a few rows back from the floor. The crowds began to disperse as people took their seats and finally the room was called to order. Only Marshal Breton remained standing. Accepting a slender wooden pointer from one of his aides he moved to a series of tables running the length of the floor.

Falco could now see that the maps portrayed the entire length of the front from the Bay of Barinthus in the south to the remote mountains north of Hoffen. These campaign maps were more detailed than the great floor map in Wrath, but this also made them more difficult to read and Falco found himself wishing he could go down to study them more closely.

'Things have changed,' began Marshal Breton, his Clemoncéan accent strong as he addressed the hall in the common tongue of Wrath. 'The war of attrition that has tested our resolve is over. The enemy has made a sudden push towards Clemoncé and several cities have already been cut off by the speed of their advance.' He proceeded to point out the locations of various cities and the enemy forces that had moved past them. 'Our scouts are reporting a surge of movement from deep within the Forsaken Lands. And now we have learned that the great Vercincallidus has fallen.'

This news was met with a collective gasp of dismay and Huthgarl froze in his seat, his face a pale mask of shock.

To the people of Beltane Vercincallidus was a living legend. He was also the main reason why Beltane had been managing to hold ground against the Possessed. His death would be a savage blow, but Marshal Breton had not quite finished.

'The death of such a great commander is a terrible loss,' he went on. 'But now our Beltonian allies have confirmed that our worst fears are true. The Marchio Dolor is heading in our direction.'

At this the hall erupted in fear and consternation. Marshal Breton raised his hands and slowly a semblance of order returned.

'There is no longer any doubt,' he told the room. 'A large Possessed army has crossed the river at the western end of Lake Viegal. The Marchio Dolor is coming north.'

'What about the Crown Prince?' asked one of the Illician commanders. 'Is the Capital in danger?'

'As yet we do not know which way the Marchio Dolor will turn. He could turn east towards Seeburg, or veer north to Hertzheim. He might follow the river Türkis to attack us here in Amboss. But...' and here the Marshal glanced in the direction of the Clemoncéan commanders. 'He might also turn west to attack the forest city of Toulwar.'

'Fossetta's in Toulwar,' whispered Bryna and Falco's eyes narrowed as he replied with a grim-faced nod. The Marchio Dolor had slipped behind their main line of defence. The damage he could now inflict was unthinkable.

The room was silent as the ramifications of what Marshal Breton was saying sank in. For the first time a large Possessed army might breach the borders of Clemoncé. And not just any army, but an army led by the Marquis of Pain himself.

'Can we oppose him?' asked an old Illician commander.

'The reports suggest his army is near a hundred thousand strong, with numerous bestiarum and several demons marching with the horde.' Marshal Breton gave a weary sigh. 'Even if we brought all our force to bear we could barely match his numbers and I will not break the Queen's armies before the enemy has even reached the border of her realm.'

Around the hall there were gasps of amazement. No one had ever faced a demon army of so great a size.

'Then we must retreat,' said one of the Clemoncéan officers and suddenly the air was filled with a different kind of tension. 'For years we have fought to preserve the Kingdom of Illicia. Maybe the time has come to think about the safety of our own.'

For their part the Illicians said nothing. To them the thought of abandoning their cities was anathema, but there was no denying that the only reason why anything of Illicia remained at all was because the armies of Clemoncé had fought and died beside them.

'I agree,' said Marshal Breton. 'I think we need to establish a new front, but our greatest stronghold is here, in Amboss, and it would be a mistake to abandon it just yet.'

'And what about Seeburg and Hertzheim?' asked one of the Illician commanders.

'Seeburg is compromised,' said Marshal Breton, his tone heavy but resolute. 'The supply lines to the city will soon be overrun. We can no longer hope to support it.'

'And Hertzheim? Is our capital city to suffer the same fate?'

'Hertzheim will soon be surrounded on three fronts,' said Marshal Breton. 'If we act quickly we could still evacuate the people before the city is cut off.'

'And is that the opinion of our great souls?' persisted the man. 'To abandon our cities and flee from the Possessed?'

As the older of the two battle mages, people naturally turned to Dominic, which was just as well because Falco appeared to be in some kind of trance. He had been painting a mental picture of the situation in his mind... the burning shadow of the Possessed, creeping like a dark fire across a world that screamed in torment, the demons like hot embers and the Marchio Dolor, a tight knot of evil driving straight for their heart. It was like a scene from his nightmares but then Dominic spoke and the image in his mind was broken.

'A battle mage would never abandon a city if there was a chance it could be saved,' said Dominic. 'But sometimes it is better to flee than to feed the enemy's appetites and swell their ranks with legions of the damned.'

'There you have it,' said Marshal Breton as if Dominic had spoken in support of his own position. 'We shall evacuate the cities of Seeburg and Hertzheim with all possible speed. And then we shall establish a new front along the Clemoncéan border, with Amboss as our last Illician foothold.'

'And if the Marchio Dolor should reach Amboss?'

'Then we shall make him pay a heavy price,' said Marshal Breton. 'But at least we will have the city's walls to protect us.'

Finally the room was quiet, sobered by the thought that they had no choice but to fall back. Normally such strategic decisions would be made by an army's most senior commander. However, in the alliance between Illicia and Clemoncé, such matters were decided by a show of hands.

'So now we move to a vote,' said Marshal Breton. 'To withdraw our forces to the Clemoncéan border, while keeping the city of Amboss at our centre. All those in favour...'

Not surprisingly it was the Clemoncéan commanders who responded first, but even here it was not without reluctance. Slowly the hands in the hall went up and even the Illician commanders seemed to accept that the end of their kingdom was at hand.

Marshal Breton breathed a sigh of relief as the hall was filled with raised hands. Only a few of the older Illician commanders could not bring themselves to vote.

'There is clearly no need for a count,' said Marshal Breton. 'The decision to withdraw is...'

'Wait!'

The commanding voice came from the entrance to the hall and Falco turned to see the emissary standing there. Covered in dust and grime from his latest campaign he strode into the hall, but Falco's eyes lingered on the darkened entrance. There was someone else waiting out of sight, someone who had no need of shadows to keep his presence concealed. Falco's eyes narrowed in recognition, but he would not betray the mysterious visitor's presence.

Despite the evening's revelations it was fair to say that every person in the hall was pleased to see the emissary, everyone, that is, apart from Marshal Breton. The Marshal watched him approach with a guarded and bitter expression. He acknowledged Sir William's many attributes, but this only made his popularity more galling.

'My Lord's pardon,' began the emissary. 'But I would like to hear Master Danté's thoughts before the people of this hall decide.'

Marshal Breton gave a scornful snort. 'Surely he's too young to advise us on such matters,' he said. 'I understand it's barely a month since he passed the Rite of Assay. Perhaps a more experienced battle mage would be better placed to judge.' His eyes moved to Dominic, but if he had hoped for the support of his countryman he was disappointed.

'I saw Master Danté oppose a demon before he'd received a day of training and he has faced many greater challenges since then,' said Dominic. 'He may be young, but you must not think him too inexperienced to speak.'

Marshal Breton looked like he was chewing on some bitter fruit.

'Very well. Let us hear the young master's thoughts. What does he think we should do?'

For a second, Falco's eyes lingered on Dominic then he turned his head to look at the emissary. A thread of tension and trust seemed to be stretched between the two men but then the emissary gave him a nod.

Speak your mind, that nod seemed to say and Falco turned to address Marshal Breton.

'We must attack the Marchio Dolor.'

Marshal Breton gaped, while the rest of the hall gave a gasp of disbelief.

'Has the young sir not being paying attention,' said a moustachioed commander from across the hall. 'The enemy's army is a hundred thousand strong, with numerous demons and bestiarum. It would not be wise to confront such a force in the open field. Better to let them break on the walls of Amboss or Toulwar.'

Falco looked at the man but his gaze did not waver.

'This demon gives strength to others,' said Falco. 'We must attack him, as soon as we are able.'

The room was filled with doubtful mutterings and even the Illician commanders balked at the idea of attacking the Marchio Dolor directly.

'Madness!' said Marshal Breton. 'Suicide!'

Even Dominic seemed uncertain of this strategy, but the emissary had learned to trust Falco's instincts.

'Could we do it?' he asked Dominic. 'If we gather all our forces we could match him in number. But could we gather enough battle mages to oppose him?'

Dominic did not answer him at first. Instead he was staring at Falco as if he were trying to discern how he could be so certain of this risky course of action.

'It would be difficult,' he said at last. 'Each of our battle mages is responsible for a territory. They cannot afford to leave these areas unprotected.'

'But we could send word if a city comes under threat,' said an Illician commander but Dominic shook his head.

'It might take days for such a message to reach us. If our battle mages were to commit themselves in the south there would be no time for them to respond if word arrived that a city was in danger.'

'And what if word could be sent more quickly,' came another voice from the entrance.

Once again the people in the hall turned to look in the direction of an unknown speaker, but this time it was not a commander or battle mage who stood in the shadowed archway but three figures in the purple robes of the magi.

Falco looked down on the face of Meredith Saker, but like him the young mage had changed beyond all reckoning. His dark eyes were still warmer than his father's, but any softness had gone from his gaze and the skin of his face was now disfigured by an ugly scar that curved from the corner of his right eye to his jaw.

By now everyone in the room had heard the story of the magi's treachery and the atmosphere in the hall became distinctly hostile, but Meredith ignored it as he walked out onto the floor.

'What if we could make sure you had time to react to an imminent threat?' he continued.

'And how could you do that?' asked Marshal Breton. 'It takes hours for the magi to send a message from one tower to another. And, in case you haven't noticed, there aren't many mage towers in the wilds of Illicia.'

Meredith did not flinch in the face of his obvious scorn. 'Toulwar, Ville de Pierre, Voisier and Hoffen,' said Meredith. 'I could send a message to any one of these cities and receive a reply within minutes.'

'Nonsense,' said Marshal Breton, more from reflex than from any understanding of the magi's art.

'Is this true?' asked Dominic, who had never heard of such a thing.

'It is,' said Meredith. 'We have magi in each of those cities who have been trained to send and receive messages instantaneously.'

'But the battle mages protect much more than just the cities. What if the outlying areas come under threat?'

561

'Then a message can be sent to the nearest city,' said Meredith. 'And my fellow magi can then relay it directly to us.'

'Could it work?' asked the emissary and Dominic pursed his lips in thought.

'If they could be sure of getting back if they were needed then there are several battle mages who would be close enough to join us.'

The emissary turned back to Marshal Breton.

'There you have it, my Lord. If we combine the armies south of Amboss we can match the Marchio's numbers and meet his demons with our battle mages.'

Once again the mood in the hall changed as the fire of hope was reignited.

'But to risk it all on the word of one young man,' said Marshal Breton and the emissary inclined his head as he conceded the point. 'What is it that makes you trust him so?'

'I do not know,' said the emissary as if he had asked himself the same question. 'But before you vote again I would ask if anyone here remembers a battle mage by the name of Aquila Danté.'

It was immediately obvious that this name struck a chord with many of the older commanders in the room.

'I remember him,' said one man with a long knightly moustache. 'He defeated two demons to save a town east of Reiherstadt.'

'I too,' said another. 'I was newly commissioned when our force was cut off in the Forsaken Lands. He fought for a week to bring us to safety.'

'And I,' said a third. 'He was injured defending our city and his dragon never left his side. It was so fierce the healers were frightened to go near him.'

'It was red,' said one of the younger commanders. 'I did not know him, but my father spoke of Aquila Danté. He said his dragon was red, like the deepest shade of blood.'

The emissary raised a hand to stall any further recollections. He looked across at Falco who was now hunched in his seat, head bowed by the tributes being paid to his father.

'You may not know the young man sitting before you,' said the emissary. 'But you knew his father.'

For all his dark armour the hunched figure of Falco looked younger than ever. But then he lifted his head and raised his eyes and the years seemed to gather about him until one could not have guessed his age.

'This is Falco Danté, son of Aquila Danté, and if he says we should attack the Marchio Dolor then I believe we should.'

The emissary's conviction proved decisive and Falco watched as the allied commanders agreed to the course of action he had suggested. As they lowered their hands Falco felt again the heat of Marshal Breton's gaze. There was anger and resentment in the Marshal's accusing stare, but there was also a kind of pity.

For several seconds Falco held the Marshal's eye. He felt no pride or satisfaction, only the terrifying weight of responsibility for what might happen if he was wrong.

97

The Dark, The Deep & The Grave

Falco could feel the eyes of the army upon him. They knew that he was the reason why they were marching south to confront the most powerful demon army ever assembled. They were now three days south of Amboss and the tension was rising as reports confirmed that the enemy was still heading in their direction, but even as the apprehension mounted so the confidence of the army seemed to grow.

On leaving Amboss they numbered barely sixty thousand troops. It would have been more but Marshal Breton refused to leave the city unguarded. However, within a day they were joined by two additional armies from Illicia's southern Leagues, pushing their numbers close to ninety thousand, and now they had learned that Prince Ernest was bringing an army from Hertzheim to meet them. He knew that the only way to save his capital city was to defeat the Marchio Dolor and so he marched with forty thousand troops and two battle mages.

Thanks to Meredith's new method of communication, three other battle mages had also agreed to join them. Two had already arrived and the third would be with them soon. With Dominic and Falco, that put their number at five, plus the two that would come with Prince Ernest. Seven battle mages and one hundred and thirty thousand troops. Surely such a massive force would be enough. That's what the commanders thought and even Marshal Breton was beginning to sound more confident.

But Falco was not so sure.

It was late evening and the army was spread out over a series of low hills. He and Sidian stood on a rocky promontory to the south of the camp. They had spent the day trying to clear the sky of dark angels. Ever since they left Amboss the enemy scouts had followed their progress in ever increasing numbers and their constant scrutiny made Falco nervous. The Marchio Dolor now knew of their strength and still he continued towards them.

Away to the south he could sense the Marchio's army like a great storm gathering on the horizon. However, the demon's army was not the only shadow converging on the land and the sense of it filled Falco with dread. Beside him, Sidian gave a low rumble of support, but there were some fears that he could only face alone. Something blacker than the Marquis of Pain was coming and Falco could not see what it was. It did not feel like the Possessed, but this fear was growing stronger and Falco was not sure how much more he could take. He wanted to shut it out, but somehow that felt like a betrayal and so he had no choice but to bear it as best he could.

Even now his fists were clenched with anxiety, but then his attention was drawn back to the present as Sidian turned his eyes to the north. Falco turned with him and there, descending towards the camp, was the distinctive shape of a dragon in flight. The final battle mage had arrived just in time for Marshal Breton's nightly briefing.

'Come on,' said Falco. 'We'd better go down to join them.'

Climbing onto Sidian's back he gripped the riding harness and together they flew down to a rocky knoll overlooking the command tent where four other dragons were already waiting. They greeted Sidian with a kind of reverence and Falco offered them a bow of respect as he turned in the direction of the tent around which the other battle mages were now gathered.

As Falco approached, Dominic introduced the final battle mage, an Illician man by the name of Armand Dietrich. With the exception of Simeon he was the oldest battle mage Falco had ever seen. His hawkish face was covered with scars and his grey hair contrasted starkly with eyebrows and a long moustache that were surprisingly dark.

'So you're Aquila's boy,' he said in a strong Illician accent. He gave Falco a searching look and then his eyes creased in a smile. 'Only battle mage I ever knew that was brave enough to marry,' he added. 'Your mother must have been an exceptional woman.'

Surprised and deeply moved, Falco just stared at him as the man reached out to take his hand before turning back to the other battle mages who were now moving into the tent. One was a woman of middle thirty years with a fierce light in her hazel eyes. Her dark hair was cut short and the design of her armour also marked her as an Illician. Her name was Blas Schneider.

Beside her was a Valentian man with deep blue eyes and a single scar crossing his right eye as it ran from hairline to jaw. His name was Lucas Vale and Falco felt a distinct surge of pride knowing that there were other Valentian battle mages contributing to the war against the Possessed.

With Dominic and himself that put their number at five and Falco had never experienced such a concentration of strength. Their combined presence provided a tremendous sense of security, but it did nothing to alleviate the sense of fear and foreboding that was now so strong that Falco was finding it difficult to think.

As he entered the tent he was relieved to see the familiar faces of Malaki, Bryna and Huthgarl. Across the way he could also see Alex standing near Jarek Snidesson. Jarek gave him a nod of acknowledgement but Alex was careful not to let his gaze drift in Falco's direction. The distance between them stung Falco with a fresh wave of regret and he wondered if they would ever be friends again.

'A bit overwhelming, isn't it?'

Falco turned to see the emissary standing beside him.

'It's not often you see so many gathered together in one place.'

The emissary gestured toward the battle mages. They had moved to speak with Marshal Breton but every now and again they would glance in Falco's direction as if they were intrigued by the strange mixture of youth and power.

'I think you make them nervous,' said the emissary and he smiled at the frown of disbelief on Falco's face. 'It's true,' he said. 'The secrets you've uncovered. The things you've achieved.'

Falco said nothing. As far as he was concerned any achievements had always come at a cost, and if anyone deserved credit for uncovering secrets it was Meredith. Looking across the tent he could see the young mage standing discreetly to one side.

'I thought you'd be staying in Wrath,' Falco had said to him when they finally had the opportunity to speak in Amboss. 'I thought the Queen had asked you to help in reforming the magi.'

'I supervised the writing of a new oath and the spells to bind it,' said Meredith. 'But I've spent most of my life shut away in a mage tower. If I have any knowledge I would like it to make a difference in the world.'

Falco could not have agreed more and once again he was struck by the change that had taken place in Meredith. He thought back to the supercilious apprentice he had known in Caer Dour, a gifted but bitter young man, trying to find himself in the lightless shadow of his father. Now here he was offering his services to generals and training older mages to use the spells that he himself had developed.

Coming back to the present Falco felt a hand on his shoulder as the emissary urged him forward.

'Come,' he said. 'The enemy is getting close and we must draw up a plan to meet him.'

Together they moved to the centre of the tent where Marshal Breton was leaning over a campaign map.

'The enemy is somewhere here,' he said, indicating an area to the southeast. 'He knows of the force that we have brought from Amboss, but still he comes on apace. Perhaps he isn't aware of the army arriving from Hertzheim.'

The Illician Commanders shared a grim smile of pride.

'In two days we shall meet the Crown Prince here,' said Marshal Breton, indicating the point where the road from Hertzheim joined the road they were on.

'And how long then before the Marchio arrives?' asked General Renucci.

'It'll be close,' said Marshal Breton. 'If we keep to our current pace we should meet the Prince in the early morning and that should give us several hours to choose our ground and deploy our troops.'

'This area just south of the junction looks good,' said the emissary as he moved in for a closer look at the map.

'Yes,' said Marshal Breton. 'The ground is level and the rough terrain to either side will guard our flanks.'

The other commanders nodded in agreement.

Suddenly the tent was filled with excitement as the commanders began to discuss their plan of battle. With Prince Ernest's troops they would outnumber the Marchio's forces and their hopes were high, but to Falco the light in the tent had suddenly grown dimmer. Looking down at the map his eyes fell on a small area between their current position and the road to Hertzheim, a high valley bordered by three distinct hills. As Falco stared at them it felt as if he was slowly being drawn into the map.

Darkness is coming...
Darkness in the earth, darkness in the deep, darkness on the hills.

The air seemed to throb with the resonance of his nightmares.

You would never have the courage
You would never have the faith

The growling voice of the Possessed was so loud that Falco was amazed that the other battle mages did not hear it. Everyone was listening to Marshal Breton but then the emissary noticed Falco's strange fugue state.

'Falco, what is it?'

The emissary's voice was full of concern, but for Falco the moment had passed. The light in the tent returned to normal and the demonic resonance was gone.

'Are you all right?' asked Malaki as he, Bryna and Huthgarl appeared at his side.

Falco waved away their concerns and moved forward to the table.

'What do they call this place?' he asked, pointing to the valley with the three hills.

'They call it Tal Der Drei Brüder,' said one of the Illician commanders. 'The Valley of the Three Brethren.'

'*So it was hills,*' thought Falco. '*It was always hills.*'

'Here,' he said out loud. 'We will meet the Marquis of Pain here.'

'Nonsense,' said Marshal Breton. 'It's too remote and there would be no reason for the enemy to pass through that region. 'No,' he continued. 'We will stop the Marchio here, just south of the road to Hertzheim.' The other commanders certainly agreed but the emissary moved to stand beside Falco.

'Why?' he asked. 'Why must we meet him there?'

'I'm not sure,' said Falco. 'I can't explain it. I just know we have to meet him there.'

Falco put a hand to his head as if at a sudden headache or dizziness.

'Are you sure you're all right?' asked the emissary.

The sense of fear in Falco's mind was suddenly stronger than ever and he felt confused and disorientated, but before he had a chance to answer, the air in the tent began to vibrate with a rumble like the roll of distant thunder. For a moment the emissary frowned, but then a smile of pure joy broke out across his face. He raced outside and people moved quickly to follow him.

As they left the tent Falco realised that the mounting noise was the sound of approaching horses. The emissary had moved a short distance to where he could see down the slope of the hill. Always a tall and broad shouldered man, he seemed to grow in stature as he looked down on the mass of cavalry now surging up the slope towards them.

Moving to join him, Falco could see what it was that had raised his spirits. Riding in broad columns were two squadrons of knights. And at the head of each they carried a banner. The first was the stylised form of three white mountains on a field of black, the insignia of the Adamanti. The second was a black horse's head on a field of silver blue, the colours of the Knights of Wrath.

In total more than eight hundred knights rode up the hill and the emissary's eyes were shining as the leaders of each came forward to greet them. In keeping with military protocol they approached Marshal Breton, but neither could resist the instinct to acknowledge the Chevalier's presence and the emissary smiled as the two knights gave him a non-too-subtle nod.

'Look!' said Bryna.

'I know... It's Lord Cabal,' said Malaki as he recognised the leader of his order.

'Yes,' said Bryna. 'But look at their helms!'

Beside her she felt Malaki tense and she could almost feel the heat of his rapidly reddening face. The Knights of Wrath were dressed in full battle armour and the left cheek of every helm was covered in crimson enamel that shone like wet blood in the warm evening light.

'Oh, blades!' groaned Malaki as Bryna smiled and Huthgarl clapped him on the back.

The two knight commanders spoke briefly to Marshal Breton, but then the leader of the Adamanti made his way over to the emissary. The two men were of similar age and both had the craggy face of a hard life well met. They embraced like old friends and then the emissary turned to Falco and the others.

'Allow me to introduce Sir Konrad Osterna,' he said. 'Lord Commander of the Knights Adamant.'

Sir Konrad's gaze was blade sharp as he looked at each of them in turn.

'The honour is mine,' he said with a bow.

His friends bowed in turn, but Falco was becoming increasingly distracted by the mounting sense of fear in his mind.

'But how do you come to be here?' asked the emissary.

'We were returning to Hertzheim when we learned that Prince Ernest was marching from the capital to join you.'

'And the Knights of Wrath?'

'We are here in case our Illician brothers forget how to couch a lance.'

They all turned to see the imposing figure of Lord Cabal standing behind them. It was the first time the emissary had heard the Lord Commander make a joke and the shock of it was writ large across his face. For a moment no one spoke as Lord Cabal cast his eyes over the emissary's companions.

'It would seem that your reputation for being able to tell the wheat from the chaff is not without foundation.'

The emissary smiled. 'It's easy to recognise quality when it's standing right in front of you,' he said.

Lord Cabal acknowledged this gracious reply and the two men clasped each other's forearms.

'We ride into a storm of hell,' he said.

'But we ride together,' replied the emissary.

The eyes of both men hardened at the thought of what lay before them and with a final look of mutual respect they moved apart.

The two Lord Commanders remained on the hill while the rest of the knights rode down to the grazing fields in the valley. As they moved off so the meeting in the tent was reconvened.

Nobody was surprised that Marshal Breton disregarded Falco's suggestion and chose the original place in which to make their stand. Even the emissary thought this location made better strategic sense. Falco could see the sense in what they were saying, but he could not get the image of the Three Brethren out of his mind. It was as if he had always known that it would end there.

But Marshal Breton had decided otherwise. In two days time they would rendezvous with the army of Prince Ernest and together they would stop the Marchio Dolor. There were still countless demons and Possessed armies throughout the Forsaken Lands, but if they could break this army and kill the enemy's chief lieutenant it could mark a significant turning point in the war.

The knights' arrival raised the morale of the entire army, but Falco felt more troubled than ever. The sense of foreboding was growing and he was now struggling to contain it. The soul crushing fear of a demon he could withstand, but this was something more.

'Falco, what's wrong?' asked the emissary as they made their way down to the lower slopes where the Irregulars were camped.

Slowly Falco became aware that people were staring at him, but he did not recognise their faces and he was suddenly overcome with the urge to run away and hide. He was breathing fast and his face was beaded with sweat.

'Are you starting with a fever?' asked Bryna but when she reached out to feel his brow Falco recoiled.

His green eyes flashed dangerously and Malaki frowned at this uncharacteristic behaviour. Even in the worst of his episodes he had never seen Falco behave like this.

The emissary was watching him carefully. He could see that this was no ordinary affliction.

'We should talk to Dominic and the other battle mages,' he said.

The emissary reached over to take Falco's elbow but he staggered away. He shook his head as if to clear his vision and raised his hands as if to fend off things that the others could not see.

'Falco,' said the emissary in a calming tone. 'It's all right. You're safe. You're with friends.'

But Falco barely heard him. His voice seemed to come from a great distance and the world around him was suddenly filled with menacing shadows. He could hear a noise in the calm air of the night, but whether it was the breeze stirring the leaves of an olive grove, or the wind whistling over some lofty mountain peak, or the sea washing against the rocks of the coast, he could not say. All he knew was that he could not bear it and he had to get away.

He saw a shape closing on him and suddenly his right hand was engulfed in flame and bolts of energy arced around his fist.

Thinking he might fall, Huthgarl had moved to catch him, but now he backed away as Falco's powers flared into life. They were all trying to think what they could do when Falco suddenly turned and stumbled away. Malaki moved to intercept him but the emissary put a hand on his arm.

'Don't try to stop him,' he said. 'Just follow him and keep him safe. I'll get Dominic and the others.'

Malaki nodded and started after him as Falco headed back towards the summit of the rocky knoll. Oblivious to Malaki's presence he was lost in a storm of guilt and fear and there was only one thing in the world that was strong enough to see him safe. Half blind and barely able to keep his feet, Falco stumbled in the direction of Sidian.

The dragon should still be waiting for him, but Falco felt like he was walking through a nightmare. He did not recognise the world around him and he could no longer remember in which direction the dragon lay. He tried to reach out with his thoughts, but they were confused and filled with self loathing. He began to panic, feeling lost and alone, but then a black shadow swooped down from the sky as Sidian landed beside him.

Far from being relieved, Falco slumped to his knees in abject terror, but Sidian grabbed him with his powerful forearms and his friends could only watch as the dragon flew off into the deepening night.

'What's happened to him?' asked Huthgarl as they stared after the departing dragon.

'I don't know,' said Malaki and with nothing else to do they went in search of the emissary.

*

The emissary was relieved to find that the battle mages were still gathered together in the command tent but as soon as he entered, he could see that something was wrong. Marshal Breton was there, but so also was Meredith and the young mage's face was paler than normal.

'What is it?' he asked. 'What's wrong?'

'It's the enemy,' said Marshal Breton. 'The Possessed are suddenly attacking all along the front.'

'We already knew that,' said the emissary. 'They're pushing towards Clemoncé.'

For a moment the emissary was confused. What did it matter if the Possessed were no longer fixated on Clemoncé? Surely that was a good thing. But then he noticed that Blas Schneider was preparing to leave.

'The Possessed are heading for the cities on the front,' said Meredith and now the emissary understood. If the battle mages continued south then the cities in their care would fall to the Possessed, but if they returned to save their cities then Marshal Breton would not have enough battle mages to oppose the Marchio Dolor.

'Do we know which cities are under threat?'

'For now it's just battle mage Schneider's,' said Meredith and Marshal Breton nodded in relief.

'That still leaves us with four battle mages,' he said. 'Plus those that will arrive with Prince Ernest.' The Marshal was clearly trying to reassure himself, but the emissary looked across at Meredith and he knew they were both thinking the same thing.

The night was yet still young.

*

Fifty miles to the south the Marchio Dolor narrowed his eyes and his lip curled in satisfaction. Through the eyes of his dark angels he had followed Marshal Breton's army as it marched south from Amboss. At first he had been scornful of its size, but as the humans advanced so their numbers grew and more Defiants came to join them. And then he learned that Prince Ernest, the whelp of Illicia, was now marching to meet them, and with him came two more Defiants with their detestable wyrms.

569

'*The fools,*' the Marchio had scoffed. '*Did they really think that he would meet them on their terms, that he would allow himself to be outnumbered?*'

These humans thought they could gather all their strength to oppose him, but he would show them that such single minded resistance would come at a cost. Taking a penitent in each fist he had plunged them into the underworld and begun to pray.

'Forget the doomed land of Clemoncé for now,' he told the demons along the front. 'Look instead to the cities. Lay them low and deliver all within unto the fires of Hell.'

Soon their cities would be transformed into smoking ruins of despair, unless their Defiants moved to defend them. The Marchio Dolor smiled. He knew the Defiants could never abandon the innocent to death and damnation. It was just one of their many weaknesses.

Night closed over the Possessed but that was no reason for them to stop. To the northeast the 'Whelp of Illicia' was getting closer. It was clear that Marshal Breton was hoping to meet the Prince and the Marchio Dolor saw no reason to disappoint him. Revelling in the prospect of what was to come, he drove his army onwards into the night.

*

Sidian carried Falco to a lofty hilltop and laid him down on a patch of level ground. The dragon had not felt so unsettled since that night on the dragon stone. Like Falco, he could feel the swelling presence of the demon army to the south but he could sense nothing of this other debilitating fear. All he knew was that he had to protect his companion soul and so he lay beside Falco and stretched out a black wing to shelter him.

On the ground beside him Falco ground his teeth and gasped with the effort of resisting the guilt, the fear and the shame. He wanted to throw himself from the mountain, drown himself in the sea or bury himself in the earth, anything to escape the wings of vengeance that beat towards him. For another hour he fought the fear until finally he could take it no more. With a final effort Falco tore the fear from his mind and cast it away. For a moment he felt as if he had abandoned a beloved friend, but he was too tired to care. He had closed his mind to the fear and finally he was able to sleep.

Sidian's posture also relaxed as he realised that Falco was now sleeping. Careful not to wake him, he moved closer so that Falco could feel the warmth of his inner heat. He still did not know what had caused him so much anguish. What he did know was that the great demon's army was still closing on them from the south and if they were going to confront it then *He That Burns With Grief* would need all the strength that he possessed.

And so he laid down his great horned head, closed his eyes and listened to Falco's breathing as he slept.

*

In the mountains of Illicia.

And the olive groves of Thraece.

And the wild coast of Beltane.

Three tormented men stared with terror into the night. For weeks now they had felt the darkness getting closer and only the presence of the child had prevented them from going mad or taking their own lives in payment for their crimes.

But now the time had come. The child had given all he could and they were left to face the final judgement on their own. For too long they had hidden themselves away, thinking that they could escape the guilt, and the grief, and the pain. But they could not.

In the darkening sky they could feel their nemeses approaching and so, with the resolve of the damned, the Disavowed went out to meet their doom.

The hermit left his cave and walked to the summit of the great cliff, so reminiscent of the place where the original crime had been committed.

The healer did not have time to reach the graveyard. He only got as far as the rocky mound where the kid goats liked to play in the sun.

And as for the fisherman, he did not have far to go. He simply walked down from his cottage to the headland where the cliffs looked out to sea.

Three broken men, resigned at last to their fate. They stared into the sky and watched as the dragons came into view. Closer they came like a winged vision of death, and not one of the men was surprised to see that the dragons were black. Were they the ghosts of murdered souls? Or just the agents of vengeance come to mete out justice, well deserved.

Over the past few days the guilt and the shame had become unbearable, but now it seemed to fade away as the curtain of their lives was about to fall.

The hermit, the healer and the fisherman knelt. As the angels of death descended towards them they bowed their heads and offered up their lives in a final act of contrition. Perhaps in death they would find some measure of peace.

Their hearts were pounding but their thoughts were clear as the wind of mighty wings stirred their hair and rocked them on their knees. Too ashamed to raise their eyes they did not look up as the dragons landed before them. They could hear the great bellows of their breathing, the scrape of steel hard claws and the swish of blade-tipped tails. They could feel the warmth of their inner fire and sense the heat of that fierce golden gaze, such strength, such beauty, killed by their own hands.

Now all the fear was washed away in tears.

'Forgive us,' they breathed.

For a moment there was silence and stillness, and then the Disavowed felt the gentle touch of something pressing against their foreheads. They tensed, as if at the kiss of death, but then they realised it was not revenge but grace and forgiveness that had been bestowed upon them.

In wonder they raised their heads and gazed upon the mirror of their souls. In disbelief they got to their feet and looked into the golden eyes of the dragons that had come in place of the ones that they had slain. In humility they opened their hearts and made a new pledge.

My life,

My strength,

My soul, I cleave to thee.

The echo of this pledge was shining in their dragons' eyes and they felt their thoughts begin to merge. And as the guilt and fear receded from their minds so they sensed the desperate need of the child and the fight from which they had hidden for so long. In their minds they saw a high valley surrounded by three hills.

'Tal Der Drei Brüder,' thought the hermit, and suddenly the Disavowed were running.

The hermit ran to his mountain home and moved through to the deepest recess of his cavern. The healer ran to the graveyard and there he began to dig and scrabble in the earth of the nameless grave. The fisherman turned from his dragon and, racing towards the sea, he threw himself from the cliffs. Through the air he fell until he broke the water in a dive just twenty yards from the pale bladder that had never marked the location of a crab or lobster pot. Down he swam, pulling himself through the water with strong strokes until his lungs began to burn for air. Too dark to see, he groped on the sea bed for a bundle wrapped in rotting cloth, so too did the healer and the hermit find a bundle of their own, a bundle of metal and leather, preserved by the magic with which it was imbued.

And the bundle was not all.

For in the dark,
And in the deep,
And in the grave,
A sword.

98

The Chevalier

At noon of the following day the army came to a halt on a vast meadow enclosed by a great curve in the river. It was the perfect place for such a large army to rest but Marshal Breton was not happy for it was also at this point that the main road was joined by the wide and dusty path leading up into the hills towards the Valley of the Three Brethren. The scouts had been using this route to keep track of Prince Ernest's army, but one of them was overdue and so they took the opportunity to rest while they waited for him to return.

Falco was sitting astride Sidian on a series of crags overlooking the army. From this vantage point he could see Marshal Breton pacing back and forth among the senior officers of the command group. The tension in the army was already high and the marshal was eager for them to move on. By this time tomorrow they would have joined with the army of Prince Ernest and then they would confront the Marchio Dolor if they still had enough battle mages to face him.

In the early hours of the morning Armand Dietrich had been called away to protect another city that was coming under threat. That left them with Lucas, Dominic and Falco plus the two battle mages that would arrive with the Prince. This was still deemed to be enough but Armand's departure did nothing to improve Marshal Breton's mood or his opinion of the venture on which they were currently engaged. Indeed the whole army was more subdued. Not only had two of their great souls now departed but word of Falco's worrying behaviour from the previous night had now spread throughout the army.

For his part Falco felt numb and exhausted. He remembered little of what had happened and he had no answers for Malaki and the emissary when they asked him what it was that had troubled him so.

All he knew was that he had lost something.

The unexplained fear had now gone, but so too had something that he had never really appreciated before, a presence that had been with him since his earliest recollections as a child. He had never known if the feelings were real or just a figment of his imagination, but whatever they were they had somehow brought him comfort.

Until the meeting in Amboss he had never heard of the Valley of the Three Brethren, but now Falco was confused. He still felt as if his destiny lay in that direction, but soon they would move past the route that would take them to this remote and windswept place.

He could not make sense of these strange sensations, but then his thoughts were arrested as one of the magi called out and Marshal Breton moved quickly to hear what had caused such alarm. Falco saw Meredith emerge from the covered wagon in which he had been sleeping and the emissary also moved towards the mage who was currently in contact with the other cities up and down the front.

Falco and Sidian swooped down from the rocks then, leaving the dragon at the side of the road, Falco worked his way through to the knot of people now gathered round the magi.

'What is it?' he asked.

'It's Maidstein,' said the emissary. 'A city some thirty miles east of Ville de Pierre. A demon army is just six hours from the city walls.'

'That's my territory,' said Lucas Vale. 'The garrison there is strong, but there's no way they can hold out against a demon.'

They all turned to look at Marshal Breton.

'Go,' he said and Lucas gave a bow.

'I am sorry,' he said and with that he raced away.

Within moments the army watched another dragon disappearing into the clouds.

Silence descended and Marshal Breton's brow was clouded with concern. With Prince Ernest's two battle mages that left them with only four to confront the Marchio Dolor and the other demons that marched with him.

'Do we turn back?' asked General Renucci.

'If we do we will only have to face this demon another day,' said Dominic.

'I agree,' said Lord Cabal.

'And I,' added Sir Konrad.

Many of the other commanders concurred, but still they turned to hear what the Chevalier had to say.

The emissary frowned in thought. He was about to speak when a murmur ran through the army and people began pointing up into the sky to the north. Turning in that direction they could all see a dragon flying towards them. At first they thought it was Lucas Vale coming back to join them, but as it drew closer they could see that this dragon was the dark blue of a winter storm cloud. Closer still and they could see that the battle mage on its back wore the bronze coloured armour of Acheron.

A space opened up in the gathered troops and the blue dragon landed in a cloud of dry grass and dust. The Acheronian battle mage was a typically large man and his dark skin gleamed in the sunlight as he hooked his hoplite helm onto his riding harness. He rolled his shoulders to ease the stiffness of several days flying and then he started towards the group of men who were clearly the leaders of this impressive force.

The soldiers parted to let him through, but others crowded forward to get a clearer view. Few had ever seen an Acheronian warrior, much less a battle mage from that realm.

The way opened up and Marshal Breton moved to meet him. He raised a hand in greeting, but the Acheronian did not reply. His dark face was set in a grim expression and it was clear that he was not the bearer of good news. He looked around at the gathered troops, but then his eyes fell on the horse-head insignia on Marshal Breton's chest. His shoulders seemed to sag and Falco had a sudden premonition of dread.

'I am looking for the Queen's emissary. The one they call the Chevalier.' His voice was deep and his accent was strong, but he made an effort to speak clearly in the common tongue.

'I am he,' said the emissary and people moved aside to let him through.

He walked forward until he stood beside Marshal Breton, his grey eyes searching the Acheronian's face.

For a moment the battle mage just looked at him as if he were measuring how well the man lived up to the stories that were told about him. He gave a barely discernible nod of satisfaction but then he sighed.

'I bring news from Navaria,' he said and all those in earshot now hung on his words, waiting to hear if the Queen had been successful or not.

'Queen Catherine saved the city of Sophia,' he said. 'The Legion du Trône prevailed against a Possessed army of much greater size.'

Marshal Breton and the other Clemoncéan commanders breathed a sigh of relief, but Falco and the emissary were waiting for the words that were caught in the battle mage's throat.

'She truly was the Queen of Wrath,' he said and suddenly the relief in Marshal Breton's eyes was gone.

Beside him the emissary had become as still as stone. He felt suddenly hollow and his breathing seemed to echo in his ears.

Slowly the battle mage opened a leather pouch at his waist and drew out a belt made from interwoven strips of black leather. But the belt was broken and the leather strips were crusted with blood. With great solemnity the battle mage stepped forward and placed the broken belt in the emissary's hands.

'I am sorry,' he said. 'Even as the battle was won, she fell.'

Like a man struck dumb the emissary looked at the straps of leather in his grasp. He opened his hands and there it was - the horse-head buckle that he had carved on the way to Caer Dour. The burnished silver was dented and scratched and there was dried blood in the crude folds of the horse's mane.

'Dead?' breathed Marshal Breton, but the emissary did not hear him.

'The Queen is dead,' went out the ripples of dismay, but the emissary did not hear them.

All across the flood plain the word was spread until some ninety thousand souls stood still in shock.

'Queen Catherine has fallen. The Queen of Wrath is dead.'

Falco stood in stunned silence as his vision slowly blurred with tears. His mind was reeling, his heart torn apart by disbelief.

'*It cannot be,*' he thought. '*She is all we have, all that holds the world together. It cannot be.*'

'King Tyramimus and all of Acheron share your grief,' said the Acheronian battle mage. 'The king has pledged our legions to come and fight beside you.' His expression and his words were sincere, but Marshal Breton just stared at him as if he were mad.

'It is too late!' he bellowed and the battle mage narrowed his eyes at the force of his accusation. 'The world has bled to death while you wallowed in your conceit. Your offer of help is too late.'

The man's dark face showed little reaction as he accepted Marshal Breton's anger. He himself had been fighting in Beltane for years, but this Clemoncéan was right. King Tyramimus had been wrong to hold back while others faced the evil of the Possessed.

A murmur of despair was now sweeping through the army as they considered what this news meant for their kingdom and the war. But Falco's thoughts were all for just one man.

He watched as the emissary walked aimlessly away, still staring down at the broken leather in his hands. Soldiers moved back from him until he was surrounded by a wall of distraught faces.

The emissary looked up from the belt and the expression on his face felt like a blade in Falco's heart. Every man there knew of the love between Queen Catherine de Sage and Sir William of Eltz. It was a story of romance and tragedy, a story that bound the emissary to these common soldiers even as they missed their own loved ones around the campfires in the night. Ever since he had taken up the post as the Queen's advisor the emissary had accepted the fact that they could never be together. But now...

But now.

The emissary's grey eyes were like the windows of a tomb.

'My life,' he mumbled and his legs seemed to buckle beneath him. 'My life entire.'

The emissary's legs gave out and he stumbled to the ground.

All around him heads were bowed and embarrassed eyes looked away. They could not bear to see this man brought low, this man who had ever been a symbol of constancy and strength.

Falco rushed to his side and tried to help him to his feet, but the emissary pushed him away. With one hand he held the sword belt that he had made. With the other, he reached up and snatched the horse-head pendant from around his neck. No longer would he be Commander of the Queen's Fourth Army. It was time for him to fight and die as she herself had done.

For all his powers Falco felt utterly helpless. He wanted to help the emissary, but then other figures moved past him and he watched as Sir Konrad and two of his fellow knights raised the emissary to his feet.

'We'll take care of him now,' said Sir Konrad and with that the Adamanti brought one of their own back into the fold.

Falco's heart ached as the emissary disappeared among his fellow knights. He wanted to go and find Malaki and Bryna, he wanted to find Sidian and fly so high that he left the world and all its tragedy far behind. But then a call went up and people began pointing up the broad track that led towards the Valley of the Three Brethren.

Careering down the slope was the scout that they were waiting for. He rode until his horse was forced to stop by the mass of soldiers now surrounding Marshal Breton

'It's the prince,' he gasped even as he slid from the saddle and pushed his way through. 'The Marchio Dolor attacked him in the night. His army is broken and retreating through the hills.'

Marshal Breton just stared at the man.

'And his battle mages?'

'One dead, one dying,' said the man. His face was pale and he gulped in air as if he had run and not ridden back to deliver his report.

'Marshal Breton!' came another shout.

As if in a daze Marshal Breton turned to see Meredith working his way towards them.

'We've received another message.'

'From where?' asked Dominic and even *his* voice was strained.

'It's Amboss,' said Meredith. 'But there's not one but three demons converging on the city.'

Marshal Breton whirled to face Falco. It seemed as if he were about to point a finger, but instead he balled his hand into a fist and closed his eyes, screwing up his face at the folly of allowing himself to follow the advice of this foolish young man.

'How long?' he asked Meredith through gritted teeth.

'Five hours... maybe six.'

Marshal Breton angled his head towards Dominic.

'Can you do it?' he asked. 'Can you get back in time?'

'Yes,' said Dominic. 'But I cannot defend against three demons. Not if they all attack at the same time.'

'I will come with you,' said the Acheronian battle mage. 'It would be an honour to fight beside you.'

'Then go,' said Marshal Breton. 'We shall be with you just as soon as we are able.'

With a quick bow, Dominic and the Acheronian hurried back to their dragons as Marshal Breton turned on Falco.

'And why are you still here?' he spat with open scorn. 'Go with your betters and see if you can repair some of the damage that you have caused.'

Falco said nothing. As Marshal Breton began to issue new orders to the army he made his way towards Sidian.

'Turn about!' cried Marshal Breton, whirling his hand in the air. 'We return to Amboss with all possible speed.'

Dazed by the storm of ill fortune that seemed to have descended upon them the army struggled to carry out his orders. But slowly the meadow stirred into action as the army reoriented itself to begin the march back to Amboss.

Over to one side Malaki, Bryna and Huthgarl watched as Falco emerged from the knights and commanders around Marshal Breton and walked towards Sidian. By now Dominic and the Acheronian battle mage were just dark shapes receding into the clouds, whereas Falco seemed slow and hesitant. He climbed onto Sidian's back and together they rose into the sky, but instead of flying north towards Amboss they flew just a hundred yards up the wide path leading into the hills.

At first no one seemed to notice, but then the commanders around Marshal Breton saw where Falco had landed and gestured in his direction. Marshal Breton's brow lowered with fury and his face flushed as he forged his way to the edge of the army.

'Where are you going?' he called out. 'Or are you so arrogant and deranged that you would face the Marchio Dolor on your own?'

Falco said nothing, but neither did he move. Through the T-shaped visor of his helm he looked down at Marshal Breton. His heart screamed at the thought of the Queen's death, but now was not the time to be laid low by grief. He could not explain the force of his conviction. All he knew was that the Marchio Dolor must be opposed.

The entire army became still as they looked at the battle mage and the black dragon standing alone on the path. They seemed to be caught in a moment of madness, but then a mounted figure moved out from the ranks of the Adamanti.

Gone was the Queen's seal and the surcoat of blue with its horse-head motif. Sir William Chevalier now wore the black and silver-white of the Knights Adamant. Without any concession to Marshal Breton he rode up the slope and stopped beside Falco and Sidian.

Seconds passed and Marshal Breton gawped at the ridiculous scene, but then the entire squadron of the Adamanti moved to follow their captain's lead. They had covered barely half the distance before Malaki, Bryna and Huthgarl rode over to join them, the Dalwhinnies and then the entire body of the Irregulars swinging round to align themselves with the direction in which Falco would lead them. Even the Exiles followed their lead with Alex Klingemann at their head.

'What madness is this?' cried Marshal Breton as General Renucci called the soldiers of the Fourth Army to do the same. 'We must retreat to Amboss!' he cried. 'It would be suicide to continue on.'

But now the Illician commanders began to order their troops in the same manner. Where the Adamanti led, they would follow, especially if there was even the slightest chance that Prince Ernest and some of his army might still be alive.

Marshal Breton looked for support from his own Clemoncéan forces but then the shadow of a mounted knight fell across him and he looked up into the face of Lord Cabal.

'I was shamed once before by men of greater courage,' said the Lord Commander, looking up at Malaki. 'I will not be shamed again.' With that he placed his own red-cheeked great-helm upon his head and led the Knights of Wrath to join their Illician brothers on the path.

For a moment Marshal Breton raged against this display of mass insurrection, but then the news from the Acheronian battle mage came back to him and all his indignation was crushed by an overwhelming sense of despair.

The Queen was dead.

All along the front the Possessed were breaking through. For more than a decade he had fought to keep the enemy at bay, but it had all been for nought. How many other armies and cities would crumble once they learned the news of Queen Catherine's death? Behind him he heard his own Fifth Army shifting and jostling as they too adjusted their position to follow Falco's lead and he no longer had the heart to oppose them.

All the world was going to hell and Marshal Breton no longer believed that it could be saved, and so he did as simple soldiers have always done since the demons of the Possessed first robbed them of their faith. He placed his trust in a battle mage.

Falco's heart might have been moved by this overwhelming show of support but he had passed beyond the reach of such emotions. It was just too painful to bear the grief of all those that they had lost. In his mind he saw an image of the Queen as they had first seen her in the orchards of Wrath, a wild, dark haired woman, sweating and breathless as she struggled to improve her skill with sword and shield, and then transformed into a vision of regal beauty on the western terrace of the palace.

'And why have you come to Wrath, Master Danté?'

Behind the armoured visage of his helm Falco wept. Through his tears he looked down at the army that was prepared to follow him and for a moment he wondered if he truly had the courage to lead them to their doom. But then the emissary stirred beside him and turned his smoke grey Percheron up the slope. Falco might not have the courage to lead them to their deaths, but the emissary had lost the one thing that he truly lived for, and he most certainly did.

99
Tal Der Drei Brüder

To Falco the march into the hills felt like walking into a dream. As the day lengthened so a thick mist had fallen, but the army pushed on until they reached the head of the pass and the way ahead levelled out. During the night the darkness had been so complete that even the enemy's dark angels could not see through it, but still the foul creatures had tormented the army with their dark presence and screeching cries. All through the night Falco had battled to keep them at bay and the blackness had been lit by his lightening and Sidian's fire. But now the night was over and the blackness had given way to an all enveloping grey.

They marched for two more hours, but still the mist covered the land like a shroud and the sound of the army's passing echoed strangely in the seemingly empty void. As the dense fog finally began to break they reached an area where the path petered out, giving way to a flat expanse of brown grass and scrub.

Falco was riding a horse beside Marshal Breton with Sidian walking a short distance away. The low cloud had been too thick for them to scout ahead and besides, with so much fear in the air Falco did not want to leave the army alone. A few yards ahead of them were two of the scouts that had been this way before. The army continued for more than a mile before they stopped.

'This is it,' said one of the scouts as Falco and Marshal Breton drew level with them. 'This is the Valley of the Three Brethren.'

'Are you sure?' asked Marshal Breton, but even as he spoke the mist continued to clear and they could see the tops of three isolated hills, one behind them to the right, another to the left and a third up ahead.

In truth it was less like a valley and more like a high plateau enclosed by three hills, but for the first time Marshal Breton could gauge the lay of the land. Close to the ground the mist was still quite thick, but the scouts had assured him that the area between the hills was level and free of significant obstacles. There was no sign of the enemy but Falco had assured him that this would be the place that they would make their stand.

Unable to say why he had allowed himself to be led here, Marshal Breton raised his arm and brought it down to left and right, his signalmen relaying the order for the army to deploy into the three divisions that had been decided upon.

General Renucci would command their right flank with the Fourth Army and one of the Illician Leagues, while the Irregulars would take the left flank with two of the larger Illician forces. His own Fifth Army would take the centre with the remaining Illician troops plus the Adamanti and the Knights of Wrath.

Without knowing the details of the Possessed force he could not risk a central push or even a single line defence. Instead he had decided to deploy in the formation of *debilis centrum*, or weak centre, but on this occasion their centre would actually be their strongest point. With luck he might be able to hold the centre long enough to enfold the enemy from the wings and then he could drive forward with massed ranks of Illician pike.

580

As the three divisions moved into position Marshal Breton rode over to Falco who had dismounted from his horse and was now standing beside Sidian and staring into the mist.

'What is it?' he asked. 'Is the enemy upon us?'

'No,' said Falco. 'This is something else.'

Suddenly there was a cry of alarm and then figures began to emerge from the mist, soldiers stumbling forward like the ghosts of broken men.

'It's the army from Hertzheim,' said Marshal Breton, his voice strained with disbelief.

Cries of concern and fear began to spread through the army as they saw the state of those who had survived the Marchio's attack. Nearly all were injured, but even those that were not were wide eyed with trauma, their gaze still haunted by the horror of what they had been through. So far gone were these poor wretches that they barely registered the presence of their kinsmen and allies. They pushed their way through the gathered ranks, lashing out and flinching from any attempt to stop them.

'So few,' said Marshal Breton as the flow of survivors began to slow.

Through the mist it was difficult to tell, but surely no more than a thousand men had managed to reach them, less than a thousand from forty.

'May the Fates have mercy,' breathed Marshal Breton, but Falco was wondering how any of them had retained the strength to flee at all.

And then he saw it, a wagon being drawn, not by mules, but by two of the finest coursers he had ever seen. But it was not the quality of the animals pulling the cart that had caught Falco's attention, it was the souls that lay within. Leaving Sidian he started towards the wagon and even though he knew what it carried he was shocked when it finally reached him.

To the front of the wagon a knight cradled the head of an unconscious man in fine robes and exquisite armour while behind them lay the mutilated figures of a dragon and a battle mage. Without hesitation Falco rushed round and climbed into the back of the wagon. Lacerated and burned the dragon was just barely alive, as was the battle mage who opened his eyes as he felt a hand on his forehead.

'Lie still,' said Falco. 'I'll see what I can do.'

The man did not know Falco, but he recognised him as a fellow soul and with the last of his strength he reached up to remove his hand.

'Save the prince,' he said and his eyes drifted towards the unconscious man at the front of the wagon.

Falco had already guessed that the unconscious man was the Crown Prince of Illicia, but now his heart lurched as the battle mage breathed his last. The man's body simply went limp and a moment later the dragon's heart also gave out as if, only together, they had had the strength to hold on.

With nothing to be done for the battle mage and dragon, Falco moved forward and placed a hand on Prince Ernest's brow. He closed his eyes and frowned at what he sensed then, placing his other hand on the prince's chest, he suffused his body with a gentle surge of healing energy.

As the wagon approached the army so a group of Adamanti rode over to guide it through. The faces of the Illician soldiers were filled with concern as they recognised the unconscious figure of their sovereign lord. The Crown Prince had suffered injuries to both body and spirit and Falco was not sure if he would survive, but that was not what the anxious onlookers needed to hear.

'He's alive,' said Falco as he jumped down from the wagon and the news quickly passed throughout the whole of the allied force.

'The Crown Prince lives,' they whispered. 'Prince Ernest is alive.'

Falco allowed them this brief moment of joy for he knew it would be short lived. Like the onset of a storm he could feel the enemy drawing closer. In the landscape of his mind it seemed like a dark sunrise, a sunrise that brought not light and warmth but fear and despair. And within the encroaching darkness he could feel the deeper shadow of demons. The Marchio himself was yet to rise above the horizon, but even now Falco could feel the force of his presence. He was the dark eye of the storm that moved towards them and Falco tried not to think of what would happen when he arrived. He could not say how many normal demons were approaching, but he knew where the first of them would strike.

Turning to Sidian he leapt onto the dragon's back.

'Signal the Irregulars to stand ready,' he called to Marshal Breton. 'The first demon will strike us there.'

'Is it him?' asked Marshal Breton. 'Is it the Marchio Dolor?'

'No,' said Falco. 'The first is just one of many. The Marchio Dolor is something more.'

Marshal Breton blanched. For all his years of experience the presence of a demon always swamped his courage and loosened his bowels. He did not know how any man could withstand such fear, let alone the fear of something greater still.

'Remember,' said Falco, drawing the Marshal back to himself. 'If you need me, sound three deep blasts of the horn. Even if I don't hear it Sidian will and we will come if we can.'

Marshal Breton nodded, glancing nervously at his signalmen before turning back to look at Falco.

'May the light shine upon your blade,' he said and Falco was taken aback by the earnestness of his tone.

'And yours,' he replied with genuine respect.

The first demon was heading towards their left flank and Falco needed to get into position to meet it, but before he moved off he looked back at a knight who sat on his smoke grey Percheron in the front rank of the Adamanti. Many of the knights were looking in Falco's direction, but the emissary was staring straight ahead. Falco reached out with his mind and now the emissary turned to look at him but there was no emotion in the steel mask of his great-helm.

'*Don't lose faith,*' Falco tried to tell him, but the emissary just looked away and Falco felt a terrible sense of loss.

Ever since the day of the trials he had relied on the emissary's presence and strength. Even when they were hundreds of miles apart he had known that the emissary was there, still fighting, still giving strength to those who looked to him for leadership. Now that man was gone and Falco felt bereft, but he could not afford to be undermined by regret or grief. The enemy would only use such things to tear his soul apart.

With a sigh he turned away and urged Sidian down the line of nervous troops. They walked past rows of spearmen now packed in tight formation to resist a frontal assault, past blocks of sword and shield ready to push forward or defend as the situation required, past squadrons of cavalry poised to strike with speed and strength. And then, just before Marshal Breton's force gave way to the Irregulars, he drew level with the Knights of Wrath.

At the head of the squadron Lord Cabal dipped his lance in salute and Falco bowed his head, but then his gaze was drawn to two knights who were yet to don their helms.

Falco returned Huthgarl's bow and then his eyes settled on Malaki. The distance was too great for them to speak, but the gaze that passed between them contained a lifetime of meaning. A tiny part of Falco still wondered if Malaki ever blamed him for everything that had happened: for the ruin of their town, the death of his father, for Quirren, and even now, for leading them to this place from which none of them really expected to leave.

But he need not have worried.

Malaki's gaze was hard and focussed, but it held a message that Falco had seen once before. Then, Falco had worried about the revelations of his noble birth, but even after everything, the message in Malaki's eyes was the same as ever.

'I am your friend, Falco Danté.
Servant, Lord or battle mage.
I will always be your friend.'

Behind the visor of his helm Falco's eyes pricked with tears. If he was able to face the agents of hell it was because he had friends like Malaki de Vane.

He gave Malaki a nod and then with a final look he continued until Sidian stood before the Irregulars. Turning round he faced the unbroken line of sword, shield and spear, which was flanked by cavalry and supported by archers. He could sense Bryna with her Dalwhinnies and Alex with the Exiles. He wished that he had been able to make his peace with Alex and he wished that he and Malaki could fight at Bryna's side, but he knew that she was not alone. She had Patrick Feckler and three hundred scoundrels who would lay down their lives for the Mistress of the Rogues. And somewhere in that great mass of troops were Lanistas Magnus and Deloix.

They were all here. All with him. And the only thing left to do was fight.

Putting his back to the Irregulars Falco turned to face into the valley. As the mist continued to lift he felt Sidian tense beneath him and then they heard it, an expanse of sound rising up and rolling towards them in waves. It was the distinctive cacophony of an army on the march, and within the approaching din they could just detect the inhuman growls and snarling of the Possessed.

*

Even though it was witnessed by a hundred of his fellow knights, Malaki was grateful that he and Falco had been able to share one last moment of intimacy. He watched as his friend moved into position and turned to scan the ranks of the Irregulars. He knew that Falco was looking for Bryna and he knew that Bryna would be sending out her heart to him.

Thinking of his wife filled Malaki's mind with fear and he tried not to dwell on what might be. Instead he thought of the vows they had made on that late spring evening and his hand moved to the scabbard that hung from his belt, the scabbard that Bryna had given him as a wedding gift.

Malaki's thoughts were interrupted as he saw Falco turn to face the mist shrouded valley. And then they heard it, the snarling cacophony of a Possessed army on the march.

With a final thought for his beloved, Sir Malaki donned his crimson enamelled great-helm, armed his shield and gripped his lance. Beneath him Fidelis shifted and stamped as the Knights of Wrath prepared to fight.

*

Peering through a forest of spears, Bryna watched as Falco moved down the line towards them. She could see him scanning the ranks of the Irregulars and she desperately wanted to catch his eye.

'Stop your fretting, lass,' said Patrick Feckler beside her. 'He knows you're here.'

Hoping he was right Bryna settled down. She thought of everything they had been through and wished with all her heart that they were back in Caer Dour in a time before the shadow of the Possessed had darkened their lives. But then perhaps the bashful blacksmith's son might never have found the courage to speak to her and she would never have known the deep joy of lying in Malaki's embrace.

Bryna's hand drifted to the quiver on her back and her thoughts returned to that late spring evening and the vows they had spoken in a circle of flowers. She turned the silver ring on her finger and raised a hand to wipe a tear from her cheek.

'Soft as shite!' cursed Paddy who despaired of such sentimentality.

Bryna shot him a look and yet despite her annoyance she was glad to have the gruff old villain beside her. She glanced at the other archers that now stood around her. They were the biggest and strongest of all the Dalwhinnies and she knew that this was no accident.

'You watch her or I'll roast your balls on a skewer,' Paddy had told them.

The expression in Bryna's eyes softened. He might be as 'rough as a badger's arse' but for all his protestations, Paddy the Feck was not entirely without sentiment.

Secure in the bosom of her adopted family Bryna looked back at Falco who was now facing off into the valley.

And then they heard it, the snarling cacophony of a Possessed army on the march.

'Here they come, the bastards!' announced Dedric Sayer and with a final thought for the men she loved, the Captain of the Dalwhinnies gave the order for the Queen's Fifth Company of Archers to stand ready.

*

Falco stared straight ahead as the noise of the approaching army grew louder and the air became tainted with the stench of hot metal and putrefaction. And then, like a nightmare emerging through the shredding veil of death, they appeared, a shimmering band of steel and darkness stretching across the valley.

584

Finally the mist evaporated completely, but it was not the warmth of the sun that burnt it away. It was the infernal heat of the Possessed, and the air was suddenly imbued with such clarity as to be almost cruel.

The enemy seemed to fill the horizon and even from half a mile away Falco could make out the dark armour and round-shields of the Sciritae and the larger figures of the black armoured Kardakae. A fringe of some six thousand skirmishers moved ahead of the main force - javelin wielding Pelts and blind Toxitae archers. Using skirmishers was a tactic employed by the armies of Acheron, Thraece and Ferocia, but the Possessed lacked the judgement and discipline for such classical manoeuvres. Driven on by mindless hate they came on too quickly and Marshal Breton would have time to punish them before the main body of the Possessed arrived.

The thought offered a vague suggestion of hope, but then Falco felt the burgeoning presence of the demon, not a lesser minion like the dozens of dark angels that hovered in the sky or the hulking bestiarum that prowled through the advancing horde, but a true demon, a vessel of the Enemy's spite.

Behind him, Falco felt the entire army recoil with shock and he literally sagged beneath the weight of so much fear, but then he squared his shoulders and took their fear unto himself.

Towards the left the towering figure came into view, almost twice the height of the troops around it. In the early morning sunlight it seemed even more obscene, as if such horrors should be confined to darkness, but no. The denizens of hell are not daunted by the sun. They are the terrors of night made flesh, abominations that have slipped the shackles of nightmare to hunt you down in the broad light of day.

Even as he stared at the demon, Falco registered the sheer size of the force now advancing upon them. It was already almost equal to their own, but he knew this was only the first wave. The Marchio's army had grown on its journey north and then it had been swollen by some thirty thousand of Prince Ernest's troops. Falco might have felt daunted by the size of the opposing army, but all his thoughts were focussed on the demon now striding towards him.

It was huge and horned and its black skin was riven with cracks that glowed and throbbed with the force of its internal heat. Its heavy head was almost wedge shaped with a chin that jutted forward like the prow of a Thraecian trireme. Walking on back-bent legs it was hunched forward as if the sheer weight of its massive shoulders bore it on. It was too far away for him to see the glowing embers of its eyes but Falco knew they were fixed upon him.

And that was good. He wanted the demon to come to him.

Between the two main armies the scattered swarm of Pelts and Toxitae were almost in range then Falco heard the signal for *Impetus Equitum* and six thousand cavalry burst out from the allied ranks to sweep away the scattered fringe of skirmishers.

The battle of Tal Der Drei Brüder had begun.

*

The drumming sound of hooves was part of the new reality that filled the emissary's mind, the dealing of death just part of the barren landscape that filled his heart. The lightly armoured skirmishers were no match for the wall of steel that smashed them into the earth and the Adamanti barely slowed as they completed their sweep and swung back behind the allied lines.

For a moment the emissary felt the urge to peel away and charge the swelling mass of the main Possessed army. It mattered not that they were many thousand and he were only one man. All that mattered was that he would meet his end. The fingers of his shield hand actually tightened on the reins but then a stab of shame shot through his gut. Catherine would never have applauded such an empty gesture of despair. She would have treated such weakness with scorn.

No.

It was enough to know that he would die this day, but he would do so in a manner that might have made her proud.

*

The knights and cavalry made short work of the skirmishers and Falco turned his thoughts back to the demon. For all the trepidation that thrummed in his veins he was sure that he and Sidian could defeat it. With luck the allies might be able to inflict some significant damage to the Possessed before the Marchio Dolor arrived on the scene, but then he felt another presence. A second demon was approaching and it would soon be threatening General Renucci on the right.

Falco was suddenly overcome with uncertainty. Somehow he and Sidian would have to stop them both. Looking from one to the other he knew there was no time to waste. Ahead of him the allied knights had cleared the ground between the two armies, but the main body of the Possessed was closing quickly. They were almost in archery range, which meant the sky would soon be full of arrows, but Falco could not wait.

Even as he heard the command for the archers to ready their bows he drove Sidian forward. Just a few powerful strides and they were airborne. If they were going to stand any chance of stopping the second demon they would need to quickly kill the first.

*

Marshal Breton watched as the cavalry completed their sweep and curved back behind the allied lines. His knights had swept through the skirmishers like threshing sticks through a field of rotting wheat and those that survived the first assault were speared or cut down by the lighter cavalry that followed in their wake. It was a daring gambit but it had paid off. The battle proper had not yet been joined and already the valley floor was littered with thousands of Possessed dead.

The marshal allowed himself a grim smile and ordered his archers to raise their bows. The enemy was now in range, but even as they prepared to shoot he saw Falco and Sidian surge forward and rise up into the sky. He wondered why Falco would attack now when they were about to fill the sky with arrows, but then he saw the second demon driving towards their right flank. Master Danté now had two opponents to face and if he did not kill the first demon quickly then General Renucci's force would be torn apart.

But still they could not lose this opportunity to weaken the enemy's ranks and trusting that the archers would try to avoid their battle mage he gave the command for them to shoot.

*

Falco and Sidian were high above the ground when they heard the collective thrum of bowstrings and a cloud of arrows burst up from the allied ranks behind him. In a sudden squall the feathered shafts whistled past them to fall like steel-pointed hail on the advancing ranks of Sciritae. These massed volleys would have a devastating effect, but Falco knew that the Possessed would not be cowed by losses. Again he wished that he could fight in the front line, protecting those he loved, but an enemy of thousands was not his to fight. His opponents were the demons of power that controlled this hellish force. The first of those was now staring up at him and its red eyes burned with all the fury of hell.

He and Sidian were now so close that they could feel the heat of the demon's gaze. Another volley of arrows streamed past them but all Falco's thoughts were for the demon. They needed to kill it, and kill it quickly, but as they came closer the demon flung up a burning arc of Baëlfire and Falco realised that this would be no easy task. He called up a protective shield but it was not quite enough to stop some of the hellish fire from burning a gash in the tip of Sidian's right wing. The dragon gave a snarl of pain and Falco felt his golden gaze focus like a lance on the demon. Then Sidian pulled in his wings and fell into a dive.

Behind them the entire army watched in awe as they descended towards the first of their hellish foes. To normal men the demons of the Possessed seemed utterly unassailable, but these normal men had a champion. Together Falco and Sidian were known as Le Cœur Noir and The Black Heart was about to enter battle.

*

Standing amid the black clad ranks of the Exiles, Alex Klingemann could hardly bare to watch as Falco dived towards the demon. Blinded by grief he had not known how to speak to him, how to tell him that he did not really blame him for what had happened to Quirren. But now it was too late. Like the rest of the army he had followed Falco on this mad gesture of defiance. But unlike them he had not done so with any sense of hope. He did not believe they would survive this day, but at least *they* had a chance of death. Unlike his brother who would spend the rest of eternity writhing in agony.

For Alex the pain was all too much. As Falco and Sidian closed on the demon he saw an arc of dark fire shoot up towards them. Falco might die at any moment and they would never have the chance to make their peace. The captain of the Exiles did not see the moment when Falco disappeared from view for his eyes were clenched and sealed with tears.

100

Demons of Fire and Flail

As the Possessed streamed towards the allied lines Falco rose up in his riding harness, ready to dismount as he and Sidian closed in for the attack, but just as he was about to leap the demon sent another gout of fire streaming towards them. Sidian avoided the attack by jinking sideways, but Falco lost his grip on the riding harness and fell thirty feet to the ground. Fortunately he was able to fortify his body, but still he was winded as he landed flat on his back amid a horde of ravening Sciritae.

Unwilling to lose his momentum Sidian continued the attack and was just reaching out with his talons when the demon grabbed a nearby Kardakae and swung the heavily armoured warrior at him. Dark armour smashed into black scales and like Falco, Sidian was sent sprawling among the Sciritae. Rushing forward the Possessed were eager to take advantage of their downed foes, but neither the battle mage nor his dragon were about to be overcome just yet.

Falco's entire body felt numbed with shock as he hit the ground but there was no time to lie in a dazed stupor. The Possessed were closing around him and he needed to move. Struggling to fill his lungs with air he twisted and rolled as half a dozen kopis swords stabbed down at him, glancing off his armour.

Kicking the legs out from under a Sciritae he managed to roll clear and get to one knee, but his shield was twisted on his arm and his own sword was still in its scabbard. For a moment the Sciritae thought him helpless and they closed in once more, but then Falco summoned his power and the Possessed had but a fractured second to realise their mistake.

A shockwave of blue energy pulsed out from Falco's kneeling form and more than a dozen Sciritae were blasted away. There could scarcely have been a more convincing demonstration of a battle mage's power, but the brightness of a Defiant is anathema to the Possessed and the proximity of the demon made the Sciritae bold. They rushed him from all sides, but now Falco had drawn his blade and the sword hummed with an ominous tone.

The first Sciritae to reach him did not even manage to land a blow before Falco severed its rancid torso at the waist. He reversed his stroke and cut a diagonal swathe through the armoured breastplate of the second. He smashed a third in the face with his shield and took the strike of a fourth on the crown of his helm before sweeping low to remove its right leg at the knee. The creature snarled as it stumbled forwards and Falco silenced it with a savage kick from one of his armoured boots. He killed another with a neck strike that spattered his face with scalding blood but there always seemed to be more. Ahead of him he could see the larger forms of Sidian and the demon engaged in a mortal struggle.

For the moment it looked as if Sidian was a match for the demon but he also had to defend against the Sciritae that struck at him from all sides and it was only a matter of time before something found a gap in the dragon's defences. Cleaving his way through the hordes of Sciritae, Falco fought his way towards them.

He had almost reached them when Sidian dodged a sweeping claw strike and grabbed the demon's forearm in his jaws. Using his great strength he pulled the demon off balance and was about to strike for its throat when a bull-sized bestiarum slammed into his side. Releasing his grip on the demon's forearm Sidian arched away from the beast's slashing tusks, but then the demon managed to get an arm around his long neck and things might have ended badly had Falco not got close enough for an attack.

From ten feet away he sent a bolt of energy spearing into the demon's side and Sidian was able to pull free of its grip. As Falco closed the remaining distance the bestiarum turned to face him, springing to the attack with an explosive burst of speed, but Falco spun away from its charge and brought his sword round in a rapid arc, hacking down to sever the creature's spine even as it went charging past.

Turning his attention back to his primary foe Falco had just enough time to raise a protective barrier as the demon threw out a wave of Baëlfire. Even inside the dome of energy Falco could feel the heat of the flames and he gritted his teeth against their devouring power. Outside his protection a number of Sciritae screamed as their flesh was consumed then, even as the dark flames died away, Falco charged forwards once more.

Having recoiled from the flames, Sidian also resumed the attack and now they could hear the sounds of battle raging behind them. The Possessed had reached the allied lines and Falco knew the second demon would soon be closing on General Renucci's position. He clenched his teeth in frustration and tried to maintain his focus. This was only the first of the Marchio's demons and they were running out of time to kill it.

*

Marshal Breton swept his eyes across the long front of the battle as the enemy tore at their defences. Unlike a normal army, the Possessed showed no fear of death or injury. With heedless abandon they threw themselves against the thickets of spears and tried to claw their way over the unyielding shield walls, but somehow the lines held.

Feeling a wave of relief he raised his gaze. Three hundred yards beyond the lines there was an intense knot of activity where Falco and Sidian were doing battle with the first of the Marchio's demons. The area was crawling with Possessed but he could just make out the larger shapes of the dragon and the demon along with the bright blue flashes of Falco's magical attacks.

Glancing over to their right flank he saw that the second demon was now getting dangerously close to General Renucci's position and with a stab of impatience he wished that Falco would hurry up and kill the first. But that was unfair. The flashes of light meant that Falco was still alive and Marshal Breton tried not to think of what would happen if he should fall.

Drawing his eyes away from the demons the marshal turned his attention back to their defences. The lines were still holding but he could see that in many places they were being forced to give ground. The front line of battle had quickly become a quagmire of black blood and gore and a grizzly bank of maimed bodies had built up in front of the defenders, requiring them to edge backwards as the Possessed used the additional height to leap over the front ranks.

The marshal knew this was only the first wave of the Marchio's force, but still he felt a surge of satisfaction at the way their soldiers had met the ferocity of the initial assault. But then one of his aides called out a warning and any sense of optimism was instantly quashed.

'Marshal Breton!' the officer cried. 'The second demon closes on the right.'

Switching his gaze back to their right flank Marshal Breton saw the massive shape of the second demon now closing on General Renucci's lines. Unlike the first demon whose skin was like the fire-blackened bark of a pine tree, the dark flesh of this monster was covered in armour and in each fist it held a weapon like a huge flail, the heads of which were elemental blocks of iron, black and angular and attached to the handles by four feet of heavy chain.

In all his years Marshal Breton had never seen so large a demon and even from so far away he could sense the creature's strength, strength that could smash its way through the walls of a castle. Above the clamour of battle he heard the faint horn call of *equitatus* and saw a unit of cavalry moving into position. General Renucci was going to try to stop the demon with a cavalry charge.

*

Knowing that they were running out of time Falco and Sidian raised the intensity of their attack and for the first time since it was born into the charnel world the demon knew what it meant to doubt. Lunging forwards it grappled Sidian and tried to drive one of its curving horns into the dragon's neck but Falco stabbed the demon in the back of its leg and Sidian was able to pull free.

Turning quickly the demon swiped at Falco's head. Its claws were like the tempered blades of a plough, and sparks flew from Falco's helm, but then Sidian attacked again and the demon felt a searing pain as the dragon's claws gouged four deep rills in the adamantine flesh of its back. Roaring in pain it struck out wildly. Falco blocked one attack with his sword and another with his shield. The demon tried for a third but Falco's blade suddenly flared with energy, slicing off two of the demon's fingers before cutting a deep gash in its thigh. The towering creature stumbled to its knees and Falco drove his blade into its chest with a thrust that grazed the demon's heart.

Disbelief erupted in the demon's mind even as it raged at the shame of its defeat. Roaring with ire it beat at Falco, its fists and claws clanging off his armour until Sidian struck it a blow so powerful that it snapped the horn from the right-hand-side of its head.

The heat went out of the demon's gaze and it slumped insensible to the ground.

As the demon collapsed Falco withdrew his sword. He was trembling with adrenaline and his body ached from the blows that the demon had rained down upon him. The battle had barely begun and already he felt exhausted, but there was no time for them to rest as Sidian struck down several of the Sciritae that were now closing on them once again.

Falco glanced down at the demon lying before him. Dark blood oozed from its many wounds and the remaining fingers on its clawed hands gouged into the earth as it tried to cling to life, but it was dying. Falco raised his sword to finish it off, but was then forced to defend himself as two Kardakae came charging towards him. He killed the first and took a numbing blow to the thigh before killing the second, but many more were now closing on their position and they would soon be overwhelmed.

'Sidian!' he cried. 'Get us out of here.'

Putting his back to Falco the dragon took a great breath then he opened his mouth and cleared the area in front of them with a sweeping burst of dragon fire. With Ferocian blades slicing the air behind him Falco leapt for Sidian's back as the dragon charged forward and surged into the air.

Screaming in demented rage the Possessed struck at the dragon's legs as they rose higher into the sky but finally they were free and clear and with barely a moment's hesitation Falco turned Sidian to the right where the second demon was now closing on General Renucci's lines.

*

General Renucci felt sick with fear as he watched the demon advancing towards them. Even hunched forward the massive creature stood more than twelve feet tall, its entire body covered in heavily pitted armour. Its ridged helm was reminiscent of an executioner's mask, its eyes glaring through the steel like the peepholes of a furnace. Beneath the mask the demon's mouth was a grinding maw of jagged teeth and it bellowed with a noise that shook the general's heart within his chest.

If they did not stop it the demon would smash his lines and the Possessed would burst through like water through a ruptured dyke. His only hope was to bring the monster down before it reached his lines, but even as the knights began their attack the general knew that they were doomed.

*

Falco looked down as General Renucci's knights closed on the demon. They barely slowed as they ploughed through the intervening Sciritae, but for all the force of their charge, he knew it would not be enough. As he and Sidian streaked over the raging battle he saw the knights in the first rank of the squadron lower their lances and lean forward in the saddle. They were just two horse-lengths short of their target when the demon swung its flails.

The head of the first enormous weapon tore through the air and several of the knights in the first rank were simply dashed aside. Their ruptured bodies were thrown into the path of those beside them and the entire line went down in a mass of tumbling limbs and broken lances.

A few of the following knights managed to maintain their course and in a series of successful strikes, four lance points searched for a gap in the demon's heavy armour. Three lances snapped and splintered, leaving barely a mark, but the fourth nicked the demon's thick hide as the rider thundered past. The man experienced a moment of satisfaction before the demon spun with surprising speed and swung a flail at his mount's rump. The horse screamed as its pelvis was shattered and the knight was spilled into a mass of Sciritae from which he did not emerge.

Twenty knights had begun the attack but now only five remained and these too would have died had a dark shape not come plummeting out of the sky. Even as it brought up its flails to crush the remaining knights Sidian slammed into the demon's back. The force of the impact knocked the massive creature off balance and it stumbled forwards as Falco leapt clear.

Drawing his body into a tuck, Falco turned in the air before breaking his fall with a series of rolls that brought him up against the body of a dying horse. He

591

caught a quick sense of the animal's agony before he came to his feet and turned to face their next opponent. The demon was by far the largest he had ever seen and even Sidian's powerful attack had not been enough to harm it. The dragon was clawing at its head and shoulders, but somehow the behemoth regained its balance with the dragon still clinging to its back.

With his claws hooked around the edges of the demon's armour Sidian opened his mouth and the demon let out a roar as its helmeted head was engulfed in dragon fire. Following his example Falco sent a dense ball of flame slamming into the creature's hip and again it staggered, but then it swung a flail over its left shoulder and Falco winced as the brutal weapon struck Sidian between his wings.

The dragon's flames were suddenly extinguished and with a growl of pain Sidian dropped from the demon's back. The armoured ridges along his spine had saved him from serious injury but Falco could sense the stiffness in his body as he reared backwards to avoid another attack that would surely have crushed his skull.

A third swing looked certain to make contact until Falco darted in to strike at the demon's left leg with all his strength. It was like hitting a solid column of iron, and even the sword that Malaki had forged struggled to penetrate the demon's hell-forged armour. Still it cut deep enough to inflict a wound and the demon felt a sharp burning pain as Falco's blade bit into its thigh. Its flail missed Sidian and the demon turned its attention to the human that barely came up to its waist. Fuelled by eternal hatred it kicked out a steel rimmed hoof but Falco whirled to one side. It swung a flail to crush him, but again Falco was too quick and the head of the flail merely thumped into the earth.

The demon felt a stab of pain at the base of its neck and turned to see the wyrm's tail snaking back from the attack. Its blade-like point had drawn blood but the injury was not enough to give this monster pause. With a howl of frustration the demon raised its fury to new heights. It clenched its fists and Baëlfire flowed down its arms until its flails glowed, and then it began to attack in earnest. Falco flung himself to the earth as a searing block of iron swept over him in a horizontal arc. Twice Sidian tried to close in, but the demon was now swinging its flails in rapid and lethal arcs and the dragon was forced to keep his distance. Fighting on opposite sides they looked for an opening and all the while the demon moved closer to General Renucci's lines.

The Possessed began to mass around the demon, as if they knew it would soon break through, and now they too began to attack. Falco stumbled as a Ferocian blade skipped off his helm. Spinning round he killed the Sciritae but the distraction cost him a moment of concentration and the head of a flail struck off the armour on his shoulder. It was only a glancing blow but still it bowled him over and left him feeling dazed.

Falco and Sidian now found themselves fighting inwards against the demon and outwards against the Possessed. There was no way they could defend against both, but fortunately there was one man on the battlefield who had seen what was happening and, from the corner of his vision, Falco saw the emissary leading a squadron of the Adamanti to their aid.

The Knights Adamant drove their charge deep into the Sciritae, but even that was not enough to stem the tide of Possessed now surrounding the demon.

They would all have been overrun had General Renucci not done the unthinkable. Following the emissary's lead he advanced his lines to enclose Falco and the demon.

At first this seemed like madness, but as the swordsmen of the Fourth Army pushed the Possessed back, Falco found that he and Sidian could concentrate more energy into their attacks. Sidian breathed out jets of fire while Falco took extra time to energise the bolts of force that he blasted into the demon's body and finally their attacks began to wear it down.

Falco caught shadowy glimpses of the demon's mind and beside the hatred and mounting frustration there was something akin to fear. The demon knew it was beaten and as its will began to waver so the substance of its mortal being grew weaker. Its dark flesh began to blister and burn beneath the relentless rake of Sidian's fire and its heavy armour no longer seemed impenetrable. With each attack Falco's bolts of magical force burned a little deeper, but now Falco could sense a new shadow forging its way into the valley. It was the shadow of an even greater Possessed army and with it came a demon whose power put all others in the shade.

The Marchio Dolor was coming and it was time to kill this demon and prepare to meet him.

Falco sheathed his sword and sent a surge of energy down into his clenched fist. He focussed the energy into a tight ball, ducked beneath another wild attack and sent it flying into the demon's chest. The dense fireball did not explode on contact, rather it punched into the heavy armour on the demon's chest and began to force its way in towards the creature's heart.

It took all of Falco's control to keep the ball of energy in place and he tried to drive it deeper even as he ducked and dodged from the demon's unending attacks. Sidian also kept up the assault, breathing fire and striking with his long tail. Falco's teeth were clenched with effort and his face was beaded with sweat, but this battle was almost over. Just a few more moments and the fireball would burst inside the demon's chest.

*

The Marchio Dolor was confused.

His dark angels had reported that only one Defiant now accompanied the army from Amboss and yet two of the Faithful had already been overcome. One was lying mortally wounded while the other showed pitiful weakness in the face of its imminent defeat.

There was nothing the Marchio could do for the colossus with the two massive flails, but the other demon was not beyond help. It would require several souls from a Gaoler's train but this demon could be brought back and made whole once more. Closing his eyes the Marchio sent his mind into the netherworld and summoned forth one of the gaolers that he had called back to join him. The gaoler in question had several strong souls upon its belt. More than enough to bring the injured demon back to full health.

Even as he moved into the valley between the three hills the Marchio opened up a rift and gated the Gaoler forward. He waited until his mind's eye saw the white demon emerge on the field of battle and then he turned his thoughts back to the Defiant who stood in his path. The Defiant who stood with a sable wyrm at his side. He had never killed a black wyrm before and he relished the prospect of destroying the strongest of its kind.

And as for the Defiant...

The man's faith was only matched by the love he felt for the humans who fought beside him. There would be some satisfaction in killing such a Defiant but the Marchio wondered if it might be possible to claim his soul.

His mind now burning with anticipation, the Marchio Dolor led his army into the Valley of The Three Brethren.

*

In truth it had not been very long, but Alex Klingemann felt as if the battle had been raging for hours. The heat radiating from the Possessed was terrifying and the stench of their rotting flesh made him gag but Alex tried to focus as the Exiles fought to hold their ground. All along the front line the fighting was the same, but the intensity of that first assault had abated and Alex began to feel as if the battle was turning in their favour. He heard a shout from behind him and at the next opportunity he stepped back, allowing the man to push forward to take his place. With such relentless fighting it was important to rotate the front ranks and the Exiles had this difficult manoeuvre down to a fine art.

Grateful for a brief reprieve Alex took a moment to cast his eye over the battlefield.

From somewhere close by, he saw a cloud of arrows shooting down the line as the Dalwhinnies did their best to support the troops on the front line. It was dangerous to bring a unit of archers so close to the fighting but Bryna had found an area of raised ground and was using the height to get a better angle for shooting at the Possessed.

There were still thousands of Sciritae in front of them, but the ranks of the enemy were definitely thinning and Alex felt a sense of elation at the thought that they might win, but then he looked to the far end of the valley where a new band of shadow now stretched across the horizon. They had weathered the first wave of darkness but a greater storm was about to break upon them.

Any sense of joy was suddenly quashed and Alex was about to re-enter the fray when something caught his eye. It was a shimmering rift, like a folded shadow in the air, halfway between the front line and the body of the first demon that Falco had defeated. Then, even as he watched, a new demon emerged from the rift and stared in contempt at the humans who battled before it.

It stood for a moment, but instead of attacking it turned towards the demon that was lying close to death on the field. Trailing behind it were a number of grisly bundles, each attached to a metal belt around the demon's waist by a long length of chain. The horrific bundles fanned out like the trailing skirt of a gown. They bumped and rolled over the ground, the chain bags snagging on stones and leaving a trail of blood in the earth.

Alex barely noticed the sudden squall of fear that surged towards him from the demon. Suddenly the fighting that raged before him seemed to recede in his mind. The one thought that eclipsed all others was that this demon was white.

Without any conscious thought Alex Klingemann pushed his way back to the front of the Exiles. There was a manoeuvre that infantry used when they

594

needed to push forward with all the strength they could muster. The manoeuvre was known as 'full force' but Alex gave the order in the language of Illicia.

'Volle Macht!' he cried and with barely a moment's hesitation the Exiles drove forward.

'Volle Macht!' he cried again and the Exiles pushed clear of the defending line of battle.

They did not know why their young commander had ordered them to advance beyond the safety of their lines, but they followed him all the same and soon they were fighting their way through a horde of Sciritae. As they progressed they fell into a defensive square as Alex led them directly towards the retreating demon. The shield and spear units on either side started to match their advance and suddenly the entire line of battle was thrown into confusion.

A little way back from the front line Lanista Magnus watched as the Exiles moved out of position.

'What the hell is he doing?' asked the veteran trainer.

'He's going to break the entire line!' replied another commander beside him.

And it was true. Just when it looked like the tide of battle was turning against the Possessed, one impetuous commander had thrown their defensive line into chaos.

'Sound the order to stand fast and consolidate,' snapped the commander and the signalmen behind him sounded their horns.

With no small measure of confusion the sword and spear units struggled to reform the line, but the Possessed pushed forward and the Exiles were suddenly cut off. For a moment it looked like they would be surrounded on all sides but then another unit moved out from the lines to cover their right flank.

'Fates curse it!' snapped the commander. 'Now the Dalwhinnies are out of position *too*.'

For a moment Lanista Magnus frowned at this uncharacteristic display of tactical stupidity. But then his gaze moved out to the new demon that had suddenly appeared on the field and he remembered what Malaki had said after the tragic attempt to save the refugees in the ravine.

Malaki had said the demon that took Quirren was white.

*

When she first saw him leading the Exiles out from the front line Bryna thought Alex had lost his mind, but then she too noticed the colour of the demon that had suddenly appeared on the battlefield. And she also noticed the pitiful bags of humanity that bumped and dragged along behind it.

'Draw swords!' she had called out to Paddy who frowned as if she were babbling nonsense, but then she had grabbed his shoulder and turned him to look out over the field.

'The demon!' she cried. 'That's the demon that took Quirren.'

A shadow of fear passed over Paddy's face at the thought of getting closer to a demon, but then a fierce light appeared in his deep set eyes. He paused for a moment and then.

'Bucklers, bonnets and blades, you luckless bastards!' he bellowed and the Dalwhinnies shouldered their bows and took up their secondary weapons. Then

595

Bryna led them out in support of the Exiles who were already fifty paces ahead of them.

Only the fact that the Possessed forces were thinning allowed them to make progress but even so it was not long before there were hundreds of Sciritae between the Dalwhinnies and the security of the allied lines.

*

Several hundred yards to the right Malaki watched in horror as the black clad Exiles moved out of position and the Dalwhinnies followed in their wake. It was too far away for him to make out the Gaoler and he could not fathom why Alex and Bryna would act in such a way.

The Knights of Wrath had just broken a block of four hundred Kardakae that had threatened to breach Marshal Breton's lines. Now Malaki blinked the gritty sweat from his eyes as he struggled to keep his wife's unit in view.

'What are they doing?' asked Huthgarl beside him.

'I have no idea,' he murmured.

As the Knights of Wrath returned to their position Malaki's heart was filled with fear.

*

Falco's mind burned with the effort of keeping the fireball in place but he knew it was almost over. Just a few more seconds and the flail-wielding demon would be dead. But he needed to be careful. The demon's flails were still swinging in wild arcs and a blow from either could be lethal. He watched as the demon raised a flail and he knew it would swing down towards him, but he also knew that he had won.

With a final effort Falco allowed the fireball to explode in the demon's chest. The massive creature convulsed as its flesh was consumed and fire burst out between the gaps in its armour.

The moment of release made Falco's head swim and he prepared to duck beneath the glowing flail that was still swinging towards him but at the last instant he felt a new presence on the battlefield. Falco recognised the Gaoler immediately and in that instant he paused. The dying demon's flail slammed into his helm and the last thing to flash through his mind was a name.

Quirren.

101

The Mercy of Patrick Feckler

A wave of despair washed over the allied forces as the cloak of Falco's protection disappeared. Marshal Breton's mouth felt suddenly dry and panic fluttered in his chest like the wings of a frantic bird.

They were lost.

Falco had fallen, and they were lost.

For an instant he felt the urge to turn his horse and flee, but he did not. He was the Marshal of Clemoncé and he could not desert the men he had brought here.

The cruel irony was that the battle had just turned in their favour. They had survived this first wave of the Possessed and were beginning to gain the upper hand. Indeed, Marshal Breton had even considered sounding the advance but now that was impossible. The demon that had appeared from the shadowy rift was not as powerful as those that Falco had killed but even so, the fear that exuded from its ash-white form made it difficult to think. And now the shadow at the far end of the valley was growing closer and the fear that came with *it* was of an altogether different magnitude.

The Marchio Dolor was upon them and Marshal Breton knew they could not stand against him. With a rush of crippling horror he realised what a terrible mistake it had been to come here. He had trusted a man less than half his age and now they would pay the price. Their defensive line was in disarray and any attempt to retreat would only end in disaster. He was about to lose the largest army that the allies had ever assembled.

Oh, shame.

Oh, shame.

In a stupor of guilt Marshal Breton could only stare into the valley as a second Possessed army surged towards them.

*

The men of the Exiles also felt the moment of Falco's fall but they had long since given up on hope, and so for them the impact of his loss was less than it was for most. With grim determination they fought their way forward, led on by a young commander who seemed to be 'possessed' by some vengeful spirit of his own.

Alex Klingemann attacked the Sciritae with a savagery that seemed at odds with the light-hearted nature of his personality. Spattered with black blood he drove the Exiles on towards the demon that walked away from them in oblivious disdain. Even with its back to them the fear from the Gaoler was like a hot wind beating at the walls of his mind, but Alex's teeth were clenched in a snarl of unwavering certainty. He would reach this demon and save his brother and nothing short of death would stop him.

Behind him the allied lines were thrown into confusion. For a while they tried to support the Exiles, but their discipline crumbled as the foundation of Falco's faith was cut out from under them. As the line fragmented they retreated back, leaving the Exiles and the Dalwhinnies adrift like islands in a sea of Sciritae, the two units growing increasingly isolated as they moved further away

597

from the main body of the army. But Alex had no thought for such things. All his thoughts were on the Gaoler and one particular bundle trailing from its belt.

Besides the mass of battered flesh, Alex caught a glimpse of dark hair and crimson cloth, the same crimson worn by Knights from the Order of the Black Eagle. That bundle of chain and dust-blackened meat was his brother. Cutting another Sciritae down he pushed forward more strongly than ever. There were still many Possessed between them but now the gaoler had stopped. Alex saw it look down at the first demon that Falco had defeated and he realised that the hellish creature was still alive.

The Gaoler drew in one of the chains from its belt. It raised the bag of tortured flesh into the air then looked down at the dying demon at its feet. Dark Baëlfire flared along its arm and suddenly the contents of the bag were consumed by flames while the unfortunate's soul was delivered into the pitiless realms of hell. At the same time a surge of dark energy flowed from the Gaoler's other hand into the body of the injured demon and slowly it began to stir.

Still glowing from the infernal heat, the horrific bag hung empty, a residue of scorched blood and charred flesh still clung to the chains, but the person within it was gone. With no thought for the soul it had just used the Gaoler let the empty bag fall and reached for another.

With a cry of despair Alex realised what was happening. The Gaoler was using the chained souls to rejuvenate the dying demon. He did not know how many it would take, but sooner or later it would draw up Quirren's chain and his brother's soul would be lost forever.

To the left of the Exiles a huge bestiarum went thundering by, but the Exiles paid it no heed. All their attention was focussed on reaching the Gaoler and so they did not notice another beast charging directly towards them from the right. Even by bestiarum standards this brute was massive and it was about to tear the Exiles apart.

*

Bryna wept as she felt the familiar cloak of Falco's protection fall away. She wept for his downfall and she wept for the fear that came rushing in to fill her mind. The only thing that allowed her to focus was the need to protect the Exiles.

Even without the fear she had never felt so exposed in a battle. Archers were not supposed to fight in close quarters with the enemy, but the Dalwhinnies were doing well. They fought with the viciousness of street fighters, but still Bryna was grateful that the Possessed were not focussing on them.

Some fifty paces ahead, the Exiles were now closing on the Gaoler and thankfully it still appeared unaware of their presence. Bryna had no idea what Alex intended to do once he reached it and suddenly the folly of their impulsive actions struck home. Behind the Dalwhinnies there was a deep mass of Sciritae, cutting them off from the main body of the army and now she could see a new mass of troops advancing towards them.

They were going to die here. She was sure of it.

A kind of paralysis crept over her and even as the Dalwhinnies continued to fight Bryna began to look for a way to escape.

'Captain!'

The shout meant nothing to her. It was a mere distraction from the instinct to survive.

'BRYNA!'

The desperation in Paddy's voice finally broke through the veil of panic and Bryna focussed on his face.

'We have to retreat!' he cried. 'We've come too far. We have to fight our way back.'

For a moment Bryna could only stare at him. She could see the feral tension in his eyes and she knew that he too was just moments away from losing control. Whipping her head round she looked back towards the allied lines, but there were now a thousand Sciritae between them and the main body of the army. She looked forward to where the Exiles had almost reached the Gaoler and then she spotted the enormous bestiarum coming in from the right. The huge creature was tossing Sciritae out of its path as it headed directly for the Exiles.

Ignoring Paddy, Bryna gripped her bow and ran to the front of the Dalwhinnies. She nocked an arrow and drew back the string.

'Suivez dix!' she cried and eight arrows followed her own, stabbing into the monster's side.

It did not even pause.

The thundering beast was now just seconds from smashing the Exiles to pieces and there was no way a mere ten arrows could stop it.

Bryna nocked another arrow then, at the top of her lungs, she cried out.

'DALWHINNIES...'

'SUIVEZ MOI!'

She loosed her arrow and the air shook with a collective 'bang' as a hundred shafts followed its course. In a dense mass the arrows tore into the bestiarum's side and it collapsed onto its chest. Its momentum carried the dead creature forward and it knocked over several of Alex's troops but the Exiles' formation held strong as they closed the remaining distance to the Gaoler.

The killing of the bestiarum cleared Bryna's thoughts and she took a moment to take stock of their situation. The Dalwhinnies were caught in a no-man's land between the first wave of Possessed and the army that now approached with the Marchio Dolor. There was no way they could fight their way free and now a mass of black armoured Kardakae was closing on their position.

'We're fucked!' said Paddy beside her and Bryna could only nod.

'We'll move over to the right,' she said, her voice surprisingly steady. 'Try to draw the Kardakae away from Alex.'

Paddy looked at her as if he did not understand how she could think of others when they were about to be reborn as Possessed.

'Come on Feckler,' said Bryna as he hesitated. 'We can still kill a few of these bastards before we're done.'

Paddy the Feck frowned. He had always thought of 'nice people' as weak, fools to be preyed upon by those of greater strength, but ever since meeting Bryna Godwin he had realised that he was wrong. Following her example he began ordering the terrified Dalwhinnies over to the right. A few Sciritae still came screaming in to attack them, but in this brief window of calm they were no real threat. But as the archers took up their new position Paddy turned to look at the wall of black steel that was now marching towards them.

'Have you ever heard of archers stopping a thousand Kardakae?' he asked.

Bryna's mouth was too dry to answer but they both knew the answer was, no.

Standing sideways to the enemy, Bryna prepared to give the order for the Dalwhinnies to shoot. Almost idly, her free hand reached back to cup the base of her quiver. A casual observer might have surmised that she was checking its weight to see how many arrows she had left, but Paddy knew she was thinking about the man who had given it to her and suddenly the unfairness of life struck at his heart.

These young people should be spawning brats on some stinking farm in the country, happy in blissful ignorance of how cruel life could be. They should not be dying on a battlefield where even their corpses would not be allowed to rest.

Paddy had never known what it meant to love someone and so he did not recognise the emotions stirring in his chest. What he did know was that if Bryna died in fear then her soul would be claimed by the Possessed, but if she died while thinking about her ballsy knight of a husband, then her soul would be put forever beyond their reach.

Almost unconsciously, Patrick Feckler drew the razor sharp knife from his belt then, as the rest of the Dalwhinnies prepared to shoot at the approaching Kardakae, his gaze moved to the pale skin of Bryna's neck.

102

To Save The Ones We Love

The darkness remained as impenetrable as ever, but slowly the silence gave way to the distant roar of the sea. Falco remembered the first time he had seen it from the rugged coast of Clemoncé, a vast expanse of blue and grey that seemed to go on forever. It was never still, never the same, the waves rolling in and drawing back like the very breath of the world.

But something was wrong.

There was no rhythm to the noise of this ocean, it just went on and on. And since when did the waves cry out in pain or echo with the grinding ring of steel?

No.

This was not the distant roar of the ocean it was the tumultuous din of war.

Hauling himself up from some great intangible depth, Falco fought his way back into the waking world. As his mind merged once more with the substance of his flesh, so the pain and the exhaustion returned. His entire body hummed like a rod of iron struck off an anvil.

He was lying on his back and he could sense movement all around him. Rolling onto his side he spat out a mouthful of blood and struggled up to one knee, wincing from the stiffness in his neck and the pain that throbbed in his skull.

Slowly he opened his eyes.

Battle was raging all about him and now he could see Sidian fighting alongside the men of the Fourth Army, but the men were struggling. They were filled with fear and they were failing. Falco knew he had to protect them, but he was still dazed by the impact of the demon's final attack. Only his helm and a burst of instinctive protection had saved him, but even so, he had come close to death and he needed a moment to collect himself.

His sword was still in its scabbard and Falco reached across his body until his fingers closed around the hilt. A distant note rang deep inside the blade and somehow it gave him strength. Grasping the handle he closed his eyes and felt the tingling sensation of power surge through his body. It began somewhere behind his eyes, washed down over his face and raised the hairs on his arms. It carried with it a deep healing warmth and as his strength returned Falco was able to gather the army beneath the cloak of his protection once more.

Slowly he climbed to his feet. He took a deep breath to clear his head and as his thoughts ran true so he recalled the last thought that had flashed through his mind before the demon's flail struck.

Quirren!

Falco's gaze snapped over to the far side of the battlefield where he could still sense the presence of the demon that had taken their friend. His thoughts came into sharp focus and he started to move, haltingly at first but then faster as the stiffness in his body was banished by need.

'Sidian!' he cried, but there was no need to call his dragon.

Of all those on the battlefield, only Sidian had known that Falco was not dead and he had been waiting for his brother to return. Slashing down two Sciritae the dragon disengaged from the battle and raced towards him.

Falco straightened his shield and watched as the dragon approached. Drawing level, Sidian dipped his wing and with only a trace of stiffness, Falco leapt for his back. Giving him barely a moment to settle himself the dragon spread his wings and took to the air. Up they soared and the spirits of the entire army soared with them.

With their combined vision Falco could see a unit of infantry directly behind the Gaoler. He did not need to see their colours of silver and black to know it was the Exiles. They were not attacking the demon, but still Falco could see sparks flying from a few individuals at the front of the depleted unit. For some reason the Gaoler appeared to be ignoring them but Falco knew that this would not last for long. Soon it would turn and the Exiles would be finished.

There was no need to convey the urgency to Sidian. The dragon's limbs were tucked in tight as he sped over the battlefield. From the corner of his eye Falco could see the vast shadow of the second Possessed army spreading up the valley. He could sense the burgeoning presence of yet more demons and now he could feel the scrutiny of the Marchio Dolor himself. The Marquis of Pain was aware of his presence and Falco felt suddenly naked and vulnerable. The enemy's chief lieutenant was trying to make sense of the human that opposed it and Falco felt as if all the secrets of his heart were being raked over and laid bare.

You would never have the courage.

You would never have the faith.

Trying to shut out the violating presence he focussed all his thoughts on the Gaoler and the faint hope of freeing Quirren from its thrall.

Knees tucked beneath the dragon's wings, he gripped the ridges at the base of Sidian's neck. They covered the half mile distance quickly, but even as Sidian came in for the attack they saw the Gaoler turn. The Exiles were scattered as the demon used one of the chained bodies to smash them aside. A small group of them was retreating while the others tried to form a wall of defence, but there was no way they could stand against the demon.

*

Sparks flew up as Alex hacked at the chain linking Quirren to the Gaoler's belt. This close to the demon he could hardly tell the difference between the fear and the terrible heat that radiated from its body. The handle of his sword felt slick in the sweat-soaked leather of his gauntlet, but then his blade made a different sound as something in the chain gave way. Another blow, and another, and with a metallic *chink* the chain was severed.

Alex's heart swelled with elation but the sense of achievement was instantly quashed as the demon turned to face him.

Someone had defiled its skirt of pain.

Someone had stolen one of its souls.

Someone was about to pay.

The Exiles recoiled in terror as the demon turned its black eyes upon them. Alex reached down to grab the chain linked to Quirren and winced from the scorching heat that turned the sweat on his gauntlets to steam. Those beside him tried to help and together they dragged Quirren away as the rest of the Exiles did their best to cover their retreat. They formed a defensive line, but then the Gaoler took hold of another chain and swung the mass of encased flesh like an enormous club.

Still dragging Quirren backwards Alex looked up as the Exiles were scattered. They could not stop the white skinned demon and now a dark shape was rising behind it. The first demon that Falco had defeated was getting back to its feet. The spent souls had done their foul work and the fear in the air grew even thicker as the injured demon was restored.

Alex knew that they were lost, but there was still one thing he could do before the Possessed claimed him. He could free his brother from his unthinkable suffering.

Looking down at the mass of flesh at his feet he raised his sword. Beneath a mask of dirt and dried blood he could just make out the shape of Quirren's face. For a moment his courage almost failed him, but then he gripped his sword in both hands with the blade pointing downwards.

As the Gaoler advanced towards him Alex Klingemann steeled his will.

'Forgive me,' he breathed and then he plunged his sword down into his brother's chest.

The blade sank deep and Quirren's lips cracked open with a gasp of pain, but to Alex's horror he did not die. The chain might have been severed but Quirren's soul was still ensnared. With a keening wail of despair Alex dropped his sword and fell to his knees. Tears flooded down his cheeks and his heart was finally devoid of hope as the Gaoler loomed before him.

The demon looked down and its eyes narrowed as if it suddenly understood the connection between this human and the soul it had tried to save. Something like amusement crept into its heavy browed gaze and then it raised one of the newly emptied bags. It had fulfilled its mission to heal the injured demon. Now it would replenish its skirt with new wells of suffering. Soon it would have two brothers trailing from its belt.

Unable to move, Alex watched as the Gaoler reached for him. He had a horrifying glimpse of the agony that lay in store, but then he felt a gust of air and the Gaoler staggered as something streaked between them. At the same time Alex saw a dragon-shaped mass slam into the black skinned demon that had just got back to its feet. That demon disappeared from view while the Gaoler stared in puzzlement at the deep gash that had suddenly appeared in its chest.

Glancing to his left Alex saw a figure rise to his feet - dark armour, barbute helm, round-shield and sword. Alex could not see the expression on his friend's face, but in some ways, the fury emanating from Falco was more terrifying than even the demons of hell.

The Gaoler was either too stupid or too arrogant to recognise the agent of its doom, but Alex knew that the monster that had taken his brother was about to die.

*

Marshal Breton hardly dared believe it as he felt the fear recede. The allied forces had begun to crumble but now they stood firm and their morale lifted as they felt Falco's reassuring presence return.

'He's alive,' said the marshal, turning to Lord Cabal who sat astride his horse close by.

'I know,' said the Lord Commander. 'But it might be too late to save the left wing.'

Marshal Breton looked over to the left where the defensive line of the Irregulars was in tatters. They had reformed into blocks but the Possessed surged around them, attacking from all sides.

'There's no way we can resist a second assault if we can't restore the line,' said Lord Cabal and Marshal Breton nodded.

'Go,' he said and with a nod Lord Cabal turned his horse away.

With a wave of his hand he drew the Knights of Wrath into formation. The aim was to sweep in front of the Irregulars and give them the chance to reform a solid line of defence. Lord Cabal's jaw was set with confident resolve. Four hundred knights were more than enough to achieve their aim. He was about to give the signal to charge when Malaki appeared beside him.

'My Lord. There are two units out of position,' said Malaki, trying to conceal the desperate need in his voice. 'The Dalwhinnies and the Exiles. They've been cut off from the army.'

Lord Cabal turned to look at the two allied units that were just visible beyond the intervening hordes of Sciritae. The Exiles were so close to the gaoler that they were clearly beyond help. The Dalwhinnies on the other hand were trapped in a relatively calm area of the battlefield, but now a block of a thousand Kardakae was closing on the archers and there was no way they would be able to stop it.

'You will never make it in time,' said Lord Cabal as he guessed what Malaki had in mind.

'But not to try...' said Malaki and Lord Cabal's eyes narrowed at the challenge implied in those four simple words.

For a moment he was on the verge of denying the request but there was something naively valiant about this young knight with the birthmark face, something that should not be denied. With a wave of his hand Lord Cabal divided his squadron of knights into two. *He* would lead one half to help the Irregulars while the other would follow the Knight of the Crimson Helm.

Malaki gave the leader of his order a bow and wasted no time in bringing his squadron to the front of the line. Ahead of him a unit of spearmen prepared to 'open the way' for them to charge through.

'Malaki!' shouted Huthgarl. 'We'll never reach them in time. There are too many Possessed between us.'

Malaki knew he was right. It would take time for them to cleave their way through the Sciritae and by then the Kardakae would have cut the Dalwhinnies to pieces. There was only one way it might be possible and Malaki could only hope that Bryna would guess what he had in mind. Turning away from Huthgarl he gave the order to sound *equitatus*.

'And sound it loud!' he bellowed.

The horns blared the signal for a cavalry charge and for a few anxious seconds Malaki waited to see if there was any reaction. Maybe the Dalwhinnies were too far away to hear the call. But then he saw movement and faces turning in his direction.

'Open the way!' he cried out and as the spearmen drew back Malaki led the Knights of Wrath into the fray.

*

The knife was steady in Patrick Feckler's hand. He knew what he was doing was right. The Kardakae were getting closer and soon there would be no time to act. He was just reaching for Bryna's neck when she turned. From the allied lines behind them she had heard the sound of horns.

Paddy paused. As ruthless as he was, he could not slit her throat while he could see her face.

'They're sounding the call for equitatus,' said Bryna.

Her eyes scanned the allied lines and then she froze.

'Malaki, no!' she breathed as she saw the spearmen open up to reveal a squadron of two hundred knights.

'The damn fool!' said Paddy as he realised what Malaki and the Knights of Wrath were planning to do. 'There's no way he'll reach us in time.'

Bryna's face was suddenly flushed with anxiety, but then a faint possibility dawned in her mind and she glanced at the approaching Kardakae before turning back to look at the mass of Possessed lying between them and the Knights of Wrath. Their arrows would have little effect against the heavily armoured Kardakae, but they could still do some significant damage to the Sciritae.

Ignoring the imminent threat, Bryna gave the order for the Dalwhinnies to turn away from the approaching Kardakae.

'Rolling volley, reducing range,' cried Bryna.

Paddy was appalled at what she intended to do but still he echoed the order.

'Mark, three hundred paces!' he bellowed. 'And don't shoot the fucking horses!' he added as the Knights of Wrath began their charge.

'Loose!' cried Bryna and the Dalwhinnies shot a volley of arrows into the mass of Sciritae between them and the Knights of Wrath.

Not all of their arrows found a mark but it was enough to ease the path for Malaki and his knights. With each volley the Dalwhinnies reduced their range, trying to match the advance of the rapidly approaching horses. The knights came on quickly, but now the Dalwhinnies could hear the stomping advance of the Kardakae. In her mind Bryna could see the wall of dark warriors looming closer, but she dared not turn round to look. She knew that if she did she would not be able to resist turning her arrows on the impending threat, but only the knights could stop the Kardakae, and only if they arrived in time.

The noise of the approaching enemy grew so loud that Bryna could barely think, but the Dalwhinnies could not stop now, the Knights of Wrath were almost through.

It was only as they finally burst through the last of the Sciritae that Paddy realised their mistake. The path the Dalwhinnies had cleared led directly to themselves. There was no way the charging knights would be able to swerve around them to reach the Kardakae. They were about to be trampled to death by their own heavy cavalry, but then he saw Bryna step forward and with a stab of horror he realised what she intended to do.

'DALWHINNIES!' cried Bryna. 'TRAVERSER, SUR MOI!'

To attempt the traverser manoeuvre at this speed was utter madness but they literally had no choice. Any second now the Kardakae would begin cleaving their way into the archers.

Teetering on the cusp of panic the Dalwhinnies faced in the direction of their insane captain and formed themselves into columns just two arm-lengths apart. Ahead of them loomed a wall of thundering horses while behind them came murder in the form of a dense block of heavily armoured Kardakae.

Ever since the training accident that killed young Daniel, Bryna had been unnerved by the drumming sound of cavalry. Just one clip from a steel shod hoof could crack a human's skull and now two hundred armoured knights were bearing down upon them at full speed. All it would take was for someone to move out of line and the manoeuvre would end in disaster.

'DOWN AND CLOSE!' Paddy roared and Bryna heard a ripple of movement as the Dalwhinnies bent down to make themselves as small as possible, burying their faces in the small of the next archer's back, but not Bryna. She was transfixed by the terrifying and glorious sight of the armoured horses thundering towards them. Behind her she heard screams of pain as the first of the Dalwhinnies were cut down by the Kardakae, but Bryna stood tall as the Knights of Wrath charged towards her.

'Ride straight, my love,' she breathed and then she closed her eyes.

*

Malaki's heart lifted as they smashed their way through the last of the Sciritae. They were going to make it. Beyond the Dalwhinnies he could see the great mass of Kardakae had almost reached the Dalwhinnies, but now the knights were flying over the ground at full attack speed.

'Now, Bryna... Do it now!' he whispered and he let out a sigh of relief as he saw the archers form into columns and bow down against the ground. All that is, save one.

Standing at the front of the Dalwhinnies he saw the slight figure of his wife, curls of auburn hair blowing in the breeze. At this speed the gaps between the archers seemed impossibly tight but they led straight through to the Kardakae and it was the only route that they could take.

'Ride straight, brothers,' thought Malaki and as he lowered his lance he glanced down at his wife. Her face was turned up towards him and even as he sped towards her, he could see that her eyes were closed.

'In the quiet of the night,' he breathed.

'And in the raging heat of battle,' echoed Bryna.

'I will love you,' they uttered together.

And the world exploded in a deafening crunch of colliding force.

*

Alex did not see the Knights of Wrath thread a lethal path through the Dalwhinnies and slam into the massed block of Kardakae. He was watching an encounter of a more intimate and terrifying nature. Feeling numb and detached he saw Falco come in for the attack. As he started forward the Gaoler dropped the chain it had been holding and thrust out both its hands. A storm of burning shale blasted towards Falco but he did not even try to avoid it. Summoning a

606

wedge of shimmering energy he surged forward. Head lowered, with sword and shield in hand, he ran directly into the screaming blizzard of brimstone.

The Gaoler hardly had time to react before Falco reached it. The nine foot demon seemed taken aback by the directness of his charge and, shutting off the flow of fire, it raised a hand to club him down, but it was far too slow to stop someone who had trained at the Academy of War. It staggered as Falco's sword cut across its thigh before whipping back to open a gash in its side. With a groan of pain the demon tried to strike Falco down with its chisel-like claws, but Falco parried the first attack with his shield and stopped the second by severing the Gaoler's right hand at the wrist.

The demon screamed as black blood gushed from the stump of its arm, but Falco was not done. Moving with lethal fluidity he delivered a deep cut to the inside of the Gaoler's right knee and as it stumbled he slashed the metal belt from around its waist. The accursed steel was no match for Falco's sword and the demon roared in outrage as its skirt of pain was cut free. Again it reached for him, but Falco avoided its grasp with ease. Dodging to one side he hacked at the demon's elbow before driving the point of his sword deep into the Gaoler's ribs. The demon slumped to its knees and as it did so Falco removed his sword, pivoted quickly, and with a backhanded blow, he struck the Gaoler's head from its neck.

The mass of bone and ash-white skin hit the ground with a thump, the Gaoler's black eyes staring at nothing as it rolled to a stop, only fixed with an expression of surprise at the swiftness of its demise.

Falco stood still as the Gaoler's corpse collapsed beside him, his body thrumming with the force of vengeance. A burst of fire caught his attention and he raised his gaze a short distance to where Sidian was currently dispatching the demon that they had previously neglected to kill.

In an avalanche of claws and steel hard scales the dragon had struck the demon, driving it into the earth. Imbued with new life the demon tried to rise, but Sidian was not about to leave it alive a second time and using all his weight he drove the demon's face into the earth. With one massive paw he grabbed the demon's shoulder; with the other he gripped the back of its coal black head. Then he opened his mouth and breathed a jet of flame into the back of the demon's neck. The demon roared and struggled to break free but Sidian did not release his grip or reduce the stream of devouring fire.

So fierce was the heat of that breath that Sidian's claws began to glow as the demon's flesh was stripped away from its bones. The dark vertebrae of its spine were laid bare then with a gristly sound of tearing the tendons gave way as Sidian snapped its neck. Only then did the dragon draw a breath and raise his head to look for Falco.

The twinned souls locked eyes and their gaze was dark as they acknowledged the force of violence that was required to defeat the demons of the Possessed. Such was the terrible power of the great souls that protected humankind. But not all the powers of a battle mage are so destructive. With a new feeling of determination Falco turned to face Alex Klingemann who still knelt over the chained body of his brother.

Returning from the realm of vengeance Falco started towards him and the force of his presence was so strong that Alex actually recoiled. But then Falco removed his helm and dropped to one knee beside Quirren's tortured body. Suddenly Alex could see the young man that he had met in Wrath, the man that had come to be his friend.

Looking down at Quirren's mangled body Falco could scarcely believe what they had done to him and tears of guilt and compassion swam in his eyes.

'He can't die,' said Alex, his voice hoarse with despair.

Falco noticed the fresh sword wound in Quirren's chest and for a moment he was puzzled. The demon that had taken Quirren was dead; surely his soul should have been released from the unholy grip of the Possessed. But then Falco understood. The Gaoler had been collecting souls, not for himself, but for another, for the demon that was now striding into the valley. But Falco did not care.

He could sense the lightless world of agony in which Quirren was trapped and he would not allow him to suffer for a moment longer. Laying down his sword Falco reached out his hand and placed it on Quirren's mangled body. Using his powers he might be able to kill Quirren but he could not bear the thought of him dying in pain and so Falco reached into his friend's tortured mind and took all that suffering unto himself.

Alex gave a sob of disbelief as he saw something in his brother's disfigured face relax. A sigh escaped his cracked lips as if the tension of unbearable torment had suddenly been released. It was too much to say that he was at peace, but Alex was able to believe that Quirren was no longer in pain.

But for Falco, the agony was now so overwhelming that his body convulsed and he almost lost control. With a trembling hand he reached for the chain trailing from the bag in which Quirren's body was encased. With a huge effort he climbed to his feet then gripping the chain he allowed the tingling sensation of power to surge in his chest.

'Stand back,' he gasped through gritted teeth, and Alex stumbled to get clear.

Falco allowed the power to build until it burned white hot and then he sent it flowing into the foul chains that imprisoned his friend. The heavy metal began to glow and the searing energy progressed until the entire mass of Quirren's body was engulfed. Falco could not believe the strength of the will holding Quirren in this anguished limbo, but he refused to be daunted. With ever increasing intensity he channelled his power into Quirren and so bright was the conflagration that Alex had to shield his eyes. His brother's body had become a mass of golden light and finally Falco could take no more.

With a great effort of will he threw back his head and screamed. There was a final flaring of light and then both Quirren and the chains that bound him were gone, transformed into a mist of silver motes falling slowly to the ground.

Falco slumped to his knees and Alex gasped as all his brother's suffering was reduced to a cloud of shining dust. Relief flooded his mind, but then Alex saw Falco fall and he hurried over to help him.

'Thank you,' he said as Falco raised his head.

Slowly the strength returned to his body and Falco placed his hand on Alex's shoulder.

'Come,' he said. 'The day's fight is not over yet.'

Alex gave a nod as the sounds of the surrounding battle registered on his senses once more. Getting to his feet he could see how far out of position the Exiles had come and now an even larger Possessed force was advancing upon them. Around him, the remaining Exiles had arranged themselves into a defensive formation, ready to fend off the new hordes of Sciritae that were approaching. Over to the right he could see the Dalwhinnies and some two hundred knights battling a huge block of Kardakae.

'Move your men towards the Dalwhinnies,' said Falco as he replaced his barbute helm. 'We need to get you back to the lines.'

Again Alex nodded and Falco was just reaching for his sword when an invisible force snatched him from the ground. His sword fell with a ringing clang and Alex could only watch as Falco landed heavily almost forty yards away. He saw his friend struggle to get to his feet, clearly disorientated by whatever it was that had grabbed him, but before he could act Falco was wrenched away once more, his body flying through the air before crashing into a mass of Kardakae.

Falco was stunned and disorientated by this mysterious attack, but still he managed to summon a burst of power to force the Kardakae back. Glancing up he saw Sidian driving through the air towards him. Relief pulsed through his mind, but then he saw the dragon plunge to the ground, torn from the sky by the same force that had taken hold of him. Fear and concern tightened around his heart as Sidian disappeared from view. The dragon failed to reappear and Falco started towards him, but then he was jerked off his feet once more.

In an ungainly heap he was dragged across the rocky ground through the advancing ranks of Kardakae who struck at him as he passed. By the time he came to a halt Falco was barely conscious. He was dazed, disarmed and confused but still he prepared to fight. He focused his power into his empty right hand, but as he got to his feet he saw that the Kardakae were drawing back.

As Falco's head began to clear he became aware that something had changed. The tumult of the battle seemed to have disappeared, replaced by an eerie quiet, punctuated only by the cries of the wounded and the shuffling of many thousand troops. Horses whinnied, distant orders were shouted and the wind sighed over the armies that faced each other in the Valley of the Three Brethren. But the fighting had ceased.

As if at some unheard signal the Possessed stopped attacking and moved back from the allied forces, they retreated just a few paces away, looming like a wave of violence just waiting to fall. It was clear that this was not the will of the Possessed warriors themselves. They raged and snarled like wild dogs straining at the leash, but they were held in check by the will of an infinitely stronger mind, a mind that wanted some calm to examine the soul that thought to oppose it.

Falco watched as the Kardakae moved back to form a curved wall around him and then he saw movement as they parted to let something through.

*

The Marchio Dolor's mind was ablaze with fury. Not only had this Defiant and his wyrm now killed another three of the Faithful, but somehow he had managed to liberate a soul from *his* dominion. Such blasphemy could not be tolerated.

The Marquis of Pain had had enough.

He hooked his fingers into the fabric of reality and with a sweeping gesture he plucked the Defiant from his feet and hauled him through the air before slamming him into the earth. The man immediately tried to rise, but the Marchio had grabbed him again and dragged him through a gauntlet of Kardakae who beat him almost senseless. The Defiant's wyrm tried to come to his aid, but the Marchio struck it from the sky and even now two of the Faithful were moving to overpower the black scaled lizard.

The noise of the battle suddenly felt like a distraction and so the Marchio called his forces to a halt. The army that had arrived with him simply stopped while those already engaged withdrew from the fighting. They railed at being restrained, but they could not go against his will.

Finally the Marchio drew the Kardakae back so that he could see this irksome Defiant for himself. Over to his right he continued to press the black wyrm into the ground, surprised at the effort it took to hold the powerful creature down. But now two of the Faithful had arrived and he released the wyrm into their unyielding grasp.

The Possessed parted before him as he walked forward to look upon the human that had caused them so much trouble. The Kardakae stood back in a great arc of steel and there on the ground was a man. Clad in armour and with a shield twisted around his left arm he swayed on his feet. Even now the Marchio could feel the force of his defiance, but after all the expectations, he was just a man.

The Marchio Dolor was almost disappointed.

He drew his sword and clenched the fist that lay beneath the shield armour on his left arm. A part of him wanted to make an example, to kill the Defiant quickly but once again he thought how much more satisfying it would be to break his spirit and claim his soul. In all the history of their conflict the Faithful had never claimed the soul of a Defiant, but the love this man felt for the humans on the battlefield might be enough to break him.

Feeling a thrill of anticipation the Marchio Dolor walked forward. It was time to test the limits of this Defiant's faith.

103

Darkness

The Marchio's army filled the valley like a dark inland sea. The defenders had managed to resist the first army that moved against them, but now they were heavily outnumbered. However, it was not the force of numbers that robbed the allied soldiers of hope, it was the massive shapes that walked amidst the horde. No fewer than six demons now strode through the heaving ranks of the Possessed. They walked upright on back-bent legs with torsos that were vaguely humanoid. Their physical forms were quite different but it was clear that they all came from the same infernal realm.

One was a winged fiend with skin that glowed like red hot coals. Two were armed with swords and covered in armour. The fourth was a wraithlike creature whose black body was wreathed in smoke. The final two were reminiscent of bulls, like the minotaurs of legend. Their skin had the mineral glint of coal and their massive claws gouged into Sidian's scales as they held the dragon fast.

And beside these six there was another, one that did not tower but stood only a foot taller than the Kardakae through which it walked. It was small compared to the other demons, but none of them could match the presence of the figure now walking towards Falco.

Feeling battered and dazed, Falco watched as the Marchio Dolor appeared with two fearsome bestiarum matching his pace like a pair of loyal hounds. One was mottled crimson and the other black, like tar. Their eyes were empty pockets of darkness and their sharp horns curved forward over muzzles filled with teeth. Their claws dug into the ground as they strained to get at Falco, but even they could not break free of the will that held them in check.

Standing fully seven feet tall the Marquis of Pain looked almost human with skin like age tarnished silver. Much of his body was covered in armour that shimmered with waves of heat. He did not carry a shield but the armour on his left arm had been extended, flaring out to either side and sweeping forward into two stabbing blades. At his waist he carried a sword that pulsed and throbbed with an angry light. The demon's horns protruded from the sides of his Ferocian helm and his eyes glowed like orbs of molten bronze.

The Marchio Dolor stopped some thirty paces short of Falco as if he in turn was studying the human who stood against him. The sense of power and authority radiating from this figure was like nothing Falco had ever known and he felt a tremor run through the foundations of his faith. The prospect of fighting such a being seemed unthinkable but still he reached for his sword.

Nothing...

His sword was not there. He had laid it down to free Quirren and dropped it as the invisible force wrenched him from the ground.

A sense of panic rose up in Falco's chest and then he saw movement to his left and watched as the two minotaur demons dragged Sidian into the clearing. They forced him down and bound him with glowing chains that the demons drew out of the earth, pulling them tight until the dragon was held firm against the ground.

Satisfied that no wyrm could break their bonds the two minotaur demons stepped back. The chains burned into Sidian's scales like branding irons, but he looked at Falco without the merest hint of submission in his fierce golden gaze. The dragon's courage made Falco's heart ache, but there were now seven demons ranged against them and he knew they could not win.

No, you cannot.

The words echoed in the cavern of Falco's mind, just as they did in the minds of every person on the battlefield. He knew the words spoke the truth but he also knew that it did not matter.

Perhaps they could not win. But they could still fight.

The Marchio Dolor frowned as he felt the power flare in the young Defiant's mind. With surprising speed Falco sent a barb of energy spearing towards the demon's chest and the Marchio barely had time to raise the shield armour on his left arm. The bolt of energy gouged a deep cleft in the enchanted steel and the demon ducked to avoid a curving arc of light that sprang from the edge of Falco's shield.

Thrusting out a hand the Marchio tried to drag him forward but this time he was ready for the invisible attack and the demon's arm shook with the strain as Falco set his feet against the earth.

Never before had the Marchio Dolor felt such a challenge to his will and he suddenly understood how this youngling had been able to defeat the Slayer. For all his youth there was a strength to this Defiant that was ageless, a strength not bound by the constraints of his human flesh. And the Marchio Dolor hated it.

With a twitch of his mind he released the hounds of hell and the two muscular bestiarum surged forward only to be stopped again, this time by the force of Falco's will. The beasts snarled and strands of silvery saliva dripped from their gnashing jaws. Their master wanted this Defiant's soul but his carcass would be theirs. They would dismember his body and strip the flesh from his tortured bones.

Falco's hand shook as he struggled to hold the beasts at bay. They were now little more than twenty feet away and if he released his grip they would be on him in an instant. For a moment he considered turning his power to the attack, but then he was forced to defend himself as a blast of burning shrapnel shot towards him from the left.

Several of the other demons began to launch their own attacks and Falco staggered as another blast almost tore the shield from his arm. Still struggling to hold the hounds at bay he summoned a sphere of magical force and strained to maintain it as attacks of fire and brimstone slammed into the shimmering globe of light. Then the ground beneath Falco split apart as the Marchio Dolor channelled his power into the earth and the flames of Baëlfire rose up around Falco.

The combined strength of the attacks was too much. Falco's protection began to fail and the hounds of hell took another step closer.

You are beaten, child, said the demonic voice in Falco's mind. *Can you not hear the sound of your failure in the screaming fear of the people you thought to save?*

Slowly Falco became aware of a growing commotion on the battlefield. The fighting had not resumed, but the air was now filled with the rising wail of fear as the cloak of his faith was stripped away. He simply was not strong enough to protect both himself and the army that now stood helpless with terror. He could hear horses neighing and snorting in fear, many breaking free of their rider's diminished control before bolting across the valley.

Panic swirled like an acid stench in the air, dissolving the courage of the soldiers on the battlefield. Too terrified even to flee, they stood in a paralysed stupor waiting for the Possessed to end their lives and claim their souls. Falco could feel their fear, but there was nothing he could do to assuage it.

Around him the dark tongues of Baëlfire rose higher, scorching the earth and licking around the sphere of his protection. To the side he could feel Sidian's presence, but even the dragon's strength was beginning to fail in the face of the evil that now filled the valley. They were doomed, and it was all his fault. He was responsible for leading them here, to this place, to this fate.

The sphere of energy surrounding him suddenly wavered. The hounds inched forward and the flames leapt up, fed by the driving winds of doubt. Falco's thoughts were suddenly filled with images of what would happen to the soldiers of Illicia and Clemoncé, to his friends.

Yes, said the voice that echoed in his skull. *You know what awaits those who oppose us.*

Tears sprang to Falco's eyes as the first clouds of despair rose up on the horizon of his mind.

But you could save them, said the voice.

Despite his inherent mistrust Falco clutched at the thread of hope implied by the Marchio's words.

'How?' he gasped and the hounds of hell moved a step closer.

Surrender yourself to me, said the voice. *Give up your soul and I swear I will let the other humans die.*

Falco almost snorted in derision. Staring into the Marchio's glowing eyes he looked for the deceit that he knew must be there, but he saw nothing. He frowned in confusion. Somehow he knew the Marchio Dolor was telling the truth.

His soul for the souls of ninety thousand others.

You would never have the courage
You would never have the faith.

Suddenly the refrain of Falco's nightmares made sense. This is what the voices had spoken of. This was the question that had haunted him all his life. Did he have the courage to surrender his own soul to save the people he loved.

Falco began to weep.

The fear was suddenly clawing at his mind. Laughing at him. Mocking him.

You would never have the courage
You would never have the faith.

To Falco's left a horse went galloping past. The beast shied away from the dark flames surrounding him and disappeared into the massed ranks of Kardakae, but Falco barely noticed it. He was faced with an unthinkable choice - to condemn ninety thousand souls to an eternity of agony, or to surrender himself to the same.

Sweat coursed down his face and his throat burned as the heat of the flames began to sear his flesh, the first touch of the fire that would claim him, or claim those he loved.

The hounds moved closer and the Marchio Dolor laughed at the agony of his decision.

It is time for you to choose, he said and Falco knew that he was right.

Any moment now the hounds would reach him and begin to tear him apart while he listened as his friends were lost to the unending torments of hell. There was only one way to save them and the thought was forming in his mind even as the sound of hoof beats loomed behind him.

All across the valley, knights and cavalrymen were fighting to control their mounts, all that is save one. Of all the horses on the battlefield only one behaved like the warhorse it was bred to be. And *it* was only able to maintain its course because of the bond that existed between horse and rider. The rider was a captain of the Knights Adamant and the horse now charging towards Falco was a smoke grey Percheron.

*

The fear was like a storm of thorns and claws tearing at his courage, but still the emissary rode on. He had once seen Falco walk into the face of evil to stand beside a man he loved. Now William Chevalier would do the same for the boy who had given them hope. Of all the battle mages he had met, only this boy made the emissary believe that they could win.

And what is faith if it is not that?

To believe in hope when all hope is gone.

Now Falco stood against seven demons of the Possessed and the emissary could not bear to see him facing the enemy alone. Without even thinking he had snatched up a lance from the chest of a dead Sciritae and driven his heels into Tapfer's flanks. Leaping over bodies and dodging other panicked horses the knight on the smoke grey Percheron charged. He saw the glowing sphere of light around Falco falter and he saw the two monstrous hounds creep closer.

With a final burst of speed he galloped past Falco and drove his lance into the face of the crimson hound. The beast died instantly as the steel point stabbed through one of its empty eye sockets to pierce its brain. The impact tore the lance from his grasp and the emissary drew his sword as the tar coloured hound leapt towards him. He leaned into Tapfer's neck as the horse reared up, but the hound's attack was too powerful and the emissary was thrown from the saddle as the smoke grey Percheron fell onto its side. Immediately the tar-skinned creature leapt upon it and with a sudden lunge it tore out the horse's throat.

The emissary rolled free as his mount came crashing down. He managed to hold onto his sword and came back to his feet just as the black hound sprang towards him, Tapfer's blood still dripping from its jaws.

As the terrifying beast lunged towards him the emissary dodged to one side and the beast went streaking past, but its sharp claws lashed out, tearing the armour from his shoulder. Blood poured down his arm but the emissary barely noticed. Again the beast lunged for him but he smacked the black fiend in the muzzle with his shield and parried a claw strike before hacking his sword into the creature's heavily muscled shoulder. His blade bit deep and the beast snarled as it spun back to face him.

He tried for another strike but the black hound surged forward and thrust one of its horns through the armour at the top of the emissary's thigh. He roared in pain as the cruel spike fractured his pelvis and tore through the ligaments of his hip, but with the hound's horn still embedded in his body he struck at the creature's neck. The monster tried to withdraw but the emissary struck again and again until the bestiarum's neck was cut clean through. The hound's decapitated body collapsed to the ground, its horn pulling free of the emissary's body by the weight of its own severed head.

Breathing heavily and almost crippled with pain the emissary ignored his defeated foes and limped forward to stand between Falco and the demon. The strength had gone from his body and the world seemed to tilt beneath him as the emissary dropped his sword and let the shield slip from his arm. With both hands he reached up to push the great-helm from his head and then he raised his gaze to look upon the Marquis of Pain. His grey eyes were filled with fear, but there was no mistaking his intentions or the strength of his resolve.

The emissary was offering his own soul in place of Falco's.

The Marchio understood this man's gesture. He understood that other humans might consider it noble, but to the demons of the Possessed such an offer was meaningless. They could claim this man's soul whether he offered it or not, but the Defiants were different.

For some reason the Defiants were able to resist both fear and despair and thus the demons were unable to claim their souls. No. Falco's soul was worth no more than any others', but the fact that the Possessed could not claim it made it a prize of maddening value.

With a growl of impatience the Demon advanced upon the emissary. His would be the first soul Possessed this day. Finally overcome by fear the emissary collapsed to his knees as the Marchio loomed over him. The demon reached out and placed a massive hand on either side of the emissary's head, just as he had with the mighty Vercincallidus. The emissary felt the searing touch of the demon's hands. He knew that he hovered on the edge of an abyss, but even now his final thoughts were for the Queen.

Had she writhed in pain as her mind was lost to desolation?

Had her life ended like this?

Yes, it had, said a voice in his mind and the emissary began to cry.

Pleased by the extent of the man's suffering the Marchio smiled. He let the flames of Baëlfire flow down his arms but stopped them just before they reached the human's head. Then he raised his eyes to look at Falco.

Now we will see which is greater, said the voice in Falco's mind.

Your love and compassion, or your fear of hell.

Your soul for the souls of ninety thousand others.

Yes or no?

Falco literally shook with the effort it took to find his voice. He knew that once he spoke the word, he could never take it back. His fate and the fate of the entire army would be decided in an instant. His mind was filled with the torment he would suffer as a consequence of his decision and the satisfaction in the demon's eyes was almost more than he could bear. But he could put it off no longer. Filled with self loathing he uttered the word.

'No.'

The Marchio Dolor frowned, but Falco's gaze did not waver. He would never forgive himself for what he had done, but he also knew that the enemy had tried to trick him. All his life he had believed that this was a choice between himself and those he loved, a choice between courage and cowardice. But this was not a question of courage, it was a question of faith. Did he have the strength to keep faith even if it condemned his friends to eternal damnation?

Even if it condemned the world?

'No,' he said again and his quiet voice resonated through all the thousands of minds on the battlefield. And then, with a huge effort of will, he added.

'You... are... defied.'

The allied army wailed in the face of their damnation, but the Marchio's mind blazed with fury.

You will burn, he said, his entire body seething with anger. *We might not be able to claim your soul but I will keep you alive for a hundred years and every hour the agony will be worse than the one that went before.*

I will stop open your ears so that you cannot shut out the screams of those that you have damned. It will feel like an eternity and the last thought in your tortured mind will be the knowledge that the suffering of those you love will never end.

Still holding the emissary's head the Marquis of Pain released the flames of hell, but they did not reach the Chevalier's flesh. Falco flooded his body with a power that denied the hateful fire. He knew it was only a temporary reprieve, but while he could, he would use his power to protect those he loved.

With an angry growl the demon flung the emissary aside and struck Falco with the full force of his mind. The sheer power of it drove Falco to one knee with a storm of screaming hatred trying to press him into the earth. He tried to rise but his strength was diminished by the realisation of what he had done. He could feel the resentment of every soul on the battlefield. The weight of it was like a mountain of guilt and Falco's strength began to crumble as the other demons added their strength to the force of the Marchio's spite.

Falco's mind was suddenly filled with images of all the people he cared about. He saw Fossetta and Simeon, Malaki and Bryna, the emissary and the Queen. He saw the man with the stubble chin and the deep brown eyes. And finally he saw a woman with green eyes and long dark hair, a woman he had never known but always loved.

'I'm sorry,' he breathed in the lightless cavern of his mind, but the faces did not hear him. He was lost to them, dead to them.

The physical pain of the demons' attacks was terrible but the psychological pain of his betrayal was worse. He might have saved himself from the clutches of hell yet still he felt himself slipping towards a bottomless chasm of despair, but then he felt another darkness converging on this place and with it came yet more phantoms from his dreams.

At first he did not recognise them, for he had never experienced their presence in the light of his waking mind, and yet he had known them all his life. In dreams he had helped them survive their own guilt and shame, and in turn they had supported him through his trials of illness, grief and nightmare. And now they had come to save him in his hour of greatest need.

Falco hardly dared believe it as a spark of hope rekindled in his breast. The force of the demons' hatred tried to break him, but now he found the strength to resist and suddenly he remembered the words that he had muttered so often in his sleep.

Darkness is coming, he would breathe as Fossetta wiped the fevered sweat from his brow.

Darkness in the earth.

Darkness in the deep.

Darkness on the hills.

And darkness was indeed coming, darkness borne upon wings of pinioned night, darkness driven mad by treachery and redeemed by grace.

Even as the demons' spite threatened to destroy him Falco braced himself against the ground and the Marchio Dolor frowned. No mortal could bear the force of evil that they drove into this human's mind and yet he remained. He had known that this Defiant was dangerous. It was time for the Faithful to cease their indulgence and kill him.

Drawing his sword the demon started forward but then some movement in the air caught his attention and he stopped. The Marchio Dolor was suddenly filled with doubt and then they appeared, three dark shapes descending onto three treeless hills, three black dragons, and between the wings of each, a man.

A hermit.

A healer.

And a man who fished the seas.

Three men lost to guilt and shame, saved by the birth of a child they had never met, a child who had somehow given them hope. That child had now become a man and that man now knelt on the valley floor, surrounded by a cabal of demons who were trying to crush his spirit. The child was almost broken, almost lost, almost but not quite yet.

Reaching out with their minds the Disavowed took the child into their embrace and Falco raised his head.

For every death and plundered soul.

For every dragon slain and battle mage bereft.

For every heart that clung to hope, and every soul consigned to hell.

Falco raised his head.

And not the fiercest flames of Hades could match the fire that burned in his bright green eyes.

A few yards to his left a black shape stirred as Sidian strained against his bonds. No wyrm could break the chains that bound him to the ground, but Sidian was not a wyrm, he was a dragon from beyond the Endless Sea and there was a series of loud chinks and pops as the chains snapped and Sidian surged to his feet.

617

Time stalled and the Valley of the Three Brethren seemed to hang on the cusp of violence, army facing army, demons facing the great souls of Wrath. And then the Marquis of Pain roared out a deafening command.

To kill and claim them all.

His fellow demons gathered their power in dark swirling clouds and the Possessed moved once more to attack. The blade of the Marchio's sword shone with a furious light and his eyes burned with hatred as he started towards Falco.

Still kneeling, Falco made no move to stop him. He braced the rim of his shield against the earth while his right hand remained empty. He was not immune to the imminent danger, he was listening, listening for a faint sound like the distant ring of steel. Even above the rising tumult he heard it and reaching back with his free hand he strained with all his might.

*

Two hundred yards away Alex Klingemann heard a metallic rattling sound at his feet. Glancing down he saw Falco's sword, still lying where he had dropped it and now he listened as the sword began to resonate with an ominous hum.

The hum rose to a screaming whine until it passed into a kind of silence. In captivated wonder Alex watched the sword raise a few inches into the air and then, like an arrow from the bow, it shot off across the ground.

*

The Marchio was almost upon him but still Falco did not move. The demon raised his sword and the infernal blade began to fall and finally Falco felt something slam into his palm, something that could withstand an edge of hell-forged steel. As the Marchio's blade came down Falco swung his sword to meet it and the demon's deathblow was deflected.

The Marchio Dolor actually staggered from the force of the impact and Falco rose to his feet. Beside him Sidian roared as he launched himself at one of the minotaur demons, while from the hilltops his kindred came swooping down, carrying with them the battle mages from Illicia, Beltane and Thraece.

All across the valley the allied forces dragged themselves back from the brink of despair and struggled to wrestle their broken formations into some kind of order. The fear of the demons was still as strong as ever, but now they were protected by the faith of not one but three battle mages. The fourth withheld his protection for *he* needed all his strength to face the demon who now attacked with such fury as the world had rarely seen.

The earth buckled, the air burned and the Marchio's sword was a livid shard of razor sharp steel. Falco ducked as the glowing blade cut a blazing path just inches above his head. He fortified his arm to take a blow on his shield and even through the disk of Missaglias steel he could feel the heat of the Marchio's blade. The demon attacked with terrifying strength, but Falco did not waver. He had faced the challenge of his nightmares and his faith remained intact.

The demon conjured Baëlfire and drove it at him in great devouring torrents, but Falco's power shed the flames like water. The strength of his defence drove the Marchio to even greater heights of rage and the demon channelled his unholy power into his sword until it scorched the air with its heat.

618

Falco could feel the hateful force in the Marchio's blade and he knew the touch of it would mean death. For all his faith, Falco knew his own strength was finite and he could not resist the demon's might much longer.

If he was going to survive this confrontation then he must end it now.

Moving with speed that belied his fatigue Falco parried two blazing sword strikes and then he struck, once to the Marchio's shoulder and again to the demon's thigh. Mercurial blood spilled onto the earth, but still the demon came on and Falco was forced to defend against another avalanche of brutal attacks. The demon sent a stream of fire towards his chest but Falco spun away, whirling round to slam his sword into the side of the Marchio's helm. His blade sheared off the demon's right horn and cut a deep gash into his arcane steel.

A spasm ran through the Marchio's body and he dropped his sword as an oily fluid seeped from his cloven skull. He tried to grapple him but Falco stepped backwards delivering a savage diagonal strike from left shoulder to right hip. So intense was the energy surging through Falco's blade that it sliced through the demon's enchanted armour. Even now the Marchio glared at him with a gaze that burned like fire, but Falco did not waver as he drew back his arm and drove his blade into the demon's chest. Dark blood welled from the Marchio's mouth as Falco's blade sank towards his mortal heart, but with the last of his unholy strength the demon reached out to grab hold of Falco, pulling him into an embrace of death as his body erupted with Baëlfire.

If he was going to die then the Marquis of Pain would take this Defiant with him.

Falco bared his teeth in agony as the dark fire engulfed him. He tried to block its awful heat but he did not have the strength to finish the demon and defend against the flames. The tendons in his neck were stretched bowstring tight and Falco screamed as he channelled all his power into the tempered blade of his sword.

Deep inside the demon's chest Falco's sword flared with the force of his faith and then his mind gave out as both battle mage and demon were lost in an explosion of dark flame and blinding incandescent light.

Slowly the cataclysm faded and in its place, darkness.

104

Of Healing, Grief & Hope

Falco woke to the murmur of voices and the sounds of people moaning in pain. He opened his eyes. Above him the sky was white and it took him a moment to realise it was the pale canvas of a tent. The air was filled with the pungent smell of ointments and herbs but it was also thick with the acrid stench of smoke and burning flesh. He became aware of figures moving around him and slowly turned his head. His vision was blurred but he could see people lying on makeshift beds while others bustled around them. He was lying in an army field hospital.

'He's awake!' said a voice from close by and Falco looked up to see Bryna sitting on the edge of his bed.

'About time!' said another voice and Alex stepped into his field of view. The teasing smile on the young Illician's face was the same as ever, but his gaze was now tinged with an enduring shadow of sadness.

Another figure appeared beside Bryna and tears welled in Falco's eyes.

'Welcome back, pastry boy,' said Malaki and Falco thought his heart might burst with joy.

He tried to sit up but his head swam and he was forced to lie back down. His body ached from head to toe and his skin felt tight and raw as if it might tear with any sudden movement. He closed his eyes against the sudden discomfort but then he felt a gentle hand on his chest and all the pain just faded away, replaced by a familiar tingling warmth.

Falco opened his eyes to see an older man standing over him. The deep brown colour of his skin and his dark ebony eyes marked him as a man of Thraece and Falco knew at once that he was a battle mage. The man had the saddest and most handsome face that he had ever seen and Falco had the strangest feeling that they had met before.

For a moment the man did not speak, but only smiled at the confusion in Falco's eyes.

'I will tell the others you have awoken,' he said, his accent surprisingly soft for one who lived at the southern extent of the world.

With a sense of wonder Falco watched him leave.

'He's been amazing,' said Bryna, coming back to sit on his bed. 'Definitely the finest healer I've ever seen.'

'He healed you after the battle,' said Malaki. 'Treated your burns.'

'You can hardly see the scars anymore,' said Alex.

Looking down at his bare arms Falco could see that his hair had been singed away and his skin was covered with faint silvery marks like swirling tongues of flame. Then all at once, the final moments of the battle came back to him.

'The Possessed?' he asked suddenly.

'Destroyed,' said Malaki.

'And the demons?'

'Dead.'

'All of them?' pressed Falco and Malaki could hear the anxiety in his friend's voice. He knew Falco was asking about one demon in particular.

'Yes,' he said. 'All of them.'

Falco's face relaxed as his mind was flooded with relief. For a moment he turned his thoughts inward and listened for the taunting spectre of his dreams but he heard only silence. Finally he opened his eyes.

'What about the army?'

'Not good,' said Malaki and Falco braced himself for the worst. 'We have near forty thousand dead, few that aren't injured and none that weren't affected by the fear.'

Falco's brow gathered in a frown of understanding. Those overcome by the fear might recover in time, but forty thousand dead! He could barely comprehend the figure but then he asked an even harder question.

'And of those we know?' he asked. 'The emissary...'

'He's alive,' said Malaki and Falco's body sagged with relief. 'Although he'll never walk properly again.'

'*But he's alive,*' thought Falco as he steeled himself to hear the names of those who had not been so lucky.

Among the names was Dedric Sayer, the foul-mouthed scoundrel from Bryna's Dalwhinnies, and Allyster Mollé, the young archer who had equalled Bryna's score on the day of the Trials. Malaki spoke of Alcaeus, the Acheronian cadet that Falco had first tried to match on the daily run up to the Pike, and Lanista Deloix the quiet academy instructor that had always moved with a lethal and feline grace.

Falco winced at the name of General Renucci and felt a surprising stab of loss to hear that Jarek Snidesson had also died. Jarek had been the bane of his early life but over the last few months they had been able to view each other with mutual respect.

But Malaki's voice had failed him at the final name.

'And Huthgarl too,' said Alex while Bryna dabbed at her eyes with her sleeve.

For a moment Falco could not believe it. He found it hard to comprehend how such strength could suddenly be reduced to nought.

'He saved us,' said Malaki, his voice thick with emotion. 'When the battle resumed the Kardakae engulfed us. We were cut off,' Malaki's gaze was inward, focussed on that terrible moment in the battle. 'But Huthgarl charged them. He forced a way through and held it open for us to break free.'

Bryna reached out to place her hand over his as the four friends remembered those they had lost. After a while they left him to rest, but Falco no longer felt tired. Beyond the tent he could feel Sidian waiting for him. The dragon's presence gave him strength and he could not wait until he was well enough to fly with him once more.

All in good time, the dragon's thoughts seemed to say. *But for now you rest.*

Falco smiled as his mind was filled with images of his own face reposed in sleep. How many times had the dragon stayed awake to watch him as he slept? A guardian of constant vigilance, a companion of endless strength.

As afternoon gave way to evening, Falco was strong enough to get out of bed and help some of the injured men around him. He was trying to ease the pain of a man who had lost his leg when a wave of weariness washed over him.

'You mustn't try to do too much,' said a familiar voice and Falco turned as Meredith Saker caught hold of his arm.

The young mage helped him back to his bed and poured him a cup of water. As the dizziness passed Falco asked him what news they had of the cities that had been attacked, but Meredith just shook his head. During the battle he and his fellow mages had lost concentration and their communication link with the other cities had been broken.

'We get the occasional image or fragmented sentence, but nothing clear,' he explained. 'All we can say for certain is that Amboss was saved.'

After Meredith had left him, Falco found that he was ready for something to eat, but the taste of the food was ruined by the charred smell of death from the piles of Possessed corpses still burning at the far end of the valley. He tried to rest but he could not sleep.

It was around midnight when he felt the presence of three men, moving through the tent towards him. Putting aside any thoughts of sleep Falco got off his bed and stood up to meet them. He had already met the healer but beside him was a tall man with weathered skin, blue eyes and a mass of thick grey hair. The third had long brown hair, shot through with broad streaks of grey. His features were craggy, his expression stern, but there was warmth in his deep brown eyes as he looked at Falco.

They did not speak, but only stood together, and what passed between them could not be expressed in words. Never in his life had Falco felt so safe as he did at that moment, standing in the presence of the hermit, the healer and the fisherman.

They could not explain the bond that existed between them and none of them felt the need to try. All they knew was that it was about twenty years since their faith had been broken and about twenty years since Falco was born. Somehow the birth of this child had echoed through their lives and given them hope. Had the Fates known that he would one day heal the rift between humans and dragons, and offer them the chance to redeem their souls?

Perhaps... but who could say?

All that could be said was that *they* would not have survived the guilt without *him* and *he* would not have survived the nightmares without *them*.

The strength of their presence lingered even after they had left, but still Falco felt restless. Hoping for a breath of fresh air he got up to leave the tent. The night was illuminated by a bright gibbous moon and Falco swept his gaze over the allied camp, calm and subdued in the aftermath of battle. But then he turned to look out across the valley where hundreds of men were still working through the night. In the cold light of the moon Falco could see row upon row of shapes laid out across the valley floor. It took him a moment to realise that they were bodies, bodies of the deceased waiting for the living to dig their graves.

The sight struck Falco to the core and he found that he could not move, but then he felt another presence and he turned to see a man beside him, a man who swayed a little as he balanced on a pair of crutches.

'There was always going to be suffering,' said the emissary. 'There was always going to be death.' He turned to look at the young man standing next to

622

him. 'But there wasn't always going to be victory, Falco. There wasn't always going to be hope.'

With so many dead it certainly did not feel like a victory but Falco could accept the truth of the emissary's words. Ever since they first met in Caer Dour there had been a strange bond between Falco and the emissary, and now they found comfort in each other's presence. For a while, they watched the work parties together and when Falco returned at last to his makeshift bed he was finally able to sleep.

By the following day Falco was feeling much better. He spent the morning doing what he could to help the injured and in the afternoon he went for a walk with the emissary.

'The healer says I need to keep moving,' said the emissary as they walked towards the edge of the camp where four black dragons watched them from the hillside. Their progress was slow and the emissary drew in a sharp breath of pain each time he caught his leg on a stone or tuft of grass. They had just decided to turn back when Falco's attention was drawn to the command tent from where Marshal Breton and several of the other surviving commanders had just emerged.

'Something's happened,' said Falco as the commanders walked towards them. With them were Lanista Magnus, Meredith Saker and two of the battle mages that Falco had met in the night.

Hobbling round on his crutches the emissary came to stand with Falco.

'What is it?' he asked as the commanders approached, but none of them seemed eager to answer.

'We've received news from Amboss,' said Marshal Breton at last.

'At least we think the message is from Amboss,' said Meredith and he too seemed reticent.

'It's actually two messages,' Marshal Breton went on.

'And they contradict each other,' added Meredith.

The emissary gave an impatient sigh, annoyed by their prevarication.

'And the messages said, what?'

'One spoke of the Queen's death and Prince Ludovico claiming the throne,' said Marshal Breton, mindful of the reaction this might provoke.

'And the other?' asked the emissary, his tone hardening at the thought of the Prince leaping onto the throne before the Queen's body was even cold.

'The other message was very faint and fragmented,' said Meredith. 'Although the mage who received thinks he could make out two words.'

'Which were?' snapped the emissary tiring of this charade.

'The first word was *Queen*,' said Meredith and he swallowed before he continued. 'We think the second word was *lives*.'

The emissary's eyes fixed him like two steel blades. Who were these fools to stir the coals of his grief?

'We could learn more if we had a quintet and a chamber of discourse,' said Meredith. 'But we are only three. We were lucky to get anything at all.'

The emissary's expression suggested that their attempts were anything but lucky.

'We can dispatch a rider to Amboss,' said Marshal Breton.

'Or a dragon,' said Lanista Magnus. 'If Amboss has news from the capital we will know it in a day or so.'

'But even they sound confused,' said Falco. 'Yes, we could send a messenger, but we might end up none the wiser.' Here he stopped and turned to the emissary. 'In a few days I could be back in Wrath. And then we'd know for certain.'

The emissary stared at him and there was a new kind of fear in his eyes, it was the fear of allowing hope back into his heart. Finally his gaze hardened.

'She is dead,' he said as if he could not bear the thought of believing her alive only to lose her all over again.

'We won't know for sure until we reach the capital,' said Falco and he felt almost cruel as he saw the desperate glint of hope in the emissary's eyes.

'I will follow you overland,' said the emissary but Falco shook his head.

'Ten days bouncing in the saddle would kill you,' he said.

'But three days of smooth flight on a dragon's back would not,' said the battle mage from Illicia. 'Erlösung would bear you, I am sure of it,' he added, and up on the hillside one of the black dragons now stepped forward.

People looked at the battle mage as if he were mad, but there was a fierce light burning in the emissary's eyes.

'We'd take it easy,' said Falco. 'And I could heal you along the way.'

'We must go directly there,' said the emissary. 'No stopping at towns or cities. I could not bear to follow a trail of rumour and speculation.' Falco nodded and the emissary went on. 'We must head directly for Wrath. Only then will we know the truth. If Prince Ludovico is on the throne then we will know that the Queen is truly dead.'

'We'll fly together,' said Falco.

'We leave at once,' said the emissary.

105

All The Hordes of Hell

Down from the high valley they flew and out over the rolling hills towards the forested kingdom of Clemoncé. Even with the gentle rise and fall of a dragon's flight Falco knew the emissary was in great pain. They rested often and Falco would do what he could to help but the emissary would never let them tarry for long. They travelled now for Wrath and the final truth of Queen Catherine's fate.

It was the morning of the third day when they first caught sight of the capital and Falco's heart sank as the distant towers came into view. The flags of turquoise and pale blue were flying at half mast. Falco's heart was beating heavily and he could only guess at what the emissary must be feeling, but even now he did not hesitate. For good or ill it was time for them to learn the truth.

For a while the city did not appear to be getting closer but then it suddenly seemed to expand until it was spread out below them. Falco had suggested that they land on the plateau so as not to alarm the people in the city but the emissary would have none of it.

'*This is going to be quite the entrance,*' thought Falco as they circled down to land on the Queen's personal terrace where a short path led to her apartments.

The palace guards were stunned by the sight of two black dragons descending towards them. The guards were placed to intercept people entering the palace via the normal routes. They had no reason to expect that someone would seek to gain access from above, but now they scurried to reach the terrace as Falco and the emissary dismounted. The emissary was clearly in pain but he wasted no time as he limped towards the door at the end of the terrace.

As they advanced, Falco could not help noticing that the palace guards were dressed, not in the pale blue and turquoise colours of the Queen, but in the green and silver livery of Prince Ludovico. Despite the pain that stabbed through his hip the emissary's face was set hard with anger as he threw open the door to the Queen's apartments.

The entrance gave onto a long room with several internal doors leading off to the sides, but the emissary moved straight towards the door at the end, which led directly into the Queen's personal chambers. The guards at the door had heard the cries of alarm and now they moved to block the two men advancing towards them.

It was clear that they recognised the emissary, but still the first guard put out a hand to stop him. Limping forward, the emissary took hold of the first guard's hand, twisted his arm and thrust him to the floor. The second guard tensed, but then he was also thrown aside as Falco made a swiping gesture with his hand. The man was momentarily stunned as the door at the end of the corridor opened and two men appeared. One was an elderly man, dressed in the grey robes of a city official. The second was Prince Ludovico himself.

The prince was in the process of thanking the man when he caught sight of Falco and the emissary. He stared in surprise, frowned as he recognised Sir William and then gasped as the emissary grabbed the front of his robes and swung him round, slamming him hard against the wall.

'You vulture!' he snarled. 'You jackal of the night.'

Struck dumb with shock the prince opened his mouth to speak, but the emissary ground his fists upwards into his jaw, while Falco looked at the guards with an expression that made it clear they would be wise not to intervene.

'How long did you wait before stealing her throne?' said the emissary, his face contorted with uncharacteristic rage. 'Did you even bring her body back to the people or is she buried beneath the fields of Valentia?'

The prince made no attempt to answer as the emissary's grip restricted his breathing.

Moving forward Falco placed a hand on the emissary's shoulder as five more guards burst into the corridor. They moved towards the emissary, but Falco's outstretched palm made them think otherwise.

'You've always been jealous,' hissed the emissary. 'Always coveted the throne *and* the woman who sat upon it. But you will never be worthy of it, just as you were never worthy of...'

'William.'

The name was softly spoken and yet it stopped the emissary with the force of a magic spell. He did not release his grip, he did not turn. He froze as if at some cold touch from beyond the grave.

'William,' the voice said again and finally the emissary found the courage to look around. And there stood a vision.

Without even thinking the emissary let go of the prince and turned towards this vision of the woman he loved. Her face was thin and her skin was pale, but there was no mistaking the light in her deep blue eyes.

Could it be?

The vision held out a hand and the emissary limped towards it. Closer now and he could see new scars on her face, but the curve in her long dark hair was the same as ever. Fearful that it would disappear at any moment he reached out to take the vision's hand. And what wonder was this, but it did not fade. Slowly the emissary allowed himself to believe that it might be true then the vision smiled and finally he could see his Queen, his Catherine.

He did not see the hollow cheeks and sunken eyes of a woman who had come close to death. He did not see the empty sleeve, pinned discreetly across the bodice of her dress. All he could see was her face. All he knew was that she was alive.

The Queen reached up and the emissary held her hand against the stubble on his cheek.

'You came back to me,' she said.

'Though all the hordes of hell should stand between us,' said the emissary and the Queen's eyes glistened with tears.

Falco felt himself overcome with wonder and then his joy was compounded as he turned to see the hunched figure of Aurelian standing beside him.

'You took your time getting here,' said the cantankerous old battle mage.

Falco could sense the sadness in Aurelian's mind and he caught a quick image of Dwimervane and Dusaule. Somehow he knew that both were gone. His heart gave a sudden spasm of loss but Aurelian put a hand on his arm and gave him a cracked toothed smile as they turned back to the emissary and the Queen.

626

'They both look knackered,' said Aurelian. 'Maybe now people will leave them in peace.'

'But her arm,' said Falco. He wondered what terrible events must have taken place for her to have suffered such an injury, but Aurelian just shrugged.

'Ah, don't worry,' he said. 'Some of the finest people I know have only one arm.'

106
The Cairn of Fallen Souls

From Hoffen in the north, to the city of Seeburg in the south, the allied forces were reeling from the enemy's great offensive. Never before had they faced such a concerted wave of attacks, but they had prevailed. The Possessed had breached the front in several places and two cities had fallen, but the Queen was confident that these could be retaken in time. There were still numerous demons and Possessed armies emerging from the Forsaken Lands, but the balance of the war had changed forever.

For all its terrible cost, Falco's victory against the Marchio Dolor had dealt the Possessed a powerful blow. The tide of darkness had turned and now the allied armies pushed forward to reclaim the land that they had lost. The soldiers of Illicia, Beltane and Clemoncé were exhausted but they no longer fought alone. What the Queen had failed to achieve in life had been accomplished by the widespread news of her death. The kingdoms were finally united.

The legions of Tyramimus marched out to join them in the east.

The people of Valentia rebelled against their cowardly king and even now their armies were flooding into Beltane, eager to regain something of the reputation for valour that they had once enjoyed.

Even the southern kingdom of Thraece was joining the fight. After years of being thwarted by the magi, Cleomenes the Younger had finally come of age. In a gesture of mercy he had killed his father, releasing him from the mindless coma in which the magi had been keeping him alive. And as for the magi themselves... the young Cleomenes had invited them to a grand feast of reconciliation, where he poisoned Veneratu Ischyrós and thirteen of his senior magi. Now a fleet of Thraecian war triremes was sailing for the coast around the beleaguered city of Svarthaven.

'The people trapped in that forsaken corner of the world may yet be saved,' the Queen had said to Falco as they stood together on the marble floor map in the Chamber of Council.

The light from the oil lamps was reflected in the polished floor and Falco watched as it played over the Queen's face. It highlighted the scars on her skin, but for all her injuries the determination in her voice was as strong as ever.

'The kingdoms have united,' she told him. 'Finally the Possessed will know what it means to face the world of Wrath.'

Falco spent almost a week in the capital, but as his strength grew so he felt the urge to return to the front. Yes, the world *had* united but this war was far from over and there would be more suffering and death before the final victory could be claimed. However, before he returned to Malaki and the others, there was one last thing he needed to do.

'I understand,' said the emissary as they faced each other on the western terrace of the palace.

'Our thoughts and our love go with you,' said the Queen who stood beside him.

628

She stepped forward to kiss him and then Falco turned away and walked towards the black dragon that waited for him at the end of the terrace. The Queen and her Chevalier watched as they rose into the sky and disappeared among the clouds.

*

Flying high above the world, Falco looked down as the forests of Clemoncé gave way to the highlands of Valentia. All through the mountains he followed the trail that led back to his home town of Caer Dour. He did not stop to look at the burnt out buildings. Instead he turned Sidian towards a dark mountain that the locals had called Mont Noir.

Up they flew until Falco could see the amphitheatre of jagged stones known as the Castle of the Winds. At the centre of the curving cliffs was a flat expanse of stone, the western edge of which fell away in a sheer cliff to the mountain slopes below. It was down the face of this precipitous cliff that Falco now took Sidian.

Down they flew to the slopes of tumbled rock and scree, and it did not take long for Falco to find what he was looking for. There, lying twisted and broken among the stones, were the decomposed bodies of a dragon and a man, still bound together in the embrace of death that had claimed them both.

Falco now understood what had taken place on that fateful night, but understanding did not assuage the grief. All through the night he toiled to extricate the bodies from the mountain's grasp and lay them in a shallow grave that he dug with his own bare hands. With great reverence he laid the remains of Darius Voltario beside the body of the dragon that had answered his call.

He gathered rocks and piled them high until the two great souls were encased in stone then he stepped back as Sidian came forward. The dragon took a deep breath and the night was illuminated by the fierce light of dragon fire, fusing the stones together into a memorial that came to be known as the Cairn of Fallen Souls.

As dawn broke across the mountains, Falco kissed his fingers and laid them lightly on the stones.

'Forgive me,' he breathed.

And deep in his soul Falco Danté finally found some measure of peace.

Epilogue

The knight removed his great-helm and raised his eyes to view the field. The Possessed army filled the valley like a forest of dark steel, but there was more. Not one but two demons strode through the seething horde and the soldiers around him could not believe that the knight was so calm.

Like hellish giants the demons towered over the normal soldiers of the Possessed and the fear that issued from them was enough to crush the courage of even the most stalwart man, but still the knight did not seem concerned. He sat there on his bay coloured destrier, the bright red birthmark showing clearly on his face, and he was not afraid.

He was not afraid because he knew they were not alone.

Turning his head he glanced up to the craggy hills that overlooked the valley. The men around him followed the direction of his gaze and suddenly their hearts were filled not with fear but with wonder, for there, at the very edge of the cliffs, was the dark shape of a dragon, and on its back a man.

The figures were silhouetted against the sky but even so the soldiers could see that the dragon was black. A ripple of astonishment swept through the Valentian army as the men recalled the stories that people told of a black dragon and the man who rode it.

'Le Cœur Noir! they whispered in the hushed tones of awe.

The knight gave a grim smile as the name spread throughout his force. The army saw a figure of rumour and legend, but the knight saw only his friend. As a child this man had been born in tragedy and lived a life of guilt, shame and illness. He had been a weakling in a world of warriors, but somehow he had managed to overcome all this to become what he was born to be.

A battle mage.

Dear reader

Thank you for buying Battle Mage. It really is very much appreciated. If you enjoyed it I would be extremely grateful if you could spare a few minutes to leave a short review on Amazon.

As a lifelong fantasy fan I must admit to being quite nervous about releasing this book. I know how passionate readers of fantasy are and I was terrified of letting you down.

I hope I didn't.

If you have any comments or would like to get in touch with me, you can say hello on Twitter: @TheFlanston

Or via my website: www.peter.flannery.co.uk

Either way it would be great to hear from you and thanks again for buying the book.

With warm regards
Peter

Peter Flannery lives in a small village in the Scottish Borders with his wife and two sons. After leaving school he studied art and design before leaving college to work in forestry. However, during an accident at work he broke his neck and, after a month on traction and a year's convalescence, he moved into horticulture before switching again to set himself up as a sculptor working for the toy industry.

A design studio in Edinburgh provided the opportunity to move from sculpting to writing, producing background stories for the company's models and games. In 2010 Peter decided to focus on his writing and in 2011 he released his first novel, a psychological thriller called First and Only. In 2012 First and Only reached No.1 in the Amazon rankings for psychological thrillers and is currently in pre-production for a movie to be shot in the spring of 2017.

Other books by Peter

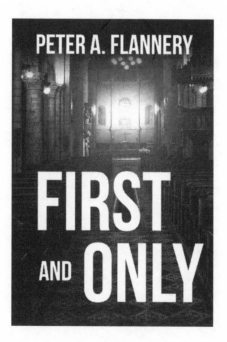